# Soaring EAGLE with MANY COUPS

# Soaring EAGLE with MANY COUPS

JAMES SAFRENO

# CONTENTS

# 1

# TRAGIC LOSS

"Did you know my Grandpa James is an Indian?" Johnny said to his friends as they looked up at the window, from which I was looking out.

"No, he isn't Johnny." "You're lying," said Sarah, his younger sister.

"I'm not lying if you don't believe me, go ask him yourself," Johnny replied angrily.

"You go with me," she said, afraid.

"Alright, I'll take you." "You guys stay here while I go with my sister," Johnny said as he grabbed his sister's hand and went upstairs.

So many years ago, and everything has gone now. But there are good memories, so I have that. To be in those mountains again, I think that is where I wish to be laid, somewhere I will not be found, I think. Look at those children down there; they have no idea what life was like back then.

"Grandpa is resting, so don't bother him; he's very old and needs his rest," said Dan.

"But Daddy, Johnny, and I need to talk to him," said Sarah, whining.

"Yeah," Johnny said.

"Ok, ok, but if your Grandpa doesn't want to talk to you, let him be."

"Grandpa, Johnny said you are an Indian," Sarah said softly.

"Johnny is right; I am a Shoshone warrior."

"See, I told you so," Johnny said.

"But Grandpa, you have blue eyes, and Indians have brown eyes," Sarah said.

"Johnny, how much has your father told you about me?"

"I didn't tell the children much about you," Dan said. "When I asked Pa, he never told me much about you."

"I can understand why he never said anything." "Your father had been through a lot, and the story is a little unbelievable even to me!" "Dan, sit down, and I will tell you and the children everything." "Everything I say is the absolute truth. I've never lied.

"It was the year eighteen fifteen, or was it eighteen sixteen when I was born, it's been so long, and I don't celebrate my birthday as the young ones do now." "I just don't remember quite when it was." "Oh well, it doesn't matter." "It doesn't change who I am, James York, also known as Soaring Eagle with Many Coups and the Earl of Worcester."

"I was born in Saint Louis, but my father, Nathaniel York, wasn't around when I was born." "He came from the east but wanted to be a mountain man." "So, he went west to the Shining Mountains, so my mother, Mary von Muller, told me." "Now, others say he was a lowlife gambler on some riverboat, but I tend to believe my mother." "My father never married my mother, so that makes me what a lot of people refer to as a bastard, as many reminded me when I was growing up." "My mother said he would come back someday, marry her, and take care of us, but I had my doubts." "Too many mountain men I met told me that most white men did not last long in those mountains unless they were very good."

"We lived in the storage room of Mr. McConnell's General Store." "It was small, but we had a stove where Mama cooked." "The stove also kept us warm." "Mr. McConnell was a robust, good man in his forties and would have let us stay there for free, but Mama felt it wasn't right to take advantage of a person's kindness." "So, Mama and I worked for him when I wasn't in school, and he gave us a little food to sustain us."

"I was small as a child, with long yellow hair and blue eyes." "I had a knack for remembering and understanding anything I read or heard, and I read every book someone let me borrow." "Mr. McConnell had a lot of customers who spoke only French, Spanish, or even Mandan, the language of an Indian tribe who lived along the banks of the Missouri River." "By the age of eight, I could speak, read, and write all these languages as well as Greek, Latin, and even German. I didn't get to use German much." "Still, I thought it useful to learn because my Mama's family was German, and my father's family was English." "My ability to speak many languages came in handy when Mr. McConnell had some customers come into the store who didn't speak English." "When I met some mountain men who spoke Spanish or French, I asked them about Pa."

"The general store had a cornucopia of goods most not so fancy like in the bigger stores, but useful items." "Mr. McConnell had a lot of customers because he was friendly, honest, and fair."

"I looked forward to going to school." "Sarah was the cute red-haired, green-eyed daughter of Mr. McConnell, two years younger than me." "She and I would go to school early."

"Sarah's mother had died in childbirth, and my Mama tried to fill in as Sarah's mother, but Mr. McConnell wanted to raise her his way and kept her near him as much as possible." "They both lived in the room above the store." "I don't know why Mr. McConnell was that way, but Sarah and I got along well."

"We left for school early because of Jack Flynn." "Jack Flynn was one of the meanest kids I ever knew." "He was a tall, strong, skinny redhead about a year older than me." "I don't think Jack ever bathed, and he smelled terrible." "He lived with a rough crowd near the river where his father worked when he wasn't drunk." "He didn't have a mother or any other kin that I heard." "The rumor was that his father had killed his mother in a drunken rage, but there was no proof." "Jack had his followers, and he intimidated most all the other kids, mostly us boys." "If you didn't do what he wanted, or just for general purposes, he'd give you a good beating." "Jack would take all or part of your lunch, and there was many a day I went hungry or had to share with Sarah because Jack stole her lunch." "He would also pick on certain kids to make fun of them." "Jack cornered one boy, a year younger than me, in the outhouse." "He forced the boy to remove all his clothing, then Jack threw his clothing up in a tree." "There that boy was, not a stitch of clothing on him, stuck in the outhouse." "Finally, he got found by his big brother and our teacher, Miss O'Brien." "His brother climbed the tree and retrieved his clothes." "When the two boys came back into the classroom, there were Jack and his friends, laughing uncontrollably." When Miss O'Brien confronted Jack, he denied it, and everyone, including the victim, was too afraid to say anything." "After school, the victim's big brother confronted Jack, who nearly beat him to death, to no one's surprise." "After that, no one tried to fight Jack." "Jack was the primary source of people calling me names because I didn't have a father."

"Grandpa, why didn't all those boys and girls tell their mothers and fathers what Jack was doing?" Johnny said.

"They did." "My Mama, Mr. McConnell, and most of the other parents met with the teacher and Jack's father." "After everybody had their say, Jack's father said there wasn't any proof, and any fight Jack was in was just to defend himself." "He also stated that they had no right to kick him out of school." "Of course, he was right in what he said." "No child who attended that school would say anything, knowing there would be a beating or worse, and so Jack stayed in school."

"With all the trouble with Jack, Miss O'Brien more than made up for it, at least to me." "Miss O'Brien was a large woman, serious about education but kind and jolly." "She seemed to take a keen interest in me and, from time to time, gave me all sorts of books to read, such as the writings of one William Shakespeare, which I can recite."

"On occasion, I would sneak into the bookstore and read what I could, or Mr. McConnell would have some books that he let me read before he sold them." "I also got to go down to Hawken's gunsmith shop from time to time, and I helped Samuel Hawken with his French and Spanish customers." "For that, he let me stick around."

"When a mountain man came into his shop, I would always ask about my Pa." "The answer was always the same: he most likely didn't use his real name." "Most mountain men used mountain names, and mountain men didn't live long." "So, my Pa was probably dead."

"Some of the mountain men were friendly, such as Louie Surveon." "Mr. Surveon didn't speak English very well, but when he found out I could speak French and had a father who was a mountain man, he treated me well." "He and others showed me how to shoot the Hawken rifle, and I got very good at it." "I was such a good shooter I was allowed to take part in some of their shooting contests, and many times I beat them." "This relationship seemed to make them like me even more." "Before Mr. Surveon left, he said, "Young one, when you get older, you find me in those mountains your father went to, and I will show you how to be a really good mountain man." "That was the last time I ever saw him."

"The winter of my eighth birthday was the coldest and wettest in some time; it was also the year Mama got sick. It started with just a cough now and then, and Mama would use a home remedy she knew to take care of it. No one thought much about it, but it got worse when mama started to have a fever, and she was bedridden. Mr. McConnell said she might have winter fever or la grippe, and maybe both, there's just no telling. He said if my mother didn't get better by the next day, he would get a doctor. Then he made something that he said his mother used to make when someone in the family wasn't feeling well. It got made from whiskey, honey, and tea, all heated over a stove. Mr. McConnell gave Mama some and told me to give her some more when she needed it.

It was cold that night, so I filled the potbelly stove as much as I could and kept the fire fed, but it was still mighty cold. Mama was shivering a lot, so I threw my blanket on her. Then after a few hours, she would start sweating, and I would have to take the blanket off. Mama went on this way all night long while Mama was mumbling in her delirium. Once or twice, I thought she mumbled out the name Nathaniel, my Pa. I was getting fatigued, and I was cold. Sometimes, during the night, I crawled into Mama's bed, hoping we could stay warm, and I could fall asleep. I woke up early the next morning as the sun was just starting to come up, and right off, I knew something was wrong. I couldn't hear Mama making any noise nor breathing, and she was cold, so I turned slowly around, and Mama had a blue look to her. I jumped out of bed and stared for a few seconds trying to figure what I was seeing. Then, as I started crying, I yelled, "Mama," followed by, "Mr. McConnell come quickly." "I think there is something wrong with Mama."

I could hear the heavy footfalls of Mr. McConnell coming down the stairs and Sarah coming after him. He went over to Mama, then turned to us and shooed us out of the room. A few seconds later, he went out of the room, went over to the store counter, wrote a note, and gave it to me then; he said, "Go to the Sheriff's office and give it to them." "Shouldn't I go to the doctor's office?" I asked.

He sighed and said, "No, James do as I told you," so off I ran.

I didn't have to go far when I ran into Deputy Johnson. Mr. McConnell and I knew Deputy Johnson for the many times he had come into the store when some drunk riff-raft from the river came in and caused trouble. I told Deputy Johnson, "Mama is real sick, and I need you to come to the store right away," and I handed him the note.

After reading the note, he told me, "Go back to the store, and I will be there shortly," so I went back to the store. Mr. McConnell wouldn't let me go back in the room where Mama was, so I waited, and soon Deputy Johnson and another man came to the store. They went into Mama's room without even saying a word to me. When everyone came out of Mama's room, the man Deputy Johnson turned his head toward me and shook it as he walked out of the store. My heart started beating hard. Mr. McConnell took me by my arm and sat me down in a chair at the rear of the store, and he and Deputy Johnson started talking to me. Tears came running down my cheeks as they told me that Mama didn't suffer and was in a better place now. Sarah, by this time, came over crying also and held my hand.

Mr. McConnell said, "I will take care of James for now until you can figure out what you are going to do." That was alright with Deputy Johnson. Otherwise, he said I would have to go to the children's home or make my way in life by myself. Before Deputy Johnson left, he told Mr. McConnell and me, "I will send the undertaker for your mother."

After Deputy Johnson left, Mr. McConnell talked to me some more, "I know it's hard to answer some questions now, but I need to know something your mother has told me little about her."

I said, still in shock, "Alright." By this time, the crying was subsiding; I felt lost and alone.

"James, do you have any relatives that you know of?" asked Mr. McConnell.

"Mama said my Pa was in the Shining Mountains."

"'Yes, but are there any others?"

"Mama said I had an aunt and uncle somewhere in Pennsylvania." "They also had a son, but I don't know of anyone else."

"Do you know if your mother has any letters from your aunt or uncle?"

"I don't know, but if she did, they would be in my Mama's keepsake box."

"One more thing, you and your mother are Catholics, am I right?"

"We were some-what Catholic, but we hadn't practiced in that religion."

"You did fine, James." "I'll take care of everything you sit here until they come to get your mother."

The undertaker came about fifteen minutes later. He was a tall, thin melancholy-looking man dressed in black who looked like he was near death himself. He didn't say a word to me; he just asked Mr. McConnell, "Where's the body?"

Mr. McConnell pointed toward the room Mama was laying. Without another word, the undertaker went in with Mr. McConnell following him. I could hear the undertaker and Mr. McConnell talking. The Undertaker looked at Mama and asked without turning around, "Who is going to pay for this?"

Mr. McConnell retorted, "Don't worry about that I don't have a lot of money, but I will pay."

The undertaker turned around and stared at Mr. McConnell, and without saying a word went outside and came back with his assistant and a coffin that was just a wooden box. They put Mama in the coffin, and they weren't too gentle about it. Then they all took Mama out of the room.

I walked into the room and sat down on the bed and just stared out into space I was numb and in total shock, then the tears came again. I sat alone in that room for hours. Neither Sarah nor I went to school that day, and I had never been absent from school. Long about noon, Sarah came into the room with something for me to eat, but I couldn't eat, and it just sat there. She left the room and told her father, and Mr. McConnell came back into the room and said, "I understand how you're feeling you're grieving." "I went through the same thing when my wife died." "You need to keep busy, so come with me." "I'm going to close the store for a few hours so that we can make some arrangements for your mother."

Mr. McConnell, Sarah, and I headed to the Catholic Church, where they had a graveyard. Mr. McConnell approached the head priest by the name of Monsignor Charles Braille, a thin old man who looked mean. He was a Frenchman, and he had a strong accent but could speak English, so Mr. McConnell didn't need me to interpret for him. Mr. McConnell explained to him that he wasn't Catholic, but Mama and I were members and about Mama dying. Mr. McConnell said, "We need a place to bury the boy's mother; she just died this morning."

The priest looked up and down at Mr. McConnell with a frown and then looked at me and asked, "You and the boy got any money?"

"No, I'm just a poor merchant who barely makes enough for my daughter and me and now James."

"Likely story, I know who you are." "You are that merchant that has that miserable little store whose clientele are those lowlife mountain men, savages, and the other riff-raft of this miserable city."

"Sir, I am an honest man and will not be talked to that way!" "Now, do you have a place to bury this poor boy's mother or not?" "You can put her where they put the rest of the lowlifes over there." "As far as services, I'm accustomed to being paid." "Since you claim you don't have any money, Father Garcia will do them; he seems to like people like you, now good-by, sir." He turned and left with Mr. McConnell's mouth being left open in shock. I think we all were left shocked by the way we got mistreated.

Just as we started to go, another priest came forward. He said, "Excuse me, I'm Father Garcia, and I heard everything that Monsignor Braille said." "I wish to apologize for Monsignor Braille behavior." "He is a bitter old man who wanted to serve in a better parish where he could make a name for himself." "What he doesn't understand is we serve where God wants us to serve." Father Garcia was a Spaniard who also spoke with an accent. He was shorter than Monsignor Braille and much younger, and his demeanor was the opposite of the Monsignors. The good priest said to me, "Don't worry about that graveyard, God loves those righteous people who got buried there, and your mother would approve being there." "Remember, God favored the poor and called them brethren." Looking at all of us, he said, "You let me know when you want the services, and we will have a wonderful service." We left feeling a lot better than when we first came, and we headed back to the store.

Before entering the store, Mr. McConnell said, "We should go through your Mama's things." I felt it was too soon, but he said, "It's better to get it over with quickly, it will be easier that way."

We went into the store, but Mr. McConnell said, "We have to eat first."

I protested, but he said it wasn't a choice. "I can't afford you getting sick on me." So as difficult as it was, we all ate. My thoughts were of Mama, who could make the most meager food taste good, and my heart sank.

After lunch, we went through Mama's things. Every item reminded me of the good times we shared, even though we didn't have much. I was feeling mighty, depressed, and lost. Mr. McConnell must have noticed because he said, "The pain will pass James."

While we were going through Mama's things, school let out, and Miss O'Brien, being a good teacher, was concerned about Sarah and me being absent. So, knowing I had never missed school, she came to the store to see what the problem was and drop off the homework we missed. We heard the bell ring as someone came into the store and a woman's voice saying, "Hello." It was from Miss O'Brien.

Mr. McConnell got up and went to greet her. "Hello Miss O'Brien"

"Hello, Mr. McConnell I've come to find out if everything is alright with Sarah and James." "I missed them today, and I also brought the work they missed."

With a sad voice, Mr. McConnell said, "There has been a tragedy, Miss O'Brien." She looked confused, concerned, and puzzled, and Mr. McConnell took her by the arm guided her to the chairs in the back of the store.

I just stood there, and as the two talked, the tears came again to Sarah and me. When Mr. McConnell finished explaining what happened, her often-cheery demeanor had melted away. With teary eyes and a soft voice, she said, "What's going to happen to James?"

"For now, he is going to stay with me until I can find his relatives who were in Pennsylvania."

"And if you can't find them?" she asked in a concerned voice.

"Deputy Johnson said he must go to the children's home."

"That just won't do; he will get eaten up there," she stated in a shocked voice.

"I'd like to keep him here, but with the store and Sarah also the amount of money I have, the authorities will never let me."

"Yes, and a single female teacher would never be permitted," said Miss O'Brien.

"Miss O'Brien, would you mind helping me with James's mother's things?"

"Certainly, I'd be happy to." With tears coming down my face, Miss O'Brien came over to me and hugged me and said, "It will be alright." She then joined us in going through Mama's things. Miss O'Brien said, "I will donate the few clothes she had."

We found the letters from my uncle and aunt. Mr. McConnell asked if he could borrow them, and that was OK with me. There were a few dollars that Mama had saved that she earned from washing and sewing. I insisted that Mr. McConnell take it for expenses, and he humbly accepted.

I found a gold locket that Mama used to wear, but I hadn't seen it for a while. I looked inside the locket, and it had a lock of light brown hair, and I wondered if it was my Pa's hair. I kept the locket and placed it on my neck and the rest of the things, such as cooking and dining items, bedding, and some cheap jewelry that wasn't worth anything. Mr. McConnell said, "You should keep these things for a while."

I offered the jewelry to Miss O'Brien, but she said, "No, you keep it."

Miss O'Brien gave me another hug and took out her handkerchief and, with tears in her eyes, left the store. We packed away the rest of Mama's things except my blanket. Mr. McConnell said, "You will sleep upstairs with us."

I'd only gone upstairs a few times, and I got touched that he offered to share their living quarters with me. I was also relieved I don't think I could sleep in that room, knowing that Mama was gone.

Mr. McConnell kept me so busy I was exhausted before I went upstairs to bed. Upstairs, Mr. McConnell fixed something to eat, but I didn't eat much. I did my homework, but my heart wasn't in it. I helped Sarah as much as I could, and then it was time for bed. I was to sleep with Sarah, and I was a little uneasy about that. Since it was winter, I had a nightshirt on, and I loved Sarah, and besides, she was more like a sister, so I thought it would be alright. I removed my clothes and laid down next to Sarah, and in a few minutes, I was out.

The next morning, I got up early, before Mr. McConnell or Sarah got up. Mr. McConnell said, "You should keep busy, and you will feel better." I went downstairs and started to clean the store, and it seemed to help.

About an hour later, Mr. McConnell came down the stairs and said, "James, you have to get ready for school. Come upstairs and get cleaned up so you can eat something before you and Sarah go."

I protested and said, "But what about Mama?"

"I'll take care of your mother's affairs; she wouldn't want you to miss any more school than you have."

I reluctantly did as he told me and went upstairs. Sarah was already dressed and eating, so I washed and sat down beside her.

We left for school, and just before we started to go inside the school building, I spotted Jack Flynn with a smirk on his face next to the entrance, and I knew there was going to be trouble, and I wasn't in the mood for it. I started to approach him when he commented, "First a bastard and now an orphan," and then he laughed.

I hung my head down and didn't say a word, but I kept walking. But Jack wasn't going to let me get away without a response. It was my turn for him to pick on, and he was taking great pleasure in taunting me. As I walked past him, he said, "It's just as well your mother is dead; she was just a disease infected whore."

I stopped in my tracks, and Sarah, with her big green eyes, looked up at me. I told her, "Take my lunch and schoolwork and go into the building."

Without a word, she did what I told her, looking back as she went. I was enraged and wasn't thinking very well when I turned around and approached Jack, who was laughing. Without saying a word, I took a swing at Jack and hit him in the nose. At first, nothing happened when I hit Jack, his head moved a little, and he stopped laughing but nothing else, then I saw a trickle of blood.

Jack's confusion at just what happened wore off quickly. He turned beet red and said, "I'll teach you!" He swung and hit me in the head, and it felt like I got hit with a fence post, and I went down. As I laid on the ground in a daze, Jack came after me like a raging bull.

Before Jack could finish his assault on me at the foot of the school's stairs, stood Miss O'Brien and, apparently, the whole school, "Jack, if you touch James, you must deal with me," said Miss O'Brien.

Sarah had run up to Miss O'Brien after she first went in and yelled with tears, "Come quickly, Jack's going to kill James!"

Jack stared at her for a few seconds, then laughed. He walked past her as if nothing happened and went into the classroom. Miss O'Brien came over to me and picked me up and asked, "Are you alright?"

I said, "Yes, but I have a headache, but it will pass." I went into the classroom; Jack was laughing under his breath. I just glanced at him and went to my seat. I had a knot on the side of my head that was turning into a bruise. The knot was near enough to my eye that it was turning black.

Jack didn't bother me the rest of the day; I guess he ran out of names to call or insult me. When I got back home, Mr. McConnell shook his head and said, "That boy is going to end up either dead or locked up somewhere for a long time."

At supper, Mr. McConnell told me Mama's services would be in two days, and I needed to let Miss O'Brien know, so she doesn't get worried when Sarah and I are not there.

The next day Jack was getting his fun by picking on someone else. I went into the classroom before the class to let Miss O'Brien know about the services.

Back in my seat, the class started, and Miss O'Brien said she had an announcement. She said, "Friday, there would be no school." "You have that day to pay your respects at the services of Mary von Muller, James' mother, if you wish." "They will be at the Catholic Church at one pm, followed by graveside services." I don't know why, but when she made the announcement, I held my head low, and I was quiet, and I kept to myself all day.

Friday came, and I didn't have anything nice to wear, but Mr. McConnell washed my clothing and mended the few holes I had. I cleaned up as well as I could and combed my hair, and I happened to be downstairs while Sarah bathed. When she and Mr. McConnell came downstairs, they looked like they were going to some fancy doings. I didn't know who would show up beside me, Sarah, Mr. McConnell, the priest, some nuns, and maybe Miss O'Brien.

When we got to the church, there were a lot of people there. Many children from my classroom and their parents, even Jack was there, although he looked and smelled the same. He stayed in the back of the church, where he wasn't causing trouble. Mr. Cooper, a mountain man I knew, showed up and brought some of his mountain men friends with him a couple I recognized. Deputy Johnson and his wife were there. Also, there were many customers of Mr. McConnell's store and even those whom Mama washed and mended clothes for them. It made me happy that so many people cared about Mama, the church got filled with people. While the services were going on, I saw Monsignor Braille with his mouth open and a shocked look on his face when he saw how many people were in the church. After the first service, Sarah, Mr. McConnell, and I got to go up first and view my Mama. I immediately started crying, and I felt Sarah's hand in mine while Mr. McConnell put his arm around me. Then Sarah began to cry, and I also saw many others in the church were using their handkerchiefs. We finally sat down, and the rest of the people came up to view Mama, and I even saw Jack coming up the side of the church and look. After the church services, we all went out to the graveyard. I got told to pick who I wanted to take Mama out to the graveyard. I chose Deputy Johnson, Mr. Cooper, and two mountain men because of my Pa; the rest were parents of those in my class. We all met at the gravesite, the priest prayed, the people sang a song, and then Mama was lowered into the ground. Many people threw flowers into the grave just before they left. When everyone was gone, but Sarah, Mr. McConnell, Miss O'Brien, the gravedigger, and I Jack, who was hiding behind a tree, came up to the grave. Without a word, he looked at all of us, threw some flowers into the grave, and ran off. I found out later that he stole the flowers from another grave.

The grave diggers filled in the grave, and Mr. McConnell put a wooden grave marker at the head of the grave. The wood marker read, "Miss Mary von Muller born June 12, 1798, died February 7, 1823, Wonderful Mother Now A Daughter of God, Rest in Peace." It got done with white letters, and the lettering was well crafted. Then Mr. McConnell put lacquer over everything and waxed the whole marker. He said it would last a very long time that way.

I thanked him and said, "Someday, I will come back and put up a stone marker." I didn't want to leave the gravesite for a while.

Mr. McConnell said, "Don't stay too long. Come back to the store when you are finished." They all left, and I was left alone, crying and drowning in my sorrows.

The next few days, Mr. McConnell kept me busy, but I never missed, a day, going to Mama's grave. Jack left me alone at school. He didn't turn over a new leaf; he just took his fun out on other children. I caught him staring at me a few times, but he never said anything to me.

What Monsignor Braille said about the store must have bothered Mr. McConnell. He started ordering things he usually didn't carry, such as perfume as well as both men's and women's fancy hats. Mr. McConnell even ordered men's and women's fancy outfits and what the mountain men called foofaraw, which is cheap jewelry and things. He stored it in the room where Mama and I slept. I thought it was foolish for him to order these things, but I didn't say anything.

It was getting on to March, and the pain of Mama's death wasn't as bad as those first days. I was getting used to sleeping with Sarah; in fact, I liked it. We were all upstairs; I had just finished washing the dishes and things when Mr. McConnell pulled out the washtub that he and Sarah bathed. He had filled the tub with warm water turned to me and said, "You haven't had a bath for more than a month, and you are starting to stink." Then he said, "Take off your clothes and get into the water."

"In front of Sarah?" I asked.

"Sarah has seen me take a bath many times, and you very well know she is more like a sister to you than a stranger, and besides, you are just a little boy," Mr. McConnell said sternly. "Now, take off your clothes, or I will!"

I knew I wasn't going to win, and he was right; I did smell. I knew this would happen sooner or later, so slowly, I started to take off my clothes. Sarah sat across from me, giggling, and I gave her a dirty look. She stopped but still had a smile on her face. Mr. McConnell gave me some soap, and I started to wash, but I guess I wasn't doing a very good job because Mr. McConnell began to bath me. I didn't mind it at all; in fact, I enjoyed it. Mama used to wash me too, and after a few minutes, I wasn't thinking about Sarah at all. I finished my bath and got out, and Mr. McConnell dried me off then told me to hop into bed, and he said he was going to wash my nightshirt.

I did as he said, and Sarah started over to the bed giggling again, but it did not last long when Mr. McConnell said, "Sarah, it's your turn."

She protested, but her father wasn't budging, so she tried crying, but that didn't work either. As her clothes got removed, of course, I had a big smile on my face. As she finished her bath, as with me, Mr. McConnell had her go to bed with nothing on so that he could clean her nightclothes, also. Mr. McConnell tucked Sarah in on her side of the bed and kissed her as he does every night, and then to my surprise, he came over to my side and did the same. Mr. McConnell lowered the light and started to wash our night things.

Sarah's hands began to wander over me, and I brushed them away and soon fell asleep. When I woke later that night, she was cuddled next to me with her arm around me, seeing no harm in it I let her and fell back to sleep.

The following weeks I became closer and closer to Sarah and Mr. McConnell not that I already wasn't, but they seemed more like family now. At school, Jack still hadn't bothered me for several weeks, but that all ended by the end of April. I was eating lunch with Sarah when Jack came up to us and said to one of his friends, "I'm hungry; it's time for me to do some shopping." When he said this, he grabbed the sandwich out of my hands and then rifled through my lunch pail.

I tried to protest, but he backhanded me and said, "Look, you waif bastard if you want worse just give me more trouble."

I didn't say anything, and he left laughing. Sarah offered a part of her lunch, but I said it was alright I won't starve, and it was back to normal for Jack for the rest of the school year.

Miss O'Brien would often come over to the store to check up on Sarah and me and bring things such as a book, cooked food, or a bit of clothing.

It was June, and the school hadn't been out but a few days when Mr. McConnell got a letter from my Uncle Henry. Miss O'Brien was there, and Mr. McConnell opened it and read it. It was short and to the point. It said, "If it weren't for unforeseen circumstances, I would have never considered inquiring about my late sister's illegitimate child. My sister was nothing but a trollop, but since I need him, have him ready, I will be there in a few weeks." Henry Muller signed it. Everybody was shocked by the tone of that letter, and we just stared at it for a few seconds.

Then Mr. McConnell said, "I think I made a mistake sending a letter to him."

"You couldn't have known," said Miss O'Brien.

"I don't want to go with him," I said.

"I have to think about what I am going to do."

"I know I'll talk to Deputy Johnson." "Maybe there is something in the law that will help." Before anybody could say anything out the door, he went.

Miss O'Brien said, "Everything is going to be alright; you will see."

Miss O'Brien stayed in the store, fixing Sarah's clothes while Mr. McConnell was gone. About an hour later, Mr. McConnell came back from seeing Deputy Johnson. His head was down; the sadness on his face told the whole story. Miss O'Brien gasped, and Sarah looked confused as to what was happening.

I just stood there, with my eyes tearing up I didn't want to leave Mr. McConnell and Sarah. Mr. McConnell began to talk in a defeated voice. "I spoke to Deputy Johnson, and he took me to an expert in law that he knew, and I got told that James's uncle has all the power under the law. "I can do nothing, I'm sorry."

I ran out of the store and down to Mama's grave and wept for hours. For the following days, my mood was sullen, as were Sarah's and Mr. McConnell's. I felt like a condemned prisoner waiting for the time.

# 2

# THE LOSS OF INNOCENCE

I was sweeping out the store when a big covered wagon came to the front of the store. I stuck my head into the store and told Mr. McConnell we had customers. He came out to greet them, not thinking who they were. A short, portly man with blond hair, a scowl on his face, and wearing what look like going to church clothes stepped off the wagon and walked to the back without speaking a word. He opened the back of the wagon and pulled a box out of the back and placed it on the ground, and then helped a lady out, and I think a boy. The woman was plump with brown hair, and she had a scowl on her face. She was complaining about how uncomfortable she was. She had a large, dark, silky dress that looked like the one the rich ladies in St. Louis wore. The boy, if he was a boy, looked younger than me. He was fat and had light brown, almost blond hair, and it looked like someone had put curls in his hair like I saw many girls have. I wouldn't have been caught dead in his clothing. It had a lot of frills, and his pants were short with high stockings. They approached Mr. McConnell, and the man said, "I'm Henry Muller; is this the vulgar bastard my sister spawned?" pointing to me.

"Sir, I do not like the language or the tone of what you are saying," said Mr. McConnell.

"I don't care what you like is this the boy or not?"

"He's Mary's child, James, and he is a good boy."

"Go get your things; we will be going in less than an hour after my wife and son get some rest." Mr. McConnell tried to be pleasant to my uncle by inviting him into the store and giving him and his family some refreshments which my uncle accepted. Mr. McConnell sent me to fix some tea for the adults and lemonade for his son and Sarah. I wasn't in the mood for anything. Mr. McConnell asked, "Are you going back to Pennsylvania, or are you going to live somewhere else?"

Shaking his head, he said with disgust, "I'm not going back to Pennsylvania." "I lost the family farm beside the land isn't much good anymore." He looked up from his tea and said in an unconvincing voice, "I got swindled." Mama had told me the truth about the farm. He was losing the farm because he was inept. That is why she left the farm. Mama tried to tell my grandfather that my uncle was incompetent and that he would ruin the farm, but all she got was the back of his hand across her face and the scorn of my uncle.

"Then, where are you going?" asked Mr. McConnell.

"I heard that the soil in the Oregon Territory is as black as tar, and you could grow a tree from an ax handle." "I also heard they are giving land away, a thousand acres per person." "That means with my late sister's bastard; I will get four thousand acres."

"The boy has a name, Mr. Muller."

"Yes, I suppose he does," he answered. "He not only will be useful for me in acquiring another thousand acres but also to help me till the land."

"But Mr. Muller, he has a great mind far beyond his age." "He could become a great man."

"Nonsense!" "He has no breeding; he is what he is."

Mr. McConnell whispered to Sarah, "Go get Miss O'Brien," and she took off. He then turned to my uncle again and said, "The Oregon Territory is very far from here, much farther than the distance you just traveled." "It has many dangers along the way Indians, animals, lack of water." "Then, there are the Shining Mountains." "You will need proper supplies."

"I have all the supplies I need." "As for those savages and wild animals, I have a rifle for them."

I finally said something. "Those horses you have attached to the wagon won't make it over the Shining Mountains, you need mules or oxen, so some mountain men told me."

"I don't listen to eight-year-old boys or lowlife mountain men," my uncle said in an annoyed voice.

Just about this time, Miss O'Brien came into the store. After introductions and an update as to where I was going, she repeated what got said earlier, "James is very intelligent far beyond most people." "It would be a total waste taking him to the wilderness."

"Madam, as I said before, I can care less about that boy's intelligence he's coming with me." "Get your things now if you have anything we are leaving now."

"But what about Mama's grave don't you want to pay your respects?"

"I can care less about your mother." "Let's go now," he growled.

"Come on, James, lets' get your things," Mr. McConnell said sadly.

As I got my things, Uncle Henry said, "What's all this it looks like junk to me."

I thought quickly and said sadly, "All this can get used for trade with the Indians and the other things I need to keep warm."

"Very well, put them in the wagon quickly I want to get out of here."

With the help of Mr. McConnell, I brought my things to the back of the wagon. Before I could put them in my aunt, Margaret said, "My precious Milford and I go first."

Uncle Henry helped them up. As he did, I gave Sarah some of Mama's jewelry, and then I started into the back of the wagon when I got stopped. Aunt Margaret said, "You are not allowed in this wagon." "Put your things in and go climb up in the front."

As I put my things in the wagon, Sarah and Miss O'Brien were crying. I felt like crying but held it back. I gave Miss O'Brien, Mr. McConnell, and Sarah, a hug and a kiss and climbed onto the wagon. My uncle climbed up and grabbed the reins, and off we went. As we moved up the street, I looked back and saw them waving at me, I waved back and saw Mr. McConnell pull out his handkerchief. I turned forward before the dam in my eyes burst; then, I held my head down, trying to control my emotions.

When the store faded from sight, my uncle said sarcastically, "I'm glad to be away from those reprobates."

I didn't say anything. I felt my uncle was too bullheaded to change his ways, and besides, I was afraid I'd get backhanded.

We traveled for many hours when we were a few miles away from Saint Louis; we found a spot to camp. I thought it was a bit early, but I wasn't going to say anything. I think my uncle was one of those people who had to learn the hard way. I got off the wagon, and my uncle said, "Remove the harness from the horses."

"I don't know much about horses and especially a horse's harness," I said.

He said, shocked, and with a bit of anger, "What?" "You live out here in the wilderness, and you don't know anything about horses?"

I said, "I didn't have any reason to learn; we didn't have a horse."

"Come over here and watch carefully." "I better not have to show you again," My uncle said harshly.

He told me to gather some wood and make a fire after he finished removing the harness from the horses. I could do that, but I had to get the flint and a knife from him. Then he told me to take the bucket and give the horses some water. I did this also while my uncle cooked. My aunt and cousin never came out of the wagon, and my uncle fed them and himself first in the wagon. I ate alone, and because my cousin ate a lot, I didn't get a lot to eat, but it was just as well it didn't taste very good.

After we ate, my uncle came out of the wagon and gave me all the plates, utensils, and everything he used to cook with then he told me to clean them. I sighed and did them without complaint.

When my uncle saw everything got done, he crawled back into the wagon, threw out my bedding, and told me to find a place to sleep away from the wagon. I laid my bedding out on the ground and wrapped a blanket around me. I didn't mind it very much I was used to lying on the floor, and I preferred to be away from them.

I could hear my uncle and aunt talking. I knew it was about me, but I didn't know just what and didn't care. Before I knew it, I drifted off to sleep.

I woke up about an hour before sunlight, and I gathered wood for a fire, figuring that's what my uncle would want. I waited well past an hour after sunrise, but no one seemed to stir. There was nothing for me to do but wait, and finally, my uncle came out of the wagon. He was about to tell me to get some wood when he saw I had already done it.

"Give some water to the horses while I fix breakfast and then harness them." "You do know how to harness them, don't you?"

"Yes, I think I can manage," I said, then I ran off to do as he spoke.

By the time I finished, my aunt, uncle, and cousin had finished eating, and he said, "Clean everything."

"Is there anything left for me?"

"No, my son said he was still hungry, and I gave him the rest."

I was mad and hungry, but again I didn't say anything. I cleaned everything, packed it away, rolled my bedding, and went to put it in the wagon. I went to throw it in the back, but every time I did, my cousin would push it out. I could hear my aunt giggling as Milford did this. My uncle got impatient and came back to see what the delay was and said, "Get on the wagon."

"Not until Milford lets me put my bedding up." He backhanded me a good one in the face, grabbed my bedding, and started to throw it in the back. Milford was up to his old tricks and began to do the same thing but stopped when he saw it was his Pa.

Then gruffly, he grabbed my arm and said, "Come with me." When we got to the front of the wagon, he shook me and said, "If you ever become unruly with your aunt or me again, I'll give you a beating you won't forget, now get up there!"

I didn't say a word, and after we had traveled for about three or four hours, we finally stopped. "Give the horses some water, but don't remove the harness." My uncle went to the back of the wagon and opened it up and let my aunt and cousin out. They had been complaining about being cooped up in the wagon too long and needed to stretch out their legs.

I gave the horses some water and joined my uncle. He gave me something that tasted like pork and a hard biscuit. It wasn't much, but I eagerly ate every crumb, I was starving. Milford was whining he wanted more, and my aunt said, "Henry get our precious more to eat." "We mustn't let him waste away."

Little chance that would happen, I thought as I drank some water to wash down the food.

My uncle went into the wagon and got some more and said, "We need to take it easy on the food."

As Milford ate, he looked at me with a smug smile on his face. I turned around and went over to a bush and relieved myself.

My uncle yelled at me, "James come over here." I went to the back of the wagon, and he handed me a chamber pot and said, "Clean it." I turned up my nose and held it out away from me. I tossed the contents behind a bush, went, and got a bucket of water to finish the job. My aunt and cousin were laughing, I'm sure at me, but I ignored them.

We rode another three or four hours when we came to a spring, and we camped there. I got told to water the horses in the spring, fill the water barrels, and get some wood, which I did. I felt sorry for the horses because they weren't getting a lot to eat. I tied a long rope to two trees and another rope to each of the horses so that rope could slide up and down the main rope, and the horses could get plenty to eat.

My uncle asked, "What are you doing there?"

I explained it to him, and he expressed himself with a surprised look and said "Smart" and walked away.

That night I got a satisfying amount of food. However, it didn't fill me Milford made sure of that, but it was satisfactory. Knowing there would be mosquitoes near the spring, I laid my bedding away from there. As I lay on the ground, I started to chuckle; I knew my uncle, aunt, and cousin were going to be all eaten up by those mosquitoes. As I said before, they must learn the hard way, they were too bullheaded to listen to me, and they should know better.

I started to think about Mama and who would take care of her grave, and Mr. McConnell, Sarah, and Miss O'Brien. I began to cry until I finally felled asleep.

I woke up later that night when everybody was asleep in the wagon, and I had to relieve myself again. But it wasn't the same as going in the bushes if you know what I mean. I walked down from the spring and away from the camp. Most of the horses were sleeping on the ground as I passed them. It was one of those warm nights I always enjoyed. I found a good spot and dropped my trousers and squatted, and relieved myself. As I was squatting there, I thought it would be a good time to bathe. So, after I had finished, I took off the rest of my clothing and jumped into the spring water. The first thing I felt was like being punctured by a million needles. The little bit of manhood I had disappeared inside of me, but, overall, it felt great. Swimming bare bottom was something I never did in Saint Louis, and I hoped to get the opportunity again.

When I finally got out, I laid on the grassy bank to dry off a bit. I started to think about the first time I had to bathe in front of Sarah and how embarrassed I was initially, and the thought made me giggle. I don't think I could take my clothes off in front of anyone else again, other than Mama, Mr. McConnell, and Sarah. So, I must bathe in private when I get the next opportunity. I got dressed and went back to my bedroll and drifted back to sleep.

The sun on my face is what woke me up, and I put on my shoes and gathered some wood. My hair hadn't dried, but it was warm, and I knew my hair would soon dry. Soon after I gathered the wood, my uncle tumbled out of the wagon's back, followed by my aunt and cousin. Uncle Henry asked, "Why is your hair wet?"

"I took a bath this morning."

"We all could use a bath," my uncle said to my aunt and cousin.

"I'm certainly not going to bathe in the spring," said Aunt Margaret.

"Frankly, Margaret, it's up to you, but it's a long way to the Oregon Territory, and you are going to get mighty dirty." "You better think about it," Uncle Henry said.

Uncle Henry turned to Milford and said, "Your mother might not take a bath, but you're going to take one."

"I don't want a bath; do I have to Mama?" Milford asked, whining.

Before Aunt Margaret could answer, Uncle Henry, said, "Yes, you do!" He took him by the arm and told me, "Where did you bathe?"

"Just up from the spring, do you want me to take you?"

"Yes," Uncle Henry answered.

So, we went back to the place I bathed, Milford whining all the way. When we got there, I asked Uncle Henry if he wanted me to leave. He said, "No, you stay here." Uncle Henry started to take Milford's clothes off. Milford complained all the way, saying he didn't want to get undressed in front of me. After Milford was stripped and trying to hide his nakedness, Uncle Henry stripped. To me, Milford and Uncle Henry seem extremely overweight my uncle and Milford having rolls of fat on them. He wasn't as hairy as Mr. McConnell, and Mr. McConnell didn't have the rolls of fat that my uncle had, Mr. McConnell had a lot more muscle. They both jumped into the water, and I started chuckling. I didn't tell them how cold the water was, and the results were predictable; they both screamed, and Milford tried to run out, but Uncle Henry stopped him. To my surprise, Milford couldn't swim, so Uncle Henry had to hold on to him. They weren't in very long when they decided to get out. Uncle Henry asked, "How did you dry yourself?"

I pointed to the patch of grass and said, "I laid there."

"You could have told me how cold it was I should beat you for that."

"It wasn't bad for me; I'm used to it, I guess."

He looked at me with unbelieving eyes but said no more. Uncle Henry got dressed and then dressed Milford like he was a baby, and we started back to camp. When we got to camp, Aunt Margaret had changed her mind and said she would bathe. I looked at Uncle Henry, but he didn't tell Aunt Margaret how cold it was. Uncle Henry told me, "You stay here with Milford and hook up the horses."

As he left, he had the first smile I'd seen on him. I got the first horse hooked up as Milford looked on, and when I started the second one, I heard the scream coming from up above the spring. It startled both

Milford and me, but I knew what it was, and I began to laugh. Milford asked, "What do you think the screaming is all about."

"Ask your mother when she gets back," I said with a smile on my face.

I got the horses hooked up, and everything packed away when my aunt and uncle came back, my aunt was madder than a wet hen. We had started late, but at least we were moving. About fifteen minutes after leaving, I heard Aunt Margaret say, "What?" in an enraged voice. She stuck her head out of the wagon and said, "You think a mongrel like you has a right to laugh at me, I'll get even with you, you mark my words." And then she went back into the wagon. Uncle Henry had a smile on his face, the second one I'd seen.

I leaned back on my seat and asked my uncle, "Why did you ask me to stay while you and Milford bathed?"

"Milford was going to have to get used to you being around." "It was better for him to quickly get over his bashfulness than a struggle over it later and you, too." "I'm not bashful except for maybe girls."

"I suppose you're right," he replied

For the next few hours, we rode in silence. We didn't stop for a noon break, and I knew it was hard for the horses. If he kept treating the horses the way he did, I don't think the horses would make it. Aunt Margaret gave Uncle Henry something to eat, but I got nothing. That didn't go unnoticed with Uncle Henry, and he said, "Margaret, give the boy something."

"I won't give him anything you get him something if you want him to eat."

Uncle Henry looked at me and said, "I don't suppose you know how to drive a wagon."

"I think if you show me, I could manage it."

"Hold the reins just like this."

I grabbed the reins, and my uncle said, "You pull to the right; the horses will go right; you pull left, and they will go left."

He then went into the wagon, and an argument started. But he came out with some food for me, and he took the reins, and I took the food.

The sun was starting to set when we finally stopped, it wasn't the best of places, but I didn't care. I told my uncle before he told me I would take care of the horses and get the wood, and he nodded. I got everything done and even got the fire going. I could see my uncle was tired, so I helped with the cooking; in fact, I did most of the cooking. When I finished, I was dead tired, but the food did taste better, and I did get enough to eat. After cleaning up, I rolled out my bedroll, laid down, and I was fast asleep.

The next morning, I had to empty the chamber pot and clean it. That's one chore I didn't like doing. We left early Aunt Margaret, and Milford didn't say a word to me, and my uncle wasn't very talkative either. About an hour after we left, Uncle Henry handed me the reins and said, "You drive." From that point on, I did more and more of the driving. And since that morning that I cooked, that became another chore I took on, but I did get to eat at least.

We finally got to the Missouri River and the town of Independence, where Uncle Henry was to get some supplies. Uncle Henry, Aunt Margaret, and Milford all went into the store. I had to stay with the wagon and horses. After a time, my relatives came out of the store arguing with the store's owner about how crooked he was to charge him outrageous prices. Then, Uncle Henry said he was a common thief. The shame was he could have gotten the same supplies a lot cheaper in Saint Louis than Independence. But as I said he had to learn the hard way, you can't tell him anything. The store owner said, "You can take your business elsewhere if you wish."

We left and followed the Missouri River west for about three hours before we stopped. I put up the horses and started dinner as I was doing this, I could hear Milford ask his father, "How much further do we have to go?"

"Yes, Henry, how much further do we have to go?" asked my aunt.

"I'm not sure, but I think it's a lot more miles."

I spoke up and said, "We aren't out of Missouri yet."

They all stared at me for a few seconds, and then Aunt Margaret said, "How would you know, have you ever been west?"

"No, but I've read a lot also talked to a lot of mountain men and the Mandan's about it." "You know you are out of Missouri when you reach the Platte River." "There is a westward bend in the Missouri River just before the Platte, and you should also see the grasslands. We should run into some Mandan soon after leaving Missouri though I don't know quite where."

"Who are the Mandan?" Aunt Margaret asked.

"They are an Indian tribe that lives along the river."

My uncle asked, "Are those savages hostile?"

"They can be, mountain men told me, but they want to live their lives as they see fit." "If we meet up with them, they will most likely just want to trade," I said.

"Nonsense, he doesn't know what he is talking about," Aunt Margaret said.

"No, I think he is right." "That book I read confirms some of what he is saying," stated my Uncle.

Milford wasn't interested in anything that was getting said. He was just interested in what I was cooking and if it was ready to eat. I let them all know the food is ready to eat, and before I could get anything, they pushed me out of the way and served themselves. I finally got my plate and ate by myself as usual, and it was just as well I was afraid Milford might take some food off my plate.

Aunt Margaret and Uncle Henry were discussing the trip as I was eating. My Uncle Henry asked, "When do you think we will be out of this miserable state of Missouri?"

"If we leave early, maybe by sundown tomorrow," I responded. I just didn't know my aunt was right about that I'd never been there before. I added, "Certainly, when we get to the bend in the river, we will know for sure."

My uncle got up early the next day. I was getting wood, but he told me, "Don't worry about a fire we will have breakfast on the trail." "We will be leaving imminently." So, I dropped the wood and got the horses hooked up. Milford and Aunt Margaret were complaining that they needed something to eat. Uncle Henry told them they would have to eat whatever we had on the trail. They both groaned but accepted what he said, and off we went. I didn't get anything to eat, nor did my uncle, but I could hear rummaging in the wagon, so I am sure my aunt and cousin ate.

We stopped sometime in the afternoon and let the horses drink and rest. My uncle went into the wagon and, in a few minutes, had some cheese, dried fruit, and meat, which he shared with me. I sat on the ground and started eating; I was starving. I placed the dried fruit beside me and begun to devour the meat and cheese when Milford walked by and grabbed my dried fruit. I yelled at him, "That's mine!" "Give it back!" He laughed and tried to run off, but I reached out and grabbed his foot. Milford tripped and fell, and he started screaming and crying so much you'd think he was dying or something.

Aunt Margaret saw the whole thing and took Milford's side, and she came over and started hitting me in the head. I put my arms up to protect myself, and I tried to getaway. Before I was successful, Uncle Henry came at me like a raging angry bull. He hit me in the face several times, and I could feel blood dripping from my nose and taste blood in my mouth. I was about to pass out when Uncle Henry grabbed my hair and pulled me up. He then pulled off my trousers and started to beat my bottom. The pain was unbearable, and after he hit me a few more times in the face, I passed out. All this time, while this was happening, Aunt Margaret and Milford were laughing.

I don't know how long I was unconscious, but when I woke, we were moving on the trail while I remained curled up next to my uncle, who was driving the team of horses. There was no question in my mind that you didn't need to be a doctor to know my uncle nearly killed me. I tried to sit up, but as I straightened up, I got dizzy again and passed out.

When I woke up the next time, it was dark out, and I was next to a tree, and my bedroll was next to me. I couldn't see very well, but by the light of the fire, I could make out my uncle, aunt, and cousin eating. My uncle and aunt were making small talk of some kind, and Milford was stuffing his face. They had no concern for me. They made my life miserable, and as I sat there, I knew I was going to run off at the first opportunity and maybe find my father if I got lucky. I sat there and watched them finish eating; of course, they brought nothing over to me. It's just as well I probably couldn't eat anyway, and I didn't want them near me. They finally retired to the inside of the wagon, and the light inside was extinguished. I wanted to cry, but it hurt a lot, and as I lay there in the dark, I could hear the river nearby. So, after about an hour when I figured they were asleep, I crawled toward the sound. Every inch of my body was hurting, but I made it. I took off all my clothing and went into the water. It wasn't as cold as the spring; however, it was cold, but it sure felt good. I washed off the blood and just sat in the cold water for about an hour then I crawled out of the water and laid on the bank and fell asleep.

Sometime later that night, I woke up and tried to stand. I wobbled a little but could stand, so I stumbled back to my bedroll and lay down again and went back to sleep.

I woke, and it was light, so I got up and started to gather wood for a fire. I found some berries, and I stuffed my mouth with them. When I got back to camp with the wood, I found my uncle's flint and knife, and I started the fire. Nothing got cleaned last night, so I started cleaning things. There were scraps left, and I ate them while I was cleaning. I watered the horses, and while I was watering the horses, I looked at my reflection in the water. My face was swollen and was black and blue. I went back to camp, and after tying up the horses, I sat down beside my bedroll and leaned back on a tree. As I sat there, I swore I would never allow someone to do that to me again.

About an hour later, my uncle came out of the wagon. He saw everything done, and then he looked at me. He went inside the wagon and got some food supplies and put them in the box. Then he came over to me and said, "If you're capable of doing those chores, then you're capable of fixing breakfast."

I stared at him without saying a word, then got up and went over to the fire to cook. When my uncle wasn't looking, I spat into the food and took satisfaction in it. I got just about finished cooking when Milford and his mother came out. Milford took one look at me and started laughing. I turned around, and with a mean look on my face took a step toward him. He stopped laughing and jumped back to his mother.

Before they could say anything, Uncle Henry said, "Shut up, Milford, and leave him alone."

I finished the food and went back to my bedroll without saying a word. When my relatives finished eating, and I cleaned everything up. I went over and rolled up my bedroll and threw my bedroll in the back of the wagon. I went over and hooked up the horses and got up in front next to my uncle, exhausted and hurting. My uncle took the reins and drove off. I sat back, not talking but thinking of my loved ones back in Saint Louis. As my uncle drove on, I could tell we weren't in Missouri anymore. My heart was hurting just as much as my body the further away from Saint Louis we got.

By noon the next day, we came to the fork of the Platte and Missouri Rivers. We stopped to water and rested the horses and then had something to eat. I still wasn't talking to anyone, and I walked off a little to get away from the others. The landscape had changed a lot instead of trees, brush, and rolling hills; it had given way to a flat sea of green grass with the bluest skies I've ever seen. I was grateful that the swelling around my eyes had gone down enough for me to see the landscape. We headed down a trail that followed the Platte River. I thought we should have followed the Missouri River, but maybe I was wrong because we were going west.

We made camp at dusk, and Uncle Henry said to me, "Keep the horses near the wagon."

Aunt Margaret interjected, "Do you have to Henry, those horses smell unbearable."

"Savages might steal them." Then Uncle Henry turned toward me and continued to talk to me, "Do you know how to shoot a rifle?"

I said, "Yes."

He continued, "We will post a guard." "I will take the first watch." "So, after we eat and you clean up, you better get some sleep." We started the fire by using some wood we brought with us and later I went to bed. I got awakened sometime during the night and handed the rifle. It was an old English flintlock more of a squirrel gun than anything else; it wasn't very good. I was kind of scared; I didn't know what to expect. About after a half-hour, I started thinking there would only be Mandan around here, and most of the time, they aren't hostile, so I relaxed a bit. My uncle was right. I figured they might not be hostile, but they might come in the night and try to steal a horse or two.

When the sun came up, I put the rest of the wood into a pile to start a fire and waited until my uncle rose. The sky shone with white cottony clouds by the time my uncle arose. He looked up at the sky and said, "Forget the fire and pack the wood, then hook up the horses we'll eat on the trail."

"No, Henry, Milford and I are hungry," my aunt said, complaining, as usual.

"It's going to rain, and I don't want to get caught in these flatlands next to the river," he replied. That's just what I was thinking, so we headed out, and sure enough, the rains came the river did rise, but we were high enough to be safe. As my uncle and I were getting soaked, he handed me the reins and said, "No need both of us getting wet." He then went inside the wagon to get out of the rain and dry off. I just sat there driving the team of horses, thinking I'm no better off than those black slaves back in Missouri. It made me tear up and reinforced my determination to take off the first chance I got.

As fast as the rains came, they left, but I got still soaked to the bone, and my long yellow hair smelled like a wet dog. We made camp that night after skipping lunch and riding through the noon break. After I finished cooking and cleaning everything, I found the driest place I could to lay down my bedroll. My uncle took the first watch, so I waited until everyone else had gone into the wagon. I found a spot up the river to strip my wet clothing out of sight of the camp, and I took a bath. When I finished, I started to put my clothes back on. However, they were still wet, so I crept back to camp and saw my uncle was sitting on the wagon smoking, which was some distance from where I was. He wasn't paying attention to me anyway. So, I laid my wet clothes on some rocks and wrapped up in my blankets and fell asleep.

I got awakened by a kick on my foot. My uncle said, pointing to my clothing, "Put on your clothes, it's your watch." He stood there waiting, and I was kind of embarrassed to get up without anything on, but he wasn't going away. I was afraid I'd get a beating if I didn't get up, so I turned my back to him, got up, and dressed quickly. He handed me the rifle and, without another word, went to the wagon.

The next morning, I used the last of the wood cooking breakfast. No one said anything about it, so I kept my mouth shut. We traveled for about an hour when I spotted two Indians on horseback looking at us, so I brought it to the attention of my uncle. He grabbed his rifle and told my aunt and cousin to stay low in the wagon. As the two riders approached us, I saw my uncle was getting nervous and was about to raise his rifle, so I said, "They may be friendly; they may just want to trade."

"Why would you say that?"

"They are not coming at us fast, and the weapons aren't armed, and besides, they have no paint on."

"You're right; I've read something about the painted faces of savages." "We will see what they want."

We stopped the wagon, and Aunt Margaret stuck her head out and asked, "Henry, what's going on?" And before Uncle Henry could say anything, she spotted the Indians. She jumped back in the wagon and said in an anxious voice, "Henry do something we're all going to get killed."

The Indians both looked at the horses and then at my uncle's rifle without saying a word. Then one rode to the back of the wagon.

My uncle got very nervous and said, "Look here, what do you two want?"

The other one came back, and I notice they looked young and skinny. One was taller than the other, and you could see the muscles in their bodies, so I would assume they were strong. Their skin was extra dark; I would think because of the sun, and both had long black hair. They were both naked except for loincloths and a strip of leather around their heads. The leather strip was to keep their hair out of their faces.

The taller one started to move his hands around, and I knew it was a way Indians talked. I asked my uncle if he knew what they were saying with their hands, and he shook his head, no, not taking his eyes off them. I waved my hands in front of me and shook my head no. They started to talk among themselves, and I recognized they were talking Mandan although a different dialect from what I understood.

I told my uncle, "They're Mandan." "I'll try to talk with them." When I said, Mandan both of their heads swung toward me, and I started talking in Mandan.

"I speak Mandan, but you speak differently than I do."

They both looked at each other, and the taller one said, "There are many Mandan some talk different, what is your name?"

"I'm called James."

"What does James mean?"

"I am not sure it is a white man's name."

"My name is Runs A Lot," the taller one said. He pointed to the shorter one and said, "This is Much Sadness."

"Who is this?" "Is he your father?" asked the taller one.

With a firm, negative voice, I said, "No, he is my uncle, my mother's brother, and my aunt and cousin are inside."

There was no hiding my hate for my relatives from them, but they didn't say anything. "My uncle's name is Henry, my aunt's name is Margaret, and my cousin is Milford, I don't know what their names mean."

My uncle asked what they were saying, and I said, "They told me their names." "That one is Runs A Lot, and the other is Much Sadness."

"Ask them what they want." I looked at Runs A Lot and said, "My uncle wants to know what you want?"

"We would like you to be our honored guests at our lodges, and maybe there is something you would like to trade for."

I turned my attention to my uncle and said, "They want us to go to their village and be their honored guests and maybe trade."

"We could use some fresh meat and vegetables; do you think we can trust them?" my uncle asked with a cautious tone.

"I got told most Indians don't lie; I believe they are honest." "You know we could also get information about other Indians who aren't as nice that we might run into," I replied.

"Shoot them both, Henry," said my aunt.

I had to think fast before my uncle did something stupid that would get all of us killed, and I said, "That wouldn't be a wise to do; there might be others around."

"You're right; we'll go to their village and trade; tell them we will follow them." I told them, and they turned their horses and headed up the river, and Uncle Henry had me follow them. Less than an hour later, we had come in sight of the Mandan village. It wasn't large about five earth mound structures, which they called lodges. I could see about twenty-five or thirty people and about sixteen or eighteen horses.

There were some trees there, and my uncle said, "We will stock up with firewood before we leave.

# 3

# A SHORT REPRIEVE

We rode up to one of the lodges. Much Sadness said, "Stay here." He and Runs A Lot then disappeared into the lodge where we parked. I told my uncle that they wanted us to wait. As we did, we attracted quite a crowd. Runs A Lot came out with an old, gray-haired man. He introduced him as Red Horse, and he was Runs a Lot's father. We got directed to go into Red Horse's lodge. My uncle was nervous about leaving my aunt and cousin alone and said, "You go; I'll stay here and stand watch." I got off the wagon and explained that my uncle was nervous about leaving my aunt and cousin alone.

I told my uncle, "This may take some time," and I went into the lodge.

It was just as well that I went in alone; it allowed me to speak freely. The lodge got brightened by the fire that was in the middle. There were a lot of furs on the ground, and he had a lance, bow, and arrows hung up on antlers. There also appeared to be some home-made cooking utensils and baskets and other things. The outside of the lodge was a dirt mound with wood sticking out like a large bowl with an opening on one side.

I waited until I was seated, I thought it would be polite, and I found out later that I was right. I sat to the left of Red Horse and when I sat Rolling Stone, the wife of Red Horse, gave everyone something to eat. It was good, and I ate like a pig. I couldn't get enough of it. As I finished, I got more I realized I wasn't being a good guest and looked at Red Horse and said, "I am sorry for the way I have eaten." "This food tastes terrific, and my uncle doesn't give me much to eat."

He laughed and said, "You eat as much as you like," I smiled and did so.

"You look like you have been in a big fight, how did you get all those marks on your face?"

I stopped eating and put my head down and said, "It was my uncle."

"You must have done something wrong."

"No, he is just mean, they are all mean." "They treat me like; I don't know what the word is, one who is taken and must do what they say, no matter what it is and can get treated any way they want."

Red Horse stared at me for a few seconds; the whole lodge was silent. Red Horse said in a grim voice, "I could make it so, they do not bother you again, and you can stay here with me."

I thought about this. I knew what Red Horse was talking about, and it would solve my problem, but they are kin, and Mama wouldn't approve. I told Red Horse, "My mother, who has died, would not have approved." "He is my mother's brother I cannot let you do this, but the thought does give me pleasure."

"They are all fools, and they will get punished if not in this world they will, in the next," said Red Horse.

"I plan to leave them and find my father, who is somewhere in the great mountains to the setting sun."

He shook his head in agreement and changed the subject.

He told me that this village was just temporary; it got made for the hunt. "My uncle wants to trade for fresh meat and vegetables." "There may be other things I don't know." "You must know I don't trust my uncle; he may try to cheat you." "I will tell him not to, but he may anyway."

"We are not stupid people; we will not let this happen."

"I will help you by running my hand through my hair if I think you are getting cheated." "I will ask you not to act angry toward my relatives, or it will be bad for me," I said.

"They will not know our true feelings." "You will tell your uncle we will trade tomorrow and that you will stay here with me that way, you will get fed well before you leave."

I told my uncle what Red Horse said, and he wasn't happy that I was to sleep with Red Horse. I told my uncle that to reject his offer would offend him, which would not be good for any of us. He relented, and he drove the wagon on the other side of the river at my aunt's demand.

I had a smile on my face when Red Horse directed me to the campfire. Many of the people in the village were there. Some of the women and children wanted to touch my hair. They were saying it shined like the sun.

We talked a lot about the Lakota, the Mandan and Lakota were related. Red Horse said, "If you meet them, they will do you harm, they do not like the white man." "Don't worry about the Lakota since they live far north; you will most likely not see them." "The Cheyenne are odd people." "There is a good chance you will see them, and sometimes they will do you harm." "Most of the time, not but don't have anything to do with them." Then he said, "If you see the Blackfeet, you are dead!"

That got my attention, and I asked Red Horse, "They will kill everybody, women, and children; they will not talk?"

"They will kill everyone and then take everything you have." Everyone there seemed to agree on what Red Horse was saying. I then said, "I have heard of the Blackfeet, but I didn't know they were that bad."

"Where do you think they will be as we travel to the setting sun?"

"After you leave the great grasslands and you see the buffalo, you will be in the greatest danger."

Someone asked, "How is it you speak, Mandan?"

"I had a friend who sometimes came to my village." "His name is Sometimes Comes; he taught me."

They all started to laugh, and Red Horse said, "Sometimes Comes has been here many times he is not right in the head."

The rest of the time, we talked about many things. We talk about how my relatives are and how to act friendly around them. We finally headed back to Red Horse's lodge. Before I went in, I saw the wagon across the river, and Uncle Henry scurrying around the wagon. I didn't see my aunt and cousin. I figured they were too afraid to come out of the wagon.

I went into the lodge and was seated next to Red Horse again. We got more food for which I was grateful, and we talked for hours. I got shown where to sleep and given a fur blanket to use. When I lay down, Rolling Stone came over to me with some concoction and said, "This is a medicine; it will heal your wounds faster." She painted my face all up and said I could wash it off when I woke in the morning.

After she finished, she asked, "Do you have wounds anywhere else?"

"On my bottom, but...." Before I could say another word, she had my trousers off, and she had rolled me over. I was entirely embarrassed, and Red Horse and Runs A Lot was laughing. After she finished, I threw my blanket over me, went to sleep, and was too ashamed to look at any of them.

The next morning, I woke up early, figuring that I would bathe before anyone rose. But when I woke, I found these people aren't like my uncle, they get up early, earlier than me. I got my trousers on under my blanket and got up, and I told everyone that I was going to bathe. They all nodded, and I went out; it seemed like the whole village was up. The medicine was dried and crusty on my body, so there was no way of getting out of bathing. I walked down the river for quite some time and then looked around. When I saw no one, then I stripped and jumped in the water. I just stayed in long enough to wash off, and then I got out and dried off. When I looked at my reflection in the water, the bruises had all but disappeared.

I walked back to Red Horse's lodge for a big breakfast. I asked Red Horse, "My uncle will get impatient when do you want to do the trading?"

"Whenever you want," said Red Horse.

"Let's wait for a little until my relatives have eaten, so I don't have to cook for them," I answered, they laughed and agreed. When I saw my uncle feeding my aunt and cousin, I waited just a little longer, so my uncle could clean everything, and then I went across the river.

I told my uncle all that got said except those negative things about him. I asked, "When do you want to do the trading; I'm to wave to them when you are ready?"

"Let's put out the things to trade now, and we can call them over."

We put out a blanket from my bedroll and put my Mama's things on it, also a little from what he had.

I told my uncle, "It would offend them if Aunt Margaret and Milford stayed in the wagon."

"I don't care if I offend those savages or not," said my aunt.

My uncle said, "I frankly don't care either."

"If you offend them, they may get hostile." "Also, if the Mandan thinks they are getting cheated, things will get nasty."

"Margaret and Milford will be out of the wagon, but the way I trade things is my business; they're just stupid savages anyway."

"They're not stupid, uncle you're not the first white man they have come across."

"You better stop sassing me, or I'll give you another beating."

"I'm not sassing you, and if you beat me again, you'll never see the sunrise again." I suppose he thought I was talking about the Mandan, but I was referring to me.

Uncle Henry changed the subject and asked, "Do you think this is enough?"

"They will tell you if they want something else and you can trade with them if you want," I said,

I waved at the Mandan, and slowly they started to come over, looking at what my uncle had. My Mama's pots and knives went fast. Someone wanted my blanket, but I let that person know that I use it to keep warm when I sleep.

My uncle thought he was getting away with cheating them, but the truth was the Mandan came out better. Some of my Mama's jewelry got also traded. Finally, Red Horse asked me to ask my uncle if he had any tobacco, coffee, or liquor.

"Red Horse wants to know if you have any tobacco, coffee, or liquor."

"I won't trade alcohol, but I can trade a little tobacco and coffee, but tell him it will be expensive."

I told Red Horse and told him to be careful.

He smiled and said, "I will trade."

I told my uncle, and he got the tobacco and coffee.

Red Horse offered him some meat and vegetables first, but my uncle wanted more.

I told Red Horse.

He turned to Runs A Lot and said to him to give me my pouch. Out of the pouch, Red Horse pulled some gold looking stones and gave one to my uncle.

My uncle's eyes popped out. He bit into it then looked at it again. He eyed the other rocks and said three, holding up three fingers.

My uncle was cheating him, so I ran my hand through my hair.

Red Horse smiled, patted me on my back, and gave my uncle two more stones. My uncle couldn't be happier. He gave Red Horse the coffee and tobacco and went to show Aunt Margaret, whose eyes lit up.

I said to Red Horse, "He cheated you." "Why did you let him?"

He laughed again and said, "I cheated him." "Those are not the yellow stones that white men want." "It is just a stone with the gray metal that white use in their rifles with a little color to make it look like the yellow stone,"

I started to laugh, and when my uncle came back, I told him that I thanked Red Horse and that he was pleased with the trade.

My uncle said he wanted to get on the trail, and I let Red Horse know. We packed everything away, and I hooked up the horses. Just before we left Red Horse, followed by Rolling Stone, came up to us and handed me a large pouch. I looked inside, smiled, and thanked him. Soon after we moved, out my uncle asked what I had in the pouch, and I told him, "Dried food, they fed me well, in fact, I got stuffed."

He thought a minute and said, "You better keep that where your aunt and cousin don't see it."

We traveled for the next three days, and the third night we camped, but the firewood that we had gathered at the Mandan camp was gone.

My uncle said, "We must do without a fire until we can get some more firewood."

I watered the horses, tied them up, and noticed what looked like a lot of large cow droppings, and I had an idea. I asked my uncle for his flint and knife; I gathered up a lot of those cow droppings and piled them up. I grabbed some dry grass, some dry twigs from a mustard plant, I cut a little hair from my head, and I kindled a fire. I moved the fire to the cow droppings, and it took fire to my uncle's amazement. I said, "I saw the Mandan do it."

When Aunt Margaret found out about it, she said it was one of the most disgusting things she ever knew. She said, "Milford and I won't eat anything cooked over that, it's filthy."

"Then both of you will go hungry," my uncle said. When supper was ready, my aunt and cousin ate without complaint.

The next night, I was starting to cook when we heard someone approach. My uncle grabbed his rifle and said, "Who's out there?"

"Just a friend Pilgrim looking for some hot coffee and maybe a meal." From the dark came a dark-skinned man dressed in buckskins. He had a beard, and he was carrying a Hawken rifle, he was a mountain man. My aunt looked at him suspiciously but didn't say anything.

To my surprise, my uncle put his rifle down and invited him in and told me, "Cook a little more for this gentleman."

I got him a cup of coffee and went back to my cooking.

He sat on the ground opposite my uncle and said, "I'm Ben Sutherland. I left the Shining Mountains, and I'm heading to Saint Louis."

"This is Margaret, Milford, and I'm Henry Muller." The mountain man looked at me, and my uncle said in a disapproving voice, "Oh, that's James York, my nephew."

"Did you walk here, Mr. Sutherland?" asked my aunt.

"Shoot, no, my horses are over yonder." "I'll get them before I lie down."

I told my uncle the stew was ready, and he spooned Mr. Sutherland a large portion, as he did for my aunt, cousin, and himself. There was little left for me, and the mountain man noticed it. "I have a lot, son, take some of mine."

"No, I'll make do with something else."

I walked away and grabbed the pouch Red Horse gave me. I could hear my uncle, and he talk about the trail ahead and Indians. The mountain man explained how dangerous some Indians were.

At that, my uncle didn't believe him and said, "Nonsense, we met up with some dirty, stupid savages awhile back, and they were as passive as I've ever seen."

Tired of the stupidity of my uncle, the mountain man said, "It's your right to believe what you want."

They talked a little more, and as they did, I rolled my bedroll out then started cleaning up things. Finally, my uncle bid him a good night and went into the wagon. The mountain man disappeared into the darkness only to reappear with three horses, two being pack horses. He unloaded the pack horses and staked all three of them. He took his bedroll and laid it next to mine, which surprised me. As he did, he said, "That uncle of yours treats you mighty bad, doesn't he?"

"Yes," I replied.

"He is going to get him, and the rest of his family killed." "You make sure you're clear of him when the trouble starts."

I shook my head yes and said, "I plan to take off and look for my father in the Shining Mountains." "Have you ever heard of a man named Nathaniel York?"

"York sounds familiar, but to be honest with you, we don't go by our Christian names." "My name in those mountains is Lone Wolf."

"How long has it been since you saw your father?"

"I've never seen him, and I'm almost nine, but my Mama said that's where he went."

"Nine years is a long time for anyone he may not be alive."

"I don't care; I'm still going to look for him."

"Those mountains are a mighty challenge for even a seasoned veteran like me, let alone a green nine-year-old." "You better be mighty careful."

At that, he rolled over and went to sleep.

When I woke up the next morning, he and his horses were gone; we packed up and left after breakfast, and the next five days were uneventful.

My aunt continued her whining, and Milford always wanted more food and tried getting mine several times. I was rationing the food that Rolling Stone gave me, so I had plenty of that.

The next day we spotted three Indians. They didn't look like Mandan, so I assumed they were Cheyenne. I'm sure they had seen us before we saw them. They didn't approach us and rode off in a different direction. My uncle didn't pay them much mind. He didn't even grab his rifle; he just grumbled, "Stupid, dirty savages."

That night at dinner, I didn't get much, so I decided to get my pouch, and it was missing. I approached my uncle, who was busy doing something, and said, "Uncle Henry, my food pouch is missing."

"I told you to keep it hid." At that, he went to the back of the wagon where Aunt Margaret and Milford were and said, "Give me James food pouch."

My Aunt tried to say, "I don't know what you're talking about."

She didn't get it entirely out when he grabbed Milford and said, "You want a beating?" In a panic, Milford quickly got the pouch and gave it to his father.

"He was holding out on us, Henry," my aunt said as an excuse.

Without a word, he gave me my pouch, empty, of course. He then said, "You more than likely didn't have much left.

"It was near full I was rationing it," I stated with a disappointed voice.

To my uncle, it was a finished event. Nothing else got done, so I went to bed hungry that night. As I laid on my bedroll, I heard my uncle yelling in the wagon, but I was not sure if it was about me.

The next morning my aunt and cousin were very cold toward me like I did something wrong. We traveled all day, and my uncle was not talking much. It was getting long past our noon break, and we hadn't stopped yet, so I asked my uncle, "Do you want to rest the horses?"

"You hungry?"

"No," I said. The truth was I was starving. However, the mood my uncle was in, I wasn't going to say anything.

"Then we keep driving until I say stop," he expressed in a surly mood.

We finally stopped that night, and when dinner got served, I got more than the usual portion. My aunt and cousin didn't protest at all, but you could see they didn't like it. The next morning, I got a larger portion of breakfast again.

I had finished cleaning up, and my uncle was tying something down when my aunt yelled at my uncle, "Henry, I need the chamber pot emptied."

"James, go dump and clean it."

Now, I was never handed the pot by any other person but my uncle. When I went to the back of the wagon and raised my arms to receive the chamber pot, Milford threw the contents in my face, and it went all over my clothing. I screamed, "It's burning my eyes." I fell to the ground rubbing my eyes. As Aunt Margaret and Milford were laughing at me, my uncle came around the corner of the wagon. He caught Milford with the chamber pot in his hands, and both him and my aunt laughing at me lying on the ground reeking of human waste. My uncle grabbed me by my arm and dragged me down to the river, and he started to strip me of my clothing. I thought I was in for another beating, but he took me into the water and splashed water into my eyes.

I said, "Milford threw it."

"Yes, I know," my uncle said in disgust.

My eyes started to clear, and my uncle got out of the water and said, "Finish washing yourself and then wash your clothes."

I watch him as he headed back to the wagon madder than a wet hen. As he approached the wagon, he heard Aunt Margaret and Milford laughing. He went to the back of the wagon and barked, "Give me that chamber pot."

As Milford was handing the chamber pot to his father, Aunt Margaret said, "What do you want with that silly chamber pot?" "Let the boy get it, Henry."

Uncle Henry didn't answer her. He took the pot and smashed it on a rock. "Henry, what are we going to do now without that pot, and I'm not going to use a bucket?"

"No, Margaret, you and Milford will use this magnificent landscape around you." "I will not!" retorted Aunt Margaret.

"Then just hold it, Margaret!" At that, he walked away, leaving Aunt Margaret and Milford with their mouths gaping open. I saw the whole thing, and I took it in with great joy.

After my clothes dried, or almost dried, we got started out traveling. For the next two weeks' things between my uncle and I seemed to get better. It may have been getting better between my uncle and me, but I hadn't forgotten the beating. I knew if he had to choose between Milford and me, it wouldn't be even a contest. Knowing this, my plans to take off hadn't changed.

It was just after noon when we heard it. The sound was like thunder, but there wasn't any storm. As we traveled farther and farther down the trail, the sound got louder, and then we spotted the dust cloud. We pulled up, got off the wagon, and walked toward the dust cloud that appeared to be coming from a valley ahead of us. When we looked into the valley, we couldn't believe what we were seeing. It was an eternal undulating sea of what I think was running buffaloes. For hours, they kept coming, and we started wondering if we were going to get across, so we could continue down the trail. Slowly the herd of buffaloes slowed down, then stopped and started grazing.

Uncle Henry said, "Let's try going across." So slowly we went I was not so confident about this being a good idea. Some of the buffalo seemed as big as a house and more powerful than anything I've seen. We made it across, and I breathed a sigh of relief.

A hundred yards from the herd when my uncle said, "Stop here and wait." "I'll be right back." He took his rifle and headed back to the herd, and I knew what he was going to do.

Aunt Margaret yelled out, "Henry, where are you going?"

He didn't answer but just kept going. I heard the boom of his rifle and just put my head down and shook it. Sure enough, the thunder started again, and my uncle came running fast. He jumped up on the wagon, half out of breath, and yelled, "Drive fast!"

I moved out and went another hundred yards, and he told me to stop. He went back to the herd. This time besides his rifle, he had a sack and a knife.

He came back with a smile on his face and sack full of buffalo meat. "Fresh meat; we need it, and besides, I wanted to see what it tastes like," my uncle said, trying to justify the danger he put us through.

At that moment, the words of the mountain man echoed in my head, "When the trouble starts to get far away if you wanted to live."

As we traveled along the trail, I reminded my uncle about what the Mandan said, "We will be in the most danger of hostile Indians after the grasslands and Buffalo."

"I think those savages are misinformed; these savages all seem docile to me." "Moreover, the only savages I've seen were those three back of the trail who cowardly ran off."

That night we had buffalo, and it surprised me it tasted good. It was leaner than beef, and to my surprise, it didn't have a gamey taste like you would get with deer.

As we traveled, the landscape started to change. We had more rolling hills with the stretches of flat grassland, much like we first moved through and trees, which made my aunt happy. We could start burning wood even though there were plenty of buffalo droppings around still. I hadn't bathed in a while, and my clothing wasn't very clean either, and my uncle was taking notice of it. I never understood why he noticed me and not my aunt and cousin. They hardly ever bathed, but of course, they never worked.

We drifted a little north of the Platte River because it was a little easier going, and Aunt Margaret was complaining. I wasn't happy about it, but the horses were getting tired, and I figured it was also better for them. About an hour or so before we regularly stopped, we came across a tributary of the Platte River. It was only four or five feet wide at the widest spot, and there were many rocks and trees there. Normally this place would have been an excellent place to camp, but it made me uneasy. What made it worse, my uncle insisted on camping out in the open away from the trees and water he hadn't forgotten about the mosquitoes.

I reminded him again about the hostile Indians. Still, he said stubbornly, "I'll tell you one last time these savages are weak, stupid and cowardly people if you want to call them people." "I don't want to hear any more about it, or I'll beat you a good one."

I was mad, but again I didn't say anything, and I wasn't going to let him beat me again. For sure, I wasn't going to lay my bedroll anywhere near the wagon. As the mountain man said, you stay away from them.

We finished the rest of the buffalo that night, and my uncle said, "I think we will stay here two nights, so the horses get rested. We must be getting near those mountains that are supposed to be so hard to cross, and I want the horses well-rested. James, you might try some fishing while we are here." I nodded my head, but by the time I clean everything up watered and tied up the horses, I was too tired to fish.

I was lying in the wooded area on my bedroll, thinking how funny it was that I could drive a team of horses, but I've never been on a horse in my life. I was short; at least I considered myself short and didn't think I could even get on top of a horse. If I did get on top of a horse, I wouldn't know what to do next to get the horse moving in the direction I wanted it to go. I noticed that there weren't many mosquitoes, and I drifted off to sleep.

When I woke up, the sun was up. I must have been more tired than I thought. I gathered up some wood and brought it up to the wagon and started a fire. My uncle came out of the wagon, grabbed the food to cook, and handed it to me. We were all eating when my uncle said, "You haven't bathed yet."

"I was very tired."

"You take those horses and water them." "Then, after you tie them up, go take a bath and wash your clothes too."

I watered the horses and tied them up, and headed toward my bedroll. I decided to take my bedroll with me, so I could lay on it as I dried. I went upstream and found a spot where it had a small sandy beach and a deep enough hole in the water where I could bathe. I was near enough to see the wagon, but there were some high rocks, trees, and bushes around to shield me from view. I laid out my bedroll and stripped off all my clothing. I decided to relieve myself first, away from where I was going to bathe, and then I jumped into the water. The water was a little cold, but I got used to it in a few minutes. It came into my mind that I wished I had soap for myself and my clothes. I wanted to get clean, so I didn't have to hear my uncle complain so much. I did make sure I washed my hair good, and as I was washing, I pulled my clothes into the water to clean them. I didn't want to get out of the water so quickly. After about a half-hour, I finally did get out. I squeezed the water out of my clothing as much as I could. I then hung my clothing on some branches to dry. I laid on my stomach to dry off and started to doze in the warming sun.

I became alert when I heard some screaming, chilling noise, and a rifle shot. I stood up and looked over the rocks that surrounded me and then froze in terror. There in front of me were eighteen or twenty screaming fierce-looking Indians; there may have been even more. They had my aunt, uncle, and cousin who were hysterically screaming. I ducked down behind the rocks. My heart was racing a thousand beats a second. I decided to hide my bedroll, so I put on my clothing quickly but quietly, except for my shirt. I hid everything else in the bushes and covered it with leaves and twigs. Then I wiped out my tracks. When I was satisfied with that, I wrapped my head in my shirt, hiding my hair. I figured my hair would be easy to spot, and my shirt would blend in with the surroundings better. I climbed a tree as far as I could go up and laid flat down on one of its limbs, and I watched.

They were treating my relatives awful, beating my uncle, and slapping my aunt. Milford wouldn't stop screaming and got hit hard, which drew blood. They tied them all up to the wagon and gagged them. They tore the wagon apart, throwing things out the back and taking great joy in finding something they wanted. One of the Indians that looked like the leader, also another, brought the horses over to my uncle was. They said something to him, pointing to the horses and then started to beat my uncle again. I'm guessing, but I think they were angry about the condition of the horses. They came across my uncle's liquor and fought over who was going to get the next drink. The more they drank, the wilder they got. They also started to eat our food and what they didn't eat they destroyed. They were there for hours, and late in the day, they began to build up the fire. Four of the Indians went looking for wood, two upstream, and two downstream. One of them came very near to me, and I thought I was going to get discovered. He even picked up some wood three feet from where I had buried my bedroll, but he didn't find it, and he didn't look up to my relief.

They stripped all the clothing of my aunt, uncle, and cousin. They burned my uncle's and cousin's clothing, but they ripped up my aunt's dress, taking many pieces of it. Then they took my aunt and spread-eagled her on the ground on her back. The Indians started taking their pleasure out on her. She would scream, and they would slap her. Finally, after about the fourth one, she stopped screaming. I don't know if she passed out or not.

Milford was crying hysterically. I could see Uncle Henry also crying and pulling at his ropes. After sixth or seven Indians pleasured themselves on my aunt, they rolled her over and started on her bottom. The rotation of Indians on my aunt wasn't going fast enough, so they grabbed Milford, laid him on his stomach, and started on him. After the third one got finished, I couldn't hear him anymore. They finally stopped and tied them back up to the wagon. Both my aunt and Mildred slumped down.

The Indian who seemed to be in charge drew his knife and started to carve on my aunt while another Indian forced my uncle to watch. They first removed my aunt's hair and kept it like it was a prize. I heard the mountain men talking about this behavior. Then they removed her nipples, her ears, and her nose. They next worked on Milford, removing his hair, then his testicles. He was making such a loud noise they removed his gag and cut out his tongue. Then they cut off his ears and nose; there was blood all over the place. Fortunately, my aunt and cousin passed out sometime during the ordeal. Then they went to my uncle and did the same to him as they did to Milford. While they were doing this, they were taking great joy in it, laughing, and dancing around.

I could feel the insides of my stomach coming up; it all made me sick. I could hear and see the screams of my aunt and my uncle's movement as they got engulfed by fire. They piled wood around them and set the wood and wagon on fire. I could hear the screams of my aunt and the movement of my uncle as they got engulfed by fire. The smell was the most terrible thing I ever smelled. It took everything I had to keep me from vomiting. When the fire died, the Indians moved south about a hundred and fifty feet from the wagon downwind of the smell and started another campfire. I laid my head down and as sick and sore as I was from being up in that tree and smelling and seeing what I saw, I drifted asleep.

# 4

# NEAR DEATH

I woke with a start and slipped on the branch I was on, ripping my trousers. I looked around and saw no one. But I was so afraid that I stayed in the tree. I could still smell that awful smell but not as bad as it was yesterday. I could see where the wagon once stood now, for the most part, almost entirely gone. I also saw where my aunt, uncle, and cousin were. They didn't even look human from where I was.

By noon I took a chance and came down from the tree ripping my trousers even more, but I didn't care. When I hit the ground, I pulled off the shirt that was on my head and bent over and started heaving. I looked over the rocks and bushes and jumped into the water, hoping that it would make me feel a little better. Once out of the water, I grabbed my shirt. Put it on and walked over to where the wagon was. I looked at my relatives, and I couldn't recognize them. Their bindings got burnt away; they had holes where their eyes and noses were. Their mouths were open like they were screaming. They had no fingers or toes, and some were missing a foot or hand. I could see bones sticking out here and there. They were all black and had ash from the wood that burnt around them and the wagon; the smell was terrible.

I knew I had to bury them. I looked for something to dig with and found a shovel, but it didn't have a handle because it got destroyed in the fire. I found a soft, sandy area near the trees and water and dug three shallow graves. I would have dug a deeper hole, but I ran into a lot of roots from the trees. I found a limb that was pliable to weave into a loop. I placed the loop around each body and dragged the body to the grave. While I was doing this, parts of their bodies would fall off. So, I took what shovel and scooped the pieces up the best way I could and deposited them in the appropriate grave. After I had everyone in their graves, I threw limbs on top of them, so it would be hard for animals to dig up. After this, I filled the graves in with dirt and put rocks on top of each grave. As I stared at what I just did, I started to vomit again.

I went over to the wagon to see what I could salvage, but I didn't see anything. There were parts of the wheels, the bottom of the wagon, a partial side, and some distorted metal. I looked around for something to carry water in, but there was nothing. I did find some discarded bits of food that were on the ground, which I picked up. The bottles that the liquor had been in were unusable smashed into small pieces. I went over to where my bedroll was and retrieved it.

I looked first to the east and then to the west, and I had to decide which way to go. I was a long way from Missouri, and the Mandan who I knew would help me. I didn't know what was ahead of me, but I believed my uncle was right when he said we must be near the Shining Mountains, so I decided to go west. I justified my decision because I was going to take off once I got to the mountains anyway.

I assessed myself and found my shoes were worn and about to fall apart, my trousers got ripped, but my shirt was still good, as was my bedroll. I went over to the water and soaked my shirt and bedroll, thinking I could suck out the water as I traveled. I crossed the stream and headed west.

I had gone a long way, and it was getting dark, so I looked for a place to sleep. I found some brush and a small tree, and I sat down next to the tree. I had no means to make a fire, so I just sat in the dark. Every noise sent shivers down my back, but after about an hour, I got used to it. I was hungry, so I ate the scraps of food I had and sucked the water out of my shirt. I had intended to stay awake all night, but I got tired and dozed off.

I woke up with the sun on my face. I slowly got to my feet and relieved myself. My shirt was almost dry, so I put it on and headed out again. I noticed that the water in my bedroll was nearly gone, but there was nothing I could do, so I kept on walking. The sky was blue with puffy clouds, and it was warm out and getting warmer. I was thirsty, so I sucked on my bedroll. There wasn't much water in it, but I did get a few trickles of water out of it. I threw the bedroll over my shoulder and kept walking. By noon I was exhausted and hot, so I sat down on a rock and rested. The bedroll didn't have any more water I could suck out of it, but it was still damp in places, so I draped it over my head to keep cool.

I started to think about my aunt, uncle, and cousin, and although I didn't like them, they were still kin. And kin or no kin no one deserved what they went through; the thought made me madder and madder. I started to think about when I first met my uncle and then when I got that beating and how he seemed to make up by trying to change his feelings about me. Then he to defend me when my aunt and cousin were doing something disgusting to me. I don't want to give the impression that I liked my uncle; I didn't. I knew if it came to a choice between me and my aunt or cousin, I'd lose every time. I was just a servant to them and nothing more.

I headed out again, and late in the afternoon, I came to a dry, rocky ravine. I looked for the safest place to cross and took the best route I could find. I went off the side, holding onto the brush as I went down. After starting down, I tripped on a loose rock, and the brush pulled free, and I fell head over heels to the bottom. I was bruised and scraped up, and I could feel blood on my forehead, but I didn't have any broken bones that I could tell, but pants got torn more, and so was my shirt. I looked for my bedroll and found it high up hooked on some brush. I tried to climb to get it, but I wasn't having much success, so I gave up on it and tried to get up on the opposite bank. With much trial, I got on the far bank and headed west. After walking about three hundred yards, my head was spinning, and I was very thirsty. I knew I couldn't go very much further without water. I decided to turn south or what I thought was south, to try to find the trail and the Platte River. I walked for hours, and it was getting late, but the moon was up, so I decided to keep on walking. Sometime during the night, I became too tired, so I collapsed and laid on my side and fell asleep.

When I woke, I just lay there thinking maybe it was a bad idea going west. I pulled myself up and started to walk some distance and noticed that I was going west instead of south. I must have gotten turned around during the night and was heading in the wrong direction. I decided to continue walking in a westward direction. If God willed it, I would find water; if not, I would be out of my misery. I stumbled west and walked many miles, and everything was spinning and blurry. I heard a buzzing just before everything turned black, and I fell facedown and passed out.

I came out of it just about sunrise; everything was still blurry, and I felt like death was near. In front of me, there seemed to be some trees. I tried to get my eyes to focus, as the trees became visible and then blurry. I heard it the babbling sound of water running over rocks. I was too weak to get up, so, with all my strength, I crawled toward the sound. I'd reach out and grab anything I could get my hand on to pull myself along. Eventually, one of the times when I was reaching out, my hand touched the water. I drew my wet hand back and pressed it to my mouth. I pushed myself a little further until I was over the water, stuck my head in, and drew in the cold sweet water. When I had enough to drink, I bathed my head and rolled over on my back and rested.

After a short time, I was able to sit up, leaning my back on a tree. I hadn't had anything to eat since those scraps of food leftover from those Indians. That wasn't much, so I was kind of weak. I knew if I didn't find something to eat soon, all the water in the world wouldn't keep me alive. Looking around, I saw many birds hanging around a bush or something just up ahead of me, so I struggled to get up, and I stumbled over to where the birds were. There was a bunch of berries in a massive bush. I could hardly believe it! I shooed the birds away and jumped into the bush, devouring handfuls of berries. After about an hour, my stomach was full. My mouth, as well as hands, was stained with the juice of the berries. I was all scratched up from the thorns on the bush, so I stripped off my clothes and walked into the water. The water felt good, and I had recovered a bit from the ordeal I had just experienced. I grabbed my clothes and washed them while I was bathing. When I finished, I hung the clothes on a tree and lay down to dry.

About an hour later, I started to put my trousers on and noticed their shape, but it was all I had, so I buttoned them up. My shirt was in worse shape than my trousers. I started to put it on anyway but stopped and went back to where the berries were and started picking more berries, placing them in my shirt. I went back to the tree I was leaning on and sat down. It was getting late, so I decided to stay another night, and I sat back, munching on the berries.

Mr. McConnell, Sarah, and Miss O'Brien came into my mind. It seemed like I hadn't seen them for a hundred years and would most likely never see them again. My mind drifted to what I was going to do tomorrow, of which way to go; I just wasn't sure. I thought of following the stream downstream, but I didn't know for sure how far I had drifted north or what I would find. Going west was a complete unknown, would I find water or food again and how near was it to the Shining Mountains? I finally decided to go up the small hill on the opposite side of the stream, survey the landscape. I then decide on which way to go, but not until I gathered more berries and took a long, deep drink of water.

The next day, after gathering the berries and drinking water, I crossed the stream and climbed the hill. In front of me, I could see what kind of looked like an island in the sky. It was the Shining Mountain still a long way off, but I could see it. I could see the stream curving to the east until I couldn't see the stream anymore, so I decided to go west. Still, to be truthful, I had decided to go west before I looked at the river.

I headed out, keeping the mountains in front of me. At the same time, back where the wagon was, from the south, the same eighteen or twenty Indians who slaughtered my relatives came. The one Indian who appeared to be in charge and a few others saw my tracks and the graves. "White child of those fools," said the leader. By the size of my tracks and the fact that I buried the bodies, they knew I was a white child and assumed I was related to the three they killed.

They followed the tracks to where I was hiding. One of the Indians pointed up the tree where a piece of ripped cloth from my trousers was hanging from the tree. The head Indian went across the river to find my tracks. It wasn't hard, he found them quickly, and then he sent out a cry, and the other Indians came over to him. "We will follow and find this boy and have our fun with him then send him to see those other fools."

I walked all day, restraining myself from eating the berries. The terrain was changing; it was a lot hillier and rocky. I got tired a lot and had to take many rests.

The Indians came to the ravine where I had fallen, and they saw my bedroll. They found a better place to cross and went on tracking me until sundown then stopped and camped.

I finally had to stop for the night I was too thirsty, hungry, and frankly worn out. I sat down and leaned against a rock and started eating the berries. They helped with my thirst and did soothe my stomach, but I was still hungry, but it didn't take long for me to fall asleep.

The next morning, I again headed west, and it was hard to walk. My goings were uphill, and by late morning I had to stop and rest. The Indians noticed my tracks went south for a while but then turned west, then north and then west. They knew I was in bad shape and expected to find me dead.

I reached the ridge of a small mountain, and there was a wide valley with some higher mountains on the other side. I noticed a dark green strip of grass on my side of the valley, and I headed for it. It was a stream about the same size as the last stream. I jumped into the water and drank until I wasn't thirsty anymore.

It was late, so I decided to stay the night. There was plenty of food around in the form of fish I could see them in the water and game also but useless to me. I had no means of catching any fish or killing any game, and even if I did, there wasn't any way to cook it.

The Indians reached the stream where I got the berries, and the leader said in amazement, "This boy would make an excellent warrior. Too bad, we must kill him." They decided to camp at the stream, and the leader said, "We will catch up with him tomorrow."

I woke up the next morning and took a deep drink of water and thought I should soak my shirt. I took off my trousers and soaked them so the water could help with the thirst I knew would come. I thought I should have soaked my trousers in the last stream but didn't think of it.

Just before I started, I looked down at myself and shook my head. I looked terrible. I was dirty, very thin, and my ribs were showing. I started laughing at the thought of Mr. McConnell, Sarah, and Miss O'Brien saw me now they would be in shock. When I reached the other side, the mountain was too steep and rocky to climb up. This time instead of heading north, I went south along the base of the mountain. The bottom of the mountain undulated back and forth, and I thought I had found a passage through the mountain a few times only to pop out into the valley again. I had sucked all the water I could out of my shirt, so I put it back on. By midafternoon, I had drained my trousers and put those on; also, it kept me cool for a while. I had walked another mile or so when I spotted the Indians.

The Indians stopped at the stream and went on. They saw my tracks turn south and traveled for about a half-hour, and then they pulled up and pointed at me, and I spotted them. I started to run. I didn't know where I got the strength to move so fast; I assume it was most likely from fear. My heart was beating so hard I thought it would jump out of my chest. I then turned down a canyon in hopes there would be a hiding place. The Indians gave chase making all kinds of noise. The canyon sloped down, and then I came to an end. There was nowhere else to run. I might have been able to climb the right side of the canyon, but it would have been slow, and I would have been out in the open easy for the Indians to catch me. The left side was almost straight up, and in front of me were boulders also dead trees from past slides, I would assume. I turned around at the entrance of the canyon were the same Indians who murdered my relatives. The Indians pulled up in front of the canyon and saw there was no way for me to escape. The leader said, "Talks A Lot come here."

He was some young-looking Indian, and it was apparent he was not that experienced and did not look very bright.

Handing him a lance, the leader said, "You go down there and count your first coup and bring back my lance with that boy's blood on it."

Seeing what was about to happen, I decided I wasn't just going to stand there as my relatives did. I looked around and found a limb from a dead tree and grabbed it. It felt good in my hands and had a suitable weight. If I got the chance, I would inflict as much damage as I could. I knew I had to outsmart them if I was to have any chance at all. I walked forward to give myself plenty of room. The Indian came with a wild scream, and the lance pointed out. The other Indians just watched with great amusement.

Meanwhile, high up on the ridge of the canyon out of sight of the Indians and me were about twenty-five more Indians watching; they were on my left.

I saw that the Indian approaching me was too high up, and the lance was in the way. I waited until the last-minute pretending like I was going to take a swing at him. Just as he was on top of me, I jumped to the other side and hit the horse in the front hooves. The horse stumbled, and the Indian flew over him, hitting his head on a rock. I ran over to him and used my club to smash his head until he was a mass of blood. The Indians at the canyon's entrance stopped making those wild screaming noises and were in total disbelief and shock. That wasn't supposed to happen, the disbelief and shock changed to anger, and two more came at me. The first one had I believe a club, and the second, about ten or fifteen feet behind the first, had a knife. I knew they wouldn't fall for the same trick, so I had to come up with something new. I grabbed the lance and club that were used for the first attack and readied myself.

High up on the ridge, the other Indians saw everything that happened and started down the side of the canyon.

The first Indian was very close to me, and I knew I had to time this just right. I had the lance in my hand, and like the last time I jumped to the opposite side, he was leaning, and he did just what I thought he would; he switched also. I jumped right back to the other side and threw the lance. I fell to the ground and rolled as I was rolling a lance from the second Indian hit the ground, just missing me. I grabbed my club, and I saw the first one falling off his horse with my lance sticking out of him. I had caught him at about the base of the throat.

The other Indians at the entrance started coming. The second Indian was coming at me with his knife, and I had my club up ready to swing. As he came, I was stepping back, not looking where I was going, and I tripped on a rock and hit my head on another large rock. Then the Indian jumped on top of me, ready to plunge his knife into me. I tried to hold the knife back, but I was too young and weak to fight him off. Everything was getting blurry, and just before the Indian plunged his knife into me, I saw an arrow sticking out of his stomach, then blood. He became weaker and fell on me, and then I blacked out.

The Indians coming into the canyon from the entrance stopped abruptly, turned around, and headed out of the canyon as fast as they could. The Indians from the top of the canyon ridge had reached the bottom and were chasing them. I don't know how far they chased them, but they killed one before the rest got away. The Indian who shot him took his hair, horse, and everything else he had, and the rest came back to the canyon.

The leader of this group threw off the Indian lying on me. He checked to see if I was alive, which I was. He then poured water down my throat and all over my face. I started to move and wake up but passed out again. All the trauma that I had gone through had taken a toll on me, and I was hurt badly.

The head Indian said, pointing to the three dead Indians, "These are his take their scalps, their horses and everything else they have while I put the boy on my horse." They all agreed and went to work with great joy.

# 5
# NEW BEGINNINGS

Carefully I was placed on the horse of the apparent leader, and we headed back to their village. When we got there, we stopped in front of a large lodge. A woman came out, and they lowered me into her arms. The whole village was stirred up by the news of the battle. The stories were already being told of it almost as soon as we got there. Every story was different according to who was telling it. It was the older and wiser ones who got believed the most. In every story told, they talked about me and the two who I killed.

During the trip to the village and while being carried into the lodge, I never woke once. I got laid on some furs, and soon after, the woman assessed me. The woman was the wife of the one who carried me on his horse. She removed all my clothing and checked out all my scrapes, scratches, and bruises. As she was doing this, her husband came in and said, "Look at his head in the back there was blood." She saw the scratch on my forehead, so she rolled me over to my side, moved my hair around, and saw the wound. She laid me on my stomach, got up, grabbed my clothing, shoes and all and said, "Take these things and destroy them they are beyond repair, and they are full of blood, dirt, and smell like those dogs you killed." She handed the clothing to her husband, and he promptly left. She then got some herbs and things, ground them, and made a paste of them. She bathed my whole body removing all blood and dirt. After this, she put the paste on the wounds I had and then bound the wounds up. She put a fur blanket on me and felt my head, and it was warm, so she forced a bitter liquid down my throat.

Hours later, because of nightmares, fever, the poison in my body, or a combination of all these things, I'm not sure which, but I was thrashing around. It was so much that the woman was afraid I would reopen my wounds. She wrapped a blanket around me with my arms inside and bound me. Much like the babies that were in the Mandan village, except there was not a board on my back. She gave me more of that bitter liquid and put a wet piece of leather on my head.

That night my fever broke, and I was less fitful, but I got kept bound up anyway. Even though the fever was gone, I still hadn't awakened by the next morning. After giving me a little water, the woman also gave me a loose, mushy mixture. By noon, the water and mushy mixture did their job, and they came out of my bottom. By the smell, there was no question on what I did. The woman untied the blanket and cleaned me up very well like I was a baby. She then put a new fur blanket on me and rebound me. She went out of her lodge and asked the old woman in the next lodge over to watch me as she cleaned the mess I made in the fur blanket. She finished cleaning everything and hung it to dry and came back inside the lodge to relieve the old woman.

The old woman looked up as she entered and said, "He is resting quietly; what are you going to do with him?"

"We haven't talked about it yet."

"You better decide he will wake up soon."

That night as she was serving her husband, food, she asked, "What will we do with the boy he will awake soon?"

"It will be up to him; we will tell him we will take care of him, but it will be his choice to stay or go."

It was all she could hope for; she had lost three boys already. Two of the boys were still young and inexperienced. One died in a hunting accident and the other when they battled their enemies. They had a baby only three weeks before I arrived, and the child died of unknown reasons. So, when I showed up, it gave the woman hope to have a child again.

It was about noon the next day when I started to wake. Everything was blurred, and I noticed I was tied up and couldn't move, and I also had no clothing on. I wondered if Mama's gold necklace was still around my neck. I was inside someplace I could see a fire and someone moving around and another sitting on the other side of the fire. I blinked my eyes several times to try to focus on them. I turned and tried to see my surroundings again. The people in this dwelling must have seen me move, and my eyes open because I heard the voice of a man say something in a language I didn't know and then pointed at me.

A woman came over to me and said something which again I didn't understand. She poured water down my throat, which I greedily drank, then washed my face and head. It was evident that these people were Indians, and since I was tied up, I must be their captive. However, I figured they were keeping me alive so that they could torture me for their amusement because of what I did to those other two Indians.

As I lay there, I started to think I should have gone southeast from the wagon to find the trail and the Platte River. I was thinking of Mr. McConnell, Sarah, as well as Miss O'Brien, then finally, Mama and the tears started coming. Why was I so foolish to think my father was still alive? I was indeed a fool. I guess I will be with Mama soon; I sure do miss her.

The woman came over to me and wiped my face again. She said something, and again I didn't understand her. She must have known I didn't understand her, and thinking about this made me mad, so I shouted in English, "I don't understand you." Then I started crying more out of frustration and being powerless.

Anyway, the woman came over again and said something while patting my head; then, she wiped my face again. She fed me something mushy that tasted a little nutty with a green flavor to it, but I was so hungry I ate everything she gave me.

"He doesn't understand what we are saying we must find a way to talk to him," the woman said with concern.

"It's a shame that Bear Slayer and his family are not here; they can speak his tongue."

"I will ask to see if anyone else knows his tongue," the man said as a matter of fact, and then he went out of the lodge.

I lay there and had a weird thought what if I had to relieve myself how am I going to tell them, and of course, right then, I did have to go. My eyes were clearing, and I could see the woman sewing something with leather. My bladder had so much pressure that I had to squeeze my manhood. I looked over at the woman and said, "I have to relieve myself."

She just smiled and nodded her head seconds later the dam broke. I wet myself, and what made things worse the mush came out the other end. It smelled bad, and I wondered if she could smell it also.

I slowly turned my head toward her, and she had already put down the thing she was sewing and gotten a towel made of leather and some water.

Then she approached me, and she untied me and removed the dirty fur blanket and started to clean me. I felt mortified I was more embarrassed than when I bathed with Sarah in front of me. I had to admit though it did feel good, especially the air hitting me. I searched for Mama's necklace, and it was there. She laid me back down, but instead of tying me back up, she put another fur blanket on me and then took the dirty things and left the lodge. Moments later, an old woman came into the lodge I assumed to guard me.

The old woman kept on talking to me, laughing at times. I just ignored her; I felt it was no use to say anything she wouldn't understand or stop anyway.

About an hour later, the other woman came back. The old woman said something to her, "He needs meat and milk do you have any left."

"I don't know I must see," the other woman said. "By the size of your breasts, I would think you have plenty of milk," the old woman said, laughing.

"I hope he will take the milk," replied the younger woman. The old woman turned to me, smiled, then left.

The woman went over to a pot, shredded some meat, and put it in a pot. Then she put water into the pot and set the pot next to the fire. My mouth watered, and I wished I could get some of that meat. I lay back and stared up at the hole on the top of the lodge to let the smoke out. I wondered how much longer I had before they would take me.

The woman came next to me and sat down and started murmuring to me. She removed her shirt, which exposed her breasts and smiled. I stared in shock; the only breast I'd seen this close was Mamas unless you count Aunt Margaret's, but I wasn't this close.

When she finished taking off her shirt, she grabbed me by the arms and sat me on her lap. She turned my head and lifted one of her breasts and placed it on my face. I tried to pull away, but I was too weak, and then I looked up at her in shock and thought I haven't been on my Mama's breast since I was five or six. Then I gave up and put my mouth on her nipple and started sucking. Sweet milk started flowing down my throat almost immediately, I looked back up to her, and she was smiling, and as I closed my eyes, she began to sing softly and rocked me. As I closed my eyes, I was thinking about how peculiar she is doing this before I was to get put to death. When I drained one breast, she gave me the other, and I didn't resist.

As the woman was nursing me, the man, who was in here before, came back into the lodge saying, "Is he better?"

"Yes, but weak."

"Spotted Buffalo's daughter Morning Star speaks his tongue; she will come later." He stopped staring and went over to the meat stewing and said, "Smells good!"

"It's for him," she said.

"It will take a lot to feed this one," he said with a smile on his face.

With a smirk, she replied, "He has also started on my other breast."

I was drifting off to sleep when the flow of milk stopped. The woman placed me back on the fur-lined ground and sat me up. I never took my eyes off her when she went over to the stewed meat and brought it over to me. She started to spoon it into my mouth, and I couldn't get enough of it. By the time she got finished feeding me, I was full for the first time since I left the Mandan. I sat back and thought they sure know how to feed you when they are going to kill you anyway.

I pulled up the fur blanket and surveyed the interior with more detail. It was much different than the Mandan's lodge; the lodge got constructed from wood poles shaped in a cone with skins wrapped around them. There were bows and arrows and three lances. There was also I think some bloody scalps, which made me nervous. I wondered if my scalp would hang with the others. Of course, there were similar cooking utensils, pots made of metal and leather. There were woven baskets, which contained things that were unknown to me. There were many furs and hides of all kinds lying around, too. Other things were hanging in this lodge, which appeared to be clothing and dried plants, which made the lodge smell good. The woman started a meal for her man, and I closed my eyes and drifted off to sleep with a full stomach.

Some people were talking and banging the cooking utensils on the pots, which woke me up. It was still light out from what I could see streaming in from the top of the lodge. My bladder had filled again, and I had to go. I looked around and saw a girl about my age and quickly pulled up my blanket, even though my body wasn't exposed. They had all stopped talking and were looking at me. I thought I should tell them again that I had to relieve myself. Maybe the woman would remember what happened the last time I told them. "I have to relieve myself, or I am going to wet my blankets and myself again."

The girl turned to the man and woman and told her something I didn't know what

The woman and man looked at each other in confusion, and the man said, "Tell him to go outside and relieve himself."

I was starting to get frustrated about how I could get them to understand when the girl said, "If you have to go, go outside."

"But I'm naked," I said. Then it hit me, "Wait, you spoke English," I said, confused.

"Yes, I speak your tongue."

I needed to attend to my bladder needs first before I found out what was going to happen to me and said, "I need something to put on before I go outside. I don't want anyone to see me with nothing on, and I'm not going to let you see me with nothing on." I know I got used to bathing in front of Sarah, but she was younger than me, besides she was like a sister.

The girl turned to the man and woman and said, "This one is an odd one, he said he doesn't want anyone to see him naked, especially me."

"Tell him how our people are, and we don't have any clothing for him yet, and if he doesn't go outside, he must wet himself." Then the woman added, "Tell him also if he wets himself, I must clean the blanket and him in front of you."

She smiled at me and said, "They said if you don't go outside, then you must wet yourself and your blanket and Turtle Woman must clean you and the blanket in front of me."

The pressure was building when she continued speaking, "Being without clothing is common with my people; you shouldn't feel uncomfortable."

I put my head down, knowing I wasn't going to last long before my bladder burst. I had no choice before I tried to get up; she said with compassion, "Wait." She removed all her clothes, and I stared with my mouth open. I thought she looked beautiful. "Now you," she said.

It was enough motivation for me; I got to my knees, and I felt very weak. I tried to stand but fell like a baby learning to walk. I tried again but fell again and looked over to all three of them. The woman called Turtle Woman turned to her man and said, "Help him until he gets his legs back. Most likely, he doesn't know where to go."

Turtle Woman's husband came over to me, grabbed my arm, and helped me to the opening of the lodge. We went outside. It took me a few seconds to adjust to the light, but when I could see well enough, I noticed no one paying me much attention. The air on my body felt good, and it was nice to be out of the lodge. He guided me to where I was to relieve myself.

We were about to pass the old woman who watched me earlier when she said, "I see he is up and about Red Elk."

"Yes, but he is as weak as a newborn colt."

The old woman replied, "He will be walking normally within a few moments when his legs get used to walking. Then Turtle Woman can leave him and come out and talk to me like she used to."

He smiled and continued beyond the village where we stopped. He pointed and then let me go as he lifted his loincloth and relieved himself, I did the same, and it felt wonderful. He then rubbed my bottom and made some gestures with his hands, which I took to mean he wanted to know if I wanted to relieve myself through the other end. I shook my head, yes, and he took out his knife. I got nervous about what he was going to do with the knife, but he squatted and softened up the soil, then he took a stick and dug a hole and pointed. I straddled over the hole squatted and relieved myself. The man then grabbed me by the arm, and we went to the river. He undid his loincloth and picked me up in his arms and went into the water. He bathed me, made sure to clean my bottom with his hand, then threw some water in my face and let me go. I dunked my head underwater and swam about ten feet before I popped up, the water felt good. I saw him swimming away from me and thought about running but knew I wouldn't get far. He swam next to me and pointed to the shore, grabbing my arm.

At the shore where he was pointing was a boy who, for some strange reason, reminded me of Jack Flynn. We swam over to the bank, and we got out to dry. The boy was a tall, strong-looking boy whom no one would want to taunt.

"Is this the boy you found?"

"Yes, he is well enough to swim," answered the man.

"He looks like he has the skin of a woman and is weaker than one," he said jealously.

The man was aware of his jealousy and said, "He isn't as weak as you think." "He has already counted coup." "He has killed two of our enemies."

"I will see how strong he is," he said in anger.

The man got up and grabbed me by the arm, said, "Grey Wolf, walk with me." He put his arm around the boy's shoulder, and we went back to his lodge. "You know if your mother weren't alive, you would be welcome in my lodge." "Your father, Grazing Deer, was a mighty warrior, and he raised you well, you would make a fine son." The boy lowered his head toward the ground, and the man continued, "What is it you wanted."

The boy raised his head and said, "My mother and I are getting low on meat; do you want to go hunting?"

The man stopped, smiled, and said," I am also low on meat. Will tomorrow morning be soon enough?"

The boy said with a smile, "Yes, I will be ready," he said as he left.

As we passed the lodges on the way back, I noticed that the outside of the lodges had paintings on them with designs, scenes of hunting, animals, and other things. We went back into the lodge I sat where I had been sleeping, and the man sat where he usually ate. I noticed the girl was still there, and I wasn't as nervous about being naked in front of her.

The woman came over and started brushing my hair. I liked her; she was very kind to me. "Ask him who he is and what his name is," the man said.

The girl started pointing and said, "This is Red Elk, this is Turtle Woman, and I am Morning Star, what are you called?"

"My name is James." "I don't know what it means." She was about to tell Red Elk and Turtle Woman, what I said when I continued, "When are your people going to torture and kill me?"

The girl looked shocked and faced Red Elk, who noticed her expression. She said, "He said his name is James." "He wants to know when we are going to torture and kill him."

They all stopped what they were doing and looked at me, and the man said, "Tell him he is our guest we will not torture or kill him, ask him why he has said these things."

Morning Star said, "Why do you think these things; you are my people's guest."

Now it was my turn to be confused, and they all noticed this also. I finally said, "I killed two of your people, your people tortured and killed my aunt, uncle, and cousin." "They did awful things and then tried to kill me." I was in tears by the time I finished saying this.

"He thinks we are our enemies, the Blackfeet that it was we who tortured and killed his family and tried to kill him."

"Tell him who we are and that we mean him no harm," Red Elk said with concern.

"It was not us who killed your family or tried to kill you." "We are Shoshone." "Red Elk saved you from being killed, and our people chased away our enemy, the Blackfeet." "It was the Blackfeet who did all those bad things; they are terrible people."

I had stopped crying and was confused. I was just about to thank Red Elk when Turtle Woman said, "Ask him if he has any family left."

"Do you have any family left?"

I sighed and said, "No, my father came to these mountains before I was born and never came back; he must be dead."

Turtle Woman gave Red Elk a yearning look, and Red Elk said, "Tell him if he wishes he can stay with us, and we will take care of him."

"Red Elk said if you would like to stay with them, they would take care of you."

I studied the offer for a few moments then asked, "Do you mean they will adopt me, be my mother and father."

"He wants to know if you are adopting him, are you going to be his father and mother."

Looking over to his wife, Red Elk said, "Tell him yes."

"Red Elk said yes."

I liked Turtle Woman, and Red Elk seemed kind also. I had no one. I couldn't go back to Saint Louis; they would put me in an orphanage, and to go off by myself would be suicide. I looked up at them with tears in my eyes and a trembling chin and said, "Alright, if they want me."

"He said yes if you want him." There was great joy between Turtle Woman and Red Elk, which made me smile; she grabbed me and held me tight.

I looked at Morning Star and said, "I must learn the Shoshone tongue." "Will you teach me?"

"Yes, I will teach you."

"He asked me to teach him our tongue, and I told him yes." "I will stay here if you wish until he can understand and speak well."

"Yes, you can stay here, but you better ask your mother and father first."

"I will be staying here until you can speak well, but I must tell my mother and father first." She left the lodge with my new mother holding me. Red Elk told Turtle Woman about going hunting in the morning; then, he left the lodge.

A few minutes later in, came Morning Star, I enjoyed the warmth of my new mother's arms; it reminded me of Mama. I got so lost in my thoughts that I reached up and stroked her face with affection. When I realized what I had done, I opened my eyes and looked at her. She had a loving smile on her face, so I snuggled even tighter.

Afterward, I sat down next to Morning Star and asked her, "How old are you?"

"Nine warm seasons have passed since my birth."

"You're the same age as me," I said with enthusiasm. I thought maybe I should bring up about the nursing Turtle Woman does to her to see what she thinks of it. "Where I come from boys my age are not on their mothers' breast, is it different here?"

"No, it is not different here, by about five or six winters boys and girls stop."

"Turtle Woman has nursed me."

"You do not like being on her breast." "I will tell her if you don't?"

"No, I like it; I just wanted to know if that was normal."

She smiled and said, "Most stop after about five or six winters, but when we are young and sick or weak like you are, our mothers will find someone to give us milk if she can." "Your mother's baby died not long ago, so she had milk still."

"She had another child?"

"She had three boys, one died in battle with the Blackfeet, one died hunting buffalo, and the last was newly born; it is unknown how he died."

My mouth was gaping open at what she told me, this new mother of mine has been through a lot.

Turtle Woman had noticed that I was looking at her with sympathy, and she said to Morning Star, "What are you and he talking about?"

"He wanted to know my age; we are the same." "He was concerned about being on your breast at his age, but he likes it."

She smiled and said, "When he is well enough, I will stop; he is too old."

"I also told him about your baby and your two boys; he is sad for you."

Turtle Woman stopped what she was doing and grabbed me and hugged me, and then said something. I couldn't understand how she could be so happy after her great loss. I still hadn't got over losing Mama.

"Why, after her great loss, does she seem to be happy?" "I lost my mother, and I am still sad about that."

"She is still sad; she will always be sad."

"I don't understand," I said in confusion.

Morning Star grabbed Turtle Woman's hand and first said to her, "He doesn't understand how we show sadness."

"Tell him, and I am not as sad now because I have a new son."

Then she said to me while holding up her hand, "This is how we show sadness."

I looked at Turtle Woman's hand and noticed that the tips of two fingers were missing, and another finger got bound with a bandage-like it was just injured. I never noticed or paid much attention to her hands, but I finally understood, and I didn't like the idea. "Your mother also said she isn't as sad now that she has a new son." I wanted to know how that worked, how people would know I was their son now. "Where I come from when you adopt someone, you have to talk to a person who decides if it is alright to adopt or not." "Then, other things must be done." "How is it done here, and how do the people know?" She smiled and said, "Here it is enough for them to ask and you to agree, and the people will know through your mother and father." "Your father has already talked to Arrow Maker, who will go around soon and tell all."

I assumed this Arrow Maker was like a town crier.

Morning Star got busy doing things with my new mother. I was getting tired, so I went over to where I slept. Now that I wasn't in any danger, I could relax, and when I did, I slipped into a dream world.

I woke at the sound of someone yelling something. Both my new mother and father were inside the lodge, and of course, so was Morning Star. They were getting ready to eat when they saw me awake. My mother said something to Morning Star, and she turned to me and asked, "Are you hungry?" I just shook my head, yes and, my father patted the ground next to him. I got up a little wobbly and walked over to where he was patting and sat down. He handed me a knife, and she some meat. I looked at the meat and then the knife wondering what I was to do with it. My father tapped me on the leg. He put one end of the meat in his mouth and then cut off a piece which he chewed and swallowed. I did the same.

I asked Morning Star, "Who was that yelling outside?"

She smiled and said, "That was Arrow Maker letting everyone know about you."

I smiled, and she must have told my new parents.

When I finished one hunk of meat, then another was given and a piece of bark with a combination of unknown vegetables. I watched how my father eats that. He ate it with his fingers, and so did I, to his great pleasure.

I asked Morning Star, "When are you going to teach me your tongue?"

"Now, if you wish," she responded.

Then she started pointing to things and saying their names in Shoshone, and I repeated them. The instruction went on all through the meal and afterward. Then she stopped and pointed at an object and asked me what it was. For everything, she pointed to I said the right word. She said, "You learn quickly."

I looked at her very seriously and said, "Ever since I was born, I remembered everything I heard or read in a book, it is a gift."

"I know many languages, and I learned them fast." I then asked her to teach me several key phrases, such as I must relieve myself; I am hungry, I am thirsty, and more. "Tell them I wish to learn all things, Shoshone, not just the language."

"He wants to know all things that are Shoshone, not just our tongue."

Red Elk said, "Tell him it must be when I get back from hunting."

"It must wait until your father comes back from hunting."

It was getting late and time to go to bed. I went over to where I slept. As I did, I asked Morning Star, "Where are you going to sleep?"

She smiled and said, "With you."

"What!" Before I could say any more, she had all her clothes off and was lying in my bed. I shrugged my shoulders and sighed, I lay down next to her, and she threw the blanket over us. As I lay there, I thought I could hear my mother and father laughing. Like Sarah's, Morning Star's hands started to wander over me, and as I did to Sarah, I brushed her hand away. With Morning Star, that didn't work because she went back to the same activity, and when I tried to brush her hand away, she brushed mine away. I gave up and let her do what she wanted. After a while, my hands were wandering over her until I fell asleep.

Sometime during the night, I woke. Everyone was sleeping, but I think what woke me was my father's snoring. I looked over at Morning Star and stroked her face and hair. Then I built up the nerve to kiss her, not like I did with Mama but different and on her lips. She awoke and smiled as did I, and I put my arm around her and fell back to sleep.

# 6

# TRANSFORMATION

When I woke up the next day, everyone was already up, including Morning Star. My father was gone; I assumed hunting. I had to relieve myself, and I knew how to tell my mother, so I said, "I have to relieve myself."

She smiled and said something I only knew one word of, "Go, you know where to go." "Do you need someone to help you walk?"

I looked over to Morning Star, and she said, "She told me you know where to go and if you need help walking."

I smiled and said, "I would like you to come." "Just in case I stumble, I could hold onto you." She told my mother what I said, and we left the lodge.

It was going to be a warm day. There weren't any clouds or wind, and I could feel the warmth on my skin. As we walked, Morning Star would point at things and tell me what they were in Shoshone. After several words, I stopped and turned to her and said, "You are very beautiful."

She first smiled and then produced a frown and said, "You are not paying attention to learning my tongue."

I laughed and repeated everything back to her in Shoshone and then English. We got to the spot where I relieved myself yesterday, and after I finished, I went over to the river to wash up.

The water was warmer than yesterday, and I asked her, "Do you want to go for a swim?"

"Boys and girls don't swim together unless they are married and alone," she said, surprised I asked.

I asked, "Why?"

She looked at me, confused, and said, "I do not know."

"Then let's go swimming."

She looked around to see if anyone was near and said, "Come with me." She grabbed my hand, and we went far upstream away from the village. She removed her clothing, and we jumped into the water.

We played in the water for about a half-hour when Morning Star said, "Your mother will be worried we better get out."

"You're right; besides, I am hungry." We got out dried and headed back. When we got back, my mother was outside, and when she saw both of us, she knew what we had been doing. She smiled and asked, "Are you hungry."

I didn't need a translation to know what she said, and I answered, "Yes," with a smile.

As I was eating, my mother said, "You are spending too much time inside." "It is time for you to stay outside more."

Morning Star translated for me, and I said, "Yes."

Outside I was introduced to everyone. Instead of Morning Star saying this is James because the people would not understand that name, she just said this is the son of Red Elk and Turtle Woman.

We were getting low on firewood for the lodge, so I told Morning Star, let's gather some wood.

She said, "Men do not gather wood."

"I am not a man; let's go."

As I was returning with the first load, we passed the old woman. I decided to get wood for her also even though Morning Star started rolling her eyes when I told her. When I brought the first load to the old woman, she didn't know what to say.

My father didn't come home that night and wasn't expected until sometime the next day. Morning Star continuously taught me how to speak Shoshone, and I was exhausted between carrying all the wood and learning the language. After having my last meal, I went over to my bed, and within a minute, I was fast asleep, and then later, Morning Star was right beside me.

About two hours after sunrise, my father came into camp with the boy he took hunting. I could see he was tired, so I did what I could to help him. I saw the other boy resented it and I didn't know why. My father talked about the hunt, and Morning Star translated what he was saying to me.

Back in the lodge, my mother told him what I had been up to, and my father turned to me and said, with Morning Star translating, "You are strong enough for me to show you how to do things, maybe next time I will take you hunting."

"I wish to make you proud of me, but there is a lot for me to learn." "I do not know how to use a bow and arrow, and I have never been on a horse." "I would love to go hunting with you, but there is a problem I do not think you are aware of," I said.

My father asked, "What is the problem?"

"When I was helping you when you returned, that boy you took with you was not happy."

My father looked at my mother and said, "What you say has truth Grey Wolf is jealous." He looked at the ground, thinking and said, "We will just have to take him with us."

I was thinking that wasn't going to work. Grey Wolf would just be competing with me and making my life miserable much as Jack Flynn did.

The next morning my fears came true. I was relieving myself when Grey Wolf came up behind me and knocked me to the ground just where I was urinating. He laughed at me and said something and walked off. I had to jump into the water and wash off.

When I got back to the lodge, Morning Star could see I was upset and asked, "What happened?"

"Grey Wolf doesn't like Red Elk is my father, but I am used to it." "There was a boy where I came from who was the same way."

All-day, Morning Star taught me the language." "That night, while I was sitting next to my father eating, my father said, "I understand you had a problem with Grey Wolf."

"Yes, but I knew another boy like him, so I am used to it."

"He has no father and had hoped I would be his father." My father asked, "What are you going to do about it?"

I replied, "What is there to do?"

"You must fight him, or he won't stop."

"He is much larger and older than me, and he is also stronger than me."

"Nevertheless, you must fight him." "It is your choice, but you will be miserable until you do."

I put my head down thinking and finally said, "How can I be strong like you?"

My father smiled and said, "I asked my father the same thing, and I will tell you what he told me to do." "Go to the stream, pick up the stones you can lift and pile them outside the lodge." "The more you pick up in one day, the stronger you will get."

The idea sounded crazy, so I asked my father, "Did it work when you did it?"

My mother started to laugh, but my father said, "Yes, it did, but you have to do everything I ask during the day."

I shook my head yes and turned to Morning Star and asked, "Will you walk beside me as I carry the rocks."

"Yes, as much as I can."

"I'll do it then," I said with conviction.

The next morning after I ate Morning Star and I went out, and she walked with me while I started picking up rocks and piling them by the lodge. After about two hours, people started noticing what I was doing, but they didn't say anything. I was tired but didn't stop, and Morning Star kept on teaching me. I saw Grey Wolf with a friend I think he was laughing at me, but he left me alone for now, and I ignored him. By noon I was dripping with sweat, and soon, after on one of my trips back to the lodge, my mother told me to come in and eat. She gave me a wet leather towel, and I washed my face and my arms and hands.

I went in and ate and asked my father, "When will I know I am getting stronger?"

He looked at me and said, "Tomorrow, if you feel sore, it will be working." "And when the rocks feel lighter, then you are getting stronger."

I smiled and went back to picking up rocks after I ate.

After about the third trip back, Morning Star said, "I need to check with my mother to see if there is anything she needs, I have been away too long."

I asked, "Do you wish me to go with you?"

She smiled and said no and then went to her family's lodge.

I continued picking up rocks, and the pile was getting larger. I had just picked up another rock when I saw Grey Wolf and some other boys waiting for me. He had his bow and arrows, and I knew there was going to be trouble. As I approached him, he said something I didn't completely understand. So, I just ignored him and kept going on. As I started to pass him, he stuck out his bow and tripped me. The large rock went flying in front of me, and I fell on it. The pain shot through me like a lightning bolt, and Grey Wolf walked off, laughing. I bent down and looked at my leg. It was bleeding. I moved it around a little, and my leg didn't appear broken, so I got up, picked up the rock again, and delivered it to the lodge.

As I headed back to get the next rock, Morning Star approached me and saw my bleeding leg and asked, "Grey Wolf?"

I said, "Yes," and kept on walking, not saying anything.

She followed me to the river where I was to get my next rock. When I got there, I started to lift the rock when she grabbed my arm and said, "Come here and sit down."

I did as she said, and she attended to my leg. I grabbed her and kissed her, smiled, and went back to carrying the rocks. That night while eating, my mother eyed the leg but didn't say anything.

"While I was eating the following morning, my father asked, "Are you sore?"

"Yes," I replied.

"Good, then it is working."

"Are you going to pick up rocks today?"

"Yes."

Just before noon, as I was coming back with another rock, my father met me at the lodge. He told me, "Put the rock down and walk with me." In his hand were a bow and arrows which he took with him and we went to the edge of the camp. There was a bank of dirt where he made a square with twigs, and he stepped back to where I was standing. I was excited I knew he was going to show me how to shoot a bow.

Grey Wolf sat down on the ground about ten feet from me with his bow and arrows, and he had a smug look on his face. I was glad my father was with me because I knew there would be trouble if he weren't. He gave me the bow and arrows and told me to hit the center of the square. I looked at the bow and arrow in confusion while Grey Wolf was laughing. I finally figured out how to string the arrow to the bow, and I pulled it back and let it fly. The string on the bow slapped against my arm, and I yelped. The arrow didn't even hit the dirt mound. If one could die of laughter, then Grey Wolf was near it. I got told to try again but hold the bow tighter I did this, and at least I hit the dirt mound. He then told me to look down the arrow's shaft, and I got nearer to the target. I got finally told to take a breath and hold it, and I hit the target to the great joy of my father. He gathered the arrows I shot and said, "When you can hit the target every time without a miss, go back there." He picked up a large rock and threw it about twelve or fifteen feet back. He then said, "Try to hit the target every time again; do this every day until it is easy for you." He turned around and walked away, but just before he left, he told Grey Wolf, "It wouldn't hurt you to help him." Grey Wolf frowned at that idea.

I started shooting the arrows but didn't get many in the target. I tried again I did better, but not all the arrows got into the target. It was getting kind of hard to try to pull back on the string of the bow. I started shooting again, taking my time and being careful, and I was having more success. I had three more arrows to get in the target area when four arrows flew past me, hitting the target dead center. I looked back and saw it was Grey Wolf, and he had picked up a stick. When I turned back to shoot more arrows, he came toward me. He hit the back of my legs, and I fell on my back, grabbing my legs. He placed six more arrows dead center, went down to the target, picked up his arrows, and walked past me, kicking dirt in my face. I was in agony for a few minutes while Morning Star tried to help me. I finally could get to my feet and walk it off.

Morning Star said, "You are going to have to do something about Grey Wolf."

"I am not ready yet," I replied

After about an hour, I went back to reshooting arrows, and I could hit the center every time. I stepped back to where my father said to stand and started reshooting arrows. I had trouble hitting the target every time, so I decided to go back to picking up rocks and try again tomorrow. I asked Morning Star to take the bow and arrows and take them back to the lodge while I went back to picking up rocks.

I got to the stream where I was getting the stones. Before I picked up the first stone, I walked into the water. The cold water felt good on my legs, and after a few minutes, I got out, picked up a rock, and headed back to the lodge. I did this for the next several hours with Morning Star at my side. It was past the time when I usually would stop. I could see Morning Star was getting tired, so I said, "Why don't you go back to the lodge and tell my mother I will quit when it is too dark to get the rocks anymore."

When I quit, it was very dark out I went to the stream one more time to bathe and soak my legs before I went back to the lodge. When I entered the lodge, my mother was about to say something, but my father stopped her. I ate and went to bed and fell asleep without saying a word.

The next morning, I was back picking up rocks. I didn't bother eating, and that afternoon I took my bow and arrows and practiced some more. I started at the short distance when I was hitting the target every time I went to the longer distance and started practicing. Morning Star didn't walk with me in the morning she had to spend some time with her mother. After about half an hour shooting at the longer distance, Morning Star joined me. She had some jerked meat, and I stopped for a few minutes to eat a little. Then I showed Morning Star how well I was doing. At the present distance, I found you had to arch the arrow a little to hit the target. I practiced another hour, then I stopped and went back to picking up rocks.

This pattern of activity went on for the next five days. Of course, Grey Wolf tormented me every day, and some days were worse than others. My father was right about the rocks. They seemed to be getting lighter, and I was running out of rocks to pick up. That night I told my father, "I have no more rocks to carry."

"I will take care of it tomorrow."

By this time, I could speak Shoshone very well, and Morning Star noticed. She said, "This will be my last night here." "You are speaking well, and my mother and father want me back." "I will miss her lying next to me, but I knew this day would come. I also knew we would see each other every day.

The next day my father joined me in my rock carrying activity. We left the lodge, and my father said, "Pick up a rock." I didn't understand why he wanted me to pick up a rock; I just deposited yesterday, but I did what he said, and I carried the rock to the stream. My father drew two lines on the bank and told me, "Put the rocks in the water between here and here. If a rock goes on the other side of the line, you go into the water and put it in the right place." He then left, and I put the first rock into the water and went back to get the next stone.

About three hours later, I was throwing into the water, a stone, and got pushed into the river. When I got out and looked around, I didn't see anyone, but I knew it was Grey Wolf. When I got back to the lodge, I stuck my head into the lodge and told my mother I was not going to eat until night. Four hours later, I was sweating but not tired. I stopped, went into the lodge, grabbed the bow and arrows, and practiced shooting until dark.

When I came back to the lodge for the day, I sat down next to my father. I looked up at him and said, "It has been three suns, and I have not missed the target once."

"I will show you tomorrow what you must do next," he replied. We ate a little, and he continued, "After you eat, take your arrows and bow to Arrow Maker and see if he can make them better." "You can use my bows and arrows to practice until Arrow Maker fixes them."

I was confused, so I asked, "I do not understand I have no bows or arrows, I use yours."

Both he and my mother were surprised and puzzled at what I was saying. My father said, "When you killed the two Blackfeet, and I killed the one on you which I counted as yours, you got all they had." He pointed at the bows and arrows and said, "This is yours, with those two lances, the war club, and scalps." "You have three knives, and the one you have in your hand is yours." "You also have three horses; you did not know this?"

It was now my turn to be surprised. I didn't know what to say, so I said, "I have three horses?"

They smiled and replied with pleasure, "Yes."

"I am going to have to learn how to ride a horse soon."

"After you finish with the rocks, I will teach you," replied my father. I smiled and shook my head, yes.

My mother said, "After you eat, I have another surprise for you."

I looked at her puzzled and asked, "What is it?"

"Wait until you eat."

I ate as fast as I could, and when I finished, I said, "What is my surprise?"

"You must wait and take your arrows and bows to Arrow Maker first," said my mother.

My disappointment was apparent. I grabbed the arrows and bows and left the lodge. My father turned to my mother and said, "You are too hard on him."

"Ha!" She smiled and said, "You should look at yourself."

I approached Arrow Maker and handed him the bows and arrows and said, "The Blackfeet made these, my father wants you to see if you can make them better."

"They are not as good as Shoshone's," he said. He patted the log next to him, and I sat down. "I do not know if I can do anything with them, but I will see.

"Now, I wish to ask you something." "I have seen how Grey Wolf treats you, why do you let him harm you?"

I put my head down and said, "He is bigger and stronger than I am; I am not sure I could beat him."

Arrow Maker said, "Some consider me as being wise, so hear what I have to say." "It does not matter if you lose; it only matters if you fight back."

"Why?" I asked.

"It will take the fun out of harming you, and he will know that there would be a price to hurt you."

I thought about this, and I knew he was right, but I told him, "I will give this more thought."

I got up and left, but instead of heading back to my lodge, I went to Morning Star's lodge. I went to the entrance of the lodge and called for Morning Star, and she came out. She looked beautiful, and I told her, "I miss you very much."

"I miss you, too."

I told her what my father said about all the things I have. To my surprise, she said she already knew it.

It was getting late by the time I got back to the lodge, and I wanted to know what surprise my mother had. "Mother, what is my surprise?"

My father said to my mother, "Maybe we should wait until tomorrow."

"No," I said in protest.

My mother and father laughed, and my mother handed me the things she made with leather. I lifted them, and they were buckskins for me to wear and moccasins for my feet. I had a big smile on my face; now, I could look like everyone else. I went over to my mother and hugged her and kiss. "You must show me how to put these on." As I put the clothes on, they felt odd because I hadn't worn anything for so long; however, I liked them.

My mother said, "I would have finished sooner, but I wanted to do my best on them, and I was busy with you."

I said, "Thank you." I ran out of the lodge. I wanted anybody still out to see me. About thirty minutes later, I came back to the lodge and sat down on my bed. My father and mother looked up and smiled. I asked my father, "Someday, will you take me hunting?"

"When you can ride a horse and can shoot a moving target."

I turned to my mother and said, "I need something to hold my knife, and I need something to hide my hair when I am hunting." I hesitated then continued saying, "And killing Blackfeet, will you make me something that will work if it is not asking too much?"

My father said to my mother, "He is right; he does need these things."

She smiled and said, "I will start tomorrow."

I slept with nothing on because it just felt better. The next morning, I decided just to wear my moccasins and loincloth. I didn't want my clothing to get dirty. I started on the rocks again. Sometime that morning, my father taught me how to make a moving target and hit it by aiming a little ahead of it. The moving target was much harder and was going to take more time to learn. As I was practicing, Grey Wolf came over to me to show how poorly I was doing with a bow and to give me more of his abuse.

It took me three and a half days to finish the rock. They stuck out in the stream like a boat dock. Several times I had to jump into the water to move a stone back over the line, but I did it without complaint. I rested for a minute, looking at my work and surveying my body for all the bruises I had from Grey Wolf's abuse. It seemed one injury would heal, and he would give me another one. Just yesterday, while I was in the water moving a rock, he threw a rock and hit me in my back. I didn't want to fight him, but I thought that I might have to. I was getting better with my arrows, also hitting the moving target about half the time.

I went back to the lodge, looking for my father. I found him talking about hunting with some other men. He turned to me, and I told him I moved all the rocks. The other men laughed, and I gave them a disapproving look.

My father said, "Let us go see." My father and the other men followed me to the rock pile in the stream. "You did well," my father said.

One of the other men, Red Hawk, said, "It will be washed away after the winter's snow," and the others agreed.

"How is your shooting," asked my father.

"I hit the target about half the time; it is more difficult; it will take time."

"You go practice for a while, and I will come and get you to show you how to ride."

As I left, I could hear the others laugh, and I felt sad at how unfit I was. I grabbed my father's bow and arrows and started to the place I was practicing. As I was crossing the camp, I spotted Morning Star carrying water and said, "I will help you with the water."

"No, it is not necessary; you are going to shoot your arrows."

"I can do...." I stopped what I was saying because out of the corner of my eye, I saw Grey Wolf throw a rock at me, and as I turned to look at him, the rock just missed me but hit Morning Star in the upper chest. She fell on her back with the water she was carrying spilling all over her. I went down to her and asked, "Are you alright, do you have pain?"

"I'll be alright," she said, trying to hide her suffering.

Something inside of me snapped, and I became enraged. As I helped Morning Star up, Grey Wolf came toward us, he felt terrible for what he did and wanted to tell her he was sorry, but at the time I didn't see it that way. To be truthful, Grey Wolf liked Morning Star very much and feared her father more when he discovered what happened. I got Morning Star entirely up on her feet, and when Grey Wolf came near, I caught him off guard. I swung and hit him right square in the face. He fell back, and before he could get up, I was on top of him swinging away. He could deflect most of the blows, but a few got in. He flipped me off him, and I went flying onto my back. Before he could get on me, I moved out of the way and was back on my feet. He started getting up, and I hit him again. He got the same look that Jack Flynn got on his face. I noticed it and didn't care; I would just outsmart him. He screamed like a wild animal and came at me. I swung at him again but missed. He hit me and split my lip, and I could taste the blood. By this time, the whole village was aware of what was happening. Every man, woman, and child were there watching and calling out battle cries.

My mother was going to stop the fighting, but my father stopped her and said, "No, let them fight; it is the only way." From behind them, Grey Wolf's mother said, "He is right."

Morning Star told her father everything that happened. He was angry but was satisfied with how I was dealing with it. Grey Wolf hit me a few more times. His punches would make Jack's feel like taps, but I blocked the pain with the rage I felt. I was surprised that I was standing up to his blows as well as I was. I fell and got up several times. But I also got a few punches in, and it was showing on Grey Wolf, and this empowered me to try harder. Out of frustration for not knocking me out quickly, Grey Wolf grabbed a stick and used it as a club. He swung, and I ducked under his club and hit him in the kidney and swept his legs. I then rolled over to where there were some sticks. By the time I got one, Grey Wolf was on me, and I used the stick to block the blow. He was furiously swinging his club, but I was able to get away and get on my feet. I couldn't let him get on top of me because, if he did, he would be too heavy to push him off, and he would finish me off. I ducked a swing and hit him in the knuckles. He dropped his club, and as I dropped my club, I got two good hits on him with my fists, one to the head and the other to the chest. He came back several times more with his blows to my head and chest. Again, out of frustration, he pulled his knife and came at me. But Arrow Maker tripped him and grabbed the knife out of his hand. He then came into my chest with his shoulder and lifted me off the ground. We both went tumbling, and I started rolling with him, not letting him pin me to the ground. We were knocking things down and even rolling through the campfire as we wrestled with each other. Through all the destruction we were causing, the people of the village couldn't care less; they were too excited to concern themselves. Our battle moved toward the stream Grey Wolf getting the better of me as we went. Streams of blood dripped down my face from mouth, nose, and several cuts I had. Grey Wolf lip got swollen, and he wasn't doing much better, blood was coming from his nose, he had several red marks on his face, and one eye was closing a little. My back was facing the bank of the stream. Grey Wolf hit me three good ones in the face. I was getting tired but could duck the fourth blow and go under his arm forcing him to turn around then I swung on him as hard as I could, and he went flying into the water, and I went in after him. The cold water energized me, and I found I could move faster in the water than Grey Wolf. Fatigue was taking over both of us; Grey Wolf's blows were becoming less frequent. We finally climbed out of the water and sat on the bank, fighting for air. Grey Wolf looked over at me and started laughing, and it surprised me, but I returned a big smile. He then said, "Maybe you did kill two Blackfeet." "I will still need to show you how to fight." I knew at that point; the fight was over, and I had survived.

Grey Wolf got up as if nothing had happened and went over to Morning Star and said, "I am sorry for hitting you with that rock I threw; it was not meant for you, please forgive me."

"There has been no harm I am not angered," she replied, and then she smiled. Grey Wolf went off with his mother, but I needed to sit for a while. The people of the village seeing the battle had ended disperse back to what they were doing and cleaning up the camp.

Both my mother and father had smiles on their faces as they and a few others came over to me. My father picked me up. I was a little wobbly, and my mother grabbed my arm and took me to the lodge. As we went, I looked up at my father and said, "Your bow and your arrows, I need to get them."

"Do not worry about them." "I will get your bow and your arrows," my father replied.

I went into the lodged and collapsed on my bed. My mother removed my loincloth and moccasins and started cleaning me up. She then applied something she made to heal my wounds. I then told my mother, "I think I will sleep a little."

"That would be a good idea," she said. I laid on my back with nothing on letting the cool breeze float over my body, and I drifted off to sleep.

# 7

# SETTLING IN

I awoke several hours later, my head throbbing, and I was sore but as hungry as a bear. Morning Star was right beside me, stroking my hair. She bent down and found a spot on my face and kissed me. I grabbed her, and with pain, kissed her back. I then asked her, "How do I look?"

"Like you fought with a wolverine."

I didn't know what a wolverine was, but I would imagine it to be a fearsome beast of some kind. As I looked at my mother, I asked, "Can you give me something to stop the pain in my head." A few minutes later, she gave me a bitter mixture to drink, and soon after, my head felt better, as did my whole body.

Morning Star said she had to go. I was going to go out with her, but my mother said, "We will be eating in a short time, Morning Star will you tell my husband," she nodded and left.

I turned to my mother and said, "Do I look as bad as Morning Star said?"

She nodded and said, "Worse!"

"I wonder what Grey Wolf looks like," I asked.

"Not as bad as you," she replied.

A few minutes later, my father came in, looked at me, and started laughing, and I admit I smiled over it even though it hurt. As my father sat down, I got up, grabbed my knife, and sat down beside him. I tried eating a hunk of meat, but it was painful because of the split lip.

My mother saw me struggling, so she said, "Shred the meat. It will be easier to eat," and I did this, and it went better.

My father said, "It should be better for you with Grey Wolf."

"I hope so; I would rather fight a wolverine than him."

My mother interjected and said, "Morning Star said he looked like a person who fought with a Wolverine."

"She is right," he replied.

After we ate, I asked for some more of that bitter water for my pain, and my mother gave me more. It was still light out, so I got dressed, grabbed the bow and arrows, and went outside. Everyone was smiling and nodding his or her head at me as I went to the place where I practiced. I was there about a half-hour when I drew back to take a shot a hand grabbed the arrow, and it was Grey Wolf. I looked at him, and he didn't look very beat up. He went down to the target and said, "You shoot about this far from the target." He then came back to me and acted like he had a bow and said, moving his arms left and right, "You do not do this." He went back down to the target and caused the target to move. He stepped to the side and said, "Shoot."

I was nervous about shooting while he was so near, but I shot anyway and hit the target. He pulled the arrow and repeated shoot, and this went on for more than an hour. My shooting improved almost a hundred percent.

I went down to him, and he said, "You did much better." He smiled and continued, "You do not look too good."

I said, "I got into a fight with a wolverine." We both laughed, and I said, "Follow me to the water."

When we reached the stream, I sat down, and Grey Wolf sat beside me. "What I did to Morning Star it was done by mistake, why did you fight?"

"I love her."

"It was not wise."

"I would do it again." There were a few moments of silence, and I could see Grey Wolf wasn't happy at how I answered. I broke the silence by saying, "Why did you mistreat me."

"Because I wanted to," he replied angrily.

"I do not think you are telling me the truth. I believe you feel if I were not here, my father would be your father."

He did not answer me but just hung his head low. I went on and said, "Suppose I wasn't here, and my father, was willing to be your father would you leave your lodge and your mother and go to my father's lodge?"

"No."

There was silence again, and then I said, "There may be a way for my father to be your father too, and you would still live with your mother."

His head popped up, and he said with interest, "How can this be?"

"It is something the whites do from where I use to live." "I will tell you more after I talk to my father and maybe a few others." Then I added with a smile, "Besides, I am not sure I want you for a brother."

He replied, "Someone has to teach you how to fight."

It was getting late, so I got up and told him, "I am going back to my lodge." "I will talk to you tomorrow, thank you for your help,"

Grey Wolf nodded, and I left. On the way back, I saw Arrow Maker and went over to him.

"Son of Red Elk, I have something for you." He went into his lodge and came out with the bows and arrows I gave him.

"Thank you; it looks like you worked hard on them." I didn't see any difference, but I didn't want to say anything. "Arrow Maker, I have something to ask you."

"What is it?"

"You know Grey Wolf wanted my father for his own?"

"Yes, I have said it," Arrow Maker said.

"There may be a way for this to happen."

"How can this be?"

"Where I come from, the whites have men who are appointed Godfathers." "I believe you would call it the Great Mystery fathers." "They take the place of a father if the father dies."

Arrow Maker said, "You did not have a Great Mystery father."

"No, I just had my mother, who died," I replied. Then I asked, "Would this Great Mystery father be accepted here?"

"It has never gotten done; I do not know."

My disappointment was easy to see, and Arrow Maker said, "It doesn't mean it cannot get done."

I smiled and said, "I will talk to my father." He nodded, and I went to my lodge.

My father was already sitting, getting ready to eat again. I hung up the bows and arrows and sat next to my father and pulled out my knife. "How did you do today with your target?" asked my father.

"I did very well, I hit the target almost all the time, but I will keep on practicing until I hit it all the time, Grey Wolf helped me."

"That was kind of Grey Wolf," replied my father.

"I have much on my mind to talk to you and my mother about," I said.

"Speak," replied my father.

There was a moment of silence, and I decided to say everything on my mind that was a concern to me, not just about Grey Wolf. "Will you consider what I have to say?"

"Of course, you are my son," replied my father.

My mother and father became very interested in what I was going to say, so I went on. "I love you both very much, maybe more than you realize."

My mother said, "We love you too."

I smiled and nodded and said, "I know it is the way of the Shoshone to have the men eat first, and the woman and children eat last, but I do not like this and wish my mother to eat with us."

My father leaned back and thought for a few seconds and said, "Do you think I do not love Turtle Woman?"

"I know you do."

There was another moment of silence, and then he said, "It would be an embarrassment if the one I love ate at the same time with us if we had a guest." He smiled at me and continued, "If we do not have guests, and if your mother wants to eat with us, it will be alright."

It made me happy he would do this for my mother and me. I went on, "What makes me sadder is my mother's hand." My father looked at my mother with confusion, and I went on, "Every time someone she loves dies, she cuts off one of her fingers to show her sadness." "I wish her to stop and not do it anymore, especially for me."

"It is our way," my mother said.

"When the mother who gave me birth died, everyone knew my sadness by the way I acted and cried." "I am still sad about that even now." "Those who didn't understand my grief if there were any, were stupid, and they do not matter."

"If you were to go to another village, how would the people know of your loss?" asked my mother.

"If I choose not to say anything, then it is my choice." "If I did tell someone, those people would know my sadness by the way I acted while telling." "My father has lost three sons, yet he has all his fingers." "How does he tell those in another village?"

My mother looked at my father, and my father said to my mother, "He has much wisdom."

"I must think about this," my mother replied.

"I have another thing to say that I believe it will be important to you both." I was trying to think about how I was going to ask about Grey Wolf, and then I said, "Grey Wolf has much sadness about not having a father."

My father said, "Yes."

Looking at my father, I said, "If you could, would you be his father, he loves you?"

"Yes, I have told him so, but it is impossible because of his mother." As my mother gave me something else to eat, they were both looking at me and wondering what I would say next.

"It is not impossible," I said.

"Then how can it be?" my father said.

"In the village I came from, many boys and girls are given what you call a Great Mystery father." "The job of a Great Mystery father is to take over as a father." "If a boy or girl loses his or her father, they will not leave their mother, but their Great Mystery father would help them learn things and take care of them, and they would feel they have a father." "I talked to Arrow Maker about this, and he said this has never got done, but it does not mean it cannot get done."

"This would be good for Grey Wolf," my father said. "You would not mind having him for a brother?"

"No," I said.

My father looked at my mother, and she nodded her head yes. "I must bring this up with the elders and see what they say." I shook my head in agreement.

We had just finished eating, and I got up, grabbed the bows and arrows Arrow Maker fixed, and sat next to my father again. "Arrow Maker repaired the bows and arrows, but I do not see the difference."

My father showed me all the changes, mostly cosmetic, but changes. I started yawning, and my father said, "Tomorrow, I will show you how to ride a horse now you go to sleep."

The next morning, I asked my father, "When will you teach me how to ride?" "If it is not soon, I will practice shooting."

"Go shoot, and I will come and get you." I went to Grey Wolf's lodge, and he was helping his mother. "Do you have time to help me with my shooting?"

"I am getting wood for my mother."

"Can I help?"

"If you wish to help, come with me." I put my bow and arrows next to his lodge and followed him. We went to a wooded area and started picking up wood for his mother. I was confused about why he was getting wood; it was a woman's job, so Morning Star told me, but I didn't say anything.

As we headed back to his lodge, I told Grey Wolf, "Tonight, you may be my brother."

He stopped and stared at me and said, "What do you mean?"

"My father will talk with the elders tonight about adopting you."

"But what of my mother?"

"You will not have to leave your mother."

"How can this be?"

"You will see tonight," I said with a smile. We went over to the place where I practiced shooting for the next several hours.

Sometime during my shooting, my father showed up. I didn't notice him standing behind me until he said, "You are doing well."

I turned around and smiled and went to him as did Grey Wolf. "I do well because of Grey Wolf."

My father put his arm around Grey Wolf, and you could tell that he loved it by the affectionate look on his face. Then my father said, "Come with me."

Grey Wolf and I followed my father until we came to two horses that were tied up. "That is your horse," my father said, touching a fine sorrel. "Get up on the horse," said my father. I looked on the right and left of the horse and decided on one side and tried to jump up without success. Grey Wolf was chuckling at what must have looked ridiculous. After I tried to jump up on the horse many times and the horse tried to move out of the way every time, my father started to come over to help me when Grey Wolf decided to help first. He pushed me out of the way, grabbed the horse's mane, and swung up onto the horse.

He jumped down and said, "Grab the mane as I did," I did as he said. "Now swing your body up, grabbing the horse with the other hand." Again, I did as he said and was almost upon the horse when he gave me a little shove up. Grey Wolf grabbed my leg, threw me off the horse, and said, "Do it again."

My father saw that he need not teach me, Grey Wolf was doing just fine. He said, "You listen to Grey Wolf; he will show you well."

After getting up and down from the horse about a dozen times, my father turned to Grey Wolf and said, "Go get your horse, and we will ride."

I didn't know if I could ride, yet I just was beginning to learn how to get up and down from a horse. Grey Wolf came with a gray appaloosa mare, and my father mounted his black and told me, "Get up on your horse." With a little trouble, I got up and looked over to my father and Grey Wolf. "Grey Wolf, move your horse so that it is in front of us." Turning to me, my father said, "Watch everything Grey Wolf does." He moved the leather rope one way, and the horse went that way. He moved the leather rope the other way, and the horse moved that way. He then turned the horse around, rode a distance from us, then turned around again and quickly came at us. He pulled up on the rope, and the horse stopped, it was very much like steering the wagon.

My father said, "Now, you do it." I moved the rope to the right nothing happened. I jerked it harder, and nothing happened again. I tried the other side with the same results. I looked at my father, and he said, "You did not look close enough." Grey Wolf was laughing again, and I felt inadequate. My father went out in front of me and said, "When you want to go right, you move your rope right, but you also press your left leg against the horse." He showed me how to move the rope, use my legs, and said, "You try it." I did, and the horse did as I wanted her to do.

"We go for a ride now," and off went my father and then Grey Wolf and then me. I was tense for a while, and my father saw it. He said, "Your horse is your friend, relax and treat her like your friend." After about a half-hour, I was more relaxed, and we stopped and got off the horses. We walked the horses for a while, then got back on them and went back to the village.

When we arrived back at the village, my father said, "Wait here with the horses." He handed me the rope that was around his horse's neck and went into our lodge. He came out with some of my mother's sweet cakes and said, "Give these to your horse, and she will know you better." I held out the cakes for the horse, and the horse inhaled them.

After I put the horses up, Grey Wolf and I went to the stream, took off all our clothes, bathed, or perhaps I should say we played in the water. As we sat on the bank drying off, I said, "After I eat, I will come and get you, and we can go listen to what the elders will speak."

"You will not have to, I will already be there," replied Grey Wolf.

I went back to the lodge and went inside to eat. After we ate, my father went to the main campfire where the other elders would meet. I was about to go when my mother said she needed water. I took a container and ran to the stream to get the water. When I got back, I told my mother I was going to where the elders were meeting. My mother said, "I will go with you."

When we got there, many were there, as I looked around, I spotted Grey Wolf as well as Morning Star. I told my mother, "I am going over there to be with Morning Star." She nodded approval, and I joined Morning Star.

The elders were sitting together with the rest of the people standing around them. Someone would say something, and the elders would comment about it. On occasion, those standing around the elders would say something, and the elders would discuss its worth. The elders were now considering moving the village and splitting into two villages. Spotted Buffalo said, "We must move game and wood are getting scarce here, and it is not healthy here; we have been here too long." Everyone seemed to agree, and he went on talking, "We must also divide into two camps so we can prepare for the snows." Again, they agreed, but what they were struggling with is who would go where. I was worried that Grey Wolf, Morning Star, or Arrow Maker would be in a different village. There was a great debate, and I whispered my concerns in Morning Star's ear.

She asked me, "Why are you so concerned where I go?"

I was stunned at her, not knowing, and I said, "I love you."

I guess others, including the elders, heard what I said, and they started laughing, but I didn't care; that's how I felt. Spotted Buffalo said, "If no one objects my lodge, Red Elks lodge, Arrow Maker's lodge, Blue Lizard's and Grey Wolf's will be in the same village."

No one objected, and my father said to me, "Do you have any objections, my son?"

"No, this is good."

"I am glad you approve," and everyone laughed again.

The discussion went on, and it got decided to leave in three days to give time to find two sites. Next, Spotted Buffalo said, "Is there anything else to be discussed."

Everyone went silent for what seemed forever, and I almost jumped in when my father got up and said, "As you know, Grazing Deer was a great warrior." Everyone made sounds of agreement. "He was almost like a brother to me." "When he died in battle with the Blackfeet, he left a wife and son behind." "I would have adopted Grey Wolf, but he would not leave his mother, which is only right." Again, everyone made sounds of agreement. "I would have brought Blue Lizard into my lodge." "Even Turtle Woman agreed with this, but Blue Lizard wanted her lodge, which is her right." "Grey Wolf wants me for his father, and I want him for my son, but I told him this is impossible even though I know he needs a father." Again, there was an agreement; my father was a great talker; I could see that. He was building a case for making Grey Wolf his son. "So, this is the problem for which there seem to be no solutions."

One Horn, an old man who is said, has great medicine and can do many things. He even sees into the future, stated in a surly voice, "If there is no solution, then why even talk about it?"

Overall, I was accepted as a member of this village and as Red Elk's son. Some were not happy I was here chief of those unhappy was One Horn. I don't know why this was so, but I was aware of this when I tried to talk to him, and he said in an annoyed voice that he didn't have time for one such as me. My father answered him and said, "I thought this was true; there was no solution until my son told me of a way."

One Horn said disrespectfully, "Anything that white mouse says has no meaning here."

I was angry, but for my father, it was an insult that he couldn't tolerate. Everyone saw the anger on his face, and he started to go for his knife when Tall As The Sky said, "Hold your tongue One Horn or you must deal with me." He then turned to my father and said, "How can this problem of Grey Wolf be fixed?" Tall As The Sky was a very tall young warrior in his early twenties, he was very strong, and he was much respected, and it got said he would be a chief someday. He knew that if my father had hurt or killed One Horn, there would have been big trouble for him. One Horn, as arrogant as he was, still had a lot of say and power with the elders, and he used it.

My father answered Tall As The Sky and said, "Perhaps my son should explain." My father motioned for me to come forward and said, "Speak, my son."

I explained to them how in my village, most boys or girls get a Great Mystery father just in case something happens to their father. I said, "This Great Mystery father would act just like a real father, but the children would not leave their mother."

"If this is so, then why are you not with your Great Mystery father now?" said One Horn sarcastically.

"I never got a Great Mystery father, my birth mother, who died, always thought my birth father would come back from these mountains, but I believe he died many years ago."

"This Great Mystery father is the white man's way and not the Shoshone way it has no place here," One Horn said in an obstinate tone. Many agreed with him, and my heart sank so much I couldn't look at Grey Wolf.

I spoke up and said, "Are we not all spirits of the land?"

Arrow Maker got up and said, "The rifle that we use to hunt is not our way, nor is the metal knife and the pots the women use all come from the white man and are not our way." "We take much from the white man and make it our way." "This Great Mystery father has never gotten done here, and it isn't our way until we make it our way." "I ask you all, what harm would this do." "Will this not do anything but good for us and Grey Wolf?" After Arrow Maker said this, he sat down, and everyone agreed with him.

Spotted Buffalo said, "I agree with Arrow Maker." "This Great Mystery father is a good thing; we shall have a vote of the elders." Everyone voted in favor of it except One Horn, and he was angry, but I didn't care. Spotted Buffalo went on and said, "Before we make this, so there are some questions I wish to ask." "Son of Red Elk, how is it after Grey Wolf did you so much harm towards you, then you and he even fought yet you still want him for your brother."

"I understood his anger toward me; he was not mad at me; he was mad because he thought I took Red Elk away from being his father." "We fought because he harmed Morning Star, your daughter, whom you now know I love." "It was not an easy thing for me to fight Grey Wolf." "He is bigger and stronger than I, and he is Shoshone." "I was so angry that day for what he did by accident to Morning Star I wanted to kill him." "I am glad I did not; I could not have lived with myself if I did." "I am not sure if I could have killed him because he is stronger and a better fighter than me." "One thing is for sure, one of us would have been dead if we both had not gotten so tired and if Grey Wolf had not spoken to me in that kind manner he did." "Since then, he has been very kind to me, showing me how to do many things like an older brother is supposed to do." "I love Grey Wolf like I love my mother and father." "No matter what happens today, he will always be my brother, and I will not fight him anymore."

When I finished, it seems like what I said had a positive effect on everyone especially, Grey Wolf. "What you did for my daughter was brave of you." "What you said about Grey Wolf is true, and I thank you for defending her." "I am also aware of your love for her, and I think she feels the same for you." I looked at Morning Star, and her face turned as red as mine, but she didn't protest, and I was happy about that. "You and my daughter will be a discussion for another time right now we need to talk about Grey Wolf."

"Grey Wolf, do you want Red Elk for a Great Mystery father and his son for a brother?"

Grey Wolf said with a joyful heart, "Yes."

"Blue Lizard, do you wish this to get done?"

With love in her heart for Grey Wolf, she said, "Yes."

"Turtle Woman, do you have any objections."

She smiled and said, "None, at all."

Spotted Buffalo looked at the rest of the elders for objections, and there were none except for the scowl on One Horn's face. Spotted Buffalo then said, "It is done."

It got decided that Grey Wolf was my brother. There was much shouting from all, including me. I went over to my father, who had a big smile on his face, and Grey Wolf joined us, and he put his arms around both of us affectionately. My mother and Blue Lizard joined us along with Spotted Buffalo, Morning Star, her mother, and her brothers. There was also Arrow Maker and his wife, Winds Blows, and Tall As The Sky.

They were all talking when, Tall As The Sky spotted the gold necklace that was my mother's, he reached for it and asked, "Where did you get this?"

Everyone had noticed and went quiet, and I said, "It was my birth mother's."

"I have seen this before, but I do not know where."

I shrugged my shoulders and said, "It is mine now that my birth mother is dead."

"I believe that it is yours." "I just wish I could remember where I saw it before."

We all started back to our lodges when Grey Wolf came up to me and said, "Be ready tomorrow we will go for a ride and bring your arrows and bow."

"If you go tomorrow you will take one of your other horses so you will know each other. I will get the horse for you," said my father.

As I watched Grey Wolf walk off with his mother, I saw Tall As The Sky looking at me. We all went into the lodge. I sat down on my bed and looked up at my father and said, "I think it went well."

"Yes, but it could have been bad with One Horn," said my father.

"Why does he dislike me?"

"One Horn does not like change when he sees the color of your skin; he sees change." "Do not feel bad about this; he does not like Bear Slayer either and sees him only as a white man," my father explained.

"What did Spotted Buffalo mean when he said that my love for Morning Star would be discussed at another time, what is there to discuss?"

"You will not need to worry about that until you are older, much older." "Spotted Buffalo is talking about what will happen when a man and a woman are in love with each other."

I was more confused than before, and I looked over to my mother to explain some of my confusion. "Your father is wise; do not concern yourself with this now." "You are young and have many other things to learn."

There was a call at the entrance of the lodge, and my father went out. A few moments later, my father came in and said, "I must leave tonight to find a new place for our village."

"What about my horse, how will I know which one to get?"

"I will leave your horse tied up outside." He gathered up some things and food and went outside with my mother, and I followed him. My father and a younger man, named Deer Slayer, were there and he got our horses and tied my horse up, a brown paint, another mare. My father and Deer Slayer took off southwest. My mother and I went into the lodge. It was late I took off my clothing to go to bed. I looked at my mother and asked, "Can I sleep with you?" She smiled and lifted her blanket, and I crawled in beside her, snuggling next to her, then I fell asleep.

# 8

# THE MAKING OF A WARRIOR

I was eating the next morning when Grey Wolf came to my lodge and called out. My mother invited him in and said, "You are the son of Red Elk and do not need to call out just come in." He smiled and shook his head in agreement. "Are you hungry?" she asked.

He smiled and said, "I am always hungry." My mother gave him something to eat. When we finished, we told my mother that we were going for a ride and would be back just before dark.

My mother asked, "Where are you going?"

Grey Wolf answered, "We will be going west." "I'll be showing him how to fight."

"You're not going to draw blood, are you?" I said cautiously.

Grey Wolf laughed and said, "Not unless you want me to."

"No, that is alright."

We both went to our horses. I turned to Grey Wolf and asked, "Do you think this horse is a good one?"

"It is a good horse," he replied. "Better than the last one, only you can tell I do not know for sure." We got on our horses, with me having a bit of a struggle, and we rode west. It could not have been a more beautiful day with a few puffy clouds, a slight breeze, but a warm day.

We rode several hours, and then we walked our horses, and I turned to him and asked, "Where are we going?"

"It is a place I found about two seasons ago." "It is my private place, but since you are my brother, I am taking you there."

We rode for another hour and came to a pond and a small waterfall. We went up an animal trail to a spot above the waterfall where there was a grassy area surrounded by trees. We tied up our horses and let them graze. You could see for miles from where we were, and the only noises were the rush of water, some birds, and a breeze moving through the trees.

After walking around a short time, Grey Wolf took off all his clothing and told me to do the same, which I did. He was thin but muscular for his age as compared to me, who had lost a lot of baby fat and had some muscle but not as much as he. His skin was brown because he was born Shoshone but lighter around the hips. I was getting browner because of the summer sun hitting my body and because most of the time, I wore just a loincloth. Grey Wolf had no scars that I could see, and I was healing from the fight we had, but I would have some scars from what my uncle and the Blackfeet had done.

He sat on the ground and told me to sit next to him. He then took out his knife and carved two sticks into crude knives. He dug a hole and added water to make mud. He found some grass and leaves that had decayed and turned black and added that to the mud.

He told me to stand up, and he touched or pointed to each area of my body and explained what would happen if you cut each area. He grabbed the back of my knee and said one could get crippled by a slicing there. He pointed at other areas of the body and said what would happen. He had me do the same to him when he had finished telling me and say what he just said to me.

He then dipped the two wooden knives into the mud. He handed me one, took the other, and said, "The mud will mark where you hit me if you can. Hold your blade up it will cause more damage if you strike your enemy."

We stood opposite each other, and I looked for an opening, and in a flash, he left a mark across my chest. I tried to jump out of the way but was too slow. Grey Wolf stepped back and said, "Now, I will show you slowly what you did wrong and how you can stop my blade watch my eyes." "They will tell you where I will move." Then slowly, he moved his wooden knife toward me and stopped. He took my free arm and showed me how to block the blade and counter strike. We practiced several different moves faster and faster, and I was blocking some but was slow on the counterstrike. Grey Wolf was running out of patience with me. "You must move faster as if your life depends on it."

"I will try harder," I said. We dunked our wooden knives into the mud and stood opposite each other, and it began again. Gray Wolf lunged at me, and I blocked him. He came at me again, and I recognized it was going to be a body strike. I blocked with my free hand and went under his arm. He turned around and was furious and said, "Why did you not strike me."

I smiled and went over to him and pointed to the back of his leg. He was shocked at what he saw. I had struck him so fast he hadn't noticed, but the blow would have crippled him.

He started laughing and said, "Do that again."

We practiced for another hour, and we were both covered with mud from the wooden knives. I still had a long way to go, but I was getting it.

We got rid of the wooden knives, and both jumped into the pond to wash off. We finally got out to dry, and I laid next to my brother. He turned to me and asked, "Yesterday, when you said you loved me, were you telling the truth?"

"I do not lie; I love you very much."

There was a moment of silence, and then he said with a soft voice, "I love you too." He put his arm around me as a sign of affection, which was a great surprise to me. A moment later, his whole character changed. He got up laughing as if nothing had happened, grabbed his bow and arrows, and said, "Come with me, we will look for food."

I got my bow and arrows, and off we went. There were a lot of rabbits where we were. He told me to lead my shot, and we both got a rabbit my first. We went back to where our clothing was, and he picked up a stick and tied a leather cord loosely at both ends. He took two flat pieces of bark, dried grass, pine needles, and another straight stick. He twisted the leather cord around the stick. He placed one piece of bark on top of the stick and the other at the bottom. On the bottom bark, he put the pine needles and dried grass, then moving the one stick with the leather cord back and forth real fast the other stick started spinning, and smoke started to come up, then a flame. He added sticks to make a campfire; it was something I'd never seen but would always remember. I watched how Grey Wolf skinned the rabbit and tried to do it myself. I didn't do as well, but with his help, I did well enough to be able to eat the rabbit after it got cooked.

As we were eating, I asked, "Do you mind if I come back here with Morning Star?" I said, giggling.

"No, you and Morning Star can come, but do not tell anyone else," he replied with a smile. "There is a cave up a little further up. You can see this place and all around." We finished eating, cleaned ourselves up, got dressed, and headed back to the village.

It was getting dark when we got back, and I was concerned that my mother would worry. I rode up to my lodge, got off the horse, found my mother and told her, "I am sorry I came back late I was slow in learning what Grey Wolf was trying to show me."

She wasn't mad and said, "At least you are safe, are you hungry?"

"No, I killed my first rabbit and ate that." "I will put up the horse, clean up and come into the lodge," My mother nodded. I handed her the rabbit fur and went to return the horse to the main herd.

After putting up the horse, I met Grey Wolf at the stream washing himself. I asked him, "Will we practice again tomorrow?"

"Yes, but here and we will do other things."

"What?"

"You will see tomorrow."

I went into the lodge, stripped off my clothes, and sat down next to my mother. She smiled at me and said, "I have some things for you."

"What are they?"

She put a small pouch around my neck as I had seen on others, and she said, "It will give you good medicine."

"What is in it?"

"Nothing, you must find things that are special for you." She then gave me a sheath for my knife and a soft leather cloth that I could wrap my hair into and tie under my chin. I hugged my mother and kissed her, and she said, "The winter snows will be here soon, and I will make warm clothing for you to wear."

"I think you do too much for me."

"You are my son; it is what makes me happy."

I stared out into space, and with a perplexing look on my face, I said, "You and my father have adopted me, but am I Shoshone?"

"Why does this trouble you, you are our son, the people as well as your father and I accept you as one of us," she said with love.

"Not all have accepted me as Shoshone?" I was talking about One Horn and his friends.

My mother continued, "Your father is wise; you should speak to him when he comes back." I looked up to my mother, smiled at her, and snuggled next to her. "I think it is time we go to bed," she said. My mother laid down, and I laid next to her and fell asleep.

The next day Grey Wolf started to show me how to fight with a wooden knife, and then he taught me how to fight with my hands and whole body. When we rested by the stream, I asked Grey Wolf what I had asked my mother, "My brother, am I Shoshone?"

He put his head down and said, "You are my brother." "I consider you a Shoshone, but I don't know if others do."

"Is there a way for me to be Shoshone?"

"I believe so, but I am not wise about this; you should talk to our father."

"I will talk to our father and maybe another also."

We went back to practicing fighting. I felt Grey Wolf was an excellent teacher. It was getting near time to eat, and we parted, but before Grey Wolf left, I said, "You spend a lot of time with me, you have other friends that you could be with."

Grey Wolf said in a disapproving tone, "You are my brother, you come first." "I do not want to talk about this anymore." I nodded my head and left.

On the way to my lodge, I saw Arrow Maker and sat down beside him. I asked him, "Am I Shoshone?"

"Some say you are because you are the son of Red Elk, and I say you are." "Others who say you are not."

"One Horn and his friends," I said.

"Yes, and others."

"Grey Wolf said there is a way for me to be Shoshone."

There was a moment of silence, and then he said, "Grey Wolf is right, but it is not easy; you should talk to your father about this."

"I will speak to him, but I wanted to talk to you too." "I better go into my lodge, thank you for being truthful with me." He nodded, and I went into my lodge to be with my mother.

The following morning Grey Wolf was showing me how to fight going over what I had learned the day before. He showed me what to do when someone heavier gets on top of you. My mind was on my father and what I would say to him about the Shoshone issue. Long before he came back, I had decided not to say anything until he had time to rest and so I continued to train.

A little after noon, Deer Slayer and my father came back to the village, and we greeted them. My father didn't look tired, but I decided to wait anyway before I said anything. My mother took his things then Grey Wolf, and I took his horse, groomed it, and let it go back to the herd.

By the time Grey Wolf and I finished the two warriors for the other half of the village arrived. It got decided to have a meeting with the elders of the village to see where we would go. The elders decided that one-half of the village would go west and slightly north, and the half I was in would go west but more south. My father mentioned the area, and I asked Grey Wolf, "Do you know this area?"

"Yes, good grass, many trees, it is in a valley, so there will be little wind; it is a good place for the winter." The meeting broke up, and we were to leave the next morning. My father went back to our lodge with my mother.

I went with Grey Wolf to his lodge; his mother wasn't at the meeting, and Grey Wolf wanted to tell her. After Grey Wolf told his mother, she said, "One place is as good as another."

I said, "I will help you pack as soon as I help my mother and father." After offering my help to Grey Wolf and Blue Lizard, I headed back to my lodge when I saw Arrow Maker along the way. I said, "Tomorrow, I will help my mother and father pack things away, then Grey Wolf' and Blue Lizard." "I will help you after I get finished with our father's lodge and Grey Wolf's too."

Arrow Maker said, "We pack tonight, so we will be on time to move."

"You will sleep under the stars?" I asked.

"Yes," he replied.

"Then I will help you tonight."

"That will be good," I smiled and left for the lodge.

My father was eating in the lodge, and he motioned for me to sit beside him as I did. "What have you been doing while I was gone?"

"Grey Wolf has been showing me how to fight and how to use a knife."

"This is good."

"He told me he loved me."

"Brothers should love each other."

I changed the subject and said, "I killed my first rabbit and ate it, but I think I need to learn how to clean and skin better." My mother held up the pitiful rabbit pelt.

My father laughed and said, "It is good that you can hunt for yourself." "You will learn how to clean and skin better."

"You will help pack for the journey tomorrow."

"Yes, and I will help Grey Wolf and Blue Lizard also." My father nodded, and I said, "Arrow Maker and his wife Crawls On The Ground will pack tonight I wish to help them, too."

My father nodded and said, "I will help too."

"They will have to sleep outside can they sleep here?" I asked.

"I will talk to them," my father answered. My father, I, and even my mother helped Arrow Maker, and Crawls On The Ground pack their things. My father invited them to stay in our lodge, which Arrow Maker accepted.

In the lodge, my parents, Arrow Maker and Crawls On The Ground, were all talking about various things. It reminded me of when I first came, and I didn't understand what they were saying, but of course, I know now what they were saying. I ignored them; it did not interest me until Arrow Maker told my father, "And did your son tell you about his desire to be Shoshone."

My father looked at me and said, "He said nothing, say more."

"I said that my wife and I say he is Shoshone, and you and Turtle Woman said the same." Some say he is and some who say he is not."

My father leaned over and said to me, "Why does this bother you?"

"I feel less of a person being in two worlds I wish to be Shoshone."

My father asked, "Why have you not told me of this?"

I put my head down and said, "I thought you would be too tired to think about this after your search to move the village." "I was going to wait until you rest."

My mother said, "He mentioned it to me."

My father thought for a second, and then Arrow Maker said, "I told him it is possible, but it will be difficult."

Again, there was a moment of silence. My father did something I never saw him do before, he turned to my mother and said, "What do you think of this?"

She said, "For me, he is a good son." "I could not ask for better, but it is yours and his decision."

My father turned back to me and said, "What Arrow Maker said is true; it is very hard. You must wait until after the snows when all the villages are one; then, the elders will decide how this can be."

I didn't say more I could see that he was in no mood to discuss this further and I could wait until the villages united again.

The next morning after we ate, we all packed everything, and then I went to Grey Wolf's lodge with my father, and we helped him. Before noon we were all heading west, I rode on my horse. I saw Morning Star walking, so I told her to join me on my horse. For the first two days, both halves of the village stayed together, but on the morning of the third day, we split in half. Strong Arm lead one group going north, and Spotted Buffalo led us south, and I also turned ten. I let my parents know, but to tell you the truth, it was uneventful. By afternoon it had clouded up and finally started to rain. We tried camping in a wooded area, but I got soaked anyway. My father made a half hut out of tree branches, as did most others. I sat between my father's legs. My mother to the side and my father draped a blanket over all of us. I was exhausted and fell asleep in my father's arms.

The next day it was breezy with intermittent showers, but we continued. That night it stopped raining, but it was cold, and I snuggled between my mother and father. The next afternoon we came to a grassy valley with trees just like Grey Wolf said. My father and I put up our lodge, and we helped Arrow Maker, then we went to Grey Wolf's lodge to do theirs. The women gathered wood, and soon a fire was going in all three the lodges. We didn't lay the furs down until the ground was dry, and then we settled down to a warm meal.

During this time, Grey Wolf continued to train me in fighting and use of the bow. We took many trips to hunt near the village. On these trips, I used both the sorrel and paint. I also used my third horse, which was a black mustang with white stockings. This black mustang was my favorite seemed to know what I wanted, and she was strong and very friendly. Grey Wolf and I went hunting for small game, and we were very successful.

The highlight of our stay in this valley was our father taking us hunting. At first, I had no luck at killing anything. Still, it was not a total loss between what my father in addition to what my brother killed; I was doing better at skinning and cleaning the game. My father said you must hit the animal just behind the front legs and be ready to shoot another arrow if it does not go down.

Grey Wolf said, "It is just like hunting a rabbit, but you have to be ready to shoot another arrow." The next time we went hunting, I got my first deer, and I was excited. After about the third or fourth kill, the thrill I experience from the first kill was gone.

I got even closer to Morning Star if that is possible. She would go for rides with me when she got a chance. The weather was getting cloudier and cold, and soon the first flakes of snow arrived. That winter was cold, but the lodge was warm, and the winter clothing my mother made also helped. It was harder to find food, greens and fruits were nonexistent, but we were managing and helping others. All meat is always shared with everyone, as was most food. We shared our food with Grey Wolf and his mother also Arrow Maker and his wife.

One cold, wintery day I was eating with my parents, and I asked, "Is it true that Arrow Maker and Crawls On The Ground do not have any children?"

"Yes, they just have themselves," said my father.

"You adopted me; can we adopt them as my grandparents?"

My mother and father looked surprised, and my mother said, "It would make them happy."

"And me too," I said.

My father leaned back and said to me, "Go get Grey Wolf and his mother also Arrow Maker and Crawls On The Ground. Ask them to come to our lodge," I then ran and got everybody.

I sat next to Grey Wolf as my father started talking. "Grey Wolf is here because he is also my son, and he has to say how he feels about what I am going to say. Arrow Maker and Crawls On The Ground have no one to take care of them, when they get too old, pointing to me, he said, "My youngest son has asked if we could adopt them as grandparents. I think it would be a good thing, Grey Wolf how do you feel about this?"

Grey Wolf said, "I think my little brother has great wisdom; I believe it is a good thing."

"What do you think of this, Arrow Maker?"

"It would warm my heart for this to happen and to give me two grandsons."

Then my father said, "And how do you feel Crawls On The Ground."

"Like my husband, I feel the same."

"And is this good with you, Blue Lizard."

"Yes," she said.

"Then, if no one objects, it is done. I will go to Spotted Buffalo and tell him of this."

"Will you make the announcement, Arrow Maker?"

"It will give me great joy."

When everyone left, my father went to Spotted Buffalo to let him know what had happened. So now I had grandparents, a brother, a father and a mother and I loved them all.

The winter came and went, and when spring came, we packed everything and went to join three other villages northeast of where we were. This village would be twice as big as when I first arrived. I would also get the opportunity to become a full Shoshone. We came to the same stream where we camped before but about fifty miles west. There were already many lodges were there, and by the time everyone showed up, there would be more than three hundred and fifty lodges set up.

Grey Wolf and I went hunting, and I asked him, "How long will we all be together?"

"About thirty suns." He held up his fingers three times to show me.

"I will ask my father again to be Shoshone."

Grey Wolf said, "I do not think you understand what you will go through."

"Whatever I go through, it will be worth it."

That night in my lodge, I asked again, "I wish to talk to you again about being Shoshone." "You said I would have to wait until we all came here."

"It will be hard for you, harder than most, because One Horn will try to prevent this."

"No matter how hard it will be, it will be worth it," I said.

My mother, who usually wouldn't say anything, said concernedly, "You are very young." "I do not wish to lose another son."

"Mother, I love you do not worry I might suffer pain and struggle much, but nothing will happen to me."

There was a moment of quiet, and then my father said, "If there is no changing your mind, I will talk to the elders tomorrow and see what can get done."

The next morning after I relieved myself, I saw Grandfather working on a bow, and I sat beside him. "Grandfather, my father, will be talking to the elders today about me becoming Shoshone."

"Yes, your father has already told me."

"Will you be there?"

"Yes, the talk will start when the sun is high up."

"Will you bring one more thing up for me?"

"What is it?"

"After I become Shoshone, I wish a name like yours or fathers' or maybe even like Grey Wolf's." "I do not want to be called the son of Red Elk or the younger son of Red Elk for the rest of my life I wish my name."

"I will bring this up." "Have you told this to your father?"

"No, I did not want to burden him with more things, I wish."

"I understand and will tell the rest of the elders."

I spent the rest of the morning with Grey Wolf. That afternoon my father headed to where the other elders were, and I started to follow, but my father turned and said, "This meeting you cannot attend. Do not be disappointed, it will be very long, and things said that you should not hear." Grey Wolf came up to me, and my father said, "You cannot attend either son; what will be said will not be meant for you to hear." What our father said didn't stop us. Grey Wolf found a tree near the meeting, and we both climbed the tree and listened on one of the tree's limbs.

Long Knife was the first to stand. He said, "What is it that Red Elk wishes to talk to us about?"

Our father stood up and said, "I have adopted two sons, one who no one questions is Shoshone." "The other who some accept as Shoshone, some do not care if he is Shoshone or not, and too many say he is not Shoshone." "My family and I feel that it is not good for him to live in two worlds." "He feels that he is less of a person, and he wants to be Shoshone."

Our father sat down, and the discussion began. Red Fox said, "He is very young and could not withstand what he must do to become Shoshone."

Arrow Maker said, "Yet he killed two Blackfeet, and I have seen him get stronger and stronger every day." To both statements, there was much agreement.

One Horn spoke, "This boy is a white child who has caused a lot of problems." "He would like to change our ways; it is bad enough for these white hunters to come to our villages, causing us great trouble." To my surprise, some agreed.

Then Tall As The Sky said, "What trouble have this boy and the white hunters caused?"

"They annoy me, and they take away from the old ways," One Horn growled, and again many agreed with him.

Our father stood up again and said, "I can understand what One Horn has said." "I can know how they have changed our ways, like the knife made of metal that One Horn wears and the metal pots his wife uses and what of his tobacco he smokes?" "Did not others see him trade with the white man?" "Yes, there have been many changes, but who would give them up?" "But my youngest son has changed nothing, and it is he who we are talking about."

The debate swung one way and then the other. This talking went on for more than an hour. Finally, those who sided with One Horn agreed to allow me to become Shoshone if One Horn would have a big say as to how this would happen. Reluctantly my father and those who supported him went along with this.

For the next hour and a half, there was a debate on what I must do. First, I had to go without clothing, and the first thing I must do was a sweat to purify myself. I had never done a sweat, and I started to ask Grey Wolf what to expect when he put his hand on my mouth, not wanting me to make any noise. If I got through the sweat, the next thing I had to go through was the gauntlet. There was a great debate about this. The only thing my father got his way about was that it was to be made up of women and done in the water. I wanted to ask Grey Wolf about this also but didn't, knowing he wouldn't let me talk. One Horn said, "If he gets past the gauntlet, he must do the long walk."

My father exploded, and he said, "Only the strongest of adults do this, and most do not survive." One Horn won this one much to the dismay of my father. I swore Grey Wolf had tears in his eyes, which worried me, but I would find out what was so bad later. I had thought that these were all the things I would have to do, as did my father.

But One Horn got up and said, "This is not all; if he gets through the long walk, he must do the Sun Dance."

Both my father and Grey Wolf were shocked at what he said as were most there. One Horn spoke on, "He is not Shoshone if he does not do this."

Tall As The Sky said, "A child has never done this, you ask too much." Most disagreed with what One Horn had said and even surprised his supporters.

However, One Horn said, "Everyone agreed that you would let me say what he has to do." Reluctantly they all agreed except for a few.

Long Knife said, "Is there anything else to discuss."

"Yes," said Arrow Maker.

"Speak then," said Long Knife.

"My grandson also wants a name such as his father's or his brother's."

One Horn was about to say something when Spotted Buffalo spoke first, "You have spoken enough One Horn, this is different." "If he survives, then he and his family will decide where to go to fast to receive a vision and get a name." "His desire to get a name will be after he has rested from the ordeal that One Horn has put him through."

One Horn was about to say something when Spotted Buffalo said, "You have no say about this, I have spoken."

At that, there was no other business, so the meeting ended with Long Knife saying to my father, "He will go through this in three suns." "If he changes his mind at any time, there will be no shame in this."

The meeting broke up, and I turned to Grey Wolf and said, "Tell me all I have to do."

Before he answered, our father said from down below us, "Both of you come to the lodge." He turned and left before I could say anything, and we both climbed down from the tree and headed to the lodge.

Grey Wolf and I entered the lodge. In addition to my mother, Spotted Buffalo and Arrow Maker were also there sitting next to my father. Grey Wolf and I sat on my bed. Everyone looked concerned, especially my mother, who looked like she was near tears.

My father spoke first, "Has Grey Wolf told you anything about what you must do?"

"No, he did not want me to make any noise."

"Do you know of anything of these trials, what they are?" my father asked me.

"I know little of it except what I learned in the white world. I know a sweat is a place where water gets poured onto hot rocks, and a gauntlet is something that one does facing many dangers."

"I will explain each trial and how they work, so you understand." "You will wear nothing; a large hole will get dug, and limbs will get placed on top and blankets on top of that like this." He formed his hands like an upside-down bowl. "There will be only one entrance which will be covered when everyone is inside." "You will go in, followed by your grandfather, Spotted Buffalo, One Horn, Running Horse, and me." "Hot rocks will get brought in as well as water to pour on the rocks, along with cleansing plants." "It will be hot for you, and you will sweat much." "You will not be allowed to drink any water while you are in the sweat lodge." "Many people inside will ask questions, then one by one each of us will leave as it becomes too hot, but you must stay." "Finally, when everyone has gone, you will be allowed to come out." "If you do not pass out, you will feel dizzy and weak, but you must go to the next trial." "You will go to the stream where there will be two rows of many women with clubs to hit you. "You must go between them from one end to the other." "They will all try to hit you, and they will swing hard." "Spotted Buffalo will choose some, but so will One Horn, and the women he picks will try to kill you." "If you are not killed or knocked out, you will go on to the next trial without rest."

"You will be blindfolded and placed on a horse with a warrior who One Horn chooses and get taken two days' ride away from this village." "You will have no clothing, no weapon, no food, and no water." "You must find your way back to the village."

"If you are alive and make it back, you must do the last trial, which is called the Sun Dance." "The only rest you will have is the time it takes to put a lodgepole up with two leather cords looped around it." "You can get a little water if you want it." "Someone will place eagle feathers in your hair; someone will paint your face, and a whistle will get placed in your mouth." "At the end of the two leather cords, there will be two sharpened tips of a deer horn; someone of your choosing will pierce your skin here and here on your chest." He pointed just above the breasts. "You will then dance toward the lodgepole and back out again, blowing your whistle." "You will go back and forth many times, and when you think you get tired, you will lean back and, without using your hands, rip the cords out of your chest." "If you cannot do it the first time, you will dance again until you get tired again, and you will try again." "All this you must-do if you fail at any trials, then all this trouble of you wanting to be Shoshone will come to an end." They all looked at me, waiting for me to say something.

I thought it was a lot for a boy to do and very challenging for a few seconds, and I would suffer much. I thought about what would happen if I declined not to do it and quickly knew that that was not an option. I would be disgraced, and very few would respect me, and of course, the same might happen to my family. I would be treated more like a woman than a man even when I got older. There is a good chance I would lose Morning Star, even though I felt she liked me, as did her family. Before I said anything, Spotted Buffalo said, "I would understand if you decided not to do this." "It is almost impossible for one who is grown, let alone you."

I looked at everyone, especially my mother, and said, "I love my family, and I love Morning Star." "I would feel less than a person if I did not do this, I am sorry, but it is not an option for me." "I must think of a way to overcome these trials."

"You are a brave child." "I am proud of you," said my grandfather.

"We will teach you all we can, these next three days to get you through these trials," said Spotted Buffalo.

"Someone must teach me how to do that dance at the end."

"Grey Wolf, do you know it?" asked my father.

"Yes, I will show my brother and other things too."

My grandfather said, "I will make the announcement."

"I do not know; he is so young," said my mother.

"He is stronger than you think and wiser than most of the warriors here." "I think he will make us proud of him," said my grandfather with pride.

I looked over to Grey Wolf and said in a melancholy voice, "I will meet you at your lodge in a few minutes I wish to speak with my mother privately first."

He left, and I looked at my mother and crawled over to her and snuggled next to her. "It will be alright; it is like the birth of a child; there is much pain at first, then great joy." I kissed and hugged my mother and said, "I love you more than I think you realize."

She held me and said, "I understand your love very well." After a few moments, I left and went to Grey Wolf's lodge.

His mother hugged me and said in a concerned voice, "I hope things go well with you."

Grey Wolf and I went down to the stream. We heard our grandfather announcing the trials I would be going through in three days. We sat on the water bank in silence for a few minutes, and then Grey Wolf said, "I think that is where the women will be."

I studied the area and said, "Let's go for a swim." I took my clothes off and jumped into the water, and Grey Wolf followed me, confused. I swam around a little and said, "How many women at the most do you think there will be on both sides?"

He stuck up ten fingers plus four more. I took a rock and placed it on the bank; then, I paced off where fourteen women would be and put another rock at the end. I checked the depth of the water from one rock to the other, and it ranged from about four feet to about three. Grey Wolf was confused at what I was doing. I swam down to him and asked, "These women, once I pass them, they cannot come after me?"

"No, they cannot."

"And will they be moving around excited while I move past them."

"I would think so."

"You stand here and tell me as I walk away from you how far the two lines of women will be." I started walking away from him, and he said stop about ten feet from him. What I was thinking might just work. "I want you to pretend there are two lines of women from that rock to that rock moving around all excited and watch what I do." I stepped back about ten feet and started running to the water. Just before I got to the rock, I dived under the water and swam nearly twenty-five feet, then came up, turned around, and looked at Grey Wolf. He looked astonished and then started laughing. I asked, "Do you think it will work?

He nodded his head yes and said, "Why did I not think of doing that?"

"You didn't know how far I could go under the water." We got out, dried off, and got dressed.

"I think we should ride around, so you know the area, and you can find your way back to the village." We were walking across the village when Grey Wolf said, "If you drink as much water as you can just before you go into the sweat lodge, it may not be as bad for you."

My father was talking to my grandfather, and we went up to him, and I asked, "Can we talk to both of you privately?"

My grandfather pointed to his lodge, and we all went in. He told my grandmother to step outside, and I said, "It will be good if my grandmother stays here also." Grey Wolf and I explained to all three of them about the sweat lodge and the gauntlet and asked what they thought.

They all smiled, and my grandfather said, "It just might work."

Then I said, "Grey Wolf and I are going to ride around and see what the area looks like, so it will be easier to find my way back."

"When you come back from your ride come to me, I will have something for the both of you," said my grandmother.

We headed west and rode for about an hour. Then we circled the village while Grey Wolf was pointing out landmarks and things, I could spot miles away. About halfway around, we stopped and rested the horses at a small stream. Grey Wolf picked up two large stones and said, "See these two stones?"

"Yes."

He hit the stones together, one glancing off the other. It left a flake with a sharp edge, and then he picked it up and used it like a knife and carved a point on a stick. "You see what I did?"

"Yes."

"It will only work on some stones; not all the best is this kind." It was a shiny black type of stone. "It is the rock that most of our arrows got made from." I pulled out an arrow, and sure enough, it was. "If you can make a fire, heat the pointed end of it, and it will make your stick harder."

We rode the other half of the circle, got off our horses, and started walking them back to the village. We walked for about a half-hour, then got back on the horses and rode them the rest of the way back to the village.

By the time we put up our horses, it was dark. We went to our grandparents' lodge, and we got told to come in. My grandmother said, "Turn around and sit down between my legs." I did as she asked, and she untied my headband and put a new one on that had been braided. It wasn't as comfortable as the one my mother made me, but it was nicer looking. She said, "I know it is not as comfortable as the one your mother made for you, but there is another reason for it other than keeping your hair back." She had another one just like it in her hand. She untied the headband at one end, and it unraveled to produce a long cord; holding the cord up, she said, "You can use this for many things like to start a fire, make a bow, a snare or even to catch fish with it." She braided the cord and removed Grey Wolf's headband and put the new one on him. "You both wear this, and One Horn will not notice." "He is not as smart as he thinks he is." With a hug and a kiss, we thanked her and left.

I was surprised that Grey Wolf kissed our grandmother; most Shoshones don't express emotions openly. Maybe some things I do are rubbing off on Grey Wolf. Grey Wolf went back to his lodge, but before he left, he told me to be ready for a long ride in the morning. I went into the lodge, and my parents didn't notice the headband, and I didn't say anything, and after I ate, I went to sleep.

The next day my brother and I did the same as the day before. When I got back, my mother said, "Tomorrow, you will come with me." She looked at Grey Wolf and said, "You can come too."

I asked, "Where are we going?"

"To show you some plants you can eat and use for healing."

"But I have shown him plants he can eat," Grey Wolf said, seeming insulted.

"You come with me, and maybe you will find more plants." Reluctantly, my brother agreed to come along, and my mother told us to have three horses ready.

The next day all three of us headed west up the stream. We stopped after about an hour, and she pointed at some willows on the bank and said, "The roots you can eat." I looked at Grey Wolf, and he shrugged his shoulders. We walked north from the river, and she pointed at some dandelions and said, "You can put the leaves in water and drink the water or eat the leaves." My mother wasn't stupid; she knew I already knew these things she was showing me. She pointed to another plant and said to me, "Do you know what that is?"

"No."

"How about you, Grey Wolf?"

"It is the stinging plant."

"And what is it good for?"

"Nothing I know of."

"Ah, there are some things that you do not know." "You cook this plant, and it does not sting anymore, and then you can eat it." We were looking for things to eat for over three hours. About half the things she showed me, I did not know. "Let us go back to the village; your father must be hungry."

We both smiled and said, "We are hungry too."

# 9

# THE TRIAL

The next morning, Grey Wolf joined me. I had eaten a lot and drank so much water I felt I was going to drown. My father had a say on where the sweat lodge would be, and it was perfect, almost opposite where I was practicing for the gauntlet. I was led out of the lodge by my father and brought to the sweat lodge. It was a typical spring day, a few clouds and a cool breeze. All the elders were there as well as most of the village. I was about to enter the sweat lodge when One Horn stopped me and tried to take my medicine bag and Mama's gold locket. I grabbed his arm first and said, "Do not touch."

It caused a stir among the village, and Long Knife stepped in and asked, "What is this all about?"

"He must remove everything," said One Horn. Long Knife examined the locket and medicine bag and said, "There is no reason for him to take off these things." I was then permitted to enter the sweat lodge. What surprised me most was that One Horn didn't say anything about my headband, thank goodness.

It was dark inside except for the light coming from the entrance. One by one, the assigned elders entered the sweat lodge with One Horn being last. One elder had water and another some plants. They sat on either side of me. It was a bit crowded, but we all fit. A small fire was lit in the middle and let burn down to red-hot coals; then hot rocks were brought in and place on the coals. Someone covered the entrance, and someone inside put water and purifying plants on the hot stones. Almost unbearably hot steam and smoke from the plants hit me. It felt like a bad sunburn, and my eyes and throat stung, and it was hard to breathe. I immediately started to sweat a lot, as did everyone else.

"Son or Red Elk, do you know who our enemies are?" asked Long Knife.

"I am told the Lakota who live far away, the Ute to the south of us and the Blackfoot and their friends who I am at war with and will kill them." "I would guess there are others."

"Yes, we have many enemies; you must learn them all."

"My father and brother will teach me." "I have a question I understand why the Blackfoot and their friends are our enemies; they are animals, but why are the rest enemies?"

Spotted Buffalo answered, "There are many reasons some hunt on our hunting grounds."

"There are many buffalo, deer, and elk, and I have met the Mandan who are related to the Lakota; they were very kind to me."

"I have said there are other reasons for them being our enemies." "If you go back to the Mandan now, the Mandan would not be so kind." "You should talk to your father about these things."

I looked up at my father and said, "When I complete these trials, I will do this."

"Who is the Great Mystery?" asked One Horn.

I thought for a few seconds about how to answer this and then said, "He is all good, creator of all, and he will help those who are worthy."

"Where did you hear this from those whites you come from?" "That is not right," One Horn said aggressively.

"What he said is, exactly what I would have said, are you going to say I am wrong or learn it from the whites One Horn?" responded Tall As The Sky disapprovingly.

One Horn was embarrassed and angry that he was challenged but wouldn't say anything too Tall As The Sky.

Sleeping Dog, a friend of One Horn, asked, "Where did my people come from?" I noticed he said my people, as did most the others, but I didn't say anything.

I took a guess, and I said, "If you are talking about many, many winters ago, long before any here were born." "I believe our people came from the north where it is freezing, and the snow and ice are always there." "This time would be when all people were the same." I could see that I was right because of the look on Sleeping Dog's face.

After more than a half-hour of questions, my grandfather got up and said, "I am going to bathe." "Good luck, my grandson!" Five minutes later, Long Knife was the next to leave. Within the next half hour, all left except my father, One Horn who appeared to be miserable but wanted to be the last one, and myself.

Finally, my father got up, put his hand on my shoulder, and said, "You have done well," and then he left, then it was just One Horn and me.

One Horn had a look of evil in his eyes, and with a smirk, he said, "You will never complete all the trials." Without me saying anything, he got up and went outside. A few seconds later, I went outside. The slight breeze felt good, but I was a bit dizzy and weak, and I knew I had to recover from the feeling quickly as someone took my arm and guided me to the stream. But I knew once I got into the water and I ducked my head under, I would feel good.

I saw the two rows of women, and they were stirring up the water. I turned to Long Knife and said, "All I have to do is get to the other end, is that right?"

"Yes."

"Does it matter how I get there?"

Long Knife looked confused and said, "No."

I stepped back about ten feet from the first two women. All the women had their clubs raised high. I started running to the water, toward the first two women. About three feet before I reached them, I dove into and under the water and swam between the women. The water was so murky that they couldn't see me. Those not in the water crowded the bank of the stream. The women in the water went silent, confused at what I did. One woman saw what I was up to and the wake in the water as I passed. She struck the water with the club. I got hit on my bottom, and it hurt, but the water cushioned the blow. Others tried to hit me but missed or just scraped me and I made it to the end and stood up. I looked over at the elders, and they, as well as most of the village, were laughing.

Long Knife called me over and said, "You are a smart young man."

"You said I could get to the other end anyway I want."

"I did, and you may come out of the water."

One Horn protested, but Long Knife said, "He has passed the first two trials, pick the one to take him for the long walk."

He picked Sleeping Dog and told him in a whisper, "You know where to take him."

He nodded and whispered, "I will not make it easy for him."

My family was all proud of me for getting through the first two trials. I was blindfolded, and my arms bound behind my back. My father became angry and demanded, "What is the meaning of this?"

One Horn said, "It is so he cannot move this blindfold."

"Spotted Buffalo grabbed my father and said, "Let it be."

Someone placed me on a horse, and Sleeping Dog got behind me. We rode off to the west. I knew it was west because I could not feel the sun's heat on either side of my face. We didn't go far when he turned. We stayed north or northeast the rest of the time.

After about four hours, Sleeping Dog stopped. He jumped off the horse, grabbed me, and threw me to the ground. I wasn't hurt, so I sat up then waited to see what would happen next. Sleeping Dog didn't give me any water, and after about a half-hour, I got lifted on the horse, stomach down, my feet facing one side and my head on the other much like game on a packhorse. It was unbearable traveling like this, but I kept my mind occupied with other thoughts to distract me. After about two hours, he rubbed my bottom and said, "You have skin like a woman," then he slapped my bottom very hard. We were still traveling north or northeast, and we went over three streams. After about three hours, I knew the sun was down because of the coolness, and we stopped.

Like before, I was thrown to the ground scraping my thigh, then dragged me to a grassy area. Sleeping dog started to make a fire, and I could smell meat, of course, Sleeping dog offered me none of it, nor did I get water. Sleeping dog finished, and when he fell asleep, I rolled over onto my stomach to relieve the pain on my thigh, and I fell asleep.

Sometime during the night, I woke with Sleeping Dog pleasuring himself on me. He raped me, and it hurt a lot, I didn't cry out but when he finished pleasuring himself and fell back asleep, and the tears came until I fell asleep again.

The next morning, I relieved myself while I lay on the ground. After Sleeping Dog finished eating, he threw me back up on the horse as the day before. As we headed out, he said, "You were just like a woman," then he laughed as I kept silent.

The day went like the day before. I got skinned up again, and that night again, I wasn't given anything to eat or drink, and it was showing on me. Sometime during the evening, he raped me again. He didn't even wait until I was asleep, and I made up my mind to deal with him when I got back to the village.

About three hours after we headed out on the third day, we crossed a stream, he threw me off the horse, and I hit the same thigh I injured earlier. Sleeping Dog said with a sneer, "I would come down there and make love to you, but I miss my lodge back at the village."

"Do yourself a favor Sleeping Dog do not be at the village when I get back." He laughed and rode off, leaving me tied up and blindfolded.

I heard the horse ride off in a different direction. When the sound faded away, I rolled over to where I heard water moving and crawled to it. I stuck my head into the water and drank until I couldn't drink anymore. I rolled onto my back and felt for a sharp rock it took a while, but I found a satisfactory one. I rubbed the leather cord that bound me on the rock for about a half-hour, and they finally broke. I removed my blindfold and let my eyes adjust to the light. I then stood up and surveyed the surroundings. I needed to find food and fast; I hadn't eaten in almost three days. I saw some dandelions and gathered up a lot of their leaves, and I stuffed my mouth with them. It was not the best of meals I have had, but it soothed my stomach. I decided to stay here for the night, so I could gather some things and look for more food. I found a sturdy straight stick about as tall as me. I walked up and down the stream. I found a second stick about the same size as the first and took that one also. To my right, I saw a lot of birds flying around the same area, so I went over to investigate them, and it was a large berry bush. I grabbed hands full and ate them; this was much better than the dandelions. I found a tree where I could break off small, flexible limbs. I brought them back to the stream. I gathered some dry wood and piled it up for a fire. Then I got everything I needed to start a fire. I didn't find a suitable rock to make a good sharp flake knife. But I did flake off a rock that was more like a saw than a knife, which gave me an idea. I started a fire by making a bow out of my headband, and then I made some snares and placed them out. I sat back and made some baskets as my mother showed me. After the baskets, I charred the ends of both sticks and rounded them on a rock. With the flake from a stone, I put a deep groove at one end of one stick and a large notch on one side. With the rough rock and the rock flake, I could make a crude point on the other stick. I heated the ends of both sticks to harden them. After I finished everything, I curled up next to the fire and fell asleep.

At first light, I went to the berry bush and filled the basket full of berries, and in the process, I got scratched up a lot. I gathered as many dandelion leaves as I could find. I found some wild onions and took them also. I walked up and down the stream until I found where Sleeping Dog first crossed. I went back to my campsite and buried my campfire, and then went to check my snares. To my surprise, I had caught two rabbits. I cleaned them and slung them on my shoulder. I did the same with the baskets and headed out.

I was thankful that the weather was cool, and there was a slight breeze. My biggest concern was water. At that time, I had no means for carrying it and knew I would get thirsty; however, I hoped to minimize the thirst with the berries. After walking for about two hours, I found another problem that I was facing. Although they were tough since I'd come to the village, my feet were nowhere near as hard as Grey Wolf's, and I was feeling it.

I walked another three hours and came to a grove of trees and decided to stop for the night. I got a fire started and ate a combination of dandelion leaves, onions, and rabbit; then I finished it off with berries. I jerked the leftover rabbit, and after I finished, since it was still light, I placed some snares out, not expecting to get anything. I looked around to see if there was any water and there wasn't. I got some pitch from some pine trees and brought it back to camp. I smeared the pitch on the bottom of my feet. I felt I could make crude moccasins out of the two rabbit pelts. I went to work doing just that, and after I finished the moccasins, I took account of what I had to eat and figured I had enough for one more meal.

I sat back against a tree and was thinking I would have to bury this fire, also. I am convinced that Sleeping Dog took me well into the Blackfoot territory. I thought about what I was going to do to Sleeping Dog for what he did to me. I knew now just how my cousin felt when they did it to him. I would not kill Sleeping Dog because he was Shoshone, but I would try to hurt him. To do this, I would have to outsmart him; he had after all over nine years on me, but he wasn't very bright. And what about One Horn, who put him up to it, what would I do to him and then I decided that more than likely nothing. One Horn's stature in the village would be lost when the people finally knew what he did,

The wind was coming up, but I was drowsy anyway and fell asleep. When I woke up in the morning, the wind was still blowing, and it was cloudy. I figured I would get rain, and that meant Sleeping Dog's tracks would disappear. I had just buried the fire and started packing up when I had to stop and dig a hole quickly because the berries and dandelions had given me the runs bad. I was squatting over the hole for some time, and when I finished, I tried to clean myself as best as I could.

I headed out again; the walking was a lot better with the moccasins. I walked for about an hour when I had an urge to go again but didn't stop walking. I just let it come out, and some ran down the back of my leg. The problem I had happened two or three times, and I was feeling dehydrated after about four and a half hours of walking. It started to sprinkle, and then there was a long and steady downpour. My backside was getting washed as miserable as the rain was; it was also good, and I did get some trickles of water to go down my throat that was refreshing.

Since I knew the tracks that Sleeping Dog left had disappeared, I decided to head south until I could see something I recognized. After having walked for six hours, I had to rest, so I sat on a rock. I looked around for shelter, but there wasn't any, so after a short rest, I started again. I walked another two hours when I came to a large hill which I climbed. There was a valley; on the other side of the valley was a stream. It had a patch of trees that extended over another lower hill. I went down to the water, drank, and then found a place to cross. I started to look for something that I could use as a shelter, and about twenty feet from the stream, I found two downed trees with a little work I could make into a dry shelter. It took me about an hour, but I had my shelter, which kept out the rain.

I found some nearly dry pieces of wood under some other trees, and with great difficulty, I could start a fire. The heat from the fire felt good since it had been getting colder with all the rain. My shelter was big enough for my whole family, but I couldn't stand up in it. I was tired and went to sleep without eating as the rain kept on coming down.

By sunup, it was still raining but not as hard. At the first chance, I left my shelter, relieved myself, and got some water to drink. Late in the morning, just before noon, it stopped raining, and the clouds parted, revealing blue skies. I took the opportunity to bathe, set some snares out, and try my luck using my gaff to get some fish. After making some mistakes trying to gaff fish, I was finally able to get three fish. I cleaned them and went back to my shelter and put them over the fire. With everything I had and the three fish, I was full for the night, and I settled down thinking about what I was going to do the next day. Gathering food was understood, but I also needed to find a way to carry water. I also decided to travel slightly southwest, still hoping to run into something I would recognize.

The next day I took my gaff and went for more fish. I was doing well by noon I had about a half-dozen fish, so I headed back to the shelter. Along the way, I checked my snares, and I had one rabbit, which I cleaned, then brought back. Back at the shelter, I dried the fish and jerked the rabbit.

Since there was still plenty of light, I took my lance also a basket and went looking for vegetables, fruits, and nuts. I headed downstream, and as I was walking, something shining in the grass caught my eye. I walked over to it, and it was a black, glassy rock about the size of a man's fist. It was the kind used for making arrow tips. Then I remembered the name of the rock it is called obsidian. I read about it in a book a long time ago. Why I didn't remember it before I don't know it was not like me. With this rock, I can make a tool for cutting, so I placed it at the bottom of the basket. I gathered dandelions since they were always abundant. I went about a quarter of a mile down the stream, and I spotted some cattails in the water, and I knew that they were edible, so I started pulling the plant up and throwing them on the bank.

I had gotten more than enough, and I began to bundle them up when I heard some noise coming toward me. I didn't have any cover on my side of the bank, so I hid the cattails among the other cattails and got behind a large rock on the other side of the stream. A man pulling two laden pack horses came up a hill and around some bushes. He was swaying back and forth like he was drunk or something. About twenty feet from me, he stopped and fell off his horse. I waited a few minutes to see if anyone else came or if he got up again, and after I thought it was safe, I went over to him. He was a short, bearded, white man about forty years old. He had two wounds on him, and I bent down to see if he was still alive; that is when he groaned and moved. It startled me, and I jumped back, and then cautiously, I went back and looked at him again. I knew whoever wounded him was near, and I had to get him out of there quickly.

I tied up his horses and left my things near them. My shelter, since I knew it was well hidden, I decided to drag him back to the shelter. I then went back for the horses and my things, and I gathered up the cattails and my basket and lance and stuck them on the packhorse. Up above my sheltered, there was plenty of grass and even pockets of water from the rainstorm. I took the horses there. I unloaded the horses and tied them up. I then broke off a branch which had leaves. I cautiously went about a hundred yards back from where he fell. I found a spot where the horses went into the water and then came out. I brushed away all tracks from the stream up into my shelter.

By the time I did all this, the sun was setting, but it was still light out. The man was still unconscious, so I removed his shirt to see how bad the wounds were. He had two holes in him, one in his chest near his shoulder, which wasn't so bad, and the other was in his stomach area, which was very bad. I was almost sure it was a fusee by the size of the hole, and there weren't any arrows used, but whatever hit him didn't come out the back. Fusees were a rifle traded to Indians to a verity of tribes, but they weren't that good. You had to be lucky or close to hit anything. The Fusee didn't have the power as the Hawken had. For his wounds, I got some spider webs to help with clotting. I bound his wounds with the leather buckskins he was wearing. I made the same medicine my mother gave me to relieve my fever; she had shown me how to make it. I knew according to what his condition was, it would not save him, the shoulder wasn't so bad, but he had a gut shot it would be a miracle for him to live. He had also lost a lot of blood, and he was pale. I thought that he would never wake up.

It was dark out, so I lit a fire I knew the smoke would spread out among the tree leaves that were overhead. After I ate, I sat back then thought that this might delay me, and there was danger here. I tried to sleep, but the old man talked crazy in his sleep. I took it that he was French by what he was saying. I looked at all his weapons, and it impressed me, he had a Hawken, an excellent one, and he also had two perfect pistols that had a great balance. He had the biggest and sharpest knife I had ever seen. It was perfectly balanced, and if I threw it, it would hit its target every time. What interested me was he had a hawk, which is a type of hatchet. I'd heard of them but never seen one. It was used for hand to hand fighting or throwing, and it was balanced and very fancy.

I don't know how I did it, but I did get a few hours of sleep before the sun came up. Although I didn't think anyone could detect my fire, I put it out anyway. I gave the man as much of my mother's medicine as possible, and by late afternoon he regained consciousness. He took one look at me and said to me weakly in broken English, "Who are you and where are your clothes?"

I responded in French, "I am the son of Red Elk, and the reason I don't have clothing on is that I am doing a trial, the long walk, to become a full Shoshone." "Who shot you?"

"Blackfeet, a lot of them." "How long have I been out you might be in danger?"

"You've been out for about one day."

"You have to help me get on a horse."

"Your wounds are terrible; you have been gut shot, and you won't last an hour."

"You're right, you take the horses and go, or they will kill you too."

"I'll take care of the Blackfeet," I said.

"You're too small, and there are too many you will get killed now go!"

"I've counted coup already by killing three." I exaggerated a little; I just didn't want to worry him.

"I can't believe that you're just a baby."

"I will tell you what, if you are feeling better tomorrow I will leave then."

"You're stubborn, and I'm too weak to force you."

"What is your name?" I asked.

"I'm called Shorty." "Why don't you have an Indian name, and what is a French boy doing here?"

"I'm not French; I'm American." "After the last of my relatives got killed by the Blackfeet, my father, a Shoshone warrior, adopted me."

"If you're not French, how do you speak French so well?"

"I speak many languages." "French is just one of them." We talked for a while and then Shorty started drifting in and out of consciousness.

When night fell, I started a small fire and then went down to the stream. I walked back to where Shorty first felled and tried to smell that aromatic smell of a campfire. I did smell something, and I didn't think it was from my campfire because I was downwind of it. I crossed the stream and climbed a tree, and then I saw it, a campfire a little short of two miles from where I was. I went back to my camp; Shorty was still out and not breathing well. I took the dark green sash that he wore around his waist and put it on myself. I then wove myself a crude hat out of the cattail stocks and stuffed my hair under it. Then I took some of the grease from the rabbit and the black ash and painted a broad black stripe that went across my eyes. I took the leftover berries and painted a line down to my chin. I then checked the pistols, and they were both loaded. I shoved them in the sash, and I took his hawk and knife. Then I draped his powder horn and shot bag over my shoulder. I finally picked up his Hawken and my lance, which I had shaved almost razor-sharp.

I headed downstream, as I walked, I knew I would have to outsmart them and not make any mistakes, or I would be as dead as Shorty would soon be. I took my time, making sure I didn't make any noise. It took me about two hours to reach the camp. I was well hidden, but I could see everything very well. There were eight Blackfeet around the fire, eating and talking and, on occasion, laughing. There was no mistaking them for anything else but Blackfeet. I could tell by the way they did their hair, and their language was the same as I had heard before. The scene gave me flashbacks to that night when they butchered my aunt, uncle, and cousin. Just watching them a rage was kindling up in me, but I waited for the best opportunity. One of the eight stood up with his fusee, and a ninth brave entered the camp and sat down around the fire. The one who stood up left the camp, and I moved to see what he was doing. I not only had the cover of the trees, but it was cloudy, and I knew the one brave would have to get his eyes adjusted to the darkness. I spotted him near the stream, squatting and relieving himself. Quietly I sneaked up behind him and sunk the hawk into his skull. He fell without a sound, and I moved out of sight to a new location where I could observe the others. After a long time, I could tell the others were wondering where their comrade was. One of them called out, and of course, there wasn't a response. The one who called out called again, then finally, the one who appeared to be the leader pointed to two others and motioned to them to find out what the problem was. I moved into a place where I could ambush them, and when they approached the dead body, I threw the knife first, which caught the first in the chest. Almost simultaneously, I threw the hawk, which landed in about the same place. They made a yell, and I retrieved the hawk and knife as quickly as I could. The whole camp was alerted, and I took up a new observation position. Three of the six had fusees, and the other three had bows. I took the Hawken and put a ball between the eyes of one of the braves with the fusee.

As soon as I shot, I moved left, and sure enough, they fired in the direction of where I was. I reloaded the Hawken real fast but couldn't raise the rifle fast enough before two of them charged. I whipped out the two pistols and shot them both at close range in the chest, killing them both. I moved again to the right and stayed down low I shot my Hawken at another who had a fusee, and the ball hit his heart this time. The last two rushed me, and the one with the bow was the nearest, in the back was the one with the fusee. They came so fast the only thing I could do was grab my lance and jam it into the stomach of the first. It startled the second one holding the fusee, for a second hesitated, which gave me time to position myself. He shot his fusee, but it got missed fire, so he pulled his knife and went after me. As he came at me swinging his knife, I whirled under his arm and, without looking back, shoved my knife into his back, and he fell but got up again. I went up to him, and although he was wounded severely, he swung and sliced my shoulder. It turned me a bit, but since I was so full of adrenaline, I couldn't feel the pain very much. I pulled my hawk out, and then as the Backfoot panic, I recognized him; he was one of them who killed my aunt, uncle, and cousin. Angrily I pulled off my crude hat and started to sing a Shoshone death song to him. He remembered me and came at me with his knife. I didn't even let him get close. I dropped him with one mighty throw of my hawk, which caught him in the chest. I looked around, and none of them were moving, and I gave a mighty victory yell.

Then, with a smile on my face, I went to the fire to see what they were eating. The Blackfoot had the hindquarter of a young deer, and I ate greedily then rested. I looked at the blood dripping down my shoulder, and it started to throb. The cut on my chest didn't have much blood, but it was irritating. After I had enough to eat, I went down to the river and bathed my wounds and bound my shoulder with some buckskin I cut off one brave. My chest didn't need anything because it had stopped bleeding before the last Blackfoot was dead. I piled all their possessions in a pile near the campfire. Then I dragged all the Blackfeet, which I killed into a circle with their heads facing the fire and scalped each one of them. I didn't care for this practice, but my father takes great stock in it as does the rest of the tribe, and besides, neither Grey Wolf nor anyone else would believe me without the scalps. I checked the feet of all the Blackfeet and took the moccasins of the one with the smallest foot. I gathered their belongings and placed them all on one of their horses and tied them all together. I jumped on the lead horse and went back to my shelter. I tied up the horses with the other three belonging to Shorty. I unloaded the one I used to carry back the Blackfeet's belongings. Afterward, I went inside the shelter to get a little sleep.

"Where you been, boy?" Shorty said weakly.

"Killing some Blackfeet."

He laughed and said, "A little thing like you; I don't believe it."

"There were nine of them; they are all dead." I produced the scalps for him to see.

I could see he was shocked at what I just did, and he said, "The angles must be protecting you." "Give me some water to drink. I'm very thirsty." I did as he asked, knowing that he shouldn't drink anything. I saw no harm since he would be dead soon.

"Are you in a lot of pain?"

"More than I've ever been in, I will be visiting the happy hunting grounds soon."

"I wish I could give you something better for your pain."

"In my things, you will find a brown and buckskin color jug, bring it to me." I found the jug and removed the cork, and it was what I thought it would be liquor. I fed it to him, and after the first few gulps, he smiled.

"When I die, all that's mine is yours." "I just ask you to bury me, so the animals don't get me."

"You have some valuable things, not just the beaver pelts, but everything else don't you have any relatives I could send them to?" I asked with compassion.

"No, what relatives I have are not worth it besides it is the trapper's code." "The first one to see a dead trapper gets his belongings." He asked for a few more sips of the liquor and then asked, "Have you ever tried it before?"

"No," I said.

"Go ahead, try some after killing nine Blackfeet you deserve some." I took a big gulp, and I wrinkled up my nose as it burned going down my throat. "Give me another." I poured some more of the liquid down his mouth. "Drink some more."

I took two more gulps. It was starting to go down a little easier, and I was getting a little peculiar. I gave Shorty more to drink, and I could see he was getting drunk, and that was helping with his pain. I drank a little more, and I think I was as bad as him. He finally asked me to lie down beside him; he hadn't been next to a warm body since he left a Crow village eight months ago. From time to time, he would ask for a sip of liquor, and I would give it to him. Then about three hours later, with a weak, hoarse voice, he asked for another drink. I gave him one drink then tried to give him another, but it just ran out of his mouth. I looked at his eyes, and they seemed dull. So, I put the backside of the knife up to his nose and saw there was no air coming out. I took my hand and closed his eyelids;

he was dead. I moved him to one side of the shelter, and I laid down on the other side and fell asleep.

The next morning, I found a soft spot and dug a hole as deep as I could, and then I placed Shorty into it. Beside him, I put his jug with what was remain of the liquor; I had no use for it. After backfilling the grave, I piled rocks on top of it and made a makeshift cross out of dried wood. I packed three of the horses with the beaver pelts and the things I took off the Blackfeet. Then I tied all the horses together, jumped on the lead horse, and headed south-southwest as I planned.

"My husband, I am worried about our son."

You could see on my father's face the worry he had. "If he does not come home soon, I will go looking for him." It had been nine days, and no one had seen me. One Horn and Sleeping Dog couldn't have been happier; they figured me dead. My father left the lodge and saw Arrow Maker and Spotted Buffalo talking to each other. He approached them and told them, "If my son does not come back soon, I will go look for him." Spotted Buffalo and Arrow Maker put their hands on his shoulder, and Spotted Buffalo said, "Give him just five more suns," he held up five fingers. "If he does not show up, I will help you look."

"Wait a minute grandpa, how would you know all of this if you weren't around?" asked Sarah.

"Yes, grandpa, I would like to know this too," said their father Dan.

"Ah grandpa has a way of knowing," said Johnny.

"Johnny is right; you must all pay attention, I said that most Indians like to tell stories, and when I got back, I got told what was said while I was gone many times." "Now, pay attention, and I will continue."

"As will I," said Arrow Maker. He continued, "If you go now, and he is still coming, it will disgrace him, and the trial will be for nothing."

"I will wait but no more after that," said Red Elk.

I kept going until night without giving the horses a rest. I found a small stream that had a trickle of water in it, and I started a fire. I went back and unloaded all the horses and used some of the food that Shorty had. It had been nine days since I left the village, and I wanted to get back before my father would come looking for me. As I sat next to the fire, I found a nice stick that would make a good club, and I started carving on it. When I got tired of doing that, I made a rifle boot out of one of the leggings from the Blackfeet.

The next day I started early. I put the club into the gun boot and held the Hawken on my lap. I rested the horses after about five hours and then rode for another six, then stopped at a fair-sized stream and unloaded the horses and started a fire. I was sure that I was out of the Blackfoot country now and felt at ease about that. But I was disappointed I hadn't recognized anything yet. I finished the work on the club and hardened it over the fire. Then I settled back for asleep. I thought about what I should do the next day. I would leave early for sure, and maybe I would run into something. I was getting impatient. It is funny that I don't think much about St. Louis anymore; home is now the village; hopefully, I was nearby. I don't know when it happened, but everything went black, and I was asleep.

When I woke, it was early morning the sun hadn't come up yet, I ate a little and put out the fire. I then loaded all my things on the horses. By the time I mounted my horse, the sun was just coming up. I rode across the stream, and just as I broke out of the trees, I stopped. To my right was the Lying Lady, a mountain range that looked like a lady who was lying down. I knew where I was, and I would be back to the village that afternoon. I went back down to the stream, got off my horse, and found some red ocher. I made some paint and painted my face like I did when I attacked the Blackfeet. I put a red and black handprint on the rear end of the horse I was riding. I retrieved five eagle feathers that I took off the Blackfeet. I put three in my hair and two on my horse I was riding and then headed out.

After a short rest for the horses, I was within three hours of the village. My mind was on Sleeping Dog; I would have to be smart again when I confronted him. The more I thought about him and the things he did to me, the madder I got. You would believe that I would be excited and thrilled that I finished the trial when I spotted the village. But the opposite was true; my whole focus was on Sleeping Dog.

At my approach, the entire village was alerted. Everyone was waiting at the edge of the village. My family was at the forefront, as was Spotted Buffalo and his wife and, of course, Morning Star, but I looked beyond them. Three Shoshone braves came out to me. When they came close enough to see me, they came to an abrupt stop and stared as I rode past them without even looking at them. The jubilation of the village stopped when they got one look at me. I stopped by my father and dropped the rope that held the other horses and, without a word, rode among the people not speaking to anyone.

I spotted One Horn, and just behind him was Sleeping Dog. I didn't go directly toward them but rode past them. I removed my club from the rifle boot and replaced it with the rifle. I circled behind Sleeping Dog, who was talking to One Horn. I took my club, and with all the strength I could muster, I slammed the club into the back of Sleeping Dog's head, and he went flying on the ground. I slid off the horse, pulled out my knife, untied the green sash, and let my two pistols and hawk drop. By this time, he got up rubbing his head madder than anyone could believe possible, which is just what I wanted him to be. He pulled his knife and came at me. I parried tripped him and sliced him on the side with the knife I now had as he fell to the ground again. He came up at me again and swung at me a few times, which I avoided each time.

My father tried to intervene, but Long Knife stopped him and said, "He is doing well enough by himself."

One Horn faded into the background, away from all the action. Sleeping Dog, because he was furious, wasn't thinking and came down with his knife to stab me. But I blocked his arm, swung under it, and came up behind him, slicing his hamstring just behind the knee. I heard Grey Wolf shouted his approval. Sleeping Dog went down with a scream grabbing his leg and dropping his knife. I turned around quickly and sliced his chest. As he laid there in agony, I said, "I told you not to be here when I got back." I walked back and retrieved my club. I tossed my knife over with my other things and went back to Sleeping Dog and slammed the club into his ribs, hearing them crack.

I was about to hit him again when Spotted Buffalo grabbed my arm. "Are you going to kill him?" he asked.

"No, just hurt him."

"He has been hurt enough." Spotted Buffalo let go of me, and as Sleeping Dog tried to get up and I hit him one more time in the jaw knocking him out. Then I threw the club away and said, "Now he has been hurt enough."

The elders approached me except for One Horn, who held back. My father said, "Son, what is the meaning of all this?"

"I see One Horn is not among you." "I think he had a hand in this also."

"One Horn come up here." Reluctantly he came up, and my father gave him a stare that could kill. I started talking, "I understand there are many challenges to these trials, and some can be very difficult. I will tell you what happened when I left here. We went toward the setting sun until we were out of sight of the village, then we changed directions. We went towards the place where there is always winter deep inside of the Blackfoot country. After almost three suns, I was thrown to the ground, tied up, and blindfolded. Sleeping Dog left throwing insults at me, and I warned him not to be here. But that is not what angered me; it is what he did before he left. After the first rest, he threw me up on the horse. I had to ride on my stomach from that point on. While riding, he rubbed my bottom and said I felt like a woman. When we stopped for the night again, I was thrown to the ground as I was every time we stopped. He dragged me to a grass area he ate and drank. I had nothing until he left me in Blackfoot lands. That first night I had to sleep on my stomach because I injured the back of my leg, and I had pain. I was awakened that night by Sleeping Dog, removing his clothing and pleasured himself on me. I did not cry out, and the next night it was the same. He would have done it one more time when Sleeping Dog dropped me off, but he wanted to get out of the area as fast as possible. "While in the sweat lodge I said, I would never kill a Shoshone, but I did not say I would not hurt one who hurt one who I loved or me."

My father was enraged and looked at One Horn with murder in his eyes. I said, "Sleeping Dog I have punished and One Horn, who I believe put him up to this, the village will punish him because everyone knows just what kind of man he is, he takes pride in his standing here."

"I had nothing to do with this," said One Horn. "I do not know anything about this; he must be lying."

My mother and grandmother came forward, and my mother said, "Let me see my son; we can tell if he is lying." She and my grandmother came up to me, bent me over, and examined my bottom and said, "He is telling the truth." Frankly, I didn't know how they could tell, but everyone believed what they said.

"I had nothing to do with this," One Horn said again in a panic.

"We will question Sleeping Dog, and I will assure you that he will tell us the truth," Long Knife said. Long Knife told someone to tie him up and take him away.

My father, satisfied at the outcome, said, "My son, tell us of all the horses and the things you have, where did you get them?"

"I was in Blackfoot land, I killed Blackfeet, and I am at war with them. I had traveled for about two days and camped near a stream." "Shortly before the sun went down, I was gathering cattails to eat." "A white man, who speaks the language of the French, was coming up the riverbank riding one horse and pulling two others. I was watching from a hidden place, and I noticed there was something wrong with him. He fell from his horse. I looked at him closely, and he had two wounds, one in the shoulder and the other in the stomach. I took him back to my camp, got his things, and gave him some medicine to help with the fever and pain, but I knew he would die. It was the Blackfeet who had done it, and I found their camp and was able, with the white man's weapons, to kill all nine. The last I made to suffer because he was one of those who killed my aunt, uncle, and cousin."

"Nine is a big number how could you kill so many?" asked Tall As The Sky innocently.

I went over to one of the pack horses and removed nine scalps. I gave them too Tall As The Sky and said, "I was smarter, faster, and quieter than they." "I will explain in more detail later, but now I wish to bathe, talk to my father and mother, then get ready for the next trial, the Sun Dance."

"Because of all that has happened, you do not have to do the Sun Dance," Long Knife said.

"No, I agreed to it, and I will do it, please have it ready soon." I turned to Grey Wolf and said, "Will you put up my horses and put my things into our fathers' lodge, I will have something for you later?" He shook his head in agreement, and I headed to the stream.

I placed my feathers and moccasins on the bank and started to bathe. Most of the black and red paint came out. There was a slight tinge on my face, but it would disappear in a day or two. I walked back to my lodge, where my mother was, and I went inside. I stood in front of my mother, trembling as my father walked in, and I said, "It hurt." A tear came down my cheek.

My father put his arm around me and said, "It is over."

My mother sat me down to attend to my arm.

"I have two more things to go through are they putting up the pole?"

"Yes, but you do not have to do this."

"It is a matter of honor and," I looked up to him and said, "pride."

"This will be very painful for you and your mother and me, but I am very proud of you, as is your mother." She shook her head in agreement.

"I have many things I wish to give some of it out."

"We will talk about that later now rest," my father said.

"Are you hungry?" asked my mother.

"A little, but I don't think I should eat until after the dance."

"He is right," reaffirmed my father.

I rested about forty-five minutes, and then I was called to come outside. All the elders were out to meet me, and I saw the pole in the center of the camp. I asked, "Before we start, can I relieve myself?" They nodded, and I headed away from the village, Grey Wolf followed.

"I do not want you to do this," Grey Wolf said somberly.

"You know I have to do this, but thank you for your concern." As Grey Wolf and I came back to the camp, we started to pass Morning Star I stopped then affectionately caressed her cheek.

I joined the elders, and one of them said, "You may choose anyone to attach the ropes, paint your face, and to place the feathers in your hair except your father."

I looked at Grey Wolf, but he was shaking his head no, then I said, "Grandfather, will you, do it?" He nodded his head reluctantly.

One of the elders took me to the pole, and at the pole, a rope got looped over, and a smaller rope was attached to the main rope. My Grandfather placed feathers in my hair, painted my face, and then attached two sharpened deer horns to the ropes. He grabbed the skin just over my left breast and pinched it hard, and then he plunged in one of the deer horns the pain was indescribable. As the blood dripped down my chest, I didn't cry out, but I squeezed my eyes shut, clenched my jaw, and gave a muted quiet moan. Grandfather passed the deer horn through my skin and muscle, and he took the deer horn and tied it back onto the rope. He then did it to the other side with the same results. My chest was completely red with blood, and my knees nearly buckled. My Grandfather stuck a whistle in my mouth and led me back so that the rope was taut. Then he said, "Dance toward the pole and then back blowing your whistle. When you are tired, lean back and try to rip the rope out through your skin without using your hands."

I started dancing toward the pole blowing my whistle, and people were singing, and drums were drumming. I wasn't a great dancer, but no one corrected me. I danced up and down for about twenty minutes and then decided to pull on the ropes. When the rope was taut, I leaned back, and the pain was traumatic. Again, I almost collapsed, but the ropes didn't pull free. I danced back and forth for another fifteen or twenty minutes and tried to break the ropes again with the same results. I went down on one knee from the pain but got right up and staggered down to the pole again. As I did, I peered down and saw my skin had torn a little. As I was dancing, the sound of the people and the drums kind of drowning out the sound of my whistle I was blowing. Then everything stopped, and I looked around. On the pole was placed another rope, and the warrior called Black Fox joined me in the dance. In the next half hour, three more joined me. I tried the ropes again, and my skin tore some more.

As I was about to start toward the pole again, they threw another rope to my right. Grey Wolf stepped up much to my shock with my grandfather helping him. I tried to protest but was too weak, and it was too late. He was already hooked up and dancing. I continued my dance, and three more times, I tried to break free of the ropes. One brave had already broken free, and on my last try, I gave it all I had and broke free. I collapsed to the ground. By the time I broke free, there must have been more than fifteen warriors dancing. I had lost a lot of blood; everything went black, and I passed out.

# 10
# Soaring Eagle With Many Coups

By sundown the next day, I woke up. There was some pain, and I was very weak and hungry. My mother saw that I was awake and asked, "How are you?"

"I have some pain, my head hurts, I feel weak, and I am hungry."

"I will get you some medicine and food that should help." "In time, you will be just fine."

"How is Grey Wolf?" "Did he free himself from his ropes?"

"Yes, he freed himself, and he is sore." "He stopped by earlier when you were still asleep."

"You mean he is strong enough to walk around?"

"You know he is older than you, and he didn't have to go through all those trials as you did." I knew he was stronger than I was, and was glad he is my brother and not my enemy.

The medicine and food I got were doing their job, and I was feeling better. My father came into the lodge with Morning Star. It just brightened up my day. "How many buffalos did he eat?" my father said to my mother.

"He just ate one Elk," my mother responded.

I took Morning Star's hand as she sat beside me. "Maybe you could stay with me until I can get better," I said mischievously.

"I do not think my mother or father would approve; we are not husband and wife." "Anyway, you look very strong to me," she said with a smile.

"Will you do something for me when you leave here?"

"Yes, what is it you wish?"

"Get Grey Wolf for me."

Morning Star left, and twenty minutes later, Grey Wolf came in with a big smile on his face. "I see you are alive," he said.

"Yes, someone has to teach you how to shoot."

"Teach me; it was I who taught you how to shoot."

"I do not mean bows and arrows." I painfully went over to where my things were stored, pulled out one of the fusees, and handed it to him.

With wonder, he said, "This is too great of a gift I have nothing for you."

"I wish nothing from you; it is yours; I am your brother." I also gave him a powder horn and a shot bag.

I pulled out another fusee and gave it to my father with a powder horn and shot bag. With a big smile, he accepted it and said, "I wish to thank you; it is a great gift."

"There is no need for you to thank me you adopted me; you are my father."

"What are you going to do with the other rifles?" my father asked.

"One is mine." I pulled out the Hawken, the two pistols, the knife, and hawk along with the powder horn and shot bag. "These are all mine, the other two rifles, I thought of giving one to grandfather and one to Spotted Buffalo." My father nodded in agreement. "The rest of the knives, you can decide what you want to do with them."

"Do you want one, Grey Wolf?"

"I will look at them and decide," Grey Wolf said.

"Mother, you choose what you want and give the rest to grandmother, and Blue Lizard." "There is some food that the white man had with my things, coffee, and tobacco, too." "Do you know what coffee is?"

My mother and father both smiled and nodded, yes.

"The Beaver furs I will keep and trade them someday."

For the rest of that day, I never left the lodge except to relieve myself. The next day I went outside. I gave grandfather a rifle with a powder horn and shot bag. He was grateful and asked me, "How are you doing?"

"I am sore and a little weak, but I am getting stronger." "Grandfather, when should I bring up to my father about getting a name?"

"Why not today it is as good as any."

I smiled and said, "I will do that."

I next went to Spotted Buffalo's lodge. Morning Star was outside, "I wish to speak with your father, is he here?"

"No, what is it you want?"

"I wish to ask him if I can make you my woman." She smiled and giggled, and I don't think she believed me. "Do you know where I can find him?"

"He is talking to Long Knife at the central fire."

I found him where Morning Star said he would be. As I went up to him, they both smiled, and Spotted Buffalo said, "How do you feel today?"

"I am fine, just a bit weak and sore."

Long Knife said, "You must pick two braves and travel to the other villages to tell them you are Shoshone now."

"I have already sent two-out, telling them you are coming."

"I would like to take Grey Wolf, but there is no one to take care of his mother."

"I will make sure his mother is taken care of," said Spotted Buffalo.

"Then the other should be your son Running Deer; he is older and wiser than both Grey Wolf and I."

"Then Grey Wolf and my son it will be," said Spotted Buffalo.

"It must wait until I receive a name, in a few days I hope it is up to my father."

"That will be just fine," Spotted Buffalo said again.

"Spotted Buffalo, I wish to speak to you privately," I said.

"I must be going anyway I have to get my horse ready for a hunt tomorrow," said Long Knife.

"What is it you want to talk to me about?"

"Can we go over by the water?"

He nodded, and we walked over to the stream and found a rock to sit on. He said, "First, I wish to tell you about Sleeping Dog we drove him away from our village." "I felt you should know this." "Now, what is it you want to speak about?"

"I wish to marry Morning Star."

He smiled and said, "I know you have a great love for her, but she and you are very young."

"What does this matter when I love her?" "I was too young to count so many coups, I was too young when I went on the long walk, and I was too young to do the Sun Dance, but I did them all."

"You are very wise for one so young." "I must give this some thought and talk to my daughter's mother also."

"I know she is too young to bear children as am I." "But in the white world, they have a step before marriage; it is called engagement." "It means Morning Star belongs to someone else, and all those who find interest in her should stay away." "If Morning Star changes her mind about me, she can still do this."

"Have you talked to Morning Star about this?"

"I told her I was going to talk to you about making her mine, but I do not think she believed me."

"Alright, I will speak to my whole family about this." "You do know there is a price for a brave marrying a woman, and Morning Star is my only daughter?"

"Yes, I do here." I handed him the rifle, shot bag, and powder horn and said, "This will be part of my payment you decide what else you wish." I stood up and said, "It will make me happy if you and your family could decide when I have received my Shoshone name." He nodded his head in agreement.

I left Spotted Buffalo to look for Grey Wolf and found him talking to a girl by the name of Falling Rock. I decided not to interfere and went over to where some boys were practicing with their bows and arrows. I sat down on a log and watched about six boys ranging from about six to nine, most of whom were very good. Every one of them was better than I was when I first started. I noticed one small boy with just a loincloth on, he was called Comes Running and was about six. He was not practicing with the other boys. I got up and sat down beside him and asked, "Why are you not practicing with the other boys?"

"My father has not yet given me a bow and arrows yet."

"Why is that?"

"We do not have much." "My father tries, but we have little."

"Come with me."

"Where are we going?"

"To my lodge." My father was eating at my lodge, and I asked, "Can Comes Running come in?" "Yes," replied my father. "Are you hungry, Comes Running?"

He nodded yes, and my father patted the ground to his right. Then he motioned me to sit on his left. My mother served both of us, and I said to my father, "I need to get my name soon, Spotted Buffalo, and Long Knife want me to visit the other villages with Grey Wolf and Running Deer."

"You will start tomorrow." "You must choose a place to get your name."

"There is a place only Grey Wolf and I know about it. I will go there." I could see my mother wasn't happy. I was leaving so soon, but I would talk to her later about it.

"Comes Running does not have a bow or any arrows I thought about giving him a Blackfoot bow and arrows."

Comes Running lit up when I suggested giving him those things, and my father noticed. "They are yours to do what you want to, but I would get the approval of Comes Running's father first, and you might as well give him a knife also."

I nodded, smiled, and asked Comes Running as we were eating, "How did you get your name?"

"My father said when there is food to be eaten, I come running, and that is how I got my name."

My mother, father, and I all laughed at what he said.

When we finished, I grabbed the knife, and bow and arrows then Comes Running, and I went to speak to his father. His father, Dancing Bear, was currying his horse when we found him. Dancing Bear was a young man, and Comes Running was his first child.

I spoke first and said, "Dancing Bear, when I killed all those Blackfeet on my long walk, I took many Blackfoot knives, bows, and arrows." "I would like to give Comes Running a knife, bow, and arrows, but my father said to ask you first."

"Your father was right to have you ask me first let me see them first."

"I handed him the items, and he examined them and said, "They are not as good as Shoshone."

"My grandfather can fix them; he fixed some for me."

He drew back on the bowstring and asked his son, "Do you want these?"

"Yes, all of the boy's practice, but me and I need to practice to become a great warrior like you."

He handed him the items and said to me, "It is a great gift I owe you much."

"All I wish for is you and your family's friendship."

"You have that without these gifts."

I smiled, and we both left, Comes Running beaming with a huge smile. We went to the place where everyone practices, and Comes Running tried his hand at shooting. As I was sitting there watching and encouraging him, Grey Wolf sat down beside me and said, "He is doing worse than you did."

"He is only six winters, and this is his first try."

He smiled and said, "I got told I will be going with you to visit the other villages."

"Yes, but tomorrow I go to get a name, the place I have chosen is that special place you took me to."

"Do you remember how to get there?"

"I am not sure; will you take me there?" He nodded, and when it started to get dark, we all went back to our lodges.

The next day when I got up, my father instructed me on what I must do to get a name. "You are not to eat; drink or sleep, and you are to stay in one spot. Do not walk around until you get an answer from your spirit guide. You shall be alone wearing nothing but may have a fire, do you understand?"

"Yes."

"When you get your vision, you will come back and tell the elders what you saw, and they will give you a name."

"Grey Wolf will go with me until I get there and then leave me."

"You must be alone; the spirit guide will not come if someone is with you."

We left about an hour later, and it took several hours to get to our destination. It turned out that I didn't need Grey Wolf to get there, but he was good company. We went up to the waterfall and then where the cave was. I tied my horse to a tree with a long rope to get to water and grass. Grey Wolf and I gathered wood for a fire, and then I told Grey Wolf that he must go back to the village so that the spirit guide could come.

When I was alone, I watched for an hour as Grey Wolf was making his way back to the village. Then he fell from my eyesight, I started my fire, stripped and laid my clothing down to sit on. I placed my weapons to the left of me just in case there was a need for them. It had been a pleasantly warm day with a few white clouds with a blue sky and an unnoticeable breeze. I listened and only heard the waterfall that was to the right of me. I did see plenty of birds and down below, to my right, some deer moving cautiously toward the water. When it got dark, I saw a night sky full of stars. It got a little chilly, but the fire kept me warm.

Sometime during the night, I got quite tired and started dozing. After doing this a few times, I splashed water on my face. I was facing east, so I saw the sun coming up. It was a beautiful sunrise. The sunlight rejuvenated me, and I could get through the day, but night came again. Soon after the sun went down, and it was dark out, I started getting tired again. This time it was earlier than the night before. Water didn't work as well as it did the night before, so I had to stand and dance around to stay awake. The next day I was thirsty and hungry. I was having a hard time trying to stay awake even during the day. Things around me didn't look right, but my spirit guide hadn't come yet. Sometime in the afternoon from far off, I could see a large bird, but I couldn't make out what kind it was, but it was staying in one area. By sundown, the sunset seemed overly orange, and as I stared at it, I could see the large bird coming nearer.

"Why are you sitting there?" came a voice to the right of me. I looked over, and I saw a boy dressed in the whitest buckskins I ever saw. He was glowing like a firefly. "Get up, fly." "Why are you sitting there?" he spoke again.

"I cannot fly; I am a boy." "Anyway, I was told to stay in one spot and wait for my spirit guide." I heard a thunderous screech, and I looked up, and the bird was near enough for me to make out that it was a huge eagle. I turned to the boy next to me and said, "You should not be here." "My spirit guide will not come if you are here."

"And what does this spirit guide look like?" said the boy.

"I do not know I would guess it would be a Shoshone warrior."

"Why would I not be your spirit guide?"

"You!"

Just then, the screech from the eagle was so loud that it sounded like cannon fire, and it went right through me. I was startled because the eagle was inches in front of me. "Get up and fly." This time the boy was to the left of me. I looked down, and my legs, arms, and whole body were turning into feathers, feathers I could see through. I stood up and flapped my arms, and sure enough, I went up. I was high up flying in circles when the boy, who I was convinced was my spirit guide, said, "Fly to the rising sun."

I didn't see him, but I could hear him. I asked him, "What is your name, spirit guide?"

"It is a name your people will know very well someday, Teancum." A few seconds later, he told me to go north and said, "What do you see?"

"I see what looks like Shoshone attacking a Blackfoot village and doing well."

Then he told me to go to the further to the setting sun again. "What do you see now?"

"I see Crow and another tribe I do not know fighting."

"That tribe is called Lakota." "Now, turn around and look at the setting sun."

"Now, what do you see?"

"A small village of Blackfeet, and they look sick."

I got told to turn south and then west. "What do you see?"

"I see many white man's cities and towns." "I also see strange machines and cattle having replaced the buffalo."

"Now let's head back," Teancum said. We stopped at a village, and he said, "Do you see what is down there?"

"Yes, a village of people who are very poor."

We headed back to my campfire, and before he left, I asked, "Teancum, what will happen to me?"

"You will live for a long time and have many children; also, there will be some sadness and some happiness." "You will be feared by some as well as admired by others, and you will have great wealth."

"Will the Indians always have sadness?"

"I see far into the future when they will find their happiness, but they will not be the same as they are now."

Everything went black, and I found myself standing next to the water. I went down and drank enough water to satisfy my thirst. I then went hunting, shot a rabbit, found some wild onions, and cooked them both. I stayed there that night, in the morning, I headed back home.

I wasn't quite at the village when Grey Wolf came out with his horse to meet me. Comes Running was running far behind him. I stopped and talked to Grey Wolf. "Did you see your spirit guide?" he asked.

"Yes, when I tell the elders what I saw, you shall hear everything." Just then, Comes Running came up to me. "Are you shooting any better?" I said to Comes Running.

"A little, but I will get better.

"Come up here." I reached down and pulled him up on my horse, and we rode around the village.

I came up to my lodge and got off my horse. My father came up to me and asked, "Did you have a vision?"

"Yes, it was strange."

"I will take your horse; you go see your mother; she has been worried."

I went into the lodge and greeted my mother. "Why, with all I have been through, were you worried?"

"I will always worry about you; you are so young and are my only son."

I smiled and sat down beside her, and she asked, "Are you hungry?"

"Yes, but I do not think I have time to eat." "My father is getting the elders together."

She handed me some roasted meat and said, "Here, the elders can wait." I laughed and took the meat and devoured it. While I was eating, my father called me, and when I didn't answer, he came into the lodge. "Why did you not answer?"

I pointed over to my mother, and she said, "He can eat first before he talks to those old buffalos."

"I will tell the old buffalos that you will come soon."

After I finished, I went to the village campfire with my mother following. I then sat opposite the elders with most of the village waiting to see what I would say. I asked my mother to sit on my right and my brother to sit on my left.

"Tell us of your vision," said Long Knife.

I got up and said, "It was on the third sunset that my spirit guide showed himself." "I was confused because he was a boy about my age; dressed in the whitest buckskins I have ever seen, his name is Teancum." "Have any of you heard of this name?" Long Knife looked at all the elders, and they all shook their heads no. "Teancum kept telling me to stand up and fly, and I said boys could not fly." "I had been watching a large eagle with a loud screech for some time before Teancum came." "Just as I was talking to Teancum, the eagle screeched such a loud noise that it went right through me, and he stood right in front of me." "I looked down at my body; it got covered with feathers, and I could see right through me. I flapped my arms like a bird, and I flew up and could fly." "The spirit guide and I flew to a battle between the Shoshone and Blackfeet, and the Shoshone were winning." "Then we saw another battle between the Crow and the Lakota, and there was no clear winner there."

"With the Lakota, there never is," my grandfather said.

"Then we were over a Blackfoot village, it was small and the people very sickly." "We were then where the buffalo are, but there were no buffalo, just white men with the white man's kind of buffalo." "There were many large white man's villages." "They were everywhere we then flew over a village." "I do not know what people they were, but they were weak and unhappy." "When we got back to the campfire, I asked if there would always be unhappiness for the people of the land." He said, "After many summers, the people will find some happiness, but they will change from what they are now." "I asked what would happen to me, and he said that there would be much happiness and sadness." "I would have much wealth, many children, and that I would live long." "He also stated that there would be some who feared me and some who honored me, and many would know of me." "I found myself next to the stream alone, so I drank water and found something to eat then rested."

The elders started to talk among themselves. Then Long Knife said, "Grey Owl will speak about this."

"Your spirit guide has shown you much." "What you have seen will come." "The Blackfeet will become weak and sick; this is good." "All the people from all tribes will suffer under the white man; this is bad, but we will resist. The people of this land, our enemies, and our friends, including the Shoshone, have brought this on ourselves. You will become a mighty warrior; this is good. Even though we will suffer under the whites, I find happiness to know this will change in the future. Did the spirit guide tell you what kind of changes there will be for us?"

"No, but things are changing all the time. My father once hunted with a bow; now, he can hunt with a rifle. I would guess that at one time, the Shoshone did not have lodges as we do now but lived in caves," I said. Many agreed with what I was saying. I asked, "And what of my name?"

There was much discussion among the elders again. Then Long Knife said, "You have made many coups, in your vision, you flew like an eagle. You will be known as Soaring Eagle With Many Coups.

# 11

# MISSED RENDEZVOUS

Long Knife asked, "Are there any more questions for Soaring Eagle With Many Coups?" No one asked any questions. "Is there anything else to talk about." Again no one said anything. "Then we are finished." He came over to me, smiled, patted my head, and walked off. My father, grandfather, and Spotted Buffalo came over to me. While my father had his arm around me, Spotted Buffalo asked, "When do you think you will be ready to leave to visit the other villages?"

I looked up at my father and said, "I think I better stay here a few days for my mother's sake."

He smiled and said, "Very well, you let me know when you wish to leave." I nodded, and Spotted Buffalo left.

The next two days got filled with Morning Star, Grey Wolf, Comes Running, my grandparents, and my parents. We went for a short hunt the next day and Comes Running wanted to come, but his father said he was still too young and needed to learn how to shoot better. Grey Wolf and I each got a deer, and we divided the meat between his mother, our grandparents, and my parents. Grey Wolf and I both felt sorry for Comes Running because he couldn't hunt with us, so we offered to take him for a swim. He accepted, and we almost drowned him.

It was the day for me to leave to visit the other villages. I told my mother and father that I was going to Spotted Buffalo's lodge and talk to him about something else, but I would come back before I left.

I went to Spotted Buffalo's lodge and asked if he was there. He was, and Spotted Buffalo invited me in. I sat on Spotted Buffalo's right and said, "How soon will it be for Running Deer to be ready to visit the villages with Grey Wolf and me?"

He looked over to Running Deer, who said with a smile, "When the sun is fully up."

"This is good." "I will tell Grey Wolf and my parents."

Morning Star was in the lodge, and I was looking at her when I said, "I have something else to talk to you about."

Spotted Buffalo noticed that I was looking at Morning Star, and he said, "Speak."

"I have talked to you about Morning Star, and you told me you would give me an answer when I came back from seeking the spirit guide."

Morning Star's head popped up, and Spotted Buffalo first looked at Morning Star, then his wife Small Moon and his two sons Running Deer and Broken Antler. Then he said, "Morning Star, do you love this one enough to be his woman."

With a meek voice, she said, "Yes."

I wanted to yell out, but I was able to keep quiet and just have the largest smile on my face that anyone ever had.

"Then she will be your woman, but it will cost you. As I have said, she is my only daughter, and she is very beautiful."

"What do you wish?" I asked.

He held up ten fingers and said, "This many horses, ten, and you can give them to me as you get them."

I smiled and said, "I already have them and will get them for you when I get back." I guessed by the expression on his face he didn't know how many horses I had. I added, "Of course, she will stay with you until I have my lodge."

"And when do you think this will happen?" he asked apprehensively.

"I would think it would take two or three seasons."

He shook his head and said, "That would be good; she will be a woman by then."

"Yes, and I will be a man, I think!" They all laughed, and I turned red, then got up and said, "I must be going." Spotted Buffalo nodded, and I went out of his lodge.

Morning Star came out after me, and I took her hand and walked off with her. "Was the amount I agreed to pay your father fair?"

"No, you agreed to pay too much."

"I was thinking he was trying to discourage me." We were silent for a few minutes, and then I asked, "Is there a ceremony when you get married?"

"Yes."

"I must talk to your father before I go," I said. "Will after the next winter be good for you to marry," I asked.

"It is not up to me to decide it is up to you."

"Then, after next winter, it will be."

"Do you think you will have a lodge in two or three years?"

"I hope to have one by then; I will be stronger by then." She smiled, and I continued, "I think I better tell Grey Wolf that I will be leaving at high sun."

"I must go back to my lodge," Morning Star said. I smiled and nodded, and she left.

I found Grey Wolf carrying firewood for his mother. "We leave at high sun. Can you be ready?" He smiled and nodded yes, and I left to tell my parents everything.

I went up to my father, who was outside talking too Tall As The Sky, and said, "I would like to talk to you and my mother before I leave." I went to the lodge, but my mother was talking to my grandmother at the next lodge over. I went over to her with my father at my side. "I will be leaving at high sun."

"I will fix you some food to eat now and some to take with you," said my mother. "I have something else to say to all of you." "About this time next year, I will marry Morning Star." "She will stay with her parents until I have a lodge of my own, in about two or three years." "Spotted Buffalo asked much for her, and I agreed to pay the amount."

"How much did Spotted Buffalo ask for?" asked my father.

"Ten horses, I don't think he knew I could pay that much."

My father sighed and said, "We learn from our mistakes." "You did pay too much." "I will talk to him and see if he will lower it."

"No, Morning Star is worth it, and I will get more horses."

"Let him alone he is a young man now and a warrior he has proven himself, besides it has been a long time since I have been to a wedding," my grandmother said, laughing.

"It is neither the wedding I am worried about, nor the price Soaring Eagle paid." "It is what comes after the wedding," my mother said.

"Yes, Yes, it will be very unusual and amusing," my grandmother said, laughing again. My father just shook his head and walked back to the lodge, as did my mother. I followed them, wondering what they meant.

I got my horse as did my brother. My mother and grandmother had given me plenty of food, and I also took my weapons, including my bow and arrows.

"Why are you taking your bow and arrows," asked Grey Wolf.

"I do not plan to do any hunting except for food for ourselves, and I want to save my powder and balls for when I have to use them." Grey Wolf looked at me and went back to his lodge to retrieve his bow and arrows.

Meanwhile, I went over to Spotted Buffalo's lodge. Running Deer was ready to go, and he was talking to his brother, Broken Antler. I went to Spotted Buffalo and said, "The marriage ceremony will be after the next snows, is that alright?"

He nodded and said, "When you get back, we will be split into smaller villages and will have moved." "Running Deer knows where." I mounted my horse as Grey Wolf joined us, and we left heading west.

We rode about a half-hour, and I asked Running Deer, "Where are we going first?"

"Too Broken Paw's village near the Snake."

I looked at Grey Wolf. He knew I didn't have any idea where or what the Snake was, and he said, "It is a large stream shaped like a snake."

I looked back over to Running Deer and asked, "How long will it take to get there?"

He smiled and said, "What is the matter?" "Do you miss my sister already?"

"I miss her always when I am not with her; I love her."

"You will soon be with her; she is already yours."

This time Grey Wolf was confused and stared at me. I told him, "After the next snows, I will marry Morning Star I have already paid a high price for her." "Did I not mention it to you?"

"No!" Grey Wolf said, surprised.

"Yes, you paid a high price for her." "You could have had her for one horse or nothing." "My father likes you," Running Deer said teasingly.

"It does not matter Morning Star is worth the price I paid for her," I replied.

"How much was paid?" Grey Wolf asked.

"Ten horses," he held up ten fingers, and a rifle, powder and balls," replied Running Deer.

Grey Wolf sighed, "This is too much." I knew I turned beet red, but I didn't say anything.

We camped by a stream, started a fire, and started eating. Earlier, we agreed to combine the food we had with us. It was just as well Grey Wolf didn't have much. While we were eating, I took the opportunity to ask, "My mother was not concerned about me marrying Morning Star or the amount I paid." "But she was concerned about what comes after the marriage." "What would make her concerned?"

Running Deer and Grey Wolf looked at each other and smiled and started laughing. "You must sleep with her," said Running Deer. I was even more confused. I didn't understand what was so funny about that; I'd slept with her before. "Why should my mother have a concern about that; I have slept with her before?"

"Like a man and a woman?" asked Grey Wolf. They both could see I was still confused, and Running Deer smiled and moved his hips back and forth, and Grey Wolf said, "Make babies now you understand?"

I was shocked and stated in a nervous voice, "But I will not be able to do that for maybe two or three seasons."

"That is why your mother is concerned," laughed Grey Wolf.

"Has Morning Star expressed any concern about this?" I asked Running Deer.

"She is curious about how you are going to achieve this, and so am I."

"I must give this some thought, but no matter what I think of, I will still marry her."

On the third day, we came upon some Crow. Running Deer spoke Crow, and he translated for us. "This is Little Bear; he is Raven, and he is Black Crow. I explained to them that you are not white and that you are a warrior at a young age."

"Tell them I would like to learn the Crow language someday," I said.

"Soaring Eagle With Many Coups said he would like to learn your language."

"Tell that white boy; I could not care less if he wants to learn Crow or not."

"Hold your tongue, Little Bear. He is a Shoshone warrior and has killed more Blackfeet than you have seen. I could see that Running Deer was angry about something.

"He would make a good woman, and I think I would like to take his horse and weapons," said Little Bear. The Crow started to move around a bit. Something was going on, and I didn't know what it was.

"He has insulted you; he said you would make a good woman, and he wants your horse and weapons."

I became enraged, shot off the horse like a cannonball, shot from a cannon, and drew my knife. I knocked Little Bear off his horse, and with the handle of my big knife, I smacked him a good one just above his left eye drawing blood. Raven and Black Crow tried to intervene on Little Bear's behalf, but Grey Wolf and Running Deer pulled their weapons on them, and they backed off. I got a few licks in, and I may have even broken his nose before he could get me off him. I came up off the ground with my blade up, and the Crow drew his knife. He swung his knife a few times but missed. In my first attempt, I slashed his upper chest near his right shoulder. One could say I was spitting fire; I was so angry. He swung at me a few more times again, missing me. But on his last swing, I went under his arm and stabbed him in the buttocks. I turned around ready for his next attack, but he was down on one knee singing. I looked up at Running Deer and said, "He is singing his death song."

"I will not kill him; I am just punishing him for his disrespect." I went to my horse and mounted it as Running Deer told Little Bear, "He will not kill you because you are Crow." "He just wanted to punish you for your disrespect." "I said he was a great warrior, and you did not believe you have paid for it now." We rode off, leaving the Crow in total shock, and I was a bit surprised that I did so well. But after all, this was over my body started to shake. I don't know why this happened. It also happened when I fought the Blackfeet and Sleeping Dog.

Back at the village, the elders held a meeting. It got decided to split the tribe and move to a new location. My father and Spotted Buffalo would go to the southeast near the valley of the bow.

It had been two days since we had the run-in with the Crow, and Running Deer said, "We must hunt for two deer. We will be coming into the village of Broken Paw tomorrow, and we should not come empty-handed." During the hunt, Running Deer decided to go off alone, and he had gotten his deer. Grey Wolf and I went together in a different direction, and Grey Wolf also got a deer, and I shot an antelope.

We came to Broken Paw's village, which was in a canyon next to a large river, which I assumed was the Snake. There was a lot of excitement in the village when we came. They were expecting us because of the other warriors Long Knife sent out. We presented the game to Broken Paw, and he kept some and gave the rest to those who needed it in his village.

He invited us into his lodge, which was as big as or larger than Spotted Buffalo's. Beforehand it was decided that I would sit next to Broken Paw, then Running Deer and finally Grey Wolf. Broken Paw said, "So you are the one we have heard about, and is it true you have killed," he put up all his fingers twice, "twenty Blackfeet?"

"I have killed many Blackfeet and hoped to kill more."

He laughed and nodded approval. I didn't correct him on the number of Blackfeet; it was something one didn't do.

"He has gone on the long walk and done the Sun Dance," Grey Wolf said, and Broken Paw just stared at me.

Running Deer added, "He has also defeated a disrespectful Crow just about two suns ago."

I told him of my spirit guide and what happened, and we talked through the night. The next day after having little sleep, we headed southwest to Strong Bow's camp.

"What is all the excitement?" Red Elk asked.

Comes Running said, "Bear Slayer and his family are coming." Red Elk walked over to Tall As The Sky and waited for Bear Slayer to come into the village. Bear Slayer got off his horse while his wife, Blue Flower, and his son, Tracking Fox, remained on their horses. "It is good to see you and your family Bear Slayer," said Tall As The Sky. "And it is good to see you again and you Red Elk," said Bear Slayer. "You and your family will stay with me, of course," said Tall As The Sky. "And you and your family will eat with my woman and me, you also Tall As The Sky," said Red Elk. Later, that night, after Bear Slayer and his family settled in, they and Tall As The Sky were all in Red Elk's lodge having a meal.

"Grandpa, there you go again, you are talking about things when you weren't there, how do you know what they said?" asked Sarah again.

Dan and Johnny also looked confused, and I said, "I don't know about you children did I not tell you that my family told me everything that went on when I got back to the village that was our way."

"But grandpa, you couldn't have known everything accurately what was said," said Dan.

"No, you are right." "I had to guess what would have happened, and I'm betting I'm very close because I know how everyone was, now let me continue with the story."

"You will be going on the buffalo hunt with us?" asked Red Elk.

"Yes, it has been a long time besides you will not find any bears there," said Tall As The Sky humorously.

"I would be honored to join you in the buffalo hunt." He didn't want to go because he knew how dangerous a buffalo hunt could be.

"It is too bad; my son is not here to meet you." "He is about the same age as your son," said Red Elk.

"I did not know you had a son that old," said Bear Slayer.

"Yes, I adopted him some time ago; he is a good son."

"He is a great warrior; he has killed many Blackfeet at such a young age," Tall As The Sky said.

"He seems to be very brave." "What is his name?" asked Bear Slayer.

"Soaring Eagle With Many Coups is his name." "He is of your people, but now he is Shoshone," replied Red Elk.

There was a moment of silence, and then Bear Slayer said, "You said he is white?"

"He was, he has yellow hair and blue eyes, but now he is Shoshone," Red Elk answered, frankly.

"Let me explain," said Tall As The Sky. "You have been adopted by our people as Shoshone." "But with Soaring Eagle With Many Coups, it was different." "He had to go through many difficult trials so hard that most men could not complete them, but he did." "Then he did the Sun Dance, which has never happened from one so young." "Because of all of my son's trials, he is not only adopted; he is Shoshone."

"Tell me about him, does he have any other family that is of his blood?"

Then Red Elk started to tell my story, "Many of the Shoshone were with me hunting elk, Tall As The Sky was with us." "We came upon about twenty Blackfeet," he put up his fingers twice, "and they were attacking my son and wanted to kill him." "My son had killed three Blackfeet, but the third knocked him out, and I finished the Blackfoot warrior off." "When I looked at my son, he was in very poor shape." "I took him back to the village, and his mother took care of him." "He did not wake for many days, but when he did, and we could speak with him." "We asked if he had any family left, and he said he did not have any family." "His father came to these mountains many years ago, but he thought his father was dead." "We asked him if he wanted to go on his way or to stay with us, and we would raise him, and he chose us."

"Most white men who come to these mountains do die within the first few years," Bear Slayer said. "It is just as well he is with you; he would be in a terrible place back with the whites besides you can train him right to survive these mountains."

"We should not have given Broken Paw that antelope," Running Deer said.

"Why is that?" I asked.

"Antelope is very tough." "The people will eat it, but it would be their last choice of meat," Running Deer said.

"I will make sure not to get an antelope for Strong Bow when it is time."

It took us about four days to get to Strong Bow's village. The village was on a flat, grassy area. Most of the trees were along the stream that went by the village. The village was a lot smaller than Broken Paw's, but the village's enthusiasm was as great as or greater than Broken Paw's village. We stayed in Strong Bow's lodge, which was smaller than my father's lodge.

The next village was Spotted Eagle's. It was about the same size as my village. Our reception at the village one could say only described as polite. There was one warrior who didn't like the fact I was Shoshone. His name is Grey Bear, and he had a familiar look to him. I found out why when someone told me that Sleeping Dog is his cousin. I explained what Sleeping Dog did to me, as did Running Deer and Grey Wolf, but he didn't believe any of us. He was getting disrespectful, so I growled, "What I did to Sleeping Dog I could do to you, watch your tongue."

Spotted Eagle said crossly, "You do not speak to Grey Bear in this way, not in my lodge, not in my village."

I looked at Running Deer and Grey Wolf, and they must have read my mind. I got up, grabbed my things as they did, and said, "You are not Shoshone." We turned and went out of his lodge. They were shocked at what I said, and we left the village.

When we had camped several miles from the village, I said I was sorry that I acted the way I did. Running Deer said, "It was not your fault they behaved poorly, I would have done the same. My father will not be pleased with what happened." Grey Wolf nodded in agreement.

"I think it would be good to watch to see if someone follows us, I said. Both agreed, and I said, "I will watch first."

We visited two more villages for the next two weeks, and then we headed back to our village.

"Now, before you, three, ask me again as I told you before, my family said what was spoken and done while I was gone."

"It is too bad you couldn't stay longer; my son would be happy to meet you," said Red Elk regretfully.

"I will be back next year, and I am sure we will meet," Bear Slayer replied.

"Will you give this to your son, Red Elk?" said Tracking Fox. Red Elk examined what Bear Slayer's son gave him. It was grizzly bear claws attached to a leather cord so one could wear it around your neck.

"I will give this to him, and he will be happy to get it." Everybody said their goodbyes and Red Elk went back to his lodge.

We were traveling through a valley about two days after we left the last village when we came upon some friendly warriors from another tribe. Running Deer and Grey Wolf, both almost at the same time, said, "They are Bannock, friends of the Shoshone." It was strange I could understand their language, but they spoke with what I could only explain as an accent. They didn't look like Shoshone; they looked more like someone from the Crow tribe.

"Are they a different kind of Shoshone," I whispered to Grey Wolf.

"Yes and no, one-time many seasons ago, long before I was born, they were Shoshone, but they broke away."

The one that spoke was Sparrow Hawk. "It is always good to meet the Shoshone, but who is this." He was pointing to me, and I said, "I am Soaring Eagle With Many Coups." I could see he was confused at the way I looked. "I am a Shoshone warrior." "I will explain why I look the way I do."

Grey Wolf and Running Deer nodded in agreement, and Sparrow Hawk said, "If you say you are Shoshone, then I believe that you are, but I would like to understand as would the rest of us." "You will come to our village and be our honored guest; it is not far from here."

His village was small, about fifteen lodges. The whole village greeted us and was very curious about me. We went into Sparrow Hawk's lodge, where he gave us food and something to drink. I explained why I am a Shoshone warrior to Sparrow Hawk, and he accepted everything I said. After we finished eating, we went to the village campfire, and I, with the help of Grey Wolf and Running Deer, told the whole story again. Grey Wolf and Running Deer built up the story some. I had noticed that from village to village, the story grew from what the truth was. I didn't correct them; it wouldn't have been polite, and it would have embarrassed them.

I had noticed that the Bannock place a body in a tree. I couldn't tell age or sex because it was the habit of most tribes to wrap a leather blanket, usually a buffalo blanket around the deceased. I said to Running Deer, "I see someone has died," as I pointed to the corpse.

He nodded and said, "Yes, he was an old man by the name of Falls A Lot, his wife died last snows, and her name was Red Morning." He didn't say any more about them, and I didn't ask.

We left early the next morning passing by Falls A Lot. It was a cold morning with a lot of clouds. Running Deer said, "It may rain today we will go for a while and then find someplace to get out of the rain." By noon, the clouds turned angry looking, and the wind kicked up. I could see Grey Wolf and Running Deer watching for a suitable place to stay before the rains came. I first saw a cave, and I pointed it out to Running Deer and Grey Wolf, who agreed to head for it. We weren't more than a hundred feet from the cave when the sky opened, and we got soaked. The cave was large, and we were able to put the horses inside. There was some wood inside, so Running Deer started a fire, and we took off our clothes to dry them. It had been raining for hours, and the sun was setting. Before it got too dark, I went out and gathered more wood. The wood was wet, so I put the wood around the fire so that it would dry. Our clothing was nearly dry, so we put them on, and we ate. We had plenty of food, so we didn't need to hunt.

It rained for two days, but finally, it ended, and it got hot. "How many suns will it take before we get back to our village?" I asked.

"Three, maybe four suns, are you in a hurry to get back to the village?" asked Running Deer.

"We have been away a long time," I replied. The next day was hotter than the day before, and we came to a good-sized stream at the midday break. I tied up my horse after watering her, stripped and jumped into the water. Running Deer and Grey Wolf didn't hesitate one second, they went in right after I did.

We finally came in sight of the village, and when the village spotted us, many came out to greet us. In the lead was Dancing Bear on his horse with Comes Running sitting in front of him. Before his father stopped, Comes Running was off the horse and running toward me. I reached down and picked him up and said, "You look much taller than you did when I left and stronger." He nodded his head yes and showed me his muscles.

"It is good to be back, Dancing Bear."

"And it is good that you are back you all must have many stories to tell."

"Yes, we have much to tell," said Grey Wolf.

"Your parents are waiting for you, let us go," said Dancing Bear. We rode into the village and received a warm welcome. I let Comes Running down, and I got off my horse and greeted my parents, as did Grey Wolf and Running Deer.

"I would assume you have many stories to tell," said my father.

"There are many stories, but I think that Grey Wolf and Running Deer can tell the stories better than I."

"We will see you tonight at the campfire." "You put up your horse and then come into the lodge."

"I will after I speak to Morning Star."

"Of course, you take your time with her."

I went over to Morning Star and put my arm around her and said, "Will you walk with me as I put my horse away?" She nodded, and as we walked, I told her how beautiful she is and how much I loved her. "I know after we are married, there is something we must do, and you are concerned about it," I said.

"Yes, we are very young," she replied.

"I would not worry about it." "You and I will be older, and you do not have to have a baby right away," I said. "Do you know how to do what we are supposed to do?" I asked.

"Yes, I think so."

"Good, you can teach me," I said, relieved.

I went down to the stream and cleaned up, walked Morning Star back to her, lodge, and then went to my lodge. When I went into my lodge, my father was sitting in his usual spot, and he patted the ground next to him, and I sat there. "So, tell me of the things that happened while you were gone," he said.

"It is best if the others tell you, but I know you want to hear from me also, I will just tell you a little, and you can listen to the rest from Grey Wolf and Running Deer later." My mother was paying attention to everything I said. "We had not gotten to the first village yet when we ran into some Crow." "One of the Crow started insulting us, especially me, and wanted to take everything we had."

"What did you do?" asked my father.

"I almost killed the one who was causing most of the problems." "If the Crow were not friends of the Shoshone, I would have killed him."

"Most villages we went to greeted us warmly, and we stayed with them overnight." "There was one village that was not that way." "In the village of Strong Bow, the people did not welcome us, and Strong Bow was annoyed that we were there." "We did go into his lodge and talked, and he said a lot of unkind things to us, especially to me." "There was another there, Grey Bear, who was very disrespectful." "We found out why they treated us poorly, Grey Bear was a cousin to Sleeping Dog, and when Sleeping Dog left this village, he went to live with his cousin." "Sleeping Dog told his cousin and the people of Strong Bow's village a lie about what happened to me, and in this village, they believed him." "All three of us tried to tell Strong Bow and Grey Bear the truth, but he would not listen to us." "When we got finished telling the truth about Sleeping Dog, they were even more disrespectful than before." "I got outraged and told Strong Bow he was no Shoshone." "Then all three of us left without sleeping in the village that night."

"On our way back to our village, we came across some Bannock warriors." My father and mother smiled, and I said, "Why did you not tell me about the Bannocks?"

"We would have informed you when we came across some, but we did not think about it," said my father.

"For such a small village, they were as kind to us as any of the other Shoshone villages if not more kind." "Most of the trip was good; we did run into some severe weather once when it rained for a long time, but we took shelter until it was over. For the rest of the details, I will leave that up to Grey Wolf and Running Deer, but I have to warn you every time they tell the story it gets bigger and bigger." They both laughed, and we started to talk about something else.

The conversation switched over to Bear Slayer. My father said, "He and his family would have liked to meet you."

"Is he Shoshone?"

"Yes, and No, he was adopted as Shoshone but not like you." "His wife is Shoshone; she is related to Tall As The Sky, and they have a son who is part white and part Shoshone." "His son's name is Tracking Fox, and he is about your age."

"I would be happy to meet them," I said.

"Tracking Fox has given you this gift." My father handed me a necklace of bear claws. "His father is a great warrior and bear hunter." I put the necklace on, and it looked good to me.

"I must think of something to give Tracking Fox." I thought for a few seconds and said, "Maybe I will give him a Blackfoot scalp." "Do you believe that is a worthy gift for him?" I asked.

"I think he will believe it is an excellent gift," said my father.

"I must give my ten horses to Spotted Buffalo for payment for Morning Star."

My mother and father looked at me, and my father said, "I talked to Spotted Buffalo while you were away, and he agreed to take only five horses, which is still too many."

"Morning Star is worth much more than ten horses to me, but I wish to thank you for talking to Spotted Buffalo." "I will take ten horses to Spotted Buffalo and let him pick the best five." My mother smiled, and my father nodded his head in agreement.

When night fell, we went to the village campfire. I had decided to give Spotted Buffalo his horses the next day. After Grey Wolf and Running Deer put on their show, it would be too late, but I intended to tell Spotted Buffalo this.

Grey Wolf was already there, so I sat next to him. "Did you tell our father what happened on our trip yet?"

"Just a little, I told them you and Running Deer would recount the story in more detail."

"You do not want to do any of the storytelling?"

"You and Running Deer do it much better than I, but if you need me for anything, I will talk." Grey Wolf nodded his head in agreement. I could see this was a great thing for him; he was enjoying it.

Spotted Buffalo and his family showed up. Running Deer joined Grey Wolf, and I motioned for Morning Star to sit next to me when she came. We waited for the rest of the village to show up, and I believe everyone was there. Spotted Buffalo quieted everyone down and said to us, "Tell us all what happened while you were on your trip." Running Deer started, and it was pure poetry coming out of his mouth. When Running Deer took a breath, Grey Wolf jumped in. Of course, they were making more out of the story than what it was. When they finished talking about the Crow, Spotted Buffalo looked at me and said, "Is this true Soaring Eagle With Many Coups."

I smiled and said, "Most of it is true, but it sounds a lot more exciting when Grey Wolf and Running Deer tell it." I thought there would be some laughter, but every eye was on me, and there was a lot of murmuring going on. I figured that many had a hard time believing a small young boy could do these things, but there wasn't an ounce of fat on me, and I was incredibly strong for my age. I also was very fast and could usually outthink most people. When they looked at me, most people underestimated me, so I had a lot of advantages. "What do you think we should do to the Crow?" Spotted Buffalo asked me.

I knew I would have to say something convincing, or the Shoshone would go to war with the Crow. I addressed the village, saying, "This Crow who showed me disrespect and tried to do us harm will not be doing that again for a very long time. I hurt him very badly, and the others showed fear. The Crow are our friends; let us not change that over a few arrogant men. I have no new wounds, and they are embarrassed that someone so small and young did this to them. I feel they have got punished enough let, there be peace with Crow."

I could see my father was mad, but, as Running Deer started talking again, he calmed down until they both came to the topic of Strong Bow. Everyone listened very carefully, especially my father. I had hoped my father wouldn't be so angry after I had talked to him about what happened, but he was. Spotted Buffalo didn't ask me what I wanted to happen to Strong Bow this time he had already decided. He said, "We will send a runner to all the villages about Spotted Eagle. When they hear about it, they shall be angered, especially Broken Paw and Long Knife."

Grey Wolf and Running Deer finished the rest of the story, and then everyone went back to his lodge.

Before Spotted Buffalo left, I approached him and said, "I will bring you the horses I promised you for Morning Star tomorrow."

"You need only bring five horses."

"I will show you ten, and you can pick which five you want."

He nodded in agreement and headed back to his lodge. I told Morning Star, "I will see you tomorrow." She smiled and nodded and followed her parents to their lodge, and I followed mine.

The next day I took ten of my horses to Spotted Buffalo. Morning Star was there with a smile on her face. When we made eye contact, I had a smile on my face also.

He looked over the horses and picked five of them. They were good ones Spotted Buffalo knew his horses. It didn't matter to me; it was worth it for Morning Star.

When he took the horses, even though we didn't have the marriage ceremony yet, we were as good as married. "When the snows melt next season, we will have the wedding ceremony," I said.

"You are as good as married now, but yes, as you have said," Spotted Buffalo replied.

"Tomorrow, I will take you to a special place where we will go when the marriage ceremony is over," I said to Morning Star. She nodded in agreement with much enthusiasm.

Grey Wolf was off hunting when we left to go to the place that Grey Wolf showed me and where I had my vision. We arrived at the small lake after a few hours of riding. She liked the area. I took her up to where I had my vision and the cave that was there. I laid out a blanket, and I brought out some food that I had. I told her, "I think you are beautiful, and I love you."

"I love you too, and I am happy that I am to be your wife."

"I think we are already married; the ceremony is just something extra."

"I believe the ceremony is more."

"You may be right; I do not know of these things." I started to play with her hair, and then I leaned over and kissed her, and she kissed me back. It was getting dark, so we regretfully headed back to the village.

The next few weeks remained occupied with hunting as well as spending time with Morning Star, and it didn't go unnoticed. I got a lot of teasing from many in the village, especially Grey Wolf and Morning Star's brothers. One day it was time to move to our winter camp, so we all packed up and left.

# 12

# THE MARRIAGE AND THE MEETING

It was a long cold winter, and we weren't in the same spot as before, we were further north. My grandmother died unexpectedly, and my grandfather, Arrow Maker, was grief-stricken. My mother was about to cut-off one tip of her finger, but I was able to stop her by reminding her that she was not blood-related, but it took some doing. We were all sad at what happened, and I felt Grey Wolf was more saddened than I, even though I was very distressed. We offered Arrow Maker to move into our lodge, but he refused, so we let him be. My mother said, "He may be this way for some time, he may come out of it and be alright, or he may die."

I brought my grandfather food and checked on him every day, as did Grey Wolf. He ate at times the food we gave him, but he often didn't eat. I told my parents about this, and they said there is nothing they could do about it. I went to Grey Wolf and said, "We must do something to help grandfather, or he will die."

"What can we do?" replied Grey Wolf.

"I do not know; maybe we have to talk to him and make him listen to what we say."

"If you think this will work, I will do it, but you must do the talking."

Our grandfather stayed mostly in his lodge, and we asked to come in, and he said, "I do not want any visitors."

"Grandfather, we do not want to be rude, but we must talk to you."

"Very well, but do not stay long," he said mournfully.

Grey Wolf and I sat opposite him, and Grey Wolf looked over to me, waiting for me to say something. I said, "I know how you feel, and I know you are sad."

"How would either of you know how I feel."

What he said made me a little angry, and I said, "It wasn't enough that I lost my uncle, aunt, and cousin the last of my blood but with the loss of my birth mother." "I am still in pain over that, and now I have lost my grandmother."

Grey Wolf jumped in and said, "And do not forget I lost my father."

"I did not mean to disrespect your losses." "I can only think about my wife."

"And our grandmother," I replied. "If you die because of what you are doing, then would it be alright for Grey Wolf and me to do the same?" "The loss of both of my grandparents would be great." Everything went silent for a few minutes, and then I said, "We will let you think about this for now, and I will bring you some food later when my mother has prepared it." We both got up, and I said just before I went out the opening, "Grandfather, I love you."

Grey Wolf said, "So do I." Then we left, and Grey Wolf and I went down to the stream.

"Do you think what we did will do any good?" asked Grey Wolf.

"I do not know, but we will find out in a few days for sure."

There was a moment of silence as I stared out into space, then Grey Wolf said, "Would you do what grandfather is doing if he dies?"

I turned my head to him and said, "I mean what I say, and I say what I mean." At that, we went to his lodge and told Grey Wolf's mother what we did.

Grey Wolf said, "Do you think it might work?"

"It could not hurt; it may bring him out of it."

"Are the two of you hungry?" We both nodded yes, and we ate and talked for a while, and then I left for my lodge.

As I walked across the camp to my lodge, I noticed that it was cold out, but it was toward the end of winter. There had been colder days, but this had been a long winter, and I would be glad when it was over.

When I entered the lodge, my father was sitting in his usual spot, and my mother was cooking. I sat down on my bed and told my parents what Grey Wolf and I did. "Will there be enough to share with grandfather?"

"There will be more than enough," responded my mother.

"Do not make very much for me; I ate at Grey Wolf's lodge."

My mother and father stared at me without saying a word, and I said, "If I did not eat Blue Lizard would have been insulted."

"You did right," said my mother.

"You do cook better than she, but do not say anything to her about it." "I would not want to hurt her feelings." Both of my parents smiled and nodded in agreement.

I picked a little at my mother's food and then brought food for my grandfather. He took the food, but I didn't know if he would eat it. This condition with my grandfather went on for several days, and in those days, it was getting warmer.

Then one sunny day, when I came out of my lodge, there was grandfather outside fixing a bow. He looked up and waved at me. At the next meal, I asked my parents if grandfather could join us in our lodge to eat. They said yes, and he agreed to join us.

The elders decided to join the other villages in three days, and I couldn't be happier. As I lay on my bed that night, I reflected on my marriage and how happy I was. I was eleven years old, and back in Saint Louis, there had been good times, but it had been nothing like this. I now had a mother and father, a brother, a grandfather, and many friends. I had never been this respected and loved, except maybe by my birth mother.

We combined into a large village again southeast of where we had the year before. This time we were at a bigger river and what made it better at this time it was warmer. I took a bath in the water, but it was mighty cold. Grey Wolf and I went hunting, and both brought back game. After a few weeks in the village, I took Morning Star for a walk and asked her, "When should we start planning for the marriage ceremony?"

"I will talk to my mother about it and see what she says."

"And I will talk to mine also." "Do you still love me and want to be my wife?"

"Yes, why do you ask me?"

"I just wanted to know if you had changed your mind."

"No, are you concerned about what we will do after the ceremony."

"No, you do not think anyone will follow us to the spot where we will go?" I said nervously.

She smiled and said, "No, would this bother you if someone did?"

"I would rather be alone with you; it is kind of a private thing like kissing."

She laughed, and so did I. We talked for a while, and then she had to go back and help her mother.

"Do not forget to speak to your mother about the ceremony."

"I will not forget." Morning Star left, and I went to find Grey Wolf.

I found Grey Wolf just leaving Falling Rock, and I went up to him and asked, "Are you going to take her for your wife?"

He smiled and said, "Maybe but not as fast as you took Morning Star."

"What is the matter? You are thirteen seasons, is it because you do not have anything to give the father for her?" I responded with a smile.

He looked at me with a perplexed look and said, "That is part of the problem."

"You are my brother; what you do not have, I will share with you what I have."

He smiled and said, "I know you would, but I wish to wait a few years to make sure she is the one I wish."

"Suppose someone else takes her you should tell her how you feel before someone else takes her."

He changed the subject, and we went swimming.

We played for about an hour he tried to drown me and me, him. To tell you the truth, I got the best of him more than he got me, and he was breathing harder than me. As we dried ourselves on the bank, I said, "You must be getting old, weak, and slow, or there is something else wrong with you." "I wore you out in there."

"No, it is none of that; you are just getting much stronger, maybe stronger than me."

"I think they should rename you, Crazy Wolf, I will never be stronger than you."

We got up and decided to get our bows and see if we could get some small game. After we got Grey Wolf's bow, we headed to our father's lodge to retrieve my bow. As we were walking, we spotted a bunch of younger boys practicing their shooting with the bow. Comes Running was one of them. "Let's go over there and see how they are doing," I said. Grey Wolf spotted Comes Running also, and he knew I was fond of him, so we went over to the younger boys.

The boys were doing very well and were playing a game. Comes Running wasn't doing as well as the other boys, but he was improving from when he first started. As we sat and watched Grey Wolf begun to tease Comes Running, "Do not make fun of Comes Running, you will hurt his feelings he is doing the best he can," I said.

Grey Wolf stopped, and I asked him, "You are better than me with the bow; what is he doing wrong?"

Grey Wolf studied Comes Running for a few seconds, and then without saying a word to me, he got up and went over to him and started telling him what to do to shoot better. Then he came back and sat down beside me. "Watch and see if he does what I said to do," Grey Wolf said.

I don't know what Grey Wolf said, but his improvement surprised even the other boys practicing with him. "Why did you not teach me as you did, Comes Running?" I asked.

"It was much more fun watching you get frustrated than to teach you as I did for Comes Running," Grey Wolf said with a smile. We got bored watching, and we left to get my bow.

We stayed together, and we were just looking for some small game. "What goes on during the marriage ceremony?" I asked Grey Wolf.

"You and Morning Star will be dressed in your best." "Someone will drape a blanket over you." "You and she will dance from different sides and join together; then, you wrap your blanket around her." "You and she will hide in the blanket still dancing, but it is a good time to kiss." "Then, you will dance up to our father and her father." "They will both pass two eagle feathers over you, and you two will be married." "Of course, there will be much happiness, excitement, and food with the people watching; then, they will also dance after the ceremony." "While everyone is dancing, you will take her into your lodge, but with you, it will be our special place." There didn't seem like there was much to this ceremony. I would have to learn the dance, but other than that, it was short and uncomplicated.

"Do you know how to do this dance, I must do?"

"No, you must ask someone else, maybe your mother or mine; they would know it."

"Why not ask our father?"

"It is not a thing a man would know or remember."

"I will ask my mother; besides, I have to ask her about the ceremony anyway."

We finished hunting and got many rabbits and game birds. We went back to the village late that afternoon. Grey Wolf went to his lodge, and I went to mine. When I went into the lodge, I gave my mother the game and pelts and sat on my bed.

"I wish to talk to you about the marriage ceremony."

"Speak, my son," my mother replied.

"I talked to Morning Star about having the ceremony, and she said she would talk to her mother, and I said the same."

"What is it you wish to know?" my mother asked.

"First, when can the ceremony be done."

"When do you want to do it?" my mother asked.

"Right now."

"There has to be some planning; we cannot do it now," replied my mother smiling. "Would you get with Morning Star's mother and decide?" My mother nodded, and I continued, "I need to learn the dance I do in the ceremony; will you teach it to me?"

She smiled and said, "Yes."

"Do you think what I have to wear is good enough for the ceremony?" Just then, my father came in and sat down in his usual spot and patted the ground next to him, so I got up and sat next to him.

"I will make you something special."

I smiled and said, "Thank you."

"What is all this talk about?" asked my father.

"He is asking about his marriage ceremony to Morning Star," replied my mother.

"Spotted Buffalo told me Morning Star asked her mother about it," said my father.

As my mother served food to my father and me, she said, "I will talk to Small Moon later about this."

My father and I talked about going hunting, and I asked, "Will you have Grey Wolf come also?"

"Yes."

"Do you wish to bring bows or the rifle?" I asked.

"Both," he replied.

I nodded my head, then had an idea and asked my father, "Comes Running has never been hunting; why not bring him along?"

"It is something his father should do," my father replied.

"Then let's invite both Dancing Bear and Comes Running."

My father smiled and said, "If you wish, you can go ask him, but what will Comes Running ride?"

"I will loan him one of my horses." "If he cannot ride yet, he can ride with me, and we will use the horse as a pack animal."

I told Grey Wolf about hunting and what I was up to with Comes Running. He said, "I will go hunting tomorrow, and I will also come with you to talk to Dancing Bear."

Grey Wolf and I found Dancing Bear in his lodge, and he invited us in. His wife, Still Water, and Comes Running were also in the lodge.

I said, "Would you speak with us privately outside?" The three of us went outside, and I told Dancing Bear, "My father and we are going hunting tomorrow." "We would like you and Comes Running to join us."

"I would be happy to go, but my son is too young."

"Your son's age is almost eight seasons." "Most boys are hunting at this age."

"I know he can shoot a bow I taught him," Grey Wolf said pointedly. Dancing Bear put his head down and said, "I do not have a horse for him to ride, even if I thought he could ride."

"I have many horses he can use one of mine." "If he cannot ride, he can ride with me, and I will use the horse for a pack animal," I said.

"Let us go into the lodge and see if he wants to go with us." Inside the lodge, when his father asked, him his father didn't quite finish what he was saying when Comes Running got excited and said yes.

"Then, will you come to my lodge before sunup tomorrow?" "I will have the horse ready for Comes Running."

Grey Wolf and I left Dancing Bear's lodge and headed to his lodge. After talking for a few minutes with him there, I went to my lodge to sleep.

The next morning my father woke me and told me to get dressed and get the horses. As I left, my mother was cooking something that smelled good. I got three horses and tied them up outside the lodge. I then went to see if Grey Wolf was up yet, and I found a horse tied up outside his lodge. I went back to my lodge to eat. My father and I were eating when Dancing Bear called out, and my father invited him in. He sat to the right of my father, and I was to his left. I patted the ground next to me for Comes Running to sit next to me. My father offered them something to eat, but they said they had already eaten. Soon after, we all went out of the lodge; Grey Wolf was approaching us with his horse. I turned to Comes Running and asked, "Do you think you can ride a horse."

"I can try," he said. I lifted him on a gentle horse of mine, and I hopped up on mine as did everyone else, and we were off. I kept an eye on Comes Running. He was having a hard time with the horse, but he was riding. I knew he would get tired sooner or later, so when we stopped for our first break, I asked him, "Do you want to ride with me?"

"No, I am doing alright," he replied.

We had gone further than I thought we would go, but my father had a place he wanted to go. By noon, I could see Comes Running got worn out, and we stopped to rest. I asked my father, "How much further to where we are going to hunt?"

"We will split up here, and when we get our game, we will meet back here." "You and Grey Wolf go that way." "Dancing Bear and I will go this way," he said.

"I will take Comes Running with me if that is alright with you, Dancing Bear." He nodded yes, and we finished eating.

After our short break, we headed to our horses. Comes Running went to his horse, but I stopped him and said, "You will ride with me." "For your first-time riding, you did very well."

There was no resistance from him. I climbed up on my horse and pulled him up, and Grey Wolf took his horse. We rode about two miles, and Grey Wolf spotted a lot of deer tracks. We got off our horses, grabbed our bows, and started following the tracks. We walked for about twenty minutes when we came to a rise, with a tree and brush line meadow just on the other side. In the meadow, there were about twelve deer. We were downwind of the deer, and Grey Wolf whispered to Comes Running, "Put an arrow in your mouth and take your time as I told you before. Pick a deer you want to shoot. Hit the deer just behind the front legs." He drew back on his bow, and I was surprised that he was strong enough to pull it back so far. Grey Wolf and I waited. It seemed to take forever for him to shoot. I was about to say something when he let go of the arrow as Grey Wolf, and I let go also. Three deer fell.

Comes Running asked, "Did I hit anything?"

"Open your eyes, you got your first deer," Grey Wolf said, laughing. Comes Running got so excited that he killed a deer he started to run over to the deer to gut it, but Grey Wolf and I were able to stop him. "We must check to make sure they are dead first." Grey Wolf gave a poke to his deer first and then said to Comes Running, "Now you check." He did as Grey Wolf, and I instructed him. Comes Running watched as we cleaned our deer, then we had him clean his. We loaded the three deer onto the horse that Comes Running had been riding, and we headed back to the rendezvous spot.

We waited for some time; then, my father showed up dragging an elk, which meant I would have to ride with my father since I was smaller than Grey Wolf. Twenty minutes after my father showed up, Dancing Bear showed up with another deer. Comes Running was so excited about killing a deer, it didn't take long for him to tell his father about the deer he shot. Dancing Bear was so delighted at his son's accomplishment that he showed him a rare expression of affection in public.

We managed to divide the four deer and one elk between the two horses. Grey Wolf was able to carry some of the meat with him, and we headed back to the village. I was riding with my father and Comes Running with his father.

Back at the village, we unloaded the deer and hanged them for us to skin. We had to skin the elk where my father killed it because it had to be cut up and divided between the horses. Comes Running was absent during this time; he was too excited telling everyone about his kill. Of course, he was making it sound a little more than what it was.

When he finally came back after telling everyone, I said, "You can use one of my horses the next time you go hunting with your father."

After my father and I finished everything, we sat down to eat. I was hungry after only eating jerked meat all day. My mother said, "I talked to Small Moon about the marriage ceremony."

My head popped up; I stopped eating and said, "What was said?"

"Ten suns, the ceremony will be held then, everything should be ready by then."

"Are ten suns alright for you, my son?" asked my father.

I smiled and said, "That would be good."

The next ten days went slowly. I told Grey Wolf, but he already knew. Grandfather had walked around and announced the marriage. I spent a lot of time with Morning Star, and my mother taught me the dance. I knew Morning Star's mother was making her a fancy dress. Also, I saw my mother making me a new set of clothes, and they were almost finished.

It was the day of the wedding, and Small Moon wouldn't let Morning Star out of the lodge or me in. I don't know why but I was very nervous about all the activities that were about to happen. My new clothes were bleached white and had some very colorful beadwork. They also included a white headband and the moccasins, which also were white and had beads. I would be wearing all my eagle feathers in my hair. The blanket turned out to be more like a robe, which was also white with much beadwork.

I went to relieve myself, I didn't need to go, but I thought it would be a good idea in case something happened and then I went to the stream to bathe.

My father and brother picked out two horses, groomed them, and put ornaments in their manes and tails. The whole village seemed to be in a festive mood. It couldn't have been a nicer day, azure blue skies without a cloud in sight. It wasn't too hot or too cold, and there was a slight breeze that you wouldn't have noticed.

Someone placed me next to Dancing Bear's lodge, and people got lined up in such a way as to leave me a path to the center of the village. My grandfather came over to me and gave me a necklace made from a shining, sky blue stones and other stones that were shining and red. Grandfather said, "This was your grandmother's; she would have wanted you to have it. I got it when I was young from a people far down from here in a land that is very hot with few trees."

"Thank you, grandfather; I will always wear it, it is beautiful."

"I gave a similar one to Grey Wolf also; I think he will marry soon."

As I was standing there with my hands to my side and thinking of Morning Star, I felt a small hand slip into mine; it was Comes Running. He had a melancholy look on his face, and I said, "This is a happy time, what is bothering you to make you look so sad?"

"You are getting married, and that means you won't have a chance to be with me," he replied with much unhappiness.

"I will not be living with Morning Star for a long time; I am still just a boy just like you." "I may indeed spend more time with Morning Star, but I will find time for you; nothing will change." "What you do not understand is that I love you very much, maybe more than you understand," I said.

Comes Running smiled at what I said, and he had a look of contentment that came on his face. He only let go of my hand when I started down toward the center of the village.

As I started down toward the village's heart, everyone was singing, and there were drums, rattles, and whistles. I got told to stroll so everyone could see me. I had a smile a mile wide, and when I finally got to the center of the village, there was Morning Star in the most beautiful dress I ever saw. I became hypnotized at her sight, and my surroundings I forgot about what was going on for a few minutes. She had a perplexed look on her face as she started dancing, and I just stood there and heard the giggles of those around me. I came out of my trance and realized I should have been dancing also. The dance was like what you would see if two birds were courting each other with a lot of spins and dips, and my blanket would open and close many times.

We danced to a point where we were only about ten feet from my father and Morning Star's father, where I open my blanket up all the way, and Morning Star danced inside my blanket. I covered both of our heads, and as Grey Wolf suggested, I give her a big kiss, and she took it all in. But afterward, she started giggling, which took something out of the moment; however, I did tell her I loved her.

I uncovered both of us but kept the blanket around her. We both danced up to our fathers. Both of our fathers passed eagle feathers over our heads and told us both to protect and support each other. When they said to have many children, many in the crowd started laughing. Morning Star and I had a hard time keeping straight faces, and I could see a faint smile on both of our father's faces. Our fathers said additional things; then, we turned around to get presented to everyone. The whole village broke out with singing and dancing.

Morning Star's and my father disappeared as did our mothers and brothers. We were watching everyone dancing and singing for about ten minutes when someone brought our horses to us. We mounted and were given a lot of food from both of our mothers, and her brothers gave morning Star blankets, and Grey Wolf brought me all my weapons.

We waved to everyone and rode off to consummate our marriage or at least to do our best according to our age. We trotted off at a good pace to show everyone we were anxious to do what newly married adults do after a wedding even though everyone knew nothing would happen. When we were out of sight of the village, we slowed down and stopped and looked at each other without saying a word. We had smiles on our faces, and we started laughing before starting again.

It took three hours to get to the spot that Grey Wolf had shown me. We went up above the lake to the cave near the place where I met my spirit guide. We both changed clothing, and I gathered firewood, enough to last us a few days. I started the fire, and Morning Star fixed something to eat. "It was a beautiful ceremony," I said.

"Yes, do the whites have as wonderful ceremonies as we?"

"Yes, but they are different." "I am happy with ours."

"That necklace is also very beautiful." "I saw your grandmother wearing it only once many years ago."

"My grandfather gave it to me, and he gave one to Grey Wolf also. I will wear it always; it will remind me of my grandmother."

As we ate, we looked at each other, thinking about how we were going to get over this awkward moment. I don't know why we were having a hard time. We got just about finished eating when I looked over to Morning Star and asked, "Are you as nervous as I am?"

"A little, I think it is foolish, and there is nothing to be nervous about." At that, I removed my clothing, and she did the same. We snuggled together on the blanket, and nature, as clumsy as nature could be, took its course until we fell asleep. We stayed there for a week, and then we headed back to the village.

When we got back, everyone greeted us warmly, but there was a bit of curiosity also. As soon as we dismounted, Morning Star was whisked away into her lodge by her mother. As I was watching this Grey Wolf, Broken Antler and Running Deer cornered me, and Running Deer said, "Well, what happened?"

"We had a fantastic time."

"No, No, I mean, how did you fill your obligation as a husband?"

I looked at them all with their smiles on their faces and said, "The same way as any husband would."

I started to walk away when Grey Wolf said, "But you are only eleven seasons."

And Broken Antler added, "My mother will check her that is what she is doing now, and everyone will know."

As I walked away, I said with confidence, "Yes, everyone will know."

My mother and father ushered me into our lodge and told me to sit on my bed. "Now, tell us what happened while you were gone." "We do not wish to be embarrassed to find out that nothing happened."

I was just about to say something when Small Moon called to come in, and my father invited her in. As she entered, she smiled at me and then said, "I have checked Morning Star, and everything is as it should be."

I smiled and stared at my parents and said, "Is there anything you need to ask me?"

"Yes, how?" asked my mother in shock.

"I guess like anyone else," I replied.

My father got up with a smile on his face and said, "He is just more man than he is a boy," he then left the lodge.

"I'm going to talk to Morning Star," with that, I left the lodge.

I found Morning Star talking to Falling Rock, and I went up to them. Both girls had big smiles on their faces, and I said, "Are you talking about me?"

"No, about Grey Wolf," said Falling Rock.

"Oh, he likes you, I think."

"Just likes?" replied Falling Rock, disappointed.

"I do not know exactly how much he loves; he is kind of shy about talking about it."

"I'll do something about that," she replied.

"Please do not tell him I said anything; he will kill me."

She left to find Grey Wolf, and I turned to Morning Star and said, "Have others been giving you trouble about our marriage as they are me?"

"What trouble are you talking about?"

"You know what we did while we were gone."

She smiled and laughed and said, "Don't worry about that; they will stop."

"Do you need anything?" "Now that we are married, I will get all that you want."

"No, I have everything I need."

"Let me know if there is anything, and I will get it." I told her I was going hunting the next day with my father and brother, and I would bring her back some meat then left.

The next three weeks were full of spending as much time as I could with Morning Star, hunting with my brother and father, and even spending time with Comes Running. Then it was time to split the village and move again. We moved west near the plains where the buffalo would be near. My grandfather, father, brother, and I all helped each other with the packing and moving. It was another beautiful day, blue skies, a slight breeze, and the sound of the village moving. As we went, I rode next to Morning Star. I couldn't have been happier.

After a week at our new village site, Grey Wolf and I went for a hunt and to see if we could find any buffalo. We each got a deer, so I was riding on the back of Grey Wolf's horse while my horse was carrying the two deer. As we were checking to see if there were any buffalo around, Grey Wolf said, "It is good to be away from the village." "Falling Rock has been giving me a lot of trouble." "Do you know anything about it?"

I gave a nervous laugh and was about to say something when Grey Wolf knocked me off his horse. "You, sitting on the ground is kind of funny, too."

I dusted myself off, and he said again, "If Falling Rock gives me trouble again, you will find yourself sitting on the ground again."

He helped me up on his horse again, and I said, "I do not know why you do not marry her." "I know you like her."

I got knocked on the ground again as he said, "I will marry her when I choose to."

He put his hand down to help me up again, and I said, "No, if I stay down here, it would not be so far to fall." He laughed and put his hand down again, wanting me to come up, and I did.

"Again, my father told me what happened while Grey Wolf and I were gone when I got back just in case you wanted to know."

"Welcome, Bear Slayer, you and Tall As The Sky will come to my lodge tonight to eat my son will be bringing home some meat," said Red Elk.

"My family and I will meet this son of yours, but first, I will settle in with Tall As The Sky then bathe, I am filthy," he replied.

"I will bathe with you," added Tall As The Sky.

"Very well, we will see you tonight," answered Red Elk.

The first one in the water was Tracking Fox, followed by Tall As The Sky, and then Bear Slayer took off his shirt and jumped in. All three swam around, Tracking Fox playing with his father more than anything else. When they finished swimming, Bear Slayer was the first one out to dry off. Soon after, Tall As The Sky came out and dried off next to Bear Slayer, but Tracking Fox continued to play in the water. As Tall As The Sky watched Tracking Fox swim, he turned to Bear Slayer to comment on Bear Slayer's son. He stopped and stared at a yellow necklace hanging around Bear Slayer's neck and said, "Can I look at your yellow necklace?" Bear Slayer took off the necklace and handed it to him.

After examining it Tall As The Sky said, "I have seen this before but not on you."

"Who have you seen it on?"

"Soaring Eagle With Many Coups, Red Elk's son."

Bear Slayer stared out into space and then finally said slowly and talked to himself more than too Tall As The Sky, "I know of only one other necklace like this."

Tall As The Sky handed Bear Slayer back his necklace, and he could see that Bear Slayer was disturbed by this revelation, so he changed the subject. "You will be going buffalo hunting with us this year?"

He was still in a stupor when he finally answered, "Yes, yes, I will go when will it be."

"On our first sighting, I hope." Tracking Fox got out, sat next to his father, and he put his arm around him.

"It is time to go back; our father and mothers will be waiting for the meat," I said. It took about three hours to get back to the village, and when we got there, I saw a boy I didn't know. "Do you know who that is?" I asked Grey Wolf.

"Tracking Fox, Bear Slayer's son." "I have not seen him for a while; he has grown." As we rode into the village, Tracking Fox spotted us and came over to us as we unloaded the deer. "You wear my necklace; you must be Soaring Eagle With Many Coups."

I looked him up and down; there was something familiar about him. He was speaking English, so I said in Shoshone, "You do not know how to speak Shoshone?"

"I speak Shoshone." "I just thought you would rather speak English since you are white."

"I am not white; I am Shoshone." "It is impolite to speak a tongue that others do not know." He was silent for a few seconds, so I continued, "The necklace you gave me is very nice." "I have something for you; I will get it later."

"No need; we have been invited to your lodge tonight to eat with you." I nodded and looked down at the necklace he gave me and said, "It is a grizzly claw, am I right?"

"Yes, my father killed the bear two seasons ago."

"It is good medicine, are you sure you want me to have it?"

"Yes," he replied. Just then, his mother called him, and he left.

"He looks to be about your age," said Grey Wolf. He also looks a little like you except for his eyes and hair."

I looked at him as he left and asked, "You think so?"

Grey Wolf nodded, and I dismissed the whole idea by saying, "There must be a lot of people who look like you too." We finished skinning the meat, and Grey Wolf took his meat, to his mother, and I took mine to my mother and Morning Star.

I sat on my bed. I thought there would be a lot of people in the lodge. Soon Tall As The Sky, Bear Slayer, and Tracking Fox came into the lodge. I patted the ground for Tracking Fox to sit by me. Blue Flower sat next to my mother, while Bear Slayer and Tall As The Sky sat to my father's right. I could have sat next to my father but thought it would be impolite to Tracking Fox, and I assumed my father felt the same. The men got their food first, then Tracking Fox and I, finally the women ate. When I had finished, Tracking Fox and I got up. I grabbed one of my scalps and said, "I am giving this to Tracking Fox." "It is a scalp from a Blackfoot warrior that I killed some time back." I could see Bear Slayer was troubled about this, but Tracking Fox couldn't have been more thrilled.

Bear Slayer asked, "Why is it you are giving this to him?"

"He gave me a necklace that has great medicine." I pointed to the necklace, and he looked even more troubled. "You do not think it is a worthy gift?" I asked.

"It is not that, it is an excellent gift, but I do not approve of the taking of scalps," he replied.

"I do not either, but it is a sign that you are a warrior, and it is the custom of the Shoshone, are you not Shoshone?"

"The Shoshone have adopted me, but I do not agree with everything they do." I looked at him for a second, then said, "Well, if you do not want him to have it, I will give him something else." He was starting to irritate me, and I think he saw it because he said, "No, it is alright my son can keep it."

I nodded and sat down in silence; I felt like I was given a blow to the head. "There is something I wish to talk to you about that does bother me more than the scalp."

"Speak."

"You have a yellow necklace around your neck would you allow me to see it?"

He held out his hand, and I said, "I never take it off."

I could see Tall As The Sky was a little befuddled at my statement as well as was my father. He was also annoyed, so I said, "But since you are my father's guest, I will let you handle it."

What I did please my father, so I took it off and handed it to him. He examined it for a few minutes, and I finally said, "It was my birth mother's she died."

He opened the locket and looked at the hair, and I said, "It is a lock of my father's hair; he perished in these mountains."

"Your father?" he said.

"Yes, I was born after he left, and he never returned."

"What makes you think your father is dead?" he asked.

"He never returned, and many mountain men who came to Mr. McConnell's store said white men do not live long in these mountains."

He handed back my necklace, and I put it on. Then he reached into his shirt and pulled out another necklace that looked identical to my mother's. He took it off and handed that one to me. I opened the locket and just stared. It had hair in it the same color as mine and my mother's. I opened the other locket and looked at my father's hair and then Bear Slayer's. They were the same color my heart started beating hard, and Bear Slayer said in English, "It's your mother's hair." "I'm your father." I was stunned as were Blue Flower and Tracking Fox, who both had their mouths open in disbelief. Tears ran down my face, and I got up, then ran out of the lodge and into the darkness.

# 13

# THE GREAT PAIN

Bear Slayer explained to Red Elk, Turtle Woman, and Tall As The Sky just what happened, they were all shocked. My mother was in a panic, and she said, "He is my son; I will not lose another."

"He knows you better than me; he is your son, but he needed to know," Bear Slayer replied sadly.

"No, it is Soaring Eagle's decision to make he is a warrior now," Red Elk said sternly. They all went out of the lodge looking for me, but I had gotten a horse and left.

I had gone to my brother's and my special place. For two days, I sat there; then, a lone rider came; it was Grey Wolf. He rode up to me and said, "I thought you would want some company." I never said a word, and he got down from his horse and said, "Our father and your mother worry as does Morning Star, you need to come back."

As I looked at the ground, I said, "Do you know who Bear Slayer is?"

"Yes, he is your birth father."

"But who do you say your father is?" Grey Wolf asked.

"Red Elk, of course," I replied.

"Then what is the problem nothing has changed."

I thought for a minute, I knew he was right but said, "What am I going to do about Bear Slayer?"

"There is only one thing you can do, be polite and tell him how you feel, and then let him make the next move."

"I nodded in agreement and said, "Let's go home."

It was dark when we got back, and my father heard me, ride up to his lodge. He came out and approached me; I hung my head low. He nodded at Grey Wolf and said to me, "Come into our lodge," which I did. There was my mother with an anxious look on her face.

"I am sorry I was distressed," I said to both in a very meek voice.

"We were worried, you should have stayed and talked about this," my father replied in a gentle voice.

"There is nothing to say you are my mother and father." I could see that this choice I made was a great relief to both of my parents. "I do not know if I should be angry with him for marrying his woman, having his boy, and not coming back to my birth mother, or I should not be mad," I said, confused.

"Maybe you should talk to him there may be a good reason for his not coming back," said my father.

"If I talk to him, I may become upset, and I may do something violent," I replied.

"You must not blame Blue Flower and Tracking Fox for any of this," said my mother with a concerned voice.

"I have no problem or anger with them," I said indifferently.

"What did Grey Wolf do or speak to get you to come back?" asked my father.

"He reminded me who my father and mother were," I said lovingly.

"Are you hungry, my son?" asked my mother.

"No."

"You better get some rest," said my father, and I then lay down and fell asleep.

The next day Tracking Fox traded glances with me but didn't say anything. I even stared at my birth father when he wasn't looking at me. I thought he was a tall man. I had wondered if I would be that tall, but I figured I took after my birth mother. They said he was a great man and an excellent warrior; I'll have to see it to believe he is. I gave him credit for keeping alive in these mountains as long as he had. At the time, I didn't know that Blue Flower, Grizzly Killer's wife, caught me staring at him for some time and then walking off.

"Soaring Eagle With Many Coups is back," said Tracking Fox as he sat next to his father eating."

Bear Slayer lifted his head and stared out into space while Tall As The Sky looked at him. "You need to talk to him; he is your son." "I saw him staring at you, and he had this sad look on his face," said Blue Flower, frankly.

"I do not know what to say; he thinks I abandoned him and his mother."

"Tell him the truth he can tell if you are lying," she replied.

"That is wise Bear Slayer," interjected Tall As The Sky.

"I will go with you, Pa," Tracking Fox said in English.

Bear Slayer stared down at his son for a few seconds then said in English, "No, this is something I have to do alone."

"Then you can explain to me about this other woman and why you have a son I knew nothing about," said Blue Flower with a bit of irritation.

"I will explain everything later when we are alone," he replied apprehensively.

"I was just leaving," said Tall As The Sky. Before anyone could say anything, he was gone.

Both Blue Flower and Bear Slayer looked at their son, and he got the hint and said in English, "I was just going." He got up and left the lodge, eating a hunk of meat.

I was down at the stream when Tracking Fox approached me and said in English, "Are you mad at me?"

I looked at him, and after a few seconds said, "No, why do you always speak English, you're Shoshone?"

"I'm half white, too." "Why does it bother you, you're white?" "Why don't you talk English?"

It irritated me that he called me white; I've tried to purge the entire white world out of me. Of course, I knew that was impossible, as I got older, I knew I would be a person of two worlds. It was hard to hide the fact that I was not white with my yellow hair and fair skin. "It's been a long time since I spoke this language." "There wasn't a lot of happiness in the white world; I prefer being a Shoshone." I patted the ground next to me, and he sat down.

"You do know you are my brother," said Tracking Fox.

"Yes, I've been told we look alike do you have a white name?"

"Zack York, what is yours?"

"James." I put my head down, then said, "James York."

"Our Pa isn't a bad person; he is very good." "There must have been a good reason why he never came back for you and your Ma." "I know he would never do that to my Ma or me," he said genuinely. I didn't say anything, and we were silent for a few minutes when he said, "What are you going to do about Pa?" "I mean, are you going to come live with us?" he asked nervously.

"I already have a mother and father; I won't be going with you." "As far as your father, I am still confused about that, but I won't kill him?"

He changed the subject and said in Shoshone, "Are all the stories I heard about you, true?"

I switched back to Shoshone and said, "I don't know what you have heard, but anything you did hear there was some exaggeration to it."

"I heard you have killed a lot of Blackfeet and been in a lot of battles."

"That is correct; you have one of my scalps."

"I also heard you did the long walk and the Sun Dance."

I took off my shirt, showed him my chest, and said, "Yes."

He touched my scars and was mesmerized at the sight of them. "Did it hurt a lot?" he asked.

"Yes, the whole ordeal I went through was very demanding."

Just then, Grey Wolf sat down next to me. "Everything good with you?" he asked.

I smiled and said, "I have not sharpened my knife, and no blood has spilled."

"Our father is coming," Tracking Fox said. Both Grey Wolf and I looked, and sure enough, he was heading right for us. I stood up and faced him.

"I wish to speak with you," Bear Slayer said to me.

"There is nothing to talk about."

"I think there is I have a lot to explain, and I owe it to you."

I looked down at my two brothers, and they both got up and excused themselves.

"Let's walk," Bear Slayer said. As we walked, I felt for my knife, and Bear Slayer took notice of it. "I know you are angry, so let's not do something that we will regret." I eased my hand off my knife and listened to him. "I met your mother after I left New York while I was waiting for your uncle Zed to meet me and take me to these mountains." "Your mother was working for and living with a wealthy French family when I met her." "She was a beautiful woman, and we spent a lot of time together, and yes, we did have relations." "When your uncle Zed came, I did tell your mother that when I found the wealth my uncle talked about, I would return and get her." "The trouble was that the wealth, uncle Zed was talking about wasn't gold or silver for which your mother and I thought it was." "It was the wealth of freedom and beauty about being your own man." "I found out what your uncle was talking about when we got to these mountains." "We were not here a week when the Blackfeet killed him." "Blue Flower's father saved my life, but he didn't come fast enough to save Uncle Zed." "When he was saving me, he was wounded very severely." "Just before he died, he made me promise that I would marry his daughter." "My love for her has grown every day since we were married."

He had finished talking, and for a few seconds, there was silence, and I would not look at him. Finally, I yelled with anger, "You promised to come back, and Mama waited for you."

He looked at me and said, "You're right." "I did promise to return, and I should have." "But you need to know at that time there were no jobs there for me." "I had no way to support your mother and to bring her here was out of the question she wouldn't have survived, you know that." "Tracking Fox came quickly, and that was another reason for not being able to go." "You should know that they wouldn't have gotten treated very kindly there either." "When I thought about your mother, I thought for sure she would forget about me and marry someone else." "She was very beautiful on the outside and inside." "She would have no problems finding someone."

I had so much anger in my heart, and I said, "Even I know no one wants a woman with a bastard child."

With that, I started to walk away from him when he said, "Had I known that your mother was pregnant, and you were born, do you think I really wouldn't have come back."

And I replied, "What do you think happens when you lie down with someone and have relations with her?" "My mother and I went through hell all those years." "I watched her die, and I buried her." I left without turning around and looking at him.

"How did it go?" asked Tall As The Sky.

"Not so good," replied Bear Slayer.

"You must try again," interjected Blue Flower.

"I think that boy wanted to kill me," Bear Slayer said.

"If he wanted to kill you, you would be dead." "You do not know him as I do." "He fights like a wolverine," said Tall As The Sky.

"He isn't mad at Ma, Pa, or me; I will talk to him; he is a nice person."

"No, you better not; he is very angry now," he replied.

"I think it is a good idea that our son talks to him; Soaring Eagle will not harm his brother."

Bear Slayer looked at his wife and said with a sigh, "Alright, but if he isn't in the mood to talk to him, let him alone."

"By the look on your face, I can tell it did not go well with Bear Slayer," said Grey Wolf.

"No," I said.

"Can I ask you a question?"

"Of course."

"You told me that before you joined us, you were going to leave your uncle and find your father." "If you were not angry at your father, then, why are you now?"

I just didn't know what to say. "There isn't any reason why I should be mad at Bear Slayer, but I am." "I am not sure how to answer you; I am confused."

"Then you must find out just what you want."

I looked up at him and said, "And they call me wise."

"Look who is coming," said Grey Wolf. It was Zack, and I knew he wanted to know how angry I was with our father.

"Are you still talking to me?" asked Zack.

"Of course, I am not angry with you," I replied.

"Our father feels sorry about what happened with your mother in the past." "He also feels terrible about your anger, are you going to hate him forever?" Zack asked.

"I don't hate him, but I don't know how long I will be angry." "What would you do if you went through what I did when I was little?"

Zack thought for a few seconds then said, "I guess I would be pretty mad, but I would forgive him." "That is what the good book says and what's more, I know him; he did not mean to hurt you or your mother."

"I have to think about this for a while." "I am very mixed up about how I feel," I said, frustrated. "I am going to my lodge; it is late, and I am hungry." Both of my brothers nodded, and I left, but I didn't go directly back to my lodge. I went to talk to Morning Star, and when I got to her lodge, I called her, and she came out. I told her everything that had transpired and then asked, "What do you think I should do?"

"I cannot say it is for you to make a decision." I looked at her, disappointed. She continued, "Why don't you go off hunting alone, so you can relax and think I know you enjoy hunting." I nodded in agreement, kissed her, and went to my lodge.

"I am going hunting alone tomorrow," I said to my parents.

"We do not need the meat," replied my mother.

"It is more than just the hunt; it is to get away so that I can relax and think."

"You are troubled by Bear Slayer?" asked my father.

"Yes, I do not know how I should feel I have much anger."

I could see the concern on my mother's face and said with a smile, "No matter what mother you two will always be my mother and father, I have already decided that."

"Perhaps I will talk to Bear Slayer to see what we can do," my father said, I nodded in agreement.

"When will you be leaving, I will have food for you?" asked my mother.

"Before first light, but there is no reason to trouble yourself."

"I am your mother; it is no trouble."

The next morning, I thought I would get up before anyone else, but my mother was fixing me something to eat. "I will be gone three or four suns, so do not worry."

"When it comes to you, I always worry."

"Is that something mothers do?"

She smiled and said, "Yes."

I took everything with me, and before the sun was up, I got on my horse and headed northwest.

"Bear Slayer I would speak with you," said Red Elk outside Tall As The Sky's lodge.

Bear Slayer exited the lodge and faced Red Elk. It was the first time they had spoken since I found out that Bear Slayer is my birth father. "It is not good that my son, I mean our son, is troubled the way he is," Red Elk said.

"I would agree," Bear Slayer replied.

"I think we need to talk and find a way to solve this problem," Red Elk said.

Bear Slayer sighed and said, "I would agree again, but I think this is bigger than the both of us."

Red Elk thought for a minute then said, "Our son went hunting to get away and think." "Perhaps we should go as well and take Tall As The Sky and Spotted Buffalo too." "Someone might come up with a solution."

"When do you want to go?

"When the sun is fully up?"

Bear Slayer nodded and said, "I will talk too Tall As The Sky about going."

Red Elk nodded and said, "I will talk to Spotted Buffalo." By noon all four then headed south. They didn't intend to stay gone for more than a day or so and then come back.

It was the morning of the third day. I had made my decision I would tell my birth father that I recognized him as my birth father and would respect him like I would any other Shoshone, but I had parents whom I loved, and I would stay with them. Furthermore, I was married, and in a few years, I would be living with Morning Star in my lodge. I figured if I left, then I would be home by early afternoon. Then I would settle this thing once and for all, and things could get back to normal.

I was just a few miles from home when I spotted thick black smoke, and my heart started pounding. I brought my horse to a full gallop, and when I got over the last rise, I saw the village was under attack. I pushed my horse so hard that it almost killed her. When I got close enough, I saw it was the Blackfeet, and I was enraged. Before I got to the village, I raised my rifle and traveling at full gallop I shot one Blackfoot warrior right between the eyes. I put up the empty rifle and pulled out my hawk. Out of the corner of my eye on my left, I saw four or five Shoshone warriors also coming at full gallop. As I went into the village, I leap off my horse before she stopped. I flew into two Blackfeet warriors swinging my hawk. I slammed into them, taking off the top part of the head of the warrior to my left and gutting the warrior to my right. I saw that Comes Running was going to be hit by an arrow when I threw my hawk and caught the warrior in the back by the spine. I noticed my two fathers, Spotted Buffalo and Tall As The Sky, had returned and were in the fight. At the same time, I saw my grandfather on the ground hurt. I went to him but had to stop by another warrior trying to kill me. I fell to the ground, rolled, and shot him with one of my pistols. When I got up, I was near Tracking Fox, and another warrior was about to kill him with a fusee. I got up and knocked my brother out of the way. I received a grazing wound to my arm that spun me around. Then I saw something that horrified me; my mother was on the ground covered with blood. I ran to her bullets and arrows, bouncing around me as I did. Grey Wolf finished off the warrior who was trying to kill Tracking Fox. I didn't know that my father, Red Elk, also saw my mother on the ground. He was going to her, but I got there first. All the life was gone from her as I stood up, I gave such loud a scream that all must have heard it. As I was screaming, I saw my father, Red Elk, get shot twice, and he fell, and I went berserk. I grabbed a lance and headed up the hill toward the Blackfeet, and every warrior I passed, I killed. Arrows and bullets didn't seem to hit me but bounced all around me. I killed five or six warriors when the Shoshone warriors saw what I was doing; they rallied behind me as did others who had come back from their hunt. As I was going up the hill, I saw one of the warriors who tortured and killed my aunt, uncle, and cousin. I headed right for him, killing every Blackfoot I came near. Then he recognized me, but by this time the Blackfeet were in full retreat, however, I pressed on. My pursuit angered the one I was after he came running down the hill at me. Before we were about to meet, I saw that there was a large rock outcropping of about two-and-a-half or three feet high on my left. He would likely go around it, but I ran upon it, and with my hawk in my right hand, I leaped up into the air and drove my hawk into the top of his head, splitting his skull in two. He didn't even know what hit him. He fell to the ground with a big thump. I retrieved my hawk and continued up the hill, not looking back at the one I had just killed. Finally, at the top of the hill, I stopped. The rest of the Shoshone warriors kept after the few Blackfeet who were left, which amounted to about sixteen or eighteen, but they escaped. I fell to my knees and dropped my hawk. I placed my face in my hands and sat there for a few minutes.

I got up and went down the hill; my head hung low. I headed to where my father was. On the way, I passed my birth father and Spotted Buffalo, not saying anything to them. The women were tending to the wounded. Blue Flower and Morning Star were with my grandfather, but no one was with my mother and father. I went over to my father, and I didn't need to check to see if he wasn't alive; it was obvious he was dead. I started to drag him to my mother. About halfway there and without a word, Grey Wolf came and helped me. I then sat on the ground next to them.

Grey Wolf said, "I will help prepare them after I get our scalps and horses. I nodded, and he left. I sat there, stunned. My mother and father were dead; my grandfather was severely wounded and might not make it, who did I have left? There was Grey Wolf and, of course, Morning Star. Who would I live with, Grey Wolf and Morning Star's parents would welcome me, but I would not feel, right with them? I looked down at my mother and father and thought that this wasn't supposed to happen. Why is everyone who I love and am so close to leaving me? The pain was unbearable. I should have died with them. I knew Grey Wolf was also hurting because he just lost another father. He was showing his pain, differently keeping busy with the scalps and horse gathering, and by doing this, he kept his pain out of his mind. Just then, I felt a gentle hand on my back. I looked around, and there was Morning Star. She could see the tears falling from my eyes, something a full-blooded Shoshone would never display in public, but right then, I just didn't care. She sat beside me, and I said in English without looking at her, "O death, where is thy sting? O grave, where is thy victory?" I do not remember where that came from, but it seemed to fit. Morning Star was confused at what I said but didn't say anything. My stomach felt dreadful, and I leaned over and vomited, I felt lost. I turned to Morning Star and asked, "My grandfather?"

"Blue Flower is with him; she is a medicine woman, but it doesn't look good for him," she replied.

I got up, walked over to him, and knelt beside him. "He grabbed my arm and said hoarsely, "Your mother, father, and I are proud of you." "I think I will be going to be with my woman soon." Tears started rolling down my cheeks as he said, "This is good; I miss her much."

"Then, all that I will have left is Morning Star and Grey Wolf."

"No, you have your birth father and your brother Tracking Fox."

I looked at Blue Flower, and she smiled at me, but I didn't say anything to her. Tracking Fox and Bear Slayer joined us, and I saw Grey Wolf kneeling by our father. "I will be back; I go to be Grey Wolf." He smiled and nodded as well as he could. I got up and went to Grey Wolf, Morning Star following.

Grey Wolf looked up and asked me, "Do you know how to prepare them for their journey."

"No, except a raised bed must be made."

He nodded and said, "We must wrap them in their finest blankets. Weapons and things of value are given them for their journey."

I nodded and said, "I wish that they get put together.

Grey Wolf agreed and said, "I will build the bed. You find the things they will take with them."

Again, I nodded, and Morning Star said, "I will wrap them in their blankets." I looked at her and nodded again. I was glad that she had volunteered to do this. I don't think I could have done it.

I went into the lodge with Morning Star and pointed to the blankets to use. I took my knife out and cut two pieces of my hair, and told her to place the hair somewhere on them. I grabbed one of my father's shields and lances also his bow and arrows. I gathered some beads my mother had and some red cloth she had traded with trappers; it was her favorite. For both, I got some herbs and other things that smelled good and told Morning Star to do what she thought best. I then left and joined Grey Wolf in constructing the raised beds.

Unnoticed to me all this time, my birth father was watching me. When I got to where Grey Wolf stood, my birth father, came and said, "I would like to help." We both nodded, and we went to the business of constructing the raised bed. When we finished, we went to get my parents with Tall As The Sky helping. Grey Wolf and I carried my mother while my birth father and Tall As The Sky took my father. Morning Star took all the things that went on the bed with them. We put my parents on top of the bed with their prized possessions. I stood there for a few minutes and then we all left. We still had grandfather to worry over. There were twelve killed and thirty-seven wounded from the village. The Blackfeet suffered one hundred and forty-two dead. I also saw that some of the eighteen who escaped were wounded. Most of the time, the outcome would have been just the opposite; this Shoshone village was fortunate.

I went back to where my grandfather lay. He was still alive but unconscious, so I sat next to him. Blue Flower spoke to Tall As The Sky and my birth father about something. I didn't know what she said at the time but found out later it was that there was no hope for my grandfather. Grey Wolf took off somewhere, but Morning Star stayed by me. After a little time had passed, she whispered in my ear that she was going to go to her parents to see what else she could do, and I nodded in agreement. It was dark when my grandfather became conscious, and said, "I have talked with your mother and father." "They are very happy they are with their sons." "They love you and want you to do what is right."

My birth father heard my grandfather talking to me and came over and sat down beside me. "I will do what they want, grandfather."

"I talked to a beautiful young lady who looks a lot like you; she said she will always be in your heart, and she also loves you." I assumed that it was my mother, and I nodded. My grandfather was quiet for a few seconds then said, "I saw and talked to my beautiful wife she waits for me, and I miss her so."

"Then go to her grandfather, do not let her wait," I said with a forced smile. He squeezed my hand, and then it went limp, and he was gone. We prepared him in much the same way as we did my parents. Blue Flower wrapped him in a blanket. Grey Wolf had gotten the wood to build the platform, and we placed him next to my father and mother.

I wasn't in the mood to talk to anyone. I went inside my lodge, and there I stayed for the next three days alone, staring out into space. Morning Star did come with food and water, but I ate and drank little. "I worry about my husband he eats little and has not been out of his lodge for three suns he won't even talk to me," Morning Star said to her father.

"I will talk to Grey Wolf and maybe Bear Slayer too," he replied.

Sorrow for my loss had changed into anger and vengeance. Spotted Buffalo had sent runners to all the villages to meet with him and to see what they were going to do. I had seen these talks before, they talked big, but in the end, they do little or nothing. This time, however, it would be different. I would see that the Blackfeet paid for what they had done.

"May I come in it is I, Bear Slayer?"

"And I, Grey Wolf?"

I didn't answer them. I knew the reason why Grey Wolf and Bear Slayer coming and, if Grey Wolf wanted to come in, he didn't need permission. The flap of the entrance of the lodge opened, and Grey Wolf stuck his head inside. I was sitting where my father used to sit, and Grey Wolf asked again, "Would it bother you if Bear Slayer and I came in and talked with you?"

Again, I didn't answer him; I didn't even look at him; I just stared out into space. There was some talk outside my lodge, and then Bear Slayer and Grey Wolf came into the lodge. I didn't offer them a seat, so they just sat opposite me. "You have not eaten for a long time, and you stay too long in your lodge. What you do is not good," my birth father said.

I didn't answer him, and there was silence for a few seconds more. Then Grey Wolf stated in a worried voice, "I have lost my grandfather and my father for the second time. It would destroy me to lose a brother too."

I looked at Grey Wolf and said, "Why are you here?" "You know why I stay in this lodge and don't eat?"

"Why are you not preparing for war, our father's spirit cries for revenge?"

"Go prepare for war I will not die, not today," I said with authority.

Without a word, they got up to leave, but before Bear Slayer went, I asked with a longing yearning voice and in English, "Wait, I wish to speak with you."

He turned around and sat back down. "What do you want to say to me? It seems you have already made up your mind what you are going to do?" my birth father said in Shoshone.

"Speak English, why are you here?" I said, confused.

"What do you mean?"

"Why did you come to my lodge?" "Why are you concerned about me?"

Without hesitation, he said, "Because you are my son despite your anger toward me."

"I am not angry with you, well not now," I said uncomfortably.

"Then why don't you come and live with me?" he asked with compassion.

"I don't think your woman, I mean your wife, would approve of this."

"I have already discussed this with her, and she has already passionately agreed."

With my head down, I said, "What of your son, Zack, he may not be happy having me around?"

"He is your brother, and from what I can tell, he is excited about you."

"I must think about this later, but I have other business to take care of, Blackfoot business," I said as a matter of fact.

My birth father put his head down and said with concern, "I don't wish you to attack the Blackfeet; it is too dangerous."

"After what has happened, you think I should just stand by and do nothing?" "I thought you were Shoshone," I said in Shoshone and with annoyance. Bear Slayer said nothing, so I said, "If I go live with you, I will do as you wish except when it comes to dealing with the Blackfeet, Grey Wolf, and Morning Star."

He was not happy, but he nodded in agreement, and I continued, "Now, I do not wish to show you disrespect, but I want to be alone; I am still mourning."

He got up and left, but instead of mourning, I was thinking how a group of warriors could attack a Blackfoot village with little or no life lost.

Many warriors from other villages were showing up at the village, and I knew there would be a council meeting the next afternoon. The council meeting would happen, but as always, there would be a lot of talking but no action, but not this time, I would see to that. Morning Star brought me water and food as always, but this time I thanked her and asked, "Do you know when they will hold the council meeting?"

"My father says that it will be tomorrow at high sun."

"Will you come and get me when this happens?"

"Yes," she said, wondering what I was going to do. I had eaten everything Morning Star gave me. Late that night, I went out of my lodge and gathered plants and clays of various colors and brought them to my lodge. I mixed three colors red, black, and yellow the way my father and Grey Wolf showed me. I got out all the eagle feathers and picked the best ones. Then I went to sleep.

I was awakened by the arrival of Morning Star with food and water again. It was late in the morning, and after she left, I dressed in my best tan buckskins, and I painted my face with a broad red stripe across my eyes with a border of black and then yellow. I braided my hair then carefully placed some eagle feathers in my hair. By this time, it was near the high sun, and I knew that Morning Star would be here to tell me the council had started. I got out my two pistols and rifle and began to clean them before I finished the last pistol Morning Star came to my lodge. I stood up, and she just stared at me in shock. When she had composed herself, she said without taking her eyes off me, "The council has started talking."

I nodded and sat back down and finished cleaning my pistol without saying a word. Meanwhile, Morning Star went to Grey Wolf, unknown to me, and was at the council meeting and told him what she had seen.

He stared at her for a few seconds, nodded, and left for his lodge. He retrieved his rifle and came to my lodge and came in. Without hesitation, he said, "Do you have any more paint?" I pointed to where I left it, and he started to paint his face. I finished with the rifle and put an eagle feather on it. I gave one to Grey Wolf, who placed it on his rifle. He asked, "Do you have any more feathers?" I grabbed a pouch and gave it to him. He braided his hair and placed a feather in his hair, also.

While he was doing this, I cleaned and sharpened my hawk and knife. I placed the two pistols, hawk, and knife in my waistband, and I looked at Grey Wolf to see if he was ready. I said, "Let's go I will do the talking."

He smiled and said, "Yes."

When we got to the council, there was a lot of shouting. Warriors were making war calls, but when Grey Wolf and I approached, everyone went silent. The crowd of people made a path to let Grey Wolf, and I approach the elders. The look on my face would have frightened a Grizzly Bear. Many throughout the village were murmuring among themselves, wondering what Grey Wolf and I were going to do.

Long Knife said, looking at both of us, confused, "What is the meaning of this?"

"I, Soaring Eagle With Many Coups, son of Red Elk, son of Bear Slayer, wish to speak," I said with a voice of thunder.

"Speak," Long Knife said, shocked.

"I have been to two of these council meetings and Grey Wolf much more." "It is always the same; we get attacked by our enemies the Backfoot, the council talks, and talks." "There are cries of war, but in the end, little or nothing happens, and our people continue to die." As I spoke, I not only looked at the elders but at the people who were at the village. "Not this time, we must attack the Blackfeet, or the Blackfeet will become surer of themselves and attack again, killing many of our people." "Perhaps your village will be next Long Knife." The whole village became excited at what I said.

"For one so young and inexperienced, you speak very bold," said Strong Bow mockingly.

I grabbed my knife but didn't pull it out. Even so, Strong Bow lunged back, and I said in an angry voice, "I kill boldly!" "Ask anyone who survived the attack on my village."

Again, were heard shouts of war and excitement. The elders started talking among themselves, but I didn't give them the chance to say anything. "It does not matter to me what the council says because my parents and grandparents cry for vengeance." "I will go in two days and attack the Blackfeet even if I have to go alone."

Grey Wolf and I turned and headed for my lodge when Long Knife said dismayed, "Wait." "We have decided we will go to war with the Blackfeet, but you must meet with us to determine how this will happen." "We will meet here after we eat tonight to discuss this." The whole village was full of excitement, and many went to ready themselves for the fight. I nodded, and I turned around and noticed my father, Bear Slayer, was perplexed at the events. I believed he hoped this would die down, and everything would go back to normal, but with the death of my loved ones, that would be impossible for me.

Back at the lodge, Grey Wolf and I were discussing what happened when I heard my father, "May I come in?"

"You do not need permission to enter my lodge; you are my father." I looked at Grey Wolf and said, "Neither do you; you are my brother, and half of this lodge is yours." He smiled sand nodded as my father came through the opening. "Spotted Buffalo and Tall As The Sky are here too," said my father. I nodded, and they all came in. I was sitting in my father's place; Grey Wolf was to my left. The rest sat to the right. "It was foolish and unwise what you did today," said Spotted Buffalo boldly.

"No, what Soaring Eagle said is wise," said Grey Wolf.

"How long must our people die before the Shoshone does something?" "If it were not for Soaring Eagle, the council would have done nothing," explained Grey Wolf.

"The Blackfeet are stronger than we are, what can we do?" added Tall As The Sky.

"My father, Bear Slayer, knows of people who live towards the rising sun who defeat an enemy who is twice as strong as they," I said.

Everyone looked at my father, who said, "What he says is true, but they had some warriors who were very skilled in the art of war."

"The Shoshone have warriors who are skilled in the art of war, and I do have a plan that I believe will work," I said.

"What is this plan you speak of?" asked Spotted Buffalo. I pulled out my two pistols, my hawk, and my knife and said, "The Blackfeet expect us to fight and argue for many days." "They will never expect us if we are to attack this soon." "I would ask you Spotted Buffalo to send runners to the Crow, Nez Pierz, and any other of our friends to see if they would join us in battle." I put my hawk down on the ground. I put my two pistols on each side of the hawk, and at the bottom, I put my knife. "We first find out where the village is." "Then, we will get there while it is still dark and place warriors out of sight here, here and here." I pointed to the two pistols and knife, I said. "When the sun starts to come up, the warriors who are where the knife is will attack slowly, picking out targets and making a lot of noise." "The Blackfeet will see us attacking and come after us making noise also." "When this happens, the warriors that are at the place where the two pistols are will attack quietly." "Most of the Blackfeet will not notice and will be trapped and killed." I looked up at everyone, and they were speechless.

Spotted Buffalo started smiling and nodding his head in agreement, and Tall As The Sky gave out a loud war cry, as did Grey Wolf. Everyone was excited and ran out of the lodge. My father stayed; he had a troubled look on his face. "You don't think it will work?" I said to him in English.

"Your plan is brilliant." "Where did you get the idea to do this?"

"From a book by General Charles Cornwallis, I believe it is called a pincer movement."

"You do know he was a British General during the War of Independence, and the British lost that war."

"Yes, but he was still a great General."

"There is something else that concerns you, I can see it in your face," I said.

"In every war, there are deaths, and I fear for your life," he replied.

"Don't worry about this my Spirit Guide said I would live unit I was very old."

"Were you not raised by your mother as a Christian?"

"Christian and Shoshone beliefs are sometimes blurred." "Was it not John the Beloved who saw Jesus sitting at the right hand of God and given instruction?" "You can call what I witnessed a Spirit Guide as the Shoshone do, or an angle like the Christians calls it; they are both the same to me." There was silence for a few seconds, and then I continued, "Are you going to join us in the battle?"

"I will go because of you, but my heart is not in it," my father said.

Just then, Grey Wolf stuck his head into the lodge and said, "The elders meet you must come." He left, and we got up and joined him.

Again, the whole village was there, and I reiterated my plan to the elders. It seemed to give confidence to them. The only change that the elders made in my plan was that instead of attacking the Blackfeet in two days, they decided to wait four days to give time to get more warriors. I could have protested and gone anyway, but it would have been disrespectful, and two more days wouldn't hurt my plan anyway.

On the night of the third day, I got the horse I wanted to ride and materials I would need to mix paint. I gave half to Grey Wolf. I went to the lodge of Tall As The Sky. I ask my father if he wanted some of my paint. There was a heated discussion between Tracking Fox and our father over going with us to fight the Blackfeet. "Pa, I am Shoshone my place is with them," he said in English.

"The answer is no, accept it," he snarled.

"Why do you wish to go?" I asked.

"Stay out of this, James, this is a family matter," my father said sharply.

I was angry, and it showed, so I turned around to leave when Blue Flower retorted, "He is family, he is your son, speak James."

"I'm sorry she is right, go ahead and ask again," my father interjected.

"Why is it you wish to go with us?" I said in Shoshone.

"Because I am Shoshone, it is my place," he replied.

"There are many Shoshone that is not going; you have no reason to go."

"You are going."

"I have a reason, and you know this very well."

"But our father is going," he said in a defeated voice.

"Pa has a reason he goes because of me."

"If you go and you die, it would be much harder for him than if I die." "He has known you longer, and your mother in her sorrow will cut off part of her finger." "While we are gone, who will protect this village?" "You are needed here: you have already counted coup." "You are right," Tracking Fox said with a new purpose.

"I have paint, do you want some?" I asked my father.

"No, I won't be wearing paint," he replied.

"How about you, Tall As The Sky?" He looked to see what I had and took some yellow.

I turned and left the lodge, and my father followed me. When we were far enough away, he said, "I want to thank you for what you said to your brother."

"I did not do it for you, I did it for me I like him, and he is my brother," I said with a bit of anger in my voice I then turned and went to my lodge.

The next day, we are supposed to leave. There were many Shoshone in the village, as well as many non-Shoshone. I painted my face the same way as before and put eagle feathers in my hair, and I also painted my horse and placed eagle feathers in her mane.

Grey Wolf came over to me and asked, "Are you ready?"

"I just have to get my weapons," I said. I turned to my brother and added, "If something happens to me, give a horse to Tracking Fox and Comes Running." He nodded, and I went into the lodge to get my weapons, food, and a blanket. I climbed up onto my horse, and Grey Wolf did the same. We rode over to where the rest of the village had gotten assembled. There were over two thousand warriors there. Every warrior got instructions for what they would do, and everyone split into three groups. Long Knife would have the group that would attack the Blackfoot village from the right. Broken Paw had the group on the left of the Blackfoot village. And Spotted Buffalo would have the group that went down to the village in the center.

Long Knife had sent two warriors to find a Blackfoot village. One day after they left, he sent three more warriors that would be ahead of us scouting for any Blackfeet who might discover us. Tall As The Sky, my father, Grey Wolf, and I were with Spotted Buffalo's group as we headed north. We made a camp that night without a fire. I stayed next to my father, and Grey Wolf was with Tall As The Sky. On the one hand, I was tired of killing, but on the other hand, I have the drive in me to kill the Blackfeet whether they harmed a loved one or me. I was getting torn apart emotionally, and a tear fell down my cheek, which didn't go unnoticed by my father.

"What bothers you?" he asked in English.

"Part of me does not wish to kill anymore."

"Then let's go back to the village you don't have to kill anyone."

"But part of me tells me that I must do this thing, so I do it, and it is tearing me apart."

He put his arm around me, and it felt good. I leaned into him for comfort. "What if I just force you to go back to the village with me?"

I tensed up and looked up at him and said, "I would fight you and kill you or at least try." "Perhaps, once I kill the last of the Blackfeet who killed my aunt, uncle, and cousin, I can stop warring with them."

He nodded and occupied himself with something else, and I went back to my thoughts.

At about noon the next day, a rider rode up to us and reported to Long Knife. It was Hidden Fox, the one who went to scout out the Blackfoot village. I got sent to meet with the elders and hear what Hidden Fox had to say. Hidden Fox said the village had about eight hundred to nine hundred lodges, a large village at the meeting. It was at the bottom of a hill next to a stream, much like my village.

I asked, "Are there many trees?"

"Yes," he replied. He informed us that we should reach the village by dark in about two days. He told us other useful information, and when he finished talking, I turned to the elders and said, "It could not be better." "If we are not detected, we should do well when we attack." "The trees will provide excellent protection."

We reached the village at night just like Hidden Fox had said. We split into the three groups and positioned ourselves, waiting for the first light. Spotted Buffalo had about four hundred in his group, and it should be enough to draw off the Blackfeet if everything went well. When the sun started coming up, I could see that Broken Paw would have added protection with the sun behind him. It would blind the Blackfeet. The village was awakening with the people relieving themselves and bathing.

Spotted Buffalo nodded too Tall As The Sky and an arrow with pitch and straw and other things set on fire, and he shot it into the lodge nearest the river. Everyone started picking off warriors, and the whole village erupted into a war fever. We were making a lot of war cries and moving slowly down the hill towards the village, and as I predicted, the whole Blackfoot village came running up the hill at us. We kept our pace picking our targets. While the Blackfeet were busy with us, Long Knife came with his eight hundred warriors from our right. Many of the Blackfeet warriors turned toward him. As they did, Broken Paw came from the left. The Blackfeet were confused and disorganized as we rushed down the hill killing Blackfeet as we went. The slaughter was unbelievable. In the first few minutes, more than three hundred Blackfeet died. As the fight progressed, the women and children ran north for protection. Even some of the warriors tried to escape but got cut off. In forty-five minutes, it was all over. The Shoshone was lucky no one got killed, and only seven got wounded, but not very bad. The Blackfeet were not so lucky, only a few lived.

Of the Blackfeet warriors that were left, the Shoshone wanted to kill them slowly, but I stopped them. Instead, I had them line up, so I could look at them. I asked my fellow warriors, "Is there anyone here who can speak the Blackfoot tongue?" A warrior, named Long Scar for obvious reasons came forward.

"I, Long Scar, was a captive with these dogs when I was a child, I can speak their tongue."

I looked at each Blackfoot warrior carefully. I sent the old warriors who were too old to fight to be with the women and children. Some protested but got forced to go with them anyway. The women, old men, and children were corralled away from the village onto open land. As I went down the line, I had three warriors yanked from the line and tied up. I called all the elders over to talk to them, and I had Long Scar standby. I told the elders, "I know you wish to kill slowly these few warriors left, and this would please me greatly, but there is a wiser thing we can do with these dogs." "Speak, what should we do with these animals?" said Long Knife.

"Let me tell them we will not kill them." "The Blackfeet should go to their other villages. Tell them that if they attack another of our villages or our friends' villages, all the tribes south of here will unite, including the Ute, and will kill all Blackfeet." "That way, they will think long before they attack us again."

The Elders talked among themselves, and then Long Knife said, "You have been wise so far." "You may do as you wish, but what of those you had tied up?"

"They are the ones who killed my white family." "They will not live long enough to see another sun," I said mercilessly. At that, our warriors cheered. When everyone quieted down, I said, "I also wish that those women and children let go with them." "Also, release the old men and anyone else you think should go." The elders nodded, and I said to Long Scar, "Tell them we will not kill them or their women, children, or their old men."

Long Scar did as I said then I said, "Tell them to go to their other villages." "Tell them if they attack our villages or our friends' villages, such as the Crow, Nez Perce, or the Bannock, all the tribes south of here, including the Ute, will kill all Blackfeet." "Tell them just like I told the elders." "As he told the Blackfeet, I brought out each of the warriors from the different tribes." I went over to the women and said, "Tell them those who have husbands still alive over there take your children and join them, they will not harm them, tell the old men to go over there also." The women did as they were told and joined their husbands. I spotted one woman who didn't look like she was a Blackfoot, so I called for a warrior to bring her out. "Tell her she does not look like a Blackfoot woman."

Long Scar asked her, and he told me, "She says she is a Ute captive, and the baby is half Ute."

"Ask her if she wants to go back to her Ute village." She nodded yes, and I said, "Take her aside and treat her well."

I headed to where the elders were, and my father joined me and asked, "What are you going to do with the woman and her child."

"I have use of her, and then I will return both to her Ute village."

"Is this wise?"

I stopped and looked at my father and said in English, "In the long run it is wise." "What do you wish me to do, kill her and her baby?"

"She wants to go back to her village," I continued to the elders as my father just stood there. I looked at the elders and warriors and said, "You can do what you want with the other women and children, but if it were me, I would let them go where they wish." "There is no honor in the killing, torturing, or taking them captive that is the Blackfoot way."

Long Knife looked at all the elders and warriors and said to Long Scar, "Tell them they can join these here or go where they wish." Long Scar did this, and all the women went to the rest of the Blackfeet.

I asked Long Scar to join me, and I went up to the three who were tied up. "Say what I say, Long Scar." He nodded, and I said, "Look at me." "Do you know who I am?" They all looked at me and talked among themselves.

"What are they saying, Long Scar?" I asked.

"The one on the left said you are the pup that got away." "The Blackfeet said other things they would have liked to do to you." "I wish not to say the words they use," he replied.

I nodded and turned my back to them. I pulled out my hawk, turned around, and sunk the hawk into the skull of the one on the left. The Blackfoot fell over onto the one next to him. I then asked four Shoshone warriors to take their horses and get on either side of them. I knocked them both onto their backs. I tied ropes around their necks and legs and handed the ropes to the warriors and told them to ride off. Those two were ripped apart much to the delight of the warriors' present.

The elders had Long Scar tell the rest of the Blackfeet to get only their water bags and what food they could carry. Broken Paw got two quivers full of arrows with two bows and rode across the valley to the low mountains about a mile away. He dropped them on the ground and came back. Then Long Scar told them to go and get the bows and arrows and don't come back here. They all left, and our warriors went to get the spoils of the battle. I looked at each dead Blackfoot to see if they were part of the murder of my uncle and his family. About an hour later, we started back to our village. We kept going until we were on Shoshone land while we were traveling the Ute woman, and her child rode next to me.

# 14

# NEW BEGINNINGS

When we camped that night, we lit a fire and had hot food. I gave some to the woman and child, and a blanket for them to sleep. I told my father that there were only four more Blackfeet left who were responsible for the death of my aunt, uncle, and cousin. He nodded with understanding at what I was telling him. I started using sign language to communicate with the Ute woman, instead of asking Long Scar to translate. I introduced my father and brother. She knew of my father and me, which was a surprise. I asked, "I have a favor to ask of you before I take you back to your people."

She gave me a look that I was familiar with; she thought I wanted to make love to her. I said, "If you think I want you to share my blanket, you are wrong. I am too young for that, and I have a woman."

"Then what is it you want," she signed angrily.

"I want you to teach me how to speak Ute and Blackfoot."

"It would take too long for you to learn." "I wish to go back to my people."

"I can learn languages very fast." "If I don't learn these languages in ten suns, that is when my father is going back to his lodge, which is near your village; I will give up and ask nothing more of you."

She thought a few seconds and signed, "I will teach you what I can for ten days at a Shoshone village."

"May we start tomorrow as we head back to the village?"

She smiled and nodded, then turned to my father and signed, "You have a strange son."

"Yes, and stubborn too."

She smiled again and nodded, and we all went to sleep.

For the next two days, she taught me both the Ute and Blackfoot languages. I offered to carry her child, who was a boy, but she said no. "Where will my son and I sleep when I get to your village?" she signed.

"In my lodge," I also replied in sign.

"You are very young to have a lodge."

"It was my adopted parent's lodge, but the Blackfeet killed my mother, father, and grandfather when they attacked our village. So now the lodge belongs to me and my brother Grey Wolf," I signed in reply.

"How will my son and I be treated at your village?"

"I would guess no one would have anything to do with you, but no one will harm you or your child." "I will see to that." She nodded, and we went on with the language lessons.

When we got to the village, I showed her to my lodge, and she and her child went in. Morning Star came running up to me. I held her tight and kissed her. I didn't care who saw it. "Who is that woman?"

"She is a Ute woman who was taken captive."

"What is she doing here?"

"She is going to teach me the Ute and Blackfoot languages." "Then I will take her back to her village." "Please be kind to her; she has been through a lot," I said.

She nodded and said, "My father said only one got killed, but our warriors killed many Blackfeet."

I nodded, and she added, "This will make you very important in this village, and you will have a voice in the council." I gave her a sad look, which she noticed right away and said, "What is the matter?"

"I cannot stay here, not with all the death."

"Where will you go?"

"With my birth father."

"In two years, I will build a lodge and come get you, will you come?"

"You are my husband, where you go, so I go."

I smiled and said, "I will be back when my father comes back next season; it will not be too long."

"When will you leave?"

"My father wants to leave in ten suns."

"Then, for the next ten suns, I will not leave your side."

I laughed and said, "Your mother and father might have something to say about that."

In the next five days, I spent a lot of time learning the two languages. Running Doe, the Ute woman, was amazed at how fast I caught on to the two languages. I found the Shoshone and Ute languages similar. I also went to Tall As The Sky's lodge and told my father that if he wanted me, I would go with him to his cabin. "But," I said, "I intend to start immediately to build my cabin for Morning Star and me."

He nodded his head in agreement. Tracking Fox and Blue Flower were thrilled that I was coming.

I said to my father, "I wish to talk to you privately outside."

"Since you are part of this family, you can speak in front of them."

I hesitated and said, "Yes, but what I wish to say, you may prefer me to talk to you first."

He said alright and then came outside with me. "I have many horses now I wish to give one to Tracking Fox, I mean Zack."

"It is good you asked me." He thought for a few seconds and then said, "Those horses you got with spilled blood, I don't approve of this."

"Not all my horses were gotten this way." "I will give him one horse that I didn't take in battle."

He smiled and, with a half-laugh, said, "You know you're very smart." "Alright, you can give him a horse." "I've meant to do it myself anyway."

"Zack, come on out here," he yelled in English, and out came Zack. "Go with James; he has something to give you."

"What?"

"You will see," I said. I turned to my father and said, "I will be dividing my father's Red Elk's things tonight, also my grandfathers." "I wish you, Blue Flower, and Zack to come to my lodge tonight as I do this." He nodded and off, Zack, and I went.

We found Grey Wolf first, and I told Zack to stay with Grey Wolf for a few minutes. I found Dancing Bear and said, "I do not know how many horses you got from the battle, but I have many horses, as you know." "I wish to give Comes Running a horse if you are not going to give him one."

"You are very kind." "I know you are a friend of Comes Running and love him very much, but I have already given him a horse."

"This is good. I just wanted to see Comes Running happy," I said.

I went back to my brothers, and we came out to where the horses were. "I am giving a horse to Tracking Fox." Grey Wolf nodded, and I said, "Pick one." Tracking Fox smiled, and he chose a young Paint. I looked at Grey Wolf, and he nodded in approval. "The paint is yours," I said.

As we headed back, I asked Grey Wolf for him and his mother to come to the lodge that night, and he agreed. Zack said excitedly in English, "I am going to tell Pa what I picked out."

"I am going to talk to Morning Star," I told Grey Wolf and went to find her. "Would you join me tonight in my lodge?" "I will be dividing my parents' things and want you to pick what you want first."

"Yes, I will be there," she said.

"I must get back to the Ute woman," I said," I kissed her and left.

I informed Running Doe of all the people who would be coming and the reason. A little past sundown, everyone went into the lodge. Grey Wolf sat to my left, and Zack sat next to Grey Wolf. My father sat to the right of me. The women sat together, although they were a little apprehensive about sitting next to Running Doe. I had taken all my grandfather's things and brought them into the lodge. When everyone quieted down, I said, "It is time to divide everything up." "How many horses do we have together, Grey Wolf?"

"With both of us, I have these many stones and three." Each stone counted as ten horses. There were twelve rocks and the three, one hundred twenty-three. "But you have more horses than I."

"No, we will divide them equally." I looked at my father and asked him, "Do you think this is a good thing to do?"

He nodded and said with a smile, "Yes."

"Then, it is done." "The extra horse is yours because I gave one horse to Tracking Fox." "When I leave, I will only take a few horses." "Will you watch my horses for me?" "If I get any foals, half will be yours."

"I will watch them, but all the foals will be yours." I was going to protest, but he put up his hand, meaning no more is to be said about this, so I just smiled.

"This lodge is larger and better than yours, it is yours if you want it, Grey Wolf."

He looked around the lodge and nodded then said, "Yes, I wish it, but what am I going to do with my old lodge?"

I looked at Morning Star and said, "Do you think your father might find someone who needs a lodge?"

"Yes,"

"Then, we will talk to him about it later."

"I thought grandfather's lodge might be used by my father when we come and visit the village." "It is big enough for all of us, and it will give us more privacy."

"He looked at Blue Flower, and she nodded. He said, "That would be good."

Before I could say anything, else Grey Wolf said, "When it is time to break down the village, I will move grandfather's lodge also."

I smiled and said, "Good." "I was going to ask you about that." "Grandfather's rifle, knife, bow, and arrows are yours." "I know you have all these things already, but now you have more." "Our father's shields and lances, I desire, but you have known him longer than I, and I have no place to put them, so they are yours."

"No, they are ours, and I will just take care of them."

I put my head down to get control of my emotions, then cleared my throat and said, "Our father's scalps which he has taken in the many battles are yours." "I have taken many scalps, but it is a thing I do not care for, and my father, Bear Slayer, does not approve, either." "You should have half of his and grandfather's eagle feathers also."

"No, you have earned them, my brother."

"As have you, do not fight with me over this Grey Wolf."

There was a moment of silence, and then Grey Wolf said, "They cannot get divided equally."

"I smiled and said, "I know what to do when the Blackfoot attack this village; Tracking Fox fought bravely." "He counted coup, and he helped protect this village when we were gone."

"I handed Zack an eagle feather, and his eyes lit up." "I whispered to my father in English, "Is this alright?"

He nodded his approval with a smile.

"Our father's bow and arrows if you have no objection I wish to have."

"I understand you keep them."

"The rest of his weapons you may have." "My mother's things I will keep." "But to be fair to you, you may have our grandmother's things,"

He nodded, and then I turned to Morning Star and said, "Of these things that are my mother's, what do you want?" She looked at the things and took a few. Then I turned to Blue Flower and said, "Would you like the rest of this?"

She smiled and said, "I will find a use for them."

"I do not think there is anything left." "Am I right, Grey Wolf?"

"I know of nothing."

I looked at my father and said, "Do we leave in four suns?"

"Yes," he said. I saw Morning Star put her head down to hide her sadness, and I said, "The sooner I go, the faster I can build our lodge, so we can both be together forever."

"What he says is true," Blue Flower said. I was grateful for what Blue Flower said, I don't like to see Morning Star sad. We talked for a while more, and everyone went back to their lodges.

On the night before I was to leave for my new home, I picked out four horses I wanted to take. Two were my favorites for riding, and the other two were strong and would be suitable for hauling logs and stones for my cabin. I also picked a horse for Running Doe, it was an older horse of no importance, and I intended to let her have it, but I hadn't told her yet. I had mastered both Ute and Blackfoot to the amazement of Running Doe, and I had packed everything I was taking, so I spent the rest of my time with Morning Star. On the morning of the day, we were to leave there; were very emotional goodbyes. It felt like someone ripped my heart out, but I had to go. Everyone knew we had to go, and we all headed south.

We had traveled for about three days. On the night of the third day, I asked my father in English, "How much further must we go?"

"We should be home in about two more days."

"When I see your cabin, I will remember where it is, and I will take Running Deer to her people."

"I will take her; it is too dangerous for you to take her."

I shook my head no and said, "It is my responsibility if something were to happen to you; it would be another loss for me." "You have Zack and Blue Flower to worry about."

"No, I can't let you do this."

"You have no choice you don't know me very well if you lost me it would be of little importance."

"You have no idea of the importance it would be."

"I am still taking her back."

"I thought you said you would do as I said except when it comes to the Blackfeet."

"I said once I came into your house, I would follow your rules except when it comes to the Blackfeet."

Our conversation didn't miss the ears of Blue Flower or Tracking Fox, and Blue Flower said to my father, "He is your son, but he is also a Shoshone warrior." "You will not change his mind; he will go no matter what you say."

My father knew he had lost this round, and he didn't say anything more about it.

All this confused Running Doe, and she asked in Ute, "Why is your father angry with you?"

"He does not want me to take you back to your village; he is afraid your people will harm me."

"Your father is wise; my people might hurt you." "Give me a horse to use, and my child and I will go alone."

"What is she saying?" asked Blue Flower.

"She agrees with Pa and wants to go to her village alone."

"I'm glad someone agrees with me," my father said.

"I can't let her do that if something happens to her and her child, the whole Ute tribe will go to war with us when she gets found, and it just isn't right."

Blue Flower nodded in agreement. "I hate to admit it, but you are right, tell her," replied my father.

"Letting you go on your own is too dangerous." "If something happens to you or your child, your people will go to war with us, and I just could not forgive myself for letting you go." She didn't say anything, so I added, "By the way, I am giving you that horse you are riding." "It is a present for staying with me and teaching me the languages." She smiled and lay down next to her child.

Sometime in the afternoon of the second day, we came upon a small lake. Beyond the lake, on a slight rise, there was a small cabin. We rode up to the cabin, and I turned to my father and said, "I will help you unload, but I won't go into your home until I come back from the Ute village."

"Aren't you tired and hungry?" "Come in and rest I won't hold you to your agreement on obeying me."

I turned to the Ute woman and said in Ute, "My father wants us to come into his lodge and eat and rest, but I think it will bring just more grief." "Are you too tired to continue to your people's village?"

"No."

"How many suns to get to your people's village."

"Maybe two suns, perhaps a little longer."

I turned back to my father and said, "No, I appreciate your offer, but I will continue as planned." "I should be back in about six days."

He wasn't happy, but he nodded his head in agreement. About forty-five minutes later, I started unloading the horses, and I changed mounts for a faster horse, and we were off.

I spoke nothing but Ute while I was with Running Doe, and as we traveled, I asked her, "Which way do we go?" She pointed the way, and we traveled until it was too dark to see. I started a fire and cooked something for us to eat. "How will your people treat your son?"

"He is still young; I think they will accept him."

"And you, will you be able to find a husband?"

"What do you mean?"

"I have heard that some people would blame you and not the Blackfeet for what happened to you."

"Maybe this happens among the Shoshone but not the Ute," she said, annoyed.

I guess what I asked was rude, so I changed the subject. "How long have you been gone from your people?"

"Near four seasons."

I asked, "Did one of the Blackfeet warriors have a scar near his eye?"

"Yes, I will never forget that one."

"They are the same ones who killed my uncle and his family and tried to kill me," I said.

We were silent for a few minutes, and then she said, "You are lucky to be alive." I nodded my head in agreement.

When we camped on the second night, Running Doe said, "My people know we are here."

"Yes, they have known since late this morning," I said.

"How did you know this?"

I smiled and said, "I am Shoshone, and I saw the Ute braves on the ridge this morning." "So why do they not approach us?" I asked.

"They are confused why you, a white boy who looks like a Shoshone, are heading to a Ute village with a woman and child."

"I guess they will find out soon."

The next morning as we rode, Running Doe said, "On the other side of this hill is a valley with a stream." "Sometimes, my people are there."

We rode into the valley and found the stream, and I asked her, "Which way should we go?"

She pointed downstream, and we traveled another hour following the river. Just as we came around the bend of the river, we got surrounded by about six Ute warriors. Of course, I knew something was about to happen. I had my rifle cocked as well as my pistols. They started signing, but I stopped them and said, "I speak your tongue as does the woman, she is Ute."

"I am Running Doe, daughter of Black Hawk."

They all looked at me, and I said, "I am Soaring Eagle With Many Coups, son of Bear Slayer."

One warrior said, "I know Bear Slayer." "Are you the one who killed everyone in a Blackfoot village?"

"I had help; Running Doe was a captive in that village." They looked at each other while the same warrior said, "From what I have heard about you, I would have expected you to be a lot bigger and older."

"Do not underestimate me because of my age or size." "I am a Shoshone warrior, and I do have many Blackfoot scalps."

"Do you have any Ute scalps?"

I stared at him and said, "Not yet, but then I am not at war with the Ute."

"You speak boldly for such a small boy."

"If I chose every one of you would be dead now," I said with a threatening tone, which angered them.

Running Doe saw this and barked, "Enough!" "I have seen him fight; he is a great warrior; he could kill every one of you." "Now, take me to my father."

They turned and headed to their village. Within a half-hour, we were in a village which was about the same size as my village.

The Warriors warned the village that we were coming, and all came out to see. In front of the people were Running Doe's mother and father. It seemed Running Doe was off her horse with her baby and into the arms of her parents before the horse stopped. As she embraced her father, she told him who I was.

"I understand that you can speak our tongue?" he said to me.

"Yes, your daughter taught it to me."

"You will come to my lodge as my honored guest." "Take care of his horses," Black Hawk said to his people.

"The horse that Running Doe rode in on I gave to her as a gift for teaching me your language."

He nodded, and as I got off my horse carrying my rifle, someone took my horse and Running Doe's horse. We walked to Black Hawk's lodge, and it was like my father's, Red Elks' lodge. I waited to get asked to sit.

Black Hawk motioned for me to sit on his left. "I am told that you attacked and killed a whole village of Blackfeet," Black Hawk said seriously.

I bent my head down and started laughing and said, "I see there is no difference between Shoshone and Ute in telling a story; the stories are greater than they are."

"You mean it did not happen?" he questioned.

"It happened, but I did have some help," I replied.

"I have seen this one fight he fights like no warrior I have ever seen," Running Doe said sincerely.

"I have heard other stories about you also, are these stories overstated also?" Black Hawk asked.

"In all stories, there is always some truth," I said.

We talked about how the same group of Blackfeet who killed my uncle and family was most likely the same who captured his daughter. I also told him about me being at war with the Blackfeet, which he thought was good. He was amazed at what I had done in my young life. He asked, "How is it you have Bear Slayer as a father, but you had another father as a Shoshone?"

"I had never met my father, Bear Slayer; he left for these mountains before I was born." "I had heard that most white men do not live long in these mountains, so I thought he was dead." "Red Elk and his wife, Turtle Woman, offered to adopt me since I had no one, and I agreed." "I found out about my father, Bear Slayer, when he visited my village with his family." "My Shoshone family was killed by the Blackfeet, during a raid on our village, I agreed to go live with him."

He nodded with understanding, and I asked a different question to change the subject. "Why is it that the Shoshone and Ute are not friendly with each other?"

"I do not know for sure, but it has something to do with the bow valley," Blackhawk said.

"My father, Red Elk, said the same thing when I asked him."

"He did?"

"Yes, no one knows what happened, and since it was a long time ago, no one remembers why they are angry with each other or why they stay bitter?"

"I do not know." "Did you ask your father about this, also?"

"Yes, and he gave me the same answer." "Something needs to get done to change this," I added.

"Yes, but I must give this some more thought."

"I must be heading back to my father's lodge, or he will worry about me," I said.

"You will stay here tonight and eat with us." "Then, in the morning, you can go back," said Black Hawk. I thanked him and was kind of happy he asked me to stay, my horse needed the rest.

The next morning when I woke up, I sat and ate with Black Hawk. I asked him, "Do you know where my father, Bear Slayer's lodge is?"

"Yes, we leave him alone if he leaves us alone."

"In time, I intend to build a lodge there also."

He smiled and said, "We will leave you alone, also." I nodded, and within an hour, I was on the trail back to my father's lodge.

I had no problem finding my father's cabin and when I rode in it was late. I tried not to make noise while I took care of my horse, but I guess my father or someone in the cabin had sensitive ears because my father came out with a rifle in hand to see what was stirring outside. I was easy to spot in the moonlight with my yellow hair. When my father saw me, he lowered his rifle and came over to me. "I thought it might be you."

"Sorry I woke you."

"It's no problem let me help you carry some of your things into the cabin." I followed him inside, and Blue Flower was up fixing me some food. I noticed she was always the peacemaker between my father and me and always tries to be kind to me.

"Are you hungry?" she asked me.

"Yes, if it isn't any trouble, I haven't eaten much while traveling back here."

At the smell of food, Zack woke and sat at the table. I put my things down and said, "I better clean up I am a little dirty." I went out of the cabin to a stream that ran behind the cabin. Removing my shirt, I bathed as well as I could. It was too dark for me to swim in the nearby lake, so this would have to do. When I finished, I grabbed my shirt and headed back to the cabin letting the warm breeze dry me off.

In the cabin, I sat at the table next to Zack, who stared at me for some reason. I found out quickly when my father said, "In this cabin, we wear a shirt to the table." I looked at my father for a few seconds wondering why he had this rule, and then without a word, I put my shirt on. The cabin was small and even more crowded with all the things that I brought back from the village. The cabin had one window, a fireplace where Blue Flower cooked food, and a water barrel. My father and his wife slept in a bed, and Zack slept on the floor.

"So how did the Ute treat you?" asked my father.

"Very well, some warriors wanted to challenge me, but after I talked to them, they had second thoughts."

Blue Flower gave me some meat and vegetables to eat with a cup of water. I looked at the cup for a few seconds I hadn't seen one in some time. I went to take out my knife when she gave me some eating utensils. Again, I hadn't seen them for some time and wasn't sure how to use them, but I did my best. The food was good, and Zack ate some also without saying a word.

"What was the name of her father?" asked my father.

"Black Hawk." My father nodded his head, and I asked, "Do you know him?"

"Yes, he is an important man among the Ute."

"I figured that out he said he leaves you alone so long as you leave him alone, and Black Hawk said he would do the same for me."

"Very nice of him," said my father, skeptically. I finally finished eating and grabbed Zack's plate and utensils, and mine and said, I will wash them. But Blue Flower said, "No, you are too tired and need to get some sleep."

I didn't argue with her I was tired and wanted to get some rest. Zack was already on the floor where he slept. I grabbed my blanket and sat on the ground on the opposite wall from him. "You can sleep with me," Zack said.

I looked at Blue Flower and my father, and they swung their head, indicating for me to sleep with Zack. So, I got up and joined him. I removed my shirt, and as I did, I looked at my father, but he didn't say anything, so I laid down, and within seconds I was sound asleep.

What woke me up the next day was Zack getting up. He and I went outside to relieve ourselves and wash up. When we came back into the cabin, I sat next to Zack at the table. "You can help Zack with his chores when you get finished eating," my Pa said.

I nodded and said, "After the chores, I would like to survey an area to build my cabin."

"Building a cabin is a mighty big job for someone as young as you," my father said.

"I've done things that no one thought I could do that was greater than this," I replied.

"Alright, I will help you if you wish me to."

"Me too," said Zack.

"You can join me after I finish the chores," I said to both my father and Zack. The chores consisted of feeding and giving water to the horses, bringing water and wood for the cabin and checking traps for rabbits.

After about three hours we were finished, and Zack said, "It's a lot quicker with two doing the chores."

I smiled and said, "Yes, you're right; now let's go find Pa."

We found him looking over by one of the horses, and I said, "Are you too busy to survey a site for my cabin."

"No, do you have a general idea where you want it?"

"Yes, about two hundred yards above your cabin."

"It's our cabin," he said.

I nodded and pointed to the general area, which was about ten feet from the stream. When we got there, Pa kicked the ground a little and said, "This is a great area but not for a cabin. Do you see those big rocks and gravel on the ground?"

"Yes," I said.

"The water has been this high before during the spring melt." "There is higher ground away from the stream over there." We walked another fifteen feet or so to the higher ground. My father said, "Build your cabin here; it's flatter, higher ground, and the soil is different, not as many rocks."

He was right; I should have known better. I won't make that mistake again. I looked around and picked up four sticks and a rock. I hammered a stick where I was standing and paced off thirty paces and put another stick in. Then I turned ninety degrees and paced off another twenty-five paces and placed another stick. I repeated this to form a rectangle and then said to my father, "This is where I will build my cabin."

"You can find some tools and things in the horse shelter." It wasn't quite a barn; just a structure for the horses could get out of the rain and snow. As we walked to the horse shelter, my father said, "I will be going hunting tomorrow, so I won't be here to help you."

I nodded, and Zack said, "Can I go with you, Pa?"

"No, not this time besides, you have chores to do."

My father went into the cabin and Zack, and I went to the horse shelter to see what I could use. "Has Pa ever taken you hunting?"

"No, not yet, I have always been too young."

"I don't think you are too young now." We got a sickle, ax, and shovel and went out to the area I marked off. I started cutting all the bushes about ten feet beyond where I had marked off while Zack used the sickle. Sometime about noon, we were called back to the cabin for lunch.

The fact that Pa wasn't going to take Zack hunting was working on my mind, so I decided to talk to Pa alone, without Zack knowing about it. I cut and removed the brush, and Zack did an excellent job cutting the grass. I was going to need the ax to cut some trees, so I needed an edge on it. I would let Zack see to that, so I would have time to be alone with Pa. "Zack, will you put an edge on the ax after we eat."

"Yes, I will do the sickle, also."

We cleaned up and went into the cabin to eat, and again Blue Flower was nice to me. The only thing I could figure is that she wanted me to like her, but she had no need for that, I started liking her long before we came to the cabin.

"Your things have made the cabin crowded," my father said.

"Yes, especially the furs, what do you think I should do with them?"

He scratched his jaw a bit then said, "Normally, I would tell you to trade them at the rendezvous, but furs don't get a good price anymore." "Give me some time to think about it." "I do have an idea, but I have to think about it for a while."

I nodded in agreement. "I do have some food things that I could give you now to use."

"Let's see them," replied my father. I searched for the leather sack with the stuff from my grandfather and parents. After a little search, I found it. I handed the bag to Blue Flower, and she started going through the things.

She pulled out some tobacco, and my father's eyes lit up. "Do you smoke, son?"

"No, I think the stuff is terrible; you can have it." He smiled and took it. She took out some salt and other spices that she said she would use. The main things that got Blue Flower and my father more excited than anything else was the tea and coffee. And there was a lot of it. I liked tea and the smell of coffee, but I could do without the taste of the coffee. What made it even better was that there were about five pounds of sugar. My mother, Turtle Woman, preferred to use honey than sugar, so there was a lot of it left.

"What is this, it looks like a stone?" Blue Flower said.

"That is hard candy." "It is sweet, and I never got around to eating it." "Why don't you give it to Zack?" "You better eat first before you try it." "Then, when you do try it, you just stick it in your mouth and suck on it; don't chew it will break your teeth," I explained.

We finished eating, and Zack went outside with candy in his mouth to sharpen the ax and sickle. When he left, I said to my father, "I wish to talk to you about Zack while he is not here."

"What about?" asked my father.

"You are going hunting tomorrow, take Zack with you."

"I cannot do that; he has chores to do."

"You know very well I could do those chores; you must take him."

"Why is it so important?"

"He is nearly as old as I am, and you have never taken him hunting; he is your son."

"He is right, I have had a concern about this for some time," voiced Blue Flower.

"He could go hunting anytime he wants to, even with you, James."

"It is not just the hunt it being with you that is important."

"Alright, I understand I will take him," Pa said, having a change of heart.

"You must tell him yourself," said Blue Flower.

He nodded and went out the door and Blue Flower, and I had big smiles on our faces.

Before I got out the door, Zack came running in all excited, "Ma, did you hear?" "Pa's going to take me hunting with him tomorrow." "He said I am almost a man and should learn to hunt like a man."

I smiled and went out the door and walked over to where the ax was, which just happened to be where Pa was. "Good idea I had taking him hunting with me," he said.

"Your idea!" "Do you get all your ideas this way?" I said.

He smiled, and I grabbed the ax, rope, and some chains and said, "I am looking for some trees about twice as wide as lodgepole trees."

"I think you will find what you want over on that ridge." "Don't you think that trees that are that small won't make a very good cabin, especially if a bear comes around?" he asked.

"I am making the cabin entirely different than what most people would make it; it will be more than strong enough."

"Alright, I hope you know what you are doing."

Just then, Zack came out and said, "What are we doing now?"

"I'm going to cut down some trees." "You need to get your horse ready for tomorrow."

I climbed bareback on my strongest horse and started off to go when my father yelled, "Go get your rifle, never be without it?"

I nodded, got off my horse, went into the cabin to retrieve my rifle, powder horn, and shot then took off again.

I found the trees I wanted, and there were plenty of them. I cut two trees and two lodge poles, hooked all four trees with a chain, and used my horse to haul them down to where I was going to build the cabin. I went back up the hill and cut down nine more trees and hauled them down to the cabin site, also. I cut the lodge poles into six four-foot lengths. Then I went and found two sticks, one about six feet and the other about three feet. I made them into marking sticks. It was getting late, and I wanted to do one more thing, so I left my tools where they lay and took my rifle and horse, to check something I saw upon the hillside. There was a trail that was just above where I was cutting trees, and on the trail were some fresh deer tracks, and they were large too. I went back and got my tools and things and put them away. Then I put my horse up and walked to the lake, where I stripped off my clothing and jumped in. I only stayed for a short time and went back to the cabin.

Blue Flower was cooking something that smelled good. "I'm sorry I didn't come out to help you, but I wanted to get my rifle cleaned and get everything together."

"That's alright, Zack, you can give me a hand when you have the time."

"Did you find the trees you wanted?" asked my father.

"Yes, there are plenty of them." I turned to Blue Flower and asked, "Do you have any leather strips I can have?"

"Yes, I think I can find some."

"What do you want them for, son?" asked my father.

"I cut down some lodge poles, and I want to use them to make sawhorses out of them," I explained. "I also need to figure out how to make a sled for moving rocks from the stream."

"What's a sled?" Zack asked.

I smiled and said, "This winter, you will find out."

He scratched his head, shrugged his shoulders, and went back to what he was doing.

"I have a drill, and you could notch and peg something that might work," said my father.

I nodded and said, "That just might work."

Dinner was ready, and we all sat down to an excellent meal. As we were eating, I asked, "I notice you have some books, may I read one?"

"Yes, but I read to the whole family," explained my father annoyed, I asked.

"If you don't want me reading your books, I won't."

"I didn't say that."

"No, but you implied it, it is ok; I will have books of my own someday," I said, not wanting to get into it with him.

My father gave me a look that could have made a grizzly run.

Blue Flower saw there was tension building between my father and me and changed the subject quickly. "How many days will you be gone, my husband?"

He turned from looking at me to Blue Flower and said, still thinking about me, "Three or four I am figuring." He then turned around quickly at me and stated in a loud, angry voice, "You make sure you do the chores."

I could see he was aching for a fight. I decided I wasn't going to have anything to do with it. Without finishing my meal or saying a word, I got up and retrieved my weapons.

"I didn't permit you to leave the table get back here."

"A Shoshone warrior does not need permission to leave," I replied in Shoshone.

As I went out the door, I said in English, "I will do your chores." I could see my father was so mad his face had turned red, but I was mad also for his talking to me that way. I slammed the door behind me, and I walked across to where the horses were. I heard the door open and my father coming at me, but I didn't turn around.

Blue Flower yelled, "No, Nate!"

As she yelled, I felt the tight grip of my father's hand on my shoulder. As he tried to spin me around in one motion, I came up with the butt of my rifle into his crotch. It bent him over, and I quickly knocked him to the ground with a blow to the head. Then I quickly turned the rifle around and pointed it at him.

Blue Flower yelled out, "No, James."

Then I heard a loud boom and felt a sting on my arm. I looked up in shock; Zack had shot me! I turned and went to the corral. I got a rope and my fastest horse, and I was out of there.

"What have you both done?" "He is your son and your brother." "You need to go after him, Nate; his wounded may be severe."

"I thought he was going to kill Pa, that's why I shot him."

Without a word, Nate dusted himself off, went and got his rifle, got on a horse, and went after me. He knew he had done wrong, that he let a little thing get out of hand.

"Now Grandpa, you weren't at the Shoshone village this time, how would you know what happened or what was said?"

"I don't know what I'm going to do with you, my mother; Blue Flower was Shoshone, and between her and Zack later, I was told everything."

I rode for about a half-hour when I stopped, I noticed the blood from my wound had clotted. I was lucky it was only a minor injury and would heal on its own. I had figured that my father would come after me, and I wasn't going to let him find me. I was still mad and didn't want to talk to him yet, maybe never. I got on my horse, made sure my tracks were covered and headed out. I rode for another hour, circled, and headed to the ridge where I had cut down the trees. When I got there, I lit a campfire, and I knew they would see it from the cabin, but I didn't care.

About four hours after my father went to look for me, he gave up and went back to the cabin. When Blue Flower heard him ride up, she and Zack came out to see what he had found. "I lost his trail and couldn't find him." "I must look in the morning," he said disappointedly.

"Maybe not," Blue Flower pointed to the hillside where there was a campfire."

"Zack put my horse up."

He got off the horse, and Blue Flower said, "Don't do something stupid and be careful he is a skilled Shoshone warrior."

"I'm not mad anymore, and I know the danger."

"Tell him I'm sorry, Pa, that I didn't mean to hurt him." He walked toward the campfire, but I saw him coming long before he got to the base of the mountain. He came up the hill, and I faded back into the dark of the trees and brush. As he came to my campfire, I worked my way around him so that I was at his back. "Come on out, I know you are out there somewhere," he said with a defeated voice.

"You would be dead if I were a Blackfoot." He turned around to see my rifle pointing at him.

"Are you going to shoot me?"

"That depends on what you are going to do."

"I'm over being angry," he said.

I lowered my rifle and went over to the fire and added more sticks. "Why don't you come back to the cabin with me? Your mother has some hot food for you, and she will tend to your wound?"

I stiffened up when he referred to Blue Flower being my mother, but I didn't say anything. "You may be over being angry, but I am not, and I have a lot to be angry about."

"Are you mad at Zack, he said he is sorry?" "He was afraid you were going to kill me." "I know he feels bad about it."

I didn't say a word; I just let him talk. He was silent for a few seconds, then said, "You must have wanted me to come here." "What do you want me to say to get you to return to the cabin?"

I lifted my head and said, "Why do you think I wanted you here?"

"You must have known we would see your campfire." "Why else would you come to this spot?"

He was right, of course; it wasn't so much I was angry at anyone; it was just that my feelings were hurt. "Go back to the cabin and take Zack hunting with you tomorrow morning." "Your chores I will do, as I have said." "I won't be going down there with you." "I have a lot of thinking to do."

He nodded and turned around to leave when I added, "I feel I am a person who has no place in this world, not St Louis in the white world, not the Shoshone village and not here."

"You shouldn't feel that way; we all love you." "Don't you notice how your mother goes out of her way to show you favor?" I stiffened again when he referred to Blue Flower as my mother, and this time he noticed it. "Does it bother you that I call Blue Flower your mother?"

A tear rolled down my cheek, and he noticed that also. I said, "I have lost two mothers I can't afford to lose another." "I like her very much; she is very kind to me, but...." I stopped in mid-sentence because I was getting too emotional.

"You need not worry about losing her; she won't die on you." "And your birth mother and Shoshone mother are still right here." He pointed to his heart and head, and I was losing it. He came over to me, lifted me gently, held me, and said softly, "Let's go home, son." I didn't resist him, so he stomped out the fire and walked me down the hill with his arm around me while I pulled my horse behind me.

When we got back to the cabin, Zack wanted to apologize, but I waved him off and said, "I don't want to talk about it." Zack put up the horse for me, and Pa took me into the cabin.

Blue Flower immediately started to work on my wound. "It is not bad; I will clean it and put something on it." As she tended the wound, she asked with concern, "Does it hurt?"

"Not now."

Zack came in and saw his mother working on my wound. He said, worried I was going to hate him, "I won't go tomorrow." "I will help you with your cabin."

"You have been waiting to go hunting with Pa too long; you go with him; I will manage with the cabin."

Blue Flower gave me food to eat, and everyone was watching me eat. I felt uncomfortable about it. "Zack, why aren't you eating with me?" He smiled and sat down next to me. Then everyone else sat down for a late snack.

# 15

# THE READJUSTMENT AND DISCOVERY

I slept in as my father and Zack left. When I did wake up, the sun had started to come up. Blue Flower was making me something to eat while I went outside to relieve myself and wash up. My arm was stiff but usable, and I went into the cabin to eat.

"How is your arm?"

"Ok, don't give me too much I am still full from last night." As I was eating, I asked, "How low are you with meat?"

"Very low, I am afraid."

"After I do some work on the cabin, I might go hunting nearby." I was silent for a moment and then said, "Why are you so kind to me when I am from another woman?"

"I love you, and you are a part of this family as you should be." "I also respect, and I am thankful for how well both of your mothers raised you," she said with sincerity.

I was stunned at what she said, and I said in a meek voice, "You know Pa wants me to refer to you as my mother."

"How do you feel about that?"

"I think it would be alright." "I mean, it wouldn't show any disrespect to either of my mothers, and you have shown me nothing but kindness."

"Then, do what makes you comfortable." "I will love you either way."

I shook my head in agreement then changed the subject." "Do you have those leather strips I was talking about yesterday?"

She nodded and got them for me, and I tied them to my loincloth.

After I ate, I went outside to do the chores. It took about four hours to do them, but I didn't care. After having my talk with Blue Flower, I felt good. When I finished, I got a two-handed plane, the ax, shovel, and a pick and went to the cabin site. I took three of the lodgepole pine sticks and tied them together, about a foot from the top, forming a tripod. I did the same with three others. I wet the leather on both tripods and let it dry. With the pick and shovel, I started to dig a trench from one stake to the other about four inches deep. When I finished, I took the ax and shaved three sides of a log with the ax. Then I used the two-handed plane to smooth it out. It was getting near noon, and I needed the saw, so I left the tools at the cabin site and went to the cabin. Before I went in, I got Pa's bucksaw and placed it on the porch. Then I washed up and went into the cabin to eat. As I sat at the table, I said, "I will be cutting the ends of the logs I have, and I will bring you the ends for firewood."

"Are you still going hunting?"

"Yes, after I laid the first log and gathered wood to make a sled." In about a half-hour, I was back at the cabin site, cutting both ends of a log. I then measured the length I needed and added about a foot on both sides and cut the log to the measured length. I then cut two six-inch notches where they needed to be and then cut and shaped another log to the same length as the first then notched it. I placed the first log in the trench and put the other log next to where I would dig another trench. After, I went looking for some wood to build a sled and found what I wanted. I put all my tools back and got my horse ready to go hunting. I went back out to pick up the wood ends and chips from the notches and brought them back to the cabin. I got all my weapons and told Blue Flower I was going to go hunting, and I should be back shortly after dark at the latest.

Before I mounted, I got a rope. I figured I would drag any game I got. I headed out and found the deer trail again. I then looked for fresh tracks and found them, and they were going up and over the hill. I followed the trail for about a half-hour, and when I got over the ridge, the trail led me to a rocky area. I could see it would be harder to find the deer for the lack of tracks. When the tracks finally disappeared, I got off my horse and walked back and forth until I could find something. In another half-hour, I found what I was looking for some broken twigs on a bush and misplaced rocks. About a hundred feet further, I found some fur on a thorny vine, and I followed the path of least resistance where I thought the deer might go, which was downhill. Finally, the rocky ground gave way to some soil, and I found the trail again. The trail led to a small grassy valley, and as I went, I saw some deer droppings. I got off my horse and took a closer look and noticed they were fresh. I knew the deer was nearby, so I decided to walk. I tied up my horse and moved as quietly as I could, and I hadn't gone far when I noticed another set of tracks. They were bear tracks, and by their size, I would guess it was a black bear. They were more likely male since there was only one set of tracks, and a female would have had cubs this time of year. Black bears are not as bad as a grizzly, but they are still dangerous. The tracks appeared to have been made sometime in the morning before the deer came through here. Since my horse didn't get skittish when I tied the horse up, I decided to continue my hunt.

About five minutes later, I was about to come out to an open grassy clearing when I spotted about fifty yards away seven deer that I could count. It was fortunate that I was downwind of them, or they would have smelled me and took off. I could see one large buck with one smaller one, and the rest were does. I aimed at the large buck, it was a long way off, but I had made many shots longer than this. I shot and hit him just behind the front legs, and he went down. The other deer ran off, but before I went over to gut the deer, I reloaded my rifle like I always do. I didn't want to be caught out here with a bear prowling around with an empty gun. After I reloaded, I walked over to the deer, and I hit it a few times with my rifle to make sure it was dead. Many a fool got killed by a stunned deer when they didn't do this. I figured the deer weighed about three hundred pounds. I would lose about a hundred pounds of that when I gutted the deer.

I had just cleaned everything out of the deer. I placed the heart, liver, and kidneys into a leather sack I had brought when I heard a large animal breaking through the brush about two hundred yards from me. Then I heard the growl, and I saw it, it was a large, old, black bear that had smelled the meat and was coming for it and me if I didn't do something about it. I figured the bear was old because it couldn't see very well. As the bear started my way, I jumped up and made myself as big as I could. The bear stopped startled and reared up on its hind legs. I took my shot and caught him on his chest near his right paw, and he fell backward. I reloaded as quickly as I could while he was still dazed. I could have used my pistols and still thought that I might have to, but they are only good at about fifty feet, and I didn't want him to be that close to me. I had finished reloading when the bear, as bad as I shot him, came after me. I reshot him, and this time I hit the bear in the neck near his left paw. The bear rolled once and lay still. I reloaded again and waited a few minutes. Then I found a long stick and went over to him. He was less than seventy-five feet from where I had been standing. I poked him, and he moved, so I shot him in the back of his neck, trying to hit his spine. He stopped moving, but I wasn't taking any chances. I reloaded and waited, then poked him again, and this time he didn't stir. I thought it best to go back and get my horse before I gutted him. I was pleased with myself because it was the first bear I had ever shot. I'd seen many bears, including grizzly but never shot one I let Grey Wolf do that. Then I brought the horse up; she was a might skittish, but I calmed her down. I went over to the bear, poked it one more time, and went to the business of cleaning the bear. Again, I kept the heart, liver, and kidneys in the same bag and hung the bag on the horse. I made a travois and put the bear and deer on it and headed back to the cabin. It was slow going, and as I went, I thought Ma would be surprised at how much meat there will be. Then I thought that was the first time in my mind I referred to her as Ma. It was getting very dark by the time I got to the hillside where I was cutting down trees. I knew Ma would be anxious, so I moved as fast as I could. The horse was also getting tired because of the weight, the terrain I had to travel, and the distance. When I got to the bottom of the hill, I got off the horse and walked it the rest of the way back to the cabin.

Ma came out of the cabin long before I got there. I assumed she heard me coming. "Sorry, I'm late, Ma I ran into some trouble." I pointed to the back of the horse where the travois was.

She smiled. I guess because I called her Ma. Then she said, "Let's see what you have there. Uh, you're just like your father killing bears and all."

"It's my first."

She put her hands on her hips and said, "We have some work to do, but first, are you hungry?"

"A might, but I would like to water and feed the horse first."

"Alright, when you get done, clean up and come in."

While I was eating, Ma started a fire outside. It would give us some light, and we could begin to dry or jerk some of the meat. When I finished eating, I went to help her hang the deer first. We had it skinned in less than thirty minutes, and I brought it into the house so that she could butcher it. I told her, "I will hang and skin the bear while you cut-up the deer."

She nodded, and I went out to complete my task. Before I had the bear half skinned, Ma had some of the deer meat cooking inside the cabin, and she had brought a lot out to dry. I finished the bear, so I brought it in the bear meat to be butchered also. She said, "Take the skins of both the deer and bear, stretch them out, and stake them to the ground." The skins got staked to scrap, and my mother saved the brains and got some ashes to cure the hides.

When I came back into the cabin, I asked if she wanted me to start another fire for the bear meat. "Yes, and when you finished with the fire, bring the bear meat out to be dried."

I did as she asked, and when she finished butchering the bear meat, she told me to build two more fires while she worked on the skins. When I finished making the other fires, she asked me to check the deer meat to see if it got finished cooking and drying. If it was, then I was to put the cooked and dried meat on the table, then cook and dry some more bear meat. I went and did what she said. Besides the meat, we kept the bear fat to make grease out of it. The grease was good for the rifles and pistols, and it was also useful to waterproof things. When she finished scraping the hides, at least enough for the night, she started to chop up the kidneys, the bear heart, and the liver into tiny pieces. Then she told me, "The deer heart and liver are good, but the bear is too strong for us to eat but not too strong for the fish." "Go down to the lake, to the far end, and throw in this chopped meat."

By the time I got back, almost everything had been cooked or dried into jerked meat. Ma had enough cooked meat to last all of us for many months. When the meat was dried enough, ma poked a hole into each piece, strung them on leather cords, and then hung them up like you would hang the clothing to dry. There they would stay for about three days. By the time I finished helping Ma, it was late, about nine or ten o'clock, I figured, and I was mighty tired. "I am going to the stream to bathe before I go to bed," I told Ma.

"Wait, and I will go down to the water with you to bathe."

I looked at her and said, "I thought Shoshone women didn't take a bath with men unless they were married to them."

"You are right, but you are a boy, and my son, it is different."

I smiled and started giggling as did she, and we both grabbed our rifles and headed to the stream. I stripped, and I was the first one in the water. As she removed her clothes, I watched her and thought Pa choose well she was very beautiful.

After bathing, we went back to the cabin. I put up my rifle, removed my clothes, and went over to Zack's and my bed. Ma said, "Why don't you crawl into bed with me." I stared at her for a second and then crawled in next to her. It was pleasant, and I snuggled up next to her like I used to do with mama in St. Louis. It wasn't very long until I was sound asleep.

The next morning, I got my chores done real fast and got out to the cabin site. This time I brought a drill to make the sled. I drilled all the holes in the rails and the top part, and I got some pine sap and sticks I could use for pegs. I assembled the sled, and I brought it down to the stream and let it soak. I then went back and started on the sides of the cabin. I squared the logs and placed notches where I needed them. I dug a trench and put the log into it connecting the front and back logs, and then I pegged both ends. On the other side, where the fireplace would go, I cut two logs about two feet long and notched them. I then cut another log six-foot-long, squared it, and notched it. I dug a trench and placed the log in it, and I pegged both ends. By then, it was time for lunch, so I cleaned up and went back to the cabin.

Before I went into the cabin, I looked at the meat drying and wondered what pa and Zack would think when they saw the stretched hides and the hanging meat. Would they be angry or happy about it? I guess the next day; I would get the answer.

I sat at the table, and Ma said, "How is the cabin coming along?"

"Good, I will haul rock from the stream this afternoon for the fireplace." "Ma, do you think Pa and Zack will be angry about the game I got yesterday?"

"No, they will be very pleased."

"I don't know Pa takes things wrong sometimes, and Zack would like to compete with me."

"You will see it will be just fine," Ma reassured me. She had cooked up a lot of deer stew with vegetables, seasoning and other things in it, it tasted incredible.

After lunch, I got my horse and headed back to the cabin site. I let the horse graze while I put in one more log. After about an hour, I had it in. I went down to the stream with the horse, sled, and stick to pry up the rocks. I put about ten rocks per load, and I dumped the stones on the cabin side I was making the fireplace.

It was on the third load of rocks that I caught a bright sparkle of yellow out of the corner of my eye. It was just at the edge of the water I scooped it up and looked at it. I read a book about minerals once, and there is this mineral called iron pyrite or fool's gold. Many people get fooled into believing that it is gold. What I had in my hand wasn't iron pyrite; it was a gold nugget about the size of a man's thumb. I dug around with the shovel to see if there was any more. I came up with five more nuggets of various sizes. I wondered if I should tell my family and decided not to inform them yet. I would look for more gold as I brought rocks up to the cabin site. I placed the nuggets I had in my possibles bag and started to haul more rock up to the cabin site. Once up to the cabin site, I dug a two by two by a two-foot hole in the corner of the cabin site and lined it with some flat rocks. I placed the gold nuggets in the hole, put a flat rock on top of the hole, and covered it with dirt. I figured as I filled my possibles bag up with gold, I would store it there. By the end of the day, I had to uncover the hole twice because my possibles bag got too full. I could see that I was going to have to make myself a kiln or furnace to smelt the gold into ingots. If my family asked what I was making, I would just tell them it is a kiln for pottery and things.

The next day I had to find limestone, sand, and gypsum to make mortar for the fireplace and the kiln, and I knew just where to find them. I worked gathering the materials until lunch, and I had three large piles of the materials. That afternoon I mixed the limestone, gypsum, and sand and made the mortar. I then laid the flooring of the fireplace with the rocks I hauled from the stream and the mortar I had made. I completed the flooring, I found an area to the left of my door to the cabin and about ten feet out, and I started to build the kiln. The kiln was going to look like a beehive about six feet wide and about the same height. I positioned it so that the wind that blew sometimes would help stoke the fire that would be burning inside the kiln, making it hotter. I got the idea by reading a Spanish book about pottery making and kilns. After I used up all the rocks, I went down to the stream and gathered some more stones, and of course, I found more gold. It made me wonder why Pa never found gold, but then again, he always went beaver hunting.

The next day I decided to start building the walls of the cabin, and when I got tired with that, I would work on the kiln. I took all the tools back and sharpened the ax and plane. I figured Pa and Zack would be back sometime the next afternoon or night, and I wanted them to see how much I had done. After supper, I helped Ma clean up. I got ready for bed. Ma offered to share her bed again, and I didn't refuse.

The next day again, I hurried and finished the chores and went out to the cabin site. I decided to haul rocks first and then work on building the walls of the cabin. I had gotten about a half dozen loads of stones when I stopped and started building the walls. By the time it was lunch, I had three rows of logs up. After lunch, I decided to work on the kiln, and by late afternoon it was about four feet high. Pa and Zack hadn't shown yet, so I took my horse and headed up the hill to cut down some more logs. By the time it was getting dark, I had brought back an additional fifteen logs. I headed back to the cabin; it was too dark to work anymore on my cabin.

Pa and Zack hadn't shown up yet, but I expected them anytime now. Ma was in distress because of their absence; it was easy to see it in her. "Anything could have held them up, remember I came back late with the game a few days ago."

"Yes, it is probably nothing they should be coming any time now."

After a few hours had passed, she became more agitated, and even I was concerned. "If they are not here by tomorrow afternoon, I will take my horse and track them I'm a good tracker and can find even old tracks where others would have a hard time at it."

"You will get two horses." "I will be going with you." I nodded in agreement, and later when we went to bed, she did not sleep well and had a restless night.

The next morning, while I did my chores, Ma, was out of the cabin looking in the direction where Pa and Zack left whenever she heard a sound that wasn't from nature. I was going to wait until that afternoon to go search for them, but I said to Ma, "If you would like, I could get the horses ready now, and we could leave early."

"No, we will wait to see if they come back this afternoon, you go work on your cabin I will come and get you."

I was on the fifth row of the cabin walls when I saw Ma coming out to where I was working. I grabbed my tools and headed toward her. When we met, she said, "It is time we go."

I nodded and started to put the tools away then I threw some water on myself, and I got the horses ready. When my eyes cleared from the water that went in them, I saw two riders coming. I grabbed my rifle and noticed one of the riders was not as tall as the other. They were coming from the direction of the lake, and then I made out who they were. I yelled for Ma, and she shot out of the cabin with a rifle in her hand. I pointed to Pa and Zack, and she gave me the rifle and went running to them. I smiled and went walking up to them, also with both rifles in my hands. Pa and Zack were both off their horses embracing Ma. I noticed that on one of the two packhorses, there was an elk and on the other a deer.

"I am sorry we are late coming back." "I ran into Othello, and we had a long talk about things I will tell you both about it later." Othello was a fellow trapper who got his name because of his love for Shakespeare.

I grabbed Pa's horse, and Ma said, "We were about to go out and look for the both of you."

"There was no danger Ma, not with Pa and me out there," Zack said with confidence.

"I am sure you are right," Ma replied.

As we started to pass the drying meat Pa stopped and looked and said, "I see someone else has been hunting."

"Yes, James has been taking excellent care of me while you have been hunting," said Ma.

"Looks like bear meat Pa," said Zack

Pa took a second look, and I said, "I happened to have a little bad luck and ran into that bear who wanted my deer."

"Why didn't you give the bear your deer?" asked Pa.

"It wasn't just the deer he wanted; he wanted me also."

"You must tell me about that bear," Zack said.

"It took three shots to kill it, and it was close."

Pa gave me a confused look he knew I was a good shot, so I said, "He was a huge bear and my first."

"Why don't you all go to the cabin and get something to eat and rest." "I will take care of the meat, horses, and your things," I said to get Pa's mind off the bear.

"Just take care of the horses and put the meat on the porch you haven't eaten yet," said Ma.

Pa and Ma went into the house, but Zack stayed and helped me.

"Did I hear, right?" "Did he call you Ma when he called you out of the cabin?" asked Nate, amazed.

"Yes, he has started calling me that ever since he came back from hunting."

"Maybe something happened when he met up with the bear."

"No, I don't think so his only concern was that you or Zack would get upset because he brought back game before you two did."

"Then what could have changed his heart about you?"

"He is a Shoshone warrior, and he does a man's work building that cabin and hunting, but he is still a boy." "I let him sleep with me while you were gone, and the way he slept, I think he misses the warmth of his mother, either mother."

"Are you saying he is making you his mother for the loss of his?"

"Yes, and I think it is wonderful."

"Are you mad at me?" asked Zack.

"No, why did you ask that?" I said.

"I did shoot you."

"It was a scratch if you wanted to kill me, you would have you are a better shot than that."

"Looks like your cabin is coming along nicely."

"Yes, I have a kiln I am building at the same time."

"What's a kiln?"

"A place to cook bowls, jugs, plates, and other stuff." Zack still looked confused, so I said, "You will see when I complete it." "After we eat, I am going to go out there and continue working."

"I'll help you if you want me to."

"Sure, there are things you can do for me, and you can see the sled I made."

We finished feeding and grooming the horses, and we both washed up before we went into the cabin. "Ma, what do you want me to do with the meat?" I asked. When I referred to Blue Flower as Ma Zack stared at me, it appeared that he was disturbed by it, but he didn't say anything.

"Just leave it out front, and after we eat, you can bring it in."

"I heard you had been a real help for your Ma while we were gone," said Pa.

Zack gave me that look again, and Ma and Pa noticed also.

"I did what I could, Pa," I said cautiously.

As Ma was giving Pa more to eat, she said, "What is wrong, Zack, and don't tell me nothing?"

"But there isn't anything wrong, Ma," he replied unconvincingly.

"I think Zack doesn't like me calling you Ma," I said as a matter of fact.

"Is this true, Zack?" asked Pa.

Zack had his head down when he replied. "I don't know Pa; it's just that she has always been my Ma."

"She still is your Ma, nothing has changed," said Pa.

"If you don't want me to call her Ma, then I won't," I interjected.

Ma and Pa stared at me for what I said, and I thought there was going to be trouble. Then Zack said, "No, I don't want that you're my brother, and she is just as much your Ma as she is mine, I will get used to it."

"Great now that is finished, we can continue to eat," said Pa.

The rest of the lunch was uncomfortable, and when I finished, I said, "I'm going down to my cabin site to continue working." I looked at Zack, but he made no effort to come with me, so I just went.

"Zack, I want to have a little talk with you," said Ma.

Ma motioned with her head for Pa to leave, and he said, "I think I will go see how much work James has done to his cabin."

I was halfway to the cabin site when I heard Pa call out, "James, wait." I stopped, and he caught up to me. "Let me carry some of those tools." I handed him the ax and the plane. Everything was silent for a few seconds when Pa said, "You shouldn't let Zack bother you; we all have a little readjusting to do."

"You know, Pa, sometimes I wonder if I made a mistake by coming here."

"Don't say that we all want you to be part of our family."

"You all have a strange way of showing it."

When we got to the cabin site, Pa changed the subject and said, "This cabin is very different, where did you come up with it?"

"It's a Dutch design I believe there are cabins like this back in the northeast."

He moved over to the fireplace and started mixing the mortar. "How did you make this?"

"It wasn't hard; the materials are easy to find limestone, gypsum, and sand." "You mix them, and it hardens up."

"What's this over here?" Pa asked, walking over to the kiln.

I said, "It is a kiln for making pottery and things it's not finished yet."

"Looks like you are going to have a nice cabin here is there anything I can do to help you?"

"I was going to have Zack square off some of these logs, but aren't you tired from your hunting trip?"

"No, I can do that for you."

We loaded a log onto the sawhorses, and I explained that I used the ax to square them, then the plane to smooth them. "I'm going to get more rocks with the sled."

"You did a good job on it."

"Thank you; Zack can use it to slide down the hill this winter." I hooked the sled up to the horse and was off to the stream. I had gotten two loads of rock and some more gold when Zack showed up. Pa had squared and smoothed the log well. I measured it and marked the places for the notches. I knew exactly how to make them, so I told Pa I would do this part.

Zack just stood there, but after a while, he finally said, "Can I help?"

I looked at Pa and was about to say I had nothing for him when Pa said, "Why don't you take over what I was doing? I'm getting a little tired."

Zack nodded, and Pa said, "James, I will help you place that log when you finish with your notches, and then I'll head back to the cabin."

I cut the niches, and Pa grabbed one end of the log. We placed it on the back wall. He looked at the tight fit all the logs had and said, "You won't have to chink these logs very much."

"No, that's one reason I like this style so much."

Pa left, and I instructed Zack on how to shape the logs. I then went back to gathering rocks. After about two hours, I had so much gold in my possibles bag; I had to store them in my secret place. Zack had finished another log, so I cut the niches, and he helped me place it. By the next day, I would have to build two ladders because the walls were getting too high. We put another log on the sawhorse, and I gave the ax to Zack. I said I wanted to check something in one of the rooms. Zack nodded, and I went to the room where the gold was. I removed the dirt and cap and placed the gold into the box. I replaced the lid and put dirt on top of it. I decided I had enough rock, so I decided to work on the kiln.

As I passed Zack, he stopped what he was doing and said, "I'm sorry for acting the way I did." "She is your mother, too; you can call her Ma."

I nodded and started again toward the kiln. Zack continued and said, "Ma wants to adopt you."

I froze in my tracks, turned around, and asked, "How do you feel about that?"

"I think it is a good idea."

I nodded and said, "I must think about that."

By the end of the day, I had completed the kiln, except for a few details. I would have to let it dry for a few days before I tested it out. "We better head back it is getting dark," I told Zack.

We gathered up the tools and headed back to the cabin. Along the way, Zack, out of the blue, said, "Do you think the next time you go hunting, you could take me with you?"

"I don't see why not."

"You must tell me about that bear you killed in more detail."

"Alright, but later I'm thinking about how I will build those ladders for tomorrow."

After dinner, before we got up from the table, Pa said he had something to say. We all turned our attention to him, and he said, "As I told you before while hunting, we ran into Othello." "While Zack slept, we talked about Beaver Trapping."

"Normally, I would bring my furs to the rendezvous to trade for the things we need, but Othello heard that what we will get for the furs is way down." "I believe this because I have been getting less and less for my furs over the past few years, and they have been quality pelts."

"So, what are you going to do?" asked Ma.

"I'm getting to that; Othello is taking his furs back east to sell." "He believes he can get double the amount there." "I don't know about double, but I know you can get more and better products." "So, I am thinking about also going east, and I am thinking of taking all of you."

"Where back east, are you going, Pa?" I asked.

"St. Louis, that's where most trappers who do trading go."

Ma and Zack were all excited, but I was concerned about something. I would like to go, but I was now thinking of my family.

"Now, there is one drawback to going that we need to talk about," Pa said. "We won't be able to visit your village Blue Flower until we get back, and we won't be able to stay long."

"How long can we visit the village?" I asked.

"Maybe two weeks."

"At least we will be able to visit," said Ma.

"Two weeks would be alright, but Morning Star and Grey Wolf would be disappointed," I said.

"So, are there any objections to going east this spring?"

"I would like to go, but I see another problem you might want to consider," I said.

"What's the other problem, son?" asked Pa.

"You forget Pa that Ma and Zack are Shoshone by blood, and they may not be treated very kindly by folks." "I don't worry about the businessmen money will keep their mouths shut." "Still, some of the common folk may make rude comments, especially to Zack."

"What does he mean, Pa?" asked Zack.

"Some people think people like Shoshone are more like animals than real people, and they believe they are better than the Shoshone." "Some people may call you and your mother names like savage and half-breed." "I don't think there will be a lot of people doing that, but some might."

"Then we will just ignore them, won't we Zack?" said Ma.

"Sure, we will, Pa," said Zack with excitement.

"I would like to buy a stone for my mother with the money I will get from my furs," I said to Pa.

"That would be a good thing, and we will all pay respect to your mother's grave," Pa said with sympathy. I didn't tell them about the gold, not yet. I would wait until I smelt it and have enough of it. "Then, we will go when the snow starts to melt, and I get some rest from trapping."

In the next few days, I gathered rocks and gold as Zack squared-off logs. One-time, Zack asked if he could change what he was doing and get some rocks. I discouraged him from doing that by telling him that it makes no sense both of us getting wet besides I know what kind and size of rock I needed.

On the third day, I asked Zack, "Do you want to do something different?"

"I sure do."

"I have three jobs that I need to complete, I need to gather a lot of wood for the kiln, I need a special mud that is at the lake, and I need a large hole dug." "What would you like to do?"

"I will get the mud."

I showed him where to get the clay and told him he could use the sled. As Zack was getting the clay, I made a second hole to store more gold, and then I went to work on the fireplace. After Zack brought the first load of clay, I made a mold for the gold out of the clay and let it firm up. I gathered wood for the kiln and loaded it up, then laid the excess by the kiln. For the door of the kiln, I used a large flat rock that I could slide back and forth with a stick. I could feel the breeze coming through the kiln, so I knew it would have a natural bellow. The mold was ready to carve. I put "Su Majestad real Felipe III de España," which means "His Royal Majesty Philip the Third of Spain." It would look like Spanish gold from about sixteen twenty. I lit the fire and made a paddle to slide the mold in and out.

When the kiln was good and hot, I put the mold in and let it bake. I also put in other objects, so I could say to my family I was testing out the kiln. I figured it would take about eight to ten hours to bake before it would be ready. That meant it would be dark out, which is good because I could have an excuse for being alone on another night while I smelt the gold.

By his fifth load of clay, I could see that Zack was getting bored, so I let him out of it. He wanted to know what was in the kiln, so I told him some test items, and he believed it. Just before we finished for the day, I threw a lot of wood in the kiln, cleaned up, and went to the cabin. I told Ma and Pa at supper that I would be out late about another three hours more feeding the fire in the kiln. I also told them I had test items in there because I knew they would ask. So out I went, Zack wanted to come, but I said it was like feeding a campfire, and it is just a one-man job, so he stayed in the cabin. After about three hours, I loaded the kiln with wood again and went back to the cabin. The fire in the kiln would burn down, and the mold would cool by the time I finished my chores the next day.

As we were doing the chores the next day, Zack asked me, "What am I going to do today?"

"Pretty much the same as yesterday," I said.

"I am going to help Ma and Pa today we need to get some fruit and vegetables."

I nodded in agreement and was happy that he wasn't going to be around. I felt the kiln, and it didn't feel hot, so I moved the stone away from the opening and took out what I had fired. Everything was as hard as a rock. The mold was perfect, and I placed it in my secret hiding spot for the gold. That night I would smelt the gold I had and hide it until the right time to tell my family. I also made some ash glaze, so I would have an excuse to be out late again that night. I looked at what I had, and I needed more logs before I could work on the cabin. I was running out of mortar also, so I had to get some more raw materials to make some more but first the logs. I went back to the cabin to get a horse, ax, chain, and rope carrying the test piece of pottery with me to show everyone. I showed the test strips to Pa and said, "I'm going to try an ash glaze on them tonight if that is alright."

"Sure, it's alright, but aren't you spending a lot of time with that kiln when you should be working on your cabin?"

"Your right Pa that's why the rest of the day, I will be chopping down logs and hauling them down to the cabin site."

"That's good."

"Will it be alright if I take your crucible with me tonight to make some shot for my pistols and rifle, so I don't get too bored?" "I'll make some for you and Zack also with my lead."

"I think that would be very considerate of you, and yes, you can use the crucible. Take the tongs also."

"Thanks, Pa, I'll go show Ma and Zack what I did." After I showed Ma and Zack, I got my horse and things; then headed to where I was cutting the trees. In between hauling the logs, I fired up the kiln and slurry-glazed the test pieces; then, I put them in the kiln. By the time I quit, I had about thirty logs piled up at the cabin site, but I knew I would need more than three times that amount to finish the walls. The rest of the time, I gathered more wood for the kiln and put my horse and tools away for the night, then I went into the cabin to eat.

After I finished eating, I took Pa's crucible, tongs, and my lead and went down to the kiln. The fire had burned down, and the kiln was cool enough to remove the test pieces. I fired the kiln back up and looked at the test strips; they came out, right. I used cobalt to turn the glaze blue. I placed them out of the way to cool off more, and I waited an hour or so until I figured the kiln was hot enough. Then I uncovered the two holes where I kept the gold. After checking to see if I was still alone, I filled the crucible with gold nuggets to the top. Then with the tongs, I placed the crucible in the kiln and shut the door. I got the mold and waited a short time while I watched to see if anyone was coming. After a brief period, I checked to see if it had melted, and it had. I carefully removed the crucible, poured the contents into the mold, added more nuggets to the crucible, and put it back into the kiln. When the gold hardened, I dropped the ingot into a bucket of water and readied the mold for the next one. After the ingot, cooled, I looked at it, and it looked perfect. I deposited it into the secret hole and continued for several hours until all the gold nuggets were gone. When I finished, I had the hole filled about halfway with ingots. I put the mold in with the ingots and covered both holes. I then scraped out the crucible with my knife to make sure all signs of gold were gone, and then I started making lead balls for the weapons. After a few hours, I figured I had made enough; besides, I was tired. I grabbed my fired strips and went back to the cabin to sleep. Everyone was asleep, but I'm sure Ma and Pa heard me come in, but I was as quiet as I could be. I put everything away, left the ceramic strips on the table, stripped out of my clothes, and then crawled in bed next to Zack, and I was asleep in seconds.

The next morning, I showed everybody the sample strips I had made. They were amazed at the color. I also gave Zack and Pa a lot of lead balls. I told them I might make one more test with the kiln before winter. At the cabin site, I dug two larger holes in the other room. I figured that I would have plenty of space to store the nuggets.

Three weeks had passed, and it was getting colder. I wouldn't be able to work late anymore, but I did have all the walls up as well as one of the three holes full of gold nuggets and another half full. I was almost ready to put the horizontal beams in for the roof, but with that, I would need help, so I would ask Pa at dinner to give me a hand. I had all the beams squared, and the walls notched, so it should go up fast with his help. I had put up all the tools, cleaned up, and went into the cabin where everyone was there.

"Today is a very special day," Pa said. Everyone had smiles on their faces; I looked at Pa puzzled, and Pa told me. "James, do you know what is so special about today?"

"No, Pa, what's this all about?" I asked.

Ma placed my favorite sweet cakes in front of me. Then she gave me something tied up and wrapped in a blanket. I looked at it, confused, and Pa said, "Happy birthday James."

I smiled and opened the blanket. It was a pair of elk moccasins for the winter. I had forgotten about my birthday I had just turned twelve.

I thanked everybody, and Zack said, "Aren't you going to eat your sweet cakes?"

I took a bite of them, and they were great, then I looked at everybody and said, "It would make me happy if I could share these cakes with all of you."

"There is no need I have enough for all of us," Ma said.

While we were eating our sweet cakes, I asked Pa, "I'm putting up the horizontal beams for the roof tomorrow, but I need some help." "Will you be able to help me?"

"I'm heading out beaver hunting tomorrow, so I can't," Pa said apologetically.

"I'll help you," said Zack.

"Alright, after chores, it shouldn't take us that long to put the beams up there are only three," I said.

Pa was gone early the next day, and Zack and I headed out to my cabin to put up the three beams after we did our choirs. I took the drill with me so that I could peg the beams in. It wasn't needed, but since I had pegged all the logs, I decided to continue with the same plan. It took us a little more than four hours to put up the beams. After lunch, I hauled more rock, and Zack was willing to shape the shorter vertical beams for the roof.

"Why do the roof beams have to be square?" Zack asked.

"Because I am going to make a different roof than what Pa has." "When I finish the cabin, it should be a lot warmer in the winter and cooler in the summer," I replied.

"I thought we were going to go hunting together," said Zack.

I looked at him for a second and then said, "Go ask Ma if she needs, or could use more meat, no use hunting if she doesn't."

When he ran off, I quickly dug up one of the holes that contained the gold nuggets and deposited what I had in my possibles bag; then, I covered it back up.

I saw Zack come running back, and when he got to me, he said, "Ma told me she could always use fresh meat and what we don't use, she will jerk."

"We will go tomorrow morning after chores," I said. I had just finished another vertical beam. With that and what Zack had done, we only had four, and we needed twenty-six in all.

"Zack, why don't you take the ax and horse and go find some cedar trees that I can make shingles out of."

Zack cheerfully accepted his next assignment, anything to get out of making the vertical beams. While he was gone, I went back to get rocks and mainly find more gold nuggets. Before Zack finished, I had filled up another hole with nuggets. When Zack arrived with his last load of cedar, I said, "It's getting late and chilly. Let's go back to the cabin for the night." We grabbed all the tools, and Zack rode the horse back to the corral while I walked. I knew I was going to have to say something soon about the gold; I just had to figure out how and when to tell them.

# 16

# THE DISCLOSURE PA'S RELIEF

"Ma, if I found a way so that Pa wouldn't have to go beaver trapping anymore, would that be good?"

"It would be good, but he must trap so we can have the white man's things." I dropped the subject and went on to something else, and when we finished talking, and supper Zack and I cleaned our weapons and got ready for the hunt the next day. We decided to go to bed early; however, it was more Zack's idea than mine because he was getting excited about the hunt and wanted to hurry things along.

The next morning after chores, we went to the same place where I got my last game, and as we were riding, I asked Zack, "Do you know what gold is?"

"I think it is that locket you have around your neck."

"Do you know what it looked like before they made this locket?"

"No, not really."

"It comes in many forms, sometimes as a shining stone."

"It is soft and melts quickly like lead," I said.

"Why are you telling me all this stuff?" asked Zack.

"Oh, it just came into my head."

Zack nodded, and I changed the subject and started to talk about the bear I shot up the trail. We entered the high mountain valley, but there was no sign of deer. We headed east because I figured that they might be moving to lower elevations. About an hour later, we ran into some fresh tracks, which led to a stream. Under a tree, there were about a dozen deer. We got off our horses and worked our way, so we were downwind and better concealed. Zack was excited, and I whispered to him, "Calm down and take your time."

Zack did exactly that, and we both took aim, and two deer fell. Zack jumped into the air with delight and started down to the fallen deer when I yelled, "Zack, stop!" Zack froze, and I said, "Never move until you have reloaded, I know Pa has told you that many times." I didn't know, but I guessed he had.

Zack said, "I'm sorry you're right," and we both reloaded our rifles.

We had cleaned the two deer and were loading one onto a horse when I spotted someone moving through the brush about two hundred yards from us. I quickly grabbed my rifle and said, "We have company." Zack grabbed his rifle, and we stepped behind a fallen tree. Three Utes came out of the bushes and were staring right at us. "I'm not looking for a fight, Zack."

"Neither am I," Zack replied.

The three Utes came closer, then they stopped and talked among themselves, pointing at us. I yelled out in Ute, "We are not looking for trouble, but we are ready for it."

Again, they talked among themselves, and one yelled out in Ute, "Are you Soaring Eagle With Many Coups?"

"I am Soaring Eagle With Many Coups, son of Bear Slayer and brother of Tracking Fox who is with me now." They looked at each other and turned and took off.

"Why didn't they attack?" asked Zack.

"I told them who we are." "Let's get the other deer tied to the horse and get out of here before the Utes change their minds," I said. We had the other deer loaded in about five minutes, and we headed back to the cabin. Fortunately, we didn't see any more Utes on our way back to the cabin, and we arrived in the late afternoon.

"Ma, we're back," Zack yelled. Ma came out of the cabin, and Zack couldn't wait to tell her about meeting up with the Utes.

"Maybe you shouldn't go hunting again until your father comes back," Ma said.

"Aw, Ma nothing happened," Zack said regretting he said anything.

"Maybe next time you won't be so much in a hurry to say anything," I said to Zack.

We unloaded the two deer and started to skin them, and by the time we finished, then cleaned up, it was time for supper.

At the dinner table, I decided to come clean about the gold and said, "Ma, do you know what gold is?"

"Yes, your father told me."

"What did he say to you?"

"Gold is the yellow necklace you have on it is very valuable."

"Yes, you're right, and do you know what it looks like before it looks like this?" I pointed to my locket.

"Your father said it is a stone found in the ground." "Why do you ask these questions?" Ma asked.

"You asked me about gold also," said Zack.

"Gold can be found on the ground or in rocks called quartz." "Other places where you might find gold are in rivers, streams, and riverbanks." "I have found a lot of gold and have melted it down to form what is called an ingot."

"Where are these ingots you have?"

"I have them hid for now if word gets out that I have found gold people will kill if they have to, to get it, and they will not care if they destroy everything while getting it." "Many whites will come here, and it will never be the same again."

"Yes, I think you are right." "Your father said men go crazy when they find gold," Ma said.

"You should also know that gold is much more valuable than all the furs that Pa could get." Ma nodded in understanding. "I think I have found a way to have this gold and trade it without anyone knowing where it came from, but I want to talk it over with Pa first."

"Are you still going to find this gold and make ingots?"

"Yes, as much as I can." "It has been too hard to hide it without you knowing." "Tomorrow, I will show you and Zack where I keep it."

Ma nodded with a concerned look on her face. The subject of gold changed, and I listened to Ma and Zack talk as I cleaned my and Zack's rifles.

The next day after chores, I got Ma and Zack and took them out to the Cabin. I dug up the four holes and showed them the gold. They couldn't believe I had that much gold. I said, "I have shown you the gold now forget I have it." "As long as I am alive do not open one of these holes to look at the gold, I'll be the only one who will open it, that way there is less chance of finding out I have it."

They both agreed, and Ma went back to the cabin while Zack and I worked on my cabin.

Knowing that Zack didn't care to square off the logs, I decided to do that, and I let Zack get the rocks. I went down to the stream with him and showed him what to look for to find the nuggets. I stayed with Zack for the first load of stones, and as we worked, we found more nuggets. Then I told him to put them in his possibles bag until we stored them in the ground. I worked making vertical beams for the next three days and had enough for one side of the cabin. Before I could take the beams and put them on the roof, I had to smelt the gold because all the holes were full. On Zack's last load, I said, "Zack, we need to get a lot of firewood; I'm going to melt the gold and pour it into the mold." As Zack excitedly started gathering wood, I went and got Pa's crucible and a bucket for water. When we had enough firewood, I started the smelting, and it took about three hours to smelt all the gold. By the time we finished, it was getting late, and we put everything away and went inside the cabin for the night.

In the next ten days, I had all the vertical beams up. It took longer because the chores took longer.

Zack and I had to bring in feed for the horses this winter, and that took some time. I started making the cross braces for the cabin when Zack said, "James, there isn't any more room for the gold, and the water is mighty cold."

"This will be the last day we will look for gold; I think it will snow soon." He agreed, and I continued to make cross braces for the rest of the day.

The next day Zack and I climbed up on the rafters and installed the cross braces. It was a four-day job because I had to peg each crosspiece. "What am I going to do now?" asked Zack.

"First, let's melt the rest of the gold and put it in the mold."

After about three hours, it was all melted. After I put the gold ingots away, I cut cedar logs about one foot long, and Zack split them into shingles. We didn't get a lot of shingles the first day, and as we walked back to the cabin to put away the tools and clean up. I said to Zack, "I think tomorrow we should bring in feed for the horses a half-day and work making shingles the other half from now on." He agreed, and for the next few days, we did just that until the snow started coming down. Even though it had started to snow, it wasn't so bad that we couldn't bring in more feed for the horses and do a few shingles. But by the following month, it was snowing heavily, and the feed gathering and shingle making came to an end for this season.

It had snowed heavily that night, and the next morning I had an excellent idea. I hooked up the sled to one of the horses and called Ma and Zack to come outside, which they did. "Get on the sled Zack," I said. He smiled and hopped on, and I climbed up on the horse. I turned around and told Zack, "Hold on tight." Off I went with Zack holding on for dear life and laughing as we went.

When we got back, I told Ma, "It's your turn Ma." She refused at first, but with a little coaxing and dragging by Zack Ma got on the sled. "Hold on, Ma," I said, and off we went. I could hear Ma screaming and laughing as I pulled her around. When we got back, Zack got on the horse, and he pulled me around. Ma just shook her head and went back to the cabin. We did this for about an hour taking turns, and then the horse got too tired, and we were getting mighty cold, so we took the horse back, wiped her down, and went inside the cabin.

This winter happened to be a very severe winter regarding snow and cold. We all worried about Pa and wondered how he was making out under these conditions, but he was wise to these mountains. Knowing this eased our concerns. We hauled wood and water into the cabin with the sled. It was a good thing we brought in extra feed for the horses, or there might have been a significant problem feeding them. We had enough food, but I thought that I would have to go out and find more game at the end of January or sometime in February. We entertained ourselves with games, then Ma and Zack wanted me to read, but I said the only book on that shelf I would read is the bible, so that's what I did.

"Trappings are mighty pitiful Nate," said Othello.

"Yes, maybe we should find another area," replied Nate.

"I think that is a good idea," said Othello.

"Then tomorrow we will head north," stated Nate.

Othello nodded his head in agreement and got closer to the fire. "You know we will be very close to the Blackfoot country or even in it," he said.

"Yes, but we have no choice if there is beaver it will be up there. Most of the Blackfeet will be wintering anyway. We will be cautious and leave early for the south before they start stirring," Nate said.

"Grandpa, your daddy, wasn't a Shoshone, so how did you know what was being said and did with him and Othello?"

"It is because my mother was Shoshone and the fact that my father lived with the Shoshones for so long he told all of us what happen and again I had to guess a lot knowing how my Pa would act and talk."

"With the price for beaver down and the pickings for the beaver being so weak, I don't think it would be worth trapping anymore, Nate," Othello stated.

"I believe you are right." "What are you going to do without trapping?" asked Nate.

"I hear Jim Bridger is going to open a trading post." "I thought I would go to the west coast and get me some land for cattle and open me a trading post too." "Then again, I could go back east and do some logging, but I am getting a little old for that," Othello said. "What about you, Nate?"

"I haven't decided yet I'll have to talk it over with my family." "One thing is for sure I won't be living back east." "According to my son James and I think he is right, Blue Flower, along with Zack, won't be treated right," Nate said.

"That leaves out logging for me; I won't put Little Girl through any bigotry from those people back there."

"I must go to St. Louis to get a good price for the furs." "I've already talked to my family about it," Nate said.

"When are you going?" asked Othello.

"Soon after I get back and rest a little, then we will go."

"Little Girl is with child, it will be too early for me to go then even though I would like to," replied Othello.

"We better turn in if we are moving out tomorrow," said Nate.

Every other day, I would go down to the cabin site to shovel out the snow that was in it, if any. Ma and Zack would look for other things to eat besides meat to give us some variety with our food. I had started the fireplace to see how it drew, and it worked perfectly. I also made a list on a piece of buckskin of the things I would like to get in St. Louis. Ma and Zack came back with little to show, and I thought I would buy some seeds for a garden for next year. "How are we doing with meat, Ma?" I asked.

"In about three weeks, I may have to send you out to find some meat."

I nodded; I wanted to do something different anyway.

"Can I go too?" Zack asked.

"I need you here, Zack," Ma said.

His disappointment was evident, but he didn't complain. "I'll go hunting with you when Pa comes back and before we go to St. Louis," I told Zack.

He nodded, but he was still disappointed that he wasn't going this time.

About three weeks later, I got everything ready for the hunt. We were already into February, and Ma told me we only had enough meat to last another ten days. I took a packhorse with me to carry what I shot. The best bet would be to find deer; they would be down low this time of year, so I headed west. The snow was deep in areas, and going was slow. I did find some tracks from time to time, but they were old, so I kept on going. After the next day of tracking, I wasn't so high in the mountains and was expecting to find traces of deer. It was by noon I had seen some fresh tracks. They were heading west, dropping into a small, protected valley. The valley floor rose and then had a sharp broad drop, and it was here I found the deer.

I got off my horse and aimed at the biggest deer in the herd. I squeezed the trigger and fired. The buck fell but so did another one which confused me, I am a good shot with the rifle but not that good. I reloaded very quickly and watched the two deer lying on the ground. Now, I'm not stupid. I know that one deer went down because of me, but someone else must have shot the other one. I scanned the area around where the deer was. I figured the second deer had to be shot by a bow because I didn't hear a rifle shot. Sure enough, I saw movement in some nearby brush and trees.

I figured the person was from some tribe, most likely Shoshone. He must know I am here someplace, so I decided to shout out in Shoshone, "I am Soaring Eagle With Many Coups, come out, I mean you no harm." No answer. Someone who was Shoshone or Crow would come out in the open. I next tried Ute, "I am Soaring Eagle With Many Coups come out, I mean you no harm." Still no answer, my heart started pounding. He may be Blackfoot, but why wasn't he attacking me? Maybe there is more than one. I decided to try to provoke him to fight me, and I said in Blackfoot, "Are the Blackfoot dogs like women who have to hide in fear of a boy who is only twelve seasons long." I readied myself for the attack, but nothing happened. I was becoming confused, and for some reason, I said in Mandan, "I am friends with the Mandan, come out." There was a movement in the trees and brush, then out pops an old man. I couldn't believe my eyes; it was Sometimes Comes, the Mandan who taught me how to speak Mandan.

I stood up and yelled in English, "Sometimes Comes, what are you doing here?"

He looked confused that I called him by name. From a distance I was from him, he didn't know who I was. "It is James York, your old friend from St. Louis."

He remembered me then, and he said as he waved me down, "Come, little one."

I grabbed my horses and went running down the hill. I dropped the reins and grabbed Sometimes Comes around the chest and gave him a big bear hug lifting him off the ground.

He looked me up and down and said, "You have grown and are very strong now."

"What are you doing here Sometimes Comes; this is a long way from your people or St. Louis?"

"Ever since you left the village of St. Louis, I do not get treated very well, and my people treat me like I am a fool."

"You're not a fool; you are a wise man." "What of Red Horse he would not treat you this way?"

"You are right, but Red Horse is an old man and cannot control the young warriors anymore."

"And you, I heard you left St. Louis with your uncle." "What are you doing here?"

"My uncle and his family were killed by the Blackfeet."

He shook his head and said, "The Blackfeet are violent people and are very bad."

"Come, let's clean our deer, and then we will talk some more." "Do you have a pack horse?"

"No."

"Then, you will put your deer on my horse, and we will go to my father's lodge."

"Your father's lodge, I thought you had no father?"

"I do have a father." "He is trapping now, but my mother, Blue Flower, and my brother Zack are there, and they will welcome you."

"You have a father, mother, and a brother?" "I am confused your mother has died, and you had no brothers."

I laughed and said, "My mother is a Shoshone woman my father married, and they had another son."

"Shoshone, the Mandan and Shoshone do not get along together."

I laughed even harder and said, "I am a Shoshone warrior of high standing; my name is Soaring Eagle With Many Coups."

He was in total shock and with a loss of words. When he composed himself, he said, "Are you this Shoshone warrior I have heard about that killed many Blackfeet."

"I have many Blackfeet scalps and will have much more. You are a friend of mine, Mandan, or no Mandan; you will be welcome in my father's lodge," I said with all sincerity.

He put his head down and said, "There is much we need to talk about, you have changed, but I will go with you because I have nowhere else to go."

I smiled and nodded my head, and we started to clean our deer. Sometimes, Comes started a fire and roasted his deer's heart and liver as I finished cleaning my deer. I loaded the two deer on the packhorse. After I finished, he offered me some liver to eat. I do not fancy liver, but out of politeness, I ate it and said, "We better leave while it is still light."

"There is a place I know that will protect us from the snow. If we leave now, we will be there before nightfall."

We arrived before dark, just as I said. There was plenty of wood because I figured that I would be using this area on the way back, so I stockpiled wood to dry out. Under the trees, there was enough grass and shelter for the horses. We both had plenty of food, and as I unloaded the horses, Sometimes Comes started a fire. As we ate, I told Sometimes Comes the whole story of how my uncle and his family came and forced me to go with him. I also told him of their deaths at the hands of the Blackfeet, my adoption by Red Elk, and Turtle Woman. I informed him about being a warrior, my marriage to Morning Star, and finally finding my father.

He shook his head and said, "You have been through a lot, but a lot of good has come from it."

I suppose he was correct, but some things I wish I had never experienced. "When was the last time you saw Mr. McConnell?" I asked.

"It has been little more than a season ago." "Mr. McConnell seems to be doing alright, but he has a hard time now when someone doesn't speak his language." "He did say he wished he had never let you go with your uncle," Sometimes Comes said.

I nodded my head and asked, "And what of Sarah, his daughter?"

"From the little I saw of her, she is growing into a beautiful girl." "Someday, she will make some man happy to have her."

"She was like a sister to me." "I miss them both," I said more to myself than to Sometimes Comes. We reminisced, and then it got late, and we slept.

We reached the small lake at the bottom of the hill from the cabin late in the afternoon. Zack was the first to see me and Sometimes Comes, and he ran into the cabin to get Ma. She came out of the cabin with a rifle in hand, which was noticed by Sometimes Comes and me. "You don't have to have that rifle, Ma, he is a friend of mine from St. Louis," I said a little embarrassed.

"When I am without you and your father, and I see a stranger coming, I always grab my rifle, just in case," she explained. She put the rifle down and continued, "Who is this one, James?"

"His name is Sometimes Comes." "He speaks English, but you need to know he is Mandan."

Ma grabbed her rifle again, and Zack went in and got his. "If you wish me to leave, I will leave," said Sometimes Comes with dignity.

"Wait, Ma, his people, have rejected him." "I know the Shoshone and Mandan don't get along well, but he is different." "If it weren't for him, I would have never learned Mandan, and it was knowing Mandan that saved my life."

Ma lowered her rifle then Zack lowered his. My heart stopped beating so hard.

"Have you ever killed a Shoshone?" she asked Sometimes Comes.

"I've never seen a Shoshone, and I don't think any Mandan I know saw a Shoshone," answered Sometimes Comes.

"If this is true, Ma, then why do the Shoshone have a problem with the Mandan?" I asked.

"Because they are related to the Dakota, and the Dakota has killed Shoshone."

"What your mother said is true, the Mandan and Dakota are related," Sometimes Comes admitted. "But, we do not follow the Dakota." "They are violent people who are sometimes friendly with the Blackfeet, who is worse."

Ma stared at him for a few seconds then said, "Let's get those deer down and skinned."

We finished skinning the deer, and Ma cooked us something to eat. "I'm guessing you will be staying here until the snow melts," Ma said.

"If you will allow me, I wish to stay."

Ma nodded then said, "Don't you try anything, or your life will end." When it was time to sleep; Sometimes Comes slept by the fire, Ma gave him a blanket, and she carried a knife to bed with her.

The next morning when Ma got up and Sometimes Comes wasn't in the cabin, she thought just as well I didn't trust him anyway. Zack was getting up when there was a bang at the door, which made me spring up. I grabbed my pistol and went over to the door. I opened it slowly and saw that it was Sometimes Comes with an arm full of wood. "You were low on wood, and I brought you some."

Ma's mouth was wide open in surprise, and he said, "I have something else for you." He went outside and brought in some greens and things to eat.

"Where did you find these things, I look every day and find nothing?" Ma asked, amazed.

"Oh, I am old and not much good for anything anymore, but ever since I was a child, I was always good at finding things to eat, even in the middle of winter."

As the days went on, Ma was getting more and more to like Sometimes Comes, especially his stories, which also held Zack spellbound. I had heard these stories many times, and they seemed to get more exciting every time he told them.

The snow was starting to melt, and you could already see some grass coming up. I expected Pa to come anytime, now, and at the dinner table, I asked Ma, "Ma, do you think if all three of us went hunting tomorrow, you would be alright?" I asked.

"How long will all you be gone?"

"If we leave tomorrow morning by early sundown, I would think."

"The streams will be high and fast you be careful, and I will be just fine alone."

"Sometimes Comes, do you know how to use a rifle?" I asked.

He nodded, and I grabbed one of my other rifles and gave it to him. I also went through my things and found an extra powder horn and shot bag and gave them to him. "They are yours to keep," I said.

"This gift is too great I have nothing in return to give you."

"You have given me the language of the Mandan."

"But you have given me a place to lodge that repaid that," He replied.

"That was not James, who gave you a place to lodge." "It was me, and that was for the deer you brought and the deer you will bring back tomorrow," said my mother.

He looked at his rifle and smiled. He shook head in agreement and with joy.

We left early the next morning after chores, and we went just about the same way as Zack and I went last summer. We took two pack horses to carry what we shot. As we passed my cabin site, I looked at the stream, and it was full up to its spring banks. No looking for gold, I thought till later in the summer. I think I will work on my cabin if Pa doesn't show. I must make lath sheeting for the roof, and that is going to take some time. It was a sunny day; the air was fresh and crisp. I figured it would warm up in the afternoon, and I would be able to strip down to my loincloth.

My Pa told the rest of my family and me about what I am about to say to you. Of course, I am going to have to do some guessing.

"Either this is the worst luck a trapper ever had, or it is the end of beaver trapping," said Othello.

"I think it is a little of both." "It is certainly the beginning of the end for beaver trapping." "I imagine there will still be rendezvous for a few years," said Nate.

"I have to tell you, either way; this is my last year." "We don't even have enough to take back east," said Othello.

"I promised my wife and boys that I would go to St. Louis." "James has a lot of furs I could sell, so that will help."

"Why don't I take yours, and you can give me a list of things you want me to bring back." "That way, you wouldn't have to make the trip, and you and your wife could enjoy the little one when he or she comes," said Nate.

"That sounds good, Nate." "The list isn't long lead, power, and coffee." "If you have enough, maybe something for Little Girl, you know some foofaraw."

"I understand; Othello, I will see what I can do." "I was planning to go to New York to see my father and mother." "They are getting old, and I don't know how much longer they will be alive but as miserable as this season is that is out," said Nate.

"When you get back, if I am not here, the things you buy for me are yours," said Othello.

"Hopefully, you will be here I'm not going to be gone that long," replied Nate

We headed east and dropped down into a valley that was much lower than where the cabin was. There were only patches of snow on the ground and plenty of green grass. Zack said, "I recognize this valley, Pa, and I came this way last time I hunted with him." We soon picked up tracks and found what we were looking for grazing about three hundred yards away. The deer had not seen us because we were downwind, but, in these valleys, the wind sometimes suddenly shifts directions, so we dared not get any closer with the horses than we were. We got off our horses and tied them up. We worked our way to within one hundred and fifty yards from the deer. We all choose what deer we were going to shoot. There were three large booms, and three deer went down.

After we cleaned and loaded the three deer Zack and I talked in Shoshone, "What is to become of Sometimes Comes?" "It is spring, and he is supposed to go," said Zack.

"Maybe he could come with us to St. Louis," I said.

"Maybe," Zack said.

"He would make a good father for Grey Wolf and a good husband for his mother," I said.

Zack started laughing and said, "It would be interesting to see how the Shoshone reacts to a Mandan." I had to smile at that thought also.

We rode on about two hours after sundown; we made it back to the cabin. After we ate, we skinned and prepared the three deer so that we could jerk the meat, then afterward; we cleaned up. As Zack and I were getting ready to go to bed, Sometimes Comes said, "Why do you two think I would not be welcome in a Shoshone village?" Zack's and my mouth fell open in shock. How did he know what we said?

"What did you both think we were doing when the two of you were away from the cabin?" "Sometimes Comes wanted to learn Shoshone, and I think I taught him well," Ma said with a smile on her face.

"We didn't mean any disrespect," I said while Zack agreed with me.

"I know, you did not show disrespect; you were just concerned about me," he said with a smile on his face.

The next day after chores, I went and worked on my cabin. I cut several lodgepole pines and split them in half. I used the two-handed plane to smooth the split side, then turned it over and used a jig to plane down the other side. Sometimes Comes and Zack cut down several cedar trees, cut the logs to length, and split them into shingles. As they were doing this, I took a break and went to talk to Ma.

"When Pa comes home, I don't think Sometimes Comes should be here," I said.

"Why?" said Ma, confused.

"Because of the gold, I don't think he should know about it."

"Where shall we send him?"

"I think I should take him to the Shoshone village; he can stay with Grey Wolf and his mother."

"Suppose the Shoshones don't want him there."

"They will listen to me, and I think Sometimes Comes will be happy there."

"When will you go?" Ma asked.

"I think I'll go tomorrow." "I will talk to Sometimes Comes at supper tonight," I replied.

Ma nodded approval, and I went back to work on the cabin.

"I have a brother called Grey Wolf in a Shoshone village," I said to Sometimes Comes as we ate.

"I know this you told me when we first met," replied Sometimes Comes.

"Grey Wolf's father died, and now he is alone with his mother, Blue Lizard. She never remarried I think you would be good for Grey Wolf and Blue Lizard."

"Oh, you do, but I am Mandan, and they are Shoshone."

"They will accept you, and once they get to know you, they will consider you one of their own."

"So, when are you going to take me to this village?"

"I was thinking about tomorrow morning after chores."

He nodded in agreement, and Zack said, "If you want to get an early start, I will do all the chores."

"That will be good; then, we will leave just before first light."

We had traveled far by the time the sun came up, and we gave the horses rest at the noon break. Sometimes Come asked, "Why suddenly you wish me to leave?"

"I told you about Grey Wolf."

"Yet, there is more."

"Alright, yes, there is more."

"Your people rejected you, the people in St. Louis mistreated you, and you say it is worse now after I left." "My father will be home soon, and then we will go to St. Louis." "In St. Louis, it will be hard for my mother and brother; it would be worse for you, they know you."

He nodded his head with understanding. I didn't tell him the whole truth but what I said was true.

"The Shoshones, once they know you, they will accept you, and then they will be like your family."

We got on our horses and rode on. On the third day, we found my village. Many from the village came and greeted us, including Grey Wolf and Morning Star. "This is Sometimes Comes he is a friend of mine and is responsible for saving my life many years ago," I told everybody in Shoshone.

"I wish to talk to your father first Morning Star, then to you, then you and your mother, Grey Wolf.

"What is it you want to talk about?" asked Spotted Buffalo.

"What I have to say is best said in private," I replied.

"We will go to my lodge and talk."

I sat to his right, and Sometimes Comes sat next to me. He sent everyone else out of the lodge while we talked. "As I said, this is Sometimes Comes; he is a good man, but he is Mandan." I paused for a few seconds to let it sink in.

Spotted Buffalo stared at Sometimes Comes, and it wasn't the friendliest look I had ever seen. "I know the Mandan and Shoshone do not get along; well, but hear me out first."

He looked at me and said, "Speak."

"He is no longer accepted by the Mandan because he is a contrary man at times, and this they don't accept." "As you know, the Mandan are near the whites, and he has visited them and tried to live with them, but he got mistreated there also."

"I know this is true because when I was with the whites, I saw this, and he had told me that when I left, it got worse." "He has been living with my family and me all winter." "At first, my mother, because of how the Shoshone feel about the Mandan did not want him with us." "But after a while, when she saw that he was a good man, she welcomed him." "It is my desire and his that he lives among the Shoshone."

When I finished, everyone was silent for a short time. I knew Spotted Buffalo was struggling with the thought of a Mandan living in a Shoshone village. "The Dakota are friends with our enemies, the Blackfeet." "The Mandan are related to the Dakota who would he fight for if we go to battle?" he asked me.

Before I could answer, Sometimes Comes said in Shoshone, "I am no longer part of the Mandan, but even if I were the Mandan have never gone to battle with the Shoshone not that I know of."

"If I am with the Shoshone, then I am Shoshone and will fight with them also die with them if I have to."

Spotted Buffalo was first shocked that he knew the language and then at what he said. "This is something I cannot decide alone." "I must call the elders together, and you two will speak, then we will decide." "You, Sometimes Comes, stay in my lodge until we are ready."

Sometimes Comes nodded in agreement and then Spotted Buffalo turned to me and said with a smile, "I think my daughter wishes to be with you." Spotted Buffalo got up as I did, and we left the lodge; he to gather the elders, and I went to be with Morning Star.

"What is it you wish to talk about?" asked Grey Wolf.

"I will speak to you and your mother later."

"Where is your family?" asked Morning Star.

"My father has not come back from trapping beaver, and when he does, we are going to the white man's village, St. Louis." "Then, we will come here, and I will bring both of you something."

"Have you been working on our lodge?"

"One more year, and it will be ready."

"Another year?"

"Yes, it is a large lodge, and I think you will like it." "It will keep you warmer in the winter."

"How long will you be here?" asked Grey Wolf and Morning Star wanted to know.

"I will head back tomorrow sometime."

"How are my horses?" I asked Grey Wolf.

"You have five more horses."

"Very good." "I'm very pleased."

"The elders meet Soaring Eagle With Many Coups," said Spotted Buffalo.

"Come, I wish to spend as much time as I can with you," I said to Morning Star.

"Spotted Buffalo, why have you gathered us?" asked Long Knife.

Spotted Buffalo walked over to Sometimes Comes and said, "This is Sometimes Comes, and he wishes to live among us." "Usually, this would not require the permission of the elders; the Shoshone would welcome him." "However, he was once Mandan, and as you know, the Mandan is an enemy of the Shoshone." "Soaring Eagle With Many Coups will tell us why he has brought him to us."

I got up and started talking, "I know the Mandan are an enemy of the Shoshone because they are related to the Dakota, my mother has told me this." "I also know the Mandan have never attacked the Shoshone, and I would guess that most in this village have never seen a Mandan before." "You have noticed that Spotted Buffalo said he was a Mandan." "The Mandan have rejected him and have driven him from their village because he is a contrary man." "I know the Shoshone are wise people, and they, as a people, honor a contrary man." "I have known Sometimes Comes when I lived with the whites." "Sometimes Comes is my friend, and it is he who taught me how to speak the Mandan language." "Knowing how to speak Mandan is what kept me alive, Sometimes Comes saved my life." "Sometimes Comes wants to live among the Shoshone." "Sometimes Comes wishes this so much he has learned our language." "He is no threat to the Shoshone; in fact, Sometimes Comes has said that if he is with the Shoshone, he is Shoshone and will fight and even die for the Shoshone," after saying this, I sat down.

Long Knife said to Sometimes Comes, "Is this true what has gotten said about you?"

"Yes, and I would think you would know that Soaring Eagle With Many Coups would never lie."

"If you lived with the whites before, why don't you live with them now?"

"The whites who live in the villages from the rising sun do not like people with my skin color and look; they treated me worse than a dog."

"I have known many whites, and they do not act this way to me," said Tall As The Sky.

I got up and said, "You have seen the white trappers and mountain men, the ones back in the white villages are just as Sometimes Comes says." "I had seen Sometimes Comes get mistreated when I lived among them, and he stated that it got worse when I left."

I sat back down, and the elders talked among themselves. Finally, Long Knife said, "We know you do not lie Soaring Eagle With Many Coups." "If you say he is a good man, then we will welcome him here among the Shoshone; this is what the elders have decided."

The meeting broke up, and Spotted Buffalo came over to me and said, "You and your friend will stay with me tonight."

"I will stay with you because you are my father now that I am married to Morning Star."

"I have other plans for Sometimes Comes, and I will let you know later about him." I went over to Sometimes Comes who was talking with others in the village and asked, "Will you be alright alone here for a while, I wish to speak to someone privately?"

He nodded yes, and I went with Grey Wolf and Morning Star to Grey Wolf's Lodge. On the way, suddenly, I was attacked by a young Shoshone warrior who jumped into my arms, it was Comes Running.

"Look at how much you have grown and so strong," I said to him. He nodded in agreement with a big smile on his face, and I continued, "I am only going to be here one day, but before I leave, I will come and see you."

He nodded and ran off, and we continued to Grey Wolf's lodge. Blue Lizard was home, so Morning Star and I were welcomed into her lodge. Grey Wolf took the place as head of the family, and I sat to the left of him while Morning Star sat with Blue Lizard. "I have something to say, and I wish you both to hear me out."

"Speak your mind, my brother."

"You Grey Wolf have heard all I have said about Sometimes Comes, that he is a very good man." Grey Wolf nodded, and I continued, "There are times you go off hunting or whatever you are doing for days, and you leave your mother alone." "I feel, and I may be wrong, that because you take care of your mother, which is good, you do not get serious with a woman."

"What he says is true, Grey Wolf," said his mother.

"I am still young," he said, annoyed that I brought it up.

"Do not be angry; I say this only out of love for you." "Sometimes Comes needs a place to live; he would make a good husband for your mother."

There was a surprised look on both Grey Wolf and his mother. Then I added, "If not a husband, maybe an uncle." "Either way, he would be a help for both of you, and you both would be a help to him."

Grey Wolf looked at his mother for some advice, but she was letting him make the decision. "I will welcome him in my lodge, and we will see how he is." "My mother must decide if she wants to marry him or not."

I smiled and said, "He will be very pleased as I am; I will go tell him."

Morning Star and I left, and I told Sometimes Comes what I had arranged. I brought him to Grey Wolf's lodge and was invited in by Grey Wolf and Blue Lizard.

Morning Star and I spent the rest of the time together. We talked about the cabin, and we became affectionate with each other.

"What do you wish me to bring back to you when I come next?" I asked.

"I will be happy with anything you bring."

I smiled, and we headed back to her lodge. When we walked into the village Grey Wolf, Morning Star's brothers, and another young warrior were playing a game to test each other's strength. Morning Star coaxed me into taking part. It was Morning Star's eldest brother and me, and Grey Wolf and Morning Star's younger brother were to go against each other. I watched Grey Wolf win with little trouble, and then it was my turn. I got told to hold a thick five-foot-long pole at one end, and Running Deer held the stick at the other end. The object of the game was to take the stick out of your opponent's hands. Or knock him off balance and onto the ground. For balance and strength, I put my right foot forward and my right hand in front of the left, and then the game began. The struggle went on for what seemed like forever. Running Deer, out of frustration of not being able to pull the pole out of my hands, or knock me down, put his whole body into it. With all my strength, I lifted him off the ground, and he lost control and fell to his side.

He was good about it and laughed. Then it was Grey Wolf's and my turn. Again, it was a mighty struggle. Many were cheering for both of us. I could see Grey Wolf getting frustrated, just like Running Deer, and he looked angry. I thought that I didn't want any hard feelings between us, so as we struggled, I started to cross my feet, and Grey Wolf caught on right away. He moved the pole so that I would trip and down I went. Grey Wolf came over and helped me up and said with a smile, "I wonder, brother, if I won by skill or you let me win to keep the peace."

"Fortunately, you will not have to find out, you wore me out, and I lost, and I am tired." Happily, he accepted what I had to say.

As Morning Star and I went to her lodge, she asked me, "Did you let him win?"

"What do you think?" "We are still brothers who love each other we both won." We talked as we ate, and afterward, I told Spotted Buffalo I was going to Comes Running's lodge and let him know I would be leaving early in the morning.

As I talked to Comes Running, I told him about my leaving. He became sad, and I told him I would bring him back something sweet when I come back. The next morning, after all the goodbyes, I headed back to the cabin, which would take me about three days to reach.

I pushed my horse, and about noontime on the third day, I rode up to the cabin. Everyone was eating lunch, so they all came out to greet me. Pa had come home the morning before, and he still looked mighty tired.

I guess I looked a little beat myself. I got off my horse, and Zack took responsibility for taking care of the horse.

"How did it go, son, your Ma told me about the Mandan?" Pa asked.

"It went well I'm sure Zack will want to hear about it, so I will go into detail later." "How did the trapping go with you, Pa?"

He put his head down and said in a sad voice, "Not well, we will need to talk about it." I looked at Ma, who was standing behind him. She shook her head, and I took it to mean they hadn't mentioned the gold.

I washed up and joined my family at the dinner table while they finished eating their meal. Ma had given me a plate full of stew, and I told the story of what happened in the village. "I told Morning Star, Grey Wolf, and Comes Running I would bring them something back when we got back from St. Louis."

Pa put his head down and said in a sad voice, "I wish you hadn't done that." "Like I told you, the trapping wasn't good this year." "I got less than half the number of furs this year as I did last year, and the price is way down." "It looks like this is the last year of trapping at least for Othello and me." "I might have to use some of your furs to get the things we need to make our life a little easier here."

I smiled and started giggling, as did Zack and Ma. Pa was confused and looked at us like we were all crazy and said, "Do you all know the seriousness of what I just said?"

We started laughing then, and I said, "Pa beaver furs aren't the only thing that is of value in these mountains."

"Like what?" he said, a little annoyed.

"Horses for one, and well, you just stay here I will bring back something that will cheer you up."

I got a shovel, went out to the cabin site, and dug up one of the gold's holes. We took off our shirts and filled them with as much gold as we could carry, and I also brought the mold. I hid the rest of the gold, and we went back to the cabin, struggling to carry our load.

I kicked at the door and said, "The table needs to get cleared off." Zack and I dumped what gold we had on the table, and Pa's eyes popped out at the sight. He picked up one of the ingots, pressed a knife into it, and left a mark.

"Where did you find this?"

"The river is full of gold; you just have to look a little," I said.

He looked at me, confused, and said, "This is Spanish Gold it has writing on it."

"Yes, Pa, it says His Royal Majesty Philip the Third of Spain." "He was the King of Spain around sixteen hundred," I explained. I then pulled out the mold and said, "I put that inscription on the gold to fool people. I found many gold nuggets in the stream and on the shore, and I smelted them in my kiln."

He looked at all the gold and said, more to himself than to us, "That's a lot of gold."

Zack and I started laughing, and Zack said, "That's only a little of it. We have a lot more still buried."

"Well, it is your gold James, you found it and made these ingots," Pa said.

"No, Pa, it's our gold; it belongs to the whole family," I said.

"That's mighty generous of you." "Again, why did you put that Spanish writing on the gold?" Pa asked.

"Because people go crazy when there is gold." "They will kill to get it, and they will come in the hundreds into these mountains looking for it, which will cause problems with all the tribes, let alone us." "They won't care if we are living here or not." "There will be people up and down the stream fouling the water and the land."

Pa nodded in agreement, then I added, "I thought that you might know someplace south of here that is special." "We can act like we came from the south and found the gold down there." "People will think the Spanish hid the gold down there intending to come back to get it."

"That just might work, at least for a while." "There is a place where someone could look for the rest of the miner's life, a great canyon." "And who knows, maybe they will find gold there," Pa said with a smile.

"Let's go get the rest of the gold and bring it back to the cabin."

"I will find a place on the floor and stack the gold, so we can put a blanket over it in case we have guests," Ma said.

Pa nodded with a smile, and we all went out to where I hid the gold.

It took almost an hour for the three of us to bring all the gold into the cabin. We put it on the table, and Ma stacked it on the floor. On the last trip out to my cabin site, we backfilled the holes to make it look like there was nothing hidden. When we all came back into the cabin and looked at the gold, I couldn't believe the amount we had.

Pa said, "How are we going to transport the gold to St. Louis." "We will need a lot of horses; the gold is very heavy."

"I thought about that, Pa, and I thought we wouldn't need that many horses." "We could make some travois, and we could get away with hauling the gold with three horses."

"It will be slow going, and those horses will still be mighty tired hauling the gold."

"As far as the horses, we can rotate the horses, and it will be a little easier for them," I said. "I guess we have about a million dollars' worth of gold here, Pa," I said.

"I think it is more than that, James, but I just don't know for sure," said Pa.

"Is that a lot Pa?" asked Zack.

"That is more than all of us would usually see in a lifetime," Pa replied.

"We must make several buckskin bags for all the gold and something to throw over those bags to disguise them."

"I will make the bags, you make the travois to carry them," Ma said.

# 17

# THE JOURNEY EAST

Ma made the buckskin sacks while Pa, Zack, and I made three travoises, not like the Shoshone kind. These were sturdier and well put together for the long distance we had to travel. Pa came up with a route that would take us to a point just before we came to Missouri, then we would turn south and then east to St. Louis, so it would look like we came from the south.

We rested the horses for about ten days, and then early in the morning on the eleventh day, we headed out before sunup. About an hour on the trail, the sun came up to a cloudless day with a slight breeze. We couldn't have had better conditions. The plan was to move the horses slowly until we got out of the Shining Mountains. Our primary concern was the Blackfeet, Cheyenne, and the Lakota, all who might attack us. The horses carrying the gold were making the best of it, but I could see it was hard for them, especially in the mountains. When we reached the plains, we rested the horses for two days before heading out again. We replaced the original three horses with three horses that were carrying the least weight when we first left the cabin. Going was a little easier for the horses, but we still traded them out every four days. On the eighth day, we rested the horses for two days.

A day after the first two-day rest Pa spotted a lot of horse tracks. I got off my horse to look, and Pa said, "They look fresh."

I checked the tracks and the grass that was trampled and said, "They are about a day-old heading south." I looked again and said, "I figure about ten horses, and they were not in a hurry." I looked up and checked the sky, and it looked like it was clouding up. I then looked at our back-trail and said, "I think we should just keep going as we have." "It looks like rain might be coming, which will help cover our tracks." "Also, it will seem like there is a lot of us, maybe a village moving." "With only ten warriors, they may not want to take the risk of attacking us because they think we are too many, even if they do see the tracks."

Pa said, "I think you are right." "We will keep on moving and keep a cold camp at night."

We traveled three more days, and when it was time to switch horses, I told Pa, "I'm going to backtrack for a while just in case someone is following us."

It had not rained yet, but the clouds were getting thicker, and I expected rain soon. If we did not have the gold, I would have taken the chance and not gone back to check, but we were very near where my uncle and his family died, and I didn't want to take any chances, and I told Pa and Ma that. "I will be back about sundown if I don't run into any trouble." Pa wasn't happy about my going, but he knew we had to make sure someone wasn't following us, so he didn't try to stop me.

I had backtracked about fifteen miles when I came to a small grassy hill. I got off my horse and staked her. I grabbed all my weapons and climbed to the top of the hill. I scanned the landscape around and saw nothing of interest, so I lay down and waited. I could see at least another five or ten miles beyond where I was because I had a clear field of view. I had planned to stay there until late afternoon then head back. It would give my horse some rest that she needed. While sitting there watching I thought it would be better if we crossed the river at the first chance we got, it would be safer on that side than the side we were on. I saw some lightning in the southwest, so I knew the rain was coming. I decided to head back; there was nothing else in sight.

I rejoined my family just before sundown and said to them, "I saw nothing, but I feel we should cross the river as soon as we can, it will be safer on the other side." "I also saw some lightning in the southwest; the storm will be on us soon.

"We will start looking tomorrow, but I have to tell you with a storm coming we may not be able to cross," said Pa.

We traveled for several hours, and then Pa saw a spot where he thought we might ford the water. He rode across first then motioned for us to follow. The water was about two-and-a-half to three feet deep, but we made it across with no problem. We continued for another hour when the rains started to come down. I didn't like getting wet, but on the other hand, our tracks washed away, which made me feel better.

As we traveled, the rain seemed to be getting heavier, and I knew Pa was looking for shelter, but there wasn't any insight. I noticed the river had risen another three feet, so we were lucky to cross when we did. After about another hour Pa pulled up. There was lightning with the rain, and out here, it is dangerous to remain in the open. Pa spotted something, and we moved toward it. It was a rocky area with some trees and brush. As we went around the trees and some large boulders, we saw a large cave. We moved toward it. It was large enough for the horses and us with room left over. Someone else had used the cave before; there were signs of a fire and some dry wood. After we had unloaded the horses, Zack and I gathered more wood so that it would dry. By the time we got back, Ma had a fire going. Zack and I stripped out of our wet clothes. When Ma and Pa saw what we were doing, they did the same.

"We'll stay here until the rains stop," Pa said.

"After we eat, we will lay everything out to dry. It looks like everything is soaked," said Ma.

"The only good thing about this rain is that our tracks are gone, and the horses will get some more rest," I said.

"I'd like to check the condition of the horses after everything gets hung out to dry," said Pa.

After our clothing dried, both Zack and I stayed in our loincloths. We figured if we had to go back out in the rain, it would be best not to wear our clothing. I slept well that night; I liked the sound of rain and the lightning; I just didn't like being out in it. It rained until early afternoon the next day; then it was off and on. Pa thought we should wait another day, which meant Zack and I had to take the horses out for water and feed them between rainstorms.

Later that night, while we ate, Pa said, "We have made more progress than I thought we would make." "I haven't seen my parents for almost fourteen years." "If we don't have any significant delays, I would like to go see them, if you all don't mind."

"Of course, we will all go see them, isn't that right, boys?" Ma said.

We both nodded, and I hoped my father's side of the family was better than my mother's.

The next day the sky was blue, so we loaded the horses and headed out. For the next week, nothing eventful happened, except we were out of the area where the Blackfeet would typically be. We now just had to worry about the Cheyenne and the Lakota. In the following weeks, we spotted about a half dozen Cheyenne who took very keen notice of us. Pa said, "Keep your rifles ready and keep going."

They followed us for about an hour, then they disappeared. I rode up to where Ma and Pa were and said, "They are setting up an ambush."

Pa scanned the area ahead of us and said, "We'll head south."

We went about five miles, and then Pa spotted a high hill and up we went. At the top was a bowl-like depression where we could stake the horses. There was plenty of grass and even some water from the past rain. The place was like a fort; we brought all our weapons to the edge of the depression and waited. It was just about sundown when we saw the Cheyenne trailing us. They were about a thousand yards away. When they were about five hundred yards away, they got off their horses and looked around.

"Maybe we should let them know we are here, Pa," I whispered.

"I'm not looking for a fight," he answered the same way.

"They aren't going anywhere soon, Pa." "If we don't try to get them to attack, they will wait until tonight and then try to sneak up here while we can't see them." "They might even figure out we are up here and attack all sides." "I have a plan that I think might work," I said.

"What do you have in mind?"

"I will sneak out the back side of this bowl and go out yonder." "If the Cheyenne attack on one of the sides, I will pick them off one at a time." "If they wait until night, I will hit them before they hit us."

"That sounds good, son, but it should be me going out the back end and picking them off."

"You're a bigger and stronger person than me and easier to see and be hit." "I can move faster, and I am a smaller target for the Cheyenne to be able to shoot me or see me." "I know how to use a bow a lot better than you, I believe."

Before he could say another word, I grabbed my bow and ran to the back of the bowl. I knew he wanted to stop me, but he wasn't fast enough. I'd rather face his anger later than risk him getting hit. I ran over the back of the bowl. I went out to about three hundred yards and walked to my right. I had found a depression in the ground and got into it, pulling my shirt over my hair, and I waited. Sure enough, about ten minutes later, here came two Cheyenne sneaking around the hill. One slowed down almost in front of me while the other kept going. The one who was in front of me crouched down when the Cheyenne did, so I reared up and shot him between the shoulder blades with an arrow. The Cheyenne made a little noise enough for the other to hear, but I had an arrow ready. When he turned around to see what the matter was, I shot him square in the chest, and he went down. Then I heard the gunfire. I quickly ran to my right to see another one heading up the hill. I let another arrow fly, but it only wounded him, but someone finished him off I figured it was Pa. I ran up the hill with another arrow ready to shoot, but it wasn't necessary. Between Ma, Pa, and Zack, they had finished the rest of them.

Zack wanted to take the scalps of the Cheyenne, but Pa said, "No, Zack, I don't approve."

"I don't care for taking scalps either, Pa, but it might be wiser if we did." "When their people find them, they will think it was a hostile tribe that fought with them and not us."

Pa looked over to Ma, and Ma said, "Zack is a Shoshone, and what James said is wise."

"I will gather their horses and belongings," I said.

Pa helped, but he wasn't happy about the whole business. When it was all done, he turned to me and said, "What you did was very foolish and dangerous.

"Yes, Pa, it was dangerous no matter who did it," I said as a matter of fact and walked off.

As we loaded up, I knew Pa was steaming and wanted to punish me for what he thought was a lack of respect. So, I just stayed away from him, hoping he would relax as we rode off.

We rode for several hours, and in that time, I could see Pa was mad because he just kept on going without rest. Just before it was dark, he stopped and said in a surly voice, "We will make camp here."

I didn't say anything and unloaded the horses while Zack and Ma started a fire. Pa and I were staking the horses together when he jerked the rope out of my hand. I stood there and stared at him, and my anger was starting to rise in me. Without looking at me with a scowl on his face, he went to where Ma and Zack made a fire. Ma and Zack saw the whole thing and were aware of Pa's anger. What they didn't know was the anger that I had. As I slowly walked behind Pa, I said in a loud voice, "Did you want to talk about it, or do you want to fight?" "Either way, this anger you have will end now."

He turned around with rage in his face, and it reminded me of my uncle just before he nearly beat me to death. Pa charged me I was angry but had my anger under control my Pa wasn't under control. Grey Wolf taught me that if you come at someone with your anger out of control, you will lose every time. I stepped to one side and swung my foot and leg into his midsection as hard as I could, and he went flying back onto the ground. It knocked the wind out of him, but to my surprise, Pa got up quickly and came at me again. This time I knew he would be mindful of my leg, and I watched as he either tried to hit me with his fist or grab me. Again, I was too fast for him. I went under his arm and kicked him in the back of the leg, and he went down again. Again, he got up very quickly and started to come after me, but there was a big boom, and we both stopped and stared at Ma, who was furious at both of us for fighting. Pa stopped, but he was so mad that he turned around and went out into the darkness.

I went over to where Ma and Zack were as she yelled out, "Nate, you come back here and talk this out."

He didn't answer; he just kept on going. We hadn't fought that bad in quite a while, and Ma turned to me and said, "You should have shown respect for your father." "You are his son, and you said you would do as he said."

What she said made me mad because I didn't see it that way. "It is not I who showed disrespect." "I agreed I would do as he said unless it had to do with the Blackfeet or anyone who was harming a loved one." "I am Soaring Eagle With Many Coups a Shoshone warrior." "Maybe you both need to understand this." I then walked off into the night; my mother being surprised I would answer her in that way.

I found a small knoll to laid down. I could still see the campfire, but I decided I best not go back tonight in fear that I might say or do something I might regret. On the Plains, your voice carries a long way, and I could hear the conversation that was going on with Zack and my mother and later with my father when he came back.

Zack had turned to Ma and said, "I have never gone against anything you and Pa have said, but you are both wrong." "Everything that James has said has been true, and he is a warrior Ma."

About a half-hour, after my father left, he came back into the camp cooled off and said to Ma, "Where is James."

"He took off after I scolded him, and he reminded me who he was."

"James, James, come back to the campfire." I heard him, but I wasn't ready to return the morning would be soon enough.

"Nate, in size, he is a small boy, but with all he has been through, he has become a man, a Shoshone warrior." "If you think back, everything he has said is true."

"I know this; I guess I have known this deep down for a long time." "I just let my anger get the best of me."

"James, James, I know I am wrong, come back to the campfire son," he yelled, but by this time I was sound asleep.

The next morning, I got up and started loading the horses. Pa came over to me to say he was sorry. I looked at him with a scowl on my face and said, "Who am I?"

Ma looked up, and the question had gotten Zack's attention.

Pa looked confused, and Ma said, "You're Soaring Eagle With Many Coups."

"Of course, you are, and you are our son," Pa said. "Look, I'm sorry for what happened yesterday." "You can be thirty years old, and I will still worry about you." "Sometimes my temper gets the better of me when it shouldn't." "It doesn't mean I don't love you," Pa explained.

Pa stuck his hand out to shake it, and I said, "I won't shake your hand." I saw the disappointment on his face, but I continued and said, in a friendly way, "I won't shake your hand, but I will hug you." I smiled and went into his arms. That was the end of the hard feelings we had with each other for the rest of the trip.

We traveled about ten days without anything happening. I was hoping to see the Mandan, but Pa had us turn south before we ran into them. With the extra six horses giving our horses more rest, we were moving faster. The three travoises that Pa, Zack, and I made were holding up well. We had a few minor repairs here and there, but overall, they did very well. We had to go easy on the water; there wasn't as much around as we had before. But all seemed to be doing very well. Four and a half days, we traveled south, and then Pa turned west.

On the morning of the second day after we turned west, we came to a small farm owned by a man named Patrick Murphy. Pa asked him, "Is there anywhere I can water all these horses?"

He spits out the tobacco he had been chewing, and with a scheming manner about him, he said, "Might be." "You got anything of value for the information."

I swung my rifle around, which he noticed, but Pa, without a word, rode off toward the west, and we followed. Before the end of the day, we ran into other people who were a lot friendlier and pointed us to where a spring was. There was plenty of grass nearby the spring, and Pa decided to stay for the night, but he said, "I don't trust these people here, we will post a watch just in case something happens."

The next morning while we were eating, I heard some riders coming and said, "Riders coming."

"You boys go hide in the brush," Pa said. Zack and I took all our weapons, including our bows. Pa and Ma grabbed their rifles and put them next to them and then waited.

When the men rode up, they had their guns drawn. There were three of them, and one of them was Patrick Murphy. "What are you doing here?" Murphy said maliciously.

"Watering our horses and resting, why do you care?" Pa said cautiously.

"This here water and land aren't for savages, white or red," he replied.

The other two were taking great pleasure in what was said. "You are going to have to pay for being here," continued Murphy with a grin.

Zack and I were able to work our way around so that we were behind them.

"We have no money, and furthermore, we got told we could come here," Pa said.

"Well, now, you have all those furs and horses and that savage whore."

I was getting outraged when I heard that. I don't think Zack knew what a whore was, or he would have exploded.

"Wait a minute Murphy," one of the riders said. "Didn't you say there were two whelps with these two when they come up to your place?"

My father and mother were now smiling, and I nodded to Zack. We both had arrows notched, and I had one in my mouth. We agreed to shoot to wound the outer two men first, which would leave Murphy in the center. I would finish him off with the extra arrow, and Zack would stand by with the rifle if needed. The first two arrows struck true, and the men went flying off their horses. I quickly notched the other arrow while Ma and Pa dove for their rifles. Murphy was so confused he didn't know what to do, and I knocked him off his horse with an arrow sticking out his shoulder. Ma and Pa, now with rifles in hand, kicked their weapons away from them as Zack and I rejoined them with our rifles.

The three men were moaning and carrying on about their wounds. Pa said, "Now what are we going to do with these three?"

I said in Shoshone, "Zack have you ever had a white scalp?"

Zack shook his head no with a smile.

"There will be no scalp-taking."

"I was just joking, Pa." "I do think we should scare them and humiliate them, though," I said.

"What did you have in mind?" Pa asked.

"I think we should take their weapons and smash them, strip them of their clothing and tie them up." "Ma can tend to their wounds if they need tending."

"I would rather heal a skunk than these three," Ma growled.

I smiled and said, "Then we can take their horses and leave them at the next farm we see."

Pa nodded in agreement, and I added, "I also think we should pretend we are going to scalp them."

"Do as you please, maybe a little scaring will do them good."

Pa and I stripped them and tied them to a tree, and Ma removed the arrows and plugged their wounds and told Pa they weren't serious. Meanwhile, Zack smashed all their weapons while the three protested and complained. Zack and I pulled out our knives and grabbed two who had hair and acted like we were going to scalp them much to their horror. I said, "Know this fool it was my brother Tracking Fox and me Soaring Eagle With Many Coups that spared your life. As we walked past the third man, Zack kicked dirt in his face, and we loaded up and left. About a mile down the creek, we threw their clothing into the water.

A little less than an hour later, we came upon a farm and told the farmer's family what happened. "It serves them right that Patrick Murphy and his friends are nothing but drunken troublemakers," Mrs. Wilely said.

"Here are their horses." "We tied them up by the spring that is about an hour from here," Pa said. "Just let their horses go; they will find their way back home, and those three can untie themselves and walk back to their places," said Mr. Wilely. Pa nodded, and Mr. Wilely added, "Don't worry about the law." "Even if we had any, they wouldn't listen to those three anyway; they have a past."

We thanked them and rode on, not stopping to talk to anyone else. We made a dry camp in a wooded area that night.

The next several days, as we traveled to St. Louis, were without incident, except for some people giving us nasty looks as we went through their towns. We entered St. Louis on a Wednesday at about ten in the morning, and I said to Ma and Pa, "It would be better if we go to Mr. McConnell's general store." "He is a little higher than other places, but he is honest, and he will help us with everything."

Pa agreed, and as we headed toward the store, things started to look familiar. I noticed things hadn't changed much, and as we got closer to the store, I started seeing people I knew; however, they didn't recognize me. As we pulled up in front of Mr. McConnell's store Pa turned to Ma and Zack and said, "Stay here and guard our things."

Before we went into the store, I could see Mr. McConnell through the window. He hadn't changed much except maybe gained a few more pounds. We walked inside, and the bell rang. My heart was beating hard, not from fear but joy.

Mr. McConnell glanced at us and continued helping a Mexican customer who could not speak English very well. He was trying to figure out just what this man wanted when I said in Spanish, "Sir, what is it you wish from this store?"

"I have a sick mule that I use to plow I need some medicine for her."

"Mr. McConnell, the man said he has a sick mule and needs medicine for her."

"We don't carry that here; he must get it at the veterinarian's down the street," he said, taken aback. "Are my eyes seeing right, is that you, James?"

"It's me, sir; I better tell him what you said." "Mr. McConnell does not carry what you are looking for, but just down the street is the veterinarian who will help you."

"Thank you very much," he said.

He left, and I turned to Mr. McConnell, whose mouth hadn't closed because he was so shocked to see me. "This is my father, Nathaniel York." "My mother, Blue Flower, and brother Zack are outside watching our things."

He shook Pa's hand and said, "You are his real father?"

"Yes, I am."

"I'm very confused and mixed-up; what happened to your uncle?"

"They are all dead; what happened is a long story."

"You must tell me everything," he said, interested.

"I will, but we have business to take care of first." "I told Pa you were an honest man who will help us."

"Yes, yes, what is it you need?" he said, eager to help.

Pa looked around and said, "Are we alone?"

"Yes, you can speak freely."

"We have a lot of furs to sell, and I need to know where to take them."

"The furs' value is down, but I know of a person who will give you a fair price for them." "I will take you to him."

Mr. McConnell went over to the door to close the store when Pa added, "I have even a more pressing need to be taken care of sooner."

Mr. McConnell stopped and turned around and said, "What is it?"

Apprehensively Pa said, "We have a lot of gold to be turned into cash."

Mr. McConnell stared at him for a second and said, "There are a lot of crooked bankers in this city, but I do know one who will deal with you honestly." "You know him, James, Mr. Warner." I nodded my head, yes, and he added, "He is a person who comes off as being stern, but he is honest."

"I remember him as being stiff and not liking children very much," I said.

"Yes, he is all business; we should go now." "I will close the store and take you down there; it is not far."

Mr. McConnell put up the "closed" sign and locked the doors. He said to Ma and Zack, "How do you do, Mrs. York and Zack." "We are going to deal with your valuables." They both returned the greeting.

Pa and I grabbed the reins of our horses, and we went down the street. "Sarah will be thrilled to see you, and she will be shocked at how much you have changed."

"I always did love Sarah, is she in school now?"

"Yes, and doing very well."

We went two blocks and then turned and went three more until we turned again. We came to the front of the bank, then Pa, Mr. McConnell, and I went into the bank. It was a huge place with a lot of customers. Mr. McConnell went up to one of the tellers and said, "We need to talk to Mr. Warner privately."

"He is a very busy man." "I will help you with your needs," he said unkindly.

"You will get him now, or when I am through with you, you will wish you were never born," Mr. McConnell said. Annoyed, he got up and went to Mr. Warner's office. Pa started laughing, and Mr. McConnell said, "Sometimes, you have to threaten these people to get what you want."

"Before I went west, I used to work in a bank in New York, I know just how he is and what you mean," said Pa.

Mr. Warner came to his door and looked us over, and you could see an annoyed look on his face. Still, he called us over to his office and said to Mr. McConnell, "This better be good, Tom." "I don't appreciate your threatening one of my tellers, and I am busy."

All three of us went into the office, including the teller. "Now, what is it you people want?"

Pa looked at the teller and said, "You're not needed here."

Mr. Warner shooed him out. When the door got shut, Pa started to talk, but I grabbed his arm and shook my head no. Then I walked over to the door and jerked it open quickly. The teller went tumbling to the floor, and Mr. Warner was outraged he got up from behind his desk and told him, "Get in your cage, you pull this stunt again, and you can look for work someplace else."

He closed the door as the teller went running back to his cage. He waited a few seconds and opened the door again, and the clerk was right where he was supposed to be. "I believe it will be alright now, what is your business?"

Pa started talking again. "We have a lot of gold, and Mr. McConnell said you were an honest banker that I can trust."

"How much gold are you talking about?" asked Mr. Warner with interest.

"With the help of my son here, it would take us a little over an hour to bring it all into your office."

Mr. Warner's mouth fell open in shock, and he said excitedly, "Is the gold in the form of dust or nuggets?"

"Ingots," Pa said.

"Then it has been smelted." "Have you seen the gold, Tom?"

"No, but I trust these people, and you know this boy, look at him closely." Mr. Warner looked at me, and he was clueless at who I was. "This is James, whom I use to send to you with the store's receipts."

"Mary's boy, yes, I remember him." "I never had any trouble with you, and you were smart too." "This is his father," Mr. McConnell added.

"Didn't know he had a father, but if what you are saying is true, then it is a pleasure to meet you."

"We need to get the gold in here," Pa said.

"I will close the bank and send my teller to the assayer and get a deputy."

"Deputy Johnson if he is still here," I said.

Mr. Warner nodded yes to my suggestion. He got up, went to the bank's lobby, and told his tellers to finish with their customers and then close the bank. He then went to the clerk that was rude to us and said to him, "Go find Deputy Johnson and bring him back here."

The teller smiled. I assumed he thought Deputy Johnson was going to arrest us, and he left in haste. He went to another free teller and said quietly to him, "Go down to the assayer's office quickly and bring him down to the bank with his equipment." When the last person left the bank, he got a handcart and told the rest of his tellers to come with him. Just before we went out, Deputy Johnson went into the bank with the teller.

"What's this all about?" asked Deputy Johnson.

I stepped forward and said with a smile, "It's been a long time, sir."

Deputy Johnson looked at me, confused, and Mr. McConnell said, "It's James York, Mary's son, and this is his father." "You passed his stepmother and brother outside."

"I'll be, I thought I would never see you again and look how much you have grown!"

"We can talk later; we have something valuable we need you to guard while we unload it." I grabbed my pistol and handed it to Deputy Johnson and said, "You may need this." He took it, and we all went outside.

Ma and Zack got down from their horses, and Pa pointed to the gold. Pa stayed with the gold while it got unloaded then placed on the cart and hauled into the bank while Ma, Deputy Johnson, Zack, and I stood guard. Even with all the help and the cart, it still took almost an hour to unload the gold. As we unloaded the gold, a man and the other bank teller came walking down the street. Zack raised his rifle, and I asked Deputy Johnson, "Is that the assayer, Deputy Johnson?"

"Yes, you can let him go."

When all the gold was in the bank, Mr. Warner had, the tellers watch the furs and horses. We all went into his office. He opened one of the bags, and the ingots poured onto his desk. Both the assayer and Mr. Warner were taking a close look at the gold. "There is something written on the ingots in Spanish."

"It says His Royal Majesty Philip the Third of Spain; he was a king in the fifteen or sixteen hundreds."

The assayer asked, "Where did you get it?"

Pa acted like he didn't want to tell, but the assayer said, "We have to have a place to put down on the paperwork."

"Alright, but you keep this quiet." "There is a great canyon about a month's ride from here to the southwest." "We found it there, and there is plenty more there." Pa played it just right, and they bought it all.

The assayer tested the gold, and he certified it as pure. "Gold has been going up and down in worth." "From a low of thirty-five dollars an ounce to forty-eight dollars an ounce. You're lucky it is now forty-eight dollars an ounce, but since it is pure and already smelted, it is even higher, about fifty-two dollars an ounce."

"I'll weigh it to see how much you have," said Mr. Warner.

"I must get back to the store." "Come back when you finish, and we will deal with your furs," said Mr. McConnell.

"How long do you think this will take, Mr. Warner?" I asked.

"With everything about an hour, I would think."

"We will come after we finish," Pa said. After about forty-five minutes, we had weighed three thousand two hundred eighty-seven pounds and fourteen ounces. Mr. Warner said, "That comes to two million seven hundred thirty-five thousand five hundred twelve dollars; you all are wealthy people. You will need to sign some papers, and I wish to know if you want to open an account here."

"Yes, we will open an account here, and we will need some spending money about fifteen thousand to start." "I have a lot of supplies to get, and my sons and wife have lists of things to purchase," Pa said.

"That's a lot of money, but we can handle it, Mr. York," he said happily. "We will need a good place to stay and to eat." "As you can see, Blue Flower is an Indian as is my son, Zack." "Frankly, you can look at how we all are, do you know of a place we can go?" he continued.

"This bank holds the note on the Le Palais Rouge, and they have a place to eat." "They will not give you any problems I will see to that." "They are two blocks further down the street." "There is a big sign on the building," Pa nodded. He was satisfied and said, "Also, what is the fastest route to New York by land or by sea?"

"By land, it will take you many weeks of hard riding and by the sea not as long," he explained.

"By sea, we go then," said Pa.

"If you are going to New York, you will need some new clothing," Mr. Warner said.

"I am not ashamed of being a Shoshone." "I will wear my good buckskins, but I will not wear a white man's city clothing," I said persistently.

"I feel the same," said Zack.

Pa looked at Ma and said, "I guess you feel the same."

"I will do what makes you happy."

"I will figure something out," said Pa.

"Let's go get your money," said Mr. Warner.

After getting the money, we went back to Mr. McConnell's store. He had lunch for us, and we sat, ate, and talked. I told him the whole story of what happened. "You know I never liked your mother's family." "I wish I could have kept you, but you know what would have happened," Mr. McConnell said.

"I understand, sir."

"But it seems it all ended up for good anyway."

"After we dispose of the furs, we have a lot of things to buy, and we will get much of them here," Pa said.

It was one-thirty, and Mr. McConnell said, "We better take care of those furs of yours and board your horses."

We took the horses down to the river and tossed the three travoises in the river and proceeded to a large building. We waited outside while Mr. McConnell went in to talk to the owner. After a few minutes, he came out with the proprietor, who was a short, balding man with three day's growth and shabby clothes. "Follow me with those furs," he said.

We went to the far end of the building where there was a large door, like a barn door. Some black men were working, maybe slaves who opened the door. The man told us to bring in the horses, and he had his men unload the furs. The man's name was Clarence White. He inspected each pelt, which took some time to do. He said, "Most are good pelts; you do know that beaver has gone down in value." "However, since you are the first to bring furs in, I will give you the best price I can." He thought for a second, then said, "Eighteen hundred for the lot of them."

It was more than Pa thought he would get, and he agreed. The man went back to his office with a smile on his face and wrote a bill of sale and handed my father a note for eighteen hundred dollars. Then he said, "You can cash that in at any bank."

Pa looked over to Mr. McConnell, who he nodded yes. Before we left, I asked Mr. White, "Sir, this is more than likely the last year for my father, trapping furs." "I am curious about how much these furs are worth when you ship them to the hat factories."

"Well, that's personal, but since this is your last year, I will get about thirty-five hundred dollars for your furs."

I nodded, and we left for the stables as we went, Mr. McConnell said to Pa, "I have to apologize to you, Mr. York." "I didn't know he gets that much of a markup."

"It doesn't matter; I got more than I thought I would, I'm satisfied."

We got to the stables, and there were a couple of black men there also. We talked to the owner, who was the blacksmith and owner of the stables. "I have to be getting back to the store, Sarah will be out of school soon, and I need to be there for her." "You will come back after you finish here?"

"Of course, Mr. McConnell, in about a half-hour or so," said Pa.

"I wish these horses to be well fed, watered, and groomed."

"Alright," said the owner.

He motioned for his men to take care of the horses, and I said, "I wish to buy a few things from you." "I need a sturdy wagon these horses can pull; it doesn't need a covered. I'll also need a flat piece of metal I can make into a stovetop, some metal doors and hinges, and these other things." I pulled out a piece of buckskin that I had written what I wanted. He wrote down all the sizes and things I wanted on a sheet of paper. "When will they be ready?" I asked.

"About two or two-and-a-half weeks after I see the money," he said.

"I may not be back for about three weeks." "With the care of the horses and the things that my son wants, how much will that cost?"

He figured it all up and said, "With all the horses and the things you wanted, about three hundred dollars will cover it, I think."

"Here is four hundred to rent four fresh horses and just make sure everything is as it should be."

He shook Pa's hand, gave him some paperwork to sign, and we rode back to Mr. McConnell's store.

"Papa, I'm home from school," Sarah said.

He came down from upstairs with a smile on his face. "Do I have a big surprise for you."

"What is it, Papa?"

"You must wait and see."

"Oh, I can't wait, tell me."

"No, I am not giving into you this time; you just wait." "Now, you go upstairs and pretty yourself up and put on a new dress, then come back down here, and maybe your surprise will be here."

Up she went wondering about what the surprise was; Papa had never acted this way before.

Less than five minutes later, we all walked into the store. Mr. McConnell said, "James, you stand right here, Sarah is upstairs getting cleaned up and doesn't know you are here."

We all had big smiles on our faces when Sarah said as she came down the stairs, "Is my surprise here yet, Papa?" She came into the store and stared at me.

A tear went down her cheek, and I said, "My sweet Sarah, you look so beautiful you take my breath away."

"James" was the only word that came out of her." She came running over and into my arms. I hugged her and kissed her. She wiped away her tears and said, "Have you come back to live here?"

"No, sweetheart, I am here just long enough to do some business, and then I am going to New York for a short time." "I will come back here to finish up the business, but I will be going back west."

She was disappointed but said, "Alright, but I want to spend as much time as I can with you while you are here."

"Oh, you mean like before you want to sleep and bathe with me?"

"You know what I mean; no one was supposed to know about that; besides, we were little children."

"If you only knew what I have been through, what we did was nothing."

Everyone else laughed, and Pa said, "Mr. McConnell, we will be staying at the Le Palais Rouge, do you know the place?"

"Oh, yes, it is a lovely place."

"Give us a couple of hours, and you and Sarah come to the place." "They have a place to eat there, and we will treat you both to dinner." "I will give you a list of things we need to order."

"We will be there, Mr. York."

I gave Sarah another hug and kiss and hugged Mr. McConnell also, and we all left.

# 18

## St. Louis

We rode back to the bank and then down two more blocks, and there it was a real grand looking place. We tied up our horses, grabbed our things, and started to walk into the hotel when a doorman said, "Sir, do you have business here."

"I am Nathaniel York; Mr. Warner has made arrangements for my family and me to stay here."

"Oh yes, Mr. York, we have been waiting for you." "I will get someone to take care of the horses; we have our stables." He called for a man to take care of our horses and take our belongings.

We crossed a large lobby to the main desk, and the doorman introduced us. Pa signed the register and said, "There will be six of us for dinner in about two hours." "We will also need to bathe before we eat."

Ma's and Zack's eyes were wide with wonder taking in all the sights as we moved through the hotel. We all were given a large room with two separate bedrooms.

"I have to relieve myself, Pa," I said.

"So, do I, Pa," said Zack

The man showing us the room opened a cabinet in both bedrooms and showed us a large chamber pot that sat under a stool with a hole in it. "We change it twice a day unless you request for us to change it more often."

"The bathwater will be up here soon, sir."

Pa nodded and tipped him, and he left. "Why did you give him money, Pa," Zack asked.

"It is just a custom they do here in the east."

Zack went into the bedroom and said to me, "How do you use that thing."

"You sit down on it and stick your manhood between your legs, and you relieve yourself, I think."

Zack removed his shirt and loincloth and tried it out. When he finished, he said, "It's strange, I don't know if I like it, but it works, I guess." "Are you going to use it?"

I nodded yes and did the same I did the same thing as he did. When I finished, I said, "I think you're right." "I don't care for it myself, but it works." I closed the lid and put it back in the cabinet.

We both put on our loincloths, and about twenty minutes later, two large bathtubs got rolled into our room with soap and oil and more towels. Pa came out of his bedroom and moved his tub into his room. I started stripping as Pa entered the room; he poured a little oil into the bathtub and went back to his room.

Zack just looked at the tub, and I said, "It's just like swimming in the lake but smaller." "Take your clothes off and get in with me." I had my clothes off, and I slipped into the tub. I smiled and said, "It's warm."

Zack got the rest of his clothing off and sat in front of me. He grabbed the soap and smelled it he was about to stick it in his mouth when I said, "That's not for eating it's for washing." He turned around and looked at me, and I said, "Give me the soap, and I will wash your back, and you can wash mine." I finished him, and I handed him the soap and told him to do me. When Zack finished, I turned around to face him, gave me the soap, and washed my front side. Then he did the same as I had done. When he finished, he sniffed his arm and wrinkled up his nose, and I laughed.

"I think we should wash our hair; will you untie my braid?" He nodded, yes. When he finished, I told him to turn around, slide forward, and hand me the soap. "Lean back, and I will hold your head as I dunk your hair in the water to get it wet." I then took the soap and scrubbed his hair, and it was filthy. I had to dunk his hair again and rewash his hair. I scrubbed so hard I thought all the black color would come out. When it was my turn, Zack had to do the same with me.

When we were all finished, I leaned my back on the tub and relaxed. Zack laid against me and said, "This bath thing is sure relaxing, isn't it?"

"Yes, it is," I replied.

When I started dozing, I told Zack, "I've had enough; if I don't get out now, I will fall asleep."

"Me too," Zack said, and we both got out and dried ourselves. We found a comb and brush for our hair, and I started combing and brushing Zack's hair. It had turned a shining black, and I told him to get up and look in the mirror. He then brushed and combed mine. It came out five shades lighter and shining. Zack put the braid back into my hair, and I put my white buckskins on the ones I used to get married. Zack put on a new pair of buckskins that Ma had made. As we went into the parlor to wait for Ma and Pa, I took a good look at the water we had bathed in and said to Zack, "It looks like a muddy water hole."

Zack and I had all our weapons on us, except for our bows and arrows.

When Ma and Pa came out of their bedroom, they looked good. Ma had the bluestone necklace that Grandpa gave me, Morning Star did not want it, and Pa had shaved. They looked at us and smiled, and Ma said, "You both look nice."

"We smell funny from that soap, I think," Zack said.

Ma and Pa smiled, and Pa said, "What are you doing with those rifles?"

"Taking them with us," Zack said.

"Put them back; you won't need them," he said.

"I don't know Pa, some of those folks are worse than the Blackfeet," said Zack.

Pa wasn't budging, so we put them back in our bedroom.

"What about the rest of those weapons?" Pa added.

I got real serious and said, "They stay," and I wasn't budging.

Pa saw that he wasn't going to win this one, so he said, "I want you to conceal them the best you can." "Now, let me tell all of you about eating habits here." "We don't eat like at Village, not even like at home; we must use a fork, knife, and spoon that they give us." "You do not touch your food with your hands." "You do not talk with food in your mouth." "If you get food on your face or hands, there will be a cloth called a napkin, which you will use." "Don't rush through your food; eat slowly."

"Seems like a person could starve eating that way, Pa," said Zack.

"What Pa says is true." "If you don't eat this way, people will think you are an animal," I said.

"Alright, we have about ten minutes before we go down to eat, are there any questions?" "No, good, if you get confused, just ask or look at James or me."

We left and went downstairs to the dining room. Pa stopped at the main desk and told the clerk, "We need the two tubs removed and the chamber pots cleaned."

"Yes, sir," said the clerk.

"When Mr. McConnell and his daughter, Sarah, show up, please send them to our table."

"I will do that, sir."

"Do you have some paper and something to write with that I can bring to the table with me," I asked.

He gave me a piece of paper and a pencil, and as we were going into the dining room Pa said, "Why did you get that for?"

"So, I could give Mr. McConnell a list of things I will need."

"Good idea, after you finish with your list, I would like to add to it."

I nodded yes, and the maître d' said, "Can I help you?"

"We have reservations for six." "It is under the name of York."

He checked us out again and said with an unpleasant look to him, "Yes, right this way."

As we followed the maître d', people stared and whispered to each other, and the maître d' took us to a dark corner near the kitchen door.

My father stopped and said, "This is the table you are giving us?"

"How about the large table next to the window?"

"That table is reserved for someone else."

I knew what the game was. I was back far enough for the maître d' to see me, and while maître d' was talking to Pa, I pulled out my pistol. When the maître d' spotted me, he knew I wasn't playing games, and his demeanor changed quickly. "Mr. York, I am sure those people won't show up tonight." "I will let you sit there."

I stuffed my pistol back into my waistband, and, as my family went to that table, I told the maître d', "We will be eating in here again." "Don't let that happen again if you don't want trouble."

"Mr. McConnell and his daughter will be joining us shortly." "Show them to our table when they come," Pa said to the maître d' as I stared at him.

"Yes, sir, I will do that."

As we were sitting there, Ma said, "James, were you going to shoot that man if he didn't give us this table?"

I didn't know Ma had seen me, and I said, "Maybe, only if he kept on being rude."

I started writing my list of things I wanted, two barrels of nails, glass for windows, some tools, books, and a large saw for milling. I think I will get a spyglass for Grey Wolf, candy for Comes Running, and what will I get for Morning Star? "Ma, what do you think Morning Star would like?"

"I don't know, maybe something that is shining." I thought perhaps a prism would be good. I was writing the list when Mr. McConnell and Sarah came in. Pa and I stood up, I grabbed Zack's arm and coaxed him up to greet Mr. McConnell and Sarah. Sarah sat between Zack and me, and her hair transfixed Zack. He had never seen red hair like hers. It took him a while to get used to my hair.

Sarah was all excited and said, "Papa told me all that happened to you." "I am happy you are alright."

"I missed you very much and always thought about you."

She noticed Zack staring at her and said, "You seem to be a very nice boy, Zack." He just shook his head yes, very slowly never taking his eyes off her hair.

Mr. McConnell, Ma, and Pa noticed also, and Pa said, "What's the matter, Zack?"

He didn't answer him but asked Sarah, "If I touch your hair, will my hand burn?"

Everyone laughed, and Sarah said, "No, silly, go ahead and feel it."

Zack reached over and felt her hair.

"He has never seen red hair before; it took him some time to get used to mine," I said.

The waiter took our order. While we were waiting for our order to come, there was a commotion at the entrance with the maître d' and three rough-looking men wanting to come in. They pushed the maître d' to the side and walked over to us, bumping into the other patrons.

"You York?" one of them asked.

I pulled out my two pistols, and I saw Zack pull his knife, but we kept them under the table. "Yes, I'm Nathaniel York." "What do you want?"

"We heard you found some Spanish gold out west, and we want to know where you found it."

"Who told you that?" asked Pa.

"A person who works down at the bank down the street now where is this gold you found we have just as much right to it as you do?"

"What is the clerk's name?" Pa asked again.

"That doesn't matter; just tell us where the gold is or else," the man snarled. All three of them showed us their guns.

"You're a fool, you are dead men and don't know it," said Pa. That was the cue for me to present my guns, and Zack raised his knife. We caught them off guard, and one of them tried to draw his pistol, but I shot him, and he went down.

"Drop them, or you're a dead man?" I said. The two released their pistols, and I said, "My Pa asked you a question what is the name of the clerk?"

"We don't know he was a short, thin man, sickly-looking with a mustache, and he wore glasses."

Just then, two deputies came in, and one of them asked what was going on.

"These three tried to do us harm." "Those men tried to pull their guns, and my son shot that one."

"What did they want?"

"We had come into some money, and they wanted it."

Just then two more deputies arrived, one of them was Deputy Johnson he said, "Those three are some low life thugs from the river, and I know these people; they are good friends of mine."

"That's good enough for me, but you must come down to the station to fill out a report." The other deputies dragged out the body and removed the other two men.

"I will do it right after we finish eating, deputy."

The deputy nodded his head that it was alright, and Pa said to Deputy Johnson, "Why don't you stay here and eat with us."

"If it is alright, I think I will." "I don't know when I will get a chance to talk to James again." I handed the list of things I wanted to buy to Pa, and as he talked, he jotted down things he wanted. I told the whole story of what happened to me after I left St. Louis. It seemed that Mr. McConnell didn't tell Sarah everything because she was shocked at what happened.

Pa explained why he never came back for Mama. There were a lot of comments on Ma's necklace. When Pa handed the list of things to Mr. McConnell, I asked him, "I know you don't have a lot of books in your store, so do you think I should go down to the bookstore and buy some there."

"That would be a good idea and easier for you," he replied.

When our food came, I noticed that Ma and Zack were having trouble using some of the utensils, but they were managing. I asked Sarah, "Is Jack still causing trouble?"

"He is worse and bigger and stronger." She hesitated for a second then continued and said, "Although I think you have grown so much, you are as tall or taller and maybe stronger."

I chuckled and said, "How is Miss O'Brien?"

"Oh, she is just wonderful."

"Sarah, don't tell anyone that I am here." "I will come down to the school tomorrow afternoon."

"I won't say a word," she said with a smile. Then she said as she giggled, "School is going to be fun tomorrow when you show up."

The dinner ended without further incident, and everybody said goodnight. It got arranged that we would meet at Mr. McConnell's store the next day.

Zack was restless in bed that night; I guessed the bed was too soft for him. The next morning when we got up, his restlessness showed, and he wasn't in a mood for being teased.

Breakfast went smoothly, and we got our horses and headed down the street. When we came abreast of the bank, Pa stopped, and he hitched his horse as we all did. "Stay here; I will take care of business here."

He went in, and I said, "I'm going in also." Before Ma could say anything, I was inside. Pa was talking to that rude teller questioning him about what happened the night before. The clerk was acting arrogant again, and Pa was losing it. "If you don't leave, sir, I will call the authorities," the teller said.

I worked my way around the bank without being seen, and when Pa had enough, he forced his way into Mr. Warner's office. I worked my way behind the teller's cages. I confronted the clerk who immediately turned around and said, "I don't have to put up with your mountain man trash of a father nor his bastard."

I was enraged, he went to grab me at the same time Pa and Mr. Warner came out of his office. I grabbed his arm and slammed him into the wall. I swung my fist and hit him with a right on his chin, then I came up with a left to the solar plexus, and he went down moaning.

Mr. Warner went over to him and barked, "You don't work here anymore."

"I will go to the authorities and have that boy arrested for assault if you fire me," the teller managed to get out. "You just go to the authorities; these people and I saw the whole thing." "You grabbed him first, and he defended himself, now what do you think the authorities will do to you for grabbing a child?" Mr. Warner said. The teller got nervous and couldn't talk. Mr. Warner added, "Now get out of my bank and don't try to get a job in a bank in St. Louis or anywhere near St. Louis, I will let everyone know about you."

He got up quickly and ran out of the bank.

"He won't go to the authorities, let me apologize to you and your son again, nothing like this will happen again." He and Pa shook hands, and he patted me on the back, and we left.

Pa never said anything to me about going into the bank, but you could tell he wasn't happy. We rode down the streets to Mr. McConnell's store and entered. Mr. McConnell was helping a customer so, while we waited, we discussed how we would do things.

"There are many places I need to go while we are in St. Louis, and I would like everyone to stick together as a family while we go to these locations," Pa said. "I know James, you have some places to go also, and we will go with you," he added.

"That's alright with me, Pa, but there is one place I would like to go alone if you don't mind."

"Where is that?" Pa asked.

"I wish to go down to the school that I used to attend by myself." "I figure you must purchase tickets to New York, and you don't need me there to do that." "That's when I could go down to the school," I explained.

Pa nodded his head in agreement, and that's when Mr. McConnell came over to us. "Mr. McConnell, I will need a place to store my things while my family and I are in New York," asked Pa.

"How long will you be gone, Mr. York?" asked Mr. McConnell.

"Oh, I don't think it will be no longer than a few weeks or so."

"Then, you can store everything where James and his mother used to sleep in the storage room."

"Of course, I will pay you for storage," Pa said.

"That's not necessary, Mr. York."

"Nonsense, you have to make a living, and I am willing I'm going to pay."

"You're very generous, sir." "What are your plans for today?" Mr. McConnell asked.

"We are going to go to various shops to get what we need that we can't get here." We talked a little longer then we headed toward the river. We first came to the glass shop, and we all went in.

"Can I help you, sir," a man asked Pa.

"Whatever my son wants, fill the order."

"I wish one hundred panes of glass, six inches by eight inches in size." "They are going across the land in a wagon, so they have to be well packed, so they don't break," I said.

"That is a lot of glass for one person." "Are you sure you need that much?" the clerk asked.

"It is a long way back to this shop." "One hundred panes are what I want."

"Alright, that will be one hundred and seventy-five dollars for the glass and another twenty for packing the glass." "That will be one hundred ninety-five dollars."

Pa pulled out one hundred ninety-five dollars and handed it to the clerk and said, "There are one hundred dollars-ninety-five." "Deliver it to Mr. McConnell's General Store." "You know where it is."

He nodded in surprise that we had that much money.

"Do you know what a prism is?" I asked.

"Yes, of course, I do," the clerk said.

"Let me see what you have."

He showed me about a dozen, and I picked one that had a beautiful shape to it, and I took it and asked Ma, "Do you wish one, Ma?"

"What is this prism?"

I showed her how it made a rainbow, and she was fascinated.

"Do you wish one, Ma?"

"Yes."

I picked another one, and I handed them to the clerk.

"That will be three dollars."

Pa gave him the three dollars, he wrapped the two prisms, and I put them in my possibles bag. As we were starting to leave, the clerk asked, "Do you want some putty for the panes?"

"What is in it that makes it putty?" I asked.

He said, "Clay, oil, and a hardener."

"No," I said, and we left.

We continued going down toward the river when Pa turned down a street and stopped at a tobacco company. "Pa the Hawken's' gunsmith shop is three doors down, is it alright if I go down there," I asked.

"Me too, Pa," said Zack.

"Yes, we will meet you down there, don't go anywhere else."

When Zack and I went into the shop, Samuel Hawken came out of the backroom of his shop to see who came in. He looked at both of us and said, "Can I help, you boys."

"I'm looking for two new rifles," I said.

"Why do you need two rifles?" asked Zack.

"I have a younger brother whose hunting abilities would greatly improve with a better rifle."

"Who?"

I said, "Zack," with a smile.

And he said, "Oh, me."

"These rifles might be a little more expensive than you two could afford," said Samuel Hawken.

"My father and mother are down the street in the tobacco shop and will be here shortly." "We have the money to pay for it," I said.

He looked at us with a bit of doubt but grabbed a rifle and said, "This is our newest rifle. It uses a cap instead of flint."

I handled it, and it felt good. I handed it to Zack, who loved it. Mr. Hawken said, "With a cap, it will fire every time." "That is what makes it better than flint."

Before he finished talking, the bell to the shop rang; it was Ma and Pa. Pa said, "Let me see that rifle." Pa looked it over, and said, "It has a good feel, but what happens when you run out of caps?"

I looked at Samuel Hawken, and he said, "Then you need to come and buy some more."

"It is hard when you live in the Shining Mountains," Pa said.

"You're right here is a flintlock," said Mr. Hawken. I liked the feel of it, it was better than mine, and I handed it to Zack.

"Can we try the rifle out," I asked.

He looked at Pa, and Pa nodded yes. We went to his rifle range in the back of his shop. Zack fired the first five shots and hit the target every time. Then it was my turn, and I hit dead center every time. I turned to Ma and Pa and asked if they wanted to try. Ma shook her head no, and Pa said, "I prefer my own."

Samuel Hawken stared at me for a long time and said, "There was one boy who used to come to my shop and shoot like that many years ago, his name was James York."

I smiled and said, "This is my father, Nathaniel York, my mother Blue Flower, and my brother Zack."

Samuel Hawken was stunned; it took him a few moments to get his speech back. "James York!" "Look how much you have grown, and you look as strong as a bull you have changed a lot,"

"It is good to see you again, sir."

"There was a time whenever a trapper would come to St. Louis, James would ask if they knew of you, Mr. York I'm glad he found you."

I turned a little red, and Pa said, "Is that so?"

"I was a different person then." "I want two of these rifles, and do you have any pistols?" I asked.

"I do," he said.

When we left there, Zack and I had new rifles, and Zack had two new pistols also.

Pa headed to the Catholic Church and said, "I think we need to take care of your mother, James."

"Yes," I said.

We came to the church, and we went to the church rectory door, which was a thick, heavy, ornate looking door with a knocker on it. Pa let me take the lead, and I used the knocker to summon someone inside. Someone from the clergy, which I didn't know, answered. He asked, "Can I help you?"

"I wish to speak to Monsignor Braille, please," I said.

"Monsignor Braille is no longer here." "Father Garcia is now in charge of this parish, and you will find him in the church unless you wish me to help you."

"No, I know Father Garcia, we will talk to him," I said.

Over to the church, we went, and at the church, I spotted Father Garcia. He had gained a few pounds, but I still recognized him. He was telling some men what repairs he wanted in the church. We all approached Father Garcia, and when he turned his attention to us, he said, "Is there something I can do for you?"

"Father, I don't know if you remember me, but I'm James York." "You helped me bury my mother, Mary von Muller, several years ago."

"Yes, I remember you, but you have changed a lot."

"This is my father, Nathaniel York, my mother, Blue Flower, and my brother, Zack." "I wish to place a stone on my mother's grave and pay someone to maintain the gravesite."

He nodded and said, "Let's go out to the gravesite." The gravesite was overgrown with weeds. The wooden marker was dirty and faded a little but still readable. Pa put the marker in place, and I tried to remove some of the weeds.

"I wish I had the money to keep this graveyard kept up, but unfortunately, I don't."

"How much would it cost to clean it up and keep it clean," Pa asked.

"I would say about two or three thousand dollars much more than we have in this parish."

"Here are five thousand dollars, get it cleaned up as soon as possible," Pa said.

"This is very generous of you, Mr. York."

"James, I'll leave you here for a few minutes to give you privacy while we go with the pastor."

I nodded, and my family went with Father Garcia to the rectory.

"I found Pa, Mama, but you know that already." "We are going to make this spot beautiful." "I'd move you, but I know you would prefer being here rather than where those rich people are." "I miss you, Mama, I wish you were here." I started crying something I hadn't done in a long time.

After a little time with Mama, I met my family at the rectory. Pa was telling Father Garcia that he expected to see progress in cleaning up this graveyard when we got back from New York.

Next, we went to the stone cutter, and I told him what I wanted and to take it to Father Garcia, who will show him where to place it. It cost a little over a hundred dollars. It would be a quality stone better than anything in the wealthy graveyard, and it would last forever. It will be red stone taller than me with the same writing on it that was on the wooden marker. It will also have a design on it, something I will look forward to seeing when we return.

After our business with the stone cutter, we went back to the hotel and had lunch. Pa said, "James, we are going to the bank to get more money, and then we will purchase tickets for the trip to New York." "It would be a good time for you to visit your school."

"Sounds good to me, Pa," I said.

"We will meet at Mr. McConnell's store when we are finished."

I nodded in agreement, and we finished our lunch.

We all left together when we got to the bank I continued to the school. It was about one in the afternoon, a beautiful day with a few clouds in the sky and a slight breeze. The school hadn't changed at all; I tied my horse up and walked into the building. I was in the cloak area, where coats and things got hung and where the lunch boxes were.

I heard Miss O'Brien quoting Shakespeare's Hamlet, "To be or not to be," said Miss O'Brien. "Now, can anyone finish what comes next?" She wasn't getting any response from anyone, so I completed the quote. "To be or not to be, that is the question: Whether 'tis nobler in the mind to suffer the slings and arrows of outrageous fortune, or to take arms against a sea of troubles and, by opposing, end them." "To die: to sleep." "No more; and by a sleep to say we end the heart-ache and the thousand natural shocks that flesh is heir to: 'tis a consummation devoutly to be wish'd." "To die: to sleep." "To sleep?" "Perchance to dream." "Ay, there's the rub; for in that sleep of death what dreams may come, when we have shuffled off this mortal coil, must give us pause." Everyone was quiet, and when I walked out into the classroom, Miss O'Brien was in shock. All eyes were on me, and Sarah had her hands on her mouth giggling.

"Only one boy could have recited that as well as you did, and that would have been James York."

"At your service, my lady," I said.

I looked around the classroom. I knew many of the boys and girls, a few were new, and of course, Jack and his followers were there. I was standing next to Jack when I entered the classroom. As I was standing there, Jack spotted my pistols and reached up to grab one. I slapped his hand away and said, "Don't touch."

Everyone was looking at Jack to see what his reaction would be. They weren't surprised to see the rage on his face. Before he could do anything, I walked up to Miss O'Brien.

"Well, James, you have certainly changed," Miss O'Brien said.

"Yes, a lot of people have said this, but inside I haven't changed that much, at least I don't think so," I said.

Miss O'Brien turned to the class and said, "Because of James's return, I am letting you go home early today, class dismissed."

Many in the class came up to me and shook my hand or made a kind comment. In the back, Jack had that look in his eyes, and he turned and went out the back of the room.

With just Miss O'Brien, Sarah, and I in the classroom, we talked for a few minutes. I told her where we were staying, which impressed her. I said, "Why don't you come to dinner with us tonight, and I will introduce you to my family."

"I will be happy to come, but don't you think you should ask your parents first?"

"They will understand and will be thrilled to meet you."

"Sarah, I will ask your father if you and he can come, also," I said.

We talked for a few minutes longer, and I said, "I have to be going." "My parents are waiting for me at Mr. McConnell's store." "I will give you a ride back to the store on my horse Sarah."

We left the school building and headed to my horse when Jack and his followers came between my horse and me. "Give up the pistols or get beat," said Jack while his followers, laughing, stood behind him.

"Years ago, that was just what I would do, but that was years ago, not now."

"I'm glad you said that now I'm going to hurt you bad."

I sighed and pulled my pistols Jack, and his followers lurched back, and I handed the pistols to Sarah along with my knife. She stepped back, and Jack and his followers got real brave again. "You have no idea who you are dealing with, Jack," I said.

"I'll know when I see you bleeding on the ground." Most of the boys and girls hadn't gone home yet. They were waiting to see what was going to happen between Jack and me. Jack was about my height now, and we weighed about the same, but I was solid muscle where Jack wasn't. Jack was furious, and he came at me without any style. It was easy for me to see what he was going to do. I sidestepped him, smashed my fist between his eyes with my right hand, and gave him a left to the head. He went flying onto his back on the ground, shaking his head. Two of his friends decided to try me, and I broke the nose of one with my right and gave a black eye to the other, sending them both to the ground. They got up and faded back into the crowd like the rest of his followers. Jack was enraged and came at me. He swung again and missed. I caught him with a blow to the eye, which closed immediately and a second blow to the mouth, which drew blood.

The crowd of kids who were watching was going crazy with excitement at the beating I was giving Jack. Jack was throwing his punches wild now, and I let him have it with a series of punches that left him a bloody mess. The last blow knocked him to the ground again. He lay there for a while, and I didn't think he was getting up, so I turned my back on him and started walking away.

I saw Miss O'Brien come running out toward us, Sarah had gotten her. As she came closer, she yelled out, "Watch out, James!"

I immediately dropped to the ground as Jack swung a large thick stick at me missing. I swept his legs and gave him one more punch to the head, which temporarily knocked him out. Miss O'Brien went over to him, saying to me, "Are you alright?"

"Yes, he never touched me."

"Someone, get some water," Miss O'Brien said. One of the boys got her a bucket of water. As she was cleaning blood off his face, Jack woke up, pushed her hand away, got up unsteadily, and took off without saying a word to anyone. As he left, Miss O'Brien said more to herself than anyone else, "That is one troubled child."

"You're still coming tonight, aren't you?" I asked.

"Yes, I will be there," she said with a smile.

Back at the store, my family was waiting there, and Sarah was telling the whole story. Pa said, trying to restrain his anger, "Couldn't you have just walked away?"

"To where Pa, he would have come after me anywhere I went."

"I find it hard to believe that you couldn't avoid this fight," he added.

I was getting irritated, and I guess Mr. McConnell saw it. He said, "Mr. York, I don't interfere with other family's business, but I feel I have to say something." "I know this boy, Jack Flynn, as does Sarah, plus I should add every parent who has a child in that school." "He is a bully, someone who will do anything to get his way." "He has hurt many a child with his reign of terror and has gotten away with it until now." "What James did was a blessing, not a bad thing." "It showed everyone that Jack is not invincible that you can stand up to him."

As Pa tried to wrestle in his mind that I was just defending myself, I said, "Yet I feel sorry for Jack, we all know how his father is." "He must have lived a miserable life since his mother passed away."

"Well, what's done is done, let's forget about this now," said Pa.

"I don't know if you will be mad, but I invited Miss O'Brien to dinner tonight," I said.

"No, we would love to meet her," said Pa. "Mr. McConnell, why don't you and Sarah join us, also?"

"We would love to come," replied Mr. McConnell.

We talked a little longer, then left.

As we got on our horses, there was a commotion going on just up the street. We all looked, including Mr. McConnell and Sarah, who were seeing us off in front of his store. It was Jack getting a terrible beating from his father.

His father was yelling, "I will teach you to lose to that sniveling, blond-haired bastard, James York."

I rode toward them over Pa's objection. Jack was a pathetic mess; he was getting beaten so severely that his father had to hold him up by his shirt to inflict the damage.

I got off my horse and said, "I'm James York; you got a problem with me?"

"Mind your own business, you lowlife bastard scum, or I will beat you, too," he replied.

"This is my business, and I am not afraid of you, you're just the town drunk."

He dropped Jack's lifeless body to the ground and came after me. He tried to grab me, but I wasn't having that. Then he took a swing at me and missed. I connected with a left to the jaw and a right just under his rib cage, which knocked him back, startling him at the strength I had.

"Well, now it looks like you might have more grit than my son has." "This beating I'm going to give you is going to be a pleasure." He came at me like an enraged bull buffalo. I stepped to the side and threw my foot into his groin, which landed him on the ground in pain. He was able to get up, and while he was attempting to do me harm, Pa and Mr. McConnell picked up Jack and brought him back to the store for Ma to attend to him. I hit Mr. Flynn in the head a few times, breaking his nose, which spewed blood, making him madder. I got sloppy, and he got me once with a good one to the head, which knocked me to the ground. He tried to take advantage of it by jumping on me, but I was too fast for him and was able to get up. After a little time, I hit him real hard to the head a few times, and he went down fighting for air.

I figured it was over and walked away when I heard a woman scream and a boom. Then I felt a sting in my arm and knocked me to the ground. There was a second boom almost at the same time as the first. When I turned back to look at Jack's father, he was lying on the ground with a red stain on his chest, and his pistol flung out to his side. I turned around again and saw Zack with his new rifle out and smoke still hanging in the air. Pa came out of the store like a shot of lightning and ran toward me. He asked, "How bad are you?"

"Not bad, Pa." "I'll just be sore for a while."

As he was helping me up, Zack and the woman who screamed, Miss O'Brien, came over to me. People were moving out into the street and checking on Mr. Flynn and seeing how I was.

The deputies also came out, and there were several them. Those standing around told the deputies what happened. One of the deputies came over to me and said to Pa, "You're Deputy Johnson's friends, aren't you?"

"Yes, we are," Pa replied.

"Are you alright young man?" the deputy asked me.

"Yes, I'll be all right," I replied.

"We got the whole story, and we know Flynn also, but we would like a statement from all of you."

Pa nodded and said, "Flynn's son is in the store. My wife is attending to him; he may be in bad shape," Pa said.

The deputy called over another deputy, and we all went into the store.

Jack was coming around, and Miss O'Brien took over with Jack while Ma worked on my shoulder. "You are fortunate the ball went through your arm without hitting your bone."

She cleaned the wound and stopped the bleeding just as the doctor came in. He looked at my arm and said to Ma, "Good job." "Just bandage him up."

Ma nodded, and the doctor went over to Jack.

After she bandaged me, she went over to Jack, and the doctor said, "What did you put on his wounds?"

"Shoshone medicine, I am a healing woman," Ma said.

"I see, well, whatever you put on him, it seemed to work," he said. The doctor stripped Jack of almost all his clothing. As he lay there, and I thought he looked more like a little boy than one who is older than me. His body was full of scars from past beatings from his father. He was dirty, with a pathetic look to him.

With a barely audible sound, Jack called me over and said, "Why did you help me after I was so mean to you all those years?"

"The truth is Jack I never hated you; I just hated the things you did." "I also believe no one should take a beating as your father gave you, especially for what I did," I said.

"What are they going to do to my father?" Jack asked.

Miss O'Brien said, "I'm sorry I have to tell you this, Jack, but your father is dead."

Jack was quiet for a minute and then said, "Good." "It is what he deserves." "I'm sure he killed my mother in a drunken rage." "What's going to happen to me?" Jack asked.

One of the deputies said, "If you have no relatives, you will go to the boys' home."

"No, he won't," Miss O'Brien stated in a loud voice. "I will take care of him; I won't let something bad happen to him like what happened to James," she added.

"And I will help also," Mr. McConnell said. Sarah and I were shocked at what they were willing to do, but Jack was the most shocked.

"Alright, they don't let single people adopt children, but at his age and who he is, they may allow it, and I don't care," the deputy said.

"He should be alright." "He will be bruised and hurting for some time, but he will recover in a few hours," the doctor said.

Pa gave him some money, and the doctor left. After the deputies got their statements from everybody, they also went.

"Where am I going to live?" Jack asked with a much stronger voice now.

"You will live with me, of course," said Miss O'Brien.

"Do you have clothing that will fit him, Mr. McConnell?" asked Pa.

"Yes, I do, Mr. York."

"Here is some money for his clothing," Pa said.

Pa tried to give him some cash, but Mr. McConnell said, "No, sir, if I am going to take care of him, the clothing will be my responsibility," he replied.

Pa nodded, and Miss O'Brien said, "We may be a little late, Mr. York. I will need time to clean up Jack and tend to his wounds with the medicine Mrs. York so graciously gave me." "Is it alright that I bring Jack with me, Mr. York?" She asked.

Pa smiled and said, "Of course, it's alright and get there when you can." "We are at the Le Palais Rouge."

Jack was standing when we said our goodbyes and left heading back to the hotel.

When we got to the hotel, Pa informed the maître d' how many people would be joining us for dinner. There was no trouble from him this time, and before we went upstairs, Pa also asked for two baths again.

In our room, we all sat down, and Pa said, "It's been one exciting day."

"I wasn't looking for trouble Pa." "I was just defending myself and trying to prevent Jack from being killed."

"I know you meant no harm, and I am not mad, but you could have been killed or seriously hurt."

"We risk our lives every day in the Shining Mountains, and I know you don't have the belief in spirit guides like I do, but my spirit guide told me I would live until I was very old."

"I will worry about all of you until the day I die." "And James, you would be surprised at what I believe about Shoshone beliefs."

"You will bathe first and alone when the water comes, and I will wash you," Ma said.

I nodded in agreement.

After we all bathed, I took a nap as Zack cleaned his new rifle. I was awakened about three hours later by Pa. My arm was throbbing as I splashed water on my face and combed out my hair. Ma rechecked my arm and said, "It looks good."

"It doesn't feel great," I said.

We started down to the dining room late because I was allowed to sleep for three hours. When we got to the dining room, all our guests had arrived, and I almost didn't recognize Jack; he had some bruises and cuts on his face. His eye was black, and there was some swelling, but he was clean with his hair combed, and he dressed nicely. He was also courteous, standing up when we came in, and not being loud.

I sat next to him and said, "Nice place, isn't it, Jack?" He only half-heard me, his eyes as big as saucers, or at least as big as they could be with a black eye, looking at everything in the dining room.

"Jack, did you hear me?" I asked.

"Uh, oh yeah, really nice place."

"You look good, Jack," I said again, trying to be pleasant myself.

"Miss O'Brien and Mr. McConnell treated me well, much better than my pa treated me." "The only bad thing is that Miss O'Brien is making me apologize in front of the class for being mean all these years."

Sarah giggled a little, and I said, "Well, it is only right, Jack, you did do some miserable things."

"Yeah, I know."

The waiter took our order, and Jack couldn't believe the taste of the food when we got our food. He ate so much I thought he was going to burst. "We will be leaving for New York the day after tomorrow," Pa said.

"So soon?" asked Miss O'Brien.

"We have to, I can only afford the time for three or four days there, and it will take us many days to get there and many days back. When we come back, we can only stay in St. Louis for a day getting the wagon loaded and taking care of last-minute business. We must get back to the Shining Mountains so that I can get some winter meat in."

We finished our meal, and again everybody said their goodbyes, and before you knew it, we were upstairs and sound asleep.

The next morning after breakfast, Pa and Ma went to an expensive clothing store for men and women. Pa tried to get me to go also, but I wouldn't having anything to do with it, nor did Zack. Pa gave Zack and me about two hundred dollars each, and we both went about our business, Zack coming with me. We agreed that we would meet back at the hotel around noon. I told Zack I wanted to buy a saw that they had in sawmills as we were riding away. On the northern end of the city, they had a sawmill, and that is where we headed.

Zack and I went to the sawmill office, where we met with a Samuel Griffin who ran the sawmill. "Mr. Griffin, my Pa and I are looking to buy a small saw blade to take with us back west something we could use to start a small sawmill with."

He pulled his pipe out of his mouth and said, "Now let me see I could have something right here that might work." He got up, and we went into the area where they sawed the wood.

"Shut the saw down for a few minutes," he told some of his workers. "It's noisy in here, and I can't hear myself think."

"Now, this here blade was the first blade they used when the sawmill first opened." "It is in excellent shape, as you can see." "I can let you have it for, let's see, oh fifty dollars."

It was round and about thirty inches in diameter. It had an excellent axle with pegs on it for water to turn the blade. And the blade was good, no rust at all. "I will take it, sir; will you box it up?" I said. "I would also like to ask you a few questions about a sawmill if that would be alright."

"Yes, let's go back to my office." "You men put that saw into a box for transport," Mr. Griffin said.

I pulled out fifty dollars, and Mr. Griffin wrote me a receipt. "Now, what is it you wish to know about a sawmill?" he asked.

"How do you manage to keep the saw from getting rusted?"

"As you can see, it not in the elements, and we also keep it oiled and covered when it is not in use."

"I would think I could substitute grease instead of oil?" I said.

"Yes, that would work," he replied.

"Sharpening the blade, how is that done?"

"You need to sharpen the blade about once a month." "You must hold the file at the same angle; about thirty-three degrees."

"Could you give me a rough drawing on how to construct a small sawmill that would fit the blade I just bought?"

"I can do better than that." He went to a closet and pulled out a box. He shuffled through some papers in the box and handed me one. "Those are the original plans for this mill before it was rebuilt and made bigger. They are yours at no cost."

I took them and thanked him. The box with the blade was sitting next to our horses. I lifted it with help from Zack, and we went back to Mr. McConnell's store.

After we stored the blade in the back of the store, I asked Zack, "Is there anywhere you want to go or anything you want to get."

"What is that good smelling shop that we pass between here and the hotel?"

I thought for a second and then said with a smile, "I know what store it is; it's the bakery."

We rode down there and got some sweets and bought some for later. We went back to the stables, and the owner showed me the wagon. I was satisfied with it, and I asked him, "Do you have any mules that you would sell or trade."

"I might, what did you have in mind?"

"We have some extra horses; maybe we could trade."

"Maybe."

"I will talk to my Pa, and when we get back from New York, if Pa wants them, maybe we can make a deal one way or another." "We will let you know when we get back."

"Alright, the pieces of metal you wanted are in the back of the wagon already," he added.

Zack and I looked in, and it was just what I wanted. "You did an excellent job." "I will tell my Pa, and we will pick everything up in a few weeks," I said. He nodded, and we left and went back to the hotel to meet Ma and Pa.

We went up to our room. While we waited for Ma and Pa to show up, Zack and I hopped on the bed and started to talk. "I got everything I wanted, how about you?" I asked.

"There wasn't much I wanted." "However, I think I would have liked to get one of those glasses that make things bigger," said Zack.

"Why didn't you say something we could have stopped and picked one up?"

"I didn't think about it at the time."

"Alright, if we get a chance, we will get one."

"Say James wouldn't it be great if you could mount one of those things on a rifle," said Zack. "Then whatever you're hunting will look all that much bigger," he added.

"Yeah, that would be an excellent idea." "If I get a chance, I must read how those things are made and adapt it to fit a rifle."

"Why don't you just talk to that Mr. Hawken about it?"

"You don't care?"

"No."

As I was thinking about it, things went silent for a few minutes. Then Zack said, "I'm ready to go back home." "I've had all I want of this city life." "I don't understand how you all can stand it."

"I'm ready to go back, but Pa wants to go to New York to see Grandma and Grandpa," I said. "You think St. Louis is bad wait till you see New York; it will be much worse," I continued.

"You have been there?" Zack asked.

"No, but I have read about it, and when I was younger, plenty of people told me about it."

Just then, the door opened, and someone came into our room. Zack and I grabbed for our weapons but put them back when we realized it was Ma and Pa, all dressed up fancy like city folk. Ma's hair looked like the white ladies. We went out to the outer room and walked around Ma and Pa. When we faced them, I started laughing. Zack became very serious and said, "You look like a white woman, and you both smell like whites."

"I think we look outstanding," said Pa.

Ma nodded her head in agreement.

"I hope you don't wear those things back home." "They won't last a day if you do," I said.

"They are just for New York and St. Louis," Pa said.

"Pa, are you trying to be someone you're not?" I asked.

"No, I'm just trying to prevent some disapproving comments." "I wish you and Zack would wear clothing like this," Pa said.

"I'd rather pack up the wagon and head back to the mountains," Zack said.

Pa was shocked that Zack was so bold with his opinion. But not Ma, she knew he was more Shoshone than white, and frankly, I think Ma didn't think much about the clothes either but was dressing this way for Pa.

We went down for lunch, and I brought up the subject of the mules, "Pa, I think if we traded for those mules, we could move faster when we go back."

"I believe you 're right, but he will most likely want two horses for one mule and money on top of that."

"Even at that, I still believe that it would be better than using horses." "Besides, I don't think it is a good idea cutting across Cheyenne country with their horses."

"Alright, let me think about it, and after lunch, maybe I will go down to those stables to look at the mules he is talking about," Pa said. I also told them my plans with the saw, and Zack told them about the sweets we brought back.

After lunch, we all went down to the stable. After looking at the mules, Pa said to the owner, "What do you want for them?"

"How much will you pay?" asked the owner, and so the dickering started.

Pa said, "I will give you those two horses for the mules."

Laughing, the owner said, "These are two good mules."

Pa pointed to two more horses and said, "I will give you those two also, two for one."

Shaking his head, no, the owner said, "These two mules are already broke to pull a wagon, like yours."

Pa looked like he was going to walk away and then said, "You drive a hard bargain, let me talk to my family first."

Pa took us aside and said, "You don't want those Cheyenne horses, do you?"

We all shook our heads no, and then pa shook his head no. Then Pa said, "I'm going to offer him the other two Cheyenne horses." "Is that alright with everyone?" We all shook our heads yes, and Pa went over to the owner, not looking very happy. Pa said, pointing at the last two Cheyenne horses, "I will give you those two horses with the four I already offered for the two mules, last offer."

"Well, I don't know," the owner started to say when pa said to us, "Alright, let's go I won't offer him any more." We all began to walk out of the stable when the owner said, "Alright, it is a deal."

Pa signed the papers, and we left. Pa had a big smile on his face, and the owner thought he got one over on Pa, but he didn't know we would have traded those horses or given them away before leaving Missouri.

The rest of the day we spent shopping for Grandma and Grandpa York. Pa didn't want to go there empty-handed. We also got the spyglass for Zack, which delighted him. We ended up at Mr. McConnell's store. He, his daughter, Jack, and Miss O'Brien happened to be there also. We said our goodbyes since we were leaving early the next morning before most folks in St. Louis would be up. We then went back to our hotel and ate a meal.

# 19

## NEW YORK

We checked out of the hotel and rode down to the stable to turn in our horses. We were going to walk down to the river to catch our boat bound for New Orleans when the owner of the barn offered to take us by buggy; mostly out of guilt from thinking, he took advantage of us. Pa gratefully accepted his offer, and soon we were on a paddleboat heading south.

The ride down the river was smooth, and the weather was good. It was partly cloudy in the day with a breeze. Ma and Zack were fascinated with the scenery along the shore and the other boats using the river. I told Pa, "People gave me a hard time about not having a Pa." "They said you were a gambler going up and down the river in one of these paddle boats."

"Did you believe them?"

"No, I was sure you went west mainly because Mama told me so." "It didn't make sense for you to come from New York just to be a riverboat gambler."

It took us longer than we figured to get to New Orleans, and when we got there, night had fallen. Pa went and checked when the next ship to New York would be. We were in luck; there would be one leaving in a few hours. We got two cabins to sleep and eat within. By first light, we were well out into the Caribbean. This ship was larger than the paddle wheel we took down the Mississippi, and it was a bit more rugged with the ship's motion going up and down and side to side. It wasn't long before Ma, Pa, and I were very seasick, but Zack took to the water like he was born for it. He was having a great time.

After some time, I said to Pa, "Maybe it wasn't such a good idea to go by sea pa."

"I know what you mean," Pa said as he and Ma heaved over the side of the ship.

"I don't understand why you don't like this ship I'm having a great time," Zack said with enthusiasm. We all looked at him in disgust and just walked away. As time passed, we did feel a little better, but our opinion about traveling by sea hadn't changed.

It was on a cloudy afternoon when we entered the port of New York. We gratefully disembarked except for Zack, who wished he could stay a few more days aboard ship. When we got our things, Ma and Pa got dressed fancy again; then Pa hailed a coach to take us to another fancy hotel. At the hotel, my father instructed the driver to wait. He told us to stay in the coach, and then he went into the hotel. He was only in the hotel a short time when he came back to the coach with another man and said, "This place will be fine, give your things to this man."

We all gave our belongings to the man who put them on a cart as Pa paid the coachman and into the hotel, we all went. The outside and inside of this hotel were beyond anything I could believe. It made the last hotel look like a dump. We got stares as we went in more for Zack and me than for Ma. I think it was the way we dressed and the fact that we were awestruck at the place. Our room was like the one in St. Louis with an outer chamber and two bedrooms. While Zack and I were looking out the window at our surroundings, there was a knock at the door, and two black men came pushing two bathtubs with a large black woman who carried towels.

"Here are your bathtubs Mr. York," said the black woman. The two black men rolled the baths into each bedroom, and the black woman gave some towels and things like soap, powder, and lotion to Ma and Pa instead of providing the towels to Zack or me. She said with a smile on her face, "I'm here to wash the boys."

Zack and I looked at each other in shock, and Zack said, "I can wash, myself, Pa."

"And I'm nearly thirteen Pa," I stated in an alarmed voice.

"In the Shoshone village, they have their customs, and both of you know what they are." "And in St. Louis, you both knew what the customs are, especially you, James." "This city is New York, and we have different habits here, and I am the one who knows them here." "In New York boys, your age gets bathed by a woman such as her, and what's more, if she doesn't bathe you, she will lose her job, isn't that so Madam?"

"To tell you the truth, I would certainly get in trouble," she replied.

"Aw, Pa," both Zack and I said together.

"You're not going to win this one boys, now go and do what she says," said Pa.

When Pa said this, Ma, who was behind Pa, moved her head in a stern motion, indicating that Zack and I would get into the bedroom and do as Pa told us. We put our heads down and went into the bedroom, the black woman following behind and shutting the door. The lady placed the towels, soap, powder, and lotion on a table next to the bed. Then she sat on the bed and called for us to stand in front of her.

She grabbed for Zack's pistols, but Zack stopped her and said, "What are you doing?"

"Undressing you, now don't give me any more trouble, or I will talk with your parents."

Zack and I both knew it was no use arguing with her, and Zack let her do as she wished. She pulled out the pistols and his knife, looked at each one of them in confusion and asked, "What do you need all these weapons for?"

"Just in case there are varmints around."

"This hotel is spotless; there are no pests here.

"I'm not talking about the four-legged ones." "I'm talking about the two-legged ones."

"There might be a few of those around I know a few myself." She said with a laugh.

She took his shirt off and looked at his loincloth and leggings and said more to herself than either of us, "Most odd-looking clothing I ever did see." She took off his moccasins, loincloth, and leggings and took him by the hand to a chamber pot, and said, "Do your business in there while I undress your brother."

She started undressing me the same way as Zack, looking at the weapons and shaking her head and said, "Varmints, huh?" I nodded my head, yes, she removed the rest of my clothes and said, "Where did you get those scars, child?"

"Many sources but mostly the Blackfeet."

"The Blackfeet, they are not from my black feet," she said.

"The Blackfeet are a tribe of Indians far to the west," I said with a smile.

"Them Blackfeet should be horsewhipped for hurting a child like you if you ask me."

"I assure you I dealt with them, and they will be dealt with again," I said seriously.

She took me by the hand over to where Zack was sitting on the chamber pot and asked Zack if he finished. He nodded yes, and she grabbed his hand and told me to do my business. She took Zack over to the tub and lifted him like a baby and placed him in the tub. She then looked over at me and said, "When you finished there, you come over to me so that I can put you in with your brother."

A few minutes later, I came over to her, and she lifted me like I was as light as a feather and put me into the tub with Zack. She started washing Zack's hair and asked, "How come you two have different colored hair?"

"Different mothers, madam," I said.

"Oh," she said, embarrassed that she asked. She finished Zack's hair and started on mine. Then she washed the rest of me, and she wasn't very gentle about it. She lifted Zack out first and dried him, then laid him on the bed with a towel wrapped around him, and then she did the same to me. After this, she unwrapped us and put lotion and powdered on us; we got mortified. She slapped us both on the bottom, grabbed everything, including the chamber pot, and left laughing.

We both looked at each other and buried our heads in a pillow. I never felt so humiliated since I had to take a bath in front of Sarah. We both got dressed in our best clothing and joined Ma and Pa out in the outer room. "I never want to go through that again," Zack growled.

"Me neither," I added.

"Well, you both look handsome," Ma said.

We both gave her a dirty look, and she acted like she was shocked.

"Alright, boys, let's go downstairs and get something to eat," Pa said.

The food seemed better than that in St. Louis, and as we finished our meal Pa said, "Shall we go see what kind of reception we will get when we visit my folks?"

It was past four in the afternoon when we left, and Pa had the doorman hail a carriage for us. Then pa told the man driving the carriage where to go and off we went.

We traveled for about thirty minutes and then stopped at a large white house; the house was across the street from a grassy area with trees, benches, and a place for children to play. Pa told the carriage driver to wait a few minutes. Pa rang the bell on the door, and a short, thin man came to the door in a few seconds. When he saw Pa, he became very excited to see him. At first, I thought it might be Grandpa, but it turned out to be the butler. We were summoned into the foyer and asked to wait. I looked around the room, and it appeared to be a beautiful place with paintings and real nice bowls and things. An older man and woman came running into the room and hugged Pa.

"This is Blue Flower, Zack, and James." "These are your grandparents, boys," Pa said. They gave Ma a hug and a kiss on the cheek and then went over to Zack and me to hugged us.

"If everything is alright, I will pay the carriage driver; if not, we can leave," said Pa cautiously.

"Of course, everything is alright, and I will pay for your carriage," Grandpa York said.

"I have plenty of money, father," Pa said.

"So, do I, and it will be my pleasure to pay him," Grandpa said. He went out and paid what the man said we owed.

When Grandpa and Pa came back into the house, we all went into a sitting room, and Grandpa ordered a maid to bring some refreshments. I wasn't hungry or thirsty, but I didn't say anything thinking it would not be polite.

"So, Nate, you made your fortune in those mountains as you told me you would." "What did you call them?" Grandpa said.

"The Shining Mountains, father, sometimes called the Rocky Mountains." "And no, I didn't make the fortune my son James did," Pa said.

"Which one is James?" Grandpa asked. I raised my hand, and Grandpa asked, "Now, young man, how did you make your father rich?"

I looked over at Pa, and he shook his head, yes, that let me reveal our secret. "I found gold, a lot of it, almost three million dollars worth so far," I said. Both Grandpa's and Grandma's mouth fell open.

"Is this true, Nate?" Grandpa asked.

"Yes, it is," Pa replied.

"I don't want it to get out; it would ruin those mountains and cause a lot of trouble," Pa added.

"Of course, we understand," Grandpa said.

"Where do you keep it, banked?" asked Grandpa.

"In St. Louis," Pa said.

Our refreshments arrived, and before Zack and I got any Grandma asked, "Would you boys like to eat in the garden."

We both looked at Pa again, and he nodded yes, and so we went outside. The maid showed us to the back of the house where there were finely cut bushes, flowers, statues, and a place to sit. And we were given milk and pastries. When we were left alone, I offered my pastries and milk to Zack, which he greedily took and devoured. We left the empty cups and explored the yard. "Strange how Grandpa and Grandma got things growing here." "You would think they would have something you could pick and eat," Zack said.

"Yeah, but I like it, it is pleasing to the eye."

We were by the window where our parents and grandparents were, and we could hear them talking.

"You look very healthy, Nate, it must be because of your wife," said grandmother.

"Blue flower has taken excellent care of the boys and me."

Blue Flower smiled and said, "Nate and the boys have taken just as much care of me as I have them."

Mother and father blew out a sigh of relief, and grandmother continued, "I didn't think you spoke English."

"Nor did I," said Grandpa.

"I speak many languages, as does Nate," Blue Flower said.

"I guessed that you are an Indian if this is true, what tribe are you from?" Father said.

"I am a Shoshone," Blue Flower said.

"All four of us are Shoshone father, James is a very well-known warrior," said Nate.

"James, he is just a boy," said Grandpa.

"Don't underestimate him father; he is very strong, wise, and a good shot with just about any weapon." Pa left out how many people I killed. Pa thought that my grandparents didn't need to know about those types of things.

"Blue Flower, have you ever seen or heard of Sacagawea," asked grandmother. "Oh yes, I know her very well, but I have not seen her for many years. That was not her Shoshone name. The last time I saw her, it was long before I met Nate, she was from another village."

"What is she like?" asked Grandfather.

"Very kind, she married a great white warrior by the name of Toussaint Charbonneau from what I understand." "She was taken away by my people's enemy, the Hidatsa, which are related to the Mandan." "Sacagawea is a Hidatsa name meaning Bird Woman." "Her brother is Cameahwait, who was the leader of another village."

"Cameahwait is Sacagawea's brother?" asked Nate.

"Yes," Blue Flower replied.

"Whatever happened to Sacagawea?" "She shouldn't be that old?" asked grandmother.

"I heard she died I do not know what of, but her children went with a white man who is raising them in the white world," said Blue Flower.

"If I am not prying, I would like to ask you about James, he does not look the same as your son Zack," said Grandfather.

"They are half-brothers." "On the way west, I met a woman in St. Louis, James's mother." "She died, and I didn't know James existed for about twelve years." "When I found, him he had been adopted by a Shoshone family who perished in an attack by another tribe." "That same tribe attacked, tortured, and killed James's aunt, uncle, and younger cousin." "Somehow, James escaped being also killed and was saved by a Shoshone warrior by the name of Red Elk." "He adopted him and raised him for several years until Red Elk's death when I found him," said Nate.

"The boy must have gone through hell," said Grandfather.

"He has been through a lot and seen a lot," replied Nate.

"It has made him a strong, wise, and independent boy who is just about to turn into a man." "So, with all the bad he has gone through, there has been some good," said Blue Flower.

"I think sometimes he is just too independent; we have butted heads at times," said Nate.

"Much like you and your father," said grandmother.

"I don't know what you mean, mother, I thought I was always an obedient son," said Nate.

"To me, Nate, but you and your father had your moments, especially just before you left."

Nate looked at his father, put his head down, and said, "I guess you are right, mother."

"So, our son is just like you, Nate, except most of the time he is right," said Blue Flower.

Nate turned red but didn't say anything, then Grandmother said, "Nate was right a lot of the time when he was at it with his father."

Blue Flower and grandmother both laughed at that while Grandpa and Pa just kept silent.

"Tell me of Zack, what kind of boy is he?" asked Grandfather.

"He is a good-natured, inquisitive boy who wants to grow up faster than he is," said Nate.

"Most boys want to grow up too fast," said grandmother.

"He has a lot of love in him for others and is very obedient." "Although with James around, he has been trying to show a little independence," said Blue Flower.

"I am afraid sometimes he is trapped between two worlds, the white and the red, which I fear will cause him great distress someday," said Nate.

"Even though James is white, the same is true with him," said Blue Flower.

"Both boys get along well together, and they are very protective of each other." "Although I don't think that either of them has a lot of patience, with each other," said Nate.

"James, there seems to be a large building back here that belongs to Grandpa's house," said Zack. We both went and investigated the place, and it turned out to be a barn with some fine-looking horses of a variety I didn't know. He also had a couple of beautiful carriages, one being better than the other. He had a lot of tack I had never seen before, especially the saddles. The building would have made an excellent cabin back in the mountains. It got put together better than the barn and corrals back in St. Louis. After looking and checking out the horses, we headed back to the house.

When we entered, Pa and Grandpa had gone into another room to talk while they smoked and drank what I figured was whiskey. Ma and Grandma were still in the same room talking, and we joined them. Zack sat next to Ma, and she put her arm around him. I sat across from them, listening to Ma and Grandma, who was talking about how Ma cures people and how she gets food and cooks it. I was bored and went to join Pa and Grandpa.

They turned toward me, and Grandpa said, "This room is for grown-ups, mostly James, we are talking about grown-up things."

I became a bit irritated and said, "I am a man I do work as a man, I hunt like a man, and I kill like a man."

"Kill, huh?" "Here is a cigar would you like to smoke it," said Grandpa.

He didn't believe I killed anyone, and I'm guessing he didn't know what I have smoked.

"Father, I told you never to underestimate him," Nate said.

I bit off one end and lit the cigar started to smoke it, and said, "I have smoked many times in counsel with the elders." "This cigar is good, better than what they smoke; it must be real tobacco."

Grandpa took the cigar out of my mouth and threw it into the fireplace and said, "I suppose you have had liquor also?"

"Yes, but I don't drink." "It muddles up one's mind, and in the mountains, that is not good," I replied.

"Muddle up, huh?" Grandpa said, laughing. "Alright, you are man enough to join us in this room," he added.

"You have some beautiful horses, Grandpa." "You have breeds I have never seen before."

"You have an excellent eye for horseflesh, young man." "Those horses are some of the best horses in New York." "Perhaps I will leave some of them to you when I die," Grandpa added.

"They will be good to breed with the rest of my herd," I said.

"Herd, you have horses?" asked Grandpa.

"Grey Wolf and I have many horses."

"Grey Wolf is that Zack's Indian name?" asked Grandpa.

"No father, Grey Wolf, was adopted by Red Elk, James's Shoshone father, which makes him James's brother."

Grandpa shook his head in understanding, and when they both had finished drinking and smoking, Grandpa said, "We should join the women before they wonder what we are up to."

"We should head back to our hotel; it is getting late," Pa said.

"Nonsense, you will stay with us," Grandma said. "You can sleep in the guest room, and the boys can sleep in your brother's and your old room," Grandpa said.

Pa looked at Ma, and Ma was leaving it up to Pa. Before Pa could say anything, Grandpa said, "I won't take no for an answer you are staying, I will send for your things."

"Grandpa, your servants, don't have a habit of washing children, do they?" Zack asked.

"Not unless we tell them to," he said.

"If you don't tell them, I'm willing to stay here, Grandpa."

Both Grandma and Grandpa looked at Ma and Pa in bewilderment, and Ma said, "The boys had a bath before they came here, and it was the job of a hotel woman to bathe them, which they did not like." "The woman washed them in a way they didn't like."

Grandma and Grandpa started laughing, and Grandma said, "You don't have to worry here." "You and James can bathe yourselves."

Grandpa called for his butler and asked Pa, "What is the name of the hotel you are at?"

"The Grand American." Pa pulled some money out and handed it to the butler, and Grandpa protested and said he would pay for it, but Pa said, "You paid for the carriage ride I will pay for my room." Pa won that one which kind of surprised me.

Grandma said, "Let me show you your rooms." We all followed her upstairs; we stopped at Zack and my room first. It had two beds in it with what I believe were toys.

"Were these yours, Pa?" Zack asked.

Pa went over, looked at them, and said with a smile, "Some of them were." "Some were your uncle Daniel's, and some were both of ours." "I've forgotten all about these."

"Can we play with them, Pa?" Zack asked.

"Of course, you can, that's why they are there," said Grandma.

The door shut, and Zack started handling the toys, but I was more interested in the books. I found one I could finish in a short period. I jumped up on the bed and started to read while Zack sat on the floor with the toys.

I don't know how many hours had passed. I was reading; there was a knock at the door. One of my Grandparents' servants opened the door and said, "It is time for dinner your family wishes your presence."

"We will be down, right after we wash," I said.

Zack and I were about to go downstairs when I decided I didn't need my pistols, and I left them on the bed, carrying my knife only, and Zack did the same. I must admit that I felt a little naked without them. We found the dining room, and we sat in the two empty chairs.

"Did you have fun playing with the toys boys," Grandpa said, looking at Zack and me.

Zack said, "Yes."

"I didn't play with them." "I'm reading one of the books that were up there."

Grandpa had a surprised look on his face as did Grandma. "What book are you reading?" Grandpa asked. "Robinson Crusoe, I think Zack would like the story; it is a good story," I said.

"I don't recognize the title, it must be Daniel's book," Pa said.

"Yes, do you read much, James?" Grandpa asked.

"They say that before I could talk if I got my hand on a book, I would read it." "I don't know if that is entirely accurate, but I do like to read almost anything, and I have read a lot of books."

Grandpa nodded and said, "Interesting." "You know Nate, I could get you a good job at the bank, and your wife would have whatever she wanted." "Also, your children would have the best of schools and make a name for themselves if you would stay here in New York."

I shook my head no, and Pa seeing it said, "I must think about it."

"For me, there is no thinking, what about Morning Star?" I said.

"Is this Morning Star a person?" asked Grandpa.

Before anyone could answer, I said, "Morning Star is my wife."

"Wife, nonsense, you're much too young to have a wife; you're only twelve," said Grandpa.

"I was married when I was ten had relations soon after that." "I have been building a cabin, and we will both live in it next year," I said.

Grandma and Grandpa were shocked, and Grandma said, "Is this possible, Nate?" "How can this be?" "No Christian minister would marry one so young?"

"He is married mother; he married young." "It is not something that hasn't happened before with the Shoshone."

"Shoshone, if it was the Shoshone who got him married, then it is not real," said Grandpa.

"It is real; Sacagawea was married to a white man when she was twelve." "When you marry in the Shoshone way, it is sacred." "Nate and I were married the same way as James," Ma said.

"Blue Flower, we didn't mean to show a lack of respect for your people," Grandpa said.

"James, why not bring your wife here?"

"She would have the best of everything," Grandpa told me in a much softer voice.

"Grandma, Grandpa you do not understand, you do have many wonderful things here, but it is like having these things in a jail cell, there is no freedom here." "You cannot trust one another; you must lock your doors." "The air is not fresh, and there is disease here." "Your people are weak and sickly, and many are unfriendly." "For the most part, it is just the opposite in the mountains, you have real freedom," I said.

"But didn't you tell me there are a lot of dangers in those mountains?" Grandma said to Ma and Pa.

"There are, but you know what they are, and one recognizes them when they come when you are good you know how to protect yourself and loved ones or avoid them altogether," said Pa.

"It sounds like you have already made up your mind," said Grandpa.

"It is not my mind to make up. I would have talked it over with my family and base my decision on what they say." "I am sure the outcome will be to go back to the mountains." "It isn't that my family or I don't love you or appreciate your offer; the fact is we love you very much, and the offer is tempting, but the call of the mountains is strong." "What we would leave behind, if we were to stay, is great," Pa said so eloquently.

"Alright, son, we understand." "You know you make those mountains sound good." "If we were younger and healthier, we might wish to go with you," said Grandpa.

"Why don't you, you're not that old, Grandpa?" "There are older people than you there," said Zack.

"Yes, Zack, I believe you, but as your father told me, you and your brother are very strong, and your Grandmother and I aren't." "Also, you hunt for your food." "I have never hunted before we buy our food at a store."

"When Mama died in St. Louis, and I had to go west with Uncle Henry, I was eight years old or younger, I was weak and didn't know how to hunt, but I learn." "Even if you didn't learn how to hunt, there would be enough of us to hunt for you." "There will be many white families coming west soon anyway, and there will be towns with stores in them, my spirit guide showed me this," I said.

"Spirit guide, what is this spirit guide?" asked Grandpa.

"Young Shoshone warriors go on something like a vision quest or have something like a prophecy." "They do this for many reasons; to get a name, they will use the rest of their lives, to get wisdom or foresight of the future."

"James got all three, and his Shoshone name is Soaring Eagle With Many Coups, coups are brave acts," Pa explained.

"I have not done this yet, Grandpa, but I will soon not for a name, I have a Shoshone name already it is Tracking Fox." "I will do it for wisdom and to see the future," said Zack.

"And what of you, Nate, have you done this vision quest and gotten a name?" asked Grandpa.

"No, but I do have a name not given by the Shoshone, but by the Cheyenne, it is Bear Slayer."

"I won't ask you how you got that name for your mother's sake," said Grandpa. "As far as your proposal James it is tempting." "However, I have too many obligations here, and most of your father's family lives here, including his brother and sisters." "Which reminds me, Nate, how long will you be able to stay here with us?" asked Grandpa.

"Three or four days at the most, and that is it."

"Then we will have a grand dinner party in two days, and I will invite all the relatives," said Grandpa.

"Yes, that will be grand, and I will make all the arrangements tomorrow," said Grandma.

The rest of the night involved grown-up talk, which Zack and I weren't interested. The food was good; Zack couldn't get enough of the sweets at the end. I ate some of mine and gave the rest to Zack.

After dinner, Zack and I excused ourselves and went upstairs, Zack, to play with the toys and me to read. It was late at night Zack had already crawled into bed and gone to sleep. I was still reading when I heard the doors of the other rooms opening and shutting. I got already stripped down to my loincloth to go to sleep soon. I decided to go down the hall to talk to Ma and Pa privately before they fell asleep. As I was walking down the hall, Grandma came up the stairs holding a lantern and spotted me.

"Child, what are you doing up at this hour you should be asleep."

"I was reading in bed and heard Ma and Pa, and I wanted to talk to them."

She put the lantern nearer to me and said, "Where did you get all those scars on your body?"

"Mostly from battles I've been in with the Blackfeet. There are others for other reasons."

She just shook her head and said, "Alright, you better get to your parents' room before they fall asleep."

I knocked on the door, and they said, "Come in."

They were already in bed, and I asked, "Can I talk to you?"

"This can't wait until tomorrow?" Pa said.

"I don't know when we will have enough privacy to talk," I said.

"Alright," Pa said. Ma patted the bed between them. I smiled and crawled up onto the bed and sat between them, and Pa put his arm around me; it was nice.

"There are a few things I want to talk about to you." "I want to say I am sorry if I made it difficult for you and Grandpa for saying I would go back if you stay here."

"I wasn't going to stay, James." "You just made me tell them quicker than what I was going to." "What you did was alright," Pa said.

"Good, there may be more trouble tomorrow with Grandma and Grandpa," I said.

"Why, what happened?" Ma said.

"Grandma saw all the scars on my body while I was walking down the hall," I said.

Pa looked at Ma and said, "That might be a problem, but I will deal with it when and if it comes up."

"At dinner, it came up about Uncle Henry getting more land in Oregon because I lived with them, do you remember that?"

"Yes, I think I do," said Pa.

"Had he gotten that land, there would have been some documentation that he owned it."

"We don't have documentation for the land around us." "Someone might try to steal it someday, and we won't be able to stop him," I said.

"We are living in an area disputed by Mexico and maybe even England as being theirs." "However, your thought is a good idea, and I will talk to a lawyer either here in New York or St. Louis before we go back home." "I will also talk to Grandpa about this tomorrow." "Alright?" Pa asked. I nodded my head in agreement, and he asked, "Is there anything else?"

"Can I sleep in bed with both of you tonight?"

"No, now go back to your bed," they both said together.

Reluctantly I went back to Zack's and my room, and it wasn't long before I was asleep.

The whole house was abuzz with the preparations for the party the next day. There were going to be about twenty-six people; they are all relatives. Everyone would sit at a long table to eat. Then there would be music and dancing after dinner. The music I would enjoy, but I didn't know how to dance at least not the white man's dance. Grandma and Grandpa tried to get us to wear some fancy clothes like Ma and Pa, but Zack and I weren't having anything to do with it. "You boys come with me I want to show you a room you haven't seen," Grandpa said.

We both followed him, and we went into a large room with a lot of books. "Are all these books, yours's Grandpa?" I asked.

"Yes, and you boys can look at any one of these books." Zack picked up a book full of maps and was thumbing through it, and I just stared in amazement at all those books. Grandpa noticed my amazement and said, "Quite a collection isn't it, James?"

"Yes, I purchased many books in St. Louis to take with me back home, but not this many I don't think." "And not as excellent of books like these."

"James, look at this, all these strange places around the world," said Zack.

Grandpa went over to Zack, took the book out of his hand, and sat down. Then he motioned for Zack and me to stand on each side of him. Pointing at a large picture of England, he said, "You see this country here?"

We both shook our heads, yes.

"This is England the York's are of royal blood, which means we are related to the king." "There is a large estate there, which belongs to me." "Someday, when your grandmother and I are gone, it will belong to one of your aunts or uncles or even your father I haven't decided yet."

"I would say your father is the frontrunner to getting it because he has more fortitude and smarts than his siblings, but don't say anything to him until you're long gone."

We both nodded our heads, yes, and he got up without saying another word and left. I stayed in there for a while, looking at as many books as I could. Zack got bored and got some toys and went outside to play.

After a while, I found a book that interested me, and I took it upstairs. I wanted to finish the first book and to get busy in the second. I was already reading the second book when Zack came into the room and asked, "Have you been here all day?"

"Yes."

"Well, it is time to eat."

"Oh, I will wait till dinner."

"It is dinner; didn't you eat lunch?"

"No."

"You better come down now, or you will starve." I left a marker in the book and washed up and went downstairs.

"We missed you at lunch, where were you?" asked Ma.

"I was reading, and time got away from me," I said.

"What are you reading, child?" asked Grandma.

"Gallic Antiquities by John Smith I found it in the library."

"That is a very hard book for a boy your age, but it is a good one if you want to know about England," said Grandpa.

"It is more difficult than Robinson Crusoe, but I am getting through it, Grandpa," I said.

"Well, if it is too boring, you don't have to finish it." "You can find another book," Grandpa said.

"Once I start a book, I always finish it." "You never know years later what you learned in it might come in handy," I replied.

"Uh, very smart," he said. Grandpa then changed the subject, and as they were talking, I wasn't paying attention to what they were saying.

Then Pa said from what I heard, "James, we will be leaving tomorrow morning early."

"Are we going home so soon?" I asked.

"Haven't you heard what we were talking about?" asked Pa.

"No, my mind was in that book I was reading and on my food."

"We are going down to a lawyer friend early tomorrow about our land, so be ready."

"I will, Pa."

"Zack, you stay here with your mother," Pa added.

Zack nodded, and after dinner, I went back upstairs to read the rest of the night.

I was up at five the next morning, and I dressed, washed, and went downstairs to join my father and grandfather, but no one was down there. So, I went back upstairs to Ma and Pa's room and knocked on the door. "What is it?" Pa said sleepily.

I opened the door and said, "I thought you told me to be up early so we could go to the lawyer's office."

"I should have told you, but city folk gets up much later than we do. Go back to bed. I will get you when we are going to go?"

I shut their door and went back to my room, but I didn't try to go back to sleep, I grabbed my book and read.

It was past seven when Zack and I got called downstairs to eat breakfast. "Are we still going to the lawyer's office?" I asked.

"Yes, we are, young man right after breakfast," Grandpa said. "I understand you were up hours earlier, James."

"Yes, early to me is way before the sun comes up but it is alright, I read while I waited."

"Most shops don't open until seven-thirty, and we must stop at another place before we go to the lawyer," said Grandpa.

"What place is that father?" asked Pa.

"The map-making shop; they will have the latest maps from the area you are living at from the government surveyor's office," replied Grandpa.

Grandpa had one of his carriages hooked up, and about a half-an-hour later, we were at the map shop. We had looked through a lot of maps when I spotted one that looked familiar. "Pa, isn't this the Yellow Stone?"

"Yes, do you have a map just south of this one?" Pa asked the clerk in the shop.

"Look, there are Longs Peak and the Three Sisters, I believe," said Pa.

"Isn't that the south fork of the Sweet River and look here, Pa this is the north fork," I said excitedly.

"Is there some significance to that river?" Grandpa asked.

"On that river is the village where Blue Flower and James came from," Pa said.

"They move from time to time, but they stay around that river," Pa added.

"Now let me see southwest of there. Our cabin should be about here," said Pa.

"I don't see the stream or lake, Pa," I said.

"You must understand the topography of maps is only as good as the information we get by the surveyors that go to these areas," the clerk said.

Grandpa and Pa just stared at him, and he said, "Oh, excuse me. Topography means...."

"It means the showing of physical features, such as rivers, lakes, mountains, and elevation," I said.

Everyone turned around and looked at me, and the clerk said, surprised, "Yes."

"Smart boy, you have there, Nate," said Grandpa.

"Yes, he is," replied Pa.

"We will take this map; do you have another?" said Grandpa.

"Yes, I do," replied the clerk.

Pa tried to pay the clerk, but Grandpa wasn't having anything to do with it, much to Pa's frustration.

We left the shop and got into the carriage, and Pa said, "Father, you are going to have to let me pay for some things."

Grandpa just laughed and said, "It is my pleasure to pay." "I haven't seen you in years, and once you leave, I may never see you again."

About twenty minutes later, we came up to a large brick building and went in. The office we went to was very busy with many people and had other doors to what I assume were other offices. "William York to see Roger Taney," said Grandpa to a clerk.

"Judge Taney is extremely busy do you have an appointment, sir?" asked the clerk.

"He'll see me if he wants to be a Supreme Court judge."

The clerk knocked at one of the doors in the office and went in. In a few minutes, he came out and said, "Judge Taney will see you, sir, right this way."

Pa and I followed Grandpa and the clerk into one room with a clerk or someone in there. Then we went into a larger room where an older man was behind a large desk with a lot of books and paper everywhere. "Bill, it is a pleasure to see you," said Judge Taney.

"This is my son Nathaniel and my grandson, James."

We both shook his hand and got directed to sit in some chairs he had in his office. "What can I do for you?" the judge asked.

"My son and his family have some land far to the west near the Oregon Territory." "The land doesn't have protected from settlers or swindlers from taking it, we need to correct this," Grandpa said.

The judge leaned back in his chair and started thinking. Then said, "There is a law that land will be deeded to each person, regardless of age, for settlement in the Oregon Territory."

"This is out of that area, east of the Territory," Grandpa said.

"That's alright it doesn't say it stops at the Oregon Territory." "I can still work something out," said the judge.

"We are very close to or in what Mexico claims as theirs," Pa said.

"That is a problem," said the judge as he leaned back to think again. Judge Taney smiled and started laughing and said, "I can still do something for you." "It most likely won't do you much good with the Mexicans, but it will be legal in the United States." "Besides, that land will probably be part of the United States someday anyway."

The judge yelled for his clerk in the outer office who came in. And he said to the clerk, "I want a legal document wrote up." "I want it to state that Mr. Nathaniel York is deeded, oh let's see, two thousand acres of land per person in his family plus what you already claim."

"You better add, regardless of age, male or female." "Especially regardless if the family member is an Indian or not if he or she is considered part of the York family," I said.

"Good ideas, Roger, you better add them just in case someone says Indians, women, or children don't have any rights," said Grandpa.

"Alright, I will have it added there is no law that I know of stating that Indians can't own land," said the judge.

"You might also add any future children born or adopted to the Nathaniel York family line," I added.

"I was going to add that young man; you seem to be a very bright person." "If you ever would like to work in this law office, I would gladly take you on," Judge Taney said.

"Now I must have some reference as to where you live, Nathaniel," said Judge Taney.

Grandpa took out one of the maps and pointed to the area. "We will note this area on the map and stamp the map. We will put in the document that there will be ten thousand acres in front of your home and the rest of the acreage around your home as the York family has marked," the judge said.

"Make me two copies," the judge added.

"Pa, I would like to have a copy also," I said.

Everybody looked at the judge, and he said, "Make that three copies." "It should take about twenty minutes or so, then we will reread it to make sure everything is correct, and then you, Nathaniel, and I will sign them." "One copy will stay here, and the others will go with you," said Judge Taney.

In the time we waited, Pa talked about the mountains and our life there. The judge seemed very interested, and I kept quiet and listened. Judge Taney offered Grandpa and Pa a drink, which they took. Just as the judge said, about twenty minutes later, the three documents came into the room. Grandpa, Pa, and the judge read the document, and all were satisfied, including me. The judge and Pa signed all three documents, and we left the office and headed for home.

Everyone was looking at the documents at home, and Pa said, "I wonder just how much land that is?"

"Over sixty-five square miles of land, Pa."

They all looked at me in surprise but didn't question my estimate. "I would say you got a good deal Nate," said Grandpa.

"Yeah," he said, still shock.

"You boys go upstairs and take your baths the maid is drawing your water now," Grandma said.

"Grandma, you said we could take our baths without help," Zack said.

"The maid is just putting water in the tub." "She isn't going to wash you although she should," Grandma replied.

We both went upstairs. Zack was feeling a little better, but I don't think he wanted to take a bath.

After we bathed, I went back to reading while Zack played with the toys. Sandwiches and milk got brought up to our room. We weren't going to get a regular lunch because of the party. It was just past six at night when Pa came to the door and said, "Get dressed in your best and no weapons. For Grandma's and Grandpa's sake, be on your best behavior, and both of you comb your hair."

Pa left without our saying anything more. Zack and I looked at each other, and Zack said, "I didn't know that we were misbehaving."

We were dressed and groomed by about six-thirty, and then we headed downstairs. There were a lot of people dressed in their finest, even Ma and Pa looked good. When they spotted Zack and me, they all stared, but I didn't care, I wouldn't be seeing them again. There were three other children there, one about Zack's and my age, but they wouldn't talk to us, and the adults didn't think Zack and I were worth talking to us. I put up with it for Ma's and Pa's sake, and at about seven, we all sat down to eat. Grandpa was sitting at the end of the table where we were seated, and Grandma was at the other end. On our side of the table, it was Ma, Pa, Zack and me. To my right were aunts and uncles, and across from us were some cousins. It was quite boring everyone talking to each other but not to Zack or me. There were a few statements said to Ma and Pa that weren't very flattering. I don't know if they caught on, but I did. There was a conversation going on across the table from us, and my relatives were speaking French. Speaking French interested me why would someone speak French unless they didn't want people to know what they were saying.

I listened to what they said, and they said, "I cannot understand it, Nate is so good-looking, and he married a dirty savage."

"Most likely, she is just a savage whore."

"I don't know how he can stand it. He could have had any woman, but he prefers her."

"If you ask me, it is like having sex with an animal."

"Look at the litter he had; even the white one looks like a lowlife."

The conversation went on and on with people around them who understood French putting in their nasty comments.

I finally had enough and said to Pa in Shoshone, "Father, I need to speak to you."

The fact I was speaking Shoshone got his attention, and he said back in Shoshone, "Speak."

"What I have to say may hurt mother's and Tracking Fox's feelings."

"Anything you have to say, you will say in front of all of us," Ma said.

"Very well, these people are speaking the French language, saying bad things about us."

"Like what?" Pa asked.

"We are nothing but dirty savages, mother is a prostitute, but they used a worse word than that." "Also, having relations with her is like having relations with an animal and much more."

Ma looked at Pa, and you could see he was mad, and Pa said, "I will deal with them."

"No, James heard what was said." "James will handle it in his way," Ma said.

Pa was not going to argue with Ma but said, "Alright, do what you think is right but no violence and let me tell Grandfather what is going to happen first."

"There will be no violence unless they try something," I said.

Grandpa could see something wrong, and Pa told him, "There is going to be a little trouble, I will explain later."

"What is it, Nate?" said Grandpa.

"Later," said Pa.

The people across the table were still at it in French, with those around us not paying attention to my family's demeanor, which was evident.

I decided to give a verbal attack in French to shock them all. Standing up and throwing my chair to the floor and in a loud, stern voice, I said in French, "Perhaps you should find out if we speak French before you speak these words of filth." "My whole family knows what you are saying." "You all don't know anything about us." "You call us animals and savages, but animals and savages have no manners, and neither do any of you." "So, who is the savage, and who are the animals?" "Look at yourselves who must hide behind the French language to speak this filth, are you cowards?"

"Look, George, this little bastard savage can speak French."

"And you call my mother a whore." "Look at you a poor excuse for a human being," I said.

"I will not have a child, let alone a lowlife savage bastard talk to my wife that way."

"The only thing keeping you and the rest of you who are involved alive now is that this is my Grandfather's house for which I will show respect." By this time, I had been speaking English, as were my relatives.

"Oh, really, what is a child going to do to me?" Cousin George said.

"You have no idea what I am capable of doing." "I have killed many for less than what you have said." "Who has made the same mistake as you are making now."

There was much laughter, some of which was nervous. Only the fools who could speak French were laughing with arrogance.

Pa stood up and said, "I would heed him." "He is strong enough and talented enough to do everything he has said, and frankly, I might just join him." "You know you're lucky you are not lying dead on the floor now." "Normally, he would not have listened to me when I told him no violence." "The only thing I can figure is that he loves and respects his Grandparents, and I think that if he did get violent, I would join him along with his brother."

"You weren't much of a fighter before you left Nate." "I can't believe you are too much to handle now," someone said.

At that, Pa was fuming, and he was about to do something when Grandpa grabbed his arm, stood up, and said to my relatives, "You will leave my house at once you are no longer welcome here." "This party was to honor my son and his family, and you have made a mockery of it." "When I investigate, all who were involved you will find you will get entirely cut off from all support, now get out!"

There was no one laughing now. Most left, including my two aunts who had nothing to say and my Grandparents, took notice of this. My father's brother, my uncle and a few cousins stayed, and my uncle said, "I must apologize to you, little brother." "I wasn't involved in their conversation, and as you know, I don't speak French, but I did laugh at your son's justified anger."

"It is the same with us; I mean no disrespect to you or your family," said a cousin. "What your son said so eloquently was correct, and I, for one, do speak French but was not involved with their disrespectful conversation."

Grandpa had the servants clear the table of all those who left. He told the rest, "Let's all come down to this end of the table and make the best out of the remainder of the evening."

My uncle asked me as he was sitting down across from me, "How many languages do you speak?"

"Nine or ten fluently and others not as good."

One of my female cousins asked, "Is it correct about you killing many people?"

Ma answered that one, "Among my people, the Shoshone, he is a great warrior." "His Shoshone name is Soaring Eagle With Many Coups; coups are acts of bravery." "He is a feared warrior by my people's enemies, and I had seen him in battle when our enemies attacked our village." "He killed many, not only with the bow and rifle but in hand-to-hand fighting with those who were much bigger than he." "He saved his brother's life as well as the lives of many others." "He has been in many battles and has always fought bravely and been victorious."

"I have seen his scars on his body since he has been here, and they are scars of battle," said Grandma.

The conversation changed to things that I had little interest in, and when it got late Zack, and I started upstairs for bed, but Grandpa stopped me and said, "Do you remember that conversation we had about England and the property I have there?"

"Yes, Grandpa, I've told no one about it," I said.

"I have made up my mind about it, and I will be giving you a piece of paper when you leave." "When you are gone three days, you can tell your family what was discussed and look at the paper." "You are not to open the paper until the three days have passed; understand?" said Grandpa.

"I will do as you say, Grandpa," I replied.

"Good boy, now off you go to bed."

Upstairs in Zack's and my room Zack was already undressed and playing with the toys. I got undressed and read, and I was still reading when Zack was sound asleep.

I was up at six, but I knew no one would be up, so I read. I wanted to finish the book before breakfast. I finished the book just before Zack, and I went downstairs to eat breakfast. I handed the book to Grandpa, and he said, "What did you think of the book, James?"

"Boring, but who knows, maybe I will use something from it when I get older."

"My exact feelings when I read it," Grandpa replied with a smile. "I have another book." "I think you will like much better, James."

"Thank you, but I don't think I will be able to finish it, Grandpa," I replied.

"Now, don't worry about that; you can take it with you."

"That is very generous of you, Grandpa."

"And you, young man, all those toys you have been playing with are yours to do with as you wish," Grandpa told Zack.

"Really!" "I can keep them?" replied Zack in excitement.

"Yes, you can," said Grandma.

"Thank you," said Zack.

"I have talked it over with your mother and Grandparents we are going back to St. Louis across the land this time."

"I will get the horses today, and we will leave sometime this afternoon." "Hopefully, we will be out of the city and at a campfire by dark."

We both nodded, I just as soon be heading back anyway. After breakfast, Grandpa took Pa to buy some horses.

# 20

# THE TRIP HOME

Pa and Grandpa came home with four beautiful horses of the same breed as what Grandpa had. One was a stallion, and the other three were mares. The horses got tied up out in front, so we could easily pack them with our belongings. They were all young. "Good breeding stock aren't they James," said Grandpa.

"Yes, sir, they are beautiful horses." "We must watch these horses very carefully, Pa, to make sure no one steals them."

"I knew you had an excellent eye for horses," Grandpa added.

We packed all our things and said our goodbyes. Grandpa handed me an envelope with papers inside and said, "Now, don't forget what I said about this."

"I won't Grandpa."

"And here is a book for you," he added.

"King Arthur," I said.

"Yes, the first real king of England, at least the England that matters."

I placed the envelope inside the book Grandpa gave me, and I packed it away and gave Grandpa and Grandma a big kiss and a hug.

Grandpa handed Zack a sack full of the toys he was playing with, and Zack also hugged and kissed them. In some ways, I felt like staying, but in others, I didn't. I will miss my Grandparents for all their kindness. We headed out, and I thought I could see tears coming from Pa's eyes as we left, but I didn't say anything.

We rode for a long time, and we finally left New York City far behind. We were heading for a place called Palmyra, where we would catch a boat to western Ohio. I felt naked without my rifle, but I knew that I would have it as soon as we reached St. Louis. We were traveling fast; these horses were better than I thought, but I still didn't believe that they would do well climbing mountains. Before we knew it one warm afternoon, we reached the outskirts of Palmyra.

We were traveling down a road just outside Palmyra. The horses were tired and needed rest when we came upon a man plowing a fielding with his two sons. So, Pa stopped and talked to him, "Good afternoon, sir." "Our horses are mighty thirsty and hungry." "I am willing to pay for some water and feed for them," Pa said.

"The water is free, but I must charge you something for the feed, times are hard now, but I will be fair."

Pa agreed, and the man introduced himself, "I'm Joe Smith, and this here is my son Hyrum and his younger brother Joseph, named after me."

"I'm Nathaniel York, this is Blue Flower, these are my sons James and Zack."

When we reached the cabin, Lucy Smith, Joe's wife, and the rest of the family came out and introduced themselves. We got invited to eat with them, and he told us that the next boat leaving for Ohio wouldn't be until the next morning. We got asked to stay the night which Pa accepted. I noticed as I am sure the rest of my family saw, they didn't have much but made do with what they did have. All the boys stayed in the barn while Ma and Pa slept in the house, which was all right with me; it was roomier out there. I liked the family, especially Hyrum and Joseph. We played games in the barn to test one's strength. It had to do with a stick, and you got put up against another. The Shoshone had a similar game, and I got put up against Joseph. I won, but it wasn't easy; he had a lot of muscle. Zack and I told the Smith boys about where we lived, and they all seemed interested, especially Joseph. I lay down and was going to read, but I was so tired and decided against it and fell asleep quickly.

After breakfast, the next day, Pa tried to give the Smiths some money, but he was putting up a fuss. Pa stuck the money into his pocket anyway, and we were off. As we left the Smith farm, I could hear Mr. Smith yell, "Mr. York, this is too much."

Pa just waved and went on, not looking back. I found out later he gave him a fifty-dollar bill, which was a lot of money.

We got on a boat at the dock, secured the horses, and off we went. It wasn't like the Mississippi or the ship traveling around Florida to New York. It was a lot smoother, but Zack took a liking to it right away. We were moving faster than if we were to ride because we were moving both day and night without rest. Then after what I would consider a short period, we landed in Ohio. Pa, Ma, and I were glad to be off the boat, and I think Zack was also. The crew was a foul, dirty bunch of creatures that you had to watch regularly, or they might try something. We planned to get to St. Louis and stay no longer than a couple of days and then head west.

We went through Ohio without incident. We never stopped at any farms or towns and didn't talk to people unless they spoke to us. There always were people who would stare at us in revulsion and spoke nasty things under their breath, but we ignored them. We also passed through Illinois with the same result until we came to the town of Commerce, a dirty, little, run-down, mosquito-infested town where we did not stay. We immediately took a paddleboat down to St. Louis. The ride on the paddleboat was much the same as the ride down to New Orleans. It looked like the same scenery as before. We reached St. Louis on Saturday at about eight in the morning. We got our belongings and horses and headed for the stable.

Pa met with the owner of the stable again, who said, "Everything is ready to go."

"Good, that is just great; I will be in St. Louis for about two days." "Please groom and feed these horses very well, and I will settle with you."

The owner looked at the horses and said, "These are excellent horses." "Do you want to sell them?" "I will give you a really good price."

"No, they are going with us," Pa said.

The stable owner wasn't happy with Pa's response, but he didn't try to bargain with Pa anymore. We got four of our other horses and rode to Mr. McConnell's store.

We entered the store, and I could hardly believe my eyes. There was Jack, working there with an apron on and a smile on his face. His wounds had all but disappeared, and he looked different, like a real well-mannered boy.

When he spotted us, he yelled, "Ma, Pa, look who's here."

Mr. McConnell came from the back room, and Miss O'Brien came down the stairs with Sarah wondering who was here. There was hugging and shaking hands, and when everyone was excitedly talking with each other. I was looking at Jack and said, "What happened to you, you look different?"

"Oh, I'm not that different," Jack said.

Miss O'Brien overheard our conversation and said, "Yes, you are; you're a very nice boy now and have many friends."

"Oh, Ma is just nice to me; they are going to adopt me," Jack said. I looked at Miss O'Brien, then Mr. McConnell, and said, "I thought you had to be married before you could adopt."

"You do James, Miss O'Brien and I are getting married, it's something we should have done with you." "We won't make that same mistake again with Jack," said Mr. McConnell.

"Congratulations, when is the big date?" asked Pa.

"It will be sometime in the future." "We haven't set a date yet." "There are some problems to straighten out first," said Miss O'Brien.

"You won't be able to teach if you are married," I said.

"I may not, those in charge haven't decided yet, but I am not worried about it," said Miss O'Brien. We talked some more and headed to the hotel, but not until we invited them to dinner.

On the way to the hotel, Pa stopped off at the bank and withdrew another ten thousand dollars. With the money Pa already had, it would be more than enough to sustain us in the mountains for many years. By that time, we would have enough gold to send another shipment. We had no problem getting a room this time, and after we bathed and went downstairs, there was no problem in the dining room. At dinner, everything seemed to be going fine, and we were all having fun when Pa pulled out an envelope and handed it to Mr. McConnell. Pa said, "This is a wedding present for you two, and also for all those years you took care of James and his mother."

He opened it up; it was a bank receipt, "What is this?" Mr. McConnell asked.

He examined the receipt, and his mouth hung open. He said as he handed it over to Miss O'Brien, "This is too much for a wedding gift."

"Oh, my lord!" Miss O'Brien said. Pa had deposited five thousand dollars into Mr. McConnell's account.

"I thought you would say that that's why I deposited it in your account." "You won't be able to do anything about it now," said Pa.

Mr. McConnell just shook his head, "I don't know what to say but what of your family?" "It should have been their choice, Nate."

"Alright, does anyone object that I gave this to them for a wedding present?"

Ma and Zack said no, but I just kept my head down, and they all noticed.

"James, do you object?" Pa said, surprise.

When I lifted my head, I had a tear in my eye, and with great emotional difficulty, I said, "I have no objection." "I am just mad at myself for not thinking of doing it myself." "You hardly know Mr. McConnell and Miss O'Brien, but I have known them almost my whole life, and I love them." "Mr. McConnell was almost like a father to me, and Miss O'Brien took over as my mother when Mama died."

I looked over to Jack, who looked uncomfortable. I said, "I didn't think I would ever say this, but since I always considered Sarah as my sister, that would make you almost my brother."

Everyone was silent and looking at me, and I continued in a sober voice, "I hope I didn't ruin everyone's dinner."

Everybody laughed, said no, and went back to talking and eating except Sarah, who was looking at me as I exchanged glances at her. She knew I was serious about what I had just said.

When dinner finished, we had made plans to visit the gravesite first thing in the morning to make sure the stone was in place, and the graveyard had been cleaned up and maintained.

While upstairs in our room, I wasn't very sleepy, so I decided to read the book Grandpa gave me. When I opened the book, the envelope that Grandpa gave me fell out. I had forgotten to give it to Pa after three days, as Grandpa had told me. I went to the outer room and told everyone to join me. When everyone was there, I said, "Grandpa told me to tell you about a conversation we had and to give you these papers." "I was supposed to say to you three days after we left, but I forgot."

"What did he tell you?" Pa asked.

"He said the York family back in England was of royal blood and that he had property there that when he died, he would pass it on." "After that trouble at the party, he said he had made up his mind, and the next day he gave me this envelope," I explained.

"What is this all about, Nate?" Ma asked.

"My father used to tell my brother, sisters, and me, stories about being related to the king of England or something and that we had property there." "We never believed him, but maybe he was telling the truth."

Pa opened the envelope and read the letter out loud, "I want to say first your mother, and I love you all, so I hope you understand why I am going to do what I have decided." "Your sisters, brother, and you never believed me when I told you about England." "I want to say to you, we are of a royal line, and we do have property there." "Your mother and I have been there, and I have someone who takes care of the estate." "The fact that none of you believed me hurt me and the thought was not to give it to any of you." "However, I changed my mind when you and your family showed up and for what happened at the party." "Your cousins will get nothing from me. I am cutting them totally out of everything." "What I'm am doing is not just because of the party; I have seen their arrogance for some time." "We will see how much arrogance they have when they see they have nothing." "Your sisters have acquired the same arrogance that your cousins have, and their demeanor at the party didn't go unnoticed." "But they are your sisters, so your mother and I have decided we will leave them something, but it will be considerably less than they think they will get."

"That leaves you and your brother." "Your brother will get the home and the business." "He will get a much smaller sum of money than what he was hoping." "And now for you, I love you, but when you left many years ago, you upset your mother and me deeply." "You didn't believe about our English background either, but I give you credit for standing up to me and having the strength to do what you wanted, and you have done well." "I won't be leaving the estate or title in England to you either." "Your wife is an amazing woman, but I doubt if she would understand what she would be getting." "Furthermore, she isn't a York by blood." "Zack is a fine boy, curious about everything, loyal to his family, and polite." "I thought about giving it to him and almost did, but he is a bit immature yet and has years to go before becoming mature." "He also lacks in his education and the ways of the world, and like his mother, I doubt if he would understand what he had." "Then there is James I was not considering him at first, but when he spoke up at the dinner party, I was most impressed." "There is a young man who will not let someone pushed him around, who seems self-educated far beyond his years, one who understands the world and would comprehend what I give him." "There is another reason why I have considered him." "I know that he is also loyal to his family and that anything he has he will give to his whole family such as he did with the gold." "For this reason, upon your mother's death and my death, James will inherit the estate and money of that estate, as well as the title which I hold, William York, Earl of Worcester." "One last thing, Nate, your brother Daniel will inherit nothing unless he brings you news personally of your mother's and my deaths." "He is to bring back a letter which I have included in the envelope signed by you or one of your family." "That is why I kept a map of where you are." "Should something happen to James, God forbid, the most senior of your family will decide who will get the inheritance." "A letter with instructions has been sent to my lawyer and the proper authorities in England."

"Here is the letter for your Uncle Daniel and a legal paper giving you everything, James," Pa said.

"Are you upset Pa, because Grandpa is right what I have belongs to the family," I said.

"No, I am not upset there wasn't anything that Grandpa had that I wanted except his love, which he has given me," Pa replied.

"We will get two metal boxes; we can keep these valuable papers and things in, one for your cabin and one for mine." "I like the way you hid the gold," Pa said to me.

I laid in bed, thinking of what Pa had read from Grandpa. I was to be an Earl, and the rest of my family will be Lords and Lady. It's going to take some explaining to make Morning Star understand what will happen.

The next day after breakfast, we went down to the graveyard. Nothing more about Grandpa's letter was said. We got to the cemetery at about a quarter to eight. The cemetery seemed cleaned very nicely, and trees and shrubs were there now. Other people were visiting long past loved ones, which were unusual because no one in the past came here because it was so depressing. Toward the back, we spotted a large red stone, and we headed for it. The stone was just what I wanted, and it was the largest in the graveyard. The fact is there were very few stones here, but it had mostly wooden markers. "It is sad, that there aren't more stone markers than there are isn't it," I said to no one in particular.

"Perhaps I can do something about that and do a little more," Pa said.

"What can you do, Pa?" I said.

"You leave that up to me," he replied.

Just then, Miss O'Brien, Mr. McConnell, Sara, and Jack showed up.

"As Ma and Pa talked to them, I said to Jack, "There is something I always wanted to ask you."

"What is it?" Jack said.

"When my mother died, I saw you in the back of the church." "Then again, I saw you behind a tree looking on, why didn't you join us or why show up at all?"

Jack put his head down and said, "I came because I wasn't allowed to go to my mother's burial." "Pa wouldn't let me, and I didn't join the rest because no one liked me, and I guess I had it coming."

As we were all talking, the priest, Father Garcia, saw all of us out in the graveyard and joined us. "What do you think of the cemetery, it's nice, isn't it?" "And now people are visiting here."

"It's very nice, but it would be better if it had more headstones and some color," I said.

"I know, but the people here are mighty poor and can't afford stones." "With our budget to maintain the graveyard, it is mighty hard," he replied.

"Maybe I can do something about that," Pa said.

Father Garcia smiled and said, "What did you have in mind, Mr. York?" Pa took him by the arm and led him away from the rest of us. I saw Pa give him a large sum of money much to the surprise and shock of Father Garcia.

After we all viewed the grave, Pa and I went to the stables to get our horses, mules, and wagon with the rest of the things we ordered while everybody else went back to the store and waited. We took the wagon and the stock down to the store. Pa grabbed one of the horses and said, "Stay here and load the wagon; I'm going to find two metal boxes for our valuables and go to the bank."

I nodded, went into the store, and told the rest what Pa said. Mr. McConnell, Jack, Zack, and I started to load the wagon while Miss O'Brien, Ma, and Sarah talked. We had the wagon almost filled when Pa finally showed up with two metal boxes and said with a smile, "It looks like I got back just at the right time." He put one of the boxes in the back and the other in the front where the seat was then helped us finishing filling the wagon. After filling the wagon with everything we had bought, we placed a tarp over it all and tied it to the wagon. Everything was ready to go. It was a large, heavy load but not too heavy for the mules, and I knew we would be traveling faster back home than when we first came to St. Louis.

We decided to meet later at a café, where they also had a bakery for our last meal with everyone because we would be leaving early in the morning. Pa decided to store our wagon and stock in the hotel's barn, and we cleaned up, rested a little, and then went to the café.

They weren't thrilled when the owners of the restaurant spotted Ma and Zack, but other than nasty stares, they didn't say anything except, "Do you have money to pay your bill?" they asked Pa.

Pa pulled out his billfold and revealed what he had on him. That shut them up real fast, and they left us alone while we ate, but I noticed that they placed us where we were away from everyone, and we did have stares.

Everyone showed up about fifteen minutes later, and we all talked while we ate. We were there about an hour and a half eating as well as talking when Pa could see the staff was getting anxious to get rid of us. "We best get going these people don't like us here," Pa explained.

He pointed at the staff, and Mr. McConnell said, "Yes, I saw how they have been acting for some time now." "It's a shame people are that way." "We will miss you and your family dearly, Nate."

"Who knows, maybe someday we will see you again," Miss O'Brien said.

"Oh, I'm sure of that," Pa said in reply but not convincingly.

As Pa was paying the bill, we left, and an arrogant person who appeared to be the owner of the place said, "Don't come back, we don't want your kind here."

"Yeah, but you sure want my money, don't you," Pa replied.

"You most likely robbed someone to get that money; that's how you lowlifes are." "You're all thieves you and that lowlife Indian whor..."

That man never finished what he was saying when Pa knocked him out with one blow and walked out.

Mr. McConnell said, "I don't blame you; I would have done the same."

We walked back to the store, pulling our horses behind us and then said our goodbyes one more time and then left. I was going to miss them, but the pain wouldn't be as bad as when I went with my uncle the first time.

Pa had paid for the room the night before, and the next morning, two hours before sunup, we left for home. It was dark out, and only an occasional person was walking up or down the street. We found out that the owner of the café tried to get Pa arrested the next day, but we were long gone, and the police dropped the whole issue.

Pa drove the wagon first, heading southwest. At noon break, Pa said, "I don't think I will go back the same way." "Just before we leave Missouri, we will head north if it doesn't look like someone followed us." "I think we can cut off a day or two doing this, and we can connect with the regular route." "I don't want to run into the same people that we did when we first came." We all agreed, and at sundown, we made camp.

The next day I woke up sore as did everyone else. "I guess it will take some time getting used to sleeping on the ground after sleeping in those soft beds," Pa said.

I drove the wagon this day, and we headed north after checking our back trail. We didn't bother to stop at any towns. We tried to avoid interacting with people as much as possible, as we did in Ohio and Illinois, and we had no trouble. In about two days, we were back on the trail that leads back home. After traveling some distance and long past Missouri, we came upon a Mandan village.

My mother was very nervous about being here, but the village was the village of Much Sadness, my old friend from years past. The people of the village didn't like the fact that a Shoshone woman was in their village. However, when Much Sadness came out of his lodge and saw me, he knew me right off, then he had great joy, and the thought of my Shoshone mother wasn't a problem among the people of the village.

I introduced my family and said they are Shoshone. "I am also a Shoshone I am called Soaring Eagle With Many Coups," I said.

Much Sadness laughed and said, "I thought it was you I have heard about you, and you are a great warrior."

I told him about Sometimes Comes and said, "Sometimes Comes now lives with the Shoshone."

"Yes, sad about him, no one listens to me now, and my people sent him away because they were tired of his foolishness." "What of your uncle and his family?" he asked.

"They are all dead, Blackfeet killed them," I said. I then told Much Sadness the whole story from beginning to end.

"I knew he had not long to live when he left here, he was a fool," Much Sadness said. We got invited to eat, and we accepted, but we told him we could not stay the night and had to be off after eating.

We left the Mandan village, and we saw no sign of anyone as we headed home for more than a week. That was just fine with us; we did not want to run into the Cheyenne again. The skies were clouding up, and we knew we were going to get wet, so we looked for shelter, but we found nothing in time.

Early the next morning, the rain came down and didn't stop for a day and a half. Of course, we got soaked, and you might know that when the rain finally stopped, we found shelter, and we stopped to dry out and rest. We started a fire and stripped out of our clothing to let them dry, and we also laid out our bedding. We stayed there overnight to give the horses a rest and to let the ground dry out.

The next day we went down the trail again. The trail was a bit muddy, and the mules had a hard time for a while, but as we traveled, the ground dried out got firmer. By the end of the day, the mud seemed to disappear. For a long time, we continued to travel without incident; we did see some old horse tracks but no people.

We finally got to the area where the buffalo would migrate up and down according to the season. Like when I first came here with my uncle, the buffalo were here again. That was dangerous because other tribes would be out hunting them, and we didn't want to run into any unfriendly tribes. Pa was trying to decide if he wanted to take the chance and cross or not when he said to all of us, "Stay here and keep your eyes open for trouble, I will be right back."

He headed south and didn't come back for about a half-hour, and when he returned, he said, "No luck that way there seemed to be more Buffalo the further south I went." "Let's see what north of here is like." When he came back, he said, "Follow me, there are fewer buffalo, and it seems safer to get across just north." We traveled about five or six miles then turned west. There were some buffalo. Like Pa said, not as many, and within about an hour, we were out of danger.

We headed back to the main trail and stayed on it for about four days. Then Pa wanted to cross the river, and after crossing the river a couple of days later, we spotted the Shining Mountains. We started moving southwest, and soon we were in the foothills. I knew that in a few days, we would be home. The mules and horses were doing fine, even the horses we got in New York. Three days later, we passed the small lake next to our cabins, and the place appeared just as we left it with a bit more grass available for the stock.

We unloaded the wagon and made room in the cabin to store everything, leaving very little room for us to live. At supper, that night, Pa said, "We will rest the stock for two weeks and then head for the village." "In two days, I will head to Othello's cabin to bring him the things that are his."

"I'll continue to work on the cabin roof after chores Pa," I said.

"I'll help Pa," Zack said.

"Very well then, we must go through our things to see what we will take to the village," Pa said.

"I will do that," Ma said. Then we all went to sleep for the next day.

# 21
# THE UTE VISIT

After I did my chores, I pulled out the things I bought for Morning Star and others in the village. I took one of the kegs of nails and brought it down to the cabin, and then I went back to get the tools and my weapons. I figured it would be best to build a platform that ran the length of the cabin high enough so that the lower roofline would be about waist high with me. It took me most of the morning to get the platform up. I could have used some help, but Pa was out looking for a deer to bring back, and Zack was busy with his toys. It was alright with me if Zack wanted to play with them, but I thought that if he continued to play with them too much, Ma and Pa would have something to say to him, and it wouldn't be pleasant. I got the first two rows of shingles on the house when Zack came and told me it was time for lunch.

"I thought you were going to help me today?" I said.

"I will go after lunch," Zack said. I came down off the roof and walked beside Zack as we went back to Pa's cabin for lunch.

"When do you think Pa will be back, Ma?" I asked.

"Soon," Ma replied.

"I could have waited to eat until Pa came home," I said.

"No, he will be tired and dirty, and I will need both of you to prepare the meat that your father will bring home."

We both nodded, and Ma changed the subject, "How are you doing on the cabin, James?"

"It took a while for me to build a platform so that I can work on the roof. But once I got it made, it went faster than I thought it would," I explained.

I ate and went back to work on the cabin. Zack finally came out to help me and asked," What do you want me to do?"

"I need more cedar cut down and brought to me, or you can start to haul rock from the stream."

He thought for a minute and then said, "I will haul rock up here."

"Watch for gold," I said. I then climbed up on the roof and started laying more shingles.

I was applying shingles for about an hour and a half when I turned around, and I spotted Pa. I yelled down to Zack, "Pa is coming." I looked up to see Pa again, but I saw about six or eight Ute warriors coming from Pa's right out of his eyesight. I came flying off that roof like a bear with its tail on fire.

I grabbed my rifle. Zack, a little confused, pulled his pistol. He had a look on his face that was asking what was going on. "Utes, a lot of them," I said. Zack's shirt was off. I grabbed it and waved it at Pa, but he didn't see me or didn't understand. So, I pulled my pistol and fired it. That got his attention and Ma's also. She came flying out of the cabin with a rifle. Pa stopped and looked over to us, and I pointed to where the Utes were coming. Both Ma and Pa understood, and Pa came flying toward my cabin since it was nearer. I had sent Zack back to the cabin to get his rifle and to protect Ma. What surprised me is that the Utes weren't giving Pa chase.

Pa made it to my cabin and was off his horse before the horse stopped. With rifle in hand, he said, "What and where is the problem?"

I pointed to the ridge and said, "There were six or eight Utes up on the ridge about to cut you off when I spotted them," I said.

"Why aren't they attacking?" Pa asked more to himself than me. I never answered him, but he said, "Let's try to make it to our cabin."

I grabbed the packhorse and got on it, and Pa grabbed the other horse, and off we went. We both made it to the house without incident. We all looked around but saw nothing, and Pa said to me, "Are you sure you saw some Utes?"

I looked at him a little angry that he would question what I saw, but before I said anything, three of the Utes showed up coming from the direction of the lake just out of rifle range.

Zack and Ma raised their rifles, but Pa said, "Wait, I think they want to talk."

"Ask them what they want, James," Pa said.

"What is it you want here?" I yelled.

"We come to talk to Bear Slayer," one of the warriors replied.

"They want to talk, Pa."

Asked them why the others hide and why do they sneak around to come here," pa said.

"I know you have others hiding why do they hide, and why do you approach us as you did."

The three looked at each other, and one said, "We are not at war with you; we heard you shooting and did not want to get shot," he said.

"Have the others come out and come slowly toward us," I said.

"Everyone, lower your guns; they just want to talk," I told my family.

As they approached, I recognized one of them; it was Black Hawk, father of Running Doe, the Ute captive that I took back to her village.

"The one on the right is Black Hawk, father of the Ute captive from the Blackfoot village," I told Pa. Black Hawk started talking and signing at the same time, but I still translated. "I have come to speak to the great Bear Slayer."

"What about?" Pa stopped signing, and he let me translate. "My father wants to know what you want to talk about."

"We wish to have a council with the Shoshone, and we want him to arrange this. We have meat to share with you, so we will not be a burden on you and your family," Black Hawk said.

"Tell him I will talk, and I have other things to talk to him about also. Also, say our cabin is too crowded to talk in, where does he wish to speak?" Pa said.

I told him about Pa's cabin and then said, "You can use my cabin, there is no roof, but the fireplace works."

Black Hawk looked at my cabin and said, "Your lodge will do.

Black Hawk and half his warriors started heading for my cabin, while some stayed behind. I said without consulting Pa, "Black Hawk."

He stopped, and I continued, "My mother is Shoshone by blood as is my brother, and I also claim to be a Shoshone as does my father." "It is not a good thing for your warriors to stay here where my mother will be."

Before Black Hawk could say anything, one of the other warriors I was standing next to said, "Who will stop us from staying here?"

With what seemed like one quick and single motion, I had pulled my knife, grabbed the warrior who challenged me, knocked him off the horse, and had the knife at his throat. Pa, Ma, and Zack had automatically cocked and raised their rifles. My quick action confused the other Utes.

I said in Ute in a tone of voice that they knew I met business, "I am a Shoshone warrior; it is I who will stop you even if I have to kill you and the rest of your people."

"Hold your weapons; we are not here to fight," Black Hawk said as he got off his horse. "He is a fool who does not know you, Soaring Eagle With Many Coups." "I will deal with him," Black Hawk said in English.

I removed my knife from his throat but slammed my fist between his eyes, knocking him out. I looked at the other Utes and said, "Consider yourselves lucky today if it weren't for Black Hawk, you would all be dead."

I turned to Black Hawk and said, "I did not know you spoke the white man's tongue."

"Sometimes, it is not good to let others know just how much you know."

I nodded and said, "Sometimes, it is dangerous if you don't."

Pa went to my cabin, and I went with him. Zack and Ma stayed back at the cabin skinning the deer Pa got and keeping an eye on the Utes. The Utes laid blankets down inside the cabin, and then everyone was sent outside, except Pa and Black Hawk. I split some shingles from some cedar logs I had and kept an eye on the rest of the Utes at the same time. The one Ute that I knocked to the ground felt it best he stayed away from me, especially after Black Hawk got through lecturing him. One Ute, however, I could see was easing toward me, and I watched him out of the corner of my eye. When he was about ten feet from me, I grabbed my rifle and gave him a glaring look.

He backed up a little and said, "I mean, you no harm." "I just wanted to talk to you."

I turned to him and lowered the rifle and said, "What is it you want?"

"I want nothing from you other than just talk." He seemed like he wanted to be friendly and to gain knowledge, which I like, but I will not let my guard down.

"I am Straight Arrow; my father is Black Hawk, and my sister is Running Doe."

I looked at him and said, "Yes, I do remember you."

"You were not this angry when you visited our village."

"I am not angry; I just don't trust any of you yet, I am Shoshone, and you are Ute," I said.

Just then, Black Hawk came out of the cabin and said to his people, "Start a fire and cook the deer." Then he went back to the cabin to talk to Pa some more.

The Utes started picking up wood for the fire. Some were about to get some of my cedar logs, and I stopped them and told them what they could have. The deer that they brought was prepared and placed on the fire, and when they did that, Straight Arrow came over to me again and said, "I will give you the heart and liver to eat when it is ready."

"To tell you the truth, I am not fond of liver and heart," I said.

"It is the best part of the deer," he replied.

"You're right, my family says the same thing, and they like the liver and heart, but I still don't."

"If it is an insult to you, I will eat it, but it is not what I prefer," I said.

"No, I do not take offense to your not eating the liver or heart." "It would be better if it is given to your father and mine anyway," he replied.

The meat was ready. Some meat the Utes brought into my cabin for Black Hawk as well as my father. Straight Arrow brought some over to me.

"What of your mother and brother?" said Straight Arrow.

"They will not come here." "I will let my father decide how to handle them."

"All those stories I have heard about you are they real?" asked Straight Arrow.

"There are many stories about me, and as you know, there is truth in all stories," I said.

He was about to ask something else when Black Hawk and Pa came out of the cabin. Black Hawk gathered his people together, and Pa came over to me and said, "Go get your mother and brother; it is safe."

"I will go tell them, but I don't think they will come."

"Tell them that I need them here."

I stared at Pa and nodded then left to get Ma and Zack. It took some convincing, but I got them to come, but they insisted on taking their rifles. The Utes offered Ma and Zack meat, which they accepted. When Ma tasted the meat, she said, "Ugh, men cannot cook, and she went back to the cabin."

Black Hawk looked at Pa, and Pa said, "All women think their cooking is the best."

Black Hawk laughed and said, "Yes, they do."

A few minutes later, Ma came out of the cabin with some bags full of spices. She went over to where the deer was. She pushed away some of the Utes who were hanging around the cooking deer. She sprinkled some spices over the deer. She then spread the coals around so that the deer wouldn't get so many flames. "Now it will taste better," Ma said.

She came over to Zack and me and sat down next to us. The Ute warriors were looking at Ma, and Black Hawk bewildered about what to do. Then Black Hawk said in Ute, "She has made it taste better. Cut some for her, Bear Slayer and me."

They did as he said and even gave some to Zack and me. "This does taste better," Black Hawk said. After they tasted what Ma had done, the rest of the Utes ate like it was their last meal.

Finally, Black Hawk went over to where his men were, and Pa came over to us. "Black Hawk and the chiefs of the other Ute villages want to meet with the Shoshone leaders to see if they can have peace," Pa said.

"This will be hard the elders the Shoshone separate at this time of year," Ma said. "I told him that it would be difficult because of that. It might take until next year for this to happen. He understood and wanted me to get things started. I also told him how we own this land now," Pa said.

"What did he say to that, Pa?" I asked.

"He did not understand how anyone could own land, but I told him that is what the whites do and that nothing will change between them and me. But other whites will come and will take the land and try to drive them off their land. He said the Utes would kill them if they try. But I told him for every one you kill five will take his place. I told him I know his people will defend the Ute land anyway. I also said that it was not only the Ute that would be mistreated by the whites, but all peoples of the land will go through the same. He asked me how I knew this, and I told him that it has already happened to the people to the rising sun." Pa explained. "I also said that the whites would not remove us from this land, and if you or the Shoshone are on this land, they will not bother you," Pa continued.

"What did he say to this, Nate?" Ma asked.

"He said he would tell the other elders what I had said and that he hopes to hear good news about the Shoshone."

We ate some more, and then Black Hawk joined us. "We must be going soon, but there is one thing I wish to know before I leave," Black Hawk said.

"What is it?" Pa asked.

"What I wish to know is for your wife, Blue Flower." "Your husband has told you why I am here?"

"Yes," Ma replied.

"You were born Shoshone and lived among them, what do you think your people will do?" asked Black Hawk.

"It is not for me to say what the elders will do; I am a woman," Ma replied.

"They will not trust the Ute, but they will want to be at peace with the Ute." "They will be cautious, but they will talk to see what the Utes have to say," I said.

"My son is right; he would know better than I," Ma said.

"The problem is not the elders of the Utes or Shoshone; it is the young warriors of the Utes and Shoshone," I added.

Black Hawk looked at me and said, "What is this problem the young warriors will have?"

"Both the Shoshone and the Ute warriors will want to test each other to see who is stronger and someone, Ute or Shoshone, will take offense at something; then, there will be violence." "Do you remember when we discussed Bow Valley, and what happened there?" "And do you remember earlier when your warrior challenged me?" I asked.

Black Hawk looked at Pa and said, "Your son speaks the truth and has much wisdom." "These are things the Utes and Shoshone must talk about, so there isn't violence."

Black Hawk and his warriors stayed for a little longer then left, leaving the rest of the meat for us.

There was still daylight, so I decided to gather more rocks and look for more gold instead of going again on the roof. Zack went back to play with his toys after leaving what gold he had found. And Pa and Ma went back to the cabin to rest and prepare the meat that Pa got. It was just about sundown when I stopped hauling rock. I dug a hole in one of the back rooms, put my metal box in it, and found the gold that Zack and I had found.

I was incredibly tired, so I headed back to the cabin. The next day I would start again on the roof. After cleaning up, Ma had some stew ready for me. Pa was in bed already, sleeping, and Zack was still playing with his toys on his bed. "If you are tired, Ma, I will clean the dishes and put everything away," I said.

"No, I know you are tired you had a big day; it will not take me long to clean up."

I crawled into bed next to Zack, which is the last thing I remember until the next day.

After chores, I started on my cabin roof again. Pa was cutting hay for the stock, and he had Zack with him after he had given him a big lecture about spending too much time with the toys Grandpa gave him. On occasion, I looked over to them, and I could see Zack was hating it and wishing he was with me instead, but I am sure he didn't say anything. By about noon, I had used up all the shingles I had made and nearly finished with one side of the roof. After lunch, I planned on taking the wagon and cutting down more cedars and hauling them back.

"I'm going to hook up the wagon and cut down more cedars, Pa."

"Good, Zack and I will give you a hand, won't we Zack?"

"Yes, Pa."

I smiled; I knew Zack wanted to play with his toys. "Pa, are you leaving tomorrow for Othello's cabin?" I asked.

"Yes, before sunup, I will be getting up extra early to load the animals," pa said to Ma.

"I will have your breakfast ready and something for you to take along for you," Ma replied.

"I'll help you load Pa," I said.

"I guess I will help too, Pa," Zack said halfheartedly.

Pa looked at Zack and said, "Such enthusiasm."

Zack put his head down in shame. I didn't say anything, but I thought Pa was a little hard on him.

All three of us hooked up the mules to the wagon, and Pa said, "Where have you been getting the cedars, James?"

"I don't know Zack has been cutting them down," I replied.

Pa looked at Zack, and Zack pointed to the area where he got the cedars, and Pa said, "We shouldn't get the cedar, or any wood from just one area unless you are going to clear the area or have no choice." "We will go to a different area that I know of," Pa said.

We traveled for a time and then came to a cedar grove and started cutting. We all took a turn, cutting and stacking the cedars in the wagon. Pa seemed to be hard on Zack, and it was showing on him. I didn't know if he was going to explode in anger or shed tears, but I knew it was coming fast. Pa was cutting a tree some distance from where Zack was cutting as I was loading. Occasionally, he would yell at Zack, and finally, I had enough. I walked over to him and said, "Why are you so hard on, Zack?"

"He has been playing with those toys too much, and he knows better," Pa replied.

"He is eleven, just a boy." "If I didn't like books more than toys, I would be playing with them."

"It makes no difference if he is eleven or twelve, he still knows better, and if you were playing with those toys as he has been, I would be getting after you too."

I got a little mad at that and said, "If you were to get after me, you know what I would do." "What's more, if you look carefully at those toys, they aren't all Uncle Daniel's toys." "I think another eleven-year-old played with them also."

Before he said anything to me, I turned and went back to loading the wagon. Pa stared at me, taken aback at what I had said. He then scratched his head, looked over to Zack, and walked over to him. I saw him talk to him, hug him, and then go back to the tree he was cutting. We worked until dusk and then headed back. Zack sat on the logs, and Pa sat next to me. I figured that I had enough cedar for the cabin and some leftover for the barn. By the time we unloaded the logs and headed back to our cabin, it was dark. "Pa, why don't you go to the cabin and rest?" "You are leaving tomorrow." "I can take care of the mules and wagon."

"Alright."

Zack stayed with me to help, and we both took care of the mules and wagon quickly.

I woke earlier than usual to help Pa pack the horses for his trip to Othello's cabin. Zack got up a bit later with all the rustling that was going on around him, and when he came out to help, we had almost finished, but he did give us some help with what we were doing. After our goodbyes, Zack and I went back into the cabin with Ma. We all ate breakfast, then Zack lay back down and said he would get up in a little bit.

"Are you ill, Zack?" Ma asked him.

"No, just a little tired," he replied.

"Alright, then you can rest after you do your chores if you are still sleepy."

Zack got up, not very happy, and went outside. I looked at Ma and said, "I never saw him this way, Ma." "He has gotten up this early before." "Maybe he is coming down with something."

"You keep an eye on him if he becomes ill, bring him to me."

I agreed and went outside to do the chores. By the time we finished, Zack was sweating a lot and listless. "Zack, come with me."

He followed me without a word, which was unusual for him. We went into the cabin, and immediately Zack lay down.

"There is something wrong with Zack Ma."

Ma felt his head and said, "You better go outside." "I will take care of Zack."

I got some tools and went out to work in my cabin. I planned to cut the cedar logs to length first and then split them into shingles. As I worked, I saw Ma come out of the cabin a few times and then go back in. By early afternoon, I had all the logs cut and was starting to make shingles. I thought about going back to the cabin to eat lunch, but then I thought about it again. I figured Ma would have her hands full with Zack, whatever was wrong with him. Typically, Ma would have called to me to come and eat, but by sundown, she hadn't called, which reinforced my belief that Ma had had her hands full all day.

I brought my tools back to the cabin and cleaned up, and went inside. Ma was tending to Zack, and I said, "How bad is he?"

"He has a fever, and he is weak."

"What can I do?" I asked.

"Nothing, I am doing all that able to be done."

"Do you wish me to track down, Pa?"

"No, it would just worry him." She turned to me and added, "You better grab some food and your blanket and sleep outside tonight."

I nodded and did as she said and headed to my cabin. I threw the blanket in the corner of the cabin, and before eating, I started a fire my fireplace, then I ate. I decided to split the rest of the cedar logs into shingles inside the cabin. The fireplace would give me enough light to do the work. It was late when I finished spitting my last shingle, and I was dead tired. I brought some more cedar kindling into the cabin with some regular pine logs that I had to burn. The smell in the cabin was great. I spread out my blanket and lay down next to the fire so that I could feed it. I stared up I could see the stars through the rafters of the cabin on this clear night. As I lay there, I was thinking of Zack. He had never been sick just like Mama, and now he is very ill, could he die? I just didn't want to think about that. Ma was a good doctor; she wouldn't let him die, but the thought worried me anyway. With all this thinking, I must have fallen asleep because the sunlight woke me up the next morning.

I went down to the stream, stripped off my clothing, and jumped into the water to bathe myself. After getting dressed, I went to the cabin to see how things were going with Ma and Zack.

When I went in, Zack was sitting at the table eating to my relief as I sat next to him, and Ma said, "Zack is better." "I do not think he should go out, so you must do his chores."

I laughed and said, "Zack will do anything to get out of his chores so that he can play with his toys."

After breakfast, I did the chores and started on my roof again. Before noon I had finished one side, moved the platform to the other side of the cabin, and began on the roof again. I had gotten a few rows done when I stopped for lunch. After lunch, I was right back on the roof. By nightfall, I had all but a small portion of the roof done. When I went back to the cabin to eat and sleep, I told Ma, "I am going to sleep in my cabin tomorrow." "By noon, the roof should get done, and I will start on the windows and doors."

"Doors?" Ma asked, wondering why I was making more than one door.

"Each of the bedrooms will have a door."

"How will the heat get into the room?" she asked.

"There will be an open space at the top of the wall because heat rises." "There will be another space under the door." "The one on the top is where most of the heat will come in."

As I ate, I looked over at Zack, who was playing with his toys. "How are you feeling?" I asked.

"Oh, I am much better; I will help you with the chores tomorrow."

"If I were you, I would put those toys away before Pa catches you with them." "You know how he feels about your playing with them too much," I replied.

"He will do chores tomorrow, but not too much; you must do most of them." "He is still too weak from the sickness, and he needs to gain his strength before we go to our village," Ma said.

"The fresh air will do him some good anyway," I replied.

I did most of the chores, and I think Zack was taking advantage of me, but I didn't mind too much. I got back on the roof, and Zack asked me, "Is there something I can do."

"You know those tools I bought in St. Louis?" I asked.

"Yes."

"You can get them for me and put them inside the cabin." Zack went and got them while I proceeded to finish the roof. After Zack got the tools, I sent him out to get firewood since I would be staying in the cabin that night.

After a couple of hours of getting firewood, I saw that he was sweating again and thought it best he got back to the cabin and rested. "Zack, you have done enough today." "You better not push it; why don't you go back to the cabin?"

He thought a minute and then said, "Maybe you're right," and he headed back to the cabin.

I had just finished putting the crown on the roof of the cabin and was coming down off the roof when I saw Pa coming. I went over to him, rifle in hand, and asked, "How was your trip?"

"Went well, I will tell you and the rest at lunch."

"When you go back to the cabin, Zack might be playing with his toys."

On Pa's face, there was a look of anger, and he was about to say something when I added, "He has been sick." "Today is the first day he has come out of the cabin for a little bit, but when I saw him getting tired again, I sent him back to the cabin." The expression on Pa's face changed from anger to concern. "Ma has been tending him; I think he will be alright by the time we go to the village." "He just must take it easy for a while."

He nodded and looked over at the cabin and said, "Looks like you have been busy."

"Yes, the roof on the outside is finished." "I will be staying in the cabin tonight to work on it from the inside." I could have worked on the cabin a little more but decided to follow Pa back to the cabin. I took the horses and told Pa I would take care of them, and he went into the cabin.

Zack had a small relapse, but he was doing alright lying in bed with his toys.

"Othello and his wife are doing fine." "They were surprised that I was able to buy so many things with the furs we had," Pa said.

"How did you convince him, Pa?" I asked.

"It wasn't easy, at first he thought the price of beaver went up and I had to stretch the truth a little." "I told him that you insisted that we divide the furs equally and that we got a good deal on the goods."

"Are they going to stay in the area?" Ma asked.

"Unfortunately, not, they are going to either California or Oregon." "I tried to change their minds, but they had their mind set in their plans."

"When are they going?" asked Ma.

"I think that by the time we get back from the village, they will have gone, or maybe after the snow melts." "It's a shame they were good friends," Pa added.

After lunch, I went back to my cabin to work on it. I could see Pa was bothered about losing Othello, but I still felt we hadn't seen the last of him yet. Making the sashes for the windows wasn't all that hard, but it was time-consuming. I had to make two for me, and one for Ma and Pa, and I decided to make them out of oak. I located some trees and took the wood I needed. I thought I would make the entranced door out of oak as I was cutting the wood. It wouldn't be easy, but it would be strong and last a lifetime. At this time, I took only enough wood for the sashes; I made myself comfortable and started work on the wood. I worked on the window the rest of that afternoon and into the night and only finish one window by the time I went to sleep. I would have to continue the window the next morning after chores.

The next morning before I started on the window, I worked on my chores. Before I finished, Pa came out and said, "Why didn't you come in for breakfast?"

"I wanted to get the chores done as fast as I could, so I could get busy on the cabin."

"I have to tell you; you are going to have to do Zack's chores also. Your mother doesn't want him out for a few days." I didn't say anything, but I'm sure Pa could see the letdown in my face. "I will tell your mother to keep something warm for you to eat when you finish the chores," Pa said.

It took me another hour and a half to do Zack's chores, and that's doing them fast." I cleaned up and went into the house to eat and spotted Zack on the bed playing with his toys.

I sat down at the table, not taking my eyes off Zack, and of course, Ma took notice. She already knew I wasn't pleased with doing Zack's chores, and she said, "It is very good of you that you love your brother so much that you would do his chores for him without complaint when he is sick." That was a dirty trick; there is nothing I could do or say when she told me that, so I started to laugh, and so did she.

I continued working on the window and had the one window finished about mid-afternoon. I made the window so that it would swing open into the cabin on small hinges, and I could latch the window shut. The glass wasn't in yet. That would come later when I got all the windows built and in. I also had to make shutters, but that would come after the windows.

As I started on the next window, Pa came into the cabin and said, "You've done an excellent job with this cabin." He walked over to the window and swung it out and back in again and said, "That's very clever of you; it will let fresh air in when you want it."

"I'm going to make yours the same way." "I figured Ma, and you would want it that way."

Pa nodded his head and said, "You know how I feel about your brother playing too much with those toys." "If he was a city boy, I might not care, but it is different here, as you know."

"I know this, Pa," I said.

He nodded again and said, "You spend a lot of time in this cabin, and lately, the time you spend working on this cabin has increased," Pa said.

I looked at him uneasily, I didn't like where this was going, and I felt it could end up in a fight. "Pa, a cabin and toys are not the same; you know that by next season I will bring Morning Star here." "I could bring her here this season, but I want the cabin a certain way, so it is more comfortable for her. After the windows and doors are in, I will slow down some. Also, someone must hunt and bring home some meat," I said with a smile on my face and the hope he would drop the subject.

"I think we can store some things down here now," Pa said.

"The glass for the windows, lead, maybe the powder and a few other things can come down here," I said.

"I think I will start hauling them down here," Pa replied. "What room is the gold in?" he asked.

I got up and showed him exactly where it was.

"How much gold do you have?" Pa asked.

"About half of the safe is full, but it isn't smelted yet," I replied.

He nodded and said, "You must show me how to smelt the gold one of these days." At that, he headed back to the cabin to haul some things down here, and I went back to working on the window.

I hadn't completed the second window, and it was dinner time. Pa had made several trips back and forth from cabin to cabin bringing things that we bought in St. Louis. Why he didn't load them in the wagon and bring them here, I will never know. I heard Pa calling me to dinner, so I put everything aside and went down to the water to clean up; without all those things Pa had stored in my cabin, his cabin will look bigger.

"I will be sleeping down in my cabin again tonight," I said.

"You must do Zack's chores again tomorrow," Ma said.

I just nodded I had figured that anyway. After supper, I went back to the cabin and worked on the window until I nodded off to sleep, finishing the second window.

The next day it was raining, but the chores I had to do, so I did them and got soaked. I didn't go back inside to eat. Instead, I went back to my cabin and checked the roof for leaks, and there weren't any. I started a fire and tried to dry off some, in hopes that the rain would let up long enough to make it back to Pa's cabin. Sure enough, in about two hours, the rain let up enough for me to get to the cabin. Inside, Pa was cleaning his rifle, and Zack was playing with his toys. Ma told me to sit at the table, and she fed me. "I did the chores, and the roof of my cabin is holding out the rain," I said to anyone interested.

"In two days, weather permitting, we are heading for the village," Pa said.

"That will be good; I should complete the windows by then. I will put the glass in when we get back." By the time I got through eating, the rains had started to come back. I ran back to the cabin and got the fire going, so I could dry off and go to work on the last window. I had the measurements of my parent's window. It would be smaller than mine, requiring less glass. By late that night, I had the last window finished. I was too tired to do anymore, so I went to sleep and slept until the first light.

The next day was cloudy with showers. I managed to get the chores done without getting too wet. Again, I had to do Zack's chores; Ma wasn't taking any chances with him getting sick again. I didn't bother going into Pa's cabin to eat, I wasn't that hungry, and I wanted to get a jump on the window glass.

As I was sitting in my cabin working on Ma and Pa's window about mid-morning, to my surprise Ma came in with something for me to eat. "Why did you not come to the cabin to eat?" Ma asked, not very happy.

"I wasn't that hungry, and I wanted to get busy on the window."

"I do not need you sick like your brother, now eat."

I stopped what I was doing and started to eat. "I'm not going to get sick by missing one meal, Ma."

"You spend too much time in this cabin."

"This window is not for my cabin; it is for your cabin." Ma came over to look at it, and I got up and showed her how the ones I've already done work. "I wish to get it finished before we leave," I said.

"When do you think you will finish?" Ma asked.

"I guess sometime tomorrow afternoon."

She nodded and said, "You make sure you come and eat lunch."

"I'll be there, Ma," I replied. She left the cabin, and I went back to work, fixing the window and picking at my food.

The next day I had finished with the window ahead of schedule and hung it before noon. I decided to go back to the oak grove and chop down enough oak for a front door and some shutters. After cutting them down and cleaning them up, I got some firewood and placed it inside the cabin.

When I about completed everything, Pa came up to me and said, "I want you to finish early and stay in the cabin tonight. You'll be getting up early to pack the horses so that we can get an early start."

"I'll just put this wood into my cabin, then clean up, and I will be right in."

Pa nodded and walked off, and I did as he said.

# 22
## THE CAVE

We loaded the horses before sunlight and had eight horses with us as we headed out. There was a slight breeze and a few clouds. I was hoping that it would not rain, but I knew better. My concern was for Zack; he was just getting over his illness, and I didn't want him to have another relapse as he did before. I'm sure Ma was thinking the same as she looked at the sky as we went.

By the next day, it was getting nasty with clouds and the wind. I knew of a cave that I thought we could get to, and so I moved up to where Ma and Pa were and said, "I know of a cave not far from here." "It isn't large enough for the horses, but it will do for us."

"You take the lead then," Pa said.

We moved fast, and within an hour, we were at the cave. Pa and I unloaded the animals as Ma and Zack gathered wood. We got a fire going just as the rains started to come down. The cave proved to be dry and warm with the fire. The horses were hobbled and standing under some trees. It was a steady, hard rain that I could see was going to last awhile. Ma and Pa were satisfied just to be next to each other and doing what an average husband and wife would do. Zack was regretting that he had left his toys at home, so he made some from what wood we had. I could tell this was not going to satisfy him if the rains kept up very long. As for me, I was bored out of my mind. After all, you could only clean and sharpen your weapons for so long. I grabbed a stick from the fire and decided to explore the rest of the cave to see what was in it.

The ceiling of the cave seemed to slope toward the back; I could touch the ceiling without jumping. There was a large boulder near the back wall that looked like it had fallen from the ceiling a very long time ago. As I looked around the boulder, I saw an opening behind it. I was curious and tried to move the stone, but I could only move it a little, not enough to see what was behind it. I thought I needed a lever so that I could move the boulder forward. Perhaps Zack could help also. I found a small branch about four inches in diameter and a little more than four feet long.

"James, what are you doing?" Pa asked.

"I'm bored, and I found a boulder in the back of the cave that looks like there is an opening on the other side, I want to see if there is."

"Alright, just don't make too much noise," Pa said.

"Zack, do you want to help me?" I asked.

"Alright." Zack got up and went to the back of the cave with me. This entire time Ma had a worried look on her face, and Pa noticed.

"What's the matter?" asked Pa. "I don't know if it is a good idea for James to move that boulder, I don't feel good about it."

"I'll stop him if you wish."

"No, it may be nothing."

"The stick is too thick to fit, I will try to move the boulder, and you slip the stick in," I said. I was able to move the boulder a little, and Zack slid the stick in. "You pull on the stick first, and I will pull the boulder with my hands, and then we will switch off." I started pulling, and Zack put his whole weight on the stick, and the boulder moved about a foot. It was enough to get behind the boulder to push, and we both did. We moved it another foot and a half, making a hole large enough to see what was behind it. There was an opening, but it was too dark to see. We went back to the fire and made some torches out of animal fat, straw, and kindling we found. It worked very well. Pa just laughed as we headed back to the opening.

I was first in, and there were what looked like steps, so I went down about six feet to a passageway that was about another ten feet long. Zack followed behind me. The wall and steps looked like they got somehow chiseled out.

We weren't that far into the cave that we could still hear Ma and Pa talking.

"They are sure quiet back there," Pa said.

"Yes," replied Ma. "James, Zack," Pa called out. There was no answer from either of us because we were too fascinated by what we were seeing. Pa and ma got up and went to the back of the cave to see what was going on.

"They must have gone down that tunnel," Pa said.

"I do not feel good about this," Ma replied.

"Let's go back to the fire to make a torch so we can see where we are going," Pa said.

The walkway was longer than I thought it would be. It made several turns until it opened out into a chamber.

"Wow! Look at how the walls and ceiling are," Zack said.

I was amazed, everywhere on the walls and ceiling were painted with bright colors. The chamber was about the size of my whole cabin. In the center, there was a kind of fire pit except instead of wood it had I think oil in it. I touched my torch to it, and it caught on fire, lighting up the whole room. At the far end of the room was something that looked like a huge elephant tusk with several smaller ones about a foot long arranged around the large ones. On the floor, there were old furs from animals I had never seen in these mountains before; some spotted yellow and black, some black, and others a brown, like a mountain lion. The pictures on the walls looked like they had a story to them. They were different than the petroglyphs I had seen having more detail. They looked like what an artist would do back east.

"There is a light, up ahead," I heard Pa say to Ma. Pa and Ma entered the chamber and were as shocked as I had been. However, I could see there was a worried look on Ma's face.

"We should leave here," Ma said.

"In a minute, I want to see this first," Pa said.

"It looks like it tells a story Pa," I said.

"This side has a lot of strange-looking elephants with hair on them and those weird cats with the long teeth like those over there," I added.

"Those are not like any elephants and cats I've seen," Pa said.

"Look at this wall Pa it has something that resembles white people at war with black people," Zack said.

"I think it represents two different tribes Zack," Pa said.

"I believe that it is more than that, Pa," I said. "Look over here these people are all black living in that strange village with that large building. And look at this, there is a large tree with a railing leading to it. White people are following the railing to the tree and beyond. They look like they are going up, some stairs, and the painting continued on the ceiling to a place that one might call heaven. Now look at this, there seems to be a canyon, and across the canyon, there are black people who look very wicked," I said.

"They look wealthy on that far side of the canyon, and the other people look like they have just enough," Zack said. "What tribe do you think they are?" he asked.

Before Pa could answer, Ma said, "Those people are of no tribe that is of today. They were the people from long ago this is a sacred place there are still spirits here we should not be here, we must go," Ma said.

"I think Ma is, right Pa, I have never seen these animals on the walls or these furs, let alone those tusks," I said.

"Alright, let's go," Pa said.

We all turned to the exit, and I looked up and said, "Wait." Everyone turned and looked at me, and I said, "Look at that picture of that boy; it is my spirit guide."

"Are you sure maybe it is someone who just looks like him," Pa said.

"No, it is him, Pa, I am certain of it," I said.

"We must go," Ma said with an anxious voice.

We left and got to where the boulder was, and Ma said, "We must seal the entrance." She started pushing on the boulder before we could react, and then we joined her. It wasn't easy, but we managed to move the boulder, so it blocked the entrance better than before.

"You two go out and get some mud so I can seal the area around the boulder even better," Pa said to Zack and me.

As Pa was caulking around the boulder, some loose dirt from above the boulder got brushed away. There were some symbols on the wall that were like the ones in the chamber. "It looks like Egyptian writing Pa like I saw in a book," I said.

"Cover that up with dirt also, Nate," Ma said.

Pa had finished, and we went back to the fire. Ma said, "I do not like it here."

"We will leave as soon as the rains stop," Pa said. It was getting late, but the rains had ceased, so we loaded up and left much to Ma's relief.

We traveled about three miles, and even though Ma was still a little nervous, we stopped to camp for the night. The next day was cloudy, but at least it was drier and warmer than it had been. Zack was doing fine, but Ma watched over him like a hen watches her chicks. The rest of the trip to the village was uneventful. We knew we were near the village when we came upon Broken Knee and Dark Horse, who were hunting.

We entered the village, and Grey Wolf was the first to greet us. We hugged each other, and he said, "I set up your lodge for you."

He could see I was looking for someone else, and he said, "She will be here soon."

I smiled and said, "I have missed her."

Just then, I spotted her running, and I went to her ignoring everyone else. We hugged and embraced each other, which she didn't like to do in public, but I didn't care, it was a silly custom anyway.

"After waiting so long, I thought you weren't coming," she said.

"Why would you think that? I said my family and I would be here, and here we are?"

To my right, there was a warrior I had not seen before. "Who is that?" I asked.

"He came to live with us from another village. He is of no importance," Morning Star said. The way she said it made me think he was trouble; if necessary, I would deal with him later.

She walked with me back to where my family was. We went to the lodge where we were to stay and unloaded the horses. Spotted Buffalo joined us and said to me, "You will stay with us, will you not?"

I looked over to my mother, and she nodded, and I said, "Wherever my wife will be, I will be too. I do need to unpack some presents that I brought for everyone."

He nodded and said to Pa, "You and your family are always welcome here, Bear Slayer." He then turned and left while Morning Star stayed with me.

Pa followed him out and told him, "You need to assemble the elders I have news of the Utes."

"What is this news you have?" asked Spotted Buffalo.

"Black Hawk, a chief of the Utes, visited my lodge. He wants to talk peace between the Ute and Shoshone."

Spotted Buffalo stared at my father for a minute. It was the type of stare I had seen before when he was thinking. "I will call the elders together for tonight. Would that be alright?" he asked Pa.

"Yes, I will be ready," Pa replied. By the time Pa rejoined us, Grey Wolf and his mother, Blue Lizard, joined us. As I was unpacking everything Morning Star as well as Grey Wolf were helping Pa, Zack and me while Blue Lizard and Ma talked.

"I am surprised I did not see Comes Running," I said to Morning Star and Grey Wolf.

"He went hunting with his father." "When he comes back and hears you are here, he will come," Grey Wolf said with a smile. "He has become an excellent hunter." "You would be surprised at how fast Comes Running has learned." "Comes Running learned faster than you," Grey Wolf added, almost laughing.

When we got finished unpacking Ma, and Blue Lizard joined us. I handed Blue Lizard different colored ribbons and some dried fruits that she couldn't get here. She was most grateful; she didn't expect to get anything. For Sometimes Comes, I gave him some tobacco. I then gave Grey Wolf a spyglass telescope. He looked at it and didn't know what to do with it. "Come outside, and I will show you how to use it," I said. Grey Wolf, Zack, Morning Star, and I went outside, and I opened the spyglass and pointed it at some trees far off. "Do you see those trees way off, Grey Wolf?" I asked.

He nodded, yes.

I handed him the spyglass and said, "Point the spyglass at those trees, close one eye and look through the spyglass at them."

He did as I said, and he couldn't believe what happened. He kept on switching his eye on and off on the spyglass. He then started to laugh and said, "This is a very good present." He handed the spyglass to Morning Star, who had the same reaction as Grey Wolf had. Zack also had a turn at it even though he had already tried it before.

I turned to Morning Star and said, "I have many things for you, but I will give them to you later."

I could see she was impatient, so I grabbed the prism out of my possibles bag and said, "This is the first present; I will give it to you now."

She took it and looked at it in confusion as did Grey Wolf. "This is an unusual stone." "It is called glass." "It is shaped in a way to make it into what is known as a prism." They were still confused, so I took the prism and grabbed Morning Star's hand. I shined the sunlight through the prism and onto her hand, and a rainbow appeared. She jerked her hand back, and I grabbed her hand again and said, "It will not harm you." They were all fascinated by the sight, even Zack, who had seen it many times.

"Both gifts are strong medicine," Grey Wolf said. As Grey Wolf started to hand the spyglass back, he said, "This is too great of medicine you should have it."

"Grey Wolf, Tracking Fox, already has one and my mother has one of those stones. I gave you one for you Morning Star and you Grey Wolf, you keep them."

They both had smiles of satisfaction. I don't think they wanted to give them up anyway; they just wanted to be polite. Blue Lizard and Sometimes Comes came out of the lodge and headed back to their lodge. Grey Wolf said, "I have things to do; I must be going." He then left and followed his mother back to their lodge.

That left Morning Star, Zack, and me. I stared at Zack, and he got the hint and said, "I know, I know you want to be alone with Morning Star." As he turned around and walked away from both Morning Star and me, we had smiles and walked in the opposite direction.

We sat on a rock and dangled our feet in the water. I kissed her, and she kissed me back. I told her I loved her, and she said the same. I was about to caress her when I heard a snap of a twig and bolted around, knife drawn. Standing there, shocked was Comes Running. I put my knife away, and as I did, I heard the brush move and saw that new warrior I met earlier, walking away with a smirk on his face. I thought that I would be more cautious of him from now on. There was something about him I just didn't like.

Morning Star had seen the look on my face and said, "Forget about him. I already told him I was married, and he is just a strange one."

"There is something I do not like about him, and there is something that bothers me about him also," I said in a strained voice.

"I do not like him either; he is very, arrogant," Comes Running said.

"I did not know you knew that word," I said to Comes Running with a smile. We all sat and talked for a while, and then Comes Running had to go back to his lodge.

Morning Star and I let her parents know we were going to eat in my lodge. I usually would have eaten with Morning Star's parents. However, Blue Lizard was cooking for my family, and I thought it would be impolite not to eat Blue Lizard's food.

After dinner, all the men went to the council meeting. At first, things brought up that just didn't interest me, so I kept quiet, but when my Pa spoke, I paid attention to what he was saying. I noticed that strange warrior, the one I didn't like, was also paying attention, and he didn't like what was being said. For the most part, the elders were interested in what Pa was saying about the Utes, which enraged that warrior even more. Most of what my Pa was saying I had heard before. What was more entertaining was how the new warrior was reacting to what Pa said. Finally, he couldn't take anymore, and he got up and said, "Enough of this foolish talk from this white man the Utes are our enemies they cannot be trusted."

"Watch your tongue, Red Hawk, Bear Slayer is our honored guest, and the tribe adopted him," said Spotted Buffalo.

"Perhaps he spends so much time with the Utes that he is now a Ute," Red Hawk replied arrogantly.

Pa was about to get up to say or do something, but I came forth first and said, "Perhaps I should cut your tongue out and feed it to the dogs."

He looked me up and down and started to laugh contemptuously and said, "Go back to your mother's breasts white pup before you get hurt."

I was fuming, and everyone was looking at me to see what I would do. Red Hawk's statement went beyond insulting, and he couldn't get away with it without a response. I tossed my pistols to Grey Wolf and drew my knife. Tall As The Sky tried to stop me by grabbing my arm, but I pushed him aside, making him lose balance and nearly fall. Red Hawk drew his knife. I was about to go after him when Tall As The Sky and Pa grabbed me. Spotted Buffalo said to Red Hawk, "Enough, Soaring Eagle With Many Coups is a Shoshone warrior and has a voice in this council. You will respect him and keep your mouth shut, or you will leave."

He started laughing again, put away his knife, stepped back, and sat down without saying another word. But I didn't remain silent; I had plenty to say concerning the Utes. "My father, Red Elk, who you all knew told me about the Utes, as did my Grandfather, Arrow Maker. At one time, the Shoshone and Utes were friendly, and they lived in peace as we do with the Crow. Then one day, while both the Utes and Shoshone were gathering wood in Bow Valley, young warriors from both the Utes and Shoshone decided to test each other, and someone was hurt. My father, Red Elk, and grandfather said it was the Utes who started this test, and it was a Shoshone who was injured."

Everyone nodded in agreement, and I went on, "Black Hawk of the Utes told me the same story, but he said it was the Shoshone who started this test, and it was a Ute who was hurt. He is the same Black Hawk who my father Bear Slayer talked to, the same Black Hawk who is the father of the Ute female I took from the Blackfeet, who many of you know. I am not sure who was to blame that day in Bow Valley, and I do not think any of the Shoshone or Utes knows it was so long ago."

I could see that Red Hawk was getting angry again because of what I was saying and because the elders were listening to me, but I didn't care and spoke on. "I will tell you I do not trust the Utes completely, nor do I think they trust us. But then again, I do not trust the Crow completely, especially around our horses, and they are our friends."

Many started laughing and shaking their heads in agreement. At this, I saw Red Hawk get up and leave, so I called Grey Wolf over, and I whispered in his ear, "Follow Red Hawk and see where he goes."

At that, Grey Wolf left, and I continued with what I was saying. "I feel it is worth a try to make peace with the Utes." "If they are our friends, we won't have to keep an eye on our backs when the Blackfeet give us troubles." "They will also make us stronger when we do fight the Blackfeet if they join us." "So, listen to what my father, Bear Slayer, has to say." "He talked to Black Hawk on the subject longer than I, and my father will tell you the truth." "I have said all I wish to say." "Again, you speak with much wisdom; we will listen to your father."

I faded back into the crowd and didn't say another word. By the end of the meeting, the elders decided to pursue this further by talking about it with other villages. They told my father they would decide after all have expressed their feelings.

It was getting late, and Grey Wolf hadn't come back yet. I was getting worried, and I walked out to where the horses were to see if I could spot him from across the valley. "It is getting late, come back to the lodge." "I am sure that Grey Wolf will be alright," Morning Star said as she joined me.

"If he is not back by sunup, I will go find him," I said, worried that something had happened to him. That night my thoughts should have been of Morning Star, but they weren't they were of Grey Wolf. Morning Star was doing a good job of trying to keep my mind off Grey Wolf, but it wasn't working, and I had a fitful night.

Morning finally came, and I got up and ate. I whispered to Morning Star in English, "I am sorry about last night. Once I find Grey Wolf, I will make it up to you."

"I know you are worried; I am not mad at you."

I kissed her and smiled then left for Grey Wolf's lodge.

"He did not come home last night," Blue Lizard said concerned.

"I am going to go find him," I replied.

Next went to Pa's lodge to get all my weapons. As I was getting them, I told my concerns to my family.

"I will go with you," Pa said.

I nodded yes, and Zack said, "I will go too."

I looked at Zack for a minute then said, "No, I need you here, if Grey Wolf comes back safe or is hurt, I want you to track us and let us know. If we don't come back by noon tomorrow, I want you to get as many warriors as you can and come get us, we will be heading North or West."

Zack agreed to stay behind. My conversation with Zack caught Ma and Pa's attention, and Pa asked, "Why not east or south?"

"I will explain on the trail."

We had just mounted when I spotted Red Hawk across the village coming in. I waited for a few minutes, staring in the area where Red Hawk came in, which confused Pa a lot. I looked at Pa and said, "If we follow Red Hawk's trail, we will find Grey Wolf."

"Why do you think that?" he asked.

"Because I told him to follow him." Before we left, Pa and I went to Spotted Buffalo's lodge where Running Deer was standing, and I said, "Keep an eye on Morning Star I don't trust Red Hawk he might start trouble."

"I will keep him away from her," Running Deer said.

We took off and followed Red Hawk's trail first West. Then, just as I figured, the trail turned north. "How did you know that Red Hawk went North?" Pa asked.

"East is where the prairie is, nothing much there. South is where the Utes are, and we know he doesn't like the Utes," I replied.

"But to the North, he might run into some Blackfeet," Pa said.

"Yes, Pa, he might, but I do not think he is very concerned about that."

At first, Pa was confused, and then he caught on and said, "Do you think he might be involved with the Blackfeet?"

"I believe he is Blackfoot, and when we find Grey Wolf, I hope I will prove it."

"What made you think he was Blackfoot in the first place?" Pa asked.

"You know how well I remember things."

"Yes."

"I've been to every Shoshone village there is, and I never saw him in any of them."

"That doesn't mean anything he could have gone hunting or something."

"I already considered that, and it is not just because I have not seen him in any of the villages," I said. "Red Hawk does not act like a Shoshone."

"What do you mean?" Pa asked.

"Shoshone, don't try to take another man's wife." "He does not have a voice with the elders because he has not proven himself yet." "Still, he expresses his opinions." "Even though I have never seen him in another village, everybody knows Bear Slayer and Soaring Eagle With Many Coups." "They would not challenge you or especially me, yet he does."

Pa thought about what I said for a few minutes then said, "You still could be wrong."

"Yes, but I have a feeling I am right."

We rode on for some time, and Red Hawk's trail kept going north. Sometime after resting our horses at an afternoon break, Pa spotted another set of tracks. I got off my horse and took a good look at them and said, "They are Grey Wolf's tracks, I can tell by the left front hoof."

We followed Grey Wolf's tracks for almost an hour. They entered a ravine, and we saw where he had stopped his horse and climbed up to a rocky outcropping. His descent from those outcroppings was not as graceful as when he went up. We decided to climb up to where he had been to see where he had been looking. "I believe he is Blackfoot, and when we find Grey Wolf, I hope I will prove it." We could see from the other side of the outcropping where there was a campfire, about a hundred and fifty yards off.

We went down to investigate. Pa felt the fire pit and said, "Still warm."

I looked around at the tracks and found Red Hawk's horse's tracks and pointed them out to Pa. We went back to our horses and continued to follow Grey Wolf's trail. It wasn't hard; not only did he leave clear tracks but deposited plenty of blood along the way.

"I should have left last night," I said in a worried voice to Pa.

"You had no way of knowing that he was in trouble."

We traveled for about a half-hour to forty-five minutes when we heard gunshots three from fusees then another from my old Hawken. It had to be Grey Wolf.

We wasted no time getting to where the noise from the shots came. Going up the hill were about a half a dozen Blackfeet. Grey Wolf hid further up in a bunch of fallen trees. We didn't have time to sneak up on them. Pa said, "You take the one on the right; I'll take the left one."

We raised our rifles and fired. Two Blackfeet warriors hit the ground. The other four turned and headed for cover, but Pa reloaded faster than me and picked off another one.

When Pa reloaded, we moved in. The numbers were more even now, and I was feeling very confident. The other three were firing at us as we moved to cover. I had an idea we were near enough for them to hear me, so I yelled out in Blackfoot, "How does it feel to know you are going to die, Blackfoot?" Sure enough, one young brave who was surprised to hear me speaking his language lifted his head, and I put a bullet between his eyes.

Pa smiled at me and said, "Smart, really smart."

A few minutes passed when one of the Blackfoot warriors said, "Who is it that speaks my language?" "I would like to know before I kill you."

"Brave words for only two of you, I am Soaring Eagle With Many Coups." "I am with my father, Bear Slayer, and the one up above is Grey Wolf, my brother."

"You did not kill the foolish one who raised his head." "He just has a minor wound," the warrior said.

"You know I am a better shot than that, and I know you know who we are," I said.

There was silence for a couple of minutes, and I turned to Pa and said, "I think one of them might be trying to work his way around to us."

"He would have to come from my side, too much open land on your side," Pa said.

"Pa, if you go over to those rocks behind us, you can pick him off no matter which way he comes from."

Pa nodded and crawled over to the rocks.

"If your brother isn't dead now, he soon will be, I wounded him badly," said the Blackfoot.

"My brother is not Blackfoot; he is strong and smart." "If he were dead, you would not have been so cautious about trying to get him." There was a loud boom from behind me and no return fire, not even an arrow. Within seconds Pa was sitting beside me and said, "Just the one left."

"Do not expect your friend to return Blackfoot," I said.

"If you are a real Shoshone warrior, fight me with knives."

"He wants to fight me with knives," I said to Pa.

"It is not necessary we will get him," Pa replied.

"I do not know how bad Grey Wolf is hurt." "We may not have the time that it will take to get him."

Pa nodded, and I said to the Blackfoot warrior, "I will fight you with knives, but you come out first without any other weapon." "I do not trust the Blackfoot your people lie." I yelled up to Grey Wolf not to fire at him, and the warrior came out, and then I went out.

When he saw me, the Blackfoot warrior started laughing and said, "You're so young you still have your mother's milk on your breath."

"There are many dead Blackfeet who smelled my breath when I took their scalps."

At that, he stopped laughing, and he charged me. I figured that he wasn't stupid and knew I would step to the right. Most would try to knock him to the ground, and he would be waiting for that. But what he didn't know was that I had no intention of moving right, but I move left where it would be awkward for him to do anything. As he came at me, he was going so fast that the warrior couldn't stop when I moved left and planted my left moccasin in the pit of his stomach, and he tumbled to the ground losing his knife.

I walked over to where his knife was and said, "Red Hawk must have picked the worst Blackfoot warriors he could find."

"I do not know this, Red Hawk," he replied as he looked up at me.

"The one who was pretending to be Shoshone in my village," I said.

"So, that is what Stands Alone is calling himself." He didn't know it, but he gave me the proof I needed to deal with Red Hawk or whatever his name was.

I kicked the knife over to him. He grabbed it and got up again and started circling me. It is an old trick that Grey Wolf taught me. By circling me, he was trying to get me to twist around in a circle to get me dizzy, so I started circling him. Frustrated that I wasn't doing what he wanted me to do, he charged me again. I ripped around him, cutting him deep on his side with my knife. He winced and grabbed his side with his free hand and came at me again. He swung at me with his knife when he came within striking distance, and I went under his arm, slicing him behind the knee. When he started going down, I grabbed his hair, pulled his head back, and sliced his throat like a deer with that he was dead.

Pa came over to me, and I said, "Maybe I should have asked him his name."

"It appeared to me you were just playing with him," Pa said.

I smiled, and we ran up to Grey Wolf, letting him know we were coming as we went. Grey Wolf was alive and conscious when we reached him. "What took you so long?" he asked with a smile being a little sarcastic.

"I was counting how many horses I would have if you didn't come back," I replied, being a little sarcastic myself.

The Blackfeet wounded him in the leg. The bullet went right through without breaking any bones. The bleeding had slowed, but he had lost a lot of blood. Pa worked on his leg and got the bleeding stopped. "Normally, I would wait a couple of days before heading back to the village, but someone might come looking for those dead Blackfeet," Pa said. "Do you think you can ride?" Pa asked Grey Wolf.

"Get me on a horse, and I will be fine," he replied.

We gathered up all the horses and things of value the Blackfeet had and much to the dismay of Pa; I scalped the Blackfeet that were there, then we headed back to the village.

We approached the heard of horses next to the village; it was dark out and startled the boy who was watching them. He was about to cry out when I stopped him. "Do not say anything to anyone about seeing us," I said. He nodded.

At that, we headed to Grey Wolf's lodge. It had to be one or two in the morning. No one saw us as Pa, and I dragged Grey Wolf into his lodge. Blue Lizard and Sometimes Comes were wide awake and up as we laid Grey Wolf down. "I will go get your mother," Pa said to me.

"Don't let anyone know Grey Wolf is back, Pa." "It might cause problems with Red Hawk if he finds out." Pa left, and I said, "I am going to take care of the horses and things we brought back."

"I will help you," said Sometimes Comes.

We released the horses to the main herd and brought everything into Grey Wolf's lodge before Ma, Pa, and Zack got back. I explained everything that happened to Blue Lizard and Sometimes Comes, who were both angry, especially Sometimes Comes.

When my family came into the lodge, Blue Lizard let Ma tend to Grey Wolf. She knew Ma was a healing woman and a good one at that. "I will kill Red Hawk for doing this to my son," Sometimes Comes said with great emotion.

Everybody was shocked that he considered Grey Wolf, his son, especially Grey Wolf, who was at a loss for words, and a tear seeped from his eyes.

"Do you think you can kill him you are up in age?" I said.

"I am no older than your father, and neither he nor you have ever seen me fight before," he said. "I am not only a Shoshone warrior but also a Mandan warrior." "Give me the honor to do this for my son," he added.

"It should be I who kills him," Grey Wolf said.

"You won't be doing much of anything for a while," Blue Lizard said, putting her foot down.

I turned to Sometimes Comes and said, "At least give me the honor to expose him for who he is, and then you can kill him." I let everyone know I was going to go to Spotted Buffalo's lodge to let him know what had happened and to let Morning Star know I was back, and I left.

When I went into Spotted Buffalo's lodge, everyone was asleep. I grabbed Spotted Buffalo's foot, and he popped up awake. "I need to talk to you," I whispered. We went outside, looked around, and then told him the whole story and what I intended to do about it.

"Are you sure he is a Blackfoot, my son?"

That was the first time he called me his son, and I said, "Without a doubt, he is a Blackfoot and means to do us harm."

"I wish to see Grey Wolf," Spotted Buffalo said.

We went into Grey Wolf's lodge, and I stayed out of the way while Spotted Buffalo talked to him. Zack was about to fall asleep, so Pa took him back to his lodge.

Spotted Buffalo had finished talking to Grey Wolf, turned to me and said, "Are you coming back to my lodge?"

I nodded yes, and he said, "I will let you and Sometimes Comes handle this, but when this starts, I will tell others that this dog must not live." He went out of the lodge and went back to his lodge.

Ma had finished with Grey Wolf and was telling Blue Lizard what to do to help him heal. "He needs his rest," Ma said to me.

"I will only be a short time, and then I will leave." She nodded and then left.

I looked at Blue Lizard, and Sometimes Comes then knelt beside Grey Wolf. "I will be alright," Grey Wolf said.

"I was worried about you, I love you," I said.

"We are brothers; brothers should love each other."

I nodded and got up and said to Sometimes Comes, "When I am ready, I will come for you."

He nodded and said, "I will be ready."

I crawled in next to Morning Star and put my arm around her. She awoke and turned around. I kissed her, and she kissed me back. "You stink, you need a bath," she said.

"It is the smell of your warrior," I replied.

She gave me a look that said she wasn't settling for that excuse, so I said, "It is late, I will bathe when the sun is up after I do something I have to do."

"We are married, and we do not do the things married people do," she said.

I was sure I knew what she was talking about, and I said, "After I do the thing I must do and bathe, everything will change, I promise."

"What is this thing you must do?" she asked disappointedly.

"I cannot tell you now, but you will understand after I get up," I replied. Morning Star wanted to know, but she accepted that I wasn't going to tell her, so she and I drifted off to sleep.

I woke late that morning. The sun had been up for hours, and Morning Star was outside with her mother. I went out to relieve myself, throw some water in my face, and to inform Spotted Buffalo and Sometimes Comes I was ready.

"Do you want anything to eat?" Morning Star asked.

"No," I said in a solemn voice. When I finished throwing water on my face, I approached Spotted Buffalo. Without saying a word, I just nodded, and he understood. I went into Grey Wolf's lodge, looked at Grey Wolf, turned to Sometimes Comes, and said, "It is time." I had my two pistols and knife, and I took the scalp of that last warrior I killed. Grey Wolf told me as we were bringing him back to the village that the last warrior that I killed was Never Miss A Shot, a poor name for one who was dead, how Grey Wolf knew his name I didn't know.

Sometimes Comes and I left the lodge, and I immediately spotted the one that the Shoshones called Red Hawk carrying wood for his lodge where he was staying. I stood in front of him about twelve feet away and pulled one of my pistols. Sometimes Comes moved to the left of me, and many Shoshone warriors went around all three of us, their weapons drawn. My Pa was there with Zack, and Comes Running was there also with bow and arrow ready.

Red Hawk stopped in his tracks, and I said in Blackfoot, "I have something that belongs to one of your friends, Never Miss A Shot." I threw the scalp down at his feet and added in Shoshone, "The rest of your companions' scalps are in Grey Wolf's lodge." "I would love to be the one who kills you Red Hawk, or should I call you Stands Alone, but it is the honor of Sometimes Comes to take your life."

Sometimes Comes pulled his knife and Stands Alone dropped the wood and pulled his knife, saying, "At least your brother is dead."

At that, Grey Wolf broke through the crowd limping and said, "I live and would kill you myself if I were not wounded." "Now, my father will kill you."

You could see the anger on Stands Alone's face, and he got into a fighting stance as Grey Wolf, and I faded back into the crowd. Stands Alone came after Sometimes Comes like a raging bull, but Sometimes Comes moved out of his way with skill and tripped him. He went sailing to the ground. But with Stands Alone's speed, he was able to trip Sometimes Comes while on the ground sending Sometimes Comes to the ground also. What Sometimes Comes lacked in speed, he made up for with skill, which surprised me, and most others present. Stands Alone tried to take advantage of Sometimes Comes on the ground but couldn't, and both men were on their feet again. Both men were looking for an advantage. At one time, Stands Alone tried to use his strength against Sometimes Comes but was surprised again when Sometimes Comes knocked him to the ground, much to my delight. Stands Alone figured he would have an easy win, but he was getting frustrated because he wasn't doing better. That's not good because you make mistakes when you are frustrated. "You do not fight like a Shoshone," Stands Alone said.

"I grew up Mandan, and now I am Shoshone," Sometimes Comes said. This revelation upset Stands Alone even more, and it showed. Stands Alone came at Sometimes Comes foolishly, and Sometimes Comes took advantage of it by slicing deeply into Stands Alone's stomach. As Stands Alone held his bleeding stomach, Sometimes Comes whipped around him and planted his knife in his back clear up to the hilt. Then with one motion, he grabbed Stands Alone's hair, pulled his head back, and slit Stands Alone's neck. He then scalped him while most of the young Shoshone ran in to count coup. Sometimes Comes, with the scalp in hand, walked over to Grey Wolf, who was sitting on the ground and gave him the scalp. He then picked up Grey Wolf and carried him back to the lodge.

Morning Star, who was standing next to me, grabbed my hand, and I smiled at her. She led me off downstream while we talked about the cabin I was making. When we had walked a little more than a mile, she stopped and said, "It is time you take a bath, you stink."

I smiled at her and completely stripped, and she did the same. We both went into the water, and she bathed me, and I washed her. We slowly caressed each other and became a truly married couple. "I loved you the very first time I saw you, and I will always love you," I said.

"I loved you too from the beginning, and I have missed you all these months you have not been with me," she said with the same love I had for her. "I wish to go back with you when you leave," she added.

"The lodge is not ready, and I made a promise to your mother and father that I would not take you with me until it was."

"It will be ready by the snow's first melt next season, and I will be here earlier than I normally am," I said. Morning Star pouted a bit, and I smiled and grabbed her by the hand, and we jumped back into the water. Then we got out, dressed, and went back to camp.

Zack was with Pa, and Pa said, "Where have you two been?"

"Bathing," I replied then smiled as Morning Star giggled.

Pa looked at Morning Star and me doubtfully and then said, "Yeah, well, if you're hungry, your mother has some food for you." "She will be back in a few minutes."

Morning Star and I went into the lodge, and Zack followed. Morning Star and I looked at Zack, and I said, "You still hungry?"

"I am always hungry; you know that," Zack replied.

Just then, Ma came into the tent and looked at me then Zack. "You can wait to eat now, go," Ma said to Zack. "Are you hungry?" asked Ma.

"I am not, but Soaring Eagle has not eaten yet," said Morning Star.

As Ma fixed something for me to eat, I wondered how much she had heard. It turned out it didn't take long before I found out. "So, you will be coming to live with my son early next season."

"Yes," said Morning Star meekly.

"Do you think a child will come before he comes or sometime after," Ma said pointedly.

"Ma, why do you say these things?" "I am not sure if I can even make babies," I said in English, embarrassed at what she said.

"You can make babies, my husband I am a woman now and know these things," Morning Star said.

I looked at Morning Star in shock as Ma stared at me like a cougar getting ready to pounce. I looked back up at Ma with a little anger that this was even getting brought up. I said, "It does not matter she is my wife, and I am more than capable of raising a family and taking care of them." I then threw the rest of my food in the fire, took Morning Star by the arm, and left before Ma could say another word.

"Gather some things we will go away for a few days," I said.

She did as I said, and as I was getting the horses ready, Pa came up to me and said, "Your mother feels sad that you are mad at her."

"I am not mad at her, Pa." "I am just angry that everybody wants to get into my business when it comes to Morning Star."

"Still, I think you should talk to your mother; where are you going?"

"Just to get away for a few days and to be alone with Morning Star."

Pa nodded and said, "Maybe it is just as well with all that has gone down; it will give everyone time to relax."

"I'll go and talk to Ma before I leave," I said.

Pa left, and a few minutes later, Morning Star came with her things. I explained to her that I was going to talk to my mother. I walked over to where my mother was and asked, "Can I speak to you?"

"Of course," she replied.

"I just want you to know I am not mad at you I am just angry at people interfering with my relationship with Morning Star." "I have decided to take Morning Star and go someplace else with her so that we can be alone," I said.

"I should not have acted the way I did, and I am happy you are not mad at me," Ma replied.

I hugged her and went back to Morning Star, and we headed out to our private spot.

Over the next five days, we became very close as time went on, I wasn't as hesitant as I was the first time, at least not for a boy my age. This lovemaking wasn't like when I was younger when it was mostly curiosity and more of a chore than anything else. Being with Morning Star is all I desired now, and she gave me great pleasure.

It was on the fifth day I had just come back with some game for Morning Star to cook. As we started to eat, I brought up the strange cave that my family and I had encountered.

"What did this cave look like?" asked Morning Star.

"It has paintings on the walls and ceiling, not like the paintings on the rocks we see sometimes or the ones on the lodges." "These had more detail and told a story, and the colors were very bright and colorful." "There were strange furs on the floor as well as bones of animals that I have never seen before," I said.

"I have heard of places where those who were here first have left their mark." "These are places that have great medicine where the Great Mystery sometimes comes, the Great Mystery protects the place," Morning Star said. "You should talk to my father about this, he can tell you better," Morning Star added. I didn't say any more about it, and the next day we headed back.

We got back late on a cloudy afternoon. Morning Star went and checked in with her mother while I sent the horses back into the main herd. While I was doing this, Pa came up to me and said, "How was your time with Morning Star?"

"Perfect, Pa."

"We want you to eat with us tonight."

"I will let Morning Star and Spotted Buffalo know." "I will come to the lodge right after I tell them and check on Grey Wolf."

After talking to Morning Star and Spotted Buffalo, I went to see Grey Wolf. I expected him to be much better but still in his lodge recovering; I could not have been more wrong.

"Grey Wolf is with Sometimes Comes hunting," said Blue Lizard.

"Already!" "It has been only a short time since he had received his wounds," I replied.

"I know, but Grey Wolf has a mind of his own, and he does as he wishes," she said.

"Please let him know I am back."

She nodded, and I headed to the river to wash up and then to my family's lodge.

As I approached the lodge, Zack was there, and he had a look to him I had seen before the look that I was in trouble for something.

"Zack, what is the matter?" I said in English.

"Oh, nothing of importance, but Pa isn't thrilled," he replied, being sheepish.

"Why isn't he happy?" I asked.

"I don't know," he replied.

He knew, and if it were about him or anyone else, he would have told me, so it must be about me. I knew there would be a confrontation at dinner. I hoped I could keep my temper.

Zack and I went into the lodge, and Zack sat on Pa's left and next to him, which was where I was supposed to sit. I was going to sit next to Zack when Pa indicated by motioning his hand for me to sit on his right. Ma was extra quiet, especially for not having seen me for many days. Ma served Pa first, but instead of Ma serving me next, Zack got served.

When Ma went to serve me, I raised my hand to stop her and said, "I rode a long way, and I am tired it is hard to control my anger." "If you have something to say, say it."

"We will raise our son our way; you do not have the right to tell him to be intimate with a girl," Pa barked.

I was shocked; I bent over and looked at Zack, who just hung his head down. Then, without a word, I got up and started to leave when Pa said, "There you go again running when you know you are wrong."

I stopped and said, "Perhaps, you should get the whole story from your son before you make such statements." "You should also know that if I did not get up to leave, you and your entire family would be dead now."

I turned to go but stopped again and said, "You are right; I don't have the right to say anything to any of you, for I am not your son and never will be." "But that is alright; I will not live with any of you ever again stay out of my way." I then left and went to Spotted Buffalo's lodge, leaving my family with their mouths open.

I asked Spotted Buffalo if I could come in. He said, "You are my daughter's husband." "You do not need permission to come into my lodge." They were all eating when I came in, and Spotted Buffalo asked, "Are you hungry?"

"Yes," I replied. Morning Star handed me some food and said, "I thought you were going to eat at your family's lodge."

"Yes, I thought you were, too," said Spotted Buffalo.

"I have no family, but Morning Star, Grey Wolf, and everyone here."

They all looked at me in surprise at what I had said. "You argued with your father again?" asked Morning Star.

"It was with all of them," I replied, distressed. Everyone in the lodge all looked at me with an expression of wanting more details. "Bear Slayer accused me of telling Tracking Fox to do something." "He then let me know it was not my place to tell him anything." "Then they told me what my place in that family was." "Even the one who said she was my mother, Blue Flower, showed me no respect."

Everyone was silent for a short time, and then Spotted Buffalo said, "Your father is a good man, and your family is good." "I am sure he will apologize to you and try to make it right."

"You do not understand this is not the first time we have fought, and it is just as you say, he does apologize and tries to make it right time after time."

"This is the way it will always be; he is never going to change." "If I forget about it and do nothing someday, I will kill him if I do not kill the whole family."

"You are angry now and are not thinking right." "Tomorrow, you will think differently," said Small Moon. Then they changed the subject, and Spotted Buffalo was talking to Running Deer about hunting.

"Just what did James mean when he said I need to get the whole story from you?" Pa asked Zack in English.

Zack told the whole story this time, and when he got finished, Pa said, "It looks like I did it again; shot my mouth off without getting James's side of it first."

"We are all at fault, and what is even worse, I think we might have pushed him too far this time he may not forgive us this time," said Ma sadly.

"I must try anyway," Pa replied.

"I'll go with you, Pa, after all, it was mostly my fault."

As we ate, Morning Star brought up the strange cave I told her.

"What is it about this cave that is strange?" Spotted Buffalo asked.

I told him about the paintings and the bones and furs. When I finished, there was a concerned look on his face, and he was staring out into space.

"You will come with me," Spotted Buffalo said sternly. He grabbed my arm, and we went outside. We headed to each of the elders' lodges, and he ordered them to follow him. I saw Pa and Zack coming toward us along the way to One Horn's lodge, who had won favor with the people of the village again.

Before Pa could say anything and without looking at him, Spotted Buffalo commanded, "Follow me."

Pa looked at me and asked, "What is going on?"

I didn't answer him and walked away.

We gathered in the center of the village where the central fire was. Spotted Buffalo told me to tell everyone about the cave. Then they turned to Zack and Pa and asked to add anything I might have left out.

"The paintings told a story," Zack said.

"What did the painting say?" Tall As The Sky asked.

My father told them what he thought they meant, and I gave my interpretation of the parts where I disagreed with him.

The elders were very serious about this, and One Horn asked, "Did you touch anything?"

"Other than light a fire in a fire pit, we touched nothing," I said.

"And how did you leave this cave?" asked Spotted Buffalo.

"We pushed the large rock in front of the opening and sealed it with mud," Pa said.

Once again, they talked among themselves. Spotted Buffalo said, "What you did is good, but you must never go back there again and never tell anyone about it."

Pa and Zack nodded, but I asked, "What is the meaning of this cave?"

Everyone looked at One Horn, and One Horn started to speak uncomfortably, "That cave is of The Old Ones', the ones who were before the Shoshone, before all people. In those days, there were mostly two peoples white skin people like yours and dark skin, darker than ours. It is said that the ones with the white skin could talk to the Great Mystery, and the Great Mystery would speak to them. The white skin people had much and were good people. The dark skin people had little and desired what the whites had. Both peoples had many warriors who fought much. The dark skin ones finally won and destroyed all the whites."

When One Horn finished, I asked, "What became of the dark skin people.

"No one knows," he replied. "That cave is bad medicine for anyone who disturbs it." "The Great Mystery protects that place," he added.

"I thought the Shoshone came from the north where it is cold when I was in the sweat lodge was this not this discussed?" I said.

"These people were not the Shoshone, so I believe they were another tribe who came from the south." "To tell you the truth, no one nor I know for sure about this. We believe we came from the cold up north, so that is what we say," said One Horn.

When the meeting broke up, Pa turned to me and said, "I wish to talk to you."

"You have nothing to say that I want to hear," I replied.

"You won't even let me apologize to you." "I promise you it will never happen again?" Pa said in English.

"Until it happens again, and then you will promise again." "Your promises are empty," I replied.

"You know how I am when I get angry, and you know I say and do things I don't mean," Pa said.

"Yes, I know this, but it wasn't just you this time, it was all of you," I said coldly.

I started to walk away when Zack said, crying, "Stop, it was my entire fault."

I tensed up and turned around and said, "You are right, it is your fault, and you're old enough to know better." I walked off into the darkness, passing Spotted Buffalo, who was watching. I could hear Pa calling to me, but I didn't answer because tears were also coming down my cheeks.

"I did not understand your language, but I could tell it did not go so well," Spotted Buffalo said.

"No, it did not," replied Pa.

"Let it be for now tomorrow after some time has passed, maybe it will be better," Spotted Buffalo said.

Pa nodded and said, "I hope so."

I didn't get back to Spotted Buffalo's lodge until late. I crawled into bed next to Morning Star, and she awoke and put her arm around me. "Everything will be alright," she said, and we both fell asleep.

The next day Morning Star had to do a few things for her mother, and I headed down to the river. I spotted Grey Wolf sitting on a rock, and I sat beside him. "I hear you have problems with your family again," Grey Wolf said.

"The only family I have, live in Spotted Buffalo's lodge and you," I said. For that statement, I got a good smack to the back of my head.

"Ow, that hurt, what did you do that for?" I complained.

"You speak nonsense when you are supposed to be wise." "Your family loves you, and you know it," Grey Wolf said.

"You were not there to see how they treated me or what they said," I replied.

"My father, Grazing Deer, and our father, Red Elk, did things and said things I did not like, but I still loved them." "The trouble with you is that you have much anger in you," Grey Wolf said.

I didn't say anything; I knew he was right, but I didn't want to go back to my family as if nothing had happened. As we were sitting there, a voice from behind me said, "Pa said we are going back home in five suns," it was Zack.

I said, "You might be heading back, but I will go when I wish if I go at all."

Grey Wolf smacked me in the back of the head again, and I snarled, "Stop that, or we will be drawing blood."

"You see, there is much anger in you," Grey Wolf said. I looked at him as if he was crazy, and he added, "I do not worry about fighting you." "You are strong but not as strong as you think." "I do not believe there would be much blood coming from me." "But from you, I think there would be a lot."

With that, he got up and limped away. When I got up to leave, I turned around, Zack was crying, and I felt terrible about it. "I am sorry if I upset you, I didn't mean to," I said.

"It's my entire fault I want things to go back to the way they were," Zack said in English sobbing.

I went up to him and put my arm around him and said compassionately, "It's not your fault, and I still love you."

"Then whose fault, is it?"

I stared at Zack for a moment and said, "A small part Ma's, part mine, and a large part Pa's."

"Pa acts that way with me too, that is just the way he is." "Remember how he did not want me to go hunting with him and the way he was acting about my toys," Zack said.

"I have to think about this Zack, but I have to tell you I do not believe that it will ever be the same."

Zack left not satisfied with what I had to say, but he stopped crying.

I sat down and started to chuck rocks into the water, not knowing what to do. I wish Pa didn't show contempt toward me when he got mad. There were other ways of dealing with one's anger. Then again, I have contempt for the Blackfeet, I guess, no not all Blackfeet just the ones who killed my family. When I get the last of them, I will not be at war with them anymore unless they show violence toward my loved ones.

There was the sound of someone clearing his throat behind me. I turned around to see Pa. "Do you mind if I sit down beside you and talk to you?" Pa asked.

"I don't own this rock," I said.

"Zack has been crying ever since you left, and Zack seldom cries, do you hate Zack?" Pa asked.

"No," I replied.

"And I haven't seen your mother cry since the death of her father." "That was more than twelve years ago." "She is crying now over the loss of a son; do you hate her?"

I looked at him to see if he was telling me the truth, and it was evident that he was. I put my head down and said in a soft voice, "No, I don't hate her, I am just a little angry with her."

"It's alright you hate me, and you're right, I have made promises to you before, only to do the same thing." "I am not perfect by any means, and I cannot say I will not make other mistakes, but with your help, I will try not to."

Mentally I was being pulled by two sides of me; one wanted to stay angry and the other wishing that nothing had happened. "I do not hate you, Pa, nor do I want to be angry, at least not now." "I wish that what happened never had happened I am so confused and lost," I said near tears.

He put his arm around me, and I nestled into him. "I wish what happened never had happened also." "It is normal for a person your age to be confused and lost sometimes." "It is all part of growing up," Pa said.

Pa and I were silent for a few minutes, and then Pa said, "What do you want to do?"

I thought for a second, then said, "I won't come back to your lodge." "It is not because of the fight we had, I am married, and you all need to accept that as true." "My place is beside Morning Star, and I would think it best I do not eat with you until we leave," I said.

"Alright, we leave in five suns if the weather holds out," Pa said.

"Zack told me this I will be there."

Pa patted me on the back, then got up and left. I sat there for a few minutes, and Morning Star came up to me and sat down. I put my arm around her as I stared into the water.

"It went well with your father?" she asked.

"Yes, it went just fine."

"Are you finished helping your mother?" I asked.

"Yes."

"Good, let's walk upstream and go swimming," I said. We walked some ways when we finally came to a small waterfall. Above that was a pool of water and a sandy beach. We stripped and went in, and it didn't take long before we were together again.

The five days passed quickly, and it was time to leave. I did not want to go but had to if I was going to finish the cabin in time. It was hard on Morning Star, but I assured her that I would return to the village at first snowmelt.

# 23

## RENDEZVOUS

By the fourth day, I was talking more, and Pa said to all of us, "I had a talk with Spotted Buffalo, and he has decided to go to the rendezvous next year." "It may be the last one, and I decided we will go also."

"He didn't say anything about it to me," I said. "I was hoping to move Morning Star into the cabin," I added.

"You can still bring her home." "The time we spend at the rendezvous will be the same amount of time we would spend if we went to the village," Pa said. I didn't say anything but got up and hunted for more wood for the fire. I knew why Pa brought this up; if he had wanted to, he could have said something long before this. Besides, he doesn't need anyone's permission to attend the rendezvous. The reason for bringing this up was to get me to talk more than I have been. He did it also to put the past into the past. I placed some wood on the fire and sat down again.

"Are you angry, James?" Ma asked cautiously.

"No," I said, confused. I looked at everyone, and all were staring at me with seeming trepidation. I said, "We were low on wood, and I was deep in thought."

"In thought, about what?" Pa asked.

I should have known he would ask, and I couldn't avoid answering. "Morning Star, the cabin, and where my life is heading," I said.

"You have a lot on your shoulders for a twelve-year-old boy," Pa said.

I stared at him for a few moments then said, "I turned thirteen yesterday, Pa."

Embarrassed, Pa said, "Oh, I knew your birthday was near, but I didn't realize it was this close I should have known."

"It doesn't matter; it is just like any other day," I said.

"It does matter, and it isn't like any other day, it is the day my son was born," Pa said. I was surprised he said that with such emotion.

I nodded and turned away before I got teary-eyed.

We finally made it back to the cabin, and everything was as we left it. Zack went out to check the stock. Pa and I unpacked while Ma got a fire started to fix something to eat. "We must go hunting in the next couple of days so that we will have enough meat this winter," Pa said.

"Just let me know, I'll be ready." When we finished unpacking and taking care of the horses, I took a quick look at my cabin. I would have to get more wood for the doors and shutters. I'll do that tomorrow and put the glass in the windows. I must move fast on all of this before the first snow comes. Between hunting and chores, it would take up a lot of my time.

The next day, I got up early and did my chores and was gone up into the hills before daylight I skipped breakfast. I figured I would cut down trees until about noon and then haul them back to my cabin. Then the rest of the day, I would install the glass, first in Pa's cabin, then mine. Before noon I had all the wood I would need, and I was hauling it down to the cabin. I had dragged the last log to the cabin when Zack came up to me and said, "Ma wants you to come and eat." I dropped what I was doing and followed Zack back to Pa's cabin.

After lunch, I got Zack to help me carry pa's window down to my cabin, and I took all the glass with Pa's help. "We are going hunting tomorrow." "Will you be ready?" Pa asked.

"I'll be ready, Pa." "And your window will be installed before we leave."

"Your mother will be happy about that," Pa added. "Bringing your glass down to your cabin has given us more room in the other cabin. Maybe you can bring more things down there to store," Pa said.

"I'm sure I can; I will do that as soon as we get back from the hunt," I answered.

I made putty for the windows, placed the glass in Pa's window frame, and inserted the cleats to hold the glass in place. Then I puttied over the cleats and smoothed everything out. It took me nearly an hour-and-a-half to do that one window, and Pa's window was smaller than mine. I placed it against the wall away from where I was working to let the putty harden up and dry. I then started on my windows. It took me an extra hour more than Pa's window did just to do one. I laid the window next to Pa's window and checked the putty on his. It was hard enough to install in the cabin, and since the sun was setting, I decided to stop working on mine for the night and install Pa's window.

Pa gave me a hand with the window, and within twenty minutes, we hung it, and it worked perfectly. "It's finished, Ma," I said. She came over to look at it, smiled, and said, "You did a great job."

"The glass will need cleaning, but do not clean it until we get back from the hunt, and I can check to see if the putty is completely dry," I explained. She nodded in agreement, and I went outside to wash up.

The next day we headed south looking for the game. Zack had a choice of going or staying, and he had chosen to stay, his toys were a big factor I believe. We had taken two pack horses to haul back the game. We had traveled for several hours without finding anything. "There is a stream near here. Let's follow the river for a while; maybe we will find some tracks," I said.

We headed southwest and found the stream. "I can remember a time when you wouldn't have even to go out hunting for the game, the game would come to you," Pa said.

"The game must have been very tame to do that," I said.

"Not tame, there was just a lot of them."

"There are some tracks here that are interesting, let's follow them and see where they lead," Pa said.

About an hour later, we came to a wooded rise. On the other side, there was a green meadow and about a dozen deer. I aimed at the right of the herd and Pa on the left. Two large bucks went down. We reloaded and went down to dress out the deer. About half an hour later, we loaded the deer and went back to the river. We followed the river for several hours; then, Pa spotted more tracks. By this time, it was late afternoon. These tracks were fresher than the last. We tied up our horses and followed the tracks on foot. It didn't take long when we saw about six or seven deer. Again, we aimed and shot, and we had two more deer. The deer were not quite as large as the last ones, but they would do. "Go back and get the horses, I will start on the deer," Pa said. Without a word, I headed back to get the horses.

I had just gathered up the horses and was heading back when I heard the boom of a pistol going off. Pulling the horses, I ran as fast as I could back to where Pa was. When I got there, he was lying on the ground clutching the back of his leg. I quickly tied off the horses and went to him.

"Snakebite, I think it was a rattlesnake," Pa said grimacing.

"What do I do?" I asked.

"You never treated a snake bite before?" he said.

"I never even saw a snake bite before," I replied.

"Cut the pant leg, and you should see two punctures there."

I did as he said and saw the two holes. "Ok, now what, Pa?"

"Cut across the punctures and suck out the poison and blood. That's enough, now go make a poultice."

I knew how to do that and got busy doing so, and after I had finished with Pa's leg, he told me to dress out the deer, which I did. When I finished dressing out the deer, Pa wasn't looking so good. I said, "If I help you, do you think you can get on your horse?"

"It will be dark soon; we should wait until morning," he replied.

"You don't look good, and if it gets too dark, I will walk in front of my horse, we will just take it slow." Before he could say anything, I got him up and managed to get him on his horse. I tried all the horses together, and we started back.

After a couple of hours of riding, it was getting so dark I couldn't see very well enough for the horses to be safe traveling. I got off my horse and walked, pulling the four horses along with me. When we came to a meadow, I rode slowly. That way, I wouldn't get so tired. I could hear animals in the brush and trees all around me, and I figured it might be wolves that smelled the deer we were hauling. I was hoping that they would not attack because of all the horses and the smell of Pa and me. But my hope was gone when they came at us. It was one of the times when we were passing through a grassy clearing. I saw four wolves to my left.

I shot the one in the lead, pulled out my pistol, and got another. The other two ran off, and I started to reload. Before I finished, the two wolves that had run off were back, and they had company. I fired my one loaded pistol and killed the one in front, and then there was a boom behind me. Pa shot another but was knocked off his horse from the recoiling rifle and the horse in a frantic state. I got one pistol loaded again to shoot another, and, at the same time, I flew off my horse knife drawn and met the last wolf. It wasn't much of a fight. The wolf bit down on my arm, but before it could apply pressure, I had my blade into her, and she dropped to the ground.

I went over to where Pa was. He was weak and very sick, but I was able to get him back on his horse. I decided to tie him to the horse so that he wouldn't fall off again. I gathered up our weapons and got out of there before another wolf showed up.

It was about an hour before sunrise, but it was getting light when we got near the cabin. I knew Ma and Zack would be up, so I pulled my pistol and fired it. Sure enough, they shot out of the cabin with two rifles. When they spotted us, they came running, and I yelled, "Pa's bad off snake bit him."

Ma took Pa's horses, and Zack took the pack horses. When we got up to the cabin, I helped Ma take Pa into the cabin. "I did what I could, Ma," I said.

"You did just fine." "Now go help your brother with the horses and deer," Ma replied as she was gathering her medicine. I did as she said, so as Zack took care of the horses we were riding, I took the deer off the packhorses and hung them to get skinned.

I had just about finished the first deer when Zack joined me. "Is Pa really bad?" he asked.

"I don't know he looks bad to me." It was full sunup when we finished with the last deer. We washed up and went into the cabin. Ma was putting hot strips of leather on Pa's leg.

"How's Pa, Ma?" Zack asked.

"He is very sick, but he will be alright," she replied.

"The deer is ready to be cut up, Ma," I said.

"Zack and I will take care of the deer you need to get some rest," Ma told me.

"I will go to my cabin and sleep there." I turned around and left she was right; I was dead tired.

I became awakened by someone grabbing my foot and shaking it. I shot up pistol cocked only to find that it was Othello. He quoted something from Shakespeare, which I couldn't make out. My head was still full of cobwebs. It confused me that he was here. I thought Little Girl, and Othello were going to California or someplace. I guess I would find out later why they were still here. When my head finally cleared, he said, "Your Ma wants you to come to eat."

I grabbed my weapons, headed down to the stream, and washed up. Then I followed Othello to the cabin. "How's Pa," I asked him.

"He's a mighty peaked if I do say so," he replied.

Little Girl and Ma were tending to Pa, who was awake. Zack was on his bed, playing with his toys. I walked over to Pa and said, "You alright?"

"Thanks to you, I am," he replied.

"It wasn't much; it was a small snake," I replied.

"Oh yeah, well, those wolves who attack us weren't so small."

That got everyone's attention, including Zack's.

"What wolves?" Ma asked.

"A few wolves attacked us, but Pa and I took care of them," I said.

"A few!" "There were at least six, if not more," Pa said excitedly. He then went and told the whole story. Ma went over to the pot in the fire and got me something to eat.

"I will sleep in my cabin tonight." "It will give you more room in here this evening," I said.

Ma turned to Zack and said, "It'd be nice if you would go down to James's cabin also."

"Can I bring my toys?" Ma nodded yes, and after I ate, we headed down to the cabin.

I started a fire in the fireplace to give light and warmth. Then I brought a log into the cabin to work on it. Zack laid the bedding in the far corner and sat down. He started to play with his toys but stopped and said, "Do you need some help?"

I smiled and said no, and there was no argument coming from him, and he went back to his toys. I figured it would be best to square the log first and then cut it into planks; it was hard work. I had squared off two sides when I finally stopped. Zack had long since put his toys away and fallen asleep, and I was soon beside him, drifting off to sleep.

The next day after chores, I finished squaring off the log and started the long process of sawing the planks, which wasn't an easy job. I found out after lunch that Othello was here for something other than a social visit. He wanted Pa to go on a beaver hunt one more time, and since I knew how Pa thought, I knew he would go. Pa looked better today. The swelling in the leg looked like it had gone down some.

I found I could cut about a plank and a half a day, and I would need two logs just to do the front door. The inner doors would be thinner and would be harder to cut, as would the shutters. By the end of the week, I had enough planks for the doors, but I still had to cut the cross pieces for all the doors.

Pa was up and about and had announced that he was going with Othello for the last beaver trapping. Little Girl and her baby would stay with us until both came back, which made Ma happy. I had little to say about his going or staying, and it didn't matter to me. Zack decided to stay with me in my cabin and let Ma and Little Girl have Pa's cabin.

A day after Pa left, I started to assemble the door, and it took me two days to get it ready; then, I hung it with Zack's help. It was getting colder, so I decided to take the chance and hang the windows before I made shutters. I was making the last of the shutters when the first snow started coming down, but the cabin was warm, warmer than Pa's cabin.

Zack made sure we all had enough firewood, which was a help to me. I surveyed the amount of wood I had and decided I would need more if I were going to put in floors and make furniture. So, for the next few days, I chopped down trees and hauled them back to the cabin during the day, and at night I worked on the cabin.

I hauled down the rest of the things I bought for the cabin and stored them in one of the rooms with Zack's help. The things I brought down from Pa's cabin made his cabin look empty, but Ma was happy to have space. The cabin was coming along nicely; I had both doors up for the bedrooms but had a problem with the rooms. There was more than enough heat even with the doors shut, but when I closed the doors, it was very dark except for a little light coming from the top of the wall and from under the doors. I would have to figure something out later. I next started on the floor, and I knew that would take me most of the winter, and I may not finish before I brought Morning Star home.

The winter dragged on, and it was a cold one. When I wasn't doing chores or hunting, I was working on the cabin floor. Ma and Little Girl came down to my cabin a few times to see the progress and were amazed at the look and warmth of the cabin.

As I was building the floor, I had to move things, or I should say Zack moved things behind me so that they would not get in the way. There was the problem of the gold and where to keep it. I solved the problem by making a small portion of the floor removable in one of the back rooms.

By early March, the floor was in place but not finished. The floor was too rough because the saw blade did not cut it smoothly. If I were to have little ones someday, it would have to get smoothed out.

It had been a hard winter, and there was plenty of snow on the ground. I figured I wouldn't be able to go to the village and get Morning Star until the end of April. The rough floor I was staring at was bothering me when Zack came into the cabin and said, "Ma wants us to come and eat."

I nodded and followed Zack back to Pa's cabin. Zack had stayed with me the whole winter. Even though he played with his toys a lot, he was still a lot of help to me. As we went into the cabin, Ma had Zack's and my plates full of food. Little Girl was already seated when we sat down, and Ma joined us after we sat down. "I figure I won't be able to go to the village until about the end of April," I said. "I think Pa should be back by then," I added.

"I think you are right," Ma answered.

"I'm bothered by the wooden floor. It is much too rough if I am going to have little ones someday, I don't know what to do," I said.

"You could just take out the wood and have dirt floors like here," Ma said.

"No, I don't want to do that," I replied.

There was silence for a few seconds, and then Little Girl said, "How do the Shoshone men make their bows smooth."

"They rub sand from the river on the wood." "I saw my grandfather, Arrow Maker, doing this many times," I said.

Everyone looked at me to see if I got the solution for my floors or not. Then I smiled. "I will remove the snow away to get to the sand as soon as I finish eating," I said.

Before I left Pa's cabin, I asked Ma, "Do you think I can use the bathing tub for a while Zack is starting to stink."

"I stink what about you?" Zack said a bit more seriously.

"You can both use the tub," Ma said.

I grabbed the tub and headed back to my cabin. I placed the bathtub in one of the back rooms and cleared out everything else from the main room of the cabin. I grabbed the shovel, an ax, and the sled that I hauled rocks with and headed for the stream with Zack following.

"I thought we were going to take a bath?" Zack said.

"Later, when there isn't so much work to do besides, I have some use for the bathwater," I replied. It was cloudy outside, and I knew another storm was coming, and I would have to get all the sand in one day. I cleared a ten by ten-foot area. The snow was the easy part, but the ice underneath is what would be hard, so I used the ax on that. When I was finished, which took several hours, Zack and I went back to the cabin to warm up. After about a half-hour, Zack and I went back to the hole, filled the sled with sand, and pulled it back to the cabin. What I did took several trips before I was satisfied, we had enough sand. I also got two rough, flat rocks and two smooth ones to use on the floor. We spread the sand on the floor and then grabbed the two rough stones and rubbed the sand into the wood. We did two passes on the floor before it was time for bed. I swept a corner next to the fireplace clean and checked the floor. It was significantly smoother than it had been, but it would need at least two more passes before I would be satisfied. Zack laid the bedding down, and we went to sleep.

I was up much earlier than Zack and did my chores instead of eating. Before I went back to the cabin, I told Zack, "When you finish with your chores, go eat and then bring me something to eat up at my cabin." He nodded, and I went back to my cabin. Since it was just me there, I threw some sand up into the loft and started sanding that. I had gotten two sandings done and started the third when Zack came in with a plate of food. I came down and ate while Zack added more wood to the fire.

When I finished, I said, "I'm going to finish off the loft first, then go back and finish off the floor." That was just fine with him; he sat back down with his toys and started playing with them. It took me about two hours to do the sanding because I had to do the steps also. I took the smooth stone and rubbed it on the loft floor, which was the last step. When I finished, the loft had a shining, smooth, and solid look to it. I told Zack to put everything up in the loft, and we went back to work on the floor. When we finished the main room, which took about four hours, we cleared out one of the back rooms and went to eat.

After we ate, we went back to work in the back room. I wanted to finish one room and get started on the other before I went to sleep. We finished the bedroom, and Zack helped me clean out the other bedroom. Then he wanted to go to sleep, and I couldn't blame him. I did the first sanding of the last room and went to bed myself.

After chores and everything else, we went to work on the last room, which took us until noon to complete. After we ate lunch, we went back and put things away. I said, "I think we should bathe. It has been some time since we last had a bath.

Zack agreed, and I put more wood on the fire, and Zack stripped and started bathing first. Zack had finished and was warming and drying himself by the fireplace while I undressed and began to bathe.

I was in the middle of my bath when the door flew open, and there stood Ma and Little Girl staring at us. It didn't faze Zack at all, but, for some strange reason, it bothered me. Maybe it was because Little Girl was there. I was uncomfortable with them being there, so I got out of the tub, dried off, and put my loincloth on while Zack stood there with nothing on.

Ma and Little Girl admired the job we did on the floor, and I said, "I'm going to take this bathwater and wash the floor, then put down a mixture that will make it shinier and protect the wood when the snow gets tracked in." After they left, I went back to working on the floor. When I finished with the tub, I had Zack take it down to Pa's cabin while I made the polish for the floor. I got just about finished making the polish out of oils, fats, bee's wax, and other things when Zack came in. "We only need one coat of this stuff." I showed him how to apply it and buff it out, and we started putting it down. I worked in the main room, and he worked on the loft and stairs. When we finished the main room and loft, we were mighty tired and went to sleep in one of the back rooms so that the polish could have time to dry completely and harden up.

The next day, we did the two back rooms, and I still had enough daylight to go up into the wooded area and get some wood to make furniture and other things. It surprised me that it took a long time to make the furniture and I wanted and the railing for the loft and stairs. Zack couldn't help me much, it was a one-man job, and it was already into April when I finished with everything I was going to do until Morning Star came. I did have cloth, and I thought of making curtains for the windows. At night, I still slept with Zack up in the loft even though I completed the bed.

The snow was finally melting, and I figured I would leave to the village in about two weeks. I got busy with the curtains, and I was clumsy at it, but within a week I had them finished and hung. The mistakes I made got hidden by how I hung them, and they looked good to me.

It wasn't a day after I finished the curtains and got them hung that Othello and Pa showed up. They didn't have a lot of beaver pelts, and they looked mighty tired. They had gotten other valuable furs, perhaps more valuable than the beaver pelts to sell at the rendezvous. Why Pa wanted to go to the rendezvous was beyond my comprehension. We had everything we needed. I suggested that we take meals in my cabin because I had a larger table with enough chairs for everyone, and they all agreed.

I let Othello and Pa rest and got busy back at the cabin. I opened the shutters that I had closed for the winter, which brought in a lot of light. At about three o'clock everybody came down to my cabin. Ma and Little Girl cooked, and Othello and Pa checked out the cabin. They were all shocked at how it came out, especially from a boy my age. I explained what my next projects would be, and we talked until it was time to eat.

"Next week, I plan to go to the village, and I will wait for you there," I said.

"If you wait an extra week, we will be going," Pa said.

"No, I promised Morning Star I would go after the last of the snow, and I intend to keep my promise."

Pa nodded and didn't argue with me for which I was grateful. "Zack, I heard you have been spending the winter in James's cabin are you planning to stay?" Pa asked.

"To tell you the truth, I like it here; it is bigger and warmer," Zack replied.

We finished eating, and Othello said, as he lit his pipe, "After the rendezvous Little Girl and I are moving on, west to the coast." "Just nothing left here for me." "Maybe I can find something in logging or something."

"We will miss you, but you can still come and visit when you have some free time," Pa said.

"Nate, what are you going to do to make it here?" Othello asked.

"You know the Shoshone and Utes have lived here for many years without trapping for beaver," Pa said.

Before Pa could say anything about the gold, I said, "I plan to build a sawmill and maybe bring up cattle from the south, I also have plenty of horses." "You know, there will be settlers here soon, and they will want those things," I said.

Pa looked at me, and I think he understood, and he said, "Yes, we have those plans and other options." Everybody finally left for Pa's cabin Zack, and I cleaned up and went to bed.

For a few days, until I left, I kept myself occupied by gathering more wood. I wanted to make more chairs and stack firewood. There wasn't much more I could do; the ground was too frozen to start laying a foundation for the barn and the water too cold to haul rocks. I asked Zack if he wanted to go with me, but he decided to go with Ma, and I took just one horse and traveled light. In four days, I made it to the village and into the waiting arms of Morning Star.

I was shocked to see Morning Star. She looked like she took on a lot of weight. "How did you gain so much weight over the winter?" I asked her in front of her family.

Her father and mother laughed, and Morning Star said, "I am not fat; I carry your son."

"How can this be?" I asked.

"You don't know how a woman gets a baby?" Running Deer asked.

"Of course, I do, at least I think I do," I said. Everybody laughed again, and I said, "I thought Morning Star and I were too young to make a baby."

"I guess you are not," Spotted Buffalo said with a smile.

"You do not want the baby?" Morning Star said anxiously.

"Of course, I want the baby; he will be my first son or daughter," I said nervously. "I don't know how my mother and father will take the news, though," I said.

"Your mother will be happy." "I know Blue Flower very well." "Your father, if he is not happy, he will be when the baby comes," Small Moon said.

"When will the baby be here?" I asked.

"Not for a while yet when the weather is warmer," Morning Star said.

"Do you have a name yet?" I asked Morning Star.

"That is for you to choose," said Morning Star.

"I must give this some thought," I replied.

For the next week, I never left Morning Star's side until she got annoyed with me being around her all the time as a deer fly. Then she told me to do something with Grey Wolf. I didn't know I could make love with her without harming the baby. I quickly found out that the baby wouldn't be in danger at all, much to my relief, but I was still as gentle as could be. Much to Morning Star's credit, she was patient with the way I was acting, understanding that this was all new to me.

My family finally came and Morning Star, many from the village, and I went to the edge of the village to greet them. When they spotted Morning Star and me, they stopped. Everyone first looked at Morning Star, then me, but it was Othello who first said something. "Looks like you are going to be a Grandpa, Nate," he said, half laughing.

Ma had a smile on her face and got off her horse as did Little Girl; she approached Morning Star and started asking her many questions about the baby. Pa's reaction was just about what Small Moon said it would be, but he didn't say anything stupid to cause a fight between him and me.

As time went by, Pa got used to the idea that he was going to be a Grandpa, and things went well with us. Zack hadn't been around as much as he usually was. I guessed he was off with some friend of his. Spotted Buffalo told Pa we would go to the rendezvous about the end of May, of course, he didn't say "May," but that is when we would go.

I didn't like the idea of Morning Star moving there so close to her time. However, I didn't have much to say about it. I was alone with Ma, and I asked her, "Do you think Morning Star should have here in the village or back at my cabin?"

"She may have a hard time having her first child; she is very young. She should have the baby here where there are a lot of women to help her," Ma replied.

"Do you think we might lose the baby?" I said worriedly.

"Anything can happen, but there are many here who have had a baby at her age, and she is strong," Ma explained. "Go out and find your brother I have some things for him to do," Ma said.

I went looking for him, but I didn't know where he went. Finally, I asked Little Man if he had seen him. "He and the girl White Doe went that way not long ago," he pointed upstream from the village. I wondered why he was with a girl he usually plays with the boys.

I followed the stream for a short distance when I heard something in a brushy area. I pulled out my pistol and cautiously crept over to where the noise was coming. As I looked through the bushes, I saw White Doe and Zack completely naked, and they weren't playing. I almost laughed Zack was as awkward as I was the first time I was alone with Morning Star. I stepped away but made plenty of noise as I left.

When I returned to the village, I waited to see when Zack and White Doe would show up. Meanwhile, Pa approached me and said, "Have you seen Zack, your mother wants him?"

"Yes, Pa, he should be here shortly."

Sure enough, Zack and White Doe appeared. "Where have you been, your mother has been looking for you?" Pa said.

"Just up the stream with a friend Pa," Zack said.

Pa looked at White Doe as she walked away, and he said a bit suspiciously, "Oh, well, go see what your mother wants."

I walked with him for some ways with a big smile on my face.

"You saw, didn't you?" Zack said in English.

"I sure did, and you better be careful, or you will have a baby too," I said.

"That will never happen." "I am too young," Zack said, sure of himself.

"That's what I thought, and you know what happened," I replied.

"You're not going to tell anyone, are you?" he asked worriedly.

"No, how did it feel?" I asked, smiling.

"You know how it felt, and I can't wait to do it again."

I giggled, shook my head, and walked off as he went into Pa's lodge.

We finally headed to where the rendezvous was going to be. Morning Star was so big with our baby; I felt she might pop. Even so, she seemed to be doing alright. It took us four days to get to the rendezvous. The Nez Perce were already there with several mountain men. As we were setting up our village, the Crow came in, and Spotted Buffalo put extra guards watching the horses. I found out that the rendezvous would start early and end that way. Zack wasn't around much, but I knew what he was doing. When everything got set up in the village, I went into Spotted Buffalo's lodge to check on Morning Star.

"How are you feeling?" I asked her.

"I will be alright; I'm just a little tired from the journey," she said.

"You leave her alone for now; she needs her rest," said Small Moon sternly. I smiled at Morning Star, kissed her, and took off with a swat on my bottom from her mother.

Jim Bridger and his Rocky Mountain Fur Company showed up three days later. I didn't know the man, but Pa knew him very well. "There are fewer mountain men this year," Pa said to Othello.

"Yeah, a lot of lowlifes here too. Maybe more trappers will show up it is early still," Othello replied. Late that afternoon, the Ohlone, a small band compared to the Shoshone, showed up. "Those are Little Girl's people." "I will be staying with them, Nate out of respect for Little Girl," said Othello.

I was surprised the Ohlone came to the rendezvous. They were from some distance away. I didn't know much about them, but they seem passive. Someone some time ago told me that they were part of a larger federation.

"I understand one must stay with their wife's family. Late tomorrow, I will be going to visit the trappers if you are interested," Pa replied.

"I surely am, I will come by to see if you are ready to go," Othello said. At that, he packed up his things, and he and Little Girl joined the Ohlone.

The next day Morning Star's mother chased me out of the lodge, so I joined Pa and Othello visiting the trappers. As we rode from one end of the trappers to the other end, Othello said to Pa, "There are a lot of pilgrims, and by the looks of it, most of them are thieves and lowlifes."

"You can say that again, I wonder what will happen next year when there aren't any more rendezvous," Pa said.

"I don't know, but I think I'm glad that I am moving to the west coast," replied Othello.

"Nate, Othello," some trapper yelled out.

Pa and Othello stopped and looked up, and Othello said, "My goodness if it isn't Jedediah Smith." Pa and Othello got off their horses, and then I did. There were six trappers in all, and some of them looked like some of them lowlifes Pa and Othello discussed.

"Come over here and take a swig of this bear piss," Jedediah said.

"I don't mind if I do," said Othello.

"Who is the young one?" Jedediah asked.

"He's my son James," Pa said.

I nodded my head, and Jedediah said a bit confused, "I didn't know you had more than one son Nate?"

"Yes, James and Zackary," Pa replied as Othello handed over the jug of alcohol, and Pa took a swig. Pa then turned to me and said, "You are old enough if you want some."

I shook my head no, and one of the other trappers, a large man I didn't like the looks of when I first saw him said, "What's the matter, you still on your mother's tit?"

I gave him a dirty look but didn't say anything, and another trapper said, "Leave the boy alone, the less he drinks, the more there will be for us."

"I'm no boy," I retorted.

Then the one trapper who started all this said snidely, "You're no man either." "I heard those tall tales about you, York, and I know they are all lies."

Pa thanked Jedediah for the drink, and he and Othello started to leave. Then, that lowlife trapper said, "I also heard you had a bastard son and a half-breed spawn from a Shoshone whore."

"You looking for a fight?" Pa said.

"I heard you are too much of a coward to fight," he replied.

I pulled my knife and said, "He isn't afraid to fight, and neither am I."

"Well now a York with some spunk," the troublemaker said.

He pulled his knife, and Pa started to swing his rifle, but the other trappers brought their rifles to bear on Pa and Othello except for Jedediah, who didn't know what to say.

"Let them fight if your son is old enough to pull a knife on a man, he is old enough to fight," said a bald trapper.

"You don't know who this young man is, fool," said Othello.

"And who do you say he is other than a baby-faced whelp?" said the bald trapper confidently.

Angrily Othello said, "The Shoshone call him Soaring Eagle With Many Coups."

"Another tall tale," said the troublemaker as he lunged at me and missed.

"I don't want anything to do with this," one of the trappers said as he lowered his rifle and left. The troublemaker lunged at me again, but he was clumsy, and I tripped him, and he went flying. I let him get up, and he was madder than a wet hen, but he was wiser, and I knew he would be more careful the next time. I wasn't paying attention, and he switched hands. He swung his left hand with the blade in it, and I moved to the right, and with his right hand in a fist, he hit me a good one, which sent me flying. I was dazed for a few seconds but still fast enough to get out of his way. I learned quickly enough not to make that same mistake. By this time, we attracted a lot of people, and they all knew it was no game. He swung again and missed, but I got him a good one in the arm, which started bleeding. By this time, he was breathing hard, which was just what I wanted, and I hadn't even broken a sweat yet. He then switched hands again, but this time I was ready for him. I stepped back, and he just missed me. Then I lunged forward with my empty fist and struck him, breaking his nose. This time he went flying, but he got up quickly, wiping the blood away. He came to me again like a desperate person, not knowing he was already a dead man. That is one thing that Grey Wolf drilled into me, while in battle, never attack someone when you feel desperate because you are already defeated when you do. He came down on me like a hammer, but I side-stepped him and sunk my knife in his chest clear to the hilt right under the sternum. He stepped back in disbelief and fell to the ground dead. The bald trapper just stared at his dead friend like the other trappers. That's when Pa knocked away his rifle and knocked him out. Jedediah and Othello pulled their rifles on the others, and they lowered their rifles and backed off.

Jim Bridger stepped forward; he had seen the whole thing and said, "You're not a bad fighter young man."

"That's because he is my son," said Pa. He looked at me then at Pa confused, Pa caught on to it and said, "I found out I had another son not very long ago."

Jim Bridger looked at the dead man and said, "Another low life." "I'm glad I'm getting out of the trapping business, and this is the last rendezvous, it's just not like it used to be."

"No, it isn't," said Othello.

"What are you going to do after this rendezvous?" asked Pa.

"Open up a trading post, it will support me in my old age," Bridger said.

"Where is it going to be?" I asked.

"I was thinking around Black's Fork on the Green River," Bridger replied.

"I know the area not very far from where we live, Pa," I said. Pa and Othello talked to Jim Bridger for some time, and I just listened.

The other trappers who supported the man I killed faded away and joined other groups of trappers. The bald one was already making excuses for why his friend was dead. "That whelp got lucky I tell you; Ben was drunk and tired from traveling here. If he hadn't been drunk, he could have taken him easy or anyone of us as far as that goes," the bald man said.

"I don't know about that if he is this Soaring Eagle, he has killed a lot of men," another trapper said.

"Are you taking his side?" asked the bald man angrily. He insulted us by not taking a drink, and he acted as if he was better than us. Anyway, even if he is this Soaring Eagle and has killed a lot of men, those men were savages, and we all know they can't fight worth a damn," the bald man added.

Many nodded in agreement, "I am going to keep an eye on him." "If I get a chance, I will make sure he wishes he was never born," he said. "I hope there are some of you I can count on when that time comes," the bald man growled.

As we were traveling back to the village, Pa said, "I don't think it is a good idea to visit the trappers; there might be more trouble."

"That's alright with me, I'm not interested in them anyway," I said.

I spent the next few weeks in the village or off hunting with Grey Wolf. Morning Star's time for delivery was changed twice, first by Ma, who said she would deliver in early July, then by her mother, who said any day, but they both said it would be a boy. There wasn't any trouble with any more trappers. Still, occasionally, when I went hunting with Grey Wolf, I saw a trapper or two watching me or even trailing me.

I wasn't sure when Morning Star would deliver so, I stuck near the village doing things to keep me occupied. It was in the morning when I was currying one of my favorite horses that there was a lot of excitement in the camp. Zack ran over to me and said, "It's time the baby is coming."

It didn't hit me at first; then, I realized it was my baby coming, and I dropped everything I had and ran to Spotted Buffalo's lodge. It seemed like everyone was there, and when I tried to go in Spotted Buffalo, and Pa grabbed both of my arms and stopped me. "It is not your place in there, let the women do their work," Spotted Buffalo said.

I paced back and forth, worried about Morning Star and the baby. At one point, I heard Morning Star Scream, and I bolted to the lodge to try to get in but was stopped again, "You can't help her son," Pa said.

"But she is in great pain; something must be wrong," I replied.

"Haven't you ever been around a baby being born before?" "The screaming and suffering are what women go through?" Othello said.

"No, the only babies I ever saw were animal babies."

Everyone looked at me in shock, not at what I said but at themselves for thinking I would have been around women giving birth. The only one who was not shocked was Sometimes Comes, he knew of the time I spent in St. Louis.

Morning Star screamed some more, and I was getting more and more upset. Pa came up to me and put his arm around me and said, "It will be alright; Morning Star couldn't be in better hands."

Time dragged on, and it seemed like the baby would never come, but someone said this was normal. It was just about dark when I heard the cry of a baby. My mouth hung open, and some tears ran down my cheeks when Ma came out of the lodge and said to me with a smile on her face, "You are a father."

"How is Morning Star?" I asked.

"You go in and see," Ma replied.

When I went in, Blue Lizard had the baby, and Small Moon was tending to Morning Star. I went to Morning Star, who was very sweaty and said, "Are you alright, I heard you scream many times?"

"I am well, just a little tired," she said. "Go see your son," she added.

Blue Lizard placed the baby in my lap, and I looked at the naked body, squirming in my arms, getting ready to cry. Small Moon wrapped a soft rabbit skin around him and said, "This will keep him warm and prevent him from crying."

As I held him, he opened his eyes, and I said to Morning Star, "His eyes are blue like mine."

Small Moon said, "Many babies' eyes are blue when they are first born, but they change."

Then thinking she may have insulted me, she said, "But perhaps this one will keep his blue eyes as his father has." I smiled, and Morning Star continued, "Your son needs a name."

"He will have two names like I have two names." "His white name will be Joseph, which means the great mystery will increase, and his Shoshone name will be...." I was going to say Red Elk in honor of my Shoshone father, but something deep inside of me stopped me.

As I seemed to be in a trance, Small Moon said, "What will his Shoshone name be?"

But I didn't answer, and Morning Star grabbed my arm, which broke my trance, and I looked at her and said a bit confused, "Hania." "His name shall be Hania, which means Spirit Warrior; it is a Hopi name." I looked at Small Moon and asked, "Do you know who the Hopi people are?"

"Yes, I have heard of them, but why do you call him by a Hopi name?" "Why not Shoshone?" she asked.

"I was going to call him Red Elk after my Shoshone father, but something inside of me said no, Hania." "I do not know the Hopi people, and I don't remember where I got the name, but that is what I feel it should be," I said.

"I think it is a beautiful name," said Morning Star. "If you don't wish to call him Hania then call him Spirit Warrior, it is the same name." "We will see which one sticks," Morning Star said. Both Small Moon and Blue Lizard smiled and agreed he would be called Hania or Spirit Warrior.

Days went on, and Morning Star became stronger and was walking around. She was still sore, but she could do the things she needed to do to care for the baby. She could also do some of the chores around the lodge. I had gone hunting with Zack and Grey Wolf, and we each brought back a deer. Being around the village so much, I got bored, so when Pa and Othello decided to trade in their furs, I decided to go with them knowing there might be trouble. That Baldheaded trapper, who was a friend of the man I killed, was making some bold statements, and some of the other trappers believed him.

Beaver pelt prices were low, and many of the trappers were grumbling. But other furs were doing alright, and Pa and Othello could buy the things they wanted. Pa gave most of the profits from the beaver and furs to Othello; we had plenty of supplies back at the cabins. I looked around and didn't see much, but I did get some ribbon and glass beads for Morning Star. Many of the trappers were eyeing me and talked under their breath, and I knew it was about me.

Pa was watching some of the marksmanship of the trappers, so I joined them. The other trappers coaxed Pa and Othello to compete with them, and they were both holding their own. It was down to four, Pa and Othello were two of them when the bald trapper pushed me aside, I believe, on purpose. An argument broke out between the bald trapper and Othello, and the other two trappers Pa stayed out of it. I thought the baldheaded man wanted a turn. Things looked like they were going to get out of hand, so I stepped forward and said, "I'll compete."

Pa said, "No, you should stay out of it."

One of the bald man's friends, who was also drunk, said, "Let the whelp shoot York, or are you afraid that killing our friend was luck."

I became so angry at what he just said I turned around and looked at him with a look that would scare any Blackfoot. Then I swung my rifle butt and connected to his forehead knocking him to the ground. "If you ever call me a whelp again, you will join your friend in hell," I said.

"Nate, this is no place for James," Othello said concerned.

"I couldn't stop him even if I wanted to." "When he is this mad, he won't listen to anyone," Pa said.

When I joined everyone, who was shooting, the bald trapper looked at his friend nursing his head. He turned to me and said loud enough so everybody could hear, "Will wonders never cease, you got lucky again if he hadn't been so drunk, he would have whipped your hide."

He didn't get the response from the other trappers he was hoping to get. Many were starting to think that maybe it wasn't luck that killed the one trapper and knocked the other to the ground.

"I will tell you what, Pilgrim, when he sobers up, send him to me, and I will send him to meet your friend," I said. Calling him a pilgrim was like him calling me a whelp, and it angered him a lot, which is just what I wanted.

Pa shot first and hit his target. Then it was my turn, but before I shot, I looked around and spotted some Shoshone warriors watching Tall As The Sky was one of them. "Watch these fools, my brothers; I do not trust them," I said in Shoshone, and they all nodded. Some of the trappers understood Shoshone, as did Othello and Pa, but I didn't care. I shot and hit the target dead center. In the next two rounds, two lost, Othello and one of the other trappers, that left just the four of us.

For the next round, they moved the target back. When Pa came up, he looked at me, then aimed and missed. Many couldn't believe it, nor could I; I had a feeling he missed on purpose. Everyone else hit the target, and they moved the target back some more.

This next shot was going to be a hard one. I would have to raise my sights a little higher than the bull's eye. A trapper who I didn't know shot first and missed. I raised my rifle and took my time, to the dismay of the bald one, I fired and hit dead center. There was a lot of chatter from the other trappers about how good a shot it was. Next, was the bald one he called up one of his friends so that he could rest the rifle on his shoulder and there was an uproar of protest over this.

"I'll allow it," I said, and everybody went quiet.

He fired, and the one who checked the target said, "It's a near miss."

The bald one protested and sent his friend down to look at the target. "It's barely in, but it is in," his friend said.

Again, there was an argument with the original one checking the target. Again, I said, "I will accept that it is in."

They moved the target back again, and the bald trapper said, "That's too far back; no one could hit that target."

Many were agreeing with him, and I said, "What do you want to do?"

Someone from the crowd said, "A moving target."

The whole crowd agreed, yelling, "A moving target."

"Alright, then a moving target it will be," I said much to the delight of the crowd. "But I wish to shoot at the far target first," I said. What I said surprised the crowd and even Pa and Othello. Again, I took my time, loaded my rifle with extra power, then waited for the breeze to stop, took aim far above the target, and fired.

The trapper checking the target yelled, "It's a clean hit."

By this time, the bald trapper knew there was a good chance he wouldn't win. A pinecone was strung up about twenty-five yards away and swung, "You got to hit it on its way back, or your shot isn't any good," some trapper said.

I knew I would have to lead my rifle ahead of the target like I used to do with my bow. When I was ready, I nodded, and the guy holding the pinecone let it go. Just when I was about to fire, the bald trapper bumped me, but I fired anyway. I hit the target, not well, but it was a hit.

When the bald trapper got up to shoot, I could already see he was going to miss and when he took his shot, and he did miss.

The crowd broke out into a loud cheer, and I received many accolades from many trappers, including the warriors from the village and Pa and Othello. But I heard the bald man say to one of his friends, "If it is the last thing I do, I will get that bastard." I believe Pa heard him too because, on the way back to the village, I told Pa that maybe I should head back to the cabin as soon as Morning Star and the baby could travel, and he agreed.

I had informed Spotted Buffalo and Small Moon that I would be leaving with Morning Star as soon as she and the baby were ready. Small Moon wasn't happy about it even though Spotted Buffalo felt this was the way it was supposed to be. I think he was going to feel the loss.

"Why don't you move the village nearer to where we are living?" I asked.

"It is very close to the Utes." "I must think about this," Spotted Buffalo said.

"You can stay at my lodge when you wish," I said.

"We will consider this, also," said Spotted Buffalo.

Three days later, I had packed everything, and we said our goodbyes, and we headed out toward home. Unbeknown to me, the trappers that had been giving me some trouble also saw us leave.

I didn't want any harm coming to Morning Star or the baby, so we traveled slowly. We had passed over many wooded hills and just finished crossing a wide, dry, brushy valley. We were now going up onto a wooded mountain ridge. The skies were clear, and there was a breeze out from the north. I had a habit of checking my back trail from time to time, it was something taught to me by my Shoshone father, and many times it paid off this time was no exception. We were halfway up the mountainside when I looked back at where we had just come. I noticed a dust cloud from the other side of the valley we had just come through. I watched it for a few minutes, and I saw it was riders following our trail.

"Someone is following us," I said to Morning Star. "We need to get over the top of this mountain before they get to the base," I added.

We traveled a little faster, made it over the top just as the sun had set, and they made it to the bottom of the mountain. We traveled a mile or two further when I found a rocky place where I could defend my family.

"Nate, those low life trappers that caused the entire problem with your son have left," said Othello concerned.

"Which way did they go?" Nate asked.

"The same direction your son went, and there are four or five of them. That's what Jedediah said."

Spotted Buffalo, Running Deer, Othello, Grey Wolf, Sometimes Comes, Tall As The Sky, Zack, and Pa got their weapons. Then they all grabbed their horses and went after the trappers at full gallop.

"I take it someone told you about what was said and done Grandpa," said Dan.

"Yes, mostly Gray Wolf, and I guess some."

I placed Morning Star and the baby high up into the rocks. She had a knife, and I gave her one of my pistols. I then gathered some brush and sticks, and I made it look like we were sleeping with a couple of blankets. I gathered some wood and started a huge fire, larger than what would be wise. I took my bow and weapons to the left of the fire. And up into a defensible place in the rocks. And I waited.

Sure enough, about a half-hour later, they came through the woods, making more noise than a herd of buffalo. Like, true pilgrims, the five of them walked up to the campfire, yelling the most vulgar comments I have ever heard. By this time, I knew the light of the campfire blinded them. Since there was no movement from our beds, the bald trapper got suspicious went over to where I had made up the beds and yanked the blankets off, and that's when I struck. I hit one of the trappers with an arrow through the neck. No one could see where it came from because they were all blinded by the fire. A second later, an arrow hit another trapper square in the chest. The last three panicked and ran for cover. One was unlucky and ran right toward me, and I pulled out my hawk and threw it. It sunk deep into his skull. I had to believe that the last two knew where I was now, so I had to be careful. I knew the bald one could shoot, but they would still be partially blind.

Just then, I heard the baby cry, as did the trappers. The last friend of the bald trapper stuck his head up for the last time. He fell back to the ground with a bullet in his head. Just then, the bald man got up and started to run up the rocks to where Morning Star and the baby were. I dropped my rifle and pursued him, but he had a jump on me. I pulled out my pistol and fired, knowing I most likely wouldn't hit him. But perhaps it would slow him down enough for me to get him. He made it to where Morning Star and the baby were before I could get to him, and there was a loud pistol boom that missed the bald trapper but startled him enough for me to leap at him with my knife. I was about to sink my knife into him when I heard a thump and felt the trapper going limp. I looked down at him; the tip of an arrow was sticking out from the center of his chest. Then I saw Spotted Buffalo with a smile on his face, and I waved to him.

I helped Morning Star and the baby down the rocky hillside to the campfire where I saw everyone else. "Looks like you had a little trouble here, but you handled it alright," said Othello.

"With the help of Spotted Buffalo," I said.

After gathering everything up and loading the five dead trappers on their horses, we all rested for the night. In the morning Pa and the rest went back to the rendezvous with the dead trappers and Morning Star, the baby, and I resumed our trek back to the cabin.

# 24

# MY END OF THE BLACKFOOT WARS

We reached the cabin in about seven days. Morning Star was more than happy with the cabin I had made. I had more than enough food at least until Ma and Pa came back. At night, I worked on some more things to sit on, like a couch that I saw at Grandpa's house. During the day, I started hauling rock for the barn and lumber mill, and of course, I found plenty of gold. Morning Star couldn't understand why I was saving it. I also did some chores around Pa's and my cabin so that things wouldn't pile up. The rest of the family showed up in about a week, and I helped unpack the horses. Ma went down to the cabin to see the baby, and Zack took care of the horses once we unloaded them. I had suggested that everyone eat at my cabin, and there was no argument from anyone, especially Ma, who was tired from the trip.

Pa sat on the couch I made he said it felt comfortable to him, and he liked it. Zack went up to the loft with his toys while Ma helped with the food. "Did Othello leave for the coast?" I asked Pa

"Yes, I don't think he will be happy there not at his age, he is a bit too old to start over," Pa replied.

Morning Star put the baby in Pa's lap and relieved Ma, who was cooking. I watched her cook and decided to make one of those stoves as they had back east. I had the metal to do it, and I didn't think it would be very hard.

"I believe we should think carefully about bringing some cattle up here. The military and settlers will be here someday, and we could get a good price for them," I said.

"With buffalo and game around, do you think that there will be that big of a demand for them," Pa said.

"With the Army coming west with the settlers, I don't think there will be enough game for everyone." "And I don't think the buffalo will last the way white people are, besides white people like beef more than buffalo and game," I said.

The baby was getting fussy, and Ma grabbed Joseph and took care of him.

"I must give this beef idea of yours some thought," Pa said.

"There is another reason why it would be a good idea to raise beef." "It will be a good cover for all the gold we find," I added.

"Did you find much when you were hauling rock for your foundations?" Pa asked.

"So much I must start smelting it soon," I said.

We came to the table to eat, I had made a basket for the baby to lie in, and he was contented.

"Zack, are you going to stay here, or are you going to sleep in my cabin?" Pa asked.

"No, this is James's and Morning Star's lodge now; it is not right for Zack to sleep here," Ma said.

"It does not bother me; Zack is no trouble; he can stay here if he wishes," I said.

"If Morning Star doesn't mind, I would like to stay here after all I did help build part of it," Zack said.

Everyone looked over to Morning Star, and she said, "I do not mind if he stays, he will be of great help."

"We have the spare room Pa, why don't you and Ma move in here it is a lot larger than your cabin," I said.

Pa looked at Ma and said, "No, I think it would be better if we stay in our cabin." "If you stay here Zack, you will have chores in this place and my place, do you understand this?" Pa asked.

"You don't understand Pa; this is York land, which includes both cabins." "Chores are to be done by all the Yorks who live on this land no matter where it is," I said. Pa nodded, he understood, and I added, "I don't expect Zack will be here for long maybe a few years, and then he will be married." "He does have an eye on a young woman in the village."

Zack gave me a dirty look, wishing I hadn't said that.

Ma and Pa looked at Zack in surprise, and Ma asked, "Who?"

"Aw, just someone I like," Zack said embarrassed.

"White Doe," Morning Star said as a matter of fact.

I was surprised that Morning Star knew, and Zack turned a dark shade of red while Ma and Pa had big smiles on their faces. If they only knew the full truth between those two, they wouldn't have been smiling.

When we went hunting someone was, there always someone with Morning Star and the baby. When Pa, Zack, and I went hunting, Ma moved in with them until we got back.

By first snow, I had the foundation for the sawmill completed, and the foundation for the barn had not gotten completed yet. Still, with the help of Zack and even Pa, I would finish it. I kept on working on the barn, even though there was snow, but it went a lot slower. I got the foundation of the barn done and some of the wall up before I stopped for the winter. When the snow came, I had plenty of gold, so I spent my time smelting it. I showed Pa and Zack how to do it, but I was a little nervous about Zack doing it without supervision. By the end of winter, we had about twice the amount of gold as we had when we went to St. Louis. I had turned fourteen some time ago, and by this point, the baby was big and growing like a weed. We all spoke to the baby in both English and Shoshone. Pa was trying to teach the baby sign language, but Ma said he was too young yet, but Pa still didn't give up.

One day, Zack and I were carrying a log for the rafters of the barn, and I notice that he was showing a lot of muscle and was getting much hairier. "Has Pa ever taught you how to fight?" I asked him.

"No, but I think I can take care of myself," he replied.

I stared at him for a few seconds, then said, "I'm sure you can take care of yourself." "Maybe if I teach you a few tricks in our free time, it will be easier for you if you need to use them."

He smiled and nodded his head in approval. Zack started to learn how to defend himself, and at first, he wasn't very good, but as time went on, he learned fast.

It was July, and both the barn and mill were just about completed. They went up quicker than the cabin even though there was more to build because Zack and I were much bigger now, and of course, Pa helped us from time to time. Also, I wasn't as fancy as I had been with the cabin.

Zack and I were sitting on a log splitting cedar for the shingles when Zack asked, "Do you think, when it is time, you could help me build my cabin?"

"Of course, we will all help," I said. Zack smiled and nodded, and I asked, "When do you think this will be, when do you want your cabin?"

"Oh, I don't believe that it will be too much longer," he replied.

I looked at him, and I was going to say something but decided not to.

About an hour later, pa came up to us and said, "Morning Star has invited your mother and me to eat with you tonight."

"You don't need an invite Pa, you can both eat with us anytime you want," I said.

Pa nodded and said, "There are a lot of things that I think we need to talk about."

"Anything serious?" I asked.

"No, just things to see how you two feel," Pa replied.

"Ok, Pa," I said. At that, he turned and left, and we went back to work.

As we were waiting to eat, Pa was playing with Joseph like he often did. Morning Star and Ma were gabbing up a storm, then laughing and looking at me for some reason. To my surprise, Zack was not playing with his toys; he was doing something with his weapons. When I thought about it, he hadn't been playing with his toys for some time. I had a book in my hand, as always, reading and, on occasion, looking at what everyone else was doing.

We all gathered to eat little Hania was in his basket asleep. Pa spoke first, "We need to think about when we will go to the village."

"I'm not thrilled to go I would like to work on the barn and mill," I said, looking over to Morning Star. I could see she wasn't happy about not going. I added, "But I know Morning Star wishes to go, and there is nothing I wouldn't do for her, so we will go whenever you want," this made her very happy.

Pa was going to set a date when Zack said, "I will be leaving next week for the village. I know you all won't be ready by then, so I will stay with someone at the village possibly Tall As The Sky or Grey Wolf until you come."

Everyone was surprised that he was so assertive and bold. I think I knew what was behind all of this, White Doe. Pa was going to object, but

I kicked him under the table and shook my head no then said, "I think I know the reason why he wishes to go so soon, and it is personal." "If you have not noticed, he is much bigger and stronger now." "He can defend himself if he needs to."

I think everyone caught on except Pa. Ma saw it and said, "Let him go, my husband, he is a man now and can make his own decisions."

I don't think Pa or anyone else could have stopped him from going, but Pa said, "Zack, it will be some time before we can get there, that isn't going to bother you, is it?"

"No, Pa, I'll be alright," he said.

Pa changed the subject, "Jim Bridger's fort and his trading post should be finished, and we will need some supplies. I think before we go to the village, James and I will go to Jim Bridger's fort and get some supplies with the wagon."

"Is there anything you want, Morning Star?" I asked her.

"You know our needs; you get what you think we need," she replied.

I smiled, and everyone knew I would get her something special. "What about you, Zack?" Pa asked.

"Lead and powder," Zack replied.

"You don't want toys?" Pa said, thinking he was funny.

"No, I've lost interest in the toys; I'm getting too old to play with them." "I'll most likely give them to Joseph to play with, at least some of them." "I might have a boy myself someday." "You could bring something sweet back, though," he said. Ma laughed at that but didn't say anything.

"We should talk about what you are doing around here, James," Pa said.

"You can talk about that later, Morning Star, and I have something to say now," Ma said with authority. Ma got all our attention, and Morning Star was smiling, and Ma said, "Morning Star has something to tell, James."

I gave her my full attention, and she said, "Hania will have someone to play with soon."

I stared at her for what felt like hours then said, "Who?"

"I thought you were the smart one she is going to have another baby," Zack said.

I looked at Zack, annoyed, and said to Morning Star, "Is it going to be a girl or boy?"

"I don't know why you would think I would know," she said.

"Well, everyone knew before," I replied.

"It is too soon to know for sure," Ma said.

I got lost in my thoughts while everyone was smiling then said, "When will the baby come?"

Ma looked at Morning Star, and their expressions changed. Ma said, "Maybe as early as March maybe earlier."

I was in a bit of shock, but at the same time, I was happy. I smiled at Morning Star, and that reassured her.

"I would like to know why you are building the barn that big." "It's bothered me for some time," Pa said.

"I have a lot of horses that I plan to bring here someday." "Those four fancy horses that we got in New York almost didn't make it through the winter we had here; they need to be in a warmer area." "The mules might be alright in the cold, but they are too valuable to chance there may be a bear attacking them or mountain lion." "Also, if I have another child after the one that is coming, I might have to find a milk cow unless Ma can help in that job," I said with a smile.

"No, not me, I am no longer able to do that," she said jokingly. "What else do you plan to do?" asked Pa.

"Build corrals, a small one around the barn, and a larger one that will stretch between your barn and mine and will connect the two." "I have an idea to make a pond in the larger corral by bringing water from the stream." "This place is going to get so big we must build a bunkhouse for hired hands, and as my family grows, I plan to add an addition to this cabin." "That's why I put that false door by the stairs to the loft." "Of course, Zack will need a cabin one of these days," I added much to Zack's approval.

"You know that's a lot of building." "It's going to take a lot of wood," Pa said. "You know that valley over on the other side of the ridge north of us?" I asked Pa.

"Yes," he replied.

"I plan to clear it of all its trees." "We need that area for grazing cattle, and that is where I will, at least at first, get the wood," I said.

"You are dead set on getting cattle aren't you," Pa said.

"I think we will be foolish if we don't but not right away, maybe in a few years." "There is a lot of work to do yet," I said.

"You seem to know what you want, and it appears to be going well with what you do, I will support your decisions," he said with sincerity.

I was touched that he didn't fight me on it and that he was willing to help. I looked over to Zack and said, "I've never asked you how you felt."

"I'm alright with anything you want to do," Zack said.

"The York family is expanding." "Which area do you want to claim as our own, Pa?" I asked.

"You're right." "Let me see..." Pa was thinking about where we should expand to next.

Zack said, "East, toward the grassland where the buffalo are."

We all looked at Zack, and Pa said, "Why?"

"There is good grazing, and besides, that's the direction where I wish to build my cabin someday."

Pa looked at me with some surprise and said, "Alright, that's where we will expand to."

I nodded approval with a smile and said, "Maybe we can register our claim at Jim Bridger's fort."

Pa nodded yes, and the conversation changed to my growing family for the rest of the night.

I concentrated on the barn roof, which I felt was the most important. When Zack left for the village, I had only a little left to do on it, and I completed that, and I had started on the mill by the time Pa and I left for Bridger's fort. The trip to the fort and back home should take about a week or a little more. There was much more work to do in the barn with the loft, stalls, doors, and things, but I decided to get the mill roof finished first.

Jim Bridger's fort came in sight in about two days. As we rode in, I noticed a blacksmith's shop, a trading post, a saloon, a crude barn, and a few other buildings I figured were for living in and storing things. There were quite a few people here from the Crow, Utes, and Shoshone. There were other mountain men that Pa knew, and when he talked to one of them, we found out there were a couple of wagon trains expected to come this way.

As we walked into the trading post, one Shoshone whipped his head around and said in Shoshone, "Soaring Eagle!" It was Running Deer, my brother-in-law. We greeted each other with a customary hug. "How is that sister of mine and my nephew, Hania?"

"The baby is growing like a weed, and so is your sister."

"What do you mean?"

"Tracking Fox didn't tell you?"

"I saw Tracking Fox at the village, but he has not said anything to me, or our family about my sister his mind is on White Doe too much I think those two will marry soon."

I looked at Pa to see if he heard, but he didn't. "Morning Star is expecting another child."

Running Deer sent up a loud whoop of joy.

"Do you know if Tracking Fox has been lying with White Doe?" I asked.

"I believe he has; he has been in a few fights also."

"What about?" Pa barked.

Pa's anger startled Running Deer, but Running Deer said, "There are others who wish White Doe's hand but not to worry Tracking Fox beat them all."

I smiled, but Pa growled, "If that boy does not look out, he is going to get that girl pregnant."

"You need not worry about that, Bear Slayer he has already asked her father for her hand."

Pa was about to blow his top when I said, "No use getting upset, Pa." "Whatever is going on, we will straighten out when we get to the village."

"He doesn't have a brain in his head," Pa said in anger.

I got serious and said, "Zack is smarter than you think, and he is old enough to make his own decisions no matter what you say to him." "When you see him, in the end, he will do what he wants, and there is nothing you can do about it."

Pa turned bright red and was going to say something more to me, but he thought he had better not, knowing how it would end up.

"We better get what we need," Pa said in a better tone.

I turned to Running Deer and said, "We will come to the village soon."

"I hope your father is not so angry when he comes."

"He will calm down he thinks Tracking Fox and I are still babies."

Running Deer smiled and went back to what he was doing.

Pa heard what I told Running Deer and said, "Until I die, you and your brother will always be my babies."

"I know, Pa."

He was calming down, and I was glad. As Pa was ordering some things, I found a few things I thought Morning Star would like and some things for the baby. I handed them to Pa and told him I needed to get something made at the blacksmith's shop and went outside.

"I need hinges for four very large barn doors and latches for the four doors. And I have a hay door up in the loft; I need hinges and latches for it. I need wire and bolts, also," I said to the blacksmith.

"I will make the latches and hinges for you, but you have to get the wire and bolts from the trading post," the blacksmith said.

"How long will it take," I asked.

"It should be ready by tomorrow morning."

I nodded and paid the blacksmith upfront, which surprised him. I was heading back to the trading post when Little Man came rushing into the compound and up to the trading post. Everyone went out of the trading post; Jim Bridger was yelling for everyone to come to him.

I grabbed Running Deer's arm and said, "Many Blackfeet are attacking white men in their moving lodges."

"You tell the Crow and see how many will fight, and I will tell the Utes." I started yelling out in the Ute language about the Blackfeet, and all the Utes were ready to fight.

"What do you think you're doing?" asked Pa.

"I go to fight the Blackfeet."

"It's not our fight; besides, we have not rested our horses."

"I will borrow a horse Pa; you know what will happen to the men, women, and children." "Also, if some whites don't go, those pilgrims will think the Utes, Crow, and Shoshone are just some more Blackfeet." "Now, I'm going; you can stay if you want."

"I'm not going to let you go by yourself; I'll go too," Pa said.

After we were all ready to go, Jim Bridger said, "Nate, I'd go with you and send more men, but I have to guard this place just in case they attack me also."

"I understand Jim," Pa said. With that we headed out, there were about fourteen of us in all.

We pushed the horses hard, and by late afternoon we could hear gunfire and war cries of the Blackfoot. We slowed and came to a rise, out of sight of what was going on. There were at least twenty-five Blackfeet and about twenty wagons in a circle.

They didn't look like they were in very good shape. Some wagons were on fire, and we could see some pilgrims lying on the ground. I said first in Shoshone then in Ute, "There isn't time to sneak up on them; we must attack them now."

My brother-in-law translated into Crow, and the other trapper knew Shoshone or Crow. I also told everyone to be careful of the whites; they may think we are Blackfeet. We cut brush and tied it behind our horses. The dust might just scare a few of the Blackfeet into thinking there are more of us.

We went charging down from the ridge, making our war cries. The whites thought they didn't have a chance, and some of the Blackfeet got confused and started to move in all directions. Before the chief Blackfoot warrior could gather everybody together, we were on them. Before the Blackfeet could get one shot off, several fell to the ground dead or wounded. It took the white settlers a few minutes to know what was going on. They finally figured it out, especially when they saw those who were white. I killed two more Blackfeet with my pistols. I didn't know where pa was, but I did see Little Man fall to the ground wounded as well as a trapper. I pulled out my knife, leaped off my horse, and knocked a Blackfoot to the ground. I had my knife buried into him clear up to the hilt before he could fight back. When I saw who it was, I had much delight; it was one of those who killed my uncle and his family. When I turned to find my horse, I saw a Blackfoot warrior about to attack Running Deer from behind. I threw my hawk, and he fell just as Running Deer was turning around. I noticed that the rest of the Blackfeet were retreating, but the Utes, Crow, and Shoshone cut them off. I went over to get my hawk and noticed another Blackfoot who had killed my uncle's family. He lay dead that left one more.

I had just gathered my weapons and noticed that the rest of our war party were off their horses and had circled the last two Blackfoot warriors. They were about to pounce on them when I yelled out for them to stop. As I walked over to them, Pa joined me. I looked at him and said with a smile, "Glad to see you are alive, but you must be getting old, I see you got wounded."

"It's a scratch; it isn't even bleeding anymore." The circle parted, and when I saw the Blackfeet, I stopped dead cold and stared for a few seconds. I said in both Ute and Shoshone, "These two are mine; all of you will understand in a moment why I do not want you to harm them; it is for me to kill them."

"What's going on, son?" Pa asked.

"You will know in a second, Pa." I then handed Pa my rifle and Running Deer, my pistols and hawk, and walked forward.

I started signing so everyone would understand me and speak in Blackfoot, "Do you know who I am Blackfoot dogs?"

"I have heard of a yellow-hair creature that has killed many of my people." "He is called Soaring Eagle With Many Coups."

"You are right; it is I who kills your people and will kill you." "Do you know why I have killed so many of your people?" I asked him.

"Because you are Shoshone," he said.

"I was not always a Shoshone think back to a white family on the grasslands next to a stream a man, a woman, and a small boy." "You tortured them to death and then burned them alive." "The yellow-haired one soiled himself at the sight of what you did, and then you tried to track him down and kill him."

He then realized who I was.

"Yes, it was I who escaped, and now you are the last and shall face the same punishment." I noticed the young boy standing next to him, stepping back as he wet himself. One of the Ute warriors grabbed him and disarmed him, and I said quickly in Ute, "Do not harm him; I have plans for him."

The older Blackfoot warrior was laughing and said, "It was a pleasure to kill your family in the way we did." "The whore was a great amusement for us, as was that boy we turned into a woman." "We would have done the same to you if we had gotten a chance." "Perhaps we would have let you live so you could have given pleasure to the whole Blackfoot village."

That was the last thing he said. He came at me with his knife, swung it, and missed, but I didn't. I sliced him across the chest, drawing blood. He was slow and made a lot of mistakes, and within a matter of minutes, I had sliced him three more times on the face, on the leg, and the arm. He was losing a lot of blood, and I kept on cutting him, much to the delight of those watching, except for Pa, who kept telling me to finish him off. He was getting weaker and stumbling due to the loss of blood. Finally, he swung at me and missed again, and I got behind him and started to scalp him alive when I heard a boom.

Pa had shot him with my rifle, and as he was reloading his rifle, he said in Shoshone, "The Blackfeet are animals; there is no need for us to be animals also."

I looked at the dead Blackfoot in my arms and then dropped him to the ground. I walked over to the Blackfoot boy, grabbed him by the arm, and started to cut away his buckskins.

"What are you going to do to the boy, James?" Pa asked, concerned.

"Don't worry, Pa. I'm not going to kill him." "I am just going to scare him and maybe humiliate him a little." "I should let everyone pleasure himself on him," I said discussed with the Blackfeet.

"If they do that you won't have to kill him, he will commit suicide," Pa said.

I didn't care until I cut away his loincloth and looked at him as did everyone else. By the looks of him, he was younger than Zack, much younger. I looked at him and said in both signing and Blackfoot, "How old are you, and who was the fool who sent you on a war party?"

"It has been almost twelve summers since my birth. The one you just fought, my uncle, brought me along, but Blackfoot boys are much braver than the boys from other tribes."

"I saw and smelled your bravery running down your leg earlier." At that, everyone laughed. I asked Running Deer to get one of the Blackfoot horses. I said in Shoshone, and I signed, "I'm letting the boy go back to his people." One of the Utes started to protest, and I signed and said in Ute, "Do the Ute people kill babies?"

The Ute friend grabbed him and said, "He is right to let the boy go; we are better than the Blackfeet."

"Do you have any relatives back at your village?"

"My mother and father, you do not remember me." "It was my mother and me that you let go when you destroyed my village."

"Then you are lucky to be alive twice, the next time you won't be so lucky." "At that, I swatted him so hard on the bottom, you could hear it clear back to Jim Bridger's fort, and it left the mark of my handprint on his bottom. Everyone laughed, and he started crying. I threw him up on his horse, grabbed the reins, and walked over to his dead uncle. I grabbed his two eagle feathers, handed them to the boy, and said, "You go back to your village and tell them you counted coup." "You must explain why you are not wearing anything and how you got the mark on your bottom." "Also, you tell your people that I am not at war with them anymore, but if they make war with me or kill one of those I love, there will not be a Blackfoot man, woman, or child left alive." "Do you understand?"

He nodded yes, sniffling, and I gave him the reins and smacked his horse on the rear end. As he rode off, you could see he was uncomfortable sitting on the horse, and everyone laughed and commented on it. I didn't sign the last thing I told the boy, and as Pa and I were walking to the wagons, I said, "I told the boy I am not at war with the Blackfeet anymore."

We had four wounded two Utes, a trapper, and one Shoshone, Little Man; we also had one dead Crow.

"Hold your fire; we are friendly!" Pa yelled at the wagon company.

"Those out there are Crow and Shoshone; they are friendly."

"There are also Utes who don't like whites but who hate Blackfeet worse." "They won't harm your either," Pa added.

The people put out the fires, but there were a lot of dead and wounded lying around. Pa knelt by a wounded woman, and I spotted a boy who was sobbing next to a man. I went to him and knelt next to him, put my arm around him and said, "Is this your father?"

"No, he is my uncle, he sobbed. "I'm all alone now," he added.

"You don't have anyone back where you come from?"

"My mother and father died of the fever I have no one."

"Not even an Aunt."

He shook his head no.

"What about these people here?" "Will, any of them, take care of you?"

"No, they all hated my uncle, called him a lowlife drunk, and I guess they are right." "They called me bad names; we only stayed with them for protection."

"Did they call you a bastard?"

Surprised, I guessed it right; he nodded his head yes.

"I used to be called that also."

"What's going to happen to me now?"

I looked at his uncle; he was dead, with half his skull blown away. I turned to him and said, "How would you feel if I adopt you?"

"You want to be my father?"

"Yes, I have one son already and one coming." "You would make a fine son also." "Your life would change a lot, and your name would change also." "But, I do wish to adopt you."

"Alright, you can adopt me."

"What is your name?"

"Christopher."

"Mine is James York, at least one of my names."

I took him by his hand and stood up and said, "We need to bury your uncle." "Which wagon is yours?"

He pointed to one where the canvas on top burnt away. Other than that, it looked to be in fair shape. We went to it, and I climbed in looking for a shovel.

"Hey there, what are you doing in there." "Those things belong to us?" an older man from one of the other wagons said.

"Why do you say that the wagon belongs to the boy's uncle?"

"Yes, but the rule is if the owner dies, it gets split up between everyone else."

"The boy is still alive."

"He doesn't count; he is just a boy."

"I say he does, but we will settle it when we get to Fort Bridger, Jim Bridger is the closest thing to authority out here."

"Now, you listen here, boy...."

He didn't get a chance to finish his sentence before I pulled my pistol out, pointed it at him, and said, "If you don't get out of here now, you will never get to the fort." That shut him up, and he walked away, talking to himself.

I smiled at Christopher as I came off the wagon with a shovel. "Would you have killed him?" asked Christopher.

"That would depend on what he would have done; the important thing is he didn't know if I would or not."

I dragged the body just beyond the wagons and started digging. Pa joined me, and I said, "This is Christopher York, your new grandson."

Pa looked at the boy, then me, and grabbed my arm, trying to get me to move away from the boy so he couldn't hear what he wanted to say.

"You can talk in front of Christopher," I said.

"Alright, have you thought this through?" "Don't you know I have enough problems with Zack," Pa said tensely.

"The only problem you have with Zack is in your mind." "Let me ask you a question; do you love Morning Star, Hania, and the baby to come?"

"You know I do," Pa said.

"And do you believe I have done well for a person of my age?" I said.

"You have done very well, better than I could hope for."

"Zack is less than a year younger than I." "He has helped build my house and fought to keep someone he loves all to himself." "I think he has done well for himself also." "Speaking of Christopher, his uncle here was the last of his family, no one in this wagon company wants him." "They hated his uncle and called him names, like a bastard." "The boy is about the same age I was and came from a similar background as I when Red Elk adopted me."

Pa put his head down and was silent for a few seconds. Then he looked at Christopher, "Welcome to the family, son." "I'm your Grandfather."

Christopher's smile was from ear to ear, and Pa said to me, "It is you who are going to have to deal with your mother and wife when you tell them."

"I don't worry about Morning Star, but Ma is a different story," I said with a smile.

Pa helped me dig the grave, and we put the body inside. We put rocks and limbs on top of the grave so that the animals wouldn't disturb it. Pa said a few words over the grave for Christopher's sake. Pa was always good at that. I explained to Pa about these people wanting the wagon and the things in it, and he agreed that it should be Jim Bridger who makes the decision.

Pa and I got the horses and tied them to the wagon. Some challenged Pa and me, but Pa set them straight real fast. "I can see why you don't want to be raised by any of those folks," Pa said to Christopher.

The sun was setting so Pa, and I got some food from the wagon and fixed something to eat. A couple of trappers joined us to eat. Most of the Indians went back to the fort.

"Pa, Christopher needs a bath really bad and his clothing, also." "There's a stream not far from here." "I would like to take him there after we eat if you think you will be alright with this wagon," I said.

"I can see he is filthy; these two men will stay with me." "He has been wounded anyway and can't ride a horse, yet I'll be alright."

"He doesn't look dirty to me," said one of the trappers as he spits out some tobacco.

"How would you know?" "You haven't bathed in at least a year," said the other trapper as he also spits some tobacco juice out. I'm glad Pa never got into chewing tobacco.

"I'll meet you sometime tomorrow before noon." "I have some things to pick up at the blacksmith's shop, and I need some wire and bolts," I said.

I found some soap and a blanket, also a little food so we would have something to eat in the morning. I put everything in a large sack with a few other things. I lifted Christopher on a horse, handed him the bag. I jumped up behind him, and off we went. Fortunately, it was a clear full-moon night, and it was light enough to travel if we took it slowly.

It was warm out, and I talked to Christopher as we rode, "I don't think I ever asked you how old you were."

"I will be nine next week," he said.

"I must get you something special for your birthday."

"Why, no one else has in the past?"

"You have to understand the way we think and do things out here is a lot different than what you are used to before." "For several years, I got raised by the Shoshone, who adopted me."

"Who are the Shoshone?"

"They are an Indian tribe as well as my family, and the Shoshone are great people." "One of the Shoshone who was fighting those bad Indians is my brother-in-law." "From the first day I lived with the Shoshone, they loved me." "At least the family that adopted me loved me as I love you now." "I am your father now and forever, and I like to do things for those I love," I said with sincerity.

Christopher was quiet for a while, and I thought I heard a sniffle coming from him. After about an hour, I asked him, "Christopher, do you know how to ride a horse?"

"I rode a little."

"Can you get on top of a horse without a saddle?"

"Not if it is a big horse like this one, I'm too little still."

"No, you're not too small I was smaller than you when I first got up on a horse, and I had never ridden a horse before."

"Okay, maybe if you show me how."

"I have a horse for you when we get to the Shoshone village; that it is just right for you." There was a long stretch of silence, and I finally said, "Is there something wrong, Christopher?"

"Do you think they will try to kill me?" he said fearfully.

"Who, the Shoshone?" Just then, I remembered how I acted when I first woke at the village. "You don't understand; I told you before the Shoshone are good people, most of them love my family and me." "Some are even our relatives, your mother is Shoshone, as is your Grandmother." "Your uncle and brother are half Shoshone, and your Grandfather and I got adopted by the Shoshone, and since I adopted you, you are now a Shoshone." "That is the way it is, those people will love you, as they do me." "However, since you are my son, some boys about your age might try to test you at times, just like if you were going to a new school, do you understand?"

"Yes, but I can't speak Shoshone how will I talk to my mother or grandmother," he said nervously.

"You will learn the language, and both your mother and grandmother speak English better than me."

He seemed more at ease after explaining about the Shoshone, and we rode for another two hours when we came to the stream. I stared at it for a little while and then crossed it. "Is this where we are going to camp?" asked Christopher.

"No, further north." We traveled another forty-five minutes when we came upon the burned-out wagon of my uncle. "That used to be your great uncle's wagon." "He and your aunt and their son I buried over there we will camp up the river, a short way." I thought I'd look at the burnt wagon when it was light." We went to the same place where I was hiding many years ago, it had a deep pool of water, suitable for bathing, and it was down low enough so a campfire wouldn't be detected.

"Watch what I do," I said. I tied the two front hooves of the horse together with a strip of leather, leaving some slack. "This is what you call hobbling the horse." "It will prevent my horse from roaming too far and still let my horse forage for food and water." I held Christopher's hand and carried the sack also other things I brought, and we went nearer to the stream.

"Watch me again," I said. I gathered some wood and twigs. Then I got some dry leaves and pulverized them into a powder. I took a little black power and my flint and started a fire. "I will show you how to do it without flint or black powder another time." After the fire was going well, we went down to the stream. I removed his shoes and found some herbs such as mint, sage, and wild onions and packed inside his shoes. "This will make your shoes smell better." I then started to undress him, but he stiffened up, and I asked, "What's the matter?"

"I have never taken my clothes off in front of anyone except maybe my Ma, and that was a long time ago."

"I understand, but it's the only way to bath just trust me it will be alright, and you will get used to it."

I removed his thin coat and took his pants off. He had a nightshirt that went to his knees. Everything was dirty and reeked of urine. It was stained and worn out. It was not worth cleaning, but he had to wear something at least at the fort. I notice that he had a severe rash. "Have you wet your pants before?"

"My uncle wouldn't let me relieve myself when we were traveling, and I had to go so bad. I wet myself a few times."

"Why didn't you just go off the side or back of the wagon?"

"I did once, but I got a good beating for it."

"I assure you anytime you have to go when you are with me, you just tell me, and I will let you go." I took a closer look in his pants and turned him around to look at his bottom, which also had a rash. Then I said, "You had to go from both ends?" he nodded yes. "Why didn't you wash yourself and your clothes when you had a chance?"

"My uncle wouldn't let me." "He said that the rain was the best bath you could get."

I guessed those people back at the wagon company got his uncle right; he was a lowlife to treat his nephew this way. I undressed, and Christopher's eyes got as big as hen's eggs. As I stood there naked, I said, "Let me guess you never saw a man naked before."

He nodded yes, I grabbed the soap and picked him up, and as I walked into the stream with him in my arms, I said, "The water will be cold, but you will get used to it as you will with everything else."

When I got him to the deep part of the stream, I told him to hold his breath, and I dunked him underwater. Then I got to a place where he could stand with his head sticking out of the water and washed him from his hair to his toes. I did this twice, being as gentle as I could where the rash was. I knew the bathing and fresh air would help heal the rash. I next bathed myself and then told him to stay in the water while I got his clothes to wash. He walked halfway out, but it was cold for him, so I said, "If you are cold, get under the water, it will feel warmer," he did as I said. Cleaning his clothing was a bigger job than I expected. They took several soakings, and scrubbing with soap, and rinsing before I was satisfied.

I placed his wet clothes on a rock, then went back in, picked him up, and carried him back to the fire. I put more wood on the fire and told him, "Stay next to the fire and keep warm while I hang up your things to dry." I brought a big branch next to the fire, wrung out his clothing, and stretched them out on the branch. As I was doing this, I noticed that Christopher was yawning, so I stretched out the blanket on a soft part of the ground. I had him lie down on it, and I lay next to him. I kissed him, pulled the blanket over both of us, and we both fell asleep. Sometime before sunup, I woke up with Christopher snuggled next to me. I looked over to the fire, which was low, and decided to get a few more hours of sleep, not wanting to wake Christopher.

When I woke up next, the sun must have been up for nearly an hour. Christopher was still sleeping next to me, so I removed the blanket gently without waking him. With the light of the day, I got a better look at his rash. It was worse than I thought Ma would have to tend to it. I covered him back up, got dressed, and restarted the fire from the hot coals. With the fire crackling, Christopher started to stir. I felt his clothing, and it was still slightly damp. Christopher stuck his head up, and I said, "Did you sleep well."

"Yes."

"Your clothes are still damp, so I won't dress you until just before we leave beside the air will do your rash some good." "Do you have to relieve yourself?"

"Yes."

"I think I have to also." I went over to him, removed the blanket, and looked at the bottom of his feet, and they were as soft as a newborn baby's foot. I picked him up, and he hugged me around the neck as I carried him to where the grass would be soft on his feet. We both relieved ourselves; I grabbed him by the hand and said, "Let's go over to where I buried my kin. I found the graves, and I could see where some animals had tried to get to the bodies, but I don't think they were successful. We then walked toward the wagon, and I picked up Christopher again so that he wouldn't step on anything. Everything was as I had left it. Except for dirt that had blown over things and some grass that had grown. I went to where the back of the wagon was, and I put Christopher down and said, "Don't you move from this spot." He obeyed me, and I looked over the wagon. I found a few hinges that I took.

Then I walked into what was left my uncle's wagon. It was up at an angle because the front wheels didn't burn away like the back. I didn't see anything inside the wagon, but for some reason, I went in anyway. I just about got to the top. When I turned around and started down, my right foot went through the floor about eight inches, but my foot didn't hit the ground. I pulled my foot out and put the handle of my hawk in. Sure enough, I heard wood; there was a false bottom to this wagon. Maybe my uncle wasn't as stupid as I thought. I took my hawk and started chopping large sections of wood away. When I had enough wood cut away to look inside, I saw three small metal boxes and one wooden one. There was also a long, round leather case with a cap on it; these things I found hardly scorched. At the other end, toward the bottom, there was appearing to be fancy women's clothes. I assume they were Aunt Margaret's and some smaller clothes, which I guess was Milford's. I thought about having Christopher wear Milford's clothes, but as I looked a little closer, they burnt beyond use. There were some beads and things on Aunt Margaret's things that were still good, so I took those. I put the hinges and beads in my possibles bag and walked over to Christopher and asked, "Do you think you can carry two of these boxes?"

"Yes."

I tucked the leather case in the waistband of my loincloth, and I gave Christopher two boxes to carry. Then, with my right arm, I lifted Christopher while carrying the other two boxes and took him to our campsite, and put him on the blanket. I piled the boxes and the leather case to the side and grabbed the sack with the food. I warmed it by the fire, and then we ate.

"Aren't you going to see what's in those things?" Christopher asked with curiosity.

"No, there isn't time now." "We will look at those things when we are with your Grandpa." "Then, we will all be surprised at what we see."

"Since I am your son now, what should I call you?"

"What are you comfortable with, sweetheart?"

"I guess Pa; would that be alright?"

"That would be fine I call Grandpa that anyway."

"What's my brother's name?"

"I guess I didn't tell you yet." "Your brother has two names, like your Grandpa, uncle, and I have." "Your brother's name is Joseph, and his Shoshone name is Hania, which means Spirit Warrior." "Your Grandpa's names are Nathanial and Bear Slayer." "Your uncle's name is Zack or Zackary, and his Shoshone name is Tracking Fox." "And I am James and Soaring Eagle With Many Coups."

As I talked to Christopher, I notice he was three shades lighter after his bath, and his hair, instead of being dark brown, was a light brown like his eyes. "We need to get you cleaned up and dressed; we have to go." "I grabbed his clothing everything was dry except his coat, so I threw that in the sack with the metal and wooden boxes and the leather case." "I kicked the fire, which was coals now, into the stream. Then I gently dressed Christopher, and after cleaning out his shoes, I put them on him and placed the blanket in the sack. I then lifted Christopher on the horse; I tied the sack to the horse and hopped up.

We traveled directly toward the fort, and I kept my eyes open for any Blackfeet. When we came in sight of the fort, the wagons were already there. When the people of the wagon company saw us, they followed Christopher and me into the fort. The Crow and Utes had left, but the Shoshone were still there. There were also a couple of Nez Perce. I took the sack and placed it inside our loaded wagon. "Pa aren't you afraid one of these people might take a snoop inside the sack?" Christopher asked me.

I looked at Christopher, smiled, pulled out my pistol, and handed it to him. I said, "If someone messes with our wagon, shoot him."

Christopher looked up at me with big eyes. At that time, Pa and Jim Bridger came out of the bar with some other trappers. I went to greet them when there was a boom from the pistol that Christopher had. I turned around real fast; rifle raised as did Pa and everyone else. Christopher, near in tears, said, "That man climbed up on the wagon, so I shot at him."

The man, hopping mad, said, "That bastard put a hole in my hat." "Who is going to pay for it?"

I took the butt end of the rifle and smacked him a good one in the forehead, and he went flying on the ground. "I'll kill the next person who messes with my wagon," I growled.

"You folks step back away from the front of this trading post," said Jim Bridger.

"But that sack is rightfully ours," said the man who I knocked to the ground.

"You want to die over a sack?" asked Bridger. "Ed, get some help and bring six chairs out here, also a table." "You people pick the ones that will represent you." "I'm not going to have you all talking at the same time," he added. Jim Bridger was no dummy; he knew how to talk to people. He knew how to win them over to his thinking, even if he had to stretch the truth a bit, and today was going to be one of his finest performances.

Upon the porch of the trading post, he put the table and a chair behind it and to the side, two other chairs. The other three chairs he had lined up on the dirt facing him. "This is a hearing to determine who owns the late Douglas Fairbank's property." As he spoke, he wrote everything down in his book. "Who are the three that represent the wagon company?"

"Bill White, Donald Twist, and Albert Friestine," the three said.

"Since Christopher is too young to represent himself, I will appoint someone." "How about you, Nate?"

"I would do it, but James would be a better person since he is adopting the boy."

Bridger looked over to me, and I nodded yes. "James York will be the boy's advocate."

"I'm James Bridger, leader of this fort." "If anyone of you wants to challenge my authority, I have a letter here from the territorial judge." "He appointed me a district judge for these parts; you're welcome to look at it." "I will tell you how this will work, I will ask questions, you three from the wagon company can ask questions, and Christopher and his advocate can ask questions." "You may all bring witnesses and evidence also." "However, first, you will all be sworn in, including any witnesses that may come forward." "Are there any questions?"

"Yeah, why do we need to be sworn in?" asked Donald Twist.

"It is the law; there is a penalty for lying, both on Earth and from the almighty above." "You got a reason to object?"

"No."

"I need a Holy Book does anyone have one?"

"I do," said a woman from the wagon company.

After Jim Bridger got the Bible, he had us all put our hands on the Bible at one time, including Christopher. He had us raise our hands, and then he said, "Do you all promise to abide by the outcome of the hearing and to swear to tell the truth so help you, God."

Everyone said, "We do."

"Since there was an issue with the sack, we will deal with that first," Jim Bridger said.

"I wish to address that sack, Mr. Bridger," I said.

"Go ahead," he replied.

"I took Christopher to a stream a few hours from here to bathe him." "I used the sack to carry soap, some food, and some rope." "This place where I took him was the same location my uncle and his family died at the hands of the same Blackfeet, the same ones that attacked the wagon company." "While rummaging through the burnt-out wagon, I found some valuables that went unnoticed when those Indians stole my uncle's things." "Those things, the soap, rope, and Christopher's coat that was still damp from being washed are the only things left in that bag." "My things and his coat are the only things that I am disputing." "The rest can be placed on the wagon and be decided together."

"How do we know you are telling us the truth?" said Albert Friestine.

"I have witnesses, my father and the two trappers that were with us," I said.

"Oh, they would take your side, they are your friends," Friestine said.

"There is another witness." "That woman over there saw what he put in the sack," Pa said.

"He is telling the truth, Albert, I saw what he put in the sack," the woman said.

"Alright, those things don't matter, let's get to the wagon and its contents," said Albert.

"Since that matter got cleared up, we will follow what James said." "Now to the wagon, you people say you have a rule about what happens if someone dies." "Is it in writing, or is it a verbal rule?"

"Verbal rule."

"And how does this verbal rule go, exactly."

"If any owner dies, his property is divided equally among the other wagons," Albert said.

"Do you all agree that is correct?"

Everyone nodded yes, and I asked Christopher, "Is what they are saying true?"

"Yes, Pa."

"We agree that is their rule," I said.

"Then the wagon and everything in it is ours," said Mr. Twist.

"No, they are not," I said. "Mr. Bridger, may I present Christopher's side for the claim of the wagon?"

"Go ahead."

"Christopher, when and where did your uncle get that wagon?"

"He got it after my Pa died back in Ohio."

"And what about the supplies in the wagon?"

"He got them in Ohio just before we left, except for some food, and things we got in Missouri just before we joined the wagon company."

"These food items that you got, how long after your uncle got those items did you meet up with the wagon company?"

"I'm not sure; I think three or four days."

"Mr. Twist, so far, do you dispute anything he has said?" I asked.

"No."

"Mr. White, we haven't heard from you yet." "I would like to ask you a few questions." "Mr. White, you seem like an honest man." "Do you have a wagon, you own wagon?"

"Yes."

"And did you leave home by yourself?"

"No, I have my wife and boy with me."

"Would your wife and boy come forward." "You have a beautiful family, Mr. White." "The clothing they are wearing was it your money that bought the clothing or the materials to make the clothing?"

"Why, yes."

"From what state do you hail?"

"The great state of Tennessee."

"Yes, I know Tennessee; it is near Missouri, where I was born."

"Yes, part of the state is right across the river."

"How old is your boy?"

"He just turned eleven."

"Fine age for a boy." "I won't ask your wife how old she is out of respect."

"I wouldn't tell you, young man, if you did," said Mrs. White, and everyone laughed.

"I imagine Mrs. White most women here would have the same response," I stated with a smile. "Now, Mr. White, do you love your family?"

"Of course, what a foolish thing to ask."

"Yes, Mr. White, because I think every man here loves his family." "Would I be right, Mr. White, that you would like to give your family all they desire and would protect them from harm with your life if necessary like you did fighting the Blackfeet?"

"Yes, Yes, of course," Mr. White said, getting a little tired of the questions.

"Just a few more questions, Mr. White." "Two days' travel west from here, your wagon company gets attacked again by the Blackfeet or another tribe, and you get killed what do you expect your wife and child to do."

"I would hope they would go on without me."

"How Mr. White, your wagon, team, and everything inside the wagon belong to the people of the wagon company, including the very clothing your wife and child have on."

Mr. White put his head down and didn't say a word, but Mr. Friestine stood up and said, "That wouldn't be true, Mrs. White would take over the property."

"Most states say women can't own anything." "This law is particularly the case in Tennessee, isn't it, Mr. White?" He nodded his head, yes, but Mr. Twist jumped up and said, "Then the boy will own it." At that point, he realized what he had said and sat down embarrassed.

"An eleven-year-old boy would own the White property a boy only two years older than Christopher." "Mr. Bridger, the wagon, and supplies got bought before they joined the wagon company." "Their rule says nothing about who can inherit the property." "However, I can understand why you have this rule." "It got made, so if a whole family loses their lives, the rest of the company can divide out the property fairly." "So, there wouldn't be any arguments if you disagree with me, let him speak?"

By this time, everyone was quiet, and no one disagreed, so Jim Bridger got up and said, "I say that Christopher owns the property."

Everyone started to leave when I yelled out, "Wait a minute!" "I have something to say that will be of interest to you all." Pa, Christopher, and I put our heads together, and I said, "Pa, we have no use for some of the stuff in that wagon."

"Yes, that team isn't worth taking care of either." "It's amazing, those horses made it this far," Pa said. "It's up to you, Christopher do you want to keep everything or give those people the things we have no use for?" I said.

"You do what you think is best, Pa," Christopher replied.

"Alright, do you want to tell them, or do you want me to tell them?" I asked Christopher.

"You tell them, Pa, you, talk better than I do."

"Gather a little nearer so you can all hear." "I will be speaking for Christopher." "I'm adopting Christopher as my son if some of you don't know this already." "First, I want to tell you the boy had a mother and father who were married, so it was just plain wrong of you to have called him a bastard." "His uncle, I won't argue with you about him; he was a lowlife." "He mistreated the boy, but it didn't give you the right to treat Christopher the way you did; it wasn't his fault." "There are things that his uncle had that Christopher has no use for them." "Things such as the team of horses and the wagon." "I'm sure there are other things in and on that wagon that Christopher doesn't want." "So, my Pa, Christopher, and I will go through what is there and give it to you people if you want it." "If you don't, maybe you can trade it to Mr. Bridger." That seemed to satisfy everyone. With the help of Jim Bridger, we went through everything and put what we wanted on our wagon.

"James, I'm going to need you to sign some papers on the boy and the property."

"Alright, Pa." "Did you get the things I ordered from the blacksmith?"

"Yes, but you must get your bolts." "There are different sizes." I took care of what I had to do with Mr. Bridger and bought some sweets for Christopher. We went looking through the wagon and took many things, like dishes, silverware, a few pictures, and other things. The rest went to those people who acted like vultures.

It was late in the afternoon, but I said to Pa, "Let's leave now, I don't want to be around these people." So, we left and headed for home with Christopher, either sitting on top of the cargo or between us. We traveled for some distance. I knew Christopher was hungry, so I gave him a pouch of pemmican, and he ate it as if his life depended on it. "Slow down, we will cook something when we make camp," I said.

We traveled for about an hour-and-a-half more, and we made a dry camp, and Pa made a stew with what we had. "When we finish eating, I wish to show you something," I said.

"I'm sure glad to be away from those people; they were pure animals," Pa said.

"Grandpa, can I have some more?"

"Why you can have as much as you wish." We finished eating in about a half-hour.

We cleaned up, and Pa said, "What is it you wish to show me?" Pa asked me.

I removed Christopher's clothing and showed Pa how bad his rash was. "That looks bad."

"You should have seen what it looked like when I washed him last night," I said.

"He should wear nothing; the air and the sun will do him good until we can have your mother look at it, and besides, he can use some sun on his body; he is as white as a ghost."

"I wasn't going to let him wear anything until gets buckskins made for him," I said.

Pa nodded his head in agreement. I told Christopher, "It is our habit to get up before the sun is up." "You need to get to bed." "Do you have to relieve yourself before you go to sleep?"

"Yes."

"Which way?"

He indicated he had to urinate, and I said, "If you don't go the other way soon, you are going to get some castor oil to help you go." After he relieved himself, I put him to bed, and he slept between Pa and me.

The next morning, about an hour before sunrise, we set out. I wrapped Christopher in a blanket and let him sleep on top of the cargo as we rode on. "When are you going to look at what you found in your uncle's wagon?" asked Pa.

"After we get settled back home." "I figure it's been there this long, a little longer won't hurt."

We traveled for two more days, and late in the afternoon, we spotted the cabin. "You might as well go to your cabin, that's where Morning Star and your mother will be," Pa said.

We rode up to the cabin. Ma and Morning Star came out with smiles on their faces and the baby in Morning Star's arms. "Who is the mouse in the blanket?" asked Ma.

I smiled and said, "This is Christopher, your grandson, and he needs doctoring." I got off the wagon, lifted Christopher down, and said, "I will explain the whole story."

Ma looked at the rash that Christopher had and said, "You can explain later." "Take him to your bed while I will get some things at your father's lodge."

I took Christopher by his hand, kissed Morning Star, and said, "I hope you are not mad."

"Why should I be mad, he will make a fine son and brother for Hania and the new baby?"

# 25

# THE LAST GOOD-BYE OR IS IT

Ma and Morning Star were tending to Christopher for some time. While Pa played with the baby like he always did, I waited until I got bored and decided to unload the wagon. I took care of the horses as soon as we got back, and the wagon was next to my barn. I carried most of the small things in and was starting on the larger things. I had a sack of beans on my shoulder when Ma came into the main room. I put the sack down, and I asked almost at the same time, Pa asked, "How's Christopher?"

"He will be alright in a few days, but he has a terrible rash. You did right James by bathing him and removing his clothing." "He is with Morning Star drinking her milk."

I smiled and said, "How did he take to it?"

"From what Morning Star told me, much the same way as you did, but he is enjoying himself now." "He will make an excellent son to you."

"He needs to learn Shoshone," I said.

"He will learn from all of us." I peeked in on him. He had curled up on Morning Star's lap nursing, and Morning Star was rocking and singing softly to him. Pa gave the baby to Ma and helped me bring in the rest of the things from the wagon.

Pa and I just sat down when Morning Star came out of the bedroom with Christopher following her.

"It looks like you need some sleep, sweetheart," I said to Christopher.

He nodded his head yes as he was yawning. I put my arm around him and said, "You will sleep up in the loft." He gave me a hug and a kiss as he did to everyone else. Then he climbed up the stairs to the loft. Within a few minutes, I heard him softly snoring.

"He will need to bathe every day in the cabin, and he should stay in the cabin as much as possible," Ma said.

"He has relieved himself from the front but has not from his bottom in many days," I said.

"I will give him something tomorrow, so he will go," Morning Star said.

"Are you going to look at what was in your uncle's wagon, the curiosity is killing me," Pa said.

I smiled and grabbed the bag with the items. I pulled out Christopher's clothing and shoes first and said to Morning Star, "Do you want these?" She looked at them and shook her head no. I cut off the buttons on his pants and threw the rest in the fire. "What about his shoes?"

"He has soft feet like a baby, we better save them until he has some moccasins," Morning Star said.

I pulled out his coat and showed it to Morning Star, who looked at Ma. Ma took the coat and said, "This is much too thin to keep him warm." "When the first snows come, he will have a coat made."

Ma handed me back the coat, and I cut the buttons off. I threw it in the fire, also. I put the three metal boxes, the fancy wooden box, and the long leather case on the table and threw the bag to the side. As Pa examined the things I had put on the table, I grabbed two ceramic cups, opened my possibles bag, and took out the hinges and threw them on the table. I took out all the beads and buttons that I had cut off my aunt's and cousin's clothing and put them in the cups. "I took these off my aunt's and cousins' fancy clothing." "I didn't bring back the clothing that was in the wagon because it was burned and soiled so bad, it wasn't worth saving."

Morning Star looked at Ma and said, "We will share these."

Pa had the wooden box in his hand, examining it when I said, "Go ahead, open it, Pa."

He smiled, unlatched the box, and said, "Oh my goodness!" "Will you look at this?" We all looked, and it was a pair of the fanciest pistols I ever saw, with gold and silver inlay on them.

Then from behind us, I heard a small voice say, "What is it, Pa?"

I turned around and said, "You should be asleep, son."

"Aw, Pa, I want to see."

"Come on down."

I grabbed the leather case next and took off the cap. I pulled out two portraits. "This one is of my Aunt Margaret, Uncle Henry, and my Cousin Milford when he was younger than I knew him." "I think this other was a picture of my grandmother and grandfather with Uncle Henry and my mother when they were about my age." The paintings were done very well and with excellent detail. There were even pictures on the walls in the background in the room that was in the painting.

Pa looked at that picture for a long time and then said, "That is your mother, alright." On the back was written "Von Muller family, 1790," and the other was "Henry Muller family, 1822."

Pa noticed the artist's name, John Trumbull, and pointed it out. "He was a very well-known artist," Pa added. "What are you going to do with the paintings, son?" Pa asked.

"Make frames for them, I suppose, and hang them, if Morning Star doesn't mind." "Christopher has some paintings also."

"What's in the metal boxes, Pa?"

"They seem to be locked," I said.

"Try the keys to the boxes we bought," Pa said.

I got the key and tried it on one of the boxes, and sure enough, it unlocked them. Inside the first box were a lot of gold coins. "How much do you think there is here, Pa," I said.

"Well, let's see." Pa dumped all the coins on the table and started to count them, and when he finished, he said, "The face value might be about five thousand dollars' worth.

"It makes me wonder why he gave up the farm back east," I said.

"I believe you told me he wasn't very bright," Pa said.

I opened the second box, and it was full of jewelry, I assume, for my Aunt Margaret. "How much do you think this is worth, Pa?"

"I don't know, but I would assume a lot more than the gold coins."

Ma and Morning Star started to put on the jewelry and admiring it as white women would. I began to open the third box as Ma and Morning Star put back the jewelry inside the box. The last box had a lot of documents, birth certificates, baptism papers, letters, a journal by Grandma, and Grandpa. Under all this was an oval painting, just big enough to fit in the box. It was a painting of my mother with her hair all made up. I looked at it for a while, and a tear seeped from my eye.

Pa also stared at it, then picked up some of the letters that had not gotten opened yet. He said, "Some of these are from your mother to either your uncle or your grandparents." "The letters got written in a language I don't know," Pa said.

"Let me see; it's German," I said. "This one letter is from a George Wythe to your grandmother," Pa said. "Now, where have I heard that name before?"

"There was a Wythe that had something to do with the Declaration of Independence." "I think he signed it," I said.

"Yes, it was George Wythe who signed the Declaration of Independence," Pa said.

Christopher leaned against me, yawning, and I said, "Alright, you have seen enough, go back up to bed." I kissed him, and he said goodnight to everyone, and up he went.

"We need to get back to our lodge and go to bed, also," Ma said. "I'll come by tomorrow and get the things that are for me, James," Pa said.

They left, and I looked at Morning Star gave her a big hug and kiss, and she said, "It is time we should go to bed, too." And that is what we did after we checked the baby and Christopher, and the lights were out.

The next day, as I was doing the chores, Pa came out and asked, "What are you going to do today."

"Since we are leaving soon, I thought I would cut down some trees in that valley I was telling you about and make some posts for the corrals."

"I will give you a hand here with your chores and help you with the posts if you help me carry my supplies down from your cabin," said Pa.

"I would have done that no matter what, Pa, but I would welcome your help," I said with a smile. We finished the chores and headed for the cabin to get the supplies. Inside, Morning Star said, "You must wait here with the baby while I help Christopher relieve himself."

Pa sat down with the baby and started playing with him. I looked at Christopher playing on the floor with Zack's toys and then at Morning Star with a confused look. She said, "He will go shortly."

I sat down beside pa and the baby and waited. Sure enough, Christopher jumped up, putting his hand on his bottom and said, "Mama, I have to go bad." Morning Star and Christopher rushed out of the cabin, while Pa and I smiled at each other. We went out to watch them. Morning Star dug a hole and had Christopher go and man, did he go! He went so much I thought his insides would come out, and as he was going, he whimpered a little from the pain of the rash. After he finished, Morning Star took him down to the stream and bathed him well. Then she brought him back to the cabin and applied more medicine to the rash. When she finished, she took over the duty of the baby. I noticed that the rash on Christopher's stomach had gone way down, and he was content now, playing with the toys.

Pa and I took his things down to his cabin and then hooked up the wagon and headed to the next valley to get wood for the posts. As we were going, I asked Pa, "Did you tell Ma about Zack yet?"

"Yes, he said with a sigh."

"What did she say?"

"Just about the same as you said, now let's change the subject."

We cut down trees for the next two days, and I had enough wood to make posts for both corrals but still needed more wood for the rails. I decided to drill three holes in each post and peg the cross rails in with a fourth that would be the cap. The going was slow, but it looked good, and I did have Pa to help. After a few days, Christopher was able to come outside, and I gave him a few simple chores to keep him busy. At night, I separated Christopher's uncle's things. I decided I needed to build a cabinet for all the china and silverware and things. I also started to read the letters that were in my uncle's box.

It turned out that George Wythe was the first cousin of my Grandmother, from his father's side of the family. So, my Grandmother's last name before she married was Wythe. Mama's letters were sad. They were all addressed to Grandma and Grandpa, and in them, she pleaded for forgiveness for leaving and asking to come back. Mama also asked for help because of me, and she asked why no one would answer her.

The Journal was different; Grandpa wrote it. As I read it from the back to the front, it spoke of how much they missed Mama and wanted her back. I wondered if that was the way they felt, why they didn't help. Then it hit me, Grandma and Grandpa never saw the letters. Uncle Henry, maybe with the aid of Aunt Margaret, hid those letters. He knew that if Mama had come back, he would not have control of the farm, and he wanted it all.

Christopher was all healed up and started hanging around Pa as much as he could. He wanted to help with anything we did. As pa and I brought the last of the wood in for the rails, he said, "I think it would be a good idea if you built the smaller corral first."

"I am thinking your right Pa, but it must wait until we get back from the village."

We headed for the village, Morning Star carrying the baby and Christopher riding with me or his Grandpa. I had considered giving him a horse to ride, but I decided to wait until we got to the village, so I could see how well he could ride. Before we spotted the village, Christopher asked me, "Pa, are you sure boys and girls my age don't wear anything?"

"Most won't." "A few of the boys might have a loincloth on."

"Do you think they might stare at me?"

"They most likely will not stare because you're not wearing anything but because they don't know you, and you're white," that seemed to satisfy him.

On the third day, we entered the village. Of course, many came to greet us, as always, and we stopped in front of my in-laws. I let Christopher down, and then I got down to help Morning Star and the baby. A young Shoshone boy, about a year younger than Christopher, was naked standing next to Christopher and looking at him by the name of Little Fox. He said, "What is your name."

"He asked you...."

That is all I got out when Christopher said, "My name is Christopher." "What is yours?"

"You understood what he said?" I asked Christopher.

"Grandma and Ma taught me a little."

"His name is Christopher." "He does not have a Shoshone name yet, and he doesn't speak our language very well yet, Little Fox," explained Morning Star.

"I will help him learn our ways," said Little Fox.

"He is our son, and he is not as strong as you, so you be careful with him," I said.

"His name is Little Fox, and he wishes to be your friend," Morning Star said.

Little Fox grabbed Christopher's arm and tried to get him to go with him.

"Pa, he wants me to go with him."

"It's alright; you can go with him; you will find us later."

Small Moon said, "Who is the little mouse?"

I smiled and said, "He is my son who I adopted, and I think he just got a Shoshone name."

"What is it?" Pa asked.

"After Ma and Morning Star's mother called him little mouse, I think Little Mouse will be his name."

Pa and everyone else laughed, and Pa said, "That's a great name for him."

I started looking around for Zack and Grey Wolf and said to no one in particular, "Where are my two rowdy brothers?"

Everyone went quiet and, from the back of the crowd, was heard, "I would imagine they are with White Doe and Falling Rock."

"Those two spend all their time with them unless they are fighting over them." "Your brother, Tracking Fox, has the marks on him to prove it."

Morning Star and the baby went with her parents to their lodge, and I helped Pa and Ma settle in their lodge. "Are you going to eat with us tonight?" asked Pa.

"No, I think it best that Christopher gets used to his other grandparents, and besides, I do not want to be around when things get heated here between you and Zack."

"Who says we will get in an argument?" asked Pa.

"Pa, I hope you do not, it would just bring heartache, but I know you, and I also know you do not like Zack growing up so quick." We talked some more, mostly about the property, and then I left.

As I walked over to Spotted Buffalo's lodge, I saw Christopher running across the village with a bunch of other boys. He looked like he was enjoying himself. I entered the lodge, and Morning Star was nursing Hania. I kissed her and stroked the baby's cheek. Spotted Buffalo talked to me about the Blackfoot battle I had, and I told him the whole story. "Your brother, Running Deer, tells a better story," Spotted Buffalo said.

"I guess I do not know how to lie, as well as he does." Everyone laughed, and we talked about the lodge, what I was doing, and Broken Antler's wife being with child.

The conversation finally turned to Christopher. "Does he wish to be like you when you were with your father, Red Elk?" Spotted Buffalo asked.

"I think he wishes to be more like Bear Slayer," I said.

"That is not true, he loves you very much, and it is you he wants to be like." "I know this because he has told me," Morning Star said.

"I know one thing for sure he loves his mother more," Small Moon said. "All boys love their mothers," Small Moon added as a matter of fact.

Morning Star said, "Little Mouse does not know what lodge we are in, and it is late; he needs to come in now."

"I'll go find him," I said. As I was walking across the village, Grey Wolf went into his lodge, so I went over to him. "Grey Wolf, it is me, Soaring Eagle With Many Coups."

"You do not need to ask to come in."

"I stuck my head inside and said I cannot go in there now; I am looking for my son."

"Your son would be with his mother."

"He has two sons now," Blue Lizard said.

Grey Wolf came outside and said, "Is it the one who is so white that he almost blinded me," he asked with a smile.

"That is him, but he will get darker in time," I said. "Come and help me find him, I wish to talk to you," I added. As we searched for Christopher, I asked Grey Wolf, "I have heard a lot about you and Falling Rock, do you marry soon?"

"In about seven suns." I stopped and looked at him. "You could have told me."

"You just got here." "What is your son's name?"

"Little Mouse, but he does not know it yet." "My mother and mother-in-law just came up with it."

"And what of Hania?"

"He is growing like a weed; he is with Morning Star." "Have you seen Tracking Fox?"

Grey Wolf started laughing and said, "Not today, but his eyes are like a raccoon's, was it you who taught him how to fight."

"Yes, did he win?"

"What do you think; he is with White Doe and has talked to her father."

"Has he announced his marriage?"

"No, I think he has waited for all of you."

"This ought to be interesting, once he tells Bear Slayer," I said. Just then, I spotted Christopher sitting next to Little Fox, throwing rocks into the stream. I pointed him out to Grey Wolf. "He does not speak Shoshone."

"Pa." Christopher jumped up and grabbed my hand.

"This is your Uncle, Grey Wolf." "You say in Shoshone Hello; Uncle Grey Wolf, my name is Little Mouse now you say it."

"Hello, Uncle Grey Wolf." "My name is Little Mouse," Christopher said.

Grey Wolf smiled and said, "I am pleased to meet my nephew, Little Mouse."

"What you said was, 'Hello, Uncle Grey Wolf.' "My name is Little Mouse." "Little Mouse is your Shoshone name." "Your uncle said I am pleased to meet my nephew, Little Mouse." Hasn't your father taught you the white man's language, yet?" I asked Grey Wolf.

"No, I have not asked, I see no point in it." "White people from the rising sun come, but they do not stay."

"They will come, I can promise you that."

"I must go back to my lodge now." He patted Christopher on the head and left.

I turned to Little Fox and said, "Little Fox, do you think you can teach Shoshone to Little Mouse and teach him our ways?"

"I will try tomorrow." "I will show Little Mouse how to shoot a bow."

"That will be good." "Little Mouse's mother wishes him now, so we have to go back to our lodge."

Little Fox turned to Christopher and said, "Goodbye."

"He told you goodbye."

"Goodbye."

I decided to stop by Pa's lodge before I headed back. When I got there, everything was quiet, so I went in first, and Christopher followed. Pa and Zack were eating, and I shrugged my shoulders. Christopher, all excited about his Shoshone name, said, "Grandma, Grandpa, I have a Shoshone name."

"Is that right, what is it?" asked Pa.

"Little Mouse."

"Do you remember how to say it in Shoshone?" I asked.

"Little Mouse."

"This is your Uncle Zack."

"Hello Uncle, how do you say Zack in Shoshone, Pa?"

"He speaks English, but his Shoshone name is Tracking Fox." Everybody smiled.

"Hello, Uncle Tracking Fox."

Zack got up and said, "I have heard all about you, and I heard you have been playing with my toys, I hope you enjoy them."

"Oh, I do."

"Go tell everyone good night," I said.

Christopher hugged and kissed everyone, including Zack, who received him warmly. Christopher went out first, and I started to go but turned to Zack and said with a smile on my face, "And I've heard a lot about your raccoon eyes and then I left.

I went into Spotted Buffalo's lodge first and sat next to Running Deer. "Where have you been, my husband?" "We thought you might have gotten lost."

"Little Mouse met his Uncle Grey Wolf, and then we said our goodnights to my family." As I was talking, Christopher sat down next to me, and everyone looked at him.

"It is the custom of the Shoshone that you do not sit with the men until you make coup." "A coup is a brave act until then you sit with your mother and Grandmother," I said, signing at the same time. "This is your Grandma, Small Moon; your Grandpa, Spotted Buffalo; and your Uncle, Running Deer." "Your uncle, Broken Antler is married and does not live in this village."

"Hello, Grandmother, Small Moon; Grandfather Spotted Buffalo and Uncle Running Deer, my name is Little Mouse." Everyone praised him and said he spoke Shoshone very well. Morning Star gave me something to eat and then fed Christopher.

"Ma, Little Fox said he would show me how to shoot a bow."

"How did you know that?" I asked. "He told me Pa, or at least I think he did." "When everyone got finished eating Morning Star nursed Christopher, and he fell asleep in her lap.

The next morning, Morning Star said, "Little Mouse you stay here, your Grandmother Blue Flower is coming, and we will measure you for some clothes."

"But, Ma, I like not having clothes on."

"You will need clothes when it gets cold and for other reasons." "What we do won't take long, and then you can play with Little Fox." Spotted Buffalo, Running Deer, and I chuckled at how he was carrying on. "Running Deer, why is it you have not found someone to marry like your brother?" I asked.

"I have found someone, but I cannot afford it yet."

"I saw you kill many Blackfeet with me; you must have many horses."

"I only got one horse, the Utes, and Crow got most of them."

"Had I known, I would have done something about it." "I, myself, killed many, and I took no horses except the one I gave to the Blackfeet boy." "How many horses do you need?" I asked.

"He held up four fingers."

"She must not be as beautiful as your sister."

"You are wrong, you paid too much for her, and I know how to reach a deal better than you do." Spotted Buffalo laughed as did Small Moon. Morning Star gave Running Deer a mean look.

Smiling, I said, "I have many horses, pick four out and get your wife." Just then, Ma came into the lodge. I got up, kissed Christopher, and said, "Good luck with the women son," and I went outside. I headed to Grey Wolf's lodge. I met him coming toward me and said, "I need a horse for Little Mouse, something small enough for him to get on, and I need it gentle something easy for him to ride."

Just then, we spotted Comes Running and called him over. "My brother's son needs a small gentle horse to ride; will you work with the horse?" Grey Wolf asked. Comes Running agreed and left to be with his friends.

I told him about Running Deer, and he was alright with it. He said, "I have come to ask you if you want to go hunting tomorrow?"

"Yes, I'll go, but first, I'll go see if my fathers need meat."

"I must go see someone after I get the horse for my nephew," said Grey Wolf.

I smiled and said, "That someone would not be Falling Stone, would it?"

He smiled and walked away.

I spotted Pa talking too Tall As The Sky and started walking over to him when Zack cut me off. "I need to speak with you," said Zack. "You said everything you have belongs to the family." "Does that mean the horses also?" he asked.

I knew right away what he was thinking and said, "Yes, but I still control what happens to the horses; what is on your mind?"

"I need some horses so that I can have White Doe as my woman."

"Does Pa know your plans with White Doe?" I asked.

"Yes."

"And how does he feel?"

"He is not very happy, but he did not fight with me."

"How many horses do you need?"

"I need six."

I acted like I was thinking then said, "I'll tell you what." "I will give you those six horses, but you hold off marrying her until next year."

He didn't like the idea, but after a few moments, he said, "Alright, I have to build a cabin anyway."

"Go pick them out, and if Grey Wolf says anything, tell him, I said it was alright." He left happy, and I went to talk to Pa.

"I would like to know if you need meat." "I'm going hunting tomorrow with Grey Wolf."

"Yes, but I would like to go if you do not mind."

"I would like to go also," Tall As The Sky said.

"Alright, we will leave at the normal time," I said.

"I saw you talking to Zack," Pa said to me.

"Yes."

"Did he ask you for something?"

"Yes, horses for White Doe's hand."

"Did you give them to him?" Pa asked in a raised voice.

"Yes." I could see Pa turning purple with anger, so before he said something, I said, "Before you get too angry and say something, you should not there is more to the story." "I let him have the horses only if he agreed to wait at least a year before he married."

"Did he agree to that?" Pa asked with hope.

"Yes, but he wasn't happy about it."

Pa thought about it for a few seconds then said to no one in particular, "That will make him a little older than fifteen." The color came back to Pa, and he said, "You did right."

"Glad you think so."

Five days passed, and while I was watching Christopher, as well as Small Fox, shooting a bow, Gray Wolf came up holding a young, small chestnut Mustang. "Little Mouse, I have something for you," Grey Wolf said.

Christopher turned around to see the horse and said, "Is the horse mine, Uncle?"

"Yes, get on her." Christopher went to the right side of the horse. He could put his arms and hands high enough that he could get up with a little effort. "You did well," Grey Wolf said, smiling. Then he added, laughing, "Better than your father did."

I didn't know if Christopher understood what Grey Wolf had said. He was just starting to understand and talk Shoshone stringing short sentences together. At first, Grey Wolf held the reins and let him get used to the horse. Then he explained to him how to make the horse go forward and stop and to go right and left. I kept asking him if he understood his uncle, and he said yes. Finally, Grey Wolf handed him the reins and told him to go slow and give it a try.

Off he went, and he was doing well and having the time of his life. When he came back, Little Mouse asked Little Fox if he wanted to ride with him, and he said yes. With great joy, both went all over the village, riding the horse. Both boy road much to the amusement of everyone, including Pa and Spotted Buffalo. Grey Wolf finally got him to get off the horse by telling him the horse must rest. He was so excited he couldn't wait to tell everyone, especially his mother and two grandmothers.

"I do not remember you being this kind to me when I was learning," I said to Grey Wolf. "He is my nephew, and you are my brother," he said with a smile, and he handed me the horse then walked off.

It was time for Grey Wolf's wedding. I went to Grey Wolf's lodge and talked to him, "Are you going to our secret spot after you marry."

He thought for a second, then smiled and said, "I did not think of that, but I think I will."

The wedding was like mine but more sensual, and Grey Wolf was less clumsy than I was, all in all, it was very beautiful. After the wedding, they went in the direction of our secret spot.

Christopher was turning darker by the day. His buckskins were ready, but he chose not to wear them, and we didn't push him. Little Fox was turning out to be his best friend, and they would ride the horse as much as they could, both taking turns at the reins. He was getting better with the bow, but for him to be good would take time, and I had decided to give him a bow and a set of arrows when we got back. Bathing Christopher wasn't a problem either; he swam with Little Fox almost every day, and he seemed to be very happy and content.

Grey Wolf and Falling Stone were gone four days, and I decided to take Christopher hunting with me. I didn't need any meat, but I figured it would be good for Christopher to learn how to hunt. Little Fox got permission to go also and Comes Running asked to go too. Although he was already a good hunter, he hadn't gone with me in some time.

We had been gone for about four hours, stopping several times to look at tracks. I explain to the boys about old tracks and droppings. Also, I told them how to determine what direction the animal was going. Most of this was something Comes Running knew already, but there were some things he didn't know. We had all just gotten off our horses to water and rest them. It was getting warm out, so I took everything off except for my loincloth. Christopher and Little Fox didn't have anything on and Comes Running had come with just his loincloth. After we finish watering the horses and Christopher and Little Fox stopped playing in the water, we traveled another half hour to forty-five minutes. I told Comes Running, "There is a large valley on the other side of that rise we will go there and circle back toward the village." As we topped the rise, we stopped and looked. There was a large wagon company coming our way.

"Pa is that the wagon company that I was on?" asked Christopher.

"No, I do not think so, this one has forty-five wagons in it, and besides the one, you were in would have been long gone by now." We rode toward the wagons, and the lead wagon stopped making the other wagons stop, and everyone pulled out their weapons.

We pulled up, and I said, "We are friendly, hold your fire."

"Alright, but don't try anything, or all of you will get shot." When we were near enough, and they saw, it was three children and me; they put their weapons away. When we rode up to the first wagon, many from other wagons crowded around us, wanting to know why we were here. "What are you children doing out here all by yourselves?" said the man in the lead wagon.

I looked at Comes Running and the people around me. Then said, pointing, "This is Comes Running, that little one is Little Fox who is a friend of my eldest son, Christopher, also known as Little Mouse, and I am James York, also known as Soaring Eagle With Many Coups." "I am teaching my eldest son how to track and hunt and who are you, sir."

"I'm Robert Cummings." "You're not that Soaring Eagle With Many Coups we have heard about, the one who wiped out a Blackfoot village?" he asked a bit bewildered.

"I am he."

There was chatter among the people around me when Christopher said, "Pa, someone is calling you."

"James, James York, it is me, Robert McConnell."

I looked up to see a portly, redheaded man trying to run toward me.

As I got off my horse, so did everyone else, I handed the reins over to Comes Running and said, "Hold on to my horse, I think I know this man." I ran at a trot and into the arms of Mr. McConnell with a big smile on my face. "What are you doing here, Mr. McConnell, and where is Sarah?"

"They are all back at the wagon."

Mr. McConnell was about to say more when Mr. Cummings said, "I hate to break up this reunion, but we have to get moving." "We need to find water and a place to feed these animals."

"I turned around and said, "Where is this wagon company headed?" I asked him.

"We are ten days out of Fort Bridger heading for Oregon," he replied.

"There is a Shoshone village about four hours southwest from here with plenty of food and water, and the Shoshone would love to trade with you," I said.

"We do need food bad, the wagon company that came before us took almost everything, but our guides said we should head northwest."

"Northwest, who are your guides?"

"Two Indians, I believe they said they were Crow." "We met them on the second day after we left Fort Bridger."

"Crow, do you have any horses missing?"

"No, I don't think so."

"The Crow are good people, but they are also the best horse thieves in this part of the country." "If you go northwest, you will run into the Blackfeet, and I guarantee that if you run into them, no man, woman, or child will be left alive." "The passage to Oregon is slightly southwest of here." "I don't know who those guides are, but they are steering you wrong." "Where are they, anyway?" I asked.

"They headed north looking for game about a half-hour before we met you," Mr. Cummings replied.

"Bob, I have had an uneasy feeling about those two from the beginning." "Let's follow this young man," said another man from the wagon company.

"He does not lie, Mr. Cummings." "He was like a son to me," said Mr. McConnell.

What Mr. McConnell said, surprised me and made me feel good.

"Alright, we will follow you, son," said Mr. Cummings. I gave Mr. McConnell another hug, and everyone went back to his wagon.

When we got on our horses, I told Comes Running and Little Fox everything that happened. "Is the hunt over?" asked Comes Running.

"Yes."

"I told my father that I would bring back a deer, I will hunt alone."

"Are you angry with me, Comes Running?"

"No, I understand why you hunt no more."

"I believe those guides that these people have are Blackfeet." "Will you stay with me for a short time before you go hunt?" "I could use your skill with the bow."

"I will wait."

"When you do go hunt in that direction," I said, pointing to the southwest." "I saw some fresh tracks, and I am sure you will kill a deer." He agreed to hunt southwest of the wagons, and I went on, "We all stay on this side of these people." "Do you understand me, Little Mouse?"

"Yes, Pa."

"He seems to be old to be your son, isn't he Mr. York?" said Mrs. Cummings.

"I adopted him; he was an orphan from the wagon company before yours."

"Do you think this is a proper life for him?" "After all, he looks like that other Indian," she said.

"Are you saying this because he is naked, and his skin has tanned brown?" "Do you also notice that he is clean, well-fed, and healthy, as well as he is happy?" "I can assure you that a few months ago, he was just the opposite."

"I didn't intend to be judgmental or rude to you, Mr. York," she said with all sincerity.

"I didn't take it that way, Mrs. Cummings." "You must understand that things out here aren't like back east." "When you get to the Shoshone village, you will find many children just like those two." "And you will find a lot of things there that you will find strange." A boy of about twelve stuck his head out of the wagon and said, "Did you say there would be naked girls there too, Mr. York."

"I did."

"You won't have to worry yourself over that, Charlie." "You won't be going anywhere near those girls," Mrs. Cummings said.

I smiled, and Mr. Cummings said, "Like Mr. York said, Matilda, things are different out here, and if the boy wants to go to the village, if this is permitted, then he can go." "I don't want to hear any more about it."

I smiled again, I could see that Mrs. Cummings wasn't happy about it, but Charlie was. I said, "Of course you know Charlie, if you do decide to look at those girls, the boys of the village will expect you to be as naked as they are."

I winked at Mrs. Cummings, and Charlie said, a little disappointed, "Oh, I didn't know that." Then he pulled his head back into the wagon. Mr. Cummings started laughing, as did Mrs. Cummings.

I turned serious and said, "Mr. Cummings, do you have a weapon ready?"

He pulled up his rifle and said, "Do you expect trouble."

"Not from the Shoshone, but maybe from the Blackfeet." "Just don't do anything unless there is shooting, or I say so."

He nodded, and I said, "I'm going to check the others." He nodded again, and I talked to each of the wagons and told them the same as I did Mr. Cummings.

When I got to Mr. McConnell's wagon, I had a big smile on my face. Miss O'Brien, now Mrs. McConnell, was sitting next to Mr. McConnell. "Sarah, Jack, look who's here," Mrs. McConnell said.

Both Sarah and Jack stuck out their heads, and Sarah squealed with Joy, "James."

She was beautiful, and then there was Jack. I was shocked when I saw him. He looked younger than Zack, not at all what I remember.

"Hello, James," he said.

"Hello Jack, we will be able to talk more when we get to the village right now; I have things to do." "Mr. McConnell, do you have a weapon?"

He had Jack hand him an old rifle, and he said, "Just this old rifle which I don't know how to use very well."

"Keep it handy; you may need it."

"Is there trouble, James?" asked Mrs. McConnell.

"There might be some I just don't know yet how much." "I have to talk to the last few wagons; I will speak to you again in the village." They all nodded, and I informed the last few wagons.

I rejoined Mr. Cummings on the south side. Nearly an hour passed, and from far off, I saw two warriors coming at us at top speed. "You two stay back behind these wagons," I said to Christopher and Little Fox in Shoshone.

"Be ready, Comes Running, but don't shoot unless you have to." He nodded.

As they approached, one of the warriors said to Mr. Cummings, "You go the wrong way you should go this way."

"I do not think we will go that way," said Mr. Cummings.

It was then that I rode into their view and rode around those who were claiming to be Crow. They both looked at each other and were very nervous. They were not Crow; I could tell by their clothing, so I said in Blackfoot, "I know, and these people know you are not Crow, you are Blackfeet, and I know you know who I am." "I would have killed you and taken your scalps, but I am not at war with the Blackfeet, consider yourselves lucky." "Had your people, who are hiding not far from here, attacked and killed these people, I would have killed every man, woman, and child that were Blackfoot." "It is not that I care for the whites, but there is someone here that is part of my family, the ones whose hair looks like fire," I said to one who I knew he was afraid of me.

Then the one who initially talked to Mr. Cummings said, "We did not know that you protected these people and had family here." "We thought these whites were the same as the last ones we attacked."

"I will give you two your lives but tell your people to get off Shoshone land, or there will be trouble now go," I said.

The two left like their tails were on fire. I turned to the Cummings and said, "They were Blackfeet, and they were setting up an ambush to kill all of you as they did to the wagon company that came before you."

Comes Running came to my side and said, "Why did you not kill them?"

"If we would have killed them, the rest of their people, who are not far from here, would have come looking for them." "There would have been too many to fight." "Did you not see how much fear they had of me?" "They will go back to their people and tell them it would be bad medicine to attack us."

Comes Running accepted what I said, and we all moved on. About thirty minutes later, Comes Running went hunting for a deer, and three-and-a-half hours later, we came in view of the village. As we got closer, many from the village came out to greet the people of the wagon company, including Pa and Spotted Buffalo. "They go to the great waters of the setting sun and wish to trade for food and our protection from the Blackfeet," I said to Spotted Buffalo.

"I know this already Comes Running has told us everything they are welcome here."

"Did Comes Running kill a deer?"

"Yes, and he is very proud of himself," said Spotted Buffalo.

"As he should be," I replied.

"You two, your mothers are looking for you." "Little Mouse, you need to take care of your horse and go see her," Pa said to Christopher and Little Fox.

"I will show these people where they may stay and make arrangements for the trade," I said. Spotted Buffalo nodded in agreement, and then I said to Pa in English, "There is someone you know in the back of this wagon company."

"Who?"

"Go back and see," I said with a smile. I watched Pa go back to where the McConnells were and saw his surprised reaction.

"You can follow me to where you can camp." "The Shoshone welcome you here," I said to Mr. Cummings.

"What about trading for food?"

"They are willing to trade." "Tonight, the Shoshone will have a council meeting and inform all the people, and I will talk to you to set up the trade." "I would advise you to keep your livestock inside your camp." "These people won't steal them, but if the Crow come around, they may try."

He nodded that he understood, and his son Charlie popped out of the wagon and said, "Can we go into the village?"

"You can but do not go inside any of their lodges unless invited." "And take the attitude to do to the Shoshones as you would want them to do to you," I said. I took the wagon company to a place just beyond the village where they circled their wagons and set up their camp.

I went over to the McConnells to help them with their things. When I got there, Sarah was already out of the wagon. I went up to her and gave her a big hug and kiss. She smiled warmly and said, "James, don't you wear clothes anymore?"

"Sarah, don't you remember we used to bathe in the same room and sleep together with nothing on, at least I have a loincloth on."

"We were just little children then." "You are grown up now, even though you do look handsome," Sarah said.

I smiled and said, "If you think I am handsome now, come down to the stream after I leave here." "I will be bathing myself and won't be wearing anything."

She smiled, and I felt a hand on my back. I turned around. It was Mr. McConnell. I gave him a warm, loving hug at just about the same time Mrs. McConnell came out of the back of the wagon. I was in her arms, giving her a hug and a kiss. "I sure have missed you all, and it is wonderful to see you." When I released my grip on Mrs. McConnell, I looked behind her, was there Jack smiling.

I stared at him in shock, back on the trail, I didn't get a good look at him, but now I couldn't believe what I saw, and everyone noticed my reaction. Jack still had his baby looks; he looked younger than Zack, much like Comes Running. He had to be more than a foot shorter than I was, and he wasn't as skinny but had put on some weight. He had no facial hair yet, although he was older than I. His red hair was nearly down to his shoulders, where it used to be sheared short. He looked very soft, much like a girl. I went over to him, hugged him and gave him a kiss, which surprised him. I asked, "Are you happy big brother?"

"Big brother?" "You look older than me," he said.

"Oh, that's just because of the rough life I live out here."

"I'm surprised you will even talk to me after what I used to do to you."

"That was a long time ago, Jack." "Now that the McConnells have adopted you, I consider you my brother, and I love you."

Tears welled up in Jack's eyes, and they started to stream down his face. I hugged him again, and he wiped his tears away.

"Did I hear you right, James?" "Are you going to bathe?" asked Mrs. McConnell.

"Yes." "After being on the trail all day, I'm filthy."

"Jack needs to bathe also; will you take him with you?" asked Mrs. McConnell.

"Yes," I said.

"We can all use a bath," she added.

"I will show you where the women bathe," Ma said as she, Pa, and Sometimes Comes approached. As they all talked, Mr. McConnell was pleased to see Sometimes Comes. Mr. Cummings and his wife and son joined our happy little group.

I finally said, "It is time for Jack and me to bathe, and besides, I wish to see Morning Star, I've haven't been home all day."

"Will there be any girls there, Mr. York?" asked Charlie Cummings with enthusiasm.

"There might be, but they would be a lot younger than you," I replied with a smile.

"In that case, Mr. York, Charlie will go with you and bathe," said Mrs. Cummings.

"Aw, Ma," Charlie moaned.

"Come on, Charlie, it will hurt only for a second," I said as I took his hand and Jack's arm.

As we headed over the open ground toward the village with my horse in tow, I said, "When was the last time you changed your clothes."

"About a month ago," said Jack.

"About the same with me," said Charlie.

"That's what I thought," I said. I made a course change to Spotted Buffalo's lodge, and as we went, I said to Jack, "You know Jack, that you will be a bit of a problem for me." "It's not your fault; it's mine, and I will deal with it."

"Why am I going to be a problem?" Jack asked.

"I had told many, including Grey Wolf, about your exploits and the trouble you gave me when we were younger." "They are going to look at you now and then look at me and think I am crazy." "There is going to be a lot of teasing, and I'm going to be the brunt of it."

"I'm sorry," Jack said.

"No need to be, like I said, it was my fault, and there will be no harm in the teasing," I replied.

We got to Spotted Buffalo's lodge, and Small Moon was sitting outside. I released the horse to the main herd and said, "This is my mother-in-law, Small Moon." "Where is Morning Star?"

"She is inside feeding Little Mouse," she replied.

"Stay here I wish to see my wife," I said to Jack and Charlie. I went inside, and Morning Star greeted me with a smile, and I kissed her. "I'm going to take a bath with two boys from the white wagon company." "Good, you need it," she said with a smile.

I said to Small Moon, "These two are going to bathe with me." "Their clothing is dirty, and it is not their way to walk around with nothing on." "Would it be possible to make them a loincloth to wear until their clothes are dry?"

She looked at both and said," Yes."

"Will it take long?"

"No, they do not have much to hide," she said, laughing.

She went back into the lodge, and Jack asked, "What did you say to her?"

"I asked her to make something for you to wear." "It will only be a short time," I replied.

In about five minutes, she came out of the lodge and handed me the loin clothes, and I said, "I will return these when their clothes are dry."

"No need, they can keep them."

I thanked her and kissed her on the cheek. In return, she giggled and gave me a love tap on the bottom.

As we headed to the stream, Charlie asked, "What did she make?"

"You will see," I said with a smile. We got to the part of the stream where everyone bathed. A few boys and men were already in the water or were drying themselves. "Alright, take your clothes off," I said.

Jack and Charlie looked around, and Charlie said, "In front of everybody?"

"Yes, of course, make it quick." "The water might be a bit cold, but once you're in, it will feel warm enough." Both sat down and removed their shoes. When Jack was down to his nightshirt, he turned to me and asked, "Everything?"

"Take everything off."

They had finally taken everything off and were trying to hide their nakedness and not doing a good job. Charlie and Jack walked slowly into the water, trying to get used to the cold. I undid my loincloth and said with a smile, "Do you boys know how to swim?"

They both turned around and said, "Yes."

"Good." I picked up all their clothing, including their shoes, and threw everything into the water.

They forgot about the cold water and their nakedness and went scrambling after everything saying, "What are you doing?"

"Your clothes are dirty and need to be washed." "Better get them before you lose them." I jumped into the water and helped them gather their clothing. They washed their clothing and place on a large rock on the shore next to the loincloths. The rest of the time was playing in the water more than anything else." Charlie's and Jack's shyness faded after a short time, and we soon got out to dry.

"What are we going to do about our wet clothes?" asked Jack.

I smiled and said, as I raised their loincloths, "A present from my mother-in-law, Small Moon." They finally put their loincloths on and headed back to their wagon company, although they struggled to walk barefooted.

As I traveled back to be with Morning Star, I ran into, Pa heading to the stream to bathe with Mr. McConnell. "The McConnells are joining us to eat." "I would like you and your family to come also."

"I will try to come, but I will talk to Morning Star first to see if she wants to, I'm sure she will," I said.

The seating was informal, so I sat to the left of Jack, Mr. McConnell sat between Jack and Pa; next was Mrs. McConnell. Ma, Morning Star, Joseph, and Christopher, Zack wasn't here yet. Ma and Morning Star were cooking, and Mrs. McConnell was trying to help, and as we were talking in walked Zack. "Where have you been?" Pa said.

"With White Doe."

"Is that so, well sit where you want, it doesn't matter," Pa said.

He looked around and decided to sit next to Christopher, much to Christopher's delight. I looked at Zack with a smile and noticed two feathers braided into his hair. I said, "Nice hawk feathers."

"You think so, I believe that they make me look really good," he replied with enthusiasm.

"Just how big is your property, Mr. York?" asked Mr. McConnell.

"Over sixty-five square miles," Pa replied.

"That is a lot of land? And you own it?" Mr. McConnell said, surprised.

"Yes, James is responsible for us owning the land; it was a wise move."

"Just what kind of land is it, if you don't mind me asking?" asked Mrs. McConnell.

"There are some mountains and meadows, a lot of trees and grasslands, a few small lakes, and several streams," Pa replied.

"I don't know if my family will approve of what I am going to propose or not, but I have a feeling they will," I said. "The property is very large, and it will get even larger as time goes on. We can use some help working the place if you want to move there instead of going to Oregon. I'm sure we will all help you build a cabin, and we will pay you a wage for helping us with the property," I added.

"I support what James just said, Mr. McConnell," said Pa.

Mr. McConnell looked at his wife and sighed, "Your offer is generous, but we have our plans." "Katherine wants to teach children again, and I think I would like to own my place and besides look at me." "I'm not in shape to do the kind of work you would need me to do."

"You would get in shape, and so would Jack, but I understand." "The offer will always be there," I said.

"As for Jack, maybe someday if he gets the desire to do that kind of work," Mr. McConnell said.

"At least you can stay with us here until your wagon company leaves." "It will be more comfortable than your wagon," Pa said.

"Jack, you can stay with us if you would like," I said.

He looked over at his mother and said, "No, I will stay with my family."

Joseph started to get fussy, so Morning Star removed her top and started nursing him. I could see that the McConnells were shocked at what Morning Star was doing. But Jack appeared to be fascinated. The McConnells tried to look away again except for Jack. When Joseph finished, Morning Star picked up Christopher and gave him the other breast, which he took hungrily. Jack had a smile on his face, but this time the rest of the McConnells could not stop staring.

I finally said, "You are going to find the customs out here a lot different than those in the east." "We have no milk cows out here, and Christopher needs milk." "When I first came to these mountains, my mother nursed me; it is the custom here." "Wherever you go, if the people in your wagon company don't have a milk cow, they will end up doing the same."

"If I offend you, I will go outside with Christopher," Morning Star said.

"No, there is no need, we will just have to learn and understand the customs," said Mrs. McConnell kindly, as she always did.

It was getting time for the Shoshone to meet. Christopher was sound asleep next to his mother, so Morning Star and I got him out of the lodge. We carried him back to Spotted Buffalo's lodge, while everyone else went to the meeting. I put Christopher to bed. Morning Star decided to stay in the lodge with him and Joseph while I went to the meeting.

Mr. Cummings was at the meeting with a few others from the wagon company. Most of the men from the village and even some Shoshone women were there. Spotted Buffalo explained to everyone that the wagon company wanted to trade for food of all types. "These people may need a guide to the great waters to the setting sun," I said.

"Ask them, my son," said Spotted Buffalo.

"Mr. Cummings, do you need a guide?" I asked him.

"Yes, but what will it cost?" he asked.

"I will guide you we will talk about price," said Sometimes Comes.

The trading was to commence about noon the next day, and everyone went back to their wagons or lodges. When I entered Spotted Buffalo's lodge, Morning Star was waiting for me. The two boys were asleep. I explained to Morning Star what was said. After talking to Spotted Buffalo, Small Moon, and Running Deer for a short time, we all went to bed.

We all went to the trade the next day. I had told Morning Star if she wanted something to let me know. I was interested in books, and I found a few other things to dress up the cabin. The trade went very well; I thought everyone seemed to be happy with what they got, and within a couple of hours, it was all over.

The next day the wagon company was to leave for the west coast, so that night, we had our last meal with the McConnells. We tried one more time to get the McConnells to come and live with us, but they were unchanging in their quest. The next day, after we said our goodbyes, we watched as they faded from our view. Everyone thought they would never see them again, but I thought differently, at least with some of them, I felt that we would cross paths again. Two weeks later, we headed back to our homes.

# 26

# THE BLACKFOOT CAPTIVE

More than two years had passed, and the barn and corrals we completed with a pond I dug from the stream. With the help of everyone, we finished Zack's cabin also. It had been easier to build than mine. It wasn't as large as mine or as fancy, although I did put a window in for him. As soon as Zack had his cabin, he married White Doe, and she was with child as was Morning Star with our fourth child.

Last year we had a daughter, but before it was her time for her birth, the baby aborted. I had found so many gold nuggets I had run out of room in the cabin where I was storing them. I had to move it to the barn. I was milling lumber now also. I made a crude shed to store the lumber we milled. I had also started on a bunkhouse, figuring I would need ranch hands in a few years. Christopher was doing many of the chores that Zack and I used to do, which was a big help. He was also handy with a rifle and often went hunting with Pa or me. Joseph was walking and doing some talking. We kept him in our room at night. Pa didn't trap anymore, but what made me happy was, he was getting into the spirit of what Zack and I felt the ranch should be.

One night, Zack and White Doe came to visit, and they were staying in my cabin in the spare bedroom. Ma and Pa were eating with us. After dinner, Ma, White Doe, and Morning Star were off by themselves talking about babies; I believe while Pa, Zack and I were talking about what we should do with the ranch. "I think I should bring the rest of my horses here, instead of leaving them at the village," I said.

"Sounds like a good idea to me," said Pa.

"Don't you think they would be safe at the village?" inquired Zack with a tone of disapproval.

"You know how I feel about the village and the Shoshone." "I have complete trust in them, and the Blackfeet haven't created any trouble for some time now." "Even the Crow seemed to lose some interest in stealing horses." "None of the tribes who populate these mountains bother me; it is the whites that seem to pass through these mountains with ever more frequency bother me." "Soon, they will be building cabins and staying." "I've heard of a settlement many miles south of here," I said.

"Most white people are honest," Pa said.

"It's the ones who aren't that I am worried about Pa." "They will steal and kill for anything they want," I replied.

"You don't think the Shoshone are strong enough to protect the horses?" Zack asked.

"They are strong enough now, but as time goes by, they will get weaker as will all tribes as more whites come," I said as a matter of fact.

I changed the subject to cattle, "I know I have brought this up before, but I feel we should buy some breeding cattle and raise them here," I said.

"I don't understand why you want to bring cattle up here son with all the buffalo, deer, and elk that are here." "I don't know who would buy them, and besides, we don't know if cattle will survive the winters this far north," said Pa.

"I would have to agree with what Pa said, James," said Zack.

"If you noticed, most of the game you have mentioned are getting harder to find except for buffalo." "However, even the buffalo doesn't seem to be as plentiful as they were." "As far as someone buying them, there will be settlers soon, and I am sure the Army will also come," I stated. "I'm not sure they will survive the winter either, but I figure that if horses can survive, cattle aren't much different," I added.

"I guess it is up to you, James." "If you are set on getting them and aren't going to change your mind, then we will get some cattle," Pa said.

"No, it isn't up to me; it is a family issue everyone has a say in it," I said.

Morning Star had heard the conversation, and she said, "If my husband's vision is correct, then the Shoshone will need some cattle." "Also, you should consider his vision."

Pa and Zack stared at her for a few seconds, then Zack lowered his head and said, "I'll go along with anything you want, James."

"It's alright with me, too," Pa said.

"I don't think it will be for a few years anyway," I said. The conversation changed to something else, then Pa and Zack started playing with the boys.

A week had passed since Zack, and his wife left for their home. Pa, Christopher, and I were working down at the sawmill. It was a hot, cloudless day, and we were sweating a lot. As for me, my mouth was dry. "Christopher, would you go fetch some water for your Grandpa and me?" I asked.

"Alright, Pa, I'll get some water for me too," Christopher replied.

I smiled as did Pa at what Christopher said. As we were stacking some boards, Pa and I heard a commotion coming from Christopher. Without understanding what he was saying, I grabbed my rifle as did Pa. Christopher came running into the mill. "Pa, some Indians are coming, and I don't think they are Shoshone or Ute."

"I shut the mill down real fast, as Pa went and looked." Christopher had grabbed his rifle, and I said as I rushed out to joined Pa, "You stay in the mill until I tell you. I think Christopher is right I don't believe that they are Shoshone or Ute, either," Pa said.

There were two of them, but they were too far away to recognize them. "We better take off to the cabin," Pa said. I agreed and called for Christopher, and all three of us ran for my cabin.

Fortunately, Ma was at the cabin. I grabbed Joseph, who was playing in front of the cabin, while Pa explained what was happening. Both Ma and Morning Star grabbed their rifles without hesitation. While everyone else stayed in the cabin, Pa and I went out to confront the Indians. I went to the right while Pa went to the left. As they started to cross the stream, they spotted us and stopped. They were closer to me than to Pa. I couldn't tell what tribe they were from, so I yelled over to Pa. "You know what tribe they are from, Pa?"

"No, but I have a feeling they may be Blackfeet."

The two warriors looked nervous; cautiously, they crossed the stream to our side and stopped. They threw their weapons onto the ground after talking with each other. Slowly Pa and I walked toward them, keeping our rifles trained on them. Pa started signing to them, "Who are you, who are your people?"

The older looking one looked at me and then back at Pa then while signing he spoke in Blackfoot. "I am Running Elk, and this is my son, Sleeping Bear." "We come in peace; we wish to talk to Soaring Eagle With Many Coups."

"You two are either very foolish or what you have to say is very important for both of you to risk your lives by coming here," I said in Blackfoot and signed.

Pa was not happy that they were here, nor was I, but I was willing to hear them out. Pa picked up their weapons, and they dismounted their horses. I guided them to the front of the cabin, and Pa yelled out to those left in the cabin, "It's alright, they have no weapons, you can come out."

Ma and Morning Star came out cautiously, followed by the children. "Who are they?" Ma said.

"Blackfeet, they want to talk about something," Pa said.

"We'll let them have their say and get rid of them." "I don't feel right about Blackfeet being here," Ma replied.

I showed them to a bench in the front of the cabin and decided to sign while I spoke in Blackfoot. "What is it you want?" I asked.

"I come from a large village." "There are many sick and near death, and many have died from a strange sickness," said Running Elk.

"What is this to me, I am Shoshone?" "If all the Blackfeet die, it will be good for everyone." "Your people have caused much trouble," I said.

"I was told that you were not at war with the Blackfeet anymore." "You even let my son live when my brother and other warriors were killed by you when they attacked some whites in their moving lodges," said Running Elk.

I thought I recognized Sleeping Bear he was the young boy that I let go, whose uncle attacked Christopher's wagon company. "I am not at war with the Blackfoot, but I do not like the Blackfoot, nor do I trust them," I said.

"What is it you want?" my father signed.

"Soaring Eagle With Many Coups has strong medicine; some say that he can do anything, and he will be successful, I was hoping he would help save my people."

"My mother is a healer, but I am not a healer, and besides, the risk to my life would be great, and for nothing, do not your people have healers?" I asked.

He looked at my mother but didn't say anything to her thinking it would be a waste of time. "We had two healers, a man and a woman, but they died early with this sickness." "To tell you the truth, they were not all that good in healing," Running Elk said.

"Neither my son nor anyone else will go to your village, so this talk has ended," Pa signed.

Running Elk raised his hand and said and signed, "I have something that I will give to Soaring Eagle With Many Coups if he comes to my village and helps my people."

"What is it that you have that I would risk my life for?" I said.

Running Elk reached into a bag and pulled out a lock of yellow hair and handed it to me. "It belongs to a boy with eyes and hair like yours, about his age," Running Elk said, pointing to Christopher. "He is a captive of my village, and I will give him to you for helping us," Running Elk added.

I knew this changed everything. I handed the lock of hair to Pa and told him what Running Elk said. Pa studied the hair, looked at me, and said, "What are you going to do?"

"I don't have much choice; I can't leave the boy there." "More than likely, they will mistreat him, and I don't think he will survive long." "It's not like what happened to me, and you know how the Blackfeet are toward most whites," I said.

"They will kill you too," said Morning Star.

"That is a chance I must take," I replied. "I know if it were me being held captive by the Blackfeet as a boy, I'd want someone to rescue me," I added.

"What can you do to help these Blackfoot dogs?" Ma asked in Shoshone with disgust.

"With your advice, medicine, and the medical book I have, I will do my best," I answered. Everyone knew there was no choice, even though everyone didn't want me to go, so there weren't any more protests.

"Christopher, go fetch that big, black medical book I have in the cabin," I told him. I turned to Running Elk and said, "I will go, but you must understand some things before I go."

He nodded yes, and I went on, "I am not a healer, my medicine is only for battle and protection." "I cannot promise you that I can help your people." "I do not want you or your people to take revenge on me." "That would not be wise of the Blackfeet," I said.

Pa signed, "If something happens to my son, many nations will go against the Blackfeet until all are dead, and I would hunt both of you down."

Sleeping Bear looked nervously at his father, and Running Elk said, "No one will harm Soaring Eagle With Many Coups."

"Your people must do everything I say when I get to your village," I said.

Christopher handed me the medical book I had gotten in St. Louis. "Tell me what this sickness looks like that your people have," I said. What he said convinced me it was measles, the fever, rash, and red eyes. I turned to the page that gave information about the sickness, and everything he said was right there. The book had a picture of what measles looked like, and I showed it to Running Elk, who showed it to his son. "Does your people's sickness look like this?" I asked.

They both nodded their heads yes.

I turned to my family and said, "His people have measles, and I had had measles when I was young in St. Louis, so I can't get it again." I turned to Running Elk and said, "Your people have a White Man's sickness." "I will try to do what I can, but you must know that since your people have not had this kind of sickness before it is deadlier than it is to the White Man." "After I gather my things, we will leave," I added.

I asked my mother to give me anything that might help and how to make more should I need it. Within the hour, I had everything together, and we were headed northwest. We were heading for the plains. I figured it would be safer there than cutting through Shoshone land. We traveled for several hours and had a dry camp. I didn't talk to the Blackfeet that much. I mainly kept to myself, however when I did speak, I told Running Elk the things I wanted to get done when I got to his village.

"When we get to your village, I want the white captive brought to me before I do anything." Running Elk agreed, and I went on, "I will need help from anyone with any understanding of healing, and we need to make shelters away from the village like this." I drew on the ground just what I wanted something like a lean-to. "In these shelters, we will put everyone who is sick, and no one is to go near them." "There will be other things that I will need." "I will ask for them when we get to the village," and Running Elk agreed to this.

We traveled some time, not seeing any tribes hostile to the Blackfeet. Then when we came to a broad valley, I saw a wide stream with a large village next to it. There wasn't much movement for a village of that size and for being late in the morning. Off to the side, I saw many graves of the Blackfoot; I would guess that a quarter of the village had died. No one noticed us until we were very near the village. The Shoshone would have been able to attack this village easily.

"Put the shelters over there where the sick will get a cool breeze and send me the things that I need, but first bring me the white captive," I said. Running Elk sent his son to get the boy and was about to show me to a lodge where I was to stay, but I said, "It would be best if I build me a place near the sick."

"I will help you," said Running Elk. We started to make a lean-to when I looked at Running Elk, he stopped, and looked up. He was looking at something behind me, and I turned around to see a naked, blond-haired boy smaller than Christopher. He was dirty and malnourished, and he had a lot of scrapes and bruises from obvious abuse. He stared at me with disbelief and shock, and his eyes started to tear up.

"Do you wish to come with me?" I said in English.

He nodded yes as tears ran down his face. "My name is James York." "What is your name?"

"Carl Kahler," he answered with a whimper.

"Come over here you're alright now, no one will hurt you anymore," I said. Carl stood next to me, and I put my arm around him, and the dam burst, and he started sobbing uncontrollably.

"You stay here and help Soaring Eagle With Many Coups while I get the others to build shelter and get the thing he needs," Running Elk said to his son.

I handed some pemmican to Carl and said, "Eat this, it is good for you, and it will fill you up for now." As we worked on the lean-to, Carl gorged himself on the pemmican. We just about finished the lean-to when two old women approached us. I stopped and looked at them and said, "What is it you want?"

"Running Elk sent us here to help." "I have a very small knowledge of medicine, and she will cook," one of the old women said.

"My mother is a Shoshone healer," I said. I went over to my things and pulled out the two mixtures my mother made and said, "Find these things." "You boil this in hot water, and you make a paste with this one." "Make a lot of it your people will need it to live." I turned to the other and said, "Do you think you can find a white man's pot?" She nodded yes, and I continued, "Cook meat and other good things to eat, but make sure what you cook has plenty of water in it." "Then add this to it." I had some salt, and she knew what it was, and I added, "You must make much until your people are well." She nodded again, and she was off.

Sleeping Bear finished the lean-to while I was talking to the women. I told him, "Make a large fire in front of this lean-to and bring plenty of wood." I looked over to where Running Elk and others of the village were making more lean-tos, and I picked up a large rock. I walked out about fifteen feet where my lean-to was and dropped it, and said to Sleeping Bear, "When you finished with the fire, make a line from here to that tree out of rocks, pine cones, or anything you can find."

"What is this for?" he asked.

"No one from your village is to go over the line unless I tell them." "It is for your people's protection from this sickness." Then I went over to where the other lean-tos were under construction. As soon as I headed over there, Carl was on my heels, grabbing at my loincloth. I knew he was afraid to be left alone, so I didn't say anything. I took his hand to reassure him.

The lean-tos for the sick went up fast and, while the healthy from the village brought the sick to the lean-tos, I took Carl down to the stream to bathe. I didn't press Carl with questions but made small talk to comfort him as he held onto me tighter than a beaver trap.

After I bathed Carl, I brought him to the lean-to, the old woman brought food, I fed the boy and then ate a little myself. I then went over to the sick to see what I could do. Some were worse than others. I gave the fever medicine to everyone and then fed them, some with solid food and some broth. However, some couldn't eat at all, and those I was most concerned about wouldn't make it. I put wet compresses on their heads, then I went back and sat down with Carl.

"You feel up to talking?" I asked Carl.

He nodded his head, yes. The sun was going down, so I wrapped him and myself in a blanket. "We will be here for some time until they are over with the measles." "Then we will leave," I said. "Do you have a family you can go to?" I asked.

"None to speak of they killed my parents and my brother," he replied.

"I have two sons and one on the way." "You are welcome to join my family, and I will adopt you as my own, but you must make that decision soon," I said.

"Are you friends of these Indians?"

"No, they are my enemies," I said.

"Then, why are you here?" Carl asked.

"I'm here because of you, or I would not have come."

He put his head down and said, "Oh."

I looked at him and said, "You are worth it."

"I have to take care of the sick ones one more time before I sleep, but you will be safe here," I said.

He looked at me nervously as I drew the blankets around his neck and walked over to where the sick was. I gave a dose of the fever-reducing medicine that Ma gave me to each one of them, whether they felt warm or not. I had to force the concoction down the throats of those who were unconscious. I changed their wet compresses, giving each one of them a new one. Lastly, I made sure each was covered with a blanket before I went back and lay down with Carl.

Carl was wide awake when I came up to him. I removed my clothes, and I crawled under the blanket with Carl. Carl snuggled next to me. As he buried his face into my side, he said, "I decided I want you to be my Pa."

I put my arm around him, then kissed him and drifted off to sleep, extremely tired. Sometime during the night, I woke up and found Carl still snuggling next to me so, I stroked his head and drifted back to sleep until morning.

In the next days, some of the healthier ones could sit up, and they looked good; many of the others were also getting better. But a few of the worst of the worst were either just hanging on or showed no change. I expected some deaths, and I told Running Elk about this. But every day, more was added to the sick from the village. Some of those who hadn't gotten the measles started to have objections about letting Carl, and I leave alive after everyone was well enough to survive. What surprised me was that Running Elk told me about this. Running Elk assured me that the numbers were small, and I need not worry yet. They would not try to do anything until they got more support from their friends.

Toward the end of the second week, two of the worst died, and the numbers of those who would like to see me dead increased. They wanted me dead even though many had recovered, and less Blackfeet were getting sick. Two days later, another died, and Running Elk came with my horse and said, "You should leave when everyone is sleeping."

"I was planning to leave anyway. Those that have recovered know what to do to help the sick."

"There is a good chance that some will come after you," Running Elk said.

"Then they will die," I replied.

He looked at me like he didn't know if I was capable or not to kill the ones who would go after me. He didn't say anymore but just turned around and walked away.

After he left, I turned to Carl and said, "Make sure you eat a lot because there might not be much to eat for some time. After you finish eating, get some sleep, we will be leaving early," I added. Carl nodded and got busy eating while I went and checked on the sick one more time, keeping an eye on those in the village. I had noticed some would stop and stare with a menacing look, and I knew time was running out fast.

It was very late, sometime after midnight, when I finally finished packing my things away. The sky was cloudy, so it was extra dark but not so dark that I couldn't survey the village. The last person up went into his lodge about an hour ago. I gently woke Carl at the same time I put my hand over his mouth and said, "Do not speak; we are leaving now."

I had arranged the blankets to make it look like someone was still sleeping, using straw for our hair and brush for our bodies. It wouldn't fool all the Blackfeet for long, but I was hoping it would fool long enough to put some distance between us the Blackfeet. I knew at first light; my ruse would become discovered.

I had lifted Carl onto the horse, grabbed the reins. I headed south, going across the stream and away from the village and the sick. "Aren't you going to ride?" whispered Carl.

"No talking, I'll ride later," I replied in a whisper. I had walked about a mile or two when I hopped up onto the horse, placing Carl in front of me. I still went slowly. I didn't need the horse to step into a hole and either break her leg or come up lame. It was too dark to check my back trail or to look for any predators. That would have to wait for first light, so I relied on my horse's sense of hearing and smell.

At first light, I moved a bit faster, and I checked my back trail. It was still very cloudy, but I didn't think it would rain. By now, I figured the Blackfeet knew Carl and I were gone. There would be some who would try to track me, and I was sure they would find me. It was impossible to cover my tracks with the boy with me, so I made sure that it would be on my terms when I met up with those Blackfeet. We headed toward Bridger's Fort because it wasn't as far as the safety of the Shoshone. In late afternoon Carl and I got off the horse to give her rest.

"Can I talk now?" Carl asked.

I smiled down at him and said, "Yes, I think it is safe to now." We started walking, leading the horse behind us.

"Are we far from home?" asked Carl.

"Depends on what you call far, I think it isn't far, but it will take us some time to get there. We are going to Fort Bridger because it is nearer.

"I've been to Fort Bridger; it's not very big," Carl said.

"No, but it will give us some protection and rest," I said as I rechecked our back trail.

Carl had noticed that I kept looking back and said, "Why do you always look back?"

"It's always good to check your back trail for dangers." "It has saved my life many times." "However, the main reason I am checking it this time is there are some Blackfeet who will try to follow and try to kill us," I said. I never believed in holding things back from anyone, good or bad. I could see that what I had said, frightened Carl. He couldn't keep his eyes off our back trail, and I added, "I am not concerned if they find us, I will take care of them."

We hadn't walked very far when I could see that Carl's feet were bothering him. They were too soft, so I lifted him on the horse while I continued to walk. After about an hour, I hopped on the horse also. It was a good thing I did because I could see the Blackfeet on my trail. I moved out fast, looking for a defensive position. There was no use trying to outrun them; the horse I had wasn't a fast one, and riding double with Carl would slow me down even more. It wasn't long before I found what I was looking for, and it would give me a clear shot at them. The Blackfeet would have to come up at me, and there was plenty of cover. Carl now knew what was going on and started sobbing uncontrollably afraid that they would capture him again. He was about the same age as Christopher but with the maturity of Joseph. I guess that is how it is with children; each has his personality. I unloaded the horse and tied her up. Then I pulled out all my weapons, including my bow, which I had taken at the last minute before I left home. I tried to calm Carl down by putting my arm around him and saying, "Everything will be ok; you will see." "You just stay behind these rocks." I didn't know what was going to happen if I had to bet the odds were against Carl and me.

I could see them better now there were about eight of them. The Blackfeet hadn't seen me yet, so that was an advantage. I pulled out one of my pistols, looked at Carl, and said, "You know how to use this?" He shook his head no as he whimpered. "You pull back on this hammer point it at one of those Blackfeet and pull the trigger, do you understand?" he nodded yes. "Only shoot when you must," I added. "You stay here and be quiet." "I am going to sneak around and try to pick a few off before I come back." He grabbed onto me, and I said, "It will be alright."

I worked my way down a ravine and hid behind a downed tree and some brush where they would have to pass near me. It wasn't long before they approached. I stuck two arrows in my mouth and strung the third. As they approached, they had no idea what was coming, which was an advantage to me. A rabbit on the other side of them ran from one bush to another, catching their attention for a few seconds, long enough to unleash my first arrow. I caught the last one in the pack squarely in the chest. As the Blackfeet shockingly peered at their downed comrade, I let my second arrow fly hitting another one of the Blackfeet in the front of the pack, and he went down. Almost at the same time, I let go of my last arrow, hitting another. Before the last arrow hit, I was running up the hill before the Blackfeet could realize where I was hiding. The last shot wasn't a clean shot, but I knew if the warrior wasn't dead, he was wounded severely. I was halfway up the hill when they spotted me and started firing at me. I dove behind a rock and just got a little skinned up. It was unbelievable what poor shots they were considering they were Blackfeet. I got a shot off with my rifle when some young, inexperienced warrior stuck up his head, and I caught him between his eyes. After the shot, I reloaded and crawled the rest of the way up the hill to where Carl was. Carl was wide-eyed and stiff as a board, holding the pistol tightly. "Are you alright?" I asked. All he could do was stare at me with his big blue eyes that were tearing up. "There were eight of them." "There are only four now," I told Carl.

There was a place on top of the hill where I could look down without being seen. As I looked down, I saw movement but couldn't get any clear shot, they were smarter now, and they were up to something. I decided to try an old trick, so I shot an arrow into some dry brush down the hill to the right of me, hoping the noise of the arrow hitting the dry brush would receive a reaction. My trick paid off one of the warriors showed himself, and I picked him off with a well-placed shot. That was another one down, but I didn't know where the other three were. I thought of trying to make a break for it, but I wasn't going to risk harm coming to Carl, and I wouldn't have gotten far anyway.

Looking down at Carl, I said, "You're doing just fine." That distraction proved almost fatal because from my left came a Blackfoot warrior firing his fusee. He hit me in the shoulder, spinning me around to the ground. However, I didn't lose my head; I came up with my other pistol and shot him in the stomach. As I did, I heard something behind me. I rolled, grabbed my rifle, and fired at another one. I hit him in the head, removing most of his face. As I got my breath, I winced with pain from the wound I had received and heard a boom from the left side. I smelled smoke from what was gunpowder. I looked over at Carl. Smoke came from the barrel of the pistol I had given him. He was shaking, staring at me. I turned around, and there lay the last Blackfoot warrior with crimson red flowing from his chest. I looked back at Carl and said, "You did very well." "That was the last one."

With some effort, I got up off the ground and walked over to Carl. With my good arm, I lifted him and hugged him. He was sobbing uncontrollably, "It will be alright." "They are all dead now," I said.

"Suppose more come," he said between his tears.

"We will be long gone and in a safe place if that happens," I replied.

I released Carl and took off my shirt to examine the wound. "Carl, you are going to have to help me." The wound looked terrible from the front, "See if you can see a hole in my back, Carl." The pain was so bad that I couldn't tell if the bullet had gone all the way through or not. The rifle the Blackfoot used was a fusee, not a very powerful weapon.

"You're bleeding from your back. I think there is a hole there," Carl said.

"Get me the water and that pouch next to the water. Now watch what I do because you must do it for my back," Carl nodded yes, but he was uneasy. I always kept medication that my mother gave me in the pouch for wounds. I used my shirt to make bandages, and I mixed the medicines with the water to make a paste. "Now watch." I washed off the blood and applied half the medicine to the wound, plugging the hole in front of me and applying a bandage. "Now, you do the back." Carl did his best, and I could see it nauseated him, but he was a good boy and did his best. It stopped the bleeding. I decided to stay here for a few hours to recuperate. "We will go after I rest a bit." I had a little jerky and gave it to Carl.

"Don't you want some?" asked Carl.

"You eat; I'll see if those Blackfeet have anything after I rest."

I rested some while Carl ate. Sometime, after I leaned back on a rock, I must have fallen asleep because when I woke, it was sundown. I looked over to where Carl was, and he was dozing, nearly asleep. My back and front were throbbing, but I ignored the pain and got up. I got Carl up and said, "We'll check these Blackfeet and see if we can use anything they have, then we will go." One by One, we checked the Blackfeet warriors. Down the hill, we found one still alive but severely wounded. The warrior looked up at me in terror. I could have killed him, but I let him live. I didn't take any of their weapons. I found some of their horses that had some food on them.

I could only find five horses, which I tied to my horse. I then mounted my horse with some difficulty. I pulled Carl up in front of me and moved out, heading south. I knew that I was risking opening my wound by riding so soon, but staying here overnight was out of the question. Some of these warriors' friends might come looking for them, and I didn't want to be here if they did.

We traveled for several hours in the dark. I knew I was risking my horse coming up lame or worse, but I wanted to put some space between the Blackfeet and us. I found a suitable place to camp, so I stopped for the night. My wound had opened again, and I did my best with Carl's help to stop it again. I was weak from the loss of blood, the rest and sleep I would get I welcomed. We had no fire, so I wrapped Carl and myself in a blanket and fell asleep with Carl snuggled next to me.

The next day we woke up late. The sun had been up for more than an hour. We both took our time while we ate something. I wasn't feeling very good, but I knew we had to go soon, so we headed south again. I was sweating a lot and figured I had a fever. About noon, we came upon a small stream. I let Carl down and told him to water the horses. I then came off the horse, nearly falling to my knees. I stumbled to the water. I splashed water all over my face and drank as much as I could. Carl had a worried look. "We will give the horses a rest here for a while," I said. I made some of the medicine that Ma gave me for fevers and took it.

"Are you going to die?" implored Carl.

"I hope not, but I am not in the best of shape," I replied.

We rested for about two hours and then headed out again. It felt like my fever had subsided some, and that gave me a little more strength. We traveled until just before dark and made a dry camp without fire again. I was bleeding a little from the front again but was able to stop the bleeding.

My fever had also come back, so I fixed some more fever medicine. I then fed Carl and ate something myself, and we were off to bed.

The next morning, I checked our back trail. It didn't look like the Blackfeet followed us again. I had made up my mind to keep going until I found a good stream because I needed to bathe my wounds, and Carl needed a bath. If I was lucky, I could stay there a couple of days to recuperate. I knew I was still in the Blackfoot country. I also knew I was nearing friendlier territory, but I didn't know if I would make it there before I stopped.

It was late afternoon when I saw what I was hoping for, a stream with trees near it; most importantly, there was protection. As I neared the stream, I told Carl, "Be quiet," and I put him on the ground. I pulled out my rifle, fired, and hit my target. Fortunately, the wound was on the opposite side of my shoulder. Even so, it was difficult for me to shoot, and it opened the wound again. Carl was stiff with fright. I looked down at him and said, "It wasn't a Blackfoot warrior I shot at, it was food, we will eat good tonight." I rode toward the deer I had just killed, while Carl walked beside me. When I tried to get off the horse, I collapsed to the ground, but I was able to get up with Carl's help. I had Carl secure the horses while I started to clean the deer. He seemed to calm down, and I had him lying on a blanket as I finished cleaning the deer, and it was hard to clean the deer with the way I was feeling. Friendly territory or not, I decided to stay here for a few days because I continued to have a fever. I was getting too weak, and my wound kept opening. As I was cleaning the deer, I noticed my wound was seeping blood again. "Go gather some wood for a fire," I told Carl. I could clean and skin the deer, but I felt Joseph could have done better. I did so poorly I wouldn't be saving the deer hide. I got the fire going and some meat on the fire. "You watch the meat cook while I tend to my wound," I said. I unwrapped my bandage, gently covering my wound, and it didn't look very good, it looked nasty. Not only was it seeping blood, but also the wound got infected and had had pus. The only good thing was that I didn't see any sign of gangrene. I let the air hit the wound while Carl and I ate. Carl ate, but he couldn't take his eyes off my wound. I smiled at him and said, "We will bathe after we eat, and hopefully, after we wash and get rest, the wound will look a lot better."

After we ate, Carl and I went down to the stream. When I got up, my head started to spin, and I felt hot, but when I got down to the river and felt the cold water, it felt good. I bathed my wound in the front and cleaned it out the best I could, even though it hurt. I told Carl, "Get the drinking water and pour it over the wound on my back." He did as I said, and I said, "If it doesn't turn your stomach, take this patch of leather, wet it, and pat my wound in the back, trying to clean it the best you can." Carl did this also, but I could see he wasn't very comfortable doing it. I finished washing up as best I could and filled the water container. As I started to walk out of the water, I yelled over to Carl and said to him as he was playing in the water, "Don't forget to wash your hair." I lay against a log, very weak, looking at Carl as I applied pressure to the open wound in front of me, which was still seeping blood. I knew I was in bad shape, and I was worried that I wasn't going to get through this one. I knew my fever had come back, and I was running out of Ma's medicine. That was another reason for me to stay here for two days to see if my wound would heal a little better.

Carl had come out of the water and sat down beside me. He smiled up at me. It was the first smile I saw him have, and he said, "Are you feeling better?"

"Sure," I stated with the best smile I could give him. I mixed some more medicine that Ma gave me, but I didn't take it. Instead, I said to Carl, "This is medicine if I get sweaty while I am sleeping and can't wake me, you pour this in my mouth."

"I thought you said you were feeling better?" he said with a worried voice.

"Oh, sure I am, this is just in case the fever comes back." "I might not even need it," I said, trying to reassure Carl. He seemed to accept my response with some doubt and started to play with some scraps of wood and rock as he dried in the sun.

By putting pressure on the wound, the wound stopped bleeding. I was very hot, most likely because of a fever, and I was also tired, and I started to doze. I awakened from my dozing by what sounded like an angel singing. I slowly turned my head toward Carl, who was oblivious that I was staring at him. He was not only singing beautifully, but he was singing in German. He had a slight accent which I hadn't asked him about, but now I knew it was German. He had his back to me, and I said in German, "You sing like an angel."

He stopped singing and looked at me curiously and said, "You speak German, I was born and lived in Germany in the city of Bamberg.

"I speak many languages, German included. I am half German on my mother's side of the family. Is Bamberg where you learned how to sing?" I asked.

"I was in a choir at the Bamberger Dom St. Peter und St. Georg," Carl replied in German.

"Is that a Church?" I asked.

"It is a huge church."

We talked for hours in German about his family who had died and his likes and dislikes. My impression was that he was very different than Christopher, living a life mostly around women and preferring doing chores that a woman would do rather than a man. I would hope this would change as time went on, but I had already decided not to push him unless necessary. After some time, Carl got tired and fell asleep, much to my relief. I also needed my rest, but before I fell asleep, I took Ma's medicine because I could feel the heat of my fever.

Throughout the night, I woke up several times in pain, but my wound wasn't bleeding. Carl was softly snoring next to me each time I woke. When the sun came up, I was exhausted and weak. I had Carl get freshwater, add wood for the fire, and heat some of the meat we had Carl did the best he could and did not complain. I didn't move around much that day. Carl entertained himself most of the day by the water. What worried me was that I had had wounds before but recovered relatively quickly, but with this wound, it was taking longer. It must have been because of the proximity of where the warrior shot me and what he shot me with, and I couldn't give my wound rest. Carl and I talked much about his past throughout the day. We spoke mostly in German, which he seemed to enjoy speaking. I knew I had a continuing fever, Ma's medicine helped, but I only had enough for one more day, so I just poured cold water over my head to keep cool.

On the third day, we were supposed to get moving. Still, I wasn't up to it, so I rested until early afternoon when I forced myself to pack the horse, gather the other horses that I took from the dead Blackfeet, and Carl then head south. It was a hot, clear day, and the heat was getting to me. At times, my eyes would get blurry, which was dangerous in this country or any other country. It was dark when we made a dry camp. I was grateful for the rest I would get. I started the fire, but Carl, who got the wood and set up camp the best he could. That night I had a fitful night, and the next morning I decided to leave as early as possible, even though I didn't feel up to it. I felt that the cool of the morning would be better than the heat of the afternoon.

We stopped at a small stream in the afternoon to water the horses and give the horses and us a rest. I poured water over my head and drank as much water as I could. I thought about staying there overnight but didn't. After about an hour, we were heading south again. By sundown, I found another small stream, and we stopped. I let Carl down off the horse, and as I got off, I fell to the ground. I was light-headed and hot with fever, too weak to do much of anything. I crawled toward the stream, Carl tried to help, but I pushed him away and said hoarsely, "I'll do this myself." I got to the water and drank, splashed water on my head, and rolled over on my back, and said, "Gather some firewood."

I don't know what happened next because everything went black. When I woke, I had a blanket on me, a fire was going, and some meat was almost heated. I looked around but only saw Carl. "Did you do all of this?" I asked him.

"I watched you do it," he replied.

"You did well," I said.

"Are you feeling better?" Carl asked.

"Not much, but we will leave late tomorrow to give me more rest."

The next day just before noon, we left for the south again. There were some welcomed clouds and a slight breeze that made conditions cooler. I had taken the last of Ma's medicine that morning, and my fever had subsided for the present. By late afternoon, I was having a hard time focusing when we were moving on a wooded ridgeline. My head was down, and from time to time, I was rubbing my eyes so that I could see well. My forehead was dripping with sweat, as it had been for the past few days. Carl was sitting in front of me as my mind started to drift from as I traveled.

"Blackfeet Pa," Carl said alarmingly.

I pushed Carl roughly onto the ground, got off the horse myself, and moved into some bushes and trees. I was confident they hadn't spotted us yet. I could see about eight warriors far down the valley. I finally could focus my eyes well enough to make out who they were, and I said to Carl, "They're Crow friendly to the Shoshone, but I don't want to meet up with them."

"Why?" asked Carl.

"They are horse thieves and that one in front is Little Bear who doesn't like me and frankly I don't care for him either. They would try to take the horses and maybe kill me also in my weakened state," I said. "It looks like they are heading to Fort Bridger like we were, but I think now I will turn toward home," I added.

"You don't look very good; you think you can make it back?" Carl asked with concern.

"No, I'm not sure, but when we get near enough if I am not able to find my way, the horse will know where to go, just let the reins drop," I answered. The Crow was out of sight, and we headed in a different direction. I was relieved in part that the Crow didn't spot us and that I decided not to go to Fort Bridger, but there was a good chance I might regret it later.

Two days had passed, my head was pounding, and my vision had worsened. The only good thing was that my wound had not reopened. I should have been one or two days away from home, but I wasn't quite sure where I was. Carl was very concerned about my condition, asking me many times during the day how I was. The answer was always the same, I'll be all right, but I wasn't very convincing. I had been so bad for the last two days that I was going into semi-consciousness at times. At one point, I put Carl on the back of the horse, and I dropped the reins, hoping I was near enough for the horse to find our home.

"Help the boy down, Nate," Ma said. Now get James down and bring him into the cabin," Ma added. I became semi-conscious and only saw a blur of people, and then everything went black again.

"Christopher, get him some clothes and feed him," said Morning Star.

"Yes, Ma," Christopher replied.

"Who are you?" Christopher asked Carl as he handed him some of my clothing from when I was his age.

"Your brother, my name is Carl."

"Welcome to the family," Christopher replied. That's your brother, Joseph; he hangs around Grandpa."

"His wound did not heal well," Ma said. "We must draw out the poison he has a fever," she added. Ma worked on me for hours, and Morning Star tried to help as much as she could as close to her delivery. Pa took care of the boys and got the story of what happened from Carl. For about three days, I was unconscious or semi-conscious. When I finally woke, the first person I saw was Morning Star. I smiled and said, "I didn't know the most beautiful woman in these parts would want to bother with someone all beat up like me."

"I can't be too choosy; there are not too many men that come by here, and my husband is a foolish man who likes to gamble with his life."

I smiled then, and she came to me and embraced me with a kiss. I started to get up, but Morning Star stopped me and said, "You're too weak you must rest and get strong, I will get you something to eat."

"What has happened to the boy, Carl?" I asked.

"Do you mean our son?" she corrected me. I smiled, and she called for Carl, "Carl, there is someone here who wishes to see you."

In walked Carl, all dressed up in one of my old buckskins. He had a big smile on his face. "Are you feeling better?" he asked.

"Couldn't be better," I replied. I looked over to Morning Star and said, "And where are Joseph and Christopher?"

"Outside doing chores with their Grandpa, Carl likes helping me in the lodge," she replied.

It was some time before I was up and around, but not so much time before Morning Star delivered a baby girl with the help of Ma and White Doe. We named her Sarah or Little Foot, her Shoshone name. This child was one girl who I could already see was going to be spoiled by her brothers and grandparents.

# 27

# CATTLE RANCH IN THE SHINING MOUNTAINS

I was in deep thought by the corrals when Pa came up to me. "It looks like you have something on your mind," Pa said.

"I do, we need to head east with the gold, and then I think we need to get serious about the cattle and bring some up here. I also believe we need to hire some help to tend this place; it's too much for all of us," I said.

Pa nodded and said, "I'll go along with what you want." "You have to fill that bunkhouse with someone anyway."

I think it should be just you and me going and have Zack and White Doe stay here watching over the women and kids," I said.

Pa nodded again and said, "Too many problems with Whites and Indians." "Also, Zack might get violent if someone said something." "He broods about this every time some White folks stare at him because he has mixed blood."

I chuckled and said, "Yeah." "Do you remember that guy trapping on our land who said something negative about his heritage?" "He almost beat him to death before you pulled Zack off him."

"Yeah, I remember he took a swing at me also," he said with a bit more seriously. "Well, he will be here in a few days; we can get things together then," Pa added.

It had been several years since I rescued Carl from the Blackfeet. He was in his teens now and had become a happy member of our family. He loved to help his mother and grandmother and had little interest in the ranch work or even in hunting. Christopher and Joseph tried to get Carl to join them. He did join them a few times, but it was to make them happy, not for himself. Sarah had become a beautiful little girl who loved playing with her dolls and following Grandpa around when she wasn't doing chores. My going east wasn't going to make Morning Star happy. She was pregnant again, and I might not make it back in time for the baby. The ranch was almost what I dreamed it would be. I could envision the cattle being here and the men I would hire tending them. Next year, I would go to the Shoshone village, get the rest of my horses, and breed them.

I saw Christopher and Joseph come riding toward the cabin like their tails were on fire yelling, "Pa, Pa, Uncle Zack, Aunt White Doe, and our cousins are coming." They have brought two strangers with them," they said, as the two boys came to a halt in a cloud of dust.

Pa asked, "What do these strangers look like?"

"One is an older man in fancy clothing with pale skin," Christopher said. "The other is a skinny man who has hair that looks like his head is on fire," Joseph said.

"That's not fire, he has red hair," Christopher said to Joseph with a disgusted voice that only a brother who loved Joseph would have said. Just then, I saw Zack and White Doe come into sight with the two strangers. At first, Pa and I couldn't make out who the two strangers were, but as they got closer, I saw Pa's jaw tighten. He knew one or two of them, and he wasn't happy. The two men got closer. I recognized who one of the men was. It was apparent the redhead was, Jack McConnell and the older one looked familiar. When they stopped in front of us, he said, "You know why I'm here, Nate?"

"Yes, Dan, I do," Pa said.

It was my uncle Daniel, and that meant that Grandma and Grandpa must have died. I looked over to Jack and said, "I didn't think I would see you again, Jack."

"So, you know who I am?" he asked.

"Of course, who wouldn't recognize you with all that red hair?" I replied.

"You all come down off those horses and rest," Pa said

As we walked toward the corrals the rest of the family joined us, Ma said, "Daniel, it is a joy to see you."

"It's nice to see you too, Blue Flower, however, I come bearing bad news," Daniel said.

Ma nodded with understanding; she knew he had bad news. She looked over to Jack and said, "And this is Jack all grown up it is a joy to see you too."

We all went into my cabin. The older kids were up in the loft while the younger ones, who had lost interest, went outside to play. "I know why you are here, Dan, so let's put that on hold."

"First, I wish to find out what brings Jack McConnell here," Pa said.

Everyone looked at Jack, who said, "Ma and Pa are dead, they died of some kind of sickness of some sort."

His statement had taken the wind right out of me. Stunned, I said, "What happened to Sarah?"

"She had gotten married a few years back and moved south, near Los Angles," Jack replied. "I sold everything I could the store had never taken off." "I sent a letter to Sarah and told her I would try to find you, folks." "I was hoping to find work and a place to live." "I don't know much about this kind of work, but I am willing to learn," he added with a voice of hope.

"You can stay here as long as you want, and you will learn from all of us," Pa said.

"Yeah, you're part of the family now, Jack," Zack said.

I was still in shock at the death of both Mr. and Mrs. McConnell and remained silent with my head down. Ma, who was sitting to the left of me, put her arm around me to comfort me. Except for Ma and Morning Star, who also knew I was hurting, the rest were talking on one subject or another, not noticing me.

The conversation finally switched to my Uncle Dan. By this time, I had recovered enough to listen carefully. "Father died first; he had a small cold and seemed fine in the beginning." "As the days passed, his color changed and he started coughing blood, he lasted about two weeks and then died," Daniel said sadly. "Mother was utterly destroyed, as you could imagine." "She wouldn't eat or sleep, and with all this stress, she had a stroke." "She lasted about a year and a half when she fell asleep one day and never woke up."

Pa was in tears, and the pain we were all feeling was overwhelming. "I need to get some air," I said and left. I grabbed the ax and got busy splitting wood.

I was splitting wood for about a half-hour when Uncle Daniel came over to me and said, "I'm sorry I upset you."

"There is no need to feel bad; it wasn't just you that upset me."

"Yes, I know, your mother told me about your relationship with the McConnell's." "You know I'm also hurting, but with time the pain eases," explained Uncle Daniel.

"I'll be alright," I said.

"That's good because there are a lot of things that you need to be acquainted with," Uncle Daniel said with relief.

I smiled at him and said, "I will be in the house around dinner time."

We had venison stew for dinner, and we talked while we ate. Uncle Daniel told me that I was Sir James now, the Earl of Worcester, and the others also had titles as Lords and Ladies. Everything was done legally and finalized back in New York and England.

After dinner, I was handed the papers establishing who I was. I also received an accounting of my holdings back in England. I saw a slight profit each year, and the person taking care of the estate deposited it in the bank. I knew I would have to go to England someday, but I had no plans now.

"How did our sisters and cousins react when they received little or nothing," Pa asked.

"Our sisters threw fits, especially their husbands." "Martha's husband was so disappointed he divorced her leaving her penniless." "Of course, I had to take her in," said Daniel. "Now, as for our cousins, they aren't talking to us." "They even went so far as to retain a lawyer, saying our father was senile or something, of course, they lost," Daniel explained.

Zack, White Doe, and their families stayed in the cabin with us while Uncle Daniel and Jack slept in the newly constructed bunkhouse. When we all gathered at breakfast, I said, "Pa and I are heading east in a couple of days."

"He is right; you can go back to your home with us, Dan." "Zack, I wish you and your family to stay here to watch over the place," Pa said.

Zack looked at Pa puzzled, and I said, "Morning Star is with child, and I don't know if we will get back in time." "Also, Jack needs to learn how to do things here."

"We will teach him, Pa," Joseph blurted out.

"All you boys would do an excellent job, but your uncle Zack has lived here longer than me, and he knows many things you haven't learned yet," I said.

Two days later, two mules and four horses got hitched to the wagon, modified and reinforced, so it could haul the gold and supplies that we placed into the wagon. We got a list of everything everyone wanted; Uncle Daniel, Pa, and I headed east, moving slowly because of the weight of everything in the wagon. We didn't stop at Bridger's Fort; the plan was not to stop at any settlement until we were safely on the other side of the Mississippi River. We did this because we didn't want anyone to know what our cargo was. However, I was still nervous because of the number of animals it took to haul everything. Our trip east was uneventful, except for one time when some Lakota started to approach us. Then they turned away when they, I assume, spotted me and or Pa. We were about to cross the Mississippi River and enter Commerce, Illinois. Looking across the river, I was surprised at how much Commerce had grown, and it looked pleasant. We crossed the river and first noticed that the people of this city were solemn. It was June thirtieth, eighteen forty-four, a hot, cloudless summer day. We saw the name of the city changed from Commerce to Nauvoo.

We rode up to a man by the name of Daniel Butler, and Pa asked, "What's going on here?" "People around here seem like they are in a daze or something."

"Our prophet and president of our church, Joseph Smith, and his brother Hyrum were murdered."

"Joseph Smith, you say?" "Is he the Smith from Palmyra New York?" I asked.

"Yes, his family lived there at one time," he replied.

"Does any of his family live here?" Pa asked.

"Yes, his mother is still alive, and he has a wife, Emma, also their children." "There are others," Daniel Butler said, getting a little suspicious of why we wanted to know.

"Where does his mother live?" Pa asked.

"I don't know if I should tell you, why do you want to know?" he replied.

"We stayed with them in Palmyra some years back; they are friends," I said. He gave us the directions to get there, and Pa said, "We should pay our respects."

We went to Lucy Smith's home and were told by a neighbor that she was most likely at her daughter-in-law's house then we were given instructions on how to get there. As we dismounted at Emma Smith's home, a woman came out, a woman came out, and Pa said, "I'm Nathaniel York, he is my brother, Daniel and my son, James." "I was wondering if a

Lucy Smith would be here with you?" Pa asked. Just as Pa asked, a strong looking elderly woman came out of the house and said, "I'm Lucy Smith."

"I don't know if you remember me, Mrs. Smith, but my family and I stayed at your home in Palmyra several years ago."

"I remember you, Mr. York," she replied.

"We came to pay our respects over the death of your sons," Pa added.

"This is Emma Smith Joseph's wife." "They're good folks, Emma," said Lucy.

"Will you gentlemen come into my home?" Emma requested.

We followed the Smiths into the house. "We won't stay long, but I would like to know how it happened, I liked Joseph," I said.

She told us the whole story, and Pa, shaking and scratching his head, said, "You mean in these days' people still think they had a right to kill him because of his beliefs."

Emma and Lucy said sadly, "They think so."

"I thought we fought a war of independence over something like this," Uncle Daniel said.

"If they knew what I believed and practiced, they might feel the same way about me," I said.

Pa sighed and said, "We must be on our way, and we wish the best for you." With that, Pa got up, and we got to the horses and the wagon and left.

We avoided going through Carthage because that's where Joseph and Hyrum died. Even so, we got stares because of the direction we came, but when they saw what clothing we were wearing, they paid us no mind thinking we were just drifting through from another place.

We headed east to the town of Springfield, and as we rode into town, we came upon a very tall man, maybe taller than Tall As The Sky. "Mister, would you direct us to the safest bank in the city," Pa asked. "Sure, follow me," the man said. Pa and Uncle Daniel got off their horses and walked beside the tall man, and Pa said, "This is my brother, Daniel York, and this is my son James, and I'm Nathaniel."

"I'm Abraham Lincoln, but most people call me Abe." "Here we are, talk to Mr. Steiner, who is the bank president." "He is all business and has no sense of humor, but he is honest." "If you need a lawyer, let me know, that is my line of work."

He excused himself while Uncle Daniel and Pa went into the bank, and I watched the wagon. It wasn't long before a stern-looking older man came out of the bank with Pa and Uncle Daniel. They both went to the back of the wagon and looked in. The older man looked like he was going to pass out. He went back inside his bank in a hurry, and soon after, there was a closed sign in the bank window. Then a bunch of clerks came running out and started to unload the wagon, much to the delight of the mules and horses, I'm sure. It took some time, but the gold got tested and weighed by the assayer. With all we had, it was worth over eight-and-a-half million dollars. We had more than enough for the cattle, and Pa gave Uncle Daniel enough money so that his sisters would each have ten thousand apiece. He also gave Uncle Daniel some money, but I didn't know how much, and I didn't care.

We crossed back to the western side of the Mississippi River and went down to Saint Louis. "It doesn't feel the same," I said to Pa.

"What doesn't feel the same?" Pa asked.

"This city; I'm going down to see Mama's grave while you go to the bank."

Pa nodded, and I said, "Withdraw at least a hundred thousand dollars from the bank."

"Why so much?" Pa asked.

"I've got a feeling if we don't, something might happen, and usually, my feelings are correct," I explained.

Pa said alright, and we parted, Pa going to the bank and me to the graveyard.

The graveyard looked nice. Trees and bushes were larger than I last remembered, and there were more graves, but Mama's headstone was still the largest. The wealthy graveyard that butted up to where the poor were and was now indistinguishable. I walked over to the church to see who was running it now. To my surprise, it was still Father Garcia, a lot older now. "You've kept the graveyard looking attractive," I said to him.

"Thank you, do I know you?" he asked curiously. I smiled and said, "I'm Sir James York." I thought I'd try out my new title.

He stared at me for a few seconds and said, "Are you that young boy who used to live at Mr. McConnell's store."

Smiling, I said, "Yes."

"You have grown and changed since I last saw you." "You know the McConnells moved away from here," Father Garcia said.

"Yes, I know, Sarah got married and is living in California." "Her father and mother died near San Francisco, and Jack is a ranch hand at my place, or he is trying to be a ranch hand."

"Too bad about Mr. and Mrs. McConnell, but I'm happy to know their children are safe," he said. "You told me you're Sir James York?" he asked, kind of confused.

"I inherited the title of Earl of Worcester when my Grandfather died," I explained. Just then, Pa approach, and I said, "Do you remember my father?"

"Yes, I do; it's a pleasure to see you again, Mr. York," Father Garcia said. We exchanged our pleasantries and then left, we had no intention of staying in St. Louis, so we headed south.

We entered the town of Popular Bluff, which was a town in southern Missouri. There was a great commotion over a black slave all in chains. Now, Pa and I didn't think it is right for someone to own someone else, but we know some people believed it is alright and had the law behind them.

"What's going on?" Pa asked a man walking toward the commotion. "The owner of that runaway slave is teaching him a lesson," he answered with excitement. We rode up to an older, stern-looking man who had started beating the large, black man with a bullwhip while being tied to a pole. As Pa watched with disgust, I got off the wagon and went over to the old man whipping his slave and grabbed his arm.

"Let's talk," I said.

Angrily, he tried to pull his arm away, but I was too strong for him. He looked down in disbelief that he couldn't escape from me, and one of his hands started to pull his pistol when Pa said while cocking his rifle, "I'd put that pistol back if I were you."

"Sir, if you just take a few minutes, I think you will like what I have to say," I said to the old man. He relented and followed me over to the wagon, and I said, "This slave, you have gives you a lot of trouble, I'm guessing."

"Yes, he is always running on me, what's your point?" he asked impatiently.

"Would you be willing to sell him to me?" "I'd give you a good price for him," I said. That got his attention, and I could see he was a shrewd man, he would want a lot.

"He is a good strong man, a very expensive slave, and you and your father don't appear to me to be able to afford him," he said.

"Appearances can be deceiving don't worry if we can pay or not, how much do you want," I replied.

Haughtily he replied, "Ok, if you want him, it will cost you a thousand dollars."

As he was chuckling and looking at people around him, I looked up at Pa, and Pa nodded. "Alright, I'll pay it," I said.

He turned around, shocked that I would meet his price. "Let's find a lawyer to draw up the papers," I added.

"Let me see the money first," he said.

I pulled out a thousand dollars and showed it to him. As he tried to grab it, I said, "You can have it after I get a paper saying he is mine.

We found a lawyer, which I had to pay for, and he drew up a bill of sale. Then Pa and I owned a slave, at least until we got out of these parts. I went over to the slave and cut him loose and said, "What's your name?"

"They call me Big Tom," he said in a deep voice.

"I'm James; this is my father, Nathaniel York." "We don't believe one should own another." "You can stay with us until we get to a place where you will be free, or you're welcome to leave if you want," I said.

"I'll stay with you until I am in a free state," said Big Tom.

"However, between now and then, I wish to make you an offer you might be interested in," Pa said.

"Big Tom, get in the back of the wagon, we won't be staying here," I said.

We entered Arkansas; Pa was driving the wagon with Big Tom beside him. "What do you plan to do now that you are free?" Pa asked Big Tom.

"Don't rightly know, maybe move up North or go out West, then try to find a job."

"We live North West of here, and we are looking for people to help out on the ranch," Pa said. "We would be willing to pay you a fair wage if you would consider working for us," he added.

"Can I ask you a few questions?" Big Tom asked.

"Sure, what you want to know?" Pa said.

"If you live up north, why are we heading south?" he asked

Pa smiled and said, "We are heading south to buy some cattle that we will move up north to build up a herd," Pa replied.

"You need to know I don't know much about cows," he said.

"Can you ride a horse and drive this wagon?" Pa asked.

"Yes, sir, I can," Big Tom answered.

"Then you will learn the rest; we will all learn," Pa said as he looked up at me.

"I will need things to be able to live up there, including a horse," he said.

"Don't worry about that, we will get them for you," Pa said.

"I can leave anytime I want?" Big Tom asked.

"You will be a free man to go or come anytime you want," Pa said.

"In that case, I would be happy to work for you," Big Tom said with a smile.

That night Pa proposed we go west for a while, at least to the Arkansas River. So, in the morning, we headed west, and after a few days, we crossed the Arkansas River and headed south. It wasn't long before we ran into about six Indians of a tribe Pa and I didn't know. They didn't look very friendly, and I tried the languages I knew with no luck. Finally, Pa used sign language, and they seemed to understand him. "I am Bear Slayer, this is my son Soaring Eagle With Many Coups, and he is our friend but only has a white name," Pa signed.

"We are Shoshone, and we are not looking for troubles," I signed. Big Tom was getting nervous, and I said to him, "If they wanted to kill us, they would have."

"Who are your people?" Pa signed. They looked at each other, then one of them signed, "We are Comanche, and we know you and your son. What are you doing here?" he asked.

"We have heard of the Comanche, and we are going south to get some of the white man's buffalo," Pa signed.

"The white man's meat does not taste as good as buffalo," the Comanche warrior signed.

"You are right, but I had a vision that the white man will someday kill many of the buffalo." "There won't be enough buffalo for everyone, so we must raise the white man's buffalo, so there will be enough to eat," I signed.

They thought for a few seconds then signed, "And what about this black one who has hair like a buffalo?"

"He was a slave of the white man; the one who owned him mistreated him and beat him like a dog." "He will go back to the land of the Shoshone with us where he will be free," I signed.

"You may travel through our lands without harm," the warrior signed. As quickly as they approached us, they left, and we continued going south with much relief that there were not going to be any troubles.

We talked to some people along the way who told us the best place to get some cattle was Sam Allen's Ranch near the Gulf of Mexico. After many days, we came to the town of Pasadena. The town had a cantina, and we rode up to it then went in. "We don't serve that kind," the bartender said, pointing to Big Tom.

"We aren't here to drink, just to get some information," Pa said. "We are looking for the Sam Allen Ranch."

"Why are you looking for Sam Allen's ranch?" someone from behind us asked.

We all turned around and sized up the man, and then Pa said, "We are looking to buy some cattle," Pa said.

The man got up from the table and came over to the bar to talk to us. "I'm Sam Allen." "How much cattle were you thinking of buying?"

"I think about six hundred would do," I said.

"This time of year, they are about thirty-five dollars a head," Mr. Allen said.

"That's high, isn't it?" Pa said.

"Yes, but as I said, they are more expensive at this time of year, and besides, I'm the only one I know of that can sell you that much cattle," Mr. Allen replied.

Pa nodded and looked at me. I said, "We also need a horse for Big Tom here."

"He's your slave?"

"No, one of our ranch hands," I answered.

"Alright, I will throw in a horse and pick out some good breeding stock."

"We have one other problem, Mr. Allen." "We need some people to drive them up north," I said.

"How far north are you going?" asked Mr. Allen.

"You ever hear of a place called the Yellow Stone?" Pa asked.

"Yes," he said, taken aback.

"We are going to a week's hard ride south of there, in a valley in the Shining Mountains," Pa said.

Sam Allen was quiet for a few moments then said incredibly, "You do know that cattle have never happened to be that far north, and I'm not sure they will be able to survive the winters up there."

"Horses survive, buffalo travels this far south from the north," I said. "I think we may lose some, but those that live will make good breeding stock," I added.

"Alright, it's your money, come to my ranch tomorrow, and I will cut your six hundred head from my main herd," Mr. Allen said.

"Where is your ranch?" Pa asked.

"Just go west of here, you will run right into it," he replied as he left. We both noticed that he didn't say he would lend us some of his men to drive the cattle north. Of course, he never said he wouldn't either.

As the three of us left the cantina, another man left also. He approached us and said, "Seniors, uno minuto," he shouted.

We stopped and turned around, and he said in broken English, "If you need someone to help you move some cattle, I will help you, I need a job."

"Do you know anything about cattle?" I asked in Spanish.

"Yes, I have worked on ranches ever since I was a boy," he replied.

"What's your name?" I asked.

"Miguel Fernandez," he replied.

I switched back to English and said, "Miguel, get your things and throw them in the wagon." "We will be at the store picking up supplies."

Miguel was an older Hispanic man with a grandfatherly look to him. He put his things in our wagon, and all four of us camped for the night outside of town.

The next morning, we went out to Mr. Allen's ranch. As we were passing over his land, we saw plenty of cattle. Miguel was telling us what he knew about the cattle, which was quite a bit. We came in sight of the ranch house which, looked like it got made of adobe with a tile roof, fancy for this country. We spotted a barn about the size of ours, corrals, a large bunkhouse, and some outbuildings. As we rode up, some of the ranch hands came up to us, and a rough-looking one said, "What's your business here?"

Before we could answer, Mr. Allen came out and said, "It's alright, Bob." "They are here to buy some cattle." "Those cattle I had you put in the west pasture are the ones they are buying."

Pa got off his horse, and the rest of us got off the wagon. "Come into my home, and we will settle up," Mr. Allen said.

Pa looked at Miguel and Big Tom and said, "Stay with the wagon and horses."

They both nodded, and we went inside. "Let me see, six hundred times thirty-five dollars that will be, oh, about, ten thousand dollars," he said.

I looked up at Pa and Pa said, "Ten thousand dollars is a lot of money, but I am not a cheating man. You're short by eleven thousand; we owe you twenty-one thousand."

It was apparent he was not an educated man and knew little or nothing about mathematics. It was also evident that he got taken back to Pa's honesty.

"We would also like to buy two horses with tack instead of one, if you can spare it," Pa added.

Mr. Allen nodded and said, "I said I would throw in one horse, so I won't charge you for that. Do you think forty dollars for the other is fair?"

"Yes, I do, Mr. Allen, and can you loan us any of your men to help drive these cattle up north, any number would be helpful."

"I must talk to my men to see if any of them are willing to go," he replied.

We left the Allen Ranch with the six hundred head of cattle and headed north. Mr. Allen could give us two of his men if we paid them double what they were getting. I had bought two rifles, among other things, in Pasadena just before we went out to the Allen Ranch. I gave one of the rifles to Miguel, but I decided to wait until we left Texas before I would give Big Tom a rifle. It might cause trouble if someone were to see a black man with a rifle. I had noticed, as Pa did, that the two men that Mr. Allen lent us didn't mix with us very well. It was up to Miguel to teach us how to move cattle. Pa and Big Tom seemed to be doing fine, but I believed my horse was catching on faster than I was. One good thing I must say about the two men, Mr. Allen loaned us; they were good at what they did.

We had traveled for many days, and we were about to enter Apache country. I handed a rifle to Big Tom, which he wholeheartedly took. The two ranch hands of Mr. Allen weren't happy at all, and one of them said, "You're not going to give that black devil a rifle, are you?"

"What I give my men is none of your business, but what you should know we are getting into some dangerous country." "If trouble starts, another rifle will come in handy," I said in disgust. He and his partner grumbled together but didn't say any more, but I could see they did not like us, especially Big Tom and me.

The next day, on a ridge, we got nervous when we spotted what I thought was Comanche. I didn't know precisely how many there were, but there were a lot of them. At one point, they started to approach but then stopped when they spotted Pa and me. They turned around and went back up the ridge. They did follow us for two days but then disappeared, and we never saw them again.

It was the night after the Comanches disappeared when the trouble started. Miguel went to relieve Big Tom, who was watching the cattle. When Big Tom carried his food on a plate past the two men that came from the Allen ranch, one of them tripped him and started laughing at him as he fell to the ground with his food splattered on his face. Pa and I lifted our heads but didn't say anything. We both wanted to see how Big Tom would handle the situation. "Hey, you lowlife, black fool, you splashed your damn food on my boot," the ranch hand said with a sneer.

"Yes sir, I'm sure sorry," Big Tom said as he got up. I should have known this is how he would react. The way he acted is how all slaves would respond to a white man. If a slave touched a white man, he would be brutally beaten or killed.

"Clean it, you dumb animal," the ranch hand said in a nasty voice.

"Big Tom, what would you do if another slave deliberately tripped you and said what that man said?" Pa asked.

"I would beat him a good one, sir," Big Tom said sincerely.

"You're a free man, Big Tom, in a territory that doesn't have any slave laws, and he is just a man like you," Pa informed him. Pa was thinking the same as me; we couldn't have Big Tom acting as a slave, not defending himself, it was a quick way of getting killed if he did.

Big Tom took a few seconds studying both Pa and me, and then a big smile appeared on his face. He turned to the one giving him all the trouble and grabbed him by the shirt and lifted him over his head, which shocked the troublemaker and his partner. Big Tom carried him down to the stream we were camped next to and threw him in; he made a loud racket all the way.

His partner grabbed his pistol, but both Pa and I grabbed ours and said to him, "Drop your pistol." "He had it coming, and you know it," Pa said.

"If it weren't for you and your friend, there wouldn't have been any trouble," I said. Big Tom, still laughing, got some more food and sat down next to Pa and me.

"This sure has been a beautiful day, Mr. York," Big Tom said with amusement.

"I can understand how you feel," Pa replied.

Meanwhile, the ranch hand came out of the water, looking like a wet cat. The ranch hand wasn't very happy but didn't say anything to Big Tom, Pa, or me. He just sat down next to his friend and went back to eating. They muttered back and forth a bit, but I didn't know what they were saying until the next day.

The next day, Mr. Allen's two ranch hands approached Pa and said, "We don't wish to work for you anymore."

"Alright," Pa said as he started to turn and walk away.

"We also came to settle up with our wages," they added.

Pa turned around and angrily said, "The deal was I would pay you twice your regular pay at the end of the drive, and the drive hasn't ended yet." "Now, if you want your money, you must complete your job and put aside your prejudices for Big Tom." "This is about Big Tom, isn't it?" Pa added.

They looked at each other, knowing they weren't going to win this one. The two ranch hands didn't say anything but just got on their horses and went out to the cattle.

I went up to Big Tom and said, "I think it would be better for you to drive the wagon today." "It will give time for those two to calm down and relax."

We had traveled for some time, and everything seemed to go very well. However, we had entered the Arapahoe country, and when the Arapahoe caught sight of us, they came down toward us. "Let me handle this." "I've had more experience with these people than you have," Pa said to me. Pa rode up to them, and I followed far enough away not to interfere with their conversation but enough to back up Pa if trouble started. "I am Bear Slayer; we are just passing through the country; we look for no trouble."

"Bear Slayer, I have heard of you." "And who is that one?" the Arapahoe warrior said.

"That is my son, Soaring Eagle With Many Coups," Pa replied.

The Arapahoe were young, but they both had heard of Pa and me. They talked among themselves. I assumed they wanted to decide what to do and still maintain face. "You may pass through our lands, but do not stop," one of the warriors said. Before Pa could say anything, they had turned around and left, and Pa rejoined me.

"If we hadn't been here, I think they would have attacked," Pa said.

"No doubt, "I replied.

We never saw another Arapahoe, but as soon as we got into Cheyenne country, the Cheyenne followed us day after day. It made us all nervous. Pa and I didn't know what they would do; the Cheyenne is so unpredictable. They followed us until we entered the Shoshone and Ute country. By that time, we were near home, and we were fortunate we didn't lose any of our herd; in fact, they looked very healthy.

"Where do you want to put the cattle?" Pa asked me.

"You know that valley north of my cabin where the small stream is?" I asked Pa.

"Yes," Pa replied.

"It's near our cabins, and it has plenty of grass and water. Also, it is warmer there in the winter because of those two hot springs that are at each end of the valley," I said.

"When will we be at your ranch?" asked one of Mr. Allen's ranch hands.

"We entered my ranch yesterday; it will take two more days to get to the valley I want the cattle in," I answered. The two ranch hands looked at each other in disbelief that Pa and I had this much land.

Two days later, we entered the valley where I wanted the cattle to be. The grass was tall in the valley, and as the cattle entered, some deer ran off. The cattle first went to the small stream and then went to graze on the grass. They seemed to take to the valley as if they knew it was home for them.

The two ranch hands rode up to my father and said, "We have brought your cattle to where you wanted them, and we want you to settle up with our wages," one of them said. "Our cabins are just over that ridge in another valley, we will settle up there," Pa replied.

Within twenty minutes, we were at my cabin, and our families came out to greet us. Of course, I immediately went into the arms of Morning Star. Morning Star was so big with a child my arms had a hard time getting around her. I was just happy to see and be with her again. As our loved one greeted us, I could see Allen's ranch hands were getting impatient, and I turned to Pa and said, "We better pay those two off and get them out of here."

As Big Tom and Miguel introduced themselves to everyone, I walked over to where the two men were and said, "I will get you your pay wait here." I piled up the cash on the table and set out two piles, more than what they had earned, and went outside with it. "Here are your wages," I said to them. They took it and started to count it, which annoyed me. They looked up at me after they counted it, and one of them said, "I think you might have shorted us."

"Either you can't figure numbers, or you're trying to pull a fast one on me." "You both have more than what you earned," I said. They both went for their pistols, seeing that I had been foolish and didn't have my rifle or pistols with me. As they drew their pistols, there was a click to the side and back of them. They both turned toward the noise, and there was a skinny redhead with his pistol cocked and ready to fire.

"James is my boss and, more importantly, my friend." "I would take it kindly if you stick those pistols back in your belt," Jack said. As Jack was talking, several other clicks were coming from my sons and the others. The two men put their pistols back into their belts and went to their horses, saddled up and left. They didn't ask for any food, and I'm not sure I would have given them any.

As they rode off, I put my arm around Jack and said, "I guess you learned some things since I've gone."

"Yes, a few things, and I presume you have forgotten a few things," he replied, referring to the fact that I was not properly armed. He was right, and I'll never make that mistake again.

In the next few days, Miguel and Big Tom were getting used to the place and teaching Jack, Zack, and my boys how to work the cattle. Zack and White Doe stayed because Morning Star was near her time. I was in the valley, helping move the cattle to a greener area when Joseph came riding over the hill like there was a Blackfoot war party chasing him. "Pa, Pa, come quick, it's Ma's time!" Joseph yelled at the top of his lungs. I didn't hesitate a second; I went at full gallop for the cabin. Zack, Miguel, Big Tom, and Jack stayed with the cattle. Joseph followed me back to the cabin.

As usual, I wasn't allowed in the cabin I tried looking in both windows, but Morning Star was in the bedroom, so all I saw was Ma and White Doe scurrying around. I paced back, and forth which amused Pa who had been watching. As time went by, everyone finally came, and I got a lot of teasing from almost everyone. It was getting darker, so, with the help of my sons, Pa started a campfire and got some food for everyone, but I wasn't interested in eating. "I don't remember it taking this long before Pa," I said.

"As I remember, Zack took a long time also," Pa replied. It was entirely dark, and one of my younger boys was dozing, and when Big Tom saw this, he picked him up and said, "You can sleep in the bunkhouse tonight," this pleased him to no end. With all my pacing and trying to peek through the windows, I finally got tired and sat next to Pa.

"It's about time you sat down, you were driving me crazy with all that pacing around," Zack said. As soon as I sat down, we all heard the wail of a baby crying. I shot up and ran to the cabin, as did everyone else but more slowly. Before I could get to the front door, Ma came out with the baby all wrapped up and placed it in my arms.

"Another boy," I said to no one.

"You better take a better look at the child, son," Ma said. I undid the blanket and looked to see if the baby was deformed or if there was another problem and not seeing anything, I looked at Ma again. She gave me a look like I was stupid or something, so I looked down again. Then I noticed that my boy was a girl, and I said in a whisper, "It's a girl." "I have a daughter!" I exclaimed a little louder.

I got to name her with a Christian name, and I decided to name her after my birth mother, Mary. Morning Star gave her the Shoshone name of Raven Spirit. I believe Morning Star gave her that name because of her shining black hair and her blue eyes.

In the days that followed, I had gone up on the ridge south of the cabin and surveyed everything I had. I couldn't have been happier, and I couldn't think of a single thing that could make my life better. As I rode down the hill, I thought how lucky I was to have met Morning Star and then the birth of our children and the adoption of the others.

# 28

# VENGEANCE IS MINE

I gathered all my family together and told them I was going to pick up supplies at Fort Bridger. I was just going to take my horse and two pack horses, and I wanted to know what they needed. Joseph and Christopher mostly wanted lead for their rifles, rope, and Joseph needed a new knife. Carl wasn't like his brothers; it was a chore to get him to work the cattle. He preferred to stay at the cabin and help his mother. He asked for things that I felt a woman would want, not the teenage boy he was. Sarah was predictable, she wanted a new doll, and if they didn't have a doll, something sweet, or maybe a ribbon for her hair. Mary was too young to want anything, but I would bring her back something anyway. Morning Star was with child again but wasn't due for some time. She gave me a list of things she wanted, also. The rest of the hands gave me a list of the items they needed. Ma and Pa heard that people were settling in the Great Salt Lake area, so they decided to look and to take Sarah with them. I figured they would be back in a day or so. Morning Star would have them when they got back.

I had decided to stop at Zack's place before traveling to the fort. When I rode up, Zack wasn't there, but White Doe was there with some of the children. "Zack should be back soon, I will fix you something to eat while you wait," White Doe said.

White Doe was a wonderful woman, but she wasn't the best of cooks. I didn't want to hurt her feelings, so I accepted. I got about halfway finished eating when Zack and one of my nephews came into the cabin. "It looks like there will be little food for Painted Horse and me," Zack said with a smile.

"You're getting fat, you don't need to be eating so much anyway," I replied with a smile.

"What brings you here?" Zack asked.

"I'm going to Fort Bridger, and I wanted to talk to you about some ideas I have," I said.

"What ideas?" asked Zack.

"I was thinking of getting all our horses that I left with Grey Wolf and bring them to our ranch," I said.

Zack thought for a minute and said, "Why do you wish to do this?"

"With the death of Morning Star's and Grey Wolf's parents, the village is getting smaller, and I think it will join another village, and it just won't be the same if you know what I mean." Again, Zack thought about it for a few seconds then said, "I know what you mean, but did you talk to Pa about it?"

"No, not yet, but I don't think he cares," I replied.

"When you want to move them, let me know, and I will help you out."

"I also was thinking of splitting the cattle and putting them on different pastures; the herd is getting very large. We have about three times the number of cattle than what we brought here. I think cattle loss will be less, and there will be more grass for them," I said.

Zack nodded in agreement and said, "Where do you want to move them?"

"I haven't decided yet," I said. "Alright, you were right about the cattle surviving here, so I assume you are right now." We talked for another hour, and then I left.

As I traveled toward Fort Bridger, I reflected on Pa and Ma and how much they have physically changed over the years. I can remember when I first saw them all those many years ago. They were not much older than I am now. They are much slower, Ma's hair is gray, and Pa's is almost white. They have a lot of wrinkles, and some of their skin hangs, but they are still healthy, and Pa is strong. However, as I think of them, I realize that there is an end to all things and all people.

By the time I came to the top of the ridge and saw the fort, it was a dark and rainy late afternoon day. Fort Bridger had a saloon that was attached to the trading post. When I entered the fort, no one was around, and I figured they were having a drink and keeping dry. I entered the trading post, and from the left of me came, "James York, get over here and have a drink with us."

"You know I don't drink Bill, but I will come over there and buy the next round if you wish," I said.

He laughed and said, "That's why I told you to come over here and have a drink." Bill was an old trapper friend of Pa's, and we had met first at one of the rendezvous when I was a child. "What's your Pa up to, James?" Bill asked.

"He went to the Great Salt Lake Valley to see if it was right about people settling there," I replied.

"It is true, James, and a strange lot of people they are," Bill replied.

"I don't remember what they call themselves, do you, Tom?"

Tom was another trapper Pa knew. He had few friends, and he was a man who had few words and liked to be left alone. "Mormons, I think," he replied.

"I've heard of those people, Pa should be back home he was due back today," I said. I didn't tell them how I knew about the Mormons. It didn't sound like they liked those people very much, and I didn't want to get into it with them.

"I don't mean any disrespect, especially after you bought us drinks, but I still think you're crazy to bring cattle up here. You haven't sold any, have you?" Bill asked.

"I don't take offense, and no, I haven't sold any. But have you noticed that the game in the mountains is getting harder to find? I believe the buffalo will be next. A lot of old trappers are shooting them for their hides from what I hear." "Besides, as more white people, like those in the Salt Valley, come they are going to want cattle, not buffalo or other game," I said.

"You're right about the game; there is still a lot of buffalo, though." "Maybe those cattle will pay off someday," Bill replied.

Just then, the blacksmith came over to us and said, "I got told to inform you that they are going to close the trading post for the night." "You better get over there and get what you need, or you must wait until tomorrow."

"I better get over there, Bill, Tom it was great to see you two again," I said as I shook their hands.

"You say hello to your father for us," Bill said.

"I'll do that," I replied. I went back to the trading post and bought my supplies and left in the rain.

After several hours, I came to an overhang, and I got off my horse and started a fire. As I was sitting next to the fire getting warm and drying off, my mind was on Morning Star and my children and the love I had for them. After I ate, I drifted off to sleep and dreamed about my family again. The next day on the trail, I started thinking about my family and was perplexed about why I couldn't get my mind off my family.

Just before noon, I rounded a mountain and stopped. A cold chill ran down my back, and I knew something was wrong. My mind went directly to Morning Star, and I took off like a shot, pulling my two pack horses. I knew if I kept up the pace I was going, I would kill the horses, but I didn't care. A feeling of dread was overcoming me. As I entered a valley, Joseph, who was hunting, spotted me and came charging toward me concerned that something was wrong.

"What's wrong, Pa?" he yelled.

I stopped and said, "Let me have your horse."

"He got off, and we exchanged horses, and I said, "Take care of the pack horses too and get everyone tending the cattle and meet me at the cabin." I didn't wait for him to answer; I took off with his horse and headed to the cabin. As I came down the hill on the opposite side of the stream that the cabin was, I could see something was wrong. At full gallop, I raced to the cabin. I was off my horse rifle in hand before the horse stopped. On the ground was my little Mary bloody and not moving. I felt her neck, but there was no pulse, and she had a hole in her chest. On the porch was Carl also bloody with a bullet in him, but he was still alive. I put a bandage on his wound to stop the bleeding. He came to for a few seconds and said, "They hurt Ma Pa," then he passed out. I looked around, and the place was a mess. I started to go into the cabin when the men and the rest of my other sons showed up. I walked into our bedroom. There was Morning Star naked, bloody and unconscious. She had cuts and burns all over her body, and it was evident that someone raped her. She opened her eyes as I was tending her, and she barely said with much difficulty, "I love you." Then she exhaled her last breath, and she was gone.

I collapsed with grief as my boys came into the room in tears. Miguel moved the boys out of the room and checked out Morning Star, but I knew it was too late. He laid a blanket over her body, grabbed my arm, and took me out of the room, and said, "Me, Big Tom, and Jack will take care of her boss," Miguel said.

Big Tom and Jack were working on Carl. There was a blanket over Mary when I went outside, and Joseph and Christopher were utterly devastated, not knowing what to do. They were worried about Carl, and although they were young men, they acted very much like young boys, crying uncontrollably. I must admit that I wasn't in much better shape. I thanked God that Sarah had gone with her Grandparents, or she would have been dead also.

Jack and Big Tom carried Carl into the spare bedroom, and then Miguel took over. I composed myself enough to ask the boys, "Where are Grandpa and Grandma?"

"They went to Uncle Zack's place with Sarah, Pa," Joseph said.

I thought about sending one of the boys after them but changed my mind and yelled, "Jack, take your horse and go to Zack's house and fetch everyone here." Without an argument, Jack got on his horse and was off. Big Tom put Mary and Morning Star in the barn and cleaned the cabin the best he could. I sat in the barn in disbelief that my little girl and Morning Star, were gone, and I just stared, as did Christopher and Joseph were still crying.

I don't know how long we sat there when we heard a lot of commotion going on outside the barn. The boys went out to investigate, but I ignored it and stayed. "It's Grandma and Grandpa with Sarah and Uncle Zack and his family," Christopher said. I didn't reply, and I don't think I heard him. I just kept staring at my beautiful wife and child in disbelief.

Pa and Zack came into the barn, and Pa put his arm around me and said, "Zack and I will bury them for you, James."

"No, I will choose the spot, and I will bury them," I said sadly without looking up.

"Alright, son, I respect that," Pa replied.

Pa left the barn, but Zack stayed and squatted next to me and growled, "Who did this thing?"

"I don't know, but when I find out who it was, they will wish they had never been born," I answered without looking up.

Zack got up and left the barn, then he got a fresh horse and headed to the Shoshone village at full gallop. "You must go and get the clothing you wish for Morning Star and Little Foot, and I must clean them up, so they can go to the Great Mystery," White Doe said from behind me. I got up, looked at her, dropped my head, and left without saying a word. As I was going, I heard White Doe start to weep as she began to clean Morning Star and Mary.

I left the barn with Pa, and my boys were at the doorway of the barn. The boys stayed there, but Pa followed me saying nothing. When I entered the cabin, Jack was in the great room, making a fire, and Big Tom left to go down to the stream to get some freshwater. I looked in on Ma, tending Carl and saw that Miguel was with her. "Will he make it?" I asked.

Ma looked up and said, "I cannot tell, but he is a strong boy, stronger than you think."

Without saying any more, I went into the other bedroom and stared at its contents. I decided to have them dress Morning Star in Shoshone clothing. Morning Star had made dresses that were bleached white and beaded for both her and Mary. They were complete with moccasins. She was going to use them for our next visit to the village. As I grabbed the items, tears seeped from my eyes. I turned around and spotted some glass beads that would look nice on them as well as some blue ribbons for their hair. I went to the barn to give the things I had collected to White Doe. I walked into the barn but didn't get far. White Doe got up and took the things I had and said, "You should wait outside."

When White Doe finished, she called me in, and I saw both lying side by side like they were sleeping. Except for a few scratches and scrapes, they both looked good, almost alive. I brought the wagon into the barn and placed Morning Star and Mary in the back of the wagon. Then I told White Doe, "I will shut the barn doors for now, so the animals don't get to them. I will prepare a place for them."

It was dark when I rode away, looking for a place for them. Ma took care of Sarah. I had brought a shovel, pick, and an ax if I needed them. There was a full moon on a cloudless night. I looked south of the cabin and stopped to stare around me. I wanted them buried somewhere that overlooked the ranch, and that you could see them from the cabin. Then I spotted the place where Morning Star and I would go to get away from everyone, and I headed for it. When I got to the area, I unloaded the horse and sent it back down below. I started a fire and just sat for a while staring out over the ranch, just like Morning Star, and I did. As I sat there, the tears started down my cheeks. The longer I sat, the more depressed I got, which caused my mind to become filled with past deaths, my mother, my Shoshone family, and now my wife and child. I sat there on the side of the mountain too numb to dig the graves; although I knew I had to do it, finally, my eyelids got heavy with sleep, and I was out.

In my sleep, I became racked with guilt that I hadn't been there to protect Morning Star and Mary. Then as I slept, suddenly, there was a bright light, so light I became blinded by the brightness of it. When, in my dream, my eyes adjusted to the light, I saw a familiar face looking over me. It was a young boy, my spirit guide, that I had seen when I was young. He said, "I have come to be with you through this night." In my dream, I nodded and lowered my eyes to Morning Star and Mary. "I told you that there would be some tragedies in your life."

I nodded again and said, "This is worse than when my mother and my Shoshone family died."

"Yes, because they died of sickness and in battle, but what happened this time was senseless, and I know what you will do," my spirit guide said.

"Will you tell me who did it?" I asked.

"You will find out soon," he replied.

There were other things we talked about, but I can't remember them now, and then I woke up with the sun coming up. I stood up and surveyed the valley, then the area. It was almost flat, and it went about ten feet back toward the hill, also another fifteen feet wide. There was a trail coming up from the valley. On the other side, it continued to go up and over the hill. There were some saplings, brush, and grass around about, so I cleared the area. As I was doing this, Ma came up the hill with some food and water. I stopped and stared at her for a few seconds, and then I went back to work.

"You must eat and drink, or you will get weak and sick."

I didn't say a word; I just kept working. It was early afternoon when Pa came up with more food and water. When he got to me, he noticed that I hadn't eaten or drunk anything. "Son, you got to eat," he said. I never answered him, I just kept working, and he went back down the hill. I was working for a short time longer when he came back, but this time he had Ma with him.

"You will eat!" "I lost my daughter-in-law and granddaughter." "I will not lose my son also," Ma said.

Pa came over and grabbed the ax out of my hand. With the motion of his head, he told me to go over and eat and drink. I ate and drank, but my heart wasn't in it. I ate in silence, and when I finished, I told Ma and Pa I wanted to be alone. Then I went back to work, and with a shovel as well as the pick, I dug a hole six feet wide and six feet long and six feet deep.

It was dark by the time I finished. Ma brought me some more food and water, and I did eat, although very little. I decided to wait and bury them when the sun came up the following morning.

The sun was high in the sky when I sat looking over the valley, dreading the knowledge that I was going to have to bury Morning Star and Mary that day. I had not left when Pa showed up with something for me to eat. As I sat there and ate, he said, "They must get buried today, James." I nodded and just stared, my depression and sorrow, being replaced with anger. When I finished eating, I got up and headed down the hill with Pa following. We didn't talk as we headed back. When we got next to the barn, my two boys, Ma with Sarah and Zack's children were, out in front of the cabin waiting for us. I didn't say anything, but my two boys joined me. I grabbed Morning Star's horse and hitched it to the wagon. There was a slight smell of decay coming from the bodies already, as I moved the wagon toward the place for their final rest. Everyone else followed us toward the hill. When I reached the bottom of the hill, I could go no further with the wagon, so I first carried Morning Star and placed her in the grave. Then I brought Mary to lie next to her mother. I decided that I would not cover them with dirt until I put some herbs on them, so they were buried with a smell that they knew. I left orders not to bury them until I came back. As I was cutting some herbs, my sons and some of Zack's children helped me. When we were about to head back with the herbs, I saw Zack, Grey Wolf, Running Deer, and some other Shoshone warriors coming at full gallop. Zack had run into them hunting as he was heading toward the Shoshone village. We all went up to the burial site where Ma was placing a blanket over Morning Star and Mary. Then we threw in the herbs and some flowers. After this, Pa read some words from the Bible. My boys and I filled in the grave with dirt.

After everyone left, it was just my boys and I holding Sarah and staring at the grave. In tears, Joseph looked up at me and said, "What are we going to do now without Ma and Mary, Pa?"

I looked at him, and everyone else and said, "We will do what your mother wanted." "She wanted for you all to grow up and be strong and healthy with large families of your own." Sarah was too confused to know what was going on. I looked down on the mound of dirt again and said, "I think it'd be good to dig up some of those flowers your mother liked I believe they are called Lupine, I believe we should plant them here." We planted the Lupine; we planted so many that you could see them from the cabin. The boys carrying Sarah finally went down to the cabin, and I was left alone at the gravesite.

I took out my knife and hawk and started sharpening both. I was figuring out what I will do to those who did this to Morning Star and Mary.

"We have found the trail of those who did this," said Grey Wolf.

I looked up, and there stood Zack, Running Deer, and Grey Wolf. I wasn't surprised at their being there; I had heard them coming up the trail.

"We must go soon if we want to get them," said Running Deer.

"Many from the village will be here soon," added Zack.

"You will not be going after them," I said. "I will be going alone, and I will kill all those animals," I added bluntly.

"She was my sister, and we all loved her," Running Deer protested.

I put my hand on Running Deer's back and said, "I understand how all of you feel, but the more that are looking for them, the easier it will be for them to find out. Then they will hide in places where we won't be able to find them. There is another problem that Tracking Fox knows very well if you go or anyone else from the village goes. Those who did this are white, they will get many whites to help them just because you are Shoshone, but with me having white skin, this will not happen," I said.

"He is right," confirmed Zack. They weren't content with what was said, but they accepted it and went down the hill.

I stayed at the gravesite and continued sharpening my knife and hawk. Then I said goodbye to Morning Star and Mary and headed down the hill toward the cabin.

Before I went through the door of the cabin, I met Ma and asked, "What is Carl's condition?"

"He is better but weak; he is a child who is not as strong as you were at his age," Ma replied.

"Has he awakened?" I asked.

Ma nodded yes and said, "He does not know about his mother or sister."

I went around her and into the bedroom where Carl was, and I knelt beside him.

"Pa, they hurt Ma and Mary," Carl said weakly.

"Yes, I know, son," I said.

"How are they doing, Pa?" Carl asked.

"Don't you worry yourself about that, you just get stronger and heal," I said sympathetically.

"That's what Grandma said," he replied.

"Carl, I need to ask you if you can tell me anything about those evil men who hurt all of you. Were they white, or were they Indians, things like that?" I asked.

"They were white Pa, and two of them were those two who helped bring the cattle here. They were looking for money or anything of value, Ma fought them, and I tried to help before they shot me. They shot Mary when she started screaming and crying and wouldn't stop. I don't know what they did to Ma except hit her," Carl said.

"Don't worry about your mother or sister, you just get better," I said. I got up and said, "I will come and see you again later; you get some rest."

When I went outside, Pa saw the anger on my face, and he asked, "How's Carl?"

"He is doing better than I thought he would, and he told me who did it," I replied.

"Who?" he asked.

By this time, everyone was gathering around us. "Those two who helped bring the cattle here," I replied.

"What are you going to do, James?" Pa asked

"Same as what you would do, kill them, kill them all," I said disgustedly. I walked to the corral and picked out my best horse. I made sure she was well watered and fed. I placed her into a stall in the barn. I proceeded to the house and cleaned my rifle and pistols. Then I got out my bow and arrows. Ma came out of Carl's bedroom, and I said, "Would you braid my feathers in my hair." She did as I asked without saying a word. I believe Ma knew what I was going to do, and she knew there was nothing she could say that would stop me.

After Ma had finished, I put a headband on. I went to my horse, braided some eagle feathers into her mane, and brought her to the cabin. I then called everyone to the cabin to talk to them. I wanted Carl to hear also, and Zack translated to Grey Wolf and Running Deer and the rest of the Shoshone. "I go to war with those who did these awful things, and I will be gone until I kill all of them, this might take some time. I will go alone; it must be this way if I am going to punish these dogs. I will take five hundred dollars, some lead, powder, and food. I want my horses that are at the Shoshone village brought here. And since there are few lodges left in the village, it would be wonderful if you would bring your lodges here, especially my brothers Grey Wolf and Running Deer.

"We will bring your horses here; we must talk to our families and think about coming here," said Grey Wolf.

"All money matters will go through Pa and Zack." "Miguel, you will remain, foreman," I said.

They all nodded in agreement.

"Pa, you be careful those men you go after will try to kill you," Christopher said.

I nodded and went into Carl's bedroom, knelt beside him, and grabbed his hand. "Ma and Mary are dead, aren't they, Pa," Carl said sadly.

I nodded yes and asked, "Did you hear me what I said about how long I'll be gone?"

"Yes."

"I want to see you up and helping out here by the time I get back, you hear me?"

"Yes, Pa, and you be careful."

I kissed Carl, got up, and said, "I love you, Carl," then I left.

"Ma, please take care of Sarah for me," I said, and she nodded yes.

"We will show you where the tracks are," Zack said. I nodded and mounted up, as did Grey Wolf and the rest of the Shoshone, then we headed to where the tracks of those murders were.

When we got to the tracks, I got off my horse and looked at them. Those murderers were also thieves; they had stolen many of my horses. I noticed my horses' tracks among those on the ground. I got back on my horse and said, "From this point on, I must go by myself." I looked at my brothers, and I could see Zack starting to tear up; to not embarrass him, I moved out with my horse not looking back.

The trail was easy to follow; they didn't even try to cover their tracks; they were traveling south, sometimes southeast. There were plenty of settlements by want to be Jim Bridgers, where they sell cheap, home-made liquor and a few trinkets. Of course, there were the bigger places like San Luis and Pueblo where they could stay a little longer. I was sure they were heading to these areas to relieve themselves of some of their plunder.

I had traveled for several hours sitting tall on my horse; I was six-foot-four, three inches taller than Pa was. I had a broader chest, and my strength was that of iron. I was a very soft, small boy when I lived in St. Louis, but I grew fast in strength and height in the Shining Mountains, I had to, or

I would have died. Both of my fathers, but mainly Grey Wolf, taught me how to fight and win. Of course, I used my intelligence and cunning to help me win most of my battles. I was a master at quickly figuring out how to use my enemy's weaknesses to my advantage and overcoming my weaknesses. This knowledge, above all, had been the primary factor in my survival.

It was getting near nightfall, and the horse and I were both tired, so I decided to make camp. As tired as I was, I knew I wasn't going to get much sleep thinking of Morning Star and my little Mary, but sometime during the darkness, I did drift off.

I was fortunate not to run into any rain. The rain clouds came on my doorstep at times when it was getting darker, but the clouds passed on, and the tracks remained. After four days, I came to a small settlement. It wasn't much of a place, just a trading post, saloon, and a corral with horses in it. I looked at the horses, and sure enough, one of them was mine. I peeked into the saloon but didn't recognize anyone, so I walked in and went to the bar. Several men were sitting at tables, drinking, and playing cards. Some of them glanced at me for a second but didn't get excited or feel threatened.

"What are you having?" asked the overweight old trapper.

"I just want information, who owns the sorrel that's in your corral?" I asked solemnly.

"Do you see that pilgrim over there dressed in black with the blue ribbon tied to his shirt?" the bartender pointed out. I didn't notice the blue ribbon when I first came in; it was Morning Stars'.

"Is he here alone?" I asked in anger.

"He had a whole passel of friends when he first came here a few days ago, but they left. Those men that he is sitting with are his friends now, I guess. What's your business with him?" asked the barkeep.

"You got a weapon behind that bar of yours?" I asked.

"I reckon I do," he replied.

"Make sure it stays there if you want to live," I said seriously.

Leaving the barkeep's mouth open, I walked over to the lowlife pilgrim. I said, "Someone told me that sorrel belongs to you," I said expressionlessly.

"What's it to you?" he smugly said, as he started to reach for his pistol.

I swung the butt end of my Hawken square in his face, breaking his nose and knocking him to the ground in a daze. One of the other three men at the table drew his pistol. Just before it cleared the table, he caught my knife in his throat, killing him. I pulled out my pistol and told the other two, "You two going to give me any trouble?"

They both backed off, and one of them said, "We don't want any trouble."

I retrieved my knife and grabbed the lowlife from the floor, and headed to the door leaving the barkeep with his mouth wide open in disbelief at what he had witnessed.

I tied up my captive outside and went to the corral for the sorrel. After latching my captive to the sorrel, we headed south. When I felt I was far enough from the settlement, I made a dry camp on some high ground. I tied the man I had captured to a tree so that he couldn't sit down. I checked my back trail and saw no one from the settlement following me. I started a fire and fixed some food. As I was eating, the lowlife became fully conscious, and he was making a lot of noise. He finally ended his foul-mouthed language and snarled, "Who are you?"

I looked at him and said, "Your executioner."

"Why? You tell me why?" he screamed.

I calmly looked up at him again and said, "I'm the husband and father of the ones you killed."

He started laughing, and I ignored him because I was about to finish my meal.

Out of frustration, he yelled, "Get it over with."

I stuck my knife in the fire, and when it turned red hot, I told my captive, "You will answer all my questions, lowlife or you will wish you had."

"I'll answer nothing," he replied stubbornly.

I got up and put the knife in front of his face and said, "No?" "Then you will die slowly and painfully." With that, I lopped off his left ear. He screamed so loud that one could hear him for miles. "Counting you, how many were there?" I asked with purpose. I had already figured there were twelve or thirteen of them, but I wanted to get him to start talking, and I thought this would be easy for him to tell me. I cut his clothing off and asked again, "How many?"

He still wouldn't answer, so I heated my knife again and touched his genitals, and he yelled out, "Thirteen."

"Give me their names," I demanded.

"Go to hell!" he replied.

I swung up with my knife and lopped off half his nose, and he yelled in pain. Again, I got my knife red hot and approached him. Before I used the knife, he said, "Ok, ok, I'll tell you anything you want." "Just don't use your knife on me again."

He told me all their names, what they looked like and where he thought they were heading. He even told me what their horses looked like and who killed Morning Star and Mary. I sat back down and started to clean my knife, "Are you going to let me go?" I told you everything you wanted, and I didn't kill that redskin wife of yours or your half-breed whelps," the captive said, starting to get a little more courage.

"I told you I was your executioner; you were there; you're just as guilty," I replied without looking up at him.

He started in with his foul language and yelling, and I finally had enough of it. I pulled out my pistol, and without looking, pointed the pistol at him and pulled the trigger. The ball went through his forehead, and he was quiet. I untied him, dragged him about a hundred and fifty yards, and left him there. I then went back to my fire, and as I was processing what I had learned, I fell asleep.

I was on the trail early the next day as I was every day. I had no pretense that my hunt was going to be easy or short, and as the days went by, my thinking came to fruition. As the days passed, the sky got cloudy, and I knew it was going to rain, but I didn't care. I knew who I was looking for and where they went. When the rains did come, I got soaked before I could find a place to get out of the storm.

The next day the rain stopped long enough for me to get back on the trail. I was still damp, but I didn't let it bother me, I kept focused on what I was doing. The rain clouds finally parted, and the heat of the day dried me off. I had traveled many days and, at last, came to the settlement of Pueblo. I looked around but didn't see any of those lowlifes. I went into the saloon and asked the barkeep if he saw those I was searching.

"I believe there were some of those fellows here a few days ago." "I think I heard them say they were heading south." "They looked like a bunch of mean troublemakers to me; I'm glad they are gone." "You seem like a decent person; why would you want to find them?" the barkeep asked.

I stared at him for a few seconds then said coldly, "When I find them, they won't be coming back." I turned and left the saloon before he could say anymore and headed toward the general store. I had in mind to get rid of the extra horse, so after I got my supplies, I asked the store owner, "Do you know of a place I can sell an extra horse I don't want anymore?"

"You can ask Bill Murray he owns the stables and corrals." "He should be there now." I headed over to the stables, and Bill Murray was inside mucking out one of the stalls. He appeared to be an ornery, older, thin man unshaved and unkempt. "Are you Bill Murray?" I asked.

He looked me up and down with what seemed to me to be an evil eye and said irritably, "What is it to you if I am?"

I never caused this man any trouble, and I felt he was putting me down. I almost turned and left, but I said in disgust, "I have an extra horse and want to sell it."

He looked me up and down again and said, "How do I know you didn't steal it."

The man was accusing me of being a thief, and I had enough of this fool. I said with irritation, "I've killed men for saying less than what you are accusing me of doing." "I wouldn't sell you this or any other horse if my life depended on it." I thought about knocking him to the ground he deserved it, but he was an old man, so I just turned and left.

As I was going, he said, "You think you're a tough guy." "You go and don't ever come back here again."

I had used all my strength to restrain my anger. I don't know why this old man was angry with me, I just wanted to sell him a horse, and I would have given him a good deal.

I continued south, thinking of the great loss of my Morning Star and my little Mary. As I thought of them, I decided I would have to lay them to rest in my mind for now. Oh, I won't completely forget my wife and child, but if I didn't put them in the back of my mind, their memory would distract me and put me in danger. For many days, I traveled south in the rain and the sun. I had gone through a few small settlements, but I was always a few days behind them; however, I was patient. I knew that sooner or later, I would catch up to them.

I ultimately came in view of a larger settlement by the name of San Luis. I checked out the town first and saw some of my horses. Also, possibly some of the horses of the men I had been looking for some time. They also had the law in this town and older, stocky man with a badge on him. I would have to deal with him first before I confronted those I wanted to kill. I decided to be honest with the deputy about what I was going to do. If he weren't cooperative, well, I would cross that bridge when I came to it.

I passed the deputy, got off my horse, and hitched the two horses to a post. The deputy came to where I was standing, and as he passed, I grabbed his arm and said, "Deputy, I would like to talk to you in private."

"What for?" he asked.

I said, "In private," as I pulled him behind the building. I explained to him what I was going to do and why.

He said, "I can understand your anger, but the law says they get a fair trial."

"I don't have time for a trial, and besides, they would kill you if you tried to take them," I said.

"Nevertheless, it's my job to keep the law here, and that's what I intend to do," he replied.

It only took one punch to the side of his head to knock him out. I dragged him away from the town; fortunately, no one saw me. I tied him up and gagged him as he was starting to come to, I said, "Understand, this has nothing to do with you, I just don't want you to get killed." "I will see you are untied when I am finished with my business here," I said to the deputy, and then I left. As usual, six of the men that I was hunting were in the saloon sitting at two tables. One of them was a ranch hand from Mr. Allen's ranch. I walked back to the stables. I told the man who owned the business there, "I'll give you five dollars in gold if you go over to the saloon." "I want you to inform the man with the red shirt on that a man is interested in buying some horses." "If he asks what I look like, tell him I'm an older, short Frenchman with brown hair." "Tell him I'm checking out the health and ages of the horses that are theirs." "When he gets up, tell him you will join him later after you have a drink." "Here is another dollar." He left with a smile on his face, and I got out my bow and several arrows. I moved to a concealed area and watched, and sure enough, it wasn't very long before two of them came out to see if I wanted to buy some horses.

"I think that mule skinner is crazy; there isn't anyone out here," said the one in the gray shirt.

"I think I will go back to that saloon and put a ball into that fool's head for sending us out here for nothing," said the guy in the red shirt. All they heard before they died was the whoosh of two arrows just before they hit their chests. I went over to them and slit their throats, then put up my bow and arrows away and headed to the saloon.

On the way to the saloon, I passed the owner of the stables and said, "I left your place a little untidy, but I will clean it up in a few minutes."

I heard him say, "Come again," but I didn't answer him and went into the saloon.

The other four were sitting together, now at the same table. I motioned the bartender to the far end of the bar. He moved without an argument, I would assume, because of the look I had on my face.

"Where are those two stupid idiots?" said the man from the Allen ranch.

"They won't be coming back, and in a few seconds, it just won't matter to you," I answered. Recognizing me, the man from the Allen ranch reached for his weapon, but he wasn't fast enough. I put a bullet between his eyes with my rifle. As I drove to the ground, I pulled out my two pistols and shot two more men. Then I pulled out my knife and flung it at the last man before he knew what was happening. I got up to reload my weapons. I did this as the rest of the people in the saloon were coming out of their hiding places. I had just finished reloading one of my pistols when one of those men, guessing I was wounded, grabbed for his pistol. As he raised his arm, I let loose with my hawk and caught him in the head. Everyone again dived for their hiding places, but they slowly came out again. I told the bartender, "You can have what they are carrying for your damages."

"Why did you kill them, if you don't mind me asking?" he said.

I stared blankly at the bartender and said, "They killed my pregnant wife and daughter and left my son for dead." I had finished reloading my weapons, then I grabbed my knife and hawk and left.

I headed back to the corrals and saw the owner staring at the two I killed.

"You can have what's in their pockets," I said. "The Appaloosa and the Paint belong to me; these two lowlifes stole them. You can have the others," I added. He nodded, and I said, "I have three horses that I want to sell, you want to buy them?" I asked.

"Where are they?" he asked.

"Two of them are the ones they took, and I'll get the third," I walked over to my other two horses and let the man look over the one I wanted to sell.

"I'll give you seventy-five dollars for all three," he said.

"Give me seventy, and I have one more thing I want you to do before I leave," I said.

He gave me seventy dollars, and I gave him a bill of sale. Then he said, "What do you want me to do?"

"Do you see those buildings over there?"

"Yep."

"Go behind them and walk about a hundred yards." "You will find a wash, and you will also locate the deputy there tied up." "Release him and tell him I'm sorry I had to tie him up, but I knew no other way, and I won't be bothering him anymore," I said.

The stable owner started chuckling and said, "I'll go right now, and you better leave before he comes looking for you."

I smiled and said, "Thanks." I got on my horse and left town heading south.

"Dan, Sarah, Johnny, what I'm about to tell you I didn't find out until I got back to my ranch, and then I guessed on a lot of it.

"Grandpa, when do you think Pa will come home?" "It's been more than two months," asked Joseph.

"I don't know I guess he will come back when he gets those men who hurt your mother and sister, and he stops hurting."

"You don't think they killed him, do you, Grandpa?" Joseph asked.

"No, I don't think so word somehow would have gotten to us if he was." "He is just will be away for some time, I would think."

Carl was up and moving around. He didn't talk much but spent most of the day at the gravesite. I'm not saying the other boys didn't go up there also; they did. But it was Carl who took care of the gravesite.

"You need to talk to Carl, he has been grieving too long," said Blue Flower to Nathaniel.

He nodded and headed up the hill toward the gravesite where Carl was. Things had changed some since I left; Grey Wolf and his family pitched their lodge on the opposite side of the stream. He and some of his children were learning to be ranch hands. Besides taking care of the cattle, there was the herd of horses now. Grey Wolf and his family preferred that over taking care of the cattle. They also preferred deer, elk, or buffalo meat over beef; to tell the truth, at times, Blue Flower and Pa also preferred it.

As Pa approached Carl, he was kneeling on the ground, talking to his mother and sister as if they were there. He put his arm around him, and tears slipped from his eyes as he leaned next to him. "I loved them a lot Grandpa, and I miss them," Carl said.

"We all do, sweetheart," his Grandpa said. My Pa usually didn't show this kind of affection with the grandkids when they are this old, but he felt Carl needed it. "We are all hurting, especially your father; it's time to let your mother and sister go and get on with your life; it's what they would want?" Pa told Carl. I don't know if what Pa said help but as brave as Carl tried to be, he completely broke down and bawled, and Pa held him closer.

As I headed south toward Santa Fe, the surroundings got more desolate, dry, and hot. I stripped down to my loincloth, which might not be so wise because it is always better to sweat than to get burned by the sun, but it sure felt good for the moment. I was getting low on water and had to find some soon. There were some low mountains to the east of me, so I headed there to find a spring or something. I went up and over the mountain ridge, and there appeared to be nothing in sight, so I headed southeast.

When I was traveling through an arroyo, I spotted some warriors from a tribe I hadn't seen before. Their clothing and looks appeared different from anything I had ever seen. I tried signing, but it seemed they didn't know sign. I tried Shoshone and Ute without any luck. Then I remembered that this was Spanish territory, so I spoke Spanish. They looked at each other and then disappeared, so I rode on. It wasn't long before these warriors came out of nowhere and were in front of me, staring. I spoke in Spanish again, "I am a Shoshone warrior, and my name is Soaring Eagle With Many Coups."

"You look like a white man to us," said one of the warriors.

"I haven't been white since I was very little; I am Shoshone."

They looked at each other and talked among themselves. "What are you doing here?" "This place is Navajo land," the warrior said.

"I am looking for some evil white men, I plan to kill them," I said.

Again, they talked among themselves and then said, "It looks like you could use some water and food."

"Yes, I could use both," I replied.

"Follow us," they said.

We went through one arroyo after another, then over some hills until came to the crest of one hill, and, looking down, I saw some dwellings next to a stream. "Are those your lodges?" I asked.

"Yes, but we call them Hogans," said one of the warriors. I ate and rested for the night with these Navajo. Their food was excellent, and we talked through the night, mostly about the Shoshone and how I became a Shoshone. They never questioned me why I wanted to kill those murderers, and I wasn't in the mood to tell them. I asked them if they saw any white men going through their lands. They said there had been many whites traveling through their lands. All in all, they treated me very well, and in the morning, they showed me the way to the settlement of Santa Fe. Santa Fe was a Spanish settlement visited by many whites. I figured they would go there first before they headed east.

I entered Santa Fe from the west; it was a dusty, desolate settlement with adobe buildings and a large church at one end. It had several canteens and a few stores and other businesses. At the end of the settlement, opposite from the church, was where the corrals were. The person who owned the place was a Spanish man who spoke no English. "Senior, give my horse some water and then feed her some corn. I don't know how long I will be," I said. I paid him and left for the mercantile for supplies.

After putting the supplies up, I went over to the cantina and talked to the barkeeper. "Senior, I am looking for six white men that would have only been here a few days."

"Did one have a scar on his face?" he asked.

"Yes, his hair is blond but darker than mine," I said. I knew the description of all those men from that first man I killed.

"Three days ago, two of those men left, then, about two hours ago, three more left. But the one with the scar is out back having fun in Carmen's casa if you know what I mean," said the barkeeper.

"I hope he paid for her services ahead of his fun," I said. I started to walk out, then stopped and said, "Did he mention what his name was when he was here?" I asked.

He thought for a minute then said, "I believe he said, Jose Marsh."

I nodded and walked out the back of the cantina. I looked around and saw a small adobe building and walked toward it. I yelled out, "Joe, Joe Marsh," then stepped to my left and pulled out my hawk.

The door to the adobe flew open, with Joe Marsh half-dressed and carrying a cocked pistol. "Who in the hell...?"

That's all he got out when my hawk hit him between his eyes. He fired off his pistol, but the shot went wild. Then the woman inside started to scream. I went over to this Joe Marsh and removed my hawk from his head. I just knew he was one of the main ones who violated Morning Star, and as I thought about this, I became enraged. I took my hawk and hacked off his head, leaving a bloody mess. I looked up at the woman who was in shock at what I had done and said, "Most people remove the head from a venomous snake." With that, I got up and walked away before the woman composed herself and said something.

"That horse needs rest, senior," said the stable owner.

"I will give her rest in a few days," I replied as I mounted my horse. I left the barn and settlement and headed east. Three of them had about a three-hour head start, but I was confident that I would catch up with them by nightfall. At least I would see their fire.

Several hours passed, and it was getting dark. I didn't think they would get as far as they got. They could have gone in a different direction, but I didn't think so. Usually, I would have stopped and rested my horse for the night, but I had decided to move on, even though it was risky. The sun was fully down, and the moon was up. I was moving slower now, walking my horse at times. As I came out of a wash, I saw the faint light of a campfire. I got as near to the fire as I could without being detected.

Three men were lying around the campfire, the ones I was looking for since I left the last town. They had no idea that I was looking for them. They were wondering where Joe Marsh was and thought he should have caught up with them by now. They then laughed and said, "Oh, he must be having fun with that senorita."

"Yeah, a lot of fun but not as much fun as we had with that feisty savage."

"Yeah, but we shouldn't have shot those two kids."

"It kind of worries me that one of those kids was white."

"Uh, let's change the subject; what got done is done."

They went back to talking about other things, and I slipped back to a safe area to decide what I was going to do next. I checked my weapons to see if I had loaded them accurately, and of course, they were. Then I headed back to their campfire. Just before I came into their sight, I cocked my rifle and yelled, "You in the camp, I'm coming in."

"Are you friendly?" one of them yelled back.

"Friend to some, but not to others," I replied.

They laughed and said, "Come on in and have a cup of coffee, Green Horn."

As I walked into the camp, I made sure I didn't look directly into the fire, and I said, "I don't drink coffee pilgrims, but I do spill blood."

When they got a look at me and heard what I said, they grabbed for their weapons, but they were too slow and partly blinded from the fire.

I shot the one on the other side of the fire square in the chest with my rifle. I fell to my left, grabbing my two pistols, and at the same time, I shot, first at the one to the left of the fire and then at the man who had his back to me when I first came in. The one on the left I shot in his throat and the other in the head. The one I shot in the head was dead, and the one I shot in the throat was bleeding a lot and fighting for air. I slammed my hawk into his skull, killing him. I went over to the one I shot in the chest; he was still alive.

"I thought you said you were friendly," he said.

"To some, but not you three," I said.

"Who are you?" he asked.

"When you kill a man's pregnant wife and child, you better kill him too," I said with disgust. I cleaned and reloaded my weapons and then put them away. Then I released the three men's horses and retrieved mine.

I was about to leave when the man I shot in the chest said, "What about me." I pulled my knife out, walked over to him, grabbed his hair, pulled it back, and slit his throat, all in one move. Then I headed east for a half hour and made a dry camp.

I got up early and headed southeast again, toward the Allen Ranch. I had decided that I would stop at the first good place with water and rest the horse and myself for three days. I had traveled about fifty miles since I left Santa Fe, through some hot, dry country, when I came upon a tree-lined stream with plenty of grass around. I, and my horse, are worn out, so I rested for the next three days.

I killed some fresh meat and regained my strength after three days of lying around. My horse and I were more than ready to move on, so we headed southeast again. I passed through some settlements where the men had passed through, so it seemed like I was on the right trail. I came to the town of Houston, which was very near the Allen Ranch, and I checked to see if anyone had seen the two men. Some had seen them but didn't have anything good to say about them. I headed for the Allen ranch early the next day. As I traveled over Allen land, I kept an eye open for the last two men but didn't see them. I rode up to Allen's ranch house, and a young woman came out. I asked her, "Is Sam Allen here?"

"No, but he should be back in a short time, I'm his niece," she said.

I got off my horse and hitched her up. I said, "I'm James York; I need to talk to him."

She stuck out her hand, which I shook, and she said, "I'm Nancy Allen."

"I'll just wait on your porch for his return if you don't mind," I said.

"No, that will be just fine," she replied.

I waited for about a half-hour to forty-five minutes, while Nancy treated me with some refreshments. Finally, Sam Allen showed up, and I got off my chair and went out to greet him. I stuck out my hand, to shake his hand, and he took it. I said, "Mr. Allen, I'm James York, I don't know if you remember me, but my Pa and I bought some cattle from you a few years back."

"I remember you; you and your Pa had some crazy idea about starting a herd way up north, how did it go?" he asked with a smile.

"Very well, the herd has increased considerably," I said.

"I'm surprised, I wouldn't think it was possible, are you here to get some more cattle?" he asked.

"No, I'm looking for two men, one of them worked for you, and I track him heading this way," I said.

"Who?" he asked.

"I think he is called Henry Miller, one of the two who helped drive the cattle north," I said.

He nodded and said, "Miller was here, but I don't know where Marsh is."

"Joe Marsh is dead," I said sternly.

"Dead, huh?" "What is your beef with those two if you don't mind me asking?"

"Those two and eleven others killed my pregnant wife and child," I answered.

He put his head down and said in a low voice, "I'm sorry to hear that."

"I fired him and the fellow who came with him two days ago."

"Do you know where they were heading?" I asked.

"I heard them say something about going north to Dallas when I paid them off."

"Thanks," I said.

"I wish I could do more for you," he said.

"Believe me; you have done plenty for me," I answered.

"Do you plan on killing them when you find them?" asked Mr. Allen.

"I've killed the other eleven, and there are just two more, killing them is my plan," I said.

"You're welcome to stay the night if you have a mind to," he said.

I thought for a few minutes and then said, "No, I appreciate your offer, but I can't rest until I get the last two, so I will move on," I replied.

He nodded and shook my hand and said, "Good luck."

I got on my horse and headed north toward Dallas. Three days later, I was going down the main street of Dallas. I was dirty and tired, and so was my horse. I headed straight for the stables to take care of my horse. She needed the rest, and she was such a good horse, I didn't want to lose her because I was pushing her too much. I didn't know that Henry Miller spotted me coming into town, and he and his partner were about to have a confrontation with me. I had just finished taking care of my horse, paid for feed, and headed for the barn door. When I stepped outside, I heard a loud boom that knocked me to the ground. Then I felt a burning sting on my shoulder. I rolled over to a nearby water trough. Another boom kicked dirt in my face, but I saw in what direction where it was coming. I pointed my rifle in that direction and waited. It wasn't long until the one on the roof popped up to take another shot, but I was ready for the man on the roof, and I fired first. I could see a red spot on his chest before he fell on his back. Just then, there was another roar from a rifle coming from another direction. There was another burning pain in my leg. I was exposed to this other person trying to kill me and didn't know where to find cover. What was worse was I was losing a lot of blood and becoming weaker. There was another boom from a different weapon, but I wasn't hit, which confused me.

"You over there don't shoot," came a voice from the same direction of the second shot. My eyes were blurry when I saw someone come over to me; then everything went black.

I woke up alone in a room sweating and dizzy; it must have been light out because I could see sunlight coming from a window. I tried getting up, but when I tried to put weight on my legs, I fell and couldn't get up again.

"You are too weak to be out of bed," said a pleasant-looking woman who came into the room and helped me back on the bed. "Now you stay there," she said.

"You're not going to get any argument from me," I replied. "Who are you?"

"I was going to ask you that, myself, I'm Becky Wagner." "My husband killed the man who was trying to kill you, my husband is the sheriff, and he brought you here."

"I'm James York."

"Mr. York, you rest for now, and I will bring you something to eat shortly," she said, then she left.

After a while, the door opened and in popped Mrs. Wagner with some food. Following her was a tall man with a large, white mustache and a rifle in his hand. "I'm Sheriff Wagner, I'd like to ask you some questions while you eat," he said.

"Alright, what do you want to know?" I said.

"Did you know who those men were who were trying to kill you?" he asked.

"I believe so, but I didn't get a good look at them," I said. "Perhaps I should tell you the whole story." "I own a large ranch up north and my family, and I live on it." "I was away on some business when thirteen men came to my ranch, and besides robbing me, they raped and killed my pregnant wife and daughter and nearly killed one of my sons." "I killed every one of them except the one you got," I explained.

"The one I shot is dead, also, but perhaps you should have let the law take care of them," he said with all seriousness.

"I am the law where I come from," I said decisively. He thought for a few moments then said, "I can't say I wouldn't have done the same, but do you have anyone around here to back your story?" he asked.

"Do you know who Sam Allen is? I asked.

"Yes, you know, Mr. Allen?" he said.

I nodded, and he said, "I'll send someone down there to check out your story while you're healing here." I nodded, and he left as I finished my meal.

I healed fast because nothing major was injured. However, it took ten days before I was strong enough to get up and dress because of the amount of blood that I had lost. I left the room and went outside to get some air, and that's where I came across Mrs. Wagner.

"I see you're feeling better, Mr. York," she said.

"Yes, I thought I would get some air and check on my horse," I replied.

"You do that, and when you get back, I will have something for you to eat," she said.

"That's very kind of you; I'll most likely be leaving soon, after I talk to your husband," I informed her. I turned around and headed for the corrals hoping the owner of the barn took good care of my horse.

After paying the bill at the stables, I brought my horse down to Wagner's home, where the sheriff and Mrs. Wagner were waiting for me. "I finally got word from Mr. Allen about you, and you check out to be alright," Sheriff Wagner said. "I see you are getting ready to leave," he added.

"Yes, I've been a burden on you and your wife long enough," I said. "I want to pay you for your troubles, here take this."

"That won't be necessary, Mr. York," Mrs. Wagner said.

"Nevertheless, I would feel better if you took it," I insisted.

"Are you going back to your ranch now that you got them all?" asked Sheriff Wagner.

"No, I'm not ready for that yet, after I pick up some supplies, I think I will just roam for a while," I said.

After I ate and said my goodbyes, I headed for the mercantile and picked up some supplies, then I headed north, thinking I would pay my respects to my birth mother.

# 29

## TIME TO PUT THE PAST IN THE PAST

I had finished sprucing up Mama's grave when I had an urge to withdraw all our money out of the bank in Saint Louis and move it north to our other bank. The feeling was so intense that I went and did just that, to the dismay of the bank manager. It took me several days to get to Springfield, Illinois, where our other bank was. The reaction of the bank manager there was quite the opposite of the one in Saint Louis. I got enough money for my needs and headed west. I had no intention of going back to the ranch for now, and I didn't know when I would, the pain was too great.

For two years, I traveled up and down the Great Plains. I avoided white people as much as possible, only staying with the Mandan and Lakota a few times. The Lakota were surprised that I would go to their village because they were enemies of the Shoshone. Still, they accepted me when I explained to them that I did not live with the Shoshone anymore. Living with the Lakota allowed me to learn their language. But I didn't care for the Lakota, to be honest, I preferred to be with the Mandan.

I didn't get in touch with any white people, but I saw plenty of them heading west in wagons. I assumed they were going to Oregon or California. I knew the various tribes would raid or attack these people to get their horses or anything they thought was of value to them. You could tell that these people were green by how some of them would wander away from the main group, especially the little ones. The way these people acted was just plain dangerous, but it was none of my business; they would have to find out the hard way.

It had started to be a very wet spring, and I was heading up north to cross over into Canada, where I hadn't been before. There were no birds in sight, and it was so quiet in the slight breeze that it gave me a relaxed feeling. I was going through some rough, volcanic country when the silence had broken by a weak moan and cry. I tried to find where the sound was coming from, but with the breeze and the sounds bouncing off the boulders, it wasn't going to be easy. The breeze was coming from the southwest, and I guessed the sound was bouncing off the boulders to the east of me, so I tried going west. The sound was not steady, but I could hear it off and on. About forty-five minutes later, I found an animal trail with fresh deer droppings on it. Shortly after that, I stopped, got off my horse, and looked on the ground. In front of me was a shoe print of a small child or a woman. I followed the footprints down the path, pulling my horse behind me. It was tricky trying to follow, or even see, the tracks. If it hadn't been for me having tracked for many years, I don't think I would have been able to see them. I had gone down a narrow opening between some large boulders. When I came out from them, I could see a large fissure on the rocky ground. The moaning cry was much louder and seemed to be coming from it. The fissure seemed unstable at its rim, and it looked like something had slipped inside. I got a rope and secured it to a smaller boulder and tested it to see if it would hold me. I then got on my stomach and crawled over to the edge. When I looked down, I saw a small, dirty boy curled up on a four-foot ledge about ten feet down. Just beyond the ledge, there was another fifty or sixty-foot drop. "Boy, can you stand up? I yelled.

"Help me," he cried.

"That's just what I'm trying to do, now stand up," I replied.

As he tried to stand, I could see his clothing had ripped by the sharp rocks. He was shaky, which meant he was either hurt or had been down there for some time, or both.

"Don't move, I'm going to lower you a rope," I said. I untied the rope, tied a loop with a slip knot on the end of it, and dropped it to the boy. "Put the rope around you and under your arms," I said.

He did as I told him, and I tightened up the rope, then crawled back and started to pull him up. It wasn't long before he popped over the top, and I said, "Crawl over to me."

He obeyed me with great difficulty, and when he was near enough, I picked him up and placed him on my horse without saying anything to him. After retrieving my rope, I hopped up on the horse behind him, and we rode out of that area. There was a small spring nearby, and I headed for it.

"Are you going to take me back to my mum?" he asked.

"I can tell from your accent that you're English." "I will get you to your parents as soon as possible," I replied. I gave him some water and some pemmican to eat until I could fix something. "What's your name?" I asked as I was making a fire.

"William Green, sir," he replied.

"I'm James York, the Earl of Worcester," I said.

"You're English, sir?" William asked.

"Yes, on my father's side," I replied.

"I thought you were an American savage," he said.

"If you are talking about the Indians, they are not savages." "Their customs are just different than yours," I replied. I took the pemmican from him and gave him some deer stew which he devoured and then I ate some myself.

"Try standing," I said. I took an assessment of William; his shirt and pants were ripped bad, and he had soiled his trousers. He had only one shoe, and it wasn't in good shape. He got scraped up in spots, and I asked, "Do you hurt anywhere?"

"No," he replied.

"You're very dirty, and you smell, and we both know why." "Your clothing is beyond repair; I'll have to get you some new clothes later." "But for now, I must give you a bath in this stream," I said. I removed his clothing and threw them in the fire. He wasn't happy about that but didn't fight me, and I said, "I know you're uncomfortable with this when I was your age, I felt the same, but you will get used to it."

I stripped to my loincloth and took him down to the stream, which was not much more than a trickle. I bathed him as best I could with the limited water. Also, I made sure the worst of his scrapes I had cleaned. He did not take very well to the coldness of the water, but he didn't fight me; in fact, he was very obedient. I was smelling kind of gamey also, so I cleaned myself up and then carried William over to the fire and wrapped him in a blanket. We talked for hours, and I found out that about three days ago, he had wandered off by himself and fallen in the crevice and couldn't get out. I figured that they had looked for him but couldn't find him, and the wagon company had to move on. I also learned that he had two sisters, one a year younger named Elizabeth, and another was two years older named Margaret. He was ten years old. He told me his father died in England and that he, his sisters and mother, came to America to start a new life. They had it rather awful in England being as poor as they were. They were heading for the Great Salt Lake with those Mormon people I had met some time back. As we talked, I noticed that William was acting kind of affectionate for the lack of words, much like Carl did. It was getting late, and William started to yawn, and to be honest, I was getting tired, so I made a bed for both of us. It wasn't long when he curled up next to me and fell asleep, as did I. I had wakened up once during the night, checked on William, who had snuggled next to me, and I fell back to sleep again.

I was awakened the next morning by large raindrops hitting my face. Still snuggled next to me was William, but he was under the blanket. "It's raining, and it's going to be a downpour, we have to find shelter," I said as William was trying to wake up. I should have known better by the way the sky looked yesterday. I knew of a small cave I had stayed in the previous winter; it was up north, but not far from here, so we headed there. There was a lot of lightning, and that got me nervous. It's not good to be out in the open when lighting is coming as close as it was now. We finally got to the cave, but we were soaked. I unloaded the horse and brought my things into the cave. The cave was too small for the horse, so I hobbled her and let her fend for herself. There was some dry wood in the cave, so I started a fire. I then stripped down to my loincloth and went outside to find some more wood to use later. I fed William, and he fell asleep laying on a blanket. When William woke, we talked some more, and he hung on every word I said. I told him of the different tribes and how they were, and I told him of some of the battles I had fought. I also asked him if he knew anything about Worcester. Other than it was in farming country, he knew little about it. He hadn't had much schooling because he had to work to help support the family when he was very young.

I decided to take him to a Lakota village to get him something to wear. It was risky, seeing that they weren't friendly, but he needed clothing, and that was the nearest place I know of to go.

It rained for almost two days, and then it stopped. I loaded up the horse and headed northeast to an area where I thought a Lakota village might be. I figured that the Lakota would find me before I found them.

William continued the habit of snuggling next to me. He stayed very near to me all the time, but I didn't mind it. "Sir, don't you think I should get wrapped up in a blanket before we enter the village?" William asked.

"Why, are you cold?" I asked, confused at what he said.

"No, sir." "With all those people we will likely run into in that village, I think I would be uncomfortable with them seeing me naked," he replied nervously.

I smiled and reflected when I had to go through the same thing. I bent down and kissed William on the cheek and said, "I had the same, uncomfortable feeling when I was your age." "You will find that in that village, most of the boys and girls wear little or no clothing." "I promise you that no one will notice that you aren't wearing anything."

William became very quiet where before he had been very talkative. This quietness went on for some time, but I didn't say anything at the time. When we stopped to rest and water the horse, William was still quiet and in deep thought. I sat him down on a log and then sat down beside him. "You seem very quiet and deep in thought." "Are you worried about having nothing on?" I asked with concern.

"No, I believe what you said." "I'm just thinking that while we go to this village, my family is getting farther away," he replied.

"Don't worry about that; we will catch up." "We can move faster and go places that those wagons can't go, which will shorten the distance between your mother and you," I said.

He put his head down, then turned his head and then looked at me with his big, light brown eyes and asked, "Why did you kiss me?"

"Why do most people kiss children in England?" I replied.

He just stared at me for a few seconds then snuggled up against me.

We remounted the horse and headed toward our destination. That night I lit a good-sized fire, I knew I was near where we wanted to go, and I hoped some Lakota would spot it. We ate and talked some more, and William seemed to want to talk about his mother a lot. When William finally got tired, instead of the usual yawning and curling up and going to sleep, he said, "I'm tired." Then he grabbed me by the neck and kissed me before lying down and shutting his eyes.

We were traveling for about three hours, and at least two of those hours, I knew the Lakota were watching us. I was within a few miles of the Missouri River when a band of six Lakota popped out in front and on the left side of William and me. Earlier, I had put William behind me, knowing something like this would happen.

Since I spoke some Lakota, I said, "I am Soaring Eagle With Many Coups I wish no trouble. I come in peace, looking for a Lakota village."

"The Shoshone are enemies of the Lakota?" he replied.

"I see you know who I am," I said.

Just then, one of the young warriors to the left of me grabbed my horse. I swung my rifle and knocked the Lakota warrior off his horse. Then I pointed the rifle at the one who was talking to me. I could feel William gripping me real tight; I figured he was scared, and I didn't blame him. The other warriors drew their bows. The one who was talking to me said with a voice that sounded like he had authority, "Put your weapons away." "What is the reason you want to go to a Lakota village?" he asked me.

"The Lakota are near where I found the boy, and I wish to trade for some clothing for him," I replied.

"Why does he need clothing?" "He looks like he is only nine seasons, and it is warm out?" he asked.

"He is white, and it is his people's custom," I replied.

"Is he one of those whites who live in those moving lodges?" he asked.

"Yes," I replied.

"These whites are stupid people they do not know how to care for their young." "They are also dangerous people, always taking, never giving, I do not trust them," he said. "Come follow us, and we will take you to our village."

I rode forward, and the one who was talking to me rode beside me. "I have heard that you have killed many Blackfoot," he said.

"I have killed many men, including white men," I answered.

"I have heard this; that is why you are still alive," he said with a large smile. "My name is Crazy Horse of the Oglala Lakota." "Someday I will be chief," he said proudly.

"I have heard of Crazy Horse," I said. What I said made him pleased that someone like me would know who he was.

About an hour and a half later, we crossed the Missouri River and into the village. We were led to a lodge and told to go in. The lodge was a typical lodge like the Shoshone's that I had seen thousands of times. There was no one in the lodge when we entered. I had William sit down, and I sat beside him. He clung to me, frightened. "Everything will be alright, you will see," I said.

"Just the same, I would rather not be here right now," he said nervously.

Just then, an old woman came in with Crazy Horse behind her. "She will make the boy's clothing." "What do you have to pay me?" Crazy Horse asked.

"Let's go to my horse, and I will show you," I said.

When I started to get up, William tried to go with me, but the old woman stopped him. "You stay here; she won't hurt you; she just wants to measure you." "I will be right back," I said.

Reluctantly he let go of me, and I went outside with Crazy Horse.

I pulled out a pistol that I had taken from one of the men I had killed a couple of years back. It was a nice pistol with engravings on it, but I liked my pistols better, so I offered it to Crazy Horse. Crazy Horse looked it over carefully, smiled, and said, "This is worth more than some boy's clothing."

"Then perhaps you can give him a knife also," I said.

He looked at the pistol then at me and nodded his head with a smile.

We went back to the lodge, and the old woman asked, "Do you want moccasins for him, he has soft feet?"

"Yes, will you make something to keep his hair out of his eyes, and Crazy Horse is giving him a knife." "Will you make something that will go around his waist to carry the knife?" I said.

She nodded yes then said, "He smells he needs a bath."

"You are right, we both need to bathe, if Crazy Horse allows it, I will wash him and myself," I said with a smile.

"He will allow this I am his mother," she said with all seriousness.

I looked at William, who was clinging to me and said, "Are you alright?"

"I'm fine now that you're back, but I was afraid when you left."

"They are just people with different ways, just like the French and English are different." It didn't look like he was buying what I was saying, so I said, "I don't think I must leave you alone anymore, so you don't have to worry."

He reached up and grabbed me around the neck as I was picking him up, and then he kissed me, and he buried his head into my chest.

We could bathe as much as we wanted. We were well-fed, but we weren't allowed to wander among the people of the village. It didn't upset William any that he couldn't mingle with others, he was still uneasy about not having anything on. After three days, the old woman came back with his clothing, and I showed him how to put them on.

There was no knife when I went to my horse. I loaded my things and then put William on the horse.

I was about to get on the horse myself when Crazy Horse approached me, "You have forgotten the boy's knife?" he said.

I took William down from the horse and handed the knife to him. He looked at it, and then, with a smile, he asked, "Is this for me?"

"Yes, and it goes right there on your hip. Or you can put it in your moccasins," I replied.

I looked at Crazy Horse and said, "Thank You."

His look completely changed, and he had a nasty scowl on his face as he stared at me and said, "I do not like white men or Shoshone." "I do not know which you are, but if I see you on our land again, I will kill you."

I didn't say anything I just put William back on the horse then got on myself, and without looking at Crazy Horse, I left.

I traveled for hours, and I knew that William was tired, but I wanted to put distance between the Lakota and us. I wouldn't have been so cautious if I had been alone, I wasn't afraid of the Lakota, but with the boy being with me I didn't want to take any chances. When it got too much for the horse, William and I got off the horse and walked. The way we were traveling went on until we came to a secure place, and it was getting dark. That night we made camp without a fire. William was so tired he fell off to sleep fast. After watching for a while and not seeing any fires or human movement, I joined William and fell asleep.

The next day we didn't push as hard as the day before. We took plenty of breaks, especially when we could get water. William was fascinated by the knife I gave him. He picked up a stick and started to carve with it, much like I used to when I was young. As the food for our night's meal was cooking, I looked over at William, singing to himself and carving on the stick. "If you continue to carve that way, you will cut yourself," I said.

He was pulling the blade toward himself instead of away. I went over to him and showed him how to carve safely and get hurt if he did it the other way.

"My mum would never let me use knives, she says they are too dangerous," William said.

"Your mother is right; they can be hazardous if you don't know what you are doing." "But, I think you have grown some since you have been out here, and a boy needs a knife to live out here," I replied. He went back to carving and singing to himself with a smile on his face.

After traveling for a couple of days, we came to the wagon trail that William's mother went down. It followed the Platte River. We crossed from one side to the other many times to shorten the distance between the wagon company and us. Many of the places we forded over, where wagons couldn't cross, but for the most part, the wagons would have to travel along the northern side of the Platte. That meant if the river went for miles in a loop, the wagons would have to go the extra miles where we didn't. We had stopped for the night when William asked, "You ever planning on marrying again?"

"Oh, I don't know; maybe, you never know what's going to happen or who you are going to meet," I replied.

"It's been some time since your wife passed." "I think it is time you start looking," he said.

I smiled and looked at him, wondering what he was up to then asked, "Do you have anyone in mind?"

"Well, it has been some time since my father died, and my mum needs a husband," he said without any trouble.

"It takes a man and a woman to like each other and then fall in love." "Then, if everything works out alright, they get married," I said.

"That will be no problem she will like you and then fall in love with you real fast, just like I did," he replied.

"You love me?" I asked doubtfully.

"Of course, and my mum will, too," he replied.

The conversation changed, and then we slept.

After a few more days of traveling, we came to a crest of a hill in the early afternoon. There was a long line of wagons, and it was William's mother's wagon company. We rode down to the lead wagon, and all the wagons stopped as we approached. A man on a horse approached us, and I said, "I'm James York, which one of your wagons is Mrs. Green's wagon?"

"I'm John Hansen; I thought you were an Indian."

"Some people would consider me a Shoshone more than a white man," I replied.

"What's your business with Mrs. Green?" he asked.

"Hello, Brother Hansen," William said as he popped his head from around me.

Mr. Hansen just stared for a few seconds in disbelief. "William, is that you?"

"Yes, sir," William replied.

"I hardly recognized you." "We all thought you were dead," Mr. Hansen said in shock.

"I'll explain later what happened, but we need to know where Mrs. Green's wagon is," I said.

"The second wagon from the end," he answered.

We rode down to the wagon as Mr. Hansen and some of the others that had heard followed. As I approached the wagon, I saw a rather good-looking woman about my age with nearly blond hair holding the reins of the wagon team. Two little girls were peering out of the front of the wagon, all wondering what was going on. "Are you Mrs. Green?" I asked.

"Yes," she said, confused.

"I have something you lost," I said.

I let William down from the horse, and Mrs. Green and the two little girls stared in shock at what they were seeing, they couldn't speak. Then the tears started to flow down Mrs. Green's face, and William said, "Hello, Mummy," as tears began flowing from his eyes.

"William!" "My God, it's my William!" she exclaimed as she cried.

I got down off my horse and helped her down, and then the two little girls, as I held the wagon team's reins, and they all embraced each other.

"I hate to break the reunion up, but we must be moving," Mr. Hansen said.

"I'm heading in the same direction." "With your and Mrs. Green's permission, I will drive her wagon," I said.

"It's alright with me." "How about you, Sister Green?" Mr. Hansen said.

"Of course, Brother Hansen, we would be honored to have him drive our team," She replied. I tied the reins of my horse to the back of the wagon. Then I helped all the Greens up into the wagon and got on myself and retrieved the reins for the team, and soon we were off.

I could hear them all talking in the back, but I wasn't listening close enough to make out what they were saying. About a half-hour went by, and Mrs. Green came out of the wagon and sat down beside me. "I want to thank you for saving William." "He told me the whole story, Brother York, and it's quite a story, he usually does not exaggerate," she said.

"Just call me James." "Why does everyone call each other brother and sister?" I asked.

"We belong to the Church of Jesus Christ of Latter-day Saints." "We believe that we are all brothers and sisters because our Father in Heaven is the father of us all," she said.

"Makes sense, I guess," I said.

"You don't have to call me sister, just call me Nancy," she said.

"We will most likely stop for the night in a couple of hours." "There is a good place to camp, plenty of water and feed for the animals," I said.

"That's good, and then I could cook you and William a good meal." "I bet you haven't had one for some time," Nancy said.

"I won't take that bet, the only food William and I had was what I cooked or what the Lakota had, and neither they nor I cook very well," I said.

"What do the American Indians eat, James?" asked Nancy.

"It varies depending on the tribe and location, but they all eat an assortment of meats that they hunt, vegetables that they can find and fruits and nuts that grow wild," I said.

"No potatoes or bread?" she asked.

"Some tribes eat a type of bread, and potatoes came from South America." "But, I don't know of any Indian using them up north here." I told her much about the various tribes, how they lived, relationships with each other. Also, how their family units were, and of course, I told her a lot about the Shoshone.

"You know a lot about these Indians, don't you?" "How did you learn so much about them?" she asked. I went silent for some time; I could see from the corner of my eye that there was a look of concern on her face. "Did I offend you, James?" she asked softly.

"No, I was just thinking of the past," I replied. I went silent again for a few seconds then continued, "When I was very young, the Shoshone adopted me." "It was a Shoshone warrior and his wife who adopted me." "I was younger than William when all that happened." "They raised me as a Shoshone, I counted coup when I was about ten, which made me a warrior, soon after I received my name, Soaring Eagle With Many Coups," I explained.

"What is a coup?" Nancy asked.

I looked at her and said, "It is a brave act." "By the time I was William's age, I had killed at least a dozen full grown-men, enemies of my people."

Nancy looked shocked, and I went on, "If I did not kill them, they would have tortured and killed me." "You should also know that by my early teens, if not younger, I was one of the most feared Shoshone, warrior there is."

She looked away, not understanding, and I asked, "Why are you shocked?" I asked. "When England went to war, didn't your people feel proud of their soldiers?" I asked.

"Yes, but they were men, not boys," she replied.

"I've read your history; there were many boys twelve and younger, not much different in the age that I was," I replied.

"It's just not the same," she said.

"What is the difference if the Shoshone are at war with Blackfeet or England is at war with the French?" She didn't say anything for a few seconds then said, "I have to think about all of this."

"You're not in England anymore; you need to adapt to the customs here." "When we get to your campsite, I won't disturb you anymore I will leave," I said.

She crawled back into the wagon, and I continued to drive the wagon team.

About forty-five minutes later, just as I predicted, we came to a stop near the river and circled the wagons. I unhitched the horses, gave them water, and placed them where the rest of the wagon company was putting their teams. By this time, William was at my side as I went up to get my horse; I told William, "I will be moving on after I water my horse."

"But I don't want you to leave," William said, crying.

"William, come over here," Nancy called, but he ignored her.

Nancy came over to William, grabbed him from behind, pulled him toward her, and said, "We have taken enough of Brother York's time, and we need to let him go." As I was about to leave, she stuck out her hand and said, "I want to thank you for everything."

I took her hand briefly and said, "Yeah," then went to water my horse. As I did, I could hear William wailing loudly.

While I was watering my horse Mr. Hansen and another man I knew, Ed Cocker, an old drunken trapper, approached me. "I want to thank you again for what you have done for the boy," Mr. Hansen said.

"Anyone would have done the same," I replied. "I would advise you to collect buffalo droppings after you leave this camp." "There won't be a lot of wood lying around." "Also, keep an eye open for the Cheyenne." "They will most likely be in this area, and they can cause trouble," I added.

"I was going to tell him about the buffalo shit, and as for those Cheyenne, you think I don't know what I am doing," Cocker said.

"No, Cocker, I don't think you know what you are doing, you're nothing but a drunk," I said in disgust.

He jumped off his horse knife drawn, but I already had my knife out before he hit the ground. "You think I am afraid of you like those no-account savages are," Cocker said viciously.

"Plenty of them dead were white men," I replied.

Before anything could happen, Mr. Hansen jumped in and said, "Enough!" "I will not have any fighting here." "Cocker, you go back to the wagon, or I will fire you now."

Cocker smiled and laughed; he said as he turned and walked off, "You're still a whelp."

"I'm sorry, Mr. Hansen, but you better watch him, or he may get you all killed," I said.

"I take no offense, Brother York." "I know he drinks too much," he replied. I hopped on my horse and headed upstream. I figured that the further I was from Cocker, the better.

"Johnny and all of you, I got the rest of what I'm going to hear from Nancy later."

"You should not have let him go, Mummy," William sobbed.

"He is a grown man William he can do as he wishes," she replied. "What's more, he has killed a lot of people; he is not good to be around," she added.

"He is a good man; he loves me, and I love him," William answered. "He told me he had to kill those people." "They were trying to kill him, or they had killed a loved one," he added. "What would you want him to do if someone wanted to kill me?"

Nancy started to think about the things I had said about adapting to this country. Also, what William said, and she had regrets at the way she treated me without getting to know me first. Nancy looked down at her crying son and didn't know what to say, but she gave it a try by saying, "Sometimes people make mistakes and I have made a big one can you ever forgive me?"

William sobbing hugged his mother and said, "I guess we all make mistakes."

The next morning, I headed west, but I hadn't traveled far when I had an urge to go back, so I acted on my urge. I decided not to go directly to the wagons but to stay my distance. I didn't want to upset William further, and I didn't want to run into Cocker. As I was traveling east, I came across a lot of Indian horse tracks about a day old. I started getting worried, so I picked up my pace. I placed my eagle feathers in my hair and put war paint on my face before I got back to the wagons. If the Cheyenne did attack, I wanted them to know I meant business. I knew I was getting near the wagon company because I heard a lot of gunfire coming from that direction.

I pulled out my bow and placed my arrows where I could get them. When the battle came into sight, I could see the people of the wagon company weren't doing very well. So, like a screaming banshee from hell, I headed straight for the wagons killing Cheyenne as I passed them. The Cheyenne were confused and shocked at the spectacle and were unable to do me harm. When I got into the compound of the wagons, there was fighting going on in there. I shot three of them with my pistols and rifle and killed another by throwing my hawk as I got off my horse.

When I spotted Nancy's wagon, I saw two Cheyenne fighting with her. William was trying to help his mother with the knife I had given him, but he got knocked down and was about to be killed until I threw my knife. It stuck in the warrior's back clear to the hilt, killing him. I threw my body against the other Cheyenne warrior, knocking him away from Nancy. As I was wrestling with him, I kicked his weapon away. Fortunately, this warrior was much smaller and weaker than I. In no time at all, I got my arm around his neck, gave his head a quick jerk to the right, and broke his neck.

"Nancy take the girls to cover, and you William protect your mother," I said quickly, joining the battle. I had reloaded my rifle and pistols when a warrior came into the compound on his horse. I dropped my rifle, pulled out my knife, jumped on the back of the horse, and slit the warrior's throat. I jumped off the horse and grabbed my rifle. The Cheyenne backed off and regrouped out of gunshot range. Instead of charging again, they stood out there, talking to each other. I grabbed my horse and went outside of the wagon compound. I went about fifteen feet and again started screaming like a banshee challenging them. The Cheyenne stared at me but did not charge me. There was much talk, and then they turned and rode away. I rode cautiously toward where they had been and saw they had indeed gone. I then removed my feathers, wiped away my paint, and headed back to the wagons.

Mr. Hansen joined me when I came into the compound, asking, "Where is Cocker, I didn't see him in the fight?"

"Under that wagon drunk," he replied as he pointed to a wagon across the compound.

Just then, William came running, jumped up, put his arms around my neck, and I pulled him up. "I knew you would come back," he said with joy.

Behind him came his two sisters and Nancy. Nancy said with humility, "I owe you dinner, will you please dine with us."

I put William down and said, "I would be happy if you want me to, but I have some business to take care of first." "William, you go with your mother, and I will join you later," I said.

I was going to thrash Cocker but, as I looked around, I saw many who were wounded, so Mr. Hansen and I dealt with the wounded first.

While the injured were being taken care of, others cleaned up the area and assessed what was needed. When Mr. Hansen and I finished with the last of the wounded, it was time to deal with Cocker, who was still drunk. I grabbed him by the leg and dragged him out from under the wagon. He got up madder than a wet hen and tried to swing his fist at me, but I easily blocked his swing and knocked him out with one punch. "What do you want to do with him?" I asked.

"Tie him up for now, and I will get some men together to decide," he said.

"I'm not part of this company, so I will leave him for you to deal with," I said.

I went over to Nancy's wagon. William was trying to start a fire; he had a little wood, so I instructed him and his sisters to gather buffalo chips that were lying in the compound. They went and did as I had told them, but the girls didn't like it. Their activity was drawing a lot of attention, but when they brought their treasures back to me, and I had added the buffalo chips to the small fire, the fire grew. Others started to do the same when they saw this. Nancy just shook her head, surprised at her three children picking up the buffalo chips and so many others, but she was also surprised at how well they burned.

"Let me get in there to cook, now that you have the fire going well," Nancy said to me as I was tending the fire.

"Be careful it is a hotter fire those chips will burn faster than wood," I said.

Margaret, being older, was helping her mother, and Elizabeth was playing with a doll. William, when he wasn't throwing a buffalo chip into the fire, he was carving with his knife. "I need to apologize to you, James I judged you wrong," Nancy said.

"Perhaps you didn't judge me incorrectly; I have killed a lot of men in my life and not only Indians," I said.

"Like whom?" she asked.

Williams' and the girls' heads popped up, and I said, "Like the ones who robbed me and killed my wife and child."

"William told me that your wife died." "I didn't know the circumstances, but it must have been devastating to you," she said.

"Yes, it was, and it's still painful, and I would imagine it will be for some time," I replied. "That's why I've been wondering all this time I've been trying to deal with it, but I think I should go back to my ranch."

"You have an estate?" she asked, surprised.

Again, the children's heads popped up. "Yes, a huge one, west of here and, I guess, another one in England in a place called Worcester," I replied, thinking it wasn't that much of a disclosure.

"Then William wasn't mistaken; you are the Earl of Worcester?" she said almost, astonished.

"Yes, my lady," I said joking and bowing.

We ate, and I explained to them how I became the Earl of Worcester.

As we were talking, Mr. Hansen approached us and said, "We decided to get rid of Cocker; his job is yours if you want it."

"Alright, but I don't wish to be paid; I'll do it for free," I said.

"It's not our way you deserve something," he said. "I have more money than you, and your people will ever see in a lifetime combined, either it's for free, or I won't do it," I said.

"You're a very stubborn man, but if you want it that way, then we will agree," he replied.

"Nancy's wagon will be the first in line, so I can continue to drive her wagon." "Have the rest of the people attach a blanket under their wagons." "As we move west, the women and children can pick up buffalo chips and throw them into the blanket. They will all have enough for a good fire when we stop," I said.

Mr. Hansen nodded and was about to turn to go when I added, "We will be moving out in about an hour." "I don't want to be here if the Cheyenne show back up with more of their friends."

When he left to inform the others, Nancy looked up to me and asked, "You think those Indians will come back?"

"With the Cheyenne, anything is possible."

We headed west with me driving Nancy's wagon in the front. We stopped late, and I instructed that the horses should not get unhitched. We would be leaving before sunrise the next morning. We had a dry camp, and I knew that we wouldn't be able to get water from the Platte River for the next two days. The camp was quiet, and it seemed that everyone ate and went to sleep early, except for the guards. This practice went on for the next two days. By the third, we had come to a stream that was a tributary to the Platte. We stopped and made camp at a good defensible place with plenty of grass and water. "We will stay here for two days to give the animals and people some rest," I told Mr. Hansen.

"I will need some men who are good shots." "I plan to go hunting to get fresh meat," I said.

"Daddy, can I go with you?" William said in earnest.

Startled, I looked at William and then at Nancy, and she said, "He loves you."

"Can he come?" I asked.

She looked down at his pleading eyes and said, "Yes, of course."

So, about an hour after we set up camp for the night, all six of us headed northwest in search of game. After several hours, we came upon some antelope tracks, not my favorite meat, but I didn't want to be searching too long. We went for a short time. I got off my horse and told everyone to get down. We followed the tracks and until we came to a rise. I told everyone to crawl to the edge. On the other side, we saw many antelopes, but we were lucky, there was also some deer. I instructed the other men to shoot the deer first, and we all chose our targets. Four deer went down along with one antelope. I looked at the person who killed the antelope. He said, "I've tasted venison before; I wanted to taste antelope."

"It's not the best of meat; it's stringy and tough but edible; I hope you enjoy it," I said. William walked beside me as we went to gut our kill, and I explained how to gut the game, and he seemed to be enjoying his time with me.

We rode double back to the wagons and loaded the game on the empty horses. I explained to Mr. Hansen that only enough meat for one meal should these people get, and the rest should be dried or jerked for use later.

William and I joined Nancy and the girls, saying, "It's a warm day, I think William and I will go downstream and bathe," I said.

"Please do you're both very dirty." "I wish the girls and I could also," she replied.

"Why don't you all come," I said.

"The girls will go, but it wouldn't be proper for a grown woman to bathe in front of a man," she said.

"Nancy, as I said before, you're not in England anymore." "You need to adapt to this country," I said. I could see Nancy was thinking about it in her mind, and then I said, "If you don't bathe, you will get sick."

"I will go with you and decide when we get there, I guess," she said.

We all walked about a mile and a half downstream, talking as we went. Elizabeth was having a hard time keeping up, so I picked her up and carried her. She put her arms around my neck, looked me in my eyes, and asked, "Are you going to be my Daddy?"

I stopped and looked at Nancy while both Margaret and William turned around and looked at both of us. Nancy raised her eyebrows and shrugged her shoulders, so I looked at Elizabeth and said, "Do you want me to be your Daddy?"

"Yes," she said then kissed me.

I looked at her and asked, "Have you talked to your mother about this?"

"Oh yes, I wouldn't have asked you if I hadn't asked Mummy first," she said.

"And what did she say?" I asked.

"She said you are handsome and would make a good daddy, but you would have to ask her first and then she would decide," Elizabeth said.

"Oh, she did, did she?" "And what do your brother and sister think about this?" I asked as we continued to walk.

"You know how I feel, Daddy," William said.

"It would feel wonderful to have a daddy again, and I feel much like William does about you," Margaret said.

I looked at Nancy and said, "You know your mother, and I must get to know each other a little more, then we will see."

We reached an area a little more than a mile from the camp. It had a sandy area and a place to dry off. I put Elizabeth down and told William to take off his clothing, and then I started to undress Elizabeth. Nancy and Margaret just stood there staring. I said to Margaret, "If you want me to be your father Margaret, then there should be no problem with you undressing." "It's only painful for a few seconds."

Slowly and reluctantly, she started to undress. I had no trouble with Elizabeth. When I finished with her, I undressed. William was already in the water, and Margaret got just about finished when I took Elizabeth by the hand, and we walked into the water. The water was only about three feet deep in the deepest area. I held onto Elizabeth and watched Margaret finish undressing. I noticed that she was starting to show signs of womanhood. I also saw Nancy staring at me, but she hadn't begun to undress. When Margaret finished undressing, she ran squealing into the water, as if to hide that she had nothing on her.

William and Elizabeth were playing together. I called them over to where I was and said, "You two take care of your sister," and I handed her over to them. I then headed toward Nancy and got out and said, "According to the children, we are supposed to be married." "Do you go into the water with your clothes on or off?" She just kept staring at me and finally said a bit confused, "What?"

"I'll start, you finish," I said and began to unfasten her dress. While she undressed, I went back into the water with the children, and then she joined us. I watched as she came in. She was a beautiful woman, at least to me. She was about a foot shorter than I with long, kind of blond, straight hair and blue eyes. She wasn't very developed up in front, much less than Morning Star was. It made me wonder how she nursed the little ones, but I liked how she looked anyway. Bathing in the stream was more play than bathing, but we all had a good time. After a half-hour of being in the water Nancy and I got out to dry, and we talked as I stroked her hair and body. We talked about various things like the ranch and how I became an earl, mostly things I already told her. Then I had an urge to kiss her, and I did, and she kissed me back. It wasn't long after that the children one by one came out of the water to dry off. Margaret laid on the opposite side of her mother from me. I put my arm around Nancy, and she snuggled next to me. It was getting late, so we all got dressed and walked back to the wagons, I carrying Elizabeth, who had fallen asleep in my arms. This bathing together would be the first of many times we would go.

The next day, everyone worked around his wagon, repairing things. There was some grumbling about not moving on. Many were anxious to get to what they called Zion, which was the Great Salt Lake. I stayed close to Nancy, and we talked a lot. Of course, when the opportunity arose, we got affectionate with each other. Later in the afternoon, Mr. Hansen came over and said, "Some of the men from the wagon company wanted to have a meeting with you."

"Alright, where do you want to meet?" I asked.

"My wagon in about ten minutes," he said.

I nodded, and he turned and left.

At the meeting, it was the usual griping; some didn't want to pick up buffalo chips, so I told them to go without a fire. Some wanted to go slower, and some faster, and no one wanted to walk outside the wagons as we traveled. I told them not to would risk losing their animals. Others didn't like my frankness; I let them know I didn't care how they felt. There were questions about what was ahead of us and if I had ever been to the Great Salt Lake, which I had. And there were questions about the various tribes we could run into; I finally asked if there were any more questions since there were none I said, "We will be moving out by dawn."

At dawn, as I said, we moved west with William at my side. Nancy and the girls were in the back of the wagon doing something. Once we had gone some little ways, the landscape leveled out quite evenly. I looked over at William and said, "I think you are old enough to learn how to drive a team of horses." "Look at how I am holding the reins with my hands and how my arms are bent." "If you want to go right, you gently pull back on the reins in your right hand, and if you want to go left, you pull gently back with the left hand. If you want to stop, you pull both hands toward you." "Do you understand?" I asked.

He nodded, and then I said, "This stick beside me is a brake to slow you down." "When you stop tie your reins to the brake, so the horses don't take off by themselves," I added. "You ready to give it a try?" I asked.

"Oh, yes, Daddy," William replied with enthusiasm.

I handed him the reins, and William reminded me how a young Shoshone looked the first time he got to ride on top of a horse. "You're doing very well; just keep them moving straight," I said, which made him feel even prouder.

"Nancy, come look at your son," I called out to her.

She poked her head out and smiled as she gazed at her son. She said, "My goodness William if I had known you knew how to drive the wagon, I would have had you do it a long time ago."

He replied with all seriousness, "I just learned mummy." I let him drive the wagon for a little more than an hour when I could see he was getting tired. I said, "Why don't you let me have those reins for now, and you can practice some more tomorrow."

He handed me the reins, and I asked, "So what did you think?"

"I liked driving the wagon a lot," he replied with a tired smile.

"You didn't get tired, did you?" I asked.

"Maybe just a little, it was my first time after all," he said.

"You did just fine, you might have some sore arms tomorrow, but that will go away with time," I said with a smile.

"I'm going to the back to rest," he said and climbed over the seat. Nancy came out and sat down beside me, and we talked about England and my life in St. Louis until the noon break.

I circled the wagons on top of a high-rise, and we took our midday break for about an hour. The horses remained hitched to the wagons. While everyone was eating and resting, I got on my horse. I told Nancy that I was going to scout for a campsite for tonight, and after the noon break, she should move the wagons west until I caught up. After I left Nancy, I told Mr. Hansen what I had told her, and I rode off.

The ground continued nearly flat and grassy. The sky was getting cloudy, and I knew we were in for some rain, but my primary concern was buffalo. I knew I was going to have to talk to these people about the buffalo. Fortunately, even though we had seen buffalo droppings, there hadn't been much to concern me. It was also fortunate that I didn't run into any tracks that were from hostile tribes. After nearly two hours, I came to a small stream, not enough water to bathe in but enough for the horses and to fill the water barrels. It would be a good place to camp for the night.

I decided to ride on, and it was a good thing I did. It wasn't long before I ran into the first significant buffalo migration path. I rode back to the wagons as fast as I could.

When I reached the wagons, the company stopped, and Mr. Hansen came out to meet with me. "Did you find a place for us to camp for the night?" he asked.

"Yes, and it's not much further to the place." "It's easy traveling, and there is a little water." "We need to talk once we get settled," I replied.

He nodded and went back to his wagon. I tied my horse to the back of Nancy's wagon, got in front, and took over the reins but not until I kissed Nancy. It took a short time to get to the campsite, we circled the wagons and settled down. I went to talk to Mr. Hansen. "We will be going through a buffalo migration path, and hopefully, there will be no buffalo." "If the buffalo are spooked, they will kill everyone in this company; there is no stopping them." "Everyone is to fix something for them to eat at lunchtime because we won't be stopping at noon." "It's not just because of the buffalo, but there will be some Indians hunting buffalo, some friendly and some not so friendly." "We will post extra guards at night starting tonight." "Everyone is to stick close to his wagon, don't let the little ones wander off," I said. "We leave at dawn tomorrow, let everyone know what I said." He nodded, and we parted, he to his wagon and me to Nancy's wagon.

The next day we headed west; most were in their wagons. We traveled for a little more than an hour, passing through the buffalo migration path without any trouble. It didn't mean that we wouldn't run into any buffalo; it meant that it was a tad safer. We traveled through the noon break like I said we ought to do. I kept my eyes open for any Indians and, of course, buffalo. It was getting late, and we needed to stop for the night. I chose a high hill with no water or grass and circled the wagons there. I instructed that we would be leaving at the same time the next day with no noon break.

"Nancy, would you mind driving the wagon for the next few days?" I asked.

"I'll do it, Daddy," William said.

"I know you would, but I need you to do something else," I replied.

"What, Daddy?" he asked.

"This area has some bad Indians, and I need you to keep watch for them." "You can't do that very well driving a wagon." "I also need you to help your sisters pick up buffalo chips so that we will have a fire tonight," I explained.

He accepted what I said, and I looked at Nancy. She said, "It will be no trouble for me to drive."

For the next few days, I scouted the area for Indians and buffalo. I saw tracks of Indians, but they were old. Once, we came to a herd of buffalo migrating south, and we had to go north for a few hours before we could cross. Some wanted to shoot the buffalo, but I was against it because it might attract some Indians. You never know when a bull buffalo would charge you, and these people were pilgrims. We had passed a few trailing buffalo, and I was scouting northwest of the wagon company when I heard a boom. I turned and headed back to the wagons as fast as I could. I saw Mr. Hansen mounting his horse with his rifle pointing at the back of the wagons, which had stopped. I followed Mr. Hansen, and we headed to where the herd was. Sure enough, a pilgrim was cleaning a buffalo cow. "What do you think you are doing?" I said.

"We need meat, so I shot one," said the pilgrim.

"You know we share everything, including meat, Brother Jeffs." "This action is a grave sin," Mr. Hansen said.

"I don't see any harm in it; now we have extra meat," he replied.

"You don't know what happened to Moses when he struck the stones too many times to get extra water?" I said.

"What's that have to do with me?" he asked angrily.

I pointed over his left shoulder, and Jeffs and Mr. Hansen looked where I was pointing. About thirty Arapaho were staring at us. Jeffs grabbed his rifle, and I pulled it out of his hand, saying, "Your rifle is empty, and you caused this trouble do you want to create some more?" I threw his rifle to the ground, then got on my horse and headed to the Arapaho. About halfway to the Arapaho, I stopped, and one of the warriors came down to meet me. "I am Soaring Eagle With Many Coups," I signed since I didn't know Arapaho.

"I am Yellow Hand, I have heard of Soaring Eagle With Many Coups," he signed back.

"These whites go to the Great Salt Lake." "They do not know the ways of the people of this land." "I told them not to hunt the buffalo, but one fool did, their people will punish him." "We look for no trouble from the Arapaho," I signed.

"These whites, they kill many buffalo and only take the hide and leave the rest to rot in the sun," he signed.

"I did not know this; it has been a long time since I have been with the Shoshone, but I did see this was to come when I was informed by my spirit guide when I was very young." "It makes me sad to know this is happening," I signed.

"With this buffalo, we will leave it for your people if you wish," I added.

"This will be good; we will not attack you, only because you ride with these whites, and we know you tell the truth," he replied.

"I will go in peace may your days be long," I signed and left.

I rode back to Mr. Hansen and Jeffs and said, "We are leaving the buffalo; get on your horses; we will go back to the wagons."

"The hell I will!" "I won't leave the buffalo I shot him, I'll keep him," Jeffs replied.

"Brother Jeffs, if you don't get on your horse right now and go back to the wagons, I will see that you excommunicated from the church," Mr. Hansen said.

"You can excommunicate me if you wish I don't care," he replied.

"I've had enough of this," I said. Then I swung the butt of my rifle, hitting Jeffs in the head and knocking him out." "I got off my horse, as did Mr. Hansen, and we both laid him on his horse." I said, "Keep him tied up for a few days, then I don't care if he comes back here."

"I'll do just that and have him excommunicated if I have my way," he replied.

I figured it was safe for me to drive the wagon. The Arapahos wouldn't attack us, and I preferred being next to Nancy; we got closer as the time went on. I didn't think something like this could happen so quickly, but I was falling in love with Nancy and, of course, the whole family. I hadn't forgotten Morning Star; she would always be in my heart, but I think if she could, she would tell me to get over it and move on.

Mr. Hanson kept Jeffs tied up for two days, and those two days he was hopping mad. Just like Mr. Hansen said, Jeffs got excommunicated from their church. Nancy told me what that meant and when they untied him, he was so angry that he said he and his family were going on by themselves. Mr. Hansen told him that it was his choice, and he left within a day, but he rejoined the company sometime later with a different attitude. I informed Mr. Hansen that the next day we would be coming to Fort Bents. He could purchase supplies there if they had the money. He informed me that few had money, and the ones that didn't would make do with what they had.

Late in the afternoon of the next day, we came to a bunch of flat-roofed, adobe buildings with Indians, mountain men, and soldiers milling around. I told Mr. Hansen, "If you have any in need of supplies, who can't pay for them make a list, and I will pay for them."

"That's mighty Godly of you, are you sure you can spare the money?" he asked.

"I have plenty of money, don't worry about that," I said.

"Then I will be back in about an hour with the list," he replied. I told Nancy, "We will be going to the trading post in about an hour." "Get the children and yourself ready and have a list of supplies you need."

She and the children were all excited, and they cleaned themselves up. In a little more than an hour, Mr. Hansen approached me with a list, and I said, "You ready to go to the trading post?"

"You want me to go, too?" he asked.

"Yes, of course, it's your list." "I'm just paying for it," I replied.

We all headed to the trading post, Nancy, at my side. There were a few others who had gone, but as Mr. Hansen said, the clear majority didn't have the money to go. "You go ahead first, Brother York," Mr. Hansen said.

"Ok," I said and handed the owner of the trading post the list of things Nancy wanted. As he was gathering the supplies, I spotted some ribbon, candy, and a fancy woman's hat. "Give me all the ribbon and candy you have and that hat," I said. I had the girls and Nancy pick out some ribbons and the children some candy for themselves. Then I gave the rest to Mr. Hansen and said, "It's always nice to get something you don't need." "Hand them out to your people," I said.

The girls were looking at some dolls, and I said, "Throw those dolls in." "Do you have a hawk?"

"We do," he said.

"Get it for me," I said.

He went into the back room, and William said, "Are you going to buy a bird, daddy?"

"No, but it is something for you," I replied.

He came out with a nice one, and I handed it to William and said, "Put it on your belt as I do."

His eyes lit up, and the trading post owner asked, "Is there anything else?"

"Do you have any rings?" I asked softly.

"What kind of rings?" he said with a loud voice.

Everyone stared at me, wanting to know what I was going to say. "The marrying kind," I replied, not being as quiet as before. I heard three little ones squealing around me.

"I think I have just what you want." "A wagon train came through here a couple of months back, and a man and his wife traded me a ring for food," he said

He handed the ring to me, and I showed it to Nancy, who tried it on and smiled. I said, "I'll take it," I said.

Nancy handed it back to me and said, "You can give it to me when you propose."

Mr. Hansen had a smile on his face when the owner of the trading post said, "Anything else?"

"Yes, whatever he has on his list," I said, pointing at Mr. Hansen. It cost me three-quarters of what I had, but it was alright with me; I could get more. We left Fort Bent the next morning and continued west.

It had been three days traveling since we left Fort Bents when William, sitting next to me, said, "Daddy, when are you going to propose to Mummy?"

"Are you asking, or is someone else asking me?" I asked.

"I am asking Daddy," he replied.

"Then I need to do some more talking to your mother about important things we need to settle, then I can propose to your mother," I said.

"When are you going to do that?" he asked.

"When I can talk to her alone," I replied. When we stopped for the night, somehow Nancy and I were left alone, and I had a good idea that William was behind the arrangement.

"Where are those children?" Nancy said to no one.

"I think William had something to do with it," I said.

"What do you mean, James?" she asked.

"He asked me when I was going to propose to you, and I told him I needed to talk to you about some matters alone first." "I think he wants to speed things up," I explained.

"Oh, and what do you want to talk about?" she asked.

"First, the children, what will my role be in their lives?" "Will you let me adopt them?" I asked.

She thought for a second then said, "They love you, especially William your role will be their father, and yes, you can adopt them if they are willing, which I would think they are," she replied.

"I don't want to replace their father, but I wish them to feel that they have one."

She put her head down and said in a sad voice, "James, my late husband was a drunk, and he was abusive." "Several times we went without food because he drank away the only money we had." "When I complained about it, he beat me." "The beatings happened not only to me but also to the children, that's why the girls were a little aloof at first until they got to know you." "Their father never gave them any of the affection they craved." "When the children and I met the Mormon Missionaries, and we decided to come to America, my husband threatened to kill us if we tried." "Fortunately, someone killed him in a pub fight over a spilled drink," she explained.

I nodded and held her and said in a soft voice, "I'm sorry you and the children had to go through all that pain."

"It's alright what else do you wish to talk about," she said, trying to change the subject.

.    "You know, even though I do tell you that I love you and the children in my heart, I will always have a love for Morning Star and my children." "I will try never to let it interfere with us, but the love is there," I said sadly, thinking of Morning Star.

"It's understandable, and I accept this; after all, you knew her since you were a child," she said understanding.

"I will take this wagon company to the Great Salt Lake, but I want to live on my ranch." "You and the children will be comfortable there; I can assure you of that," I said.

"I will live where my husband wishes to live, but I joined this church because I believe it is true, and I want the children to be in this church," she said as a matter of fact.

"That's alright with me; a person has a right to believe anything he or she wishes," I replied.

"I am hoping you will consider joining this church, also." "If you only read the Book of Mormon, I think you would join us in our faith," she said cautiously.

I looked at her uncomfortably and said, "My family got the Book of Mormon as a gift many years ago, and I have read it." "I have not only met Joseph Smith and his family; I have stayed at their home." "They are an exceptional family, and I see nothing wrong with the book." "However, the Shoshone raised me differently than you were, and I don't know if I could ever shed the beliefs I have because of this."

She knew I was uncomfortable with the conversation of religion, so she put her arm around me and asked, "Is there anything else?"

"To tell you the truth, yes, I don't know how my family, especially my children, will react when they find out we are married." "You also need to know that Morning Star was a Shoshone, and I have relatives who are Shoshone." "Some of them are living on the ranch," I said warily of how she would react.

"I knew Morning Star was an Indian by her name." "As you say, Indians are people too, so it doesn't bother me." "Your family's reaction to the children and me, I would expect them to be shocked that you married and felt awkward about me." "That would be natural, and the children and

I will feel awkward, also." "But once we get to know each other, I would think everything will smooth out," she replied.

I stared out into space thinking, and she raised her eyebrows, expecting me to say something which snapped me back into reality. "I said there isn't anything else."

I pulled out the ring and said, "Will you marry me, Nancy," I said nervously.

"Yes, James, I will marry you, but is that how you proposed to Morning Star?" she asked.

"No, I loved Morning Star from the first time I met her, and she loved me." "I had told her, as she had said to me, how much we loved each other." "We were always together; even many times at night, we would sleep together." "One day, I went to her father's lodge; I think I was ten or eleven years old." "She, as well as her whole family, was there, and I told her father that I wished to marry her then her father said what she would cost, which were many horses, but she was worth it," I explained.

"You mean you had to pay for a wife?" Nancy asked.

"This is the custom of many Indian tribes, and you must have counted coup also, coup means to have done a brave act." "This process is expected not only from the father of the bride but the future wife." "I had counted coup many times already, so that was no problem." "At the time, I did have the number of horses her father wanted, and I think he did not believe I could get them." "To make a long story short, we got married the Shoshone way," I explained.

"It seems quite young for you to marry." "Surely you didn't consummate the marriage until you were much older," Nancy said, surprised at my age.

"It was young, even for a Shoshone, but we got permission, and we did consummate the marriage, the best way we could for our age." "To be honest with you, she was more mature than I was as far as knowing how to do things." "She had to show me how to have relations with her," I said with fond memories.

She looked at me, shocked, and said, "You don't expect the children to marry and have relations as young as you did, do you?" she asked nervously.

"Of course not, what happened to me was meant for me." "My children back on the ranch were not even thinking about marriage when I left." "Most of them are men or near men by now," I said, surprised she even asked.

"Well, that's a relief, so when do you want to get married?" Nancy asked.

"I'll leave that up to you," I said.

"I'll talk to Brother Hansen to see when he can marry us," she said.

"Fine with me," I replied.

As soon as Nancy left to talk to Mr. Hansen, the children showed up with big smiles on their faces, "I guess you three heard everything," I said.

"Everything daddy," Elizabeth said, giggling as did the other two.

"Ah, go get cleaned up for dinner," I said.

While the children were gone, Nancy came back with Mr. Hansen, and Mr. Hansen said, "I understand you two want to be married."

Just then, Nancy spotted the children before she could say anything I said, "They already know they heard our whole conversation."

Nancy smiled, and I turned to Mr. Hansen. He continued, "I could marry you now, but I would rather you wait and meet with our prophet, President Brigham Young, who will marry you at the Great Salt Lake."

"Why do you want me to meet him?" I asked.

"If I'm correct, you have a large ranch, don't you?" he asked.

"Yes," I said.

"You have cattle there, maybe horses?" he asked.

"We have large herds of cattle as well as horses, and we also have a lumber mill, amongst other things," I said.

"We need all those items, Brother York," he said.

"They are for sale if we can agree on a price," I said.

"President Young will be fair with you," he said. I looked over to Nancy and asked, "Can you wait?"

"Yes," she replied.

"Then we will wait," I said to Mr. Hansen.

During the time we traveled to the Great Salt Lake, I became more and more in love with Nancy and the children, if that was possible. I told her everything about the ranch, including the gold. And I told her about all my relatives living or dead. On the way, we saw some Indians, but they never troubled us, I recognized most of them as friendly. We continued into the Salt Lake Valley, and by mid-afternoon on a sultry, cloudy day, we arrived. It was like a parade with people greeting us with songs and cheers. The people directed us to a place to camp near a stream that emptied into the Great Salt Lake. It's funny the last time I had been here there was nothing here but a few trees and brush. Now I saw a town and some farms here and there.

About two hours after we settled in, Mr. Hansen came to our wagon with a man by the name of George Cannon. "Brother York, Sister Green I want you to meet George Cannon, he is one of President Young's counselors," Mr. Hansen said.

I shook his hand and said, "It's an honor to meet you, sir."

"The pleasure is mine, Brother York, Sister Green."

"I understand you two wish to get married, and then there is some business you want to discuss with President Young," said Mr. Cannon.

"That's right, sir, the sooner, the better, I want to make us all a family, and I also want to go home as soon as possible," I said.

"President Young can marry you tomorrow and perhaps also talk to you about your business." "Would that be alright?" he said.

"That would be fine, is it alright with you, Nancy?" I said.

"Yes," she said.

"Then tomorrow it is," said Mr. Cannon as he excused himself and left.

The children were squealing with joy in anticipation of tomorrow, as was Nancy, and I must admit I was feeling quite good, also.

The next morning it was a bright and warm day. We walked upstream perhaps two miles or more to give Nancy and the family privacy as we bathed. I tried to clean my clothing the best I could. The girls dress in lovely dresses, and although we had to fight with William, his mother had him dress into a fine, black suit. Someone lent Nancy, a wedding dress, and when I saw her, she looked like an angel. Brigham Young sent a wagon for us, and we all climbed in and headed for the place in the settlement where we were to be married. Several people joined us as we went down the streets to the home of Mr. Young. When he came out to greet us, I notice he was a tall man, about ten years older than I. Mr. Young had long hair, and when he spoke, he spoke like one with authority. We shook hands and had a firm grip and a pleasant smile.

"Brother York, Sister Green, and who do we have here?" he said, referring to the children.

"This is Elizabeth, William, and Margaret." "After the wedding, I wish to adopt them as my own," I said.

"We will do that Brother York if everyone is willing," he said with enthusiasm as Nancy and the children confirmed their desires. "I thought we would have an outside Marriage to allow this vast crowd to enjoy the ceremony," he said

"It will be alright with me." "How about you, Nancy?" I said, and she nodded.

The wedding was beautiful, but if pressed, I would have preferred the Shoshone way. After the wedding, several people brought food; even the Youngs brought a cake. People also brought instruments to play music, and a party commenced. It was a lot of fun. As it was going on, Mr. Young brought Nancy, the children, and me into the house where we first signed papers of our marriage and then the adoption papers.

"I know we have business to talk about, but let's leave that until tomorrow." "You come back here, and we will talk," Mr. Young said.

"That seems appropriate to me," I said. Then we all went outside and enjoyed the party.

That night we all slept outside as a family. It was too awkward to consummate our marriage with the children there. I had no problem with it, but Nancy did so early in the morning before the children woke up, we went off alone. The experience was like the first time with Morning Star and me.

"Daddy, where did you and Mummy go?" asked William.

"Oh, we were just making each other feel good," I said.

"You could have done that here, Mummy, and we could have helped both of you," William said.

"They were having sex silly," Margaret said as a matter of fact.

William turned red, and Elizabeth started to giggle. He said, "Oh, I guess we couldn't help."

"Making love would have been a better choice of words, Margaret, and where did you get those ideas?" Nancy said, a bit alarmed.

"I don't know Mummy; I guess someone told me that's what mummies and daddies do when they get married after all I am twelve," she said.

"Why don't we change the subject." "This day is supposed to be happy," I said.

"Yes, while your daddy is gone to talk to President Young, we will clean and pack the wagon so that we can be on our way," Nancy said to the children.

I cleaned up, got on my horse, and headed over to Mr. Young's home.

"Sir, is it inconvenient for you to meet with me now?" I asked Mr. Young.

"No, no, come right in," he replied. "This is Brother Porter Rockwell," Mr. Young said.

"We know each other, President Young," Porter said.

"It's been a long time, Porter," I said as I shook his hand. He had long dark hair and a beard. He had a rough look to him, just as I remembered him.

Porter left, and Mr. Young showed me to a chair. "I understand you have a large herd of cattle and horses." "I also heard that you have a lumber mill, and you are willing to sell us some lumber," he said.

"Yes, I have those things, and they are for sale, but I want you to understand something." "I could sell them without my family discussing it, but I wish to make them part of the business deal, so there aren't any hard feelings in the family." "You will only have to deal with my father, my brothers Zack, Grey Wolf, and me." "How many are you interested in buying?" I asked.

"To start Brother York maybe about three hundred head of cattle." "That would include a bull and about seventy-five horses." "I am also in need of about a thousand board-feet of pine." "I'll write down the sizes before you leave." "And do you have any hardwood?" President Young asked.

"When I left the ranch, I didn't have any cut." "But I can have what you need in about two weeks after I start milling," I said.

"That will be just fine," he said. "Now, we don't have a lot of money to be spending because of the way we came to this valley, but we want to be fair," he said.

"You can save some money if you come to get the items yourself." "If I must bring them here, it will cost you more, but either way, we will also be fair," I said.

"Then, sir, we will come to get it ourselves," he replied.

We shook hands, and I drew him a map of how to get to the ranch.

"I would like to talk to you about one more thing if I may," said Mr. Young.

"Alright, what is it?" I replied.

"You know your wife and the children; belong to the church I belong to also." "They will be isolated at your ranch and separated from us, and they may drift away, that is a concern of mine," he said.

"My family back on the ranch have lived there most of their lives, and yet we still pray and read the bible often." "The Smiths gave the Book of

Mormon to us years ago, and whatever I read stays in my head, so I know this book very well." "I don't think I could change my beliefs that I have." "I do believe that one has a right to believe what they want." "Since my family believed in your church, I will support them in their faith, but I don't think I will convert."

"I would still feel better if you would join our church." "After all, we must consider your family, especially your children," Brigham Young said.

"Yes, you are right, but there are some things that I have trouble with, such as plural marriage, which goes against in the Book of Mormon." "The fact that in Nephi Three, it said that Christ came down and announced that he was Jesus Christ." "This passage doesn't make sense; Jesus and Christ are Greek words, and Jesus' last name wasn't Christ, and isn't the Book of Mormon translated word for word without change?" I said. "Let me answer your concerns, first, isn't it true that your Indian friends sometimes take more than one wife, and in the bible, many had more than one wife?" "Yes, you are right about Jesus' name, but the Book of Mormon is for our time and not back in their time, so Jesus used the name we would be familiar with."

"I'll tell you what; when you send someone to my ranch, send someone who can preach to my family and my hired hands." "It will give me time to think about it, and I can talk to my family about it," I replied. We shook hands and parted, and the next day we headed to the ranch in the wagon.

"Daddy, how much farther do we have to go?" asked Elizabeth.

"To tell you the truth, we reached the ranch about an hour ago, but we won't be at the house until late afternoon tomorrow," I said.

Everyone heard what I said. William and Margaret stuck their heads out of the back of the wagon. Nancy said, "Elizabeth, you come back here with your brother and sister. I want to sit by your Daddy." Elizabeth crawled back into the wagon, and Nancy came out, sat down beside me, and I kissed her. "I didn't realize you owned so much land or how beautiful it is," she said.

"I need to tell you it's not just mine; the whole family owns it," I said.

"Do you have papers for it?" she asked.

"Oh yes, I made sure of that years ago," I replied. We traveled for a few more hours, talking about where the different tribes lived.

"Where do you pick up supplies?" she asked.

"Before I left, we got supplies at Fort Bridger. However, my father has been to the settlement at the Great Salt Lake," I answered. We made a dry camp that night and went to sleep altogether. The children had a hard time falling to sleep because of the excitement of getting to their new home.

Just like I said, it was late afternoon when Pa's and my cabins came into sight. I also saw some Shoshone lodges across the stream. Pa was the first to spot us coming. "Blue Flower, Carl, Sarah, we have company!" Pa said as he grabbed his rifle. Ma and Carl went out of my cabin, rifle in hand, staring at us coming.

Then I could hear Carl say, as he ran toward me, "Pa, it's Pa!" He met me just as I passed Pa's cabin.

I stopped the wagon and got off. I hugged Carl and said, "My, have you grown!" "You look like you are two feet taller." He looked up at Nancy and the children and said, "Looks like this family has grown too Pa."

"Yes, it has," I said. "This is Nancy, and this is Margaret, William, and Elizabeth," I said, pointing to each of them.

Carl climbed up to the front of the wagon and said with a kiss on her cheek, "I'm Carl." "So, you are my new Ma, and they are my brother and sisters, welcome to the family."

I climbed back on the wagon and drove the wagon up to the cabin, thinking that had gone well. I jumped off and helped Nancy get down, and Carl helped the children down. I hugged and kissed Ma and Pa, then went over to Sarah and lifted her and said, "I'm home."

"I can see that, and who are these lovely people?" Ma asked.

I smiled and said, "This is my wife, Nancy, and our children William, Margaret, and Elizabeth." "I was married about a week ago, in the settlement next to the Great Salt Lake," I said.

"James, you can put the horses away and unload the wagon, but my daughter and grandchildren must be hungry and need to freshen up," said Ma, not taking no for an answer.

"Carl, get on a fresh horse and go get everybody," I said.

"Yes, Pa," he said, and then off he went.

"I'll give you a hand with your things," Pa said.

Sarah went into the house with Ma, and I said to Pa, "Thanks for the help there is a lot we need to talk about," I said.

"I would think there would be," replied Pa.

Pa and I put up the horses, and as I did, my eyes drifted up to where I buried Morning Star. There was a patch of flowers that shined from the hillside, and it made me feel good.

We started to unload the wagon when everyone showed up in a cloud of dust. I hugged my boys and my brothers Zack and Grey Wolf, who happened to be with the cattle. I also shook the hand of all the hired hands that were more like family. "So, where is this new Ma Pa?" asked Christopher.

"In the cabin with your Grandma with your new brother and sisters," I said.

"It seems like there are enough out here to help you, Pa. Christopher and I are going to see our new Ma and brother and sisters," said Joseph smiling. Before I could say anything, they left for the cabin, and the rest unloaded the wagon. Then the hired hands went back to the cattle, and Pa, my two brothers, and I went to the cabin to get acquainted with Nancy and my new son and daughters.

# 30

## WORCESTER

I told my family what I had been doing over the years while I was gone and that the murderers of Morning Star and Mary were all dead. I also told them about how I came across William and how I fell in love with Nancy and the children. "The day after Brigham Young married us, he wanted to talk to me about buying some cattle as well as horses and lumber."

"How much?" Pa asked.

"Three hundred head of cattle with a bull, seventy-five horses, a thousand board feet of pine and five hundred board feet of hardwood. Do we have enough animals and pine?" I asked.

"Yes, we have more than enough, and we can cut enough hardwood in less than two weeks.

"He also talked to me about joining his church," I said.

"You didn't tell me this, James," Nancy said.

"I didn't want to concern you with it until I worked it over in my mind," I replied.

"What do you wish to do, James?" Ma asked.

"I still don't know many of their beliefs are like Shoshone beliefs, so I don't know what the harm it would be, besides Nancy and the little ones belong to this church."

"You have to do it for yourself, not for us, James," Nancy said.

"This is the church that the Smiths started, and they were good folks, so if they believe in the bible, I don't see anything wrong with it," Pa said.

"I have time to think about this before I make a decision," I said.

We changed the topic of the conversation to Grey Wolf, and Zack said, "We have a bit of a surprise for you, at least Grey Wolf does."

I looked at Grey Wolf, who said, "I do not see why Zack has made a fuss over this."

"Made a fuss out of.... Wait, you spoke English, the white man's tongue," I said, shocked.

"I thought it would be best if I am to live here, I should learn to speak this way," Grey Wolf said.

The inside of the cabin hadn't changed much. No one slept in the bedrooms. Carl slept in the loft, while my other two boys slept with the hired hands. Sarah stayed with Ma and Pa, so I decided that the two girls would sleep in Morning Stars' and my old room, and Nancy and I would take the other. William would sleep in the loft with Carl, and that made him happy. I think Carl will welcome the company; Sarah wanted to stay with Ma and Pa, who she was used to now. When everyone left, and everyone was in bed, including Nancy and me, we started talking. "This is a beautiful home you have made," Nancy said.

"You like it, and what about the children?" I asked. "William sees this place as another adventure, but I just don't know about the girls I do know they all love you," Nancy replied.

As the days passed, Nancy fit in, and William was fascinated with his uncle, Grey Wolf. He would follow him around everywhere he went; I think Grey Wolf was eating it up. The girls stuck around the house a lot, and they didn't like to get dirty. They bathed at least once, if not more, every day. Margaret enjoyed the books that I had and would read to Elizabeth often. Ma tried to get them to do things outdoors, like collect herbs and greens. They did do as she said, but their heart wasn't in it. They enjoyed their one-on-one time with their mother and me. My hope was they would get used to their environment in time. Sarah concerned me; she acted like I was a stranger. Ma said it would take time for her to come around. I spent plenty of time at Morning Stars' and Mary's gravesite, and Nancy even joined me at times. The rest of the time, I was at the mill milling hardwood.

About two weeks after I came home, ten men rode up to the cabin. One was driving a large wagon, Carl grabbed his rifle, and I said, "It's alright Carl, they're friends."

"Brother York, we have come from Salt Lake to buy the items you talked to President Young about, I'm Robert Gubler.

"Pa, is he an uncle or something?" Carl asked.

"No, the people in their church call everybody brother and sister," I said.

"Why don't you all come into my home, so we can discuss business in a more relax setting?" I said.

"Brother Nelson and I would be happy to come in, but I think the rest of the men would want to see the items we wish to purchase," said Mr. Gubler.

"Carl, take these people to the mill first and then tell Grandpa to come to the cabin. Then show them where the horses are and bring them to the cattle. Tell your uncle Zack and your uncle Grey Wolf to come to the cabin, also," I said.

By this time, Nancy and the girls were standing in front of the cabin, watching what was going on. Carl got on a horse and took the men to the locations they wanted to see. Mr. Gubler and Mr. Nelson got off their horses and joined me in the cabin.

"This is Nancy and my daughters Margaret and Elizabeth," I said.

"It's a pleasure Sister York and what beautiful daughters you have," said Mr. Gubler.

"If you don't mind, I would like to wait until my Pa and brothers come." "It shouldn't take long," I said. About forty-five minutes later, Pa and my brothers showed up, and I made the introductions.

"We paid thirty-five dollars a head for the cattle; we had to pay to drive them to the ranch as well as hire men to take care of them." "I feel sixty-five dollars a head for the cattle is a fair price," I said.

"That's much too high for us, how about forty dollars a head?" "It should give you a five-dollar profit per head," Mr. Gubler said.

"Seems a little low to me, considering how much money we spent getting them up here and then taking care of them." "How about sixty dollars a head?" Pa said.

"We'll come up to forty-five dollars a head, and that will hurt," Mr. Nelson said.

I looked at both and said, "No more dickering, fifty dollars a head, or there's no deal, and that's it," I said firmly.

Mr. Gubler looked at Mr. Nelson and said, "May we go outside and talk in private."

"Sure, take all the time you need," Pa said.

"Do you think our price is too high?" Zack asked.

"No," Pa replied as they walked back in.

"We will pay your price if we may modify it a little." "We will give you five thousand in cash and credit in our stores for ten thousand to buy what you wish," Mr. Gubler said.

"Why should we do this?" "We buy our supplies from Fort Bridge," said Pa.

"I will guarantee our prices will be lower, and the quality will be better." "We also have a larger variety," replied Mr. Nelson.

"This arrangement might be good for Grey Wolf," I said.

"What do you want to do, son," Pa said.

"I think we take this deal I don't see any difference if we pay cash for supplies or get credit," I said.

"Do you two agree?" Pa asked Zack and Grey Wolf.

Zack nodded, but Grey Wolf said, "I do not understand everything that is said, but I will agree with what you say."

"What it means is that you can go to the white man's village next to the Great Salt Lake and get what you want just by asking," I said.

Grey Wolf smiled and nodded, and I added, "You put this in writing, so when we come, all we have to do is show the paper," I said to the two men.

"We will do that and now about the horses: fifty dollars a head, three thousand in credit, and the rest in cash," Mr. Gubler said.

"I think that will work, even though it is mighty cheap." "The horses are worth seventy-five dollars, if not more, back east." "I want you to understand that if you buy later, they will be much higher," Pa said. Pa looked at us, and we all nodded.

I said to Grey Wolf, "It means we can buy more at the village of the white man."

Grey Wolf nodded, and we went on talking about the lumber with Mr. Gubler. He said, "I know President Young said a thousand board-feet of pine, but we recalculated we need fifteen hundred board-feet of pine do you have enough?"

I looked at Pa, and he said, "Yes, we do."

"I was thinking fifty cents a board-foot for the pine and hardwood," said Mr. Nelson.

"No, no, fifty cents a board-foot for the pine is alright, but the hardwood is much harder to mill." "It will be seventy-five cents a board-foot for that, and we are firm on that," Pa said.

"Alright, Brother York, we will pay that price." "It is still a good deal, and we will pay you that in cash," Brother Gubler said, satisfied with the outcome. We all stood up, and Pa and my brothers were about to leave when Mr. Gubler added, "We also came to speak with you about joining our church."

I looked at Pa and my brothers and said, "Why don't you wait until tonight? I will have everyone here to listen to what you have to say." "Then everybody can decide what they want to do," I said.

"That sounds good to me," said Mr. Nelson. After this, we all went out to see what they bought.

That night the family and ranch hands gathered in front of the cabin where we built a large fire. Mr. Nelson spoke first on the history of the church, and then he gave a testimony of what he believed. Then Mr. Gubler started to talk, and to my surprise, he spoke to Grey Wolf directly. "Brother Grey Wolf, Brother Nelson, told you of the history of our church, I will tell you about the Book of Mormon." I was the only one who had read the book other than Nancy and little ones. Everything he said, I recalled and wondered why he was going over it. Grey Wolf and Ma both said, "We got raised in the customs of my people, and we will not change, but as my son has told you, one can believe what they want."

"We are disappointed, but we understand." "We still love you and will pray that someday you will change your mind."

"Do you remember that cave we entered many years ago; it is just like their beliefs?" "So, let him continue, and you can decide what you want to do."

When Mr. Gubler finished what he had to say, he gave a testimony of his beliefs, as did the rest of the men who came. When Mr. Gubler finished what he had to say, then he also gave a testimony of his beliefs, as did the rest of the men who came. Then Mr. Gubler said, "If you believe what the rest of these men and I said, do you wish to become baptized and join this church?"

I got up and said, "As for me, I will not join this church and get baptized at this time, I love my new family, but at this time I don't wish to join, you all can choose if you want to or not." At that, everyone went and rested for the night. Some talked about what these men had said as they left.

The next day about noon, I walked past Pa's cabin to the lake, and it looked like no one wanted to join this church. The people from the Salt

Lake were there, and so were Nancy and the little ones, except for William. "Where is William?" I asked Nancy.

"I don't know, most likely with your brother, I would guess."

I turned to Mr. Gubler and said, "I'm sorry; no one came to join your church."

"No, it is your and their choice."

I was about to go back to the cabin when Jack came and said, "Those men have convinced me that their beliefs are correct, and I think my mother and father would approve so I will become baptized."

Ma and Pa were watching with Sarah. No one else came, even though I felt others wanted to but decided to wait and think about it for a little longer.

The men from Salt Lake had gone, and the years passed. We had other buyers for the horses, cattle, and wood beside the Mormon Church. The Army also bought some. In my free time, I hunted for gold, and there was plenty of it. One day when I was working at the mill, Carl came running. "Pa, we have company coming."

"Who?" I asked.

"Don't know pa, but they have a girl," he replied. Sure enough, there were two men and a young lady from Salt Lake.

"Have you come to buy something?" I asked them as they got off their horses.

"No, Brother York, we do not need anything," they replied. "We have been sent by President Young to talk with you," they added.

Just then, Nancy, Ma, and the girls came back from gathering herbs and wildflowers. "These people are from the Great Salt Lake," I told Nancy and everyone else.

"Why don't you all come into the house, you must be tired and hungry," Nancy said. The girls went about playing, and Ma went back to her cabin as we sat down and got acquainted and then had some refreshments.

"Brother York, President Young wishes you to marry Martha," said Mr. Scofield. I looked at Nancy then at Martha and back again to Scofield. I stated with a smile, "Martha is beautiful but also very young, even younger than most of my sons, and I am already married to someone I love."

"As you already know, Brother York, we believe in plural marriage." "President Young wishes you as well as Martha to join in marriage," said Mr. Scofield sternly.

"You do not wish to talk to me in this tone of language; the consequences could be harsh," I replied angrily.

Nancy didn't say anything, but she wasn't happy, either, but she let me handle it. "Let's everyone calm down and talk this over, there is no need in getting upset," said Brother Sorensen trying to keep the peace.

I looked over to Martha and said, "Why do you wish her to marry me anyway when there are men who are her age and who are single?" I asked.

"Because the prophet wants you to, Brother York," said Mr. Scofield contemptuously.

"You have a death wish, mister," I said with venom.

"Bob, go sit on the chair behind me and don't say another word," said Mr. Sorensen. Unhappily, he went and sat down, grumbling to himself. Mr. Sorenson continued, "I wish to apologize to you, Brother York." "I assure you that he will be dealt with back at Salt Lake." "President Young would never have allowed this; I can assure you." "You are wrong about the men, though; there are not many among us in our faith there is the importance of being married," he said.

"She is young, don't you think?" "With all the people coming to the Great Salt Lake, there should be a young man for her," I said.

"For every man, there are twenty women." "Most men come already married to the Great Salt Lake," he replied.

"You two are talking and not considering the feelings of Martha," Nancy said concerned. We looked over at Martha, and she had her head down, and we both knew she was upset.

"I'm sorry, Sister Arnold," said Mr. Sorenson.

"As am I," I said.

"What do you want, sister?" asked Mr. Sorenson.

She lifted her head and, with a soft voice, said, "If he doesn't want to marry me, he shouldn't."

"It's not that I don't want to marry you, I just don't think it would work out or that you would be happy," I said.

She lowered her head again, and Mr. Sorenson, and I looked at each other without saying anything. Then I looked at Nancy, leaned my head backward, and closed my eyes, and then it came to me.

"You know Martha; I have four sons; three are old enough to be married." "Why don't you stay with us and see if you and they have any interest in each other," I said.

She lifted her head, smiled, and said, "That sounds like a very good idea," she said.

"Yes, that is a good idea, why didn't I think of that myself?" Mr. Sorenson said happily.

"But the prophet wants her to marry Brother York, and I will report this if he won't," Mr. Scofield said smugly.

"Shut up, Bob," Mr. Sorenson said.

"Martha, you will be welcome here." "However, Mr. Sorenson no offense to you, but I want you two to get on your horses and get off my property," I said.

They left, and I moved the girls up into the loft, which pleased them, and I gave Martha their room. As far as Carl and William, if they didn't want to sleep in the loft with their sisters, they could sleep with their brothers.

Carl was at the mill, William, Joseph, and Christopher were with the cattle. None of them knew anything about Martha yet. When they all came home to eat, I said, "You boys go to the lake and take a bath we have a guest, a female guest."

"So why do we have to take a bath for a girl, Daddy?" asked William.

Before I could say anything, his brothers grabbed him and said, "You'll know in a few years."

When they all came back from their baths, Nancy and I brought Martha out in front; I said, "Boys, this is Martha." "She will be staying with us until she finds a man to marry."

Christopher and Joseph came rushing up to her to greet her. I noticed that Carl lagged and wasn't as enthusiastic as his brothers. Of course, William wasn't interested at all, saying, "I don't see why we had to take a bath over a girl."

"William, because it is polite," said his mother.

Christopher and Joseph hung around Martha like a moth to a candle, but Carl didn't seem very interested. I got Nancy outside to talk to her about it, "Did you notice Carl?" "I know he is not as rugged as his brothers, but it concerns me that he shows no interest in Martha." "She is beautiful and pleasant, and it seems odd that he doesn't take notice," I said.

"Perhaps he just hasn't matured as fast as his brothers have," she replied.

"Normally, I would say you are right, but he seems soft makes me think he is what the French would call the Shoshone men who are like him, berdache more woman than a man," I said concerned.

"James, perhaps you should talk to him, but regardless of what he is, remember we love him," Nancy said.

"Of course," I said.

We went inside and notice Carl was sitting by himself while his two brothers were still hanging around Martha, who was eating it up. William had gone to his Uncle Grey Wolf's lodge. He and his family were teaching him the Shoshone language and ways. I sat down next to Carl and put my arm around him while Nancy busied herself. "Let's go for a walk Carl," I said.

We got up and went outside and headed for the stream. Carl was very quiet, so I asked, "Do you have something on your mind?"

"Not really, Pa," he replied.

"Not really means to me that you do have something on your mind but don't want to talk about it," I said.

"Yes, Pa," he replied shyly.

"I have noticed over the years that you do not have the same interests as your brothers, and you are not as rough," I said.

"I try to be Pa," he said cautiously.

"I also see you don't have much interest in Martha like your brother's do." "Do you prefer men over women?" "We all will love you anyway, even if you do," I said.

"I like girls, Pa; it's just Christopher and Joseph are much stronger than I as well as they're better looking." "I don't have a chance," he answered emotionally louder and with a tear in his eye.

I put my arm around him and said, "I love you, but I have never lied to you or sugar-coated anything, am I right?"

"Yes, Pa," he said much more softly.

"Then listen to me; you are very good looking." "When people are around you, they feel very comfortable to be with you." "You have a boyish look to you which is good, many girls like that and I think Martha likes that also."

"You think so, Pa?" he asked.

"Yes, and you are strong, it's a different kind of strength than your brothers have, but even if you weren't strong, it isn't the most important thing in getting a girl." "If you are interested in Martha, use your talents and what you know to get her." "Don't concern yourself with your brothers' abilities." "No matter what happens, they will love you just like your mother and me," I said.

"Alright, Pa," he said warmly.

We got up and walked back to the cabin. As we did, I said, "By the way, your sisters will be sleeping up in the loft." "You can sleep with them or your brothers," I said.

"Alright, Pa," he replied, and we went into the cabin.

We went inside, and both Joseph and Christopher were making fools of themselves around Martha. Carl walked up to her, grabbed her hand, and said, "Would you like to go for a walk?" Christopher and Joseph stood up and looked at Carl in shock. Carl kept his eyes on Martha and said, wanting his brothers to hear, "Alone."

"Yes, I would," she replied with a smile and then left with Carl.

"Why didn't we think of that?" said Christopher.

"I didn't think Carl would have the nerve to talk to her," Joseph said.

"Yeah," confirmed Christopher.

"Yep, I think everything is just going to be fine," I said as I smiled and put my hands behind my head.

A few months later, we all went to the Great Salt Lake, and Carl was married to Martha. Christopher and Joseph met their future wives. Then we all headed back to the ranch but not until Nancy, and I visited a doctor.

Nancy and I were trying to have a child without any luck, so we went to a doctor. "I cannot see anything wrong with either of you," said Doctor Williams.

"So, what do we do?" I asked.

"You two are getting older, and I imagine the work on your ranch is not the easiest line of work." "Why don't you both go somewhere where you can relax?" "I understand you can afford it," said the doctor.

"We will do that," I said.

"I must tell you one more thing because of your age; you must be very careful when you get pregnant." "You, Nancy, might die if you decide to risk it; this should be the last child you have, Nancy." "It's too dangerous to have any more, but it doesn't mean you can't adopt or have a child by another, younger woman."

What he said didn't sit right with me. He might be right, but it was the way he said it, we thanked him anyway and left. "Do you still want to have a child; I wouldn't want anything to happen to you?" I asked.

"I'm stronger than you think I will be just fine," She replied.

As we neared the ranch, it came to me where we should go to relax, England, Worcester. I told Nancy what I was thinking and told her not to say anything until I talked to Ma, Pa, and my brothers.

I sat down in Pa's cabin with both Ma and Pa and said, "As you know, Nancy has been trying to get pregnant without luck." "The doctor in Salt Lake said we should go someplace where we could relax, get away from any troubles, and be comfortable." "I was thinking of going to Worcester."

"You have to do what you think is best." "We can take care of this place." "You know that we York's are getting to be a very large family," Pa said.

"I think it is time to take possession of the estate anyway." "I believe we will take my daughters with us, maybe William, too, if he wants to go, although I doubt that he does." "The girls think this life is not for them, but they put up with it except for Sarah she who I believe doesn't want to go." "Now that Margaret and Elizabeth are older and don't care for this place, we thought we would give them a break and take them with us," I said.

"How long will you be gone?" Ma asked.

"I don't know; it could be two or three years with traveling time." "I won't leave for another year, so I can send letters to the people there, letting them know I am coming."

Nancy and I talked to William as well as the girls, as predicted Margaret and Elizabeth were thrilled. But William wanted no part of it; the family would look after him. Anyway, he spent most of his time with his uncles or grandparents. Sarah didn't want to go and said she would stay with her grandparents too; besides, she had her eye on a boy from another ranch.

The letter got sent out, and the year seemed to pass by rapidly. In the early spring, we headed east with a load of gold that had been mined and smelted. We rode into Springfield, Illinois early in the afternoon, and I went directly to the bank and deposited the gold and to withdraw a large sum of money. I also made arrangements that if I needed any more money, I could get it with a signature and a password through the mail. We just stayed in Springfield overnight, and as we had dinner, we heard the news of a possible civil war, but I didn't pay any mind to it. The next day we headed to New York to see my Uncle Daniel and to get clothing and a boat to England.

We went to Grandpas' old house in New York, where Uncle Daniel was living. He was thrilled to see us and asked us to stay in his home until we could arrange passage to England. "How's your father doing?" he asked.

"He's doing fine," I replied. I noticed that he didn't ask about Ma or Zack, and I also noticed that even though he was near Pa's age, he looked old and sickly.

The girls enjoyed the lifestyle of New York, and Nancy was just content to be with me. I didn't care for New York at all, but I put up with it. Uncle Daniel helped get us passage to England on a ship that was going to leave in a few days. He also took us shopping for proper clothing. As we were shopping, the rumor of war was a hot topic, more so here than in Springfield. Uncle Daniel was gracious during our stay with him, allowing us to leave our weapons, horses, and things in his care, and when we boarded the ship, he was there to see us off.

I had forgotten how sick I got the last time I went on a ship, and this time was no different. It took about two and a half miserable weeks to get to England, at least they were miserable for me but not Nancy or the girls, they seemed to fare a lot better. We docked at the Port of London two and a half weeks after we left New York, and I wished it could have been sooner. The plan was to spend the night in London and then make arrangements to go to Worcester and Hanbury Hall, the home of the Earl of Worcester. I thought that New York was the worst city to live in, but I was wrong, London was far worse. It had its' nice areas like New York, but it had far more dreadful areas where the poor lived. There were many more people there also, and the rich were far more arrogant than those in New York, even more than my relatives. But even the poor and those who wanted to be rich were arrogant. London made me miserable because of the people and conditions; I couldn't wait to leave London. However, I did ask Nancy and the girls, "Do you want to visit the place where you lived before, we go on to Worcester?"

There was a resounding no from all three of them, and Nancy said, "There are too many bad memories there, and everybody we knew is either dead or gone."

I arranged for a coach to take us to Worcester the next morning. People in London informed us it would take about four or five days to get there, depending on the weather. If the weather in London were any indication of how nasty weather will be, this trip to Worcester will be long. We stayed at comfortable inns as we traveled, not as nice as the place where we stayed in London, of course, but they were warm and clean. The further we were from London, the better the weather got. Also, the landscape became more rural, much more to my liking. The girls spent the time speculating what

Worcester would be like when they got there. As the countryside changed, they became more critical of the place. On the third day, I asked the driver, "Have you ever been to Worcester?"

"Several times, sir," he replied.

"What can you tell me about the place?" I asked.

"It's a very old and poor village." "Worcester has a lot of farming and livestock, but most of it belongs to the Earl Sir," he said.

"Are there a lot of people," I asked.

"It's a large community, sir," he answered.

"Did I hear you, right?" "You said most of the livestock and farming belongs to the Earl?" I asked again.

"Yes sir, are you thinking of living there, sir?" he asked.

"Yes, for a few years, maybe." "Do you know where Hanbury Hall is?" I asked.

"Yes sir, that's the home of the Earl of Worcester," he said.

"Do you know who the Earl of Worcester is?" I asked with a smile.

"I never saw him, sir, but I hear he lives overseas somewhere," he said.

"You have seen him you are speaking to him, I am James York, Earl of Worcester," I replied.

"My Lord forgive me for not knowing I am not a wise man," he said apologetically.

"There is nothing to forgive; you just didn't know." "Please don't call me Lord or Sir." "I am James, a man going home, just like you," I said, then shook his hand.

The news of Worcester didn't make my daughters happy. They were even speculating that we would be living in a barn, although I don't think they were serious. My Daughters' gloom changed when the coach rode up to Hanbury Hall. Hanbury Hall is a three-story, large mansion made of brown brick, with outbuildings in a lighter color nearly the same size. The grounds looked like a large park, like I saw in St. Louis and New York, with animals grazing on them. Nancy and the girls were ecstatic, and when several servants came out, they were speechless.

"I would assume sir; you are the Earl of Worcester?" one of the servants said.

"I am, and you are?" I asked.

"Edward Gifford, I'm the administrator of your estate, sir," he replied.

"I will want to talk to you after I settle in." "Let me introduce you to Nancy, my wife, and my daughters, Margaret, and Elizabeth." "Make arrangements for lodging and food for the driver and have someone take care of his horses," I added.

He instructed one of the other servants to take care of the driver. I shook the driver's hand, and then we all went into the house. The girls had their large bedrooms, which were very striking, and the girls were thrilled as they settled in. Nancy was ecstatic when she saw our room, which was bigger than our whole cabin. After we ate, I figured we would take a tour of the house and the estate in general. As we settled in and changed our clothing for something more comfortable, Nancy and I talked about almost everything.

About an hour after we settled in, there was a knock at our bedroom door, it was Edward. "Sir, lunch has been prepared for you, Lady York and your children," he said from the other side of the door.

"Edward, come in," I said.

He opened the door, and I said, "We need you to show us where to go."

"Yes, sir," he replied.

We followed him down the hall to gather the girls and then downstairs we went. As we went, I said, "You will be eating with us, Edward."

"Oh, no sir, that wouldn't be proper," he replied, shocked that I had asked.

"Proper or not, I still wish you to sit down at the table with us." "There is much to talk about, and I like to speak while I eat," I said as Nancy smiled.

"Yes sir," he replied, not very happy.

Edward sat down with us, but I could see he was uncomfortable, and I said, "Edward, you need to relax." "I am indeed the Earl, but I did not grow up as an aristocrat, nor have I ever had servants." "I feel my family, and I are no better than anyone in Great Britain, including you and the staff."

"Sir, may I speak frankly?" Edward asked.

"I wouldn't have it any other way," I replied.

"I know you grew up as an American, and in America, they have their customs, but you are now in Great Britain, and we have our customs." "You are a nobleman, and if you lower yourself to my level, you will find you will have a difficult time." "It is what our people are used to, and I urge you not to do this for your sake as well as your family's," he said.

Nancy grabbed my hand, I smiled at her and said to Edward, "Mr. Gifford, am I right that for years you have been taking care of everything, staff, upkeep, and the finances of this estate?" I asked.

"Yes sir," he said, wondering where I was going with this conversation.

"I'll tell you what I'm going to do, sir; I will do my best with your help to adjust to the customs of Great Briton." "As for Nancy and my daughters, who are better bread than I, I can't speak for them will that make you happy?"

"Yes, sir, it would make me very happy," he replied.

"I have only one request that in private, you will conduct yourself a little more informally."

"Yes, sir."

He started to get up when I said, "Mr. Gifford, I know what we agreed to, but I need to talk to you, so please remain seated." He sat back down, and I continued, "After lunch, I need you to assemble the staff, in here will be fine." "My family and I then wish a full tour of the estate and, in particular, this home. Then I want to meet with you privately for a full financial report of my holdings and any concerns, needs or troubles that there might be," I said.

"Yes, sir," he replied.

The staff got lined up in the dining room, and I said, "Thank you for coming; you have done an excellent job here." "If you have any concerns or needs, I wish to know about them." "Just tell Mr. Gifford, and he will tell me about them, and I will try to resolve them." "Now, are there any questions you want to ask me?"

No one said anything, so I turned to Mr. Gifford, and he dismissed the staff. Then we were taken on a tour of the estate, except for the local town and homes I discovered that I owned. I also found out that the estate was larger than I thought. We went into the main house and to the study. While Nancy and the girls went about doing something else, Mr. Gifford gave me a list of all the income per year and what the profit was after expenditures, and it was substantial. I had more wealth than all the money we had in America, ten times over. "There is something you should know, sir, the town is impoverished and run-down, as are the people in your homes, sir," Mr. Gifford said concerned.

I thought for a few seconds then said, "Tomorrow, we will go into the town." "I want to see for myself."

"Yes, sir," he replied.

The next day I had Nancy and the girls stay home and go for a ride on one of the many beautiful horses that we had, while Mr. Gifford and I took a carriage to the town. When I saw the town, it was worse than I thought. Buildings were run-down or empty, sewage in the cobblestone street, young men hanging around with nothing to do, and older men and women looking much older than what they should. I saw skinny children playing, not noticing that they were destitute, as children would. They all looked sickly and malnourished, and many of the people stared curiously at us. "The place looks like it was gasping for its last breath," I said to Mr. Gifford.

"Yes, sir, it is in horrible shape," he replied.

We stopped near the town center, and I turned to Mr. Gifford and said, "If I own this place, how did it get in such bad shape when you were taking care of it?" I asked.

"Sir, your Grandfather only authorized me to spend funds on Hanbury Hall, not anywhere else." "When you became the Earl, I didn't get any different instructions," he explained.

"Why didn't you write I would have given that authorization?" I said.

"It was my understanding that you were a woodsman, sir." "I didn't know where to send a letter," he said.

"Yes, it is hard to send mail to where my family and I live," I replied sadly. I asked, "Is there anyone here that the people look up to and listen to?"

"Except for you, sir, there is the vicar of the church." "His name is Charles Quinn," he said.

"Let's go see him," I said. Mr. Gifford told the driver where to go, and we headed to the church.

We approached the church, which was in bad condition, but it was in better shape than the rest of the buildings in the town. On the side of the church was a small house where the vicar and his wife and children lived. Mr. Gifford and I got out and knocked on his door. A woman opened the door and said, "Mr. Gifford, please come in." We sat down at a table while the woman yelled, "Charles, please come here, Mr. Gifford is here, and he has brought a gentleman."

A gangly, unshaved, slightly graying man came into the room with an apron. "It's a pleasure to see you, Mr. Gifford, and who do we have here?" he asked.

"This is Lord James York, Earl of Worcester," he replied.

Both the vicar and his wife bowed, and the vicar said, "It is an honor, sir, to have you visit this humble house."

"The pleasure is mine; Vicar Quinn, please sit down and relax." "I have some things to talk to you about," I said. "It's my understanding that

I own most of everything around here, and I am alarmed at the condition of my property as well as the people who live here."

"Yes, My Lord things are bad, the people here are impoverished," the vicar said.

"If I have your permission, I wish to speak at this Sunday's services," I said.

"You need no permission, my lord," he said.

"Good, I also want you to choose two or three other people, besides yourself." "To meet with me tonight to talk about the situation with this town at Hanbury Hall, let's say about five," I said.

"I will do that, My Lord," he replied.

"Come up with a list of needs for this town and these people," I added.

"Very well, My Lord," he said.

"We need to be going and let you get organized thank you for your hospitality, Mrs. Quinn," I said. Then Mr. Gifford and I got up and left for home.

On the way home, I turned to Mr. Gifford and asked, "How did I do?"

"You were excellent, My Lord, but the day is not over," he said with a smile.

When we got home, Nancy and the girls were still out, so I went into the library and saw what I had to read.

We had an early dinner Nancy and the girls were all excited about their day of riding. "Daddy, you should take a ride with us; it's was just wonderful," Margaret said.

"When I get time, I will do just that, but there are things I must do first," I said.

"What things, James?"

"Some people from the town will be coming here in about a half-hour to discuss how I can help the town and the people," I said.

"Is the condition of the town real poor?" she asked.

"Yes, far worse than I had thought," I replied.

"Daddy, do you believe that we can have a party sometime?" asked Margaret, apparently not listening to what I had just said.

"Yes, Daddy, a party would be such great fun," Elizabeth said with excitement.

"I will talk to Mr. Gifford about it and see what he has to say," I said.

"We will need party dresses, Daddy," said Margaret.

"Oh, yes, daddy," confirmed Elizabeth.

"I'm sure Mr. Gifford can handle all of it," I said with a smile.

While we were finishing up eating three people from the town arrived, Mr. Gifford showed them to the study until I could join them. "I'm sorry I am late, gentlemen and madam, dinner detained me," I said.

"It is entirely alright, My Lord," said Vicar Quinn. "Let me introduce everyone, this is Mrs. Bowman, she is the town midwife, and she does most of the doctoring around here." "Mr. Nils, here is our smithy, and he takes care of any sick animals." "Finally, this is Mr. Hawks, he is the miller, and his wife is a fine baker if I do say so myself."

"Please be seated," I said." "Mr. Gifford started to leave, and I said, "Please stay, Mr. Gifford, I will need your input since you have run this estate for so long."

"Yes, My Lord," he replied.

A servant came in with tea and some cookies or what Nancy and the girls would call biscuits. "I wish to transform this town and the surrounding area into something of beauty and improve the welfare of the people, which is my desire." "Where to start and how to get it done is what we need to talk about," I said as an opening statement. "When Mr. Gifford and I went into the town, I saw a lot of people just standing around." "Why weren't they working?" I asked.

"There just isn't any work, My Lord," said Vicar Quinn.

"All who want to work will have a job cleaning up and repairing the town," I said. "And why isn't there more farming or grazing of animals?" I asked again.

"The land is yours, My Lord, there is little land to farm or raise animals," said Mr. Nils.

"That is a waste of land, we will set aside areas for farming and for raising livestock, and we will take twenty percent of the profit." "The rest goes to those working the land," I said to Mr. Gifford.

"Where are the people going to get the seed and livestock, My Lord," said Vicar Quinn. I thought for a few seconds and then said, "I will purchase the livestock and seed according to what the people want." "They can pay it back slowly with their profits." "I also want to start other enterprises in the town bringing in much-needed funds." "I am concerned about the health of the people." "Why are they so sickly looking?" I asked.

"I would say, My Lord, it is because of filth, poor housing, and a lack of food and medicine," said Mrs. Bowman.

"I can assure you the filth and poor housing will be taken care of when we hire those who are unemployed," I said. I thought for a few seconds then added, "We will repair one of those empty buildings and turn it into a type of store where, if you can't pay, you can still have enough food to get you by until you can." "I will have food delivered here, also." "I think a certain percentage of food from the locals should be donated to keep the place running," I said. "Also, since you, Mrs. Bowman, do most of the healing here, I think we will expand your home, giving you a place to heal people and to store medicines that I will pay for if that is alright with you," I said.

"That would be wonderful, My Lord," she replied.

We talked for an additional hour, then I concluded by saying, "I am from America, as you may know." "Mr. Gifford is instructing my family as well as me on how we should conduct ourselves with my status in life." "My daughters wish to have a party or two sometime, and I think it would be wonderful if we could have one party in which the locals will be the guests." "How do you feel about this, Mr. Gifford?"

"As you wish, My Lord."

"I will talk more about this later, Mr. Gifford," I said.

"Yes, My Lord." They all left for their homes, and I sat down in the drawing-room with my family and asked Mr. Gifford to join us.

"Mr. Gifford, how well do you think things went tonight?" I asked.

"Very well, My Lord."

"I talked to Mr. Gifford about having a party with the local people, and I think we will do this after things get going in the town," I said to my family.

"Is it possible that we also can have a party with the nobility, or would it be a disaster because of where we came from?" I asked Mr. Gifford.

The girls were getting all excited when Mr. Gifford said, "Let me work with all of you for a period." "Then perhaps we can have the party with the local people, then I think you will do just fine, My Lord, with the nobility."

In the days leading up to Sundays' services, someone placed in town was a notice that I was going to talk to all, and the four people who had come to Hanbury Hall spread the news, also. By the time Sunday came, the Church was overflowing when my family and I walked in. Vicar Gifford gave a fine sermon and then invited me to stand up and talk to the people. "I have a desire to improve this town and the homes in my estate." "I will hire anyone who desires to work to clean up, make repairs and improvements, and maintain everything." "All supplies that are needed,

I will pay for them." "Once a building can be cleaned up and repaired, and an addition will be built to Mrs. Bowman's home to help people with medical problems." "I will buy food items for the store and sold to you at cost, and those who can't pay, no one will you turned away." "We will give you the food, and I will also buy medications so that Mrs. Bowman can help heal the sick." "I am going to let those who wish to raise crops and livestock on my holdings to do so." "I will only charge you twenty percent of your profits, and another five percent of your profits will go into the store to feed the people of the town." "I will also pay for the livestock and seed, which can be paid back slowly with your profits." "I also wish to start a school, not just for the little ones but for all who want to learn." "I wish to bring in other businesses so that money can flow into this town." "Finally, all debts owed Hanbury Hall by any of you are forgiven." "Are there any questions?" I concluded.

There was a lot of noise and excitement in the congregation, and finally, one man got up and said, "My Lord, what is the catch?" "What do you want from us for all of this?"

"There is no catch I just want your happiness and well-being," I said.

"No one does anything for free, My Lord," another man said.

"You're right by improving this town; it will increase the value of the estate and bring more people here." "Also, by improving your health and by enhancing you financially, it will make the goods which get produced on the estate sell better and for a higher price."

"When will this all start?" a lady asked.

"Today is Sunday, so it is a day of rest." "Tomorrow, if the committee could get together here at the church, if you wish to work, talk to them.

"Vicar, you and the committee can make a list of things you need and bring them to Hanbury Hall so that we can get them." "Meanwhile, use what you have here to clean up and repair the town." "You should first start on one of the empty buildings, Mrs. Bowman's home, the general cleanup of the town, and the church, then the most in need." "Vicar, find out who wishes to farm and graze animals on Hanbury Hall land and have them come up to Hanbury Hall," I said.

The people seemed happy and satisfied, and after the services, my family and I went home.

"Mr. Gifford, could you find a map of my estate or have one drawn?" "It doesn't have to be perfect or large, but I want it to show the location of all buildings, roads, and streams?" I asked.

"Yes, My Lord," he replied.

"I need it done as quickly as possible," I added.

"Yes, My Lord," he replied again.

About a half-hour later, he came back with a map of the estate that he had found in the library. I unrolled and reviewed it, pointing to certain areas. I asked Mr. Gifford, "Is the land here and here good enough to farm or graze animals?"

"My Lord, I know nothing about agriculture."

"Is there anyone on the staff who does?" I asked him.

"Perhaps the stable master, My Lord, I believe his father was a farmer," he replied.

"Good, send someone for him," I said.

"Very well, My Lord," he replied and left the room.

About twenty minutes later, both were back, and we were bent over a table looking at the map. "Are the areas here and here good for farming and grazing of animals?" I asked the stable master, pointing to the two areas that I asked Mr. Gifford about.

"Yes, My Lord, this area here with the pond would be best for livestock. I know this area over here across the road would be best for farming. My grandfather used to farm this area, which produced abundant crops," said the stable master.

"Very well, thank you for your help; you may go back to what you were doing," I said.

"It's been my pleasure, My Lord," he said, then left.

"I plan to go horseback riding tomorrow." "If the vicar sends someone up here, show them the areas we have chosen." "Then make the list of what they will need," I said to Mr. Gifford.

"Yes, My Lord."

Late the next morning, I asked Nancy and the girls if they wanted to go riding, but they were having dresses made, and it was going to take most of the day. No one came to the Hall about making use of the land that I had designated. But I was confident that Mr. Gifford could handle it if someone came while I was out riding. The kitchen help packed me a large lunch just in case I got hungry. I decided to wear my buckskins and, even though I left most of my weapons with my uncle in New York, I did have my knife. I felt kind of naked with nothing else and would have to rectify that soon. The stable master gave me a beautiful thoroughbred horse, much taller, and faster than the Mustang that I was used to riding. Still,

I would put some of my Mustangs against this horse any day. I thought I would ride in a circle surveying the land, which was extensive. After about two hours, I had gone through a lot of open fields, meadows, and wooded areas. It was very different from the Shining Mountains.

I finally stopped by a stream to eat, even though I wasn't very hungry. I thought it would be a shame to waste food. As I got the food, I heard a voice coming from upstream, so I put the food back and remounted my horse to investigate who it was. I traveled little ways and saw two small boys about nine and eleven years of age, fishing, and from their looks, they had to be brothers. They looked very skinny and dirty with long brown hair. As I rode up to them and got off my horse, they looked scared, and I said, "Have you boys had any luck catching anything?"

Without saying anything, they both nodded their heads yes.

I was surprised that they could catch anything with what they had. "Do you two know who I am?" I asked.

Both, nearly in tears, nodded their heads yes. Then the oldest one, half crying, said, "We didn't mean any harm, My Lord."

"There is no reason to be afraid I am not angry with either of you," I said. "Why are you fishing here?"

"Because we are hungry, My Lord," the little one said.

"Let me see what you have caught and what you are fishing with," I said.

They showed me three trout, which amazed me. I had the boys sit on the ground, went and got the food prepared for me, gave most of it to them, and ate the rest myself. They were surprised that I did this and hesitated to eat it but only for a few seconds before devouring what I had given them.

"Thank you, My Lord," they both said almost at the same time.

"You boys can come here anytime you want to fish without getting into trouble," I said.

They both smiled and said, "Thank you, My Lord."

I noticed that they were sticking some of the food in their clothing, and I asked them why. The boys indicated that they had other brothers and a sister who were also hungry. "Do you two have any pockets in that clothing you have?" I asked.

"Yes," they said as they showed me. I pulled out two five-pound notes and gave each of them one and said, "That should feed your family for a while." "You two boys come by Hanbury Hall tomorrow, and I will give you proper fishing equipment." "I have to leave now," I added.

"Thank you, My Lord," they both said as I left.

I rode into the town toward Vicar Quinn's home; I noticed more people were smiling as I rode through the town. I also noticed that there weren't any men loafing around, and there was activity in one of the buildings. People seemed to be cleaning up the town, and there wasn't a foul smell like there had been.

I met the vicar talking to someone, and I approached them. They both turned to greet me. "How are things going?" I asked.

"Very well, My Lord. I sent several lists of things we need to Hanbury Hall," replied Vicar Quinn.

"That's good, I would like it if you could just order what you need instead of my staff doing it," I said.

"Yes, My Lord, we will be better able to do that once the store has food, and someone runs it," said Vicar Quinn.

"Did you order the supplies to fill the store?" I asked.

"Yes, My Lord," the vicar replied.

"And have you hired enough people to do the work that is needed?" I asked.

"Yes, My Lord," he replied again.

"Very well keep me posted on the progress and when the store opens," I said.

"Yes, My Lord, we will do that," he replied.

I was about to leave when I thought of one more thing, "Was there anyone interested in farming and raising livestock?"

"Yes, My Lord, they were sent to Hanbury Hall, and Mr. Gifford took care of them," he replied.

I got on my horse and said, "Let's not forget to get Mrs. Bowman set up, and I want a school set up, I will supply it."

"Yes, My Lord," he said as I rode off.

The next day the two boys had come to Hanbury Hall, and I had given them some fishing gear. I had the kitchen provide them with enough food to feed an army. In the next few months, the supplies had come. The town was changing for the better. All the buildings, inside and out, were being repaired and painted white and brown. Installed in town was a sewer system, and people were growing small vegetable gardens in their yards. It got decided to raise sheep in the fields allotted, and a large field of wheat opposite the grazing area a farmer planted. The people looked a lot healthier, and we found someone to teach the basics of education for which another building was restored and turned into a school. There were other empty buildings restored and turned into businesses. I had told the vicar to have another mill built so the wheat from the field on my estate will for little or nothing get milled, and I also told him to repair the road with cobblestones.

At Hanbury Hall, I hired a teacher from London to teach the girls. Also, to help at the school in the town when he had the time. I also hired a seamstress so that Nancy and the girls would have plenty of clothing.

"Daddy, I thought we were going to have a party," Margaret complained.

"You're right, go get Mr. Gifford, and we will arrange it," I told her.

She scampered out of the room as fast as she could, and in a few minutes, she came back with Nancy, Elizabeth, and Mr. Gifford.

"I think it is time for a party, Mr. Gifford," I said.

"Yes, My Lord." "Could I assume your party will be with the town people?" he said.

"Yes, we will see how that goes first before we have one for the nobility," I said.

"May I suggest, My Lord, that we have it in six weeks, so the people can buy or make proper clothing, and we can get things together?" he asked.

I looked at Nancy and the girls, and they didn't seem to object, so I said, "That would be fine, Mr. Gifford."

"Very well then, My Lord, I will get started with it," he said, and then excused himself.

Mr. Gifford decorated Hanbury Hall very festively. Mr. Gifford informed me that it would be decorated more elaborately, according to the nobility's taste. The decorating was more than it was for the people of the town, who would feel uncomfortable with elaborate decorations. I didn't know if he was right or wrong, Hanbury Hall looked quite fancy to me. What made me most happy was the joy Nancy and the girls were having. The people started coming at about five o'clock in the evening. They seemed like a happy, lively lot. Many brought their children, which was alright with me. I enjoyed the children and let Mr. Gifford know that they should be allowed to come. The important thing was that there were boys and girls the same age as my daughters, which pleased Margaret and Elizabeth immensely. I felt completely comfortable with these people. They were my type of people, but I wished I could say they were comfortable with me. The truth was that they couldn't look at me as if I were anything but nobility. I talked to Nancy, and she felt the same way, but the girls hadn't noticed at all. They were too busy with children their age, especially the boys.

The party ended at about ten o'clock. Nancy and I were disappointed that we couldn't have made inroads in our relationships with the people of the town. "My Lord, they will always think of you and the Lady as being out of their class," said Mr. Gifford.

"You're most likely right, Mr. Gifford. At least the girls didn't seem to have any trouble with the boys," I said.

"Yes, My Lord, but their parents will not let them associate with your daughters for fear that you wouldn't approve," said Mr. Gifford.

"You don't know my daughters, if they are interested in anyone, they will pursue them," I said with a smile.

"Yes, My Lord," he replied with a smile.

# 31

## TRIP BACK TO AMERICA

Two months later, another party was getting arranged, this one with the nobility, which I had never met. Like what Mr. Gifford said, Hanbury Hall got decorated even more elaborately than before, so much so that the first one looked like a barn dance compared to this one. Of course, Nancy and the girls were excited, but I think the one who was the most excited was Mr. Gifford. As for me, I was a little apprehensive. These weren't my type of people, and as long as we had been here, you would think one of these people would have visited.

Because of the long distances, some of these people had to travel; many were staying at Hanbury Hall. Mr. Gifford sent an invitation to everyone who was of nobility, including Queen Victoria. Mr. Gifford said that was the proper thing to do. To my surprise, the Queen informed us that she was coming; however, Prince Albert, her husband, had other duties. The Queen arrived a few days before the party, and of course, we gave her the best room we had. She was a short, slightly overweight, pleasant-looking woman, with brown hair. There was no mistaking; by the way, she carried herself that she was the Queen. The first day and the next morning, she ate her meals in her room, hardly ever coming out. I went upstairs to her room, guarded by two guards, and as I tried to knock on her door, but I got blocked by the two guards. "I wish to speak to the Queen," I said politely.

"State your business," one of the guards said.

What the guards said irritated me, and I said more forcefully, "I am the Earl of Worcester, and this is my home. Now, one or both of you will go in and ask the Queen if I may speak to her, or I will knock both of you out and go in unannounced."

They just looked at me, a bit concerned, and I was about to keep my promise when the door opened, it was the Queen. "It's alright, come in James, and we will talk," she said. I looked at both guards with a bit of anger and walked in and shut the door behind me. "Please, sit James," she said. She sat down opposite me and asked, "Now, what is it, you wish?"

"Excuse my demeanor; You're Majesty, I don't know how a nobleman acts because of my background." "I have come because I was concerned about your health, we haven't seen you since your arrival," I said.

"I assure you, I am alright now, but to tell you the truth, I was sick even before I left London, so there is no need to worry. I also want you to be aware that I know of your background before you came here, you lived a rugged life," she said.

"Yes, Your Majesty," I replied.

"Have you ever wondered why I came to your party, James?" she asked.

"I was surprised I didn't think I was of any significance to having the pleasure of your presence," I replied.

She smiled and said, "If you were any other Earl, I wouldn't have come, but I have heard of the work you have done with the town, and the fact I know of your background persuaded me to come."

"Your Majesty, have you ever been to Hanbury Hall and explored the countryside?" I asked.

"I have only been here once as a small child." "We stayed overnight," she replied.

"Are you up to going for a horseback ride and take a tour of the property, and perhaps, the town?" I asked.

Again, she smiled and said, "It's been a long time since I was on horseback, and I think it is time I do it again." "I would be delighted, give me an hour to put on proper clothing."

"Very well, Your Majesty, I will get things arranged," I said, then excused myself and left.

I got into my buckskins, and as I was dressing, Nancy came in and said, "Why are you dressed like that?"

"I'm going horseback riding with the Queen do you want to come?" I asked.

"No, I have too much to do before the party, have a nice ride though," she replied with a smile then left the room.

I stuck two pistols in my belt and put my knife in its sheath, and then I went to talk to the stable master. "Ready me a horse and one for the Queen be mindful of her size. Then bring them up to the front of the house," I said to him.

"Yes, My Lord," he replied.

I went back to the house to wait for the Queen. It wasn't very long before she descended the stairs, wearing riding clothes I'd seen other nobility wear.

"You look wonderful, Your Majesty," I said.

"You think so, James?" "I wonder what Albert would say," she said, half chuckling.

"I would think he would say the same thing," I replied.

The Queen's guards were joined by two more, protesting her going. She stopped and turned around then said rather forcefully, "James is more than capable of protecting me." "I do not need you hovering over me all the time now, go."

"Your Majesty is correct; my husband is a great warrior back in America and has the strength of many men, I have seen it," Nancy said as I smiled.

"Very well, Your Majesty," one of the guards said, not too happy.

I kissed Nancy and went out of the door with the Queen.

The stable master was standing with the two horses. I went to help the Queen up onto her horse when I notice the horse had a side-saddle. "Why do you have a side-saddle on the Queen's horse?" I asked the stable master.

Before the stable master could answer, the Queen said, "Riding any other way, James wouldn't be proper for a lady of my status."

I nodded, helped her up onto the saddle, and then got on my horse. We headed in the same direction as I had the first time. We talked about many things, mostly about me and my life in the mountains. After riding for a while, we came to that same stream where the two boys were fishing. Sure enough, they were there again. "Catch anything, boys?"

I got off my horse and helped the Queen down. "Yes, My Lord." "We caught a lot of fish," the older one said.

"And they are beauties," said Queen Victoria.

"Yes, my Lady," said the older one, again with a smile on his face.

I smiled and said, "Do you two know who this lady is?" I asked.

Both boys examined the Queen very carefully and looked at each other as if to say, is she who I think she is? They bent over at the waist, and the older one said, "We're sorry, Your Majesty, for not recognizing you at first."

She went over to them, lifted them, and said, "It's alright." "No need to apologize."

"How did you two know who the Queen was?" I asked the boys.

"We have a picture of her Majesty in the school, My Lord," the younger one answered.

We talked with them for a few minutes longer, then mounted up and left. As we rode into the town, the first thing we saw was men building a cobblestone road and people cleaning up. To say we created quite a stir would be an understatement. Unlike the two boys, most knew who my companion was as we rode up to the vicar's home Mrs. Quinn being outside watching our approach.

We dismounted, and with her mouth hanging open and in a half-trance, Mrs. Quinn directed us to the Church where her husband was. As we headed for the church, Mrs. Quinn followed, as did a large crowd from the town. Vicar Quinn was in the front of the church cleaning something, and he had his back to us when we entered.

"Vicar Quinn, I have someone for you to meet," I said with a smile.

"Oh?" "Who would that be, My Lord?" he asked as he turned around and almost passed out. "Your Majesty!" "It is a great honor for you to visit our small town and church," the vicar said, bent over with respect.

"Small, yes, but with significant improvements, I am well pleased," she said as she smiled and took his hand. As she talked to the vicar, the whole church filled up with the local people. The Queen turned around and said, "You should all be proud of yourselves for all the improvements you have made." "The Earl has told me you have a medical facility and a school here, where you didn't have one before this pleases me immensely." "I am sure the town will grow someday to be one of the largest and finest communities in the United Kingdom." "Again, I wish to give you my thanks for your efforts and to encourage you to continue to make improvements," Queen Victoria told the people.

"Your Majesty, the one responsible for all that has happened here, is the Earl of Worcester." "Without his generous help, all this would not have been possible," said Mrs. Bowman sincerely.

I whispered to the Queen, "That's Mrs. Bowman the healer and midwife of the town she exaggerates my part in this town."

"James, you are too modest, but I know what you mean." "I'm very aware of the Earl's part in making this happen." "He is why I am here, but I am also mindful of the fact that without your skills and talents, this town would not be doing as well, either," she explained.

"It is getting late, and we need to be off to Hanbury Hall now," I said to the townspeople. Then we excused ourselves and left for Hanbury Hall.

When we arrived at Hanbury Hall, the Queen's guards were anxiously waiting. The Queen looked at me and said, "James be grateful you're not a king."

"But, Your Majesty, I am a York who rules over a patch of land about the size of Wales," I said with a smile.

She smiled and giggled a little and said, "You know what I mean." She went upstairs to her room, and that would be the last time I saw her until the party

All the people who were staying with us had arrived. I didn't care much for them, except for the Queen. The others would hardly associate with my family and me, and they acted like it was an honor to me that they had come. I think the word I am searching for to describe them is snooty. I asked Mr. Gifford, "Is this the attitude I am to expect from my guests?"

"I'm afraid, My Lord, from most of them, it is," he said.

Is it my diction or my background?" I asked him.

"I would say mostly your background." "Your diction has improved immensely, and I hardly detect anything wrong with it, My Lord," he replied.

As I thought, I had a perplexed look. Mr. Gifford said, "If I may say, My Lord, without offending you, these people are selfish, self-centered snobs who have nothing better to do than talk bad about each other." "Most of them think they are smart because they went to fancy schools, but they aren't." "You have more knowledge than they will ever have, and you are quite the opposite of them." "I would suggest you dazzle them with your mind, My Lord." "They won't know how to react."

"Thank you, Mr. Gifford," I replied and left.

There was to be a banquet first, and then there was an entertainment of music with dancing. Each person would come into the ballroom to mingle before dinner. Their names got announced as they entered the ballroom. My family and I would be second to the last to come in, then the Queen, which many didn't realize was at Hanbury Hall.

"Your Royal Highness Henry Granville Fitzalan-Howard, Duke of Norfolk and his wife, Duchess Augusta.

"Lord Alan Plantagenet Stewart and his wife, Lady Arabella Arthur."

The names were called out one by one. Finally, they called out, "Lord James York, Earl of Worcester and his wife, Lady Nancy and daughters,

Lady Margaret and Lady Elizabeth." I noticed that most barely gave a glance at Nancy and me. My daughters got more than one glance by the young men of their age. Of course, who wouldn't look at them? My daughters were very beautiful. Nancy and I tried to mingle with the guests, but we were getting a lot of cold shoulders, and I was starting to regret having a party with these ingrates.

"Her Majesty, Queen Victoria!" That got everybody's attention as she waltzed in. It seemed like several people tried to clamber around her, trying to get her attention. But she spotted Nancy and me standing alone, and she ignored them and came over to us.

"I was afraid they would treat you this way, but let me assure you, not all of the nobility is as rude as they are," the Queen said.

"Perhaps they are just a bit shy, and they will warm up when they get to know us," Nancy said optimistically.

"Perhaps, but if they don't, they will know how displeased I am," she replied.

Dinner began, and The Queen sat at the head of the table. My family and I sat to the right to her since we were the hosts. Then the highest-ranking member of nobility sat to her left, and the rest being seated by their ranking. I noticed that it was much like entering a Shoshone lodge for dinner.

My servants served the first course according to rank, and people started talking to each other, mostly in French, but there was some German and English. However, they weren't talking to Nancy or me. The girls had some boys talking to them, and a family member would give him a dirty look, but it didn't stop them. I figured that they thought that I couldn't understand the conversations that were in French and German, but of course, I did, as did the Queen, who was not pleased. They were talking about Hanbury Hall and the improvements with the estate and the town. They said they couldn't understand why the Queen would come to a party when my family and I came from a backward background. If the Queen's looks could kill, there would have been many dead people at the dinner table. You would think that they would stop with this negative talking, seeing how the Queen reacted, but their conversation was getting worse. It reminded me of an incident many years ago. When I was small at my grandfather's house, how his guests were bad-mouthing my mother, father, brother, and me. I was rather pleased with myself because I was controlling my temper, as long as the conversation was about me. But then it was starting to be directed at Nancy and the girls. My anger was starting to well up. Nancy noticed it, and so did the Queen. I was about to explode when the Queen thundered so everyone could hear, "I understand James, you can speak, read and write several languages." "Is this correct?"

"Yes, Your Majesty," I said, confused.

"How many and what are the languages, James?" she asked wisely. "Eleven or more: several Indian languages, Latin, Greek, Spanish, German, Hebrew, French and of course English," I said, understanding now what she was doing.

"I also have heard you have read Chaucer, the entire works of Shakespeare, Plato and Aristotle, Cicero and Hugo," she said with a smile.

"Yes, Your Majesty and many others," I said.

"I guess I owe you an apology," said His Royal Highness George Sutherland-Leveson-Gower, Duke of Sutherland.

"There is no guessing about it; you and everyone here owe the whole York family an apology, and I am not pleased."

The rest of the dinner was very quiet. However, during the entertainment and dance, many came up to us and talked, making Nancy happy. But for me, these were just not my kind of people. The party ended, and everyone finally left by the next day, which was just fine with me. The only one I would miss is Queen Victoria; however, she did invite our family to her palace.

As time passed, the girls were getting many suitors, both commoners and nobles. I warned the two of them about those who might be users and told them that it didn't matter if they were the poorest of the suitors or the richest bad people could get found in both. I told them to choose wisely and get to know them before it went too far. Nancy and I got invited to some smaller dinner parties I didn't want to go but went anyway to make Nancy happy. To me, these parties were, for the most part, made to gossip and be nosey. Many would ask how I became so wealthy, and I told them the truth. They also wanted to know my past, which pained me to tell them because I became homesick, which Nancy knew. After a few years, the girls got invited to their suitors' homes for dinners or parties, and they were eating it up. The girls seemed to put life in the Shining Mountains far behind them, and I knew they would never go back. What concerned me more was if Nancy would follow me back to our home in America.

Elizabeth was the first to bring a young man home to ask me if it would be alright to marry her. He was from the nobility, his father being a Lord. He was very good looking but not very strong looking; however, I had to remember how he grew up.

"What do you do for work?" I asked.

"I went to school to learn accounting," he replied with a smile.

"I didn't ask you that, how are you going to support my daughter?" I said.

"My family has money, sir," he said.

"I would assume your family has money because your father has worked hard to acquire it." "Once they pass on and you run out of money, where will you get the money to support my daughter?" I asked.

"To tell you the truth, I haven't thought about it," he replied.

I looked at him for a few moments then said, "I tell you what I will do, you tell me the last person you dated before my Elizabeth." "Let me talk to your parents, and I will need to speak to some friends for advice, then talk to Elizabeth in private and then I will make my decision, is that reasonable?"

"Yes, sir, I'll make arrangements for you to talk to my parents right away," he replied. He then told me the name of the young lady he had dated or what it turned out to be, just talked to, and there was no dating involved. After he left, I spoke to Mr. Gifford about this young man and then the vicar in the town. Neither could tell me much except Mr. Gifford said that his parents seemed to be good people, and he never heard anything bad about the young man. I then wrote to the Queen for advice about this young man. My concern was that Elizabeth wasn't as level-headed as her sister. I was afraid she might get into something she would regret; Nancy agreed with me.

Two days later, Lord James Kenneth Howard and Lady Louisa came to Hanbury Hall to discuss their son's marriage to my daughter. "Lord James, it appears your son is a fine person; however, my concern is that he has never had employment," I said.

"He is our only child, and we have more than enough money," he replied.

"It's not just the money, Lord James." "We are also quite wealthy, but an idle mind and body can get into a lot of mischief," said Nancy.

"From what I understand, sir, you earned your wealth, and you know what it is to work," I said.

"Yes, and I understand what you are saying about my son," he replied.

"Lady Louisa, what kind of child was your son growing up, and how is he now?" asked Nancy.

"He was a delicate, timid, intelligent, and affectionate child." "He didn't have very many friends, and the ones he had were much like him or are adults much older than him." "I would say that he struggles with his shyness and his passivity." "He is also embarrassed by his naiveté," she said.

"Elizabeth is just the opposite, it makes me wonder how they ever got together," I said.

"Your daughter and our son met at the party that you had some time back." "I believe she is the first girl he has expressed any interest in," said Lady Louisa.

"Yes, I remember he was very excited that she showed any interest in him." "He asked me a lot of questions about girls when we got home that night," Lord James said.

I looked over to Nancy to see what she was thinking. She smiled and nodded. I said, "Have your son come and talk to me again next week, and I will give him my answer," I said.

When we finished talking, they left. We waited until Margaret and Elizabeth were home, then we had a family meeting.

"Elizabeth, why do you care for this young man he is just the opposite of you?" "He is shy, and I don't think he has very much experience with girls," I said.

"That's what I like about him, daddy." "Those other boys are either conceited, they want your money, or want to get me in bed."

"What do you think of this boy Elizabeth wishes to marry," Nancy asked Margaret.

"Elizabeth is right about most of those rich boys, but James is different." "I think he will be alright," Margaret said.

I walked over to the fireplace and stared into the fire for a moment, when Elizabeth asked, "Well, will you let me marry him?"

"I'll make that decision when I get an answer from the letter I sent to the Queen," I said.

"You wrote the Queen?" asked Elizabeth, surprised. I turned around and said, "Yes, she should know him almost as well as his parents, and I value her opinion."

I got a long letter from the Queen, and it said pretty much what I already knew." "Soon after I received the letter, Elizabeth's suitor came for my answer. "I did get a letter from the Queen about you, young man." "I know you want an answer from me, and I will give you that answer after a question or two I have for you," I said.

"If we all decided to go back to the wilds of America, would you go, and how would you cope, knowing that you are a bit soft?" I asked.

"I will go wherever my wife wishes to go and yes you are right, I guess I am soft, but I can learn," he replied.

I nodded and said, "Hanbury Hall is larger than your parents' home; would you be willing to have the wedding here?" I asked.

"Yes, sir," he replied.

"Where do you intend to live here at Hanbury Hall or your parents' home?" I asked.

James looked at Elizabeth, and I could tell they hadn't thought about it. Elizabeth said, "Both places, daddy."

"Very well, but let me tell you one more thing." "I like you, James, how could I not like you with a name the same as mine." "But if you harm my daughter you will most likely lose your life do you understand me?" I said.

"Yes, sir," he replied, a bit tense.

"Then welcome to the family," I said with a smile.

"Thank you, sir, you won't regret it."

"I'm not one who makes wedding plans, and I assume your father isn't, either." "Have your mother contact Elizabeth's mother to decide what they and you want to do," I told James and Elizabeth.

The wedding was very beautiful. But no matter how it was, if Elizabeth was happy, I was happy. The Queen, with much regret, couldn't come but sent a beautiful gift. Elizabeth's brothers and grandparents couldn't come either, for reasons I didn't quite understand, and it was a great disappointment. No sooner than Elizabeth's wedding was over, and they were on their honeymoon; Margaret was getting attention by a steady suitor but not from the nobility. Before this young man came to me for my daughter's hand, I went to the town and asked the vicar about this boy. He told me he came from a good family and he hadn't heard anything bad about him. He suggested I talk to Mrs. Bowman, who knew about everything about everyone in the town. I thanked him and left for Mrs. Bowman's home.

"He is a hard worker with a soft heart. He has gone out with other girls but has never been serious with any of them until he met your daughter, My Lord," said Mrs. Bowman. "He is the type of young man who you like the first time you meet him. The children of the town adore him," she added.

"He is a big man, is he prone to violence?" I asked.

"He has been in some fights growing up and never lost." "He doesn't take any abuse from anybody, but those fights have been few," Mrs. Bowman replied.

"Do you think he would ever strike a woman?" I asked.

"No, I don't think so, My Lord," she said cautiously.

"I feel that this is my main fear and that he would try to dominate my Margaret, who is a free spirit at heart," I said. We talked a little more, and I excused myself and left.

Over the next few days, my mind worried over this young man Margaret was seeing. He seemed like a good person, but I just didn't know. I would have to, if necessary, approach him differently than my son-in-law, James. I talked to Nancy about my concerns about him, and she didn't seem as concerned as I, but I just wanted to make sure, and two months later, I got my chance.

I was relaxing in the library reading a book when Margaret and Edward Nils, a son of the town's blacksmith, walked inside. "Daddy, Edward would like to talk to you," Margaret said with a smile.

I looked at her, then him, and said, "Speak what's on your mind."

"I wish to marry your daughter, sir," he said proudly.

I stared at him for a few seconds and then said to Margaret, "Edward and I are going to go for a little walk, and then Edward or I will give you my answer."

I smiled and said to Edward, "I need to change clothing first."

Margaret and Edward were waiting for me in the foyer. When Margaret saw me, her mouth fell open. I was wearing my buckskins with my knife at my side. "Why are you dressed like that, daddy?" asked Margaret, concerned.

"Because it is comfortable, sweetheart," I answered with a smile.

"Don't do anything foolish," she replied as I went out the door with Edward.

I turned around and said in Shoshone, "I do nothing foolish when it comes to my family." She had learned enough Shoshone from her grandmother and uncle to understand what I said.

We headed across an open field toward a thicket of trees and a trail that led to the town. As we walked, we talked, "Has Margaret told you about my background?" I asked.

"She said you were a frontiersman, and you grew up with some American Indians," he replied.

"It's a bit more than that," I said. "Where do you and Margaret plan to live?" I asked.

"Margaret wants to stay at Hanbury Hall," he said.

"And how do you feel about that?" I asked.

"I am a man, and I feel I should provide a shelter for my wife, not live off the wealth of relatives," he replied.

"If you were in the mountains of America, I might agree with you, but you're not, and I don't think you have the funds to build or buy a house here." "So, I think your best choice is to live at Hanbury Hall," I said. We walked further, and as I talked, I tried to rile him up, and it seemed to be working. "I hear, you are considered a tough guy in the town, that you never lost a fight," I said. I gave a contemptuous laugh and said, "Everyone you must have fought must have been an old man, a child, or was it a woman, you don't look very strong to me."

Edward was fuming he looked like an enraged bull, then he said in anger, "If you weren't Margaret's father, I would show you how tough I am."

"Don't let that stop you, or are you all talk like that lowlife father of yours?" I said, taunting him.

That's all it took, he took a swing at me, but I blocked his arm and gave him a good one between his eyes, which he took stumbling back in surprise. He recovered quickly, and I gave him a few more hits to the head and one to the ribs. He got me a few times, and he hit hard, but I had got hit harder before, so they did not affect me. After about a half-hour of exchanging blows, the toll on him was showing its effects, and he was getting winded. Finally, he was swinging wildly, and I stopped playing with him and knocked him out. I picked him up and carried him to the stream that ran through my property and dropped him in the water, which revived him quickly then I sat down. With a smile, I said as he walked out of the water, disgusted with himself. "The only other problem I have with you marrying Margaret is your lack of control when you get mad." "It would be bad for you if you hurt Margaret; otherwise, you would make a good son-in-law."

"Is that what this was all about?" he asked as he sat down beside me.

I nodded, and he said with all sincerity, "As mad as I may get, I would never harm Margaret or any loved one."

"You tried to harm me," I said.

"Of course, you're not a loved one," he said with a smile.

"You got a point there." "I tried pushing you as much as I could, but remember there will be times Margaret will get on your nerves too," I said.

"Yes, sir, I know that," he replied.

"Come, let's go down to the town and talk to your parents and make arrangements for your mother and my Nancy to get together so they can speak about the marriage arrangements." "It would be a good thing to have your family up to Hanbury Hall for dinner, and then they can talk all they want, what do you say?" I asked.

"That sounds good, sir, but my family can be rowdy at times," he replied.

"I just gave you a hell of a beating, and I was only playing with you; how do you think your family is going to cause me problems?" I stated. He smiled and then started laughing, and we continued toward the town.

It got decided to have a wedding where both the nobility, relatives of the groom and people of the town would attend. It would be a very different wedding than the one Elizabeth had. We had invited the family left in America, but again, they had excuses why they couldn't come. It didn't make sense; I thought that I would have to investigate this later. The one happy thing that happened is that Queen Victoria and Prince Albert were coming.

The day of the wedding Hanbury Hall was decorated festively. All the nobility was informed that there would be common people and to expect protocol mistakes. It was a beautiful wedding as well as a great reception. Still, I felt as uncomfortable as I did at Elizabeth's wedding, and I thought Nancy felt the same way. The nobility gave us the feeling we weren't at their level, and the commoners felt they weren't at my level, so Nancy and I were in limbo. There was one exception to this, Queen Victoria and Prince Albert treated us very well. The one good thing was that the girls were accepted, for some reason, in both classes.

Days after the wedding, when Margaret and Edward were on their honeymoon and Elizabeth and James were living at James's parents' house, Hanbury Hall became very lonely.

It was painful not having any real friends but as painful as it was for me, I couldn't imagine how hard it was for Nancy.

I had been writing Pa and Ma trying to find out what was going on, without any success. So, after two years of trying to find out what was going on, I started writing my boys and asking them then I got a letter from Carl and everything came out. The ranch was all right and doing well; that wasn't the problem; the problem was Ma and Pa; they were both ill and had been for some time. Pa was in the worse condition, but they didn't want Nancy and me to worry and leave the life they thought I had here.

I showed the letter to Nancy, who asked, "What do you want to do about it?"

"I think we need to have a meeting with Elizabeth, Margaret, and their husbands, Mr. Gifford, too."

Everyone came into the drawing-room, and I said, "Mr. Gifford, I know how you wish to do things properly, but for this moment, I want you to be more like a friend." "Frankly, Nancy and I always felt you were more like family."

"Yes, My Lord," he replied.

I smiled at his response then read out loud the letter sent by Carl. I looked around the room for any comments. Mr. Gifford said, "My Lord, it is your mother and father; you must go back to the wilds of America to be with them; it is the only proper thing to do."

"Of course, James, you know wherever you go, I will follow," Nancy said lovingly, and I squeezed Nancy's hand in return.

Then something unexpected happened. Elizabeth's James said meekly, "I am not very strong, as you know, father, but I feel the same as mother, and I wish to follow you to America if you have me."

"I too," said Edward boldly, "I'd follow you to the depths of hell if you wish."

I looked at the girls then back to their husbands and said, "And what of your wives."

"Daddy, there is no need to ask me it's Grandma and Grandpa," Margaret said.

"Me neither Daddy," replied Elizabeth.

"There is something you need to know, Daddy." "Elizabeth and I were going to surprise everyone; we are both with child," said Margaret.

Once the commotion of the news ended, I said, "Then you two can't go." "You both know what's involved in getting there."

"Daddy, we will reach the ranch long before the babies come, so we are going." "Besides, we are Yorks and as strong as any Shoshone woman," said Elizabeth. I could see that James and Edward looked concerned, so I asked, "Are you two having second thoughts about this?"

"No father, Elizabeth knows better than I what she is getting into, but I am concerned," James said.

"I don't think we should tell our parents about the babies until we get to America." "There will be fewer problems with them," said Edward.

James agreed and then I turned my attention to Mr. Gifford and said, "As I told you, Mr. Gifford, I consider you family do you wish to go with us?"

"Perhaps, if I were a younger man, My Lord, I would have loved to go, but I am too old and not rugged enough to survive the trip." "It would be best to stay, and I serve you here," he replied.

My family or I told those who needed to know that we were leaving, and in four days, we were off to London to book passage to America. As before, the trip across the Atlantic did not go well for me. Even with the seasickness I had, I would have preferred porting in New Orleans, but with the civil war that was going on now, I figured it would be safer to port in New York. When we arrived in New York, there was a problem. Since Great Britain was supporting the south, the New York port officials didn't want the ship to port in New York. But it was a Dutch ship which happened to port in London for a brief period. So, after a lot of argument, we could come ashore. Then there was another problem, Edward and James were British citizens. That was also solved when they decided that they would allow them into the country since they married my daughters. Thank God, they didn't know that Nancy and the girls had immigrated years before.

By the time everything was completed, it was late, so we stayed in a nice hotel while I planned to buy some horses and supplies. I could have stayed with relatives, but I was in a hurry to get to the Shining Mountains, and I just didn't want to deal with them. Anyway, I figured they already knew about Ma and Pa, and if they were interested, they would have traveled west to see them. It was bad enough that I had to stop by my uncle's home to retrieve my weapons, but it was necessary.

I tried to get horses, and it wasn't easy, but I got seven horses, enough for each of us with a packhorse. The horses weren't in very good condition, and they cost me three times as much as they should have, as did the supplies.

I stopped at my uncle's home to pick up my weapons. An old butler answered the door and informed me that my uncle was in the hospital, deathly ill. I felt bad about my uncle, so we all went to visit him. When I saw him, my heart sunk at his sight. "Tell your father I am sorry I can't go to him and let him know that I love him," said my uncle.

"I'm sure he will understand, and I am certain he loves you also," I said.

"Your father was right for going west; the life he chose was a much healthier life than the one your grandfather, and I chose." "You tell him this, James," requested Uncle Daniel, having a hard time breathing.

Later, I asked the doctor what was the matter with him. He was utterly baffled, but years later, I found out he had cancer. Two letters got sent back to England, letting the in-laws know of the pregnancies, and then we were off, heading west. As we traveled, we saw plenty of troops along the way. We rode into the city of Dayton, Ohio, and so far, Edward fared well, but James got worn out. One could only imagine how he felt when Elizabeth told him how far we still had to go. While James and the women rested, Edward and I went to find more supplies with luck and some fresh horses. At the corrals, I purchased seven new horses in a lot better shape than the ones we had; of course, I had to pay a lot more than what the horses were worth again. As I was receiving my bill of sale, I noticed six or seven soldiers, who looked like they had been drinking, eyeing us. That old instinct came over me, indicating there was going to be trouble.

"Edward prepare yourself for a conflict with those soldiers I can feel it my bones," I said.

"I had the same feeling," he said.

"Let me do the talking if they confront us," I said.

He nodded, and I told the owner who had sold me the horses, "Feed them well, my family, and I will pick them up in the morning."

He agreed, then Edward and I started to walk away when, as I had predicted, the soldiers interrupted our progress. "Why aren't you two lowlifes in uniform," said one of the soldiers with three stripes.

"I don't see how that's any of your business," I replied.

"We are making it our business," he replied confidently.

"Father, he has a thick skull as well as little brain matter; just knock him out and let's be on our way," Edward said.

"Oh, a Limey bastard!" "You people are helping those scums in the south," he replied hostilely.

"Look, friend, he is my son-in-law, and I'm not looking for trouble," I said.

I started to go around him to leave, and he grabbed me. I didn't hesitate for a second; I swung and caught him square in the face, which knocked him down. Then the others came in, and the fight with Edward and I commenced. As I knocked one of the soldiers down, another would get up. They got a few punches in, but they got the worst of it, and Edward was thoroughly enjoying himself. After about thirty minutes, I thought it was all over when a dozen of their buddies showed up. We did our best, but they were wearing us out, and just when I thought they were going to get the best of us, I heard a pistol go off, then the soldiers backed off.

Some officers and higher-ranking noncommissioned officers approached us. A Major Pratt asked sternly, "What's going on here?"

None of the soldiers would answer, so I said, "There was a dispute over the reason I wasn't in uniform and the fact that my son-in-law is British."

The Major looked at me, then at his drunken men, who were trying to stand straight up and asked the Sergeant, "What business is it of yours to question these men?"

"None," said the Sergeant.

"Sergeant Murphy put these men in the stockade until I decide on a fitting punishment," said the Major.

"Yes, Sir," replied the Sergeant.

The Sergeant took away the drunken soldiers, and the Major turned to me and said, "My apologies, sir." He stared at me for a few moments, and before I could say anything, he added, "Do I know you, sir?"

"I'm not sure; you do look familiar; my name is James York."

He smiled and said, "You're Soaring Eagle With Many Coups, aren't you?"

"Yes, I said, confused.

"I was a captain at Fort Bents when we bought horses from you," he said. Then the memory of him came back to me, and he said, "If you two join the Union Army, I can guarantee you both commissions, after seeing how well you fight. And you, Mr. York, are legendary; you both would be an asset."

"No, my place is in the mountains, and besides, I was born in St. Louis, it doesn't seem right." "I have no hard feelings for the people in the north or the south," I replied. We talked a little longer then Edward, and I left to find the rest of the family who was not happy with the confrontation we had.

We left the next morning, and I decided not to enter any large cities except for Springfield, Illinois, where I withdrew a large sum of money. I didn't want to rest for long until I got to the Plains, where we could take a day or two for rest. I could see James was struggling to cope with a situation of our trek west, but he wasn't complaining aloud. It was funny how he was trying to keep clean. I think the others also knew that staying clean was almost impossible, at least the clean James got accustomed to being. We finally got to the Mississippi River then discovered there was no ferry to carry us across. We had to travel north to find a safe place to cross, which took over a day to find. On the other side of the Mississippi River, we traveled to Kanesville, Iowa, now known as Council Bluffs. We rested there for two days because James wasn't doing well and needed the rest.

"This will be the last town we will see until we get to the ranch." "We will be eating and sleeping outdoors." "Do you think you have the strength to endure the hardship?" I asked James.

"Father, I will not leave Elizabeth; I will be just fine; I'm getting stronger every day." "I've gotten this far; I'll make it all the way," he replied.

"Alright, we will see how you do, but don't put your health in danger. The first time it gets too much for you, let me know," I said. Two hours later, we headed west. I not only kept an eye on any danger that might be around us, but I also kept my eye on James. By the end of the week, I thought I was going to have a problem with James, but he surprised not only me but all of us at how well he started to adapt. Both Edward and James were amazed at how much game there was and the fact that it belonged to no one. They were also astonished at their first sighting of buffalo. But things got tense when some warriors appeared on the ridge of a hill. They could have been Lakota or maybe Cheyenne, but we were a little far east for them. They followed us for a day or two and then disappeared, which made me even more nervous. I had bought rifles for everyone who didn't have them before we crossed the Mississippi River. But James and Edward had little experience with how to shoot. I found a place on the high ground that had plenty of protection. I told everyone that I was going out to scout around for any trouble and that they were to post a guard, I would be back in the morning.

I headed east for a short time and then circled from where my family camped out. After several hours, I smelled smoke in the air from a campfire, so I tied my horse up and headed toward where it was coming from on foot. It wasn't long before I spotted about a dozen or more Lakota. I waited for one of the warriors to leave the campfire to relieve himself, and then I sneaked up to him and knocked him out. I dragged him away to a place where the rest of the warriors couldn't hear me talking to him; then I revived him. I could speak enough Lakota that I didn't have to sign. "Do you know who I am?" I asked the warrior.

"You will soon be a dead, white man," he replied.

"You are a fool." "I am Soaring Eagle With Many Coups, a Shoshone warrior, and you are very near to where my people are," I said forcefully. At that, he tensed, and I continued, "You tell those fools you came with that if you attack me, the Shoshone nation and I will go to war with your people, and I will kill every one of them." "Do you understand me?" He nodded, and I knocked him out again. Then I headed to my horse and went back to my family.

"We are leaving now," I said.

"But it is dark," replied James, my son-in-law.

The others agreed, but Nancy said seriously, "If your father says it is time to leave, we leave."

We headed west at a slow pace. As the sun came up, I kept my eyes on my surroundings, searching for any Lakota that might try to sneak up on us. At noon break, I checked my back trail to see if anyone followed, and I didn't see anything. By sundown, I figured they had taken my threat to heart and had left us alone, but Edward and I kept guard all night. By noon the next day, I felt more at ease. They would have attacked us if they were going to, so we slowed down some and made camp early that night.

After several days of heat, dust, and rain, we made it to the border of the ranch. James and Edward were amazed that the family owned so much land. They were also astounded at the beauty of the mountains and, of course, the ranch. As we circled the small lake and went up to the cabins, it was Carl who first spotted us. Carl's emotions were totally out of control, and we could see tears streaming down his cheeks as he yelled, "Pa, Ma, it's Ma and Pa!" "They're back!"

# 32

# MY WANING YEARS

William came running across the creek from his Uncle Grey Wolf's lodge. He had grown a foot taller and looked more like a Shoshone than an English white man. What concerned me was that there was no sign of Ma and Pa. Nancy got off her horse to hug William. "Mother, I am so happy to see you." "I missed you a lot," William said in perfect Shoshone.

"William, are you speaking Shoshone?" Nancy asked.

"Oh, Mummy, I forgot that I was speaking Shoshone since I speak it all the time, I'm sorry," he said.

"It's alright you just surprised me at how well you can speak Shoshone," Nancy replied.

As the children and I got off their horses, I made the introductions, "These are your brothers-in-law, James and Edward." "And this is Carl and William," I said. "Where are Grandma and Grandpa?" I asked William and Carl.

"In their cabin Pa with Martha." "Pa, they are not in very good shape," replied Carl.

I looked around and saw two small cabins down the valley and assumed they were my boys' homes. Then I said to William and Carl, "William, go tell the others we are here, and Carl put up the horses, will you?" They did as I asked, and the rest of the family and I walked to Pa's cabin. "Perhaps it is better if you all stay outside while your mother and I go in first," I said grimly. They all nodded, and Nancy and I went into the cabin.

It was dark inside Ma was lying on a bed on the floor while Pa was in bed, and Martha was tending him. When Ma spotted us, her face showed joy, and she motioned for me as well as Nancy to come to her. We went to her and kneeled by her side. I placed my hand on her face and then kissed her. "You should not have come; we are old and not important," Ma said.

"You sound too much like a Shoshone I have never believed in the Shoshone way for the old."

She smiled, and I asked, "Why have you not used your medicines to heal you and Pa?"

She slowly shook her head and said, "This kind of sickness, you cannot cure with any medicine, Shoshone or white man's."

"What are you trying to say?"

She smiled and said, "Your father and I will soon join our fathers and mothers."

With horror on my face and my eyes tearing up, I said, "I do not believe this; I will not let this happen."

"You cannot stop it, my son," she replied.

"James, Nancy, is that you?" Pa asked weakly.

I got up and stood by Pa, while Nancy stayed with Ma. I said, "I'm here, Pa, I saw Uncle Daniel; he sends his love."

"I heard that he is sick also," Pa said.

"He's not doing so well, Pa." "What is this sickness you have?" I asked.

"The doctor from the Great Salt Lake City said it is called cancer," replied Martha sadly.

"How did they get this cancer?" I asked again.

"The doctor doesn't know," Martha said.

"What kind of medicine are you giving them?" I asked Martha.

"The doctor said there is no medicine, but if they feel pain, I'm to give them this, it's called laudanum," she replied.

I kneeled next to Ma again and asked, "Ma, have you ever seen this kind of sickness among the Shoshone?"

"Yes, but not many," she replied.

"How did you treat them," I asked.

"With kindness and then we let them go to The Great Beyond." "Do not worry, my son, your father, and I have lived a good life," Ma said.

"I do not accept this," I said, upset. I got up and went outside, where the whole family was waiting.

I looked at Zack, then Grey Wolf, and said in a grim voice, "We must talk, let's go."

"Aren't you going to talk to your boys?" asked Zack.

"Later, now I must speak with you about Ma and Pa," I replied.

We walked off toward the corrals talking in Shoshone, "Ma and Pa said there is nothing that can get done to cure them, and I do not believe this."

Zack and Grey Wolf looked at each other. Grey Wolf put his hand on my arm and with sad eyes said, "There is no one among the Shoshone or any other tribe that can do anything, and the white medicine man said the same." I hadn't shed any tears since the death Morning Star and my daughter until now. I was frustrated at the inability to do anything.

"James, all we can do is to make them comfortable," Zack said with compassion.

Pa got laid to rest next to Morning Star as well as my dear Mary, and a week later, Ma died, and we placed her next to Pa. It wasn't the Shoshone way, but I figured Ma and Pa would want it this way. The death of Morning Star and Mary had taken a lot out of me, but that was many years ago when I was young, so I recovered, but the pain was always there. The death of Ma and Pa was different; it would take me much longer to recover from this.

Elizabeth and Margaret had their babies, both girls. They were named Victoria, for Margaret's baby and Anna, for Elizabeth's. Nancy, it turned out, was also pregnant, and the child would be our last. She gave birth one month to the day after Elizabeth delivered. It was a boy, and we named him Nathaniel, after Pa. Carl and Martha took over Ma and Pa's cabin. It wasn't long before they had little ones to fill the cabin. I didn't understand why it had taken them so long to start a family. The only thing I could figure was that Carl needed to grow up a little more. Sarah was to marry a young man from the next ranch over.

After the babies were old enough to travel, I said to Nancy, the girls, and their husbands, "You all need to decide whether you want to stay here or go back to Worcester." "As for me, I will be staying; this is where I belong."

"Wherever my husband goes, I go," replied Nancy.

I could see on James's face that he wanted to go back as would Elizabeth, but James did not say anything, so Elizabeth did, "We will go back, Daddy." "I hope you and mother will visit from time to time."

"You can bet on it, Sweetheart," I replied.

"I need a little time to think about it, father," said Edward. The next day Edward decided to go back to Worcester, explaining it would be better for the baby and his extended family.

By the end of the week, we were heading east without Nancy. She decided the trip would have been too much trouble for the baby. So, she said her goodbyes back at the ranch. There wasn't much change on the journey east from when we first came. We stayed away from larger cities. The civil war was nearly over, and the north had won. I had written a letter to Mr. Gifford explaining what I wanted for Worcester and Hanbury Hal. He was to let me know of any needs or troubles he might have. I also informed the girls and their husbands what I had written to Mr. Gifford and what I wanted for Worcester and Hanbury Hall. They sail off toward England at about nine o'clock in the morning. As they left, I felt very lonely.

Before I left New York, I went to see Uncle Daniel. I rode up to his house with my three horses in tow and knocked at his front door. An old butler I didn't recognize answered, "Yes? What is it that you want?"

"I'm here to see Daniel York," I said. Before he could answer, a woman said at the same time she looked at me, "What is it he wants, Douglas?" "You know vagabonds like him are supposed to come to the side door."

"I'm here to see Uncle Daniel York." "I'm James York, Earl of Worcester," I said a little irritated.

"Oh, come in, I'm Penelope Bugger." "My father died three months back, and my husband and I inherited his estate," she said coldly.

"I will be going then," I said abruptly.

I turned around and left before she could say another word. As I headed west, I was able to sell the extra horses for a good price, and it wasn't long before I crossed the Mississippi River. The ride back was lonely and uncomfortable. I occupied my mind with the past and all I had gone through, both good and bad. I saw a few wagon trains and an occasional Indian, but I avoided them. I had wondered what the rest of my life would be. I wasn't interested in the ranch anymore, nor the gold that was on it. But I did have a responsibility to my family, so I would do my best with a smile, no matter how I felt. I had some neighbors nearby that I hadn't bothered to visit; perhaps I would see them. Then I should meet this boy who wanted to marry Sarah.

I was nearing the natural migration trails of the buffalo when I smelled death and spotted vultures. I came over a rise and down in the valley below were hundreds of dead buffalo rotting in the sun. I rode among carcasses of the buffalos in total shock. The buffalo hides got taken, but everything else had remained left to rot, what a waste, I thought. Who could have done this? As I rode among the dead buffalo, I saw about fifteen Cheyenne warriors riding toward me on the ridge on the opposite side of the valley. I raised my rifle, just in case, and stood my ground as they approached. I spoke some Cheyenne, so I said, "I'm Soaring Eagle With Many Coups, and my father was Bear Slayer."

They all looked at each other, and it was clear that they knew who I was, so I asked, just in case they thought I killed the buffalo, "Who did this?"

They looked at me, not knowing quite what to say. One, who appeared to be a Cheyenne leader, said, "White men kill for the hides alone." "If we find them, we will kill them."

I nodded and said, "If I find them first, you will not have to kill them, they will be dead."

They nodded, also, then, without saying another word, they left. Most tribes that hunt buffalo believe the buffalo is not only for food and things they can make from the animals. The buffalo is a very sacred animal that they honor in their religions. Their anger is because the white man insulted the buffalo and destroyed what the tribes depended on to survive. I had mixed feelings about it; I did not rely on the buffalo, and my beliefs were somewhat unclear. However, I do remember a blond-haired boy many years ago, who got a warning that this would happen by his spirit guide.

I continued to head west soon; the Shining Mountains rose before me. Usually, I would feel great pleasure at seeing the mountains, but not this time, so many years had gone now so much had changed. Oh, I had joy for Nancy, the boys, and the rest of the family. However, not the ranch nor the mountains. It was a rainy day as I rode toward my cabin. I didn't even look at Ma and Pa's cabin as I passed it, but I did look up at the graves when I got off my horse.

William came out of the cabin and said, "I will help you take care of the horse, daddy."

"That would be a great help, son," I said. William and I took care of the horse in silence and then headed for the cabin with William carrying most of my gear. In the cabin, I told Nancy about the trip, especially the buffalo. She could see I was tired, so she didn't press me on anything. I checked in on the baby while Nancy put something on the table for me to eat. I was quiet while eating, and when I had finished eating, I went directly to bed.

Over the next few days, weeks and months, everyone saw that I had lost interest in the ranch they could all see it. Finally, as I was sitting in front of the cabin, Nancy came up to me and said, "It appears you have a lot on your mind, that you have lost interest in doing anything."

"Everything has gone; everything has changed; there are no new horizons for me," I replied without looking at her.

"Then what do you want to do?" she asked.

Looking at her, I said, "I don't have a clue." I thought for a second, then added, "I guess all that is left is helping our children and family to do well."

"You know that will be a significant job that should keep both of us busy."

As time passed, more and more people came west. As they did, they found gold in Colorado, near Pike's Peak. It made me a little nervous living so near the strike. It wasn't like the gold strikes in California, which was much further away. But, then again, there was the silver strike in Nevada. With all this gold and silver being found all around me, I found some try mining on the ranch, but we chased them off every time they tried. There was plenty of gold still on the ranch. Zack and I only found a fraction of it. We hired more ranch hands and built another, much larger bunkhouse and converted the old bunkhouse into an addition to the cabin. I did let some of the men search for gold in their free time if they gave us twenty percent of what they found. It worked out quite well for us, increasing our wealth to a point where we didn't need to worry about money even if we had to at all. We only had trouble with one man who did little work because he decided he was going to prospect, and no one was going to stop him; of course, he was mistaken. Before I was going to fire him and throw him off our property, he must have gotten wind of it because he had taken off with all the gold he had found. When I demanded twenty percent of what he had, he refused and tried to kill me. That was a big mistake on his part. I ended up with all the gold, and he ended up with a cold grave.

As the people from the east came west, they killed many buffalos, and the tribes fought back for their survival. Of course, the military came to protect the whites. The whites made reservations for the several different tribes, usually, on the worst land, there was. Many of the tribes were too weak to fight back and did as the military told them. They went on these reservations to starve and die; this included the Shoshone. I went to see Tall As The Sky, who was now the leader of a large Shoshone band and talked to him about what was happening. I invited him and the rest of the Shoshone to move to the ranch. I guaranteed him that the remainder of the people would not be bothered if they stayed on the ranch; they would always have food since I had plenty of cattle. He told me that he would talk it over in the council with the people of the village to decide if they would accept my offer. As it turned out, a small portion of the Shoshone took up my offer and made a small village to the north of my ranch. Grey Wolf and the few Shoshone who came to the ranch years ago, joined them.

As the railroad and telegraph headed west and more towns and cities sprung up all over the country. One day at the ranch, we got a visit from Lieutenant Charles Woods and some of his men. "I'm looking for James York," the Lieutenant said.

"You found him," I said.

"You're a much older man than I thought, Mr. York. Nevertheless, I have got ordered to recruit you to be our scout and tracker," he said.

"There are several much younger men you could choose from," I replied.

"It is my understanding that you are the best, and the information I have says that you used to live with the savages," he said rather ignorantly.

"I am a Shoshone warrior, as are my brothers, and the Shoshone are not savages," I said a bit irritated. "You came out of your way to come here." "Why?" I asked.

"We have been having trouble with one savage, I mean warrior, by the name of Chief Joseph." "He left the reservation, and he and his followers are defying the U.S. government by doing so." "My orders are to bring him back, one way or another," the Lieutenant said.

"Thunder Rolling Up The Mountain is his real name." "He is a Nez Perce, and the Nez Perce are friends of the Shoshone."

"The Crow is their friends also, but they wouldn't help them," said an older sergeant that I had seen before.

"I am not a Crow; the Crow forget their friends if it benefits them the Shoshone don't," I said firmly.

"Then you won't go?" the Lieutenant said, aggravated.

I shook my head, no.

The Lieutenant turned and told the sergeant, "Come on, let's go; we are wasting our time here." "I might as well warn you, Mr. York; the U. S. government may end our buying of your goods because of this," the Lieutenant said in a threatening tone.

"I don't need the government's money, but if they decide to buy from someone else, they will pay more and get lower quality," I said sternly. I knew the government wouldn't stop buying from me, and I also knew the lieutenant knew this, too. He turned and left, sometime later, I heard that they got Chief Joseph and the Nez Perce people, just before they entered Canada.

As the years passed, Nancy and I made trips back to Worcester and Hanbury Hall. Every time we visited, it seemed like Worcester would grow a little bigger. On the last trip we would make, Nancy and I had noticed that Mr. Gifford was having a difficult time doing his job. We talked this over with Margaret and Edward because they lived at Hanbury Hall all the time, and they confirmed what Nancy and I thought. We agreed that I would ask Mr. Gifford to speak with me in the study.

"You know, Mr. Gifford, that I always thought of you like family," I said.

"Yes, My Lord," he replied.

"We are all getting older, and in age, we tend to have a difficult time," I said.

"Yes, My Lord," he said.

"Hanbury Hall will always be your home for as long as you wish," I said.

"Thank you, My Lord," he said, relieved.

"I want you to hire a reliable assistant you can train for that day when you can no longer work," I added.

"I can do the work, My Lord," he replied.

"I know you can now, but while you still can work." "I want you to train someone to make your life a little easier," I insisted.

"Yes, My Lord," he said a little unhappily.

"Do not fret he will not replace you; this is your home for the rest of your life," I said.

"Yes, My Lord," he replied a little more at ease.

Nathaniel was all grown up now. He was gone most of the time because of a girl on the Markus Ranch south of here. Sarah had married, and she and her husband moved to California. Unfortunately, Sarah was never very close to Nancy or me, and I never heard much from her. As predicted, the Military still bought cattle, horses, and lumber from us, to tell you the truth they increased the amount. The Shoshone flourished on the ranch, many working for us so that they could buy goods.

As Nancy and I were getting older and slowing down some, Nancy came to me and wanted to talk about the ranch. "We, or at least I am getting too old to continue working and living on the ranch, and I feel we should find a house in Salt Lake City or Denver and move there. The boys can take care of this place, at least the ones who wish to stay here," Nancy said.

Years ago, I would have put up a fight, but I lost interest in the ranch when Ma and Pa died, so I said to Nancy, "We can take a trip to both of those cities as soon as I talk to my brothers if you would like," I said.

She smiled and said, "Yes."

I hadn't seen Grey Wolf for some time. William had said he was sick, so I went to talk to him first.

"I hear you are sick, my brother," I said.

"I am old and should go the way of our ancestors," Grey Wolf said.

"Do not talk foolishly, Grey Wolf." "You will be just fine and will live a much longer life," I said concerned.

"What is it that brings you here?" he asked.

"I am looking for a lodge in the white man's city." "Do you wish to come and live with us," I asked?

He thought for a few seconds and then said, "No, my place is here; you go and find yourself a place." We talked for a short time, and then I left for Zack's home.

I found Zack instructing one of his boys to break a horse. "I just saw Grey Wolf, and he doesn't look good," I said sadly.

"Yes, I saw him yesterday he was talking about dying," Zack said.

"What did you tell him? I asked.

"I told him he was too strong and stubborn to die." "But I think he knows I was just trying to comfort him; he knows he is going to die," Zack said.

I did not want to believe this, so I changed the subject and said, "Nancy and I are going to consider buying a home in the Denver or the Salt Lake area."

"Why?" he asked.

"Nancy is having a hard time living on the ranch, and I'm slowing down some myself," I replied. Zack nodded, and I said, "Are you interested in doing the same?" "It would be nice to have someone I can talk to nearby."

He didn't even hesitate to reply, "James, I am half Shoshone by blood, and looks and my wife is full Shoshone." "You know we would not get treated very well." "This ranch is the place where I wish to be." "I know you lost interest in it after Ma and Pa died, and that is alright." "So, you go, and I will stay here; anyway, someone has to run this place."

With tears in my eyes, I hugged him, said my goodbyes, and left to go back to the cabin to talk with our children.

"Your mother and I are going to buy a home in Denver or Salt Lake." "We are getting too old to live here," I said to the children. "Your uncle Zack will be staying to help run the ranch, and, of course, all of you are also capable of running the ranch," I continued. "Now, it is your choice if any of you would want to join us," I said.

"Martha and I will go, also, Pa. We are not doing much good here, anyway," Carl said. Joseph, Christopher, and William all understood why we were moving, but they decided to stay.

After they all left to do their choirs, I looked around the ranch at all I had done. The memories were many. Upon the ridge, I could still see the graves of my loved ones with the beautiful bright plants and flowers that we all planted so many years ago. I will say my goodbyes before we leave. The valley was dotted with cabins now, from my children and their children. All decided that William would take over my cabin; he would be married soon anyway. There were many good memories of this place, along with many bad memories. But I felt that the good outnumbered the bad. The ranch was very peaceful now that the Blackfeet were too weak to cause any troubles. Then there were the Utes until a few years ago; they were too busy dealing with the Mormon settlers. I'm not sure what the outcome was, but I do know the settlers were still there.

A week after the meeting with the children, Nancy, Margaret, Carl, and I left for Denver on a cloudy day. It took us some time to get to Denver from our ranch. Along the way, we passed smaller ranches and the occasional traveler. However, we never stopped and talked, except maybe to say hello. Denver was high up in the mountains, and we arrived there on a cold, dark, cloudy day. Right away, we saw that it was a somewhat wild city with many lowlifes in certain areas. We checked into a hotel and went to get something to eat. We noticed people were unfriendly, rude, and in many cases, thought they were better than anyone. It didn't help that Carl and I were in buckskins and our wives dressed in home-made clothing, as were many women who lived on ranches. "Maybe we should buy some store-bought clothes," Nancy said, concerned.

"Wearing fancy clothing will make things worse when those snobs find out who we are," I said.

"I would rather get accepted for who we really are," Carl said.

The next day we were directed to a person named Mark Henderson who could help us look at some homes or home sites if we decided to build a house. To get to his office, we had to pass through some rough areas of Denver. I wasn't too thrilled with that. We had stabled our horses, so we walked to Mr. Henderson's office. It wasn't very far anyway, and I figured we all needed to get the exercise to work the kinks out of our bodies. We hadn't gone far when we heard the insults and mockery coming from drunks and lowlife troublemakers. We all ignored it until some young, stupid toughs tried to get physical with us.

"Well, look what we got here, boys, a bunch of settlers all dressed up like mountain men," said one of the lowlifes.

"Yeah, and look at the womenfolk, even the old one looks good," said another.

By this time, I was getting irritated, and Nancy, Margaret, and Carl knew it. I tried to walk past them, but the one who was causing the most problems put his hand on my shirt. That was a big mistake on his part with my left hand, I removed his hand, and with my right, I came down on his jaw. The pop was so loud, as his jaw broke that it surprised even me. When the man went down, one of his friends came at me with his knife and pulled my knife. Then there was a boom of a pistol, and the man went down.

To my surprise, Carl was standing there with a smoking pistol and an angry look on his face. The rest of the troublemakers ran, much to our relief. I didn't want any more trouble. I went over to check on the two injured men, and both were moaning, but they would live. We waited around for any authorities to come. However, none did, so we continued, leaving the two men lying on the ground, and Forty-five minutes later, we were at Mr. Henderson's office.

"Mr. York, the type of home you wish only can get found where the high society of Denver is." "You and your family would never be suitable for the high society people," said Mr. Henderson smugly.

"My father is the Earl of Worcester, if he isn't part of your high society then no one is, don't judge us by our clothing," Carl said angrily.

Mr. Henderson stood up and looked at us arrogantly then said, "If you are the Earl of Worcester, Mr. York, then go live in Worcester."

I was about to get up and knock him out, but Nancy grabbed my arm. I looked at Nancy and said, "Let's go I didn't like Denver at first sight when we entered this den of reprobates." Mr. Henderson's mouth was hanging open at what I said as we left and headed back to the hotel.

The next morning it was raining, and after picking up some supplies, we headed west to the Great Salt Lake. After two days of traveling, the rains hadn't stopped. I wasn't feeling well, so we looked for some shelter and found it under an overhang. I was running a fever and was also very weak. Carl managed to start a fire, and we had plenty of food, so we rested there for two days when my fever finally broke. I was still weak when we saddled up and continued to move west. As we went, I became concerned we might run into some Utes, and in my weakened state, I didn't know what would happen. We were friendly with them, but they were now fighting with the settlers in the Salt Lake Valley also they might not recognize me because of my age and the time that had passed since I had contact with them.

The rains had stopped when we finally dropped into the Sanpete Valley. The sun was warm, and it felt good on my body. We had been lucky and hadn't run into any Utes. I wasn't quite sure how far we were south of Salt Lake City, so we turned north and hugged the tree line next to the mountains. It wasn't the safest thing to do because of the Utes, but there would be fresh water and plenty of firewood. After camping for the night, we headed north again and came to a town by the name of Manti. Manti was a farming community with a large structure was under construction upon a hill. As we entered the town, we attracted a lot of stares, but we didn't pay any attention to them. We needed supplies, so we stopped at the only general store that was there.

The lady who was clerking in the store wasn't rude but not friendly, either. I was curious about the large, ornate structure, so I asked, "Who owns that large building under construction on top of the hill?"

"God," she replied.

"God?" I said.

"It's the house of the Lord, our temple, she replied.

"Like the one, they are building Salt Lake City?" Nancy asked.

"Yes, but it will be smaller," she answered. "Are you saints?" she asked, not believing so.

"I'm not, but my wife and daughter-in-law are," I said with a smile.

Just then, there was a familiar voice behind us, "James, is that you?"

We all turned around; it was Jack McConnell. Some years back, Jack and Big Tom found enough gold to make a comfortable life for themselves.

Since the Civil War was over, Big Tom decided to head southeast to find his family and maybe buy a small farm for himself. Jack went west looking for a place to settle down, which ended up being this town of Manti. Miguel died of a heart attack about a year before they left, and he was buried at the ranch since we knew of no relatives he had.

"Yes, it is me, and this is Nancy and my daughter-in-law Margaret and of course, you know Carl."

"Carl! I can't believe you have grown so much, and now you are married," Jack said.

"What are you doing here, James?" he asked.

"We are heading to Salt Lake City to find a place to live." "Nancy and I are getting too old for the ranch."

"How long will you be here?" Jack asked.

"Not long, just enough time for us to get some supplies and something to eat."

"Since there is no place to eat yet in this town, you will all eat with us," Jack said.

"Us, you mean your clerk?" I said, confused.

"No, no, Jenny is my wife; I should have told you I'm sorry about not introducing you to her," he explained.

We ate a meal with Jack and his wife and talked about the old times. After leaving Jack, it took us four days to get to Salt Lake City. After checking into a hotel, we went to a man who handled property; his name was Mr. Henry Walker. He was a pleasant man who always had a smile and a kind word. Most of the people in Salt Lake City seemed to treat us with respect and courtesy. I felt they did this, not because they knew me, which I didn't think they did, but this was just the type of people they were, at least to us. I only had been in the city a few times, and that was for business or a wedding or two, many years ago. I had already made up my mind that this would be the city for us because we got treated so well. We also wanted to be here because of the proximity to the ranch, which I wanted to be near. We searched for a place for two days, and finally, late on the second day, we found something we all liked.

The location of the house was on one corner of a ten-acre lot. It was a large home for Salt Lake City. It had four bedrooms and what Mr. Walker told us were maid quarters, a dining room, parlor, library, a room that we could use for an office, a sitting room, a large kitchen with a pump, and a wet room. I had no intention of farming the ten acres, even though it had water running through it; that just wasn't me. I thought I could have some fruit trees or maybe a vegetable garden. However, nothing else unless Carl and Margaret wanted something, and I didn't believe that they did. We also had a large fancy barn in the back, much like Grandpa had. We all decided that Carl and Margaret would live in the house with Nancy and me while we had a home built next door for them. It would have to be a big house because we found out Margaret was pregnant again, and I had a strong feeling it wouldn't be the last child. We hired a maid and cook; the house wasn't Hanbury Hall, but for Salt Lake City, it was very fancy, and we were happy with it.

Years ago, I had gone east and brought all our wealth to Salt Lake City for safekeeping and convenience. We had plenty of money to work with, and we furnished according to our taste and bought a carriage. I needed to go back to the ranch to bring the rest of our belongings to the home in Salt Lake. It got decided that Nancy would stay behind with Carl as well as Margaret, and I would take a rented wagon to fetch our things. Nancy wasn't pleased about this but finally agreed when I pointed out that it wasn't very far to the ranch.

I was feeling good as I traveled toward the ranch. I thought we had made the right decision leaving the ranch and settling in Salt Lake City. It was a sunny day, and I was daydreaming of everything I had done in getting this house and setting it up. Daydreaming was something I had not done since when I was younger, and it was a bad habit now. I should be paying more attention to my surroundings. Fortunately, I didn't run into any problems during the time while I was not paying attention. I made camp for the night next to a cliff that sloped into a mountain valley.

I started a fire and fixed something to eat, then sat back and rested. It was late when I was looking over the valley. I spotted something far off and coming nearer fast as if it was floating or flying toward me. It came so quickly that I thought it was going to hit me, so I grabbed for my pistol. I was too slow, and whatever it was, seemed to go right through me. I was so startled that it stunned me; I didn't know how to react. Then I heard a voice behind me, "Soaring Eagle With Many Coups, why do you have your weapon out? Do you not know who I am?" the voice said.

I swung around and saw a boy who looked familiar, dressed in white buckskin. Then it hit me; he was my spirit guide. Before I could say anything, he said, "You must move quickly back to your lodge where your brothers are, one of your brothers doesn't have long."

The word "long" faded off into the night breeze, and he was gone. I didn't hesitate I hitched my horses up to the wagon and slowly headed out. Usually, a person would question what had just happened. However, I wasn't an ordinary person, and relying on my instincts had paid off many times.

When the sun came up, I could move much faster; I quickly made it to the ranch. No one was around, or at least I didn't see anyone. Out of the corner of my eye, I saw movement in the bunkhouse. I got off the wagon and went over to see who I had seen. "Ted, where is everybody?" I asked the ranch hand.

"Mr. York, everybody is with your brother, Grey Wolf, he is in a bad way," he said, surprised to see me.

"You stay here for now and take care of my wagon and horses," I said as I got on another horse and headed to Grey Wolf's lodge.

There were several horses, men, women, and children standing around Grey Wolf's lodge. I went inside Zack, Grey Wolf's wife, his children, and, of course, Grey Wolf, lying on the ground. Grey Wolf was gaunt and slipping in and out of consciousness. When I kneeled beside him, and he came around, Grey Wolf smiled at me then said hoarsely, "I knew you would be here."

"Of course, I am here I am here to make you better," I replied.

He smiled again and said, "I knew you were coming, and I am to go the way of our ancestors because your spirit guide told me."

"How did you know he was my spirit guide?" I asked.

With difficulty, Grey Wolf said, "Many years ago, before you came to our village, I had a younger brother who died." "Your spirit guide was my brother; he had a different name then." "He told me about you and that I would join him."

With that, he closed his eyes and, to my broken heart, never opened them again. His body was prepared the Shoshone way and was placed by his children in a place where no one would know, at his request.

After spending some time with my children and Zack and his family, I loaded up the wagon with help and headed southwest with my head hung low. I was in Salt Lake City in about a week. After unloading the wagon, I sat down and explained all that happened to my family. Nancy could see that it had taken a lot out of me. In the days following, talking to my family, I became very despondent and never really got over the death of Grey Wolf.

As the years passed, many things changed in the Salt Lake City area. A large temple was still getting built, and many new buildings were going up. Christopher decided to move to Salt Lake City, and we built a home for him on my property. It wasn't a month after Carl moved into his home that William showed up at my house. I was sitting in the parlor with William when he said sadly, "It's just not the same without Uncle Grey Wolf, Carl, you, and mother."

"How do your wife and children feel?" I asked.

"The same," he replied.

"What do you want to do?" I asked, knowing what he was going to say.

"We were thinking of moving here with you and Carl," he replied.

I nodded and said, "Leave your wife and little ones here and go get your things."

We built another house for William and his family next to Carl's home, and now there were four families of York's.

Several years had passed; I didn't leave the property much. I gardened some or worked with the horses we had. One day, Joseph, who was the last son living on the ranch, showed up with that look that meant there was trouble. "Pa, we need to talk."

"I can see by the look on your face that it isn't good, so what is it?"

"It's Uncle Zack, one night he went to sleep, and he never woke up," Joseph said with tears streaming down his cheeks.

I just stared at him as my heart sank, then everything went black.

I woke up in bed in a dimly lit room with Nancy and my family standing around me. "I'll be alright, just let me be alone," I said hoarsely.

Everyone left except Nancy, who stayed and comforted me, which I appreciated. I didn't think things could get much worse in my life, and I went deeper into my depression with the death of my brothers. If it weren't for my Nancy, I would have felt entirely alone. I didn't talk to many people, and when I had to talk, the conversation wasn't long. By this time, I had hung up my buckskins and weapons and wore city clothes frankly; I didn't care anymore.

Two years had passed; my grandchildren had children. The ranch was still turning a hefty profit, and more and more of my family were moving to Salt Lake City. The first snows had fallen when my dear Nancy fell sick. Our servants fetched the doctor. After the doctor examined her, he approached William and me while we were waiting for his diagnosis. The doctor said, "Perhaps if Nancy was a younger woman, I could have more hope for her, but at her age, there is not much I can do."

"What are you saying about my mother, doctor?" asked William, concerned.

Before the doctor answered, I knew what he was going to say. "Your mother is dying, and there is nothing I can do except make her comfortable."

I stiffened up and said, "How long?"

"It could be days, weeks, months, maybe a year but no longer.

I had William send word to his sisters, and they arrived just in time. I never left Nancy's side after the doctor told us of her prognosis. One stormy day, with a clap of thunder, Nancy gave up her last breath, and I felt entirely alone. From that day forward, I never went outside; I stayed mostly in one or two rooms. My health failed somewhat; I wasn't the same young man I used to be, and I only had my memories left to me. I knew I still had my children and grandchildren. However, they were from another generation and had their own lives, so I isolated myself. As time went on, I got forgotten, except to be known as the old man in the window. I got that name from sitting next to the window for hours. Looking out at the world and thinking of the past.

"That's my story, Dan." "I can see by the look on your face that you are having a hard time believing it," I said a little disappointed.

"Well, it is quite a story, grandpa," Dan said.

"Let's leave and let grandpa get some rest kids," Dan said to Johnny and Sarah. I stared at them as they went out into the hall, then I heard Sarah say, "Daddy, I believe the story that grandpa told us."

"I know you do, but grandpa is very old, and sometimes old people like grandpa get confused about things and make them up," Dan said to the children.

"You three get back in here," I barked. All three of my grandchildren walked into my room, and Dan was about to apologize, I thought, but I didn't let him. "So, you think I am confused," I said. I walked over to a chest I used when I traveled to England and opened it on the table. Next, to the chest, I pulled out my buckskins, Hawk, pistols, Hawken, and what Blackfoot scalps I had kept. I then walked away and pointed to the items on the table. Dan and the children examined the items, and they were amazed, as were the children.

"Are these real?" Dan said, pointing to the scalps.

"Of course, they are," I said.

"I guess your story is true, grandpa," Dan said, astonished.

"I told you so," said Sarah.

After they left, I looked at the things I had put on the table. I put on my buckskins, and they felt good. I loaded my pistols and rifle and put the pistols on my belt along with my hawk and knife, and they all felt great. I then did something I hadn't done in a long time. I went outside and went into the barn. I picked out a horse, and with a little difficulty, I saddled the horse.

Before I got on the horse, Christopher came into the barn and said with concern, "Where do you think you are going, pa?"

"For a ride and don't try to stop me, it could get messy," I replied bluntly.

I got on my horse, and Christopher asked, "Are you coming back home?"

I smiled and giggled a bit and said in Shoshone, "Yes, I am going home." With that, I left the barn and headed for the Shining Mountains. As I did, I could see Joseph, Carl, and the grandchildren come running to my home, but I didn't stop. I figured one of my servants had informed my family of my departure.

"I'm a writer, and years later, I had written everything that grandpa had said or what happened when he wasn't around," said Dan.

"Where is he going?" Carl asked Christopher.

"Pa said he was going for a ride, but he said he would come home,"

"Did he say he would come home, or he was going home?" Joseph asked in alarm.

"I'm not sure he could have said going home; he said it in Shoshone," Christopher replied.

"He is not coming back," Carl said.

Joseph nodded in agreement and said, "We better go after him."

"I doubt if you will ever find him, Dad," Dan said to his father.

"As I write my grandfather's story, I pieced together from others that saw him what Grandpa said and did, and like Grandpa, I also took a good guess of what he would do and say.

I left the city behind me and headed up a deer trail and over the mountain, then dropped into a mountain meadow. I had only intended to go for a short ride, but when I got to the second mountain ridge, something drove me forward. I didn't know where I would go, maybe to that spot where I saw my spirit guide in my youth, and I made love to Morning Star or maybe to the Yellow Stone, perhaps to a Shoshone Village. It had been a long time since I had some of their cooking. The sun was setting, but I rode on with joy in my heart.